D0311188

THE REAL RILEY MAYES

RACHEL ELLIOTT

BALZER + BRAY

Imprints of HarperCollinsPublishers

HARPER
alley

Balzer + Bray is an imprint of HarperCollins Publishers.
HarperAlley is an imprint of HarperCollins Publishers.

The Real Riley Mayes
Copyright © 2022 by Rachel Elliott
All rights reserved. Manufactured in Bosnia and Herzegovina.
No part of this book may be used or reproduced in any manner whatsoever without written
permission except in the case of brief quotations embodied in critical articles and reviews. For
information address HarperCollins Children's Books, a division of HarperCollins Publishers,
195 Broadway, New York, NY 10007.
www.harperalley.com

Library of Congress Control Number: 2021948580
ISBN 978-0-06-299574-2 (pbk.) — ISBN 978-0-06-299575-9

The artist used brush pens, markers, and Bristol paper to create the illustrations for this book.
Typography by Dana Fritts. Hand-lettered by Rachel Elliott.
22 23 24 25 26   GPS   10 9 8 7 6 5 4 3 2 1
❖
First Edition

Dear brilliant team at HarperCollins,
trusty literary agent Susan Hawk,
Kentucky Foundation for Women,
fabulous feedback group,
writing, illustrating, and
comic- making friends everywhere,

supportive family, and
loving partner, Carol—

This book exists because of you.

Thank you,
Rachel E.

CHAPTER 1

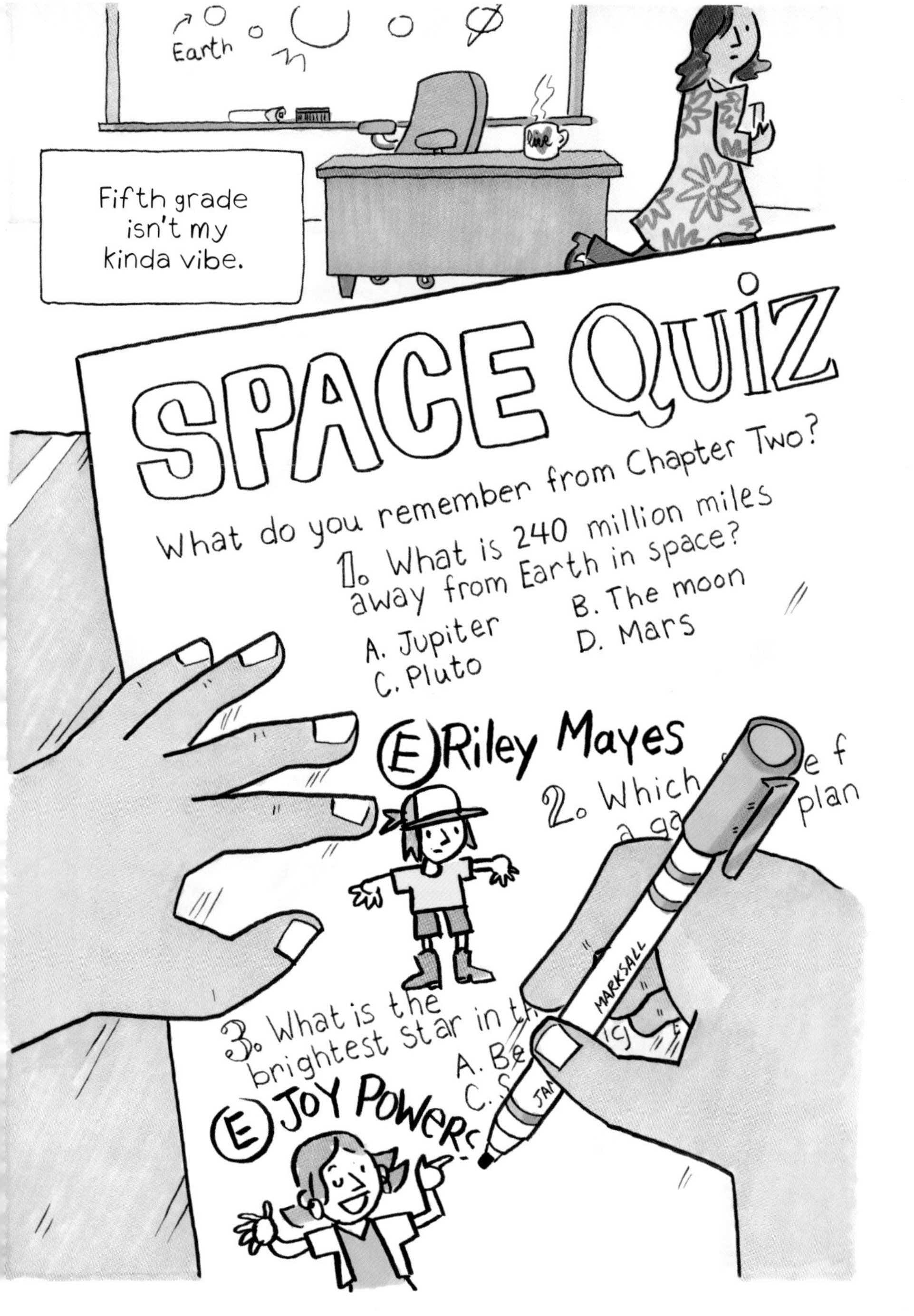

Earth
Fifth grade isn't my kinda vibe.
SPACE QUIZ
What do you remember from Chapter Two?
1. What is 240 million miles away from Earth in space?
A. Jupiter
B. The moon
C. Pluto
D. Mars
(E) Riley Mayes
2. Which
3. What is the
(E) JOY POWERS
MARKSALL

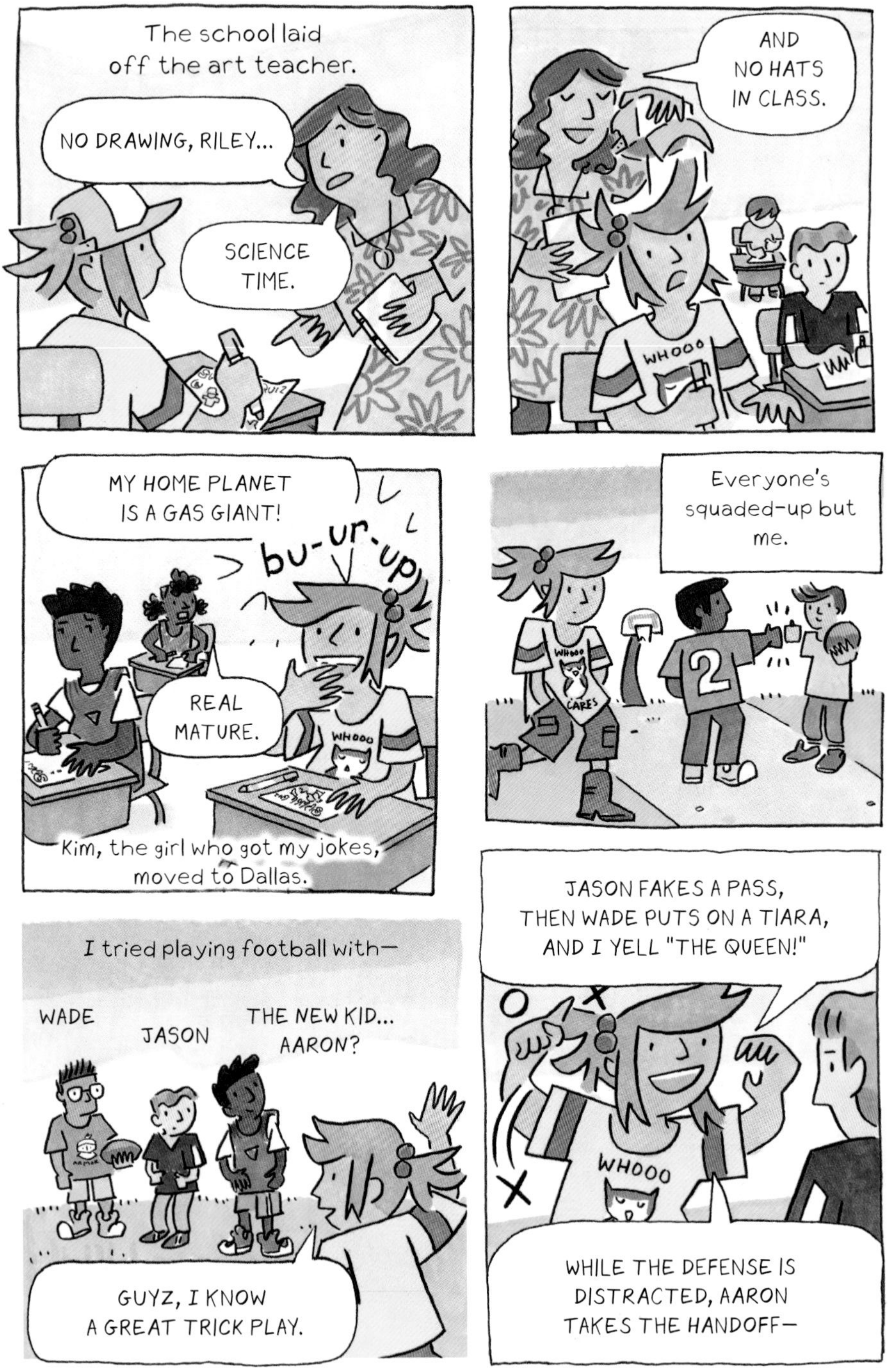

The school laid off the art teacher.
NO DRAWING, RILEY...
SCIENCE TIME.
QUIZ
AND NO HATS IN CLASS.
WHOOO
MY HOME PLANET IS A GAS GIANT!
bu-ur-up
REAL MATURE.
WHOOO
Kim, the girl who got my jokes, moved to Dallas.
Everyone's squaded-up but me.
WHOOO
CARES
2
I tried playing football with—
WADE
JASON
THE NEW KID... AARON?
GUYZ, I KNOW A GREAT TRICK PLAY.
JASON FAKES A PASS, THEN WADE PUTS ON A TIARA, AND I YELL "THE QUEEN!"
WHOOO
WHILE THE DEFENSE IS DISTRACTED, AARON TAKES THE HANDOFF—

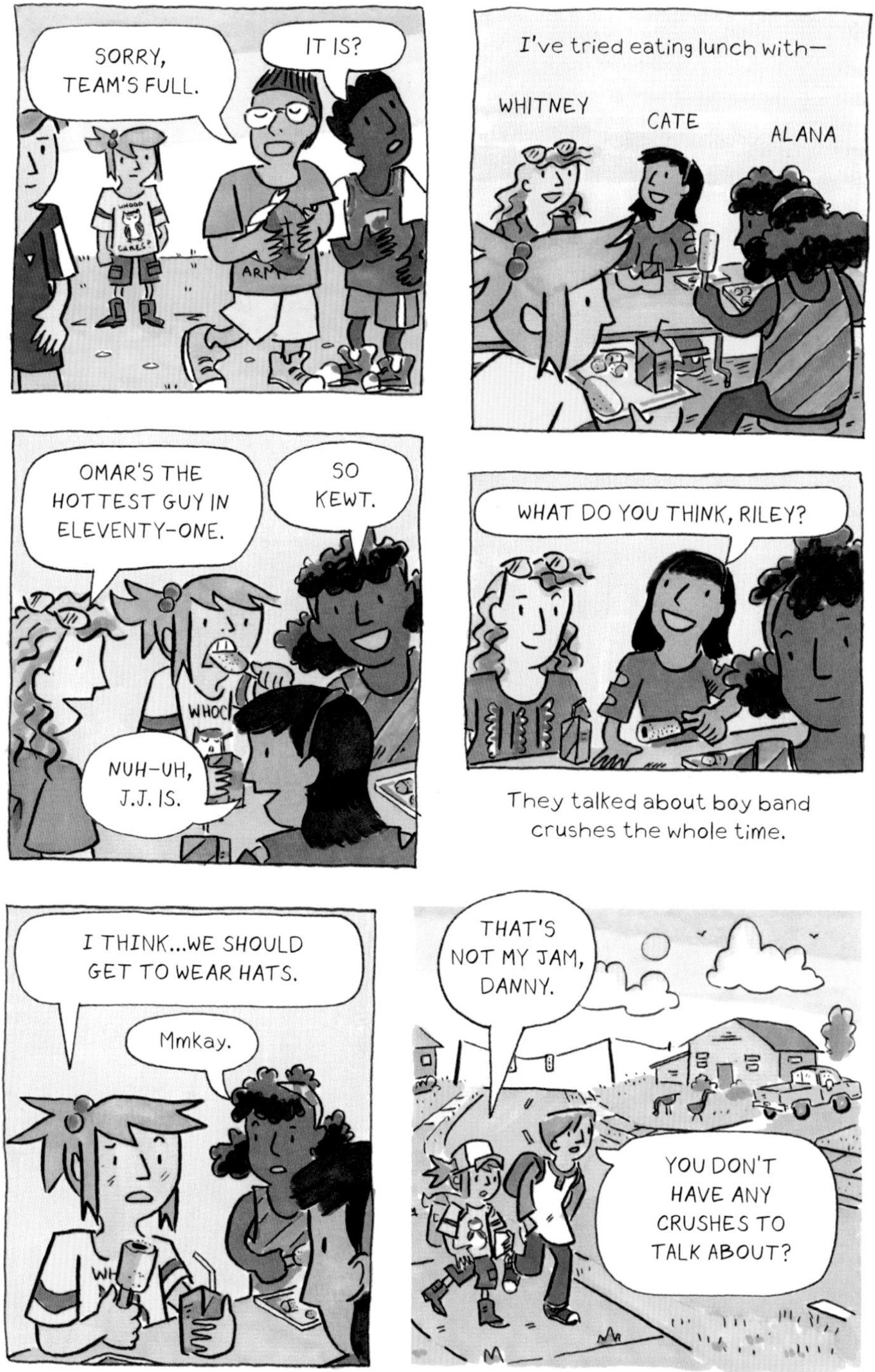
SORRY, TEAM'S FULL.
IT IS?
ARM
I've tried eating lunch with—
WHITNEY
CATE
ALANA
OMAR'S THE HOTTEST GUY IN ELEVENTY-ONE.
SO KEWT.
NUH-UH, J.J. IS.
WHAT DO YOU THINK, RILEY?
They talked about boy band crushes the whole time.
I THINK...WE SHOULD GET TO WEAR HATS.
Mmkay.
THAT'S NOT MY JAM, DANNY.
YOU DON'T HAVE ANY CRUSHES TO TALK ABOUT?

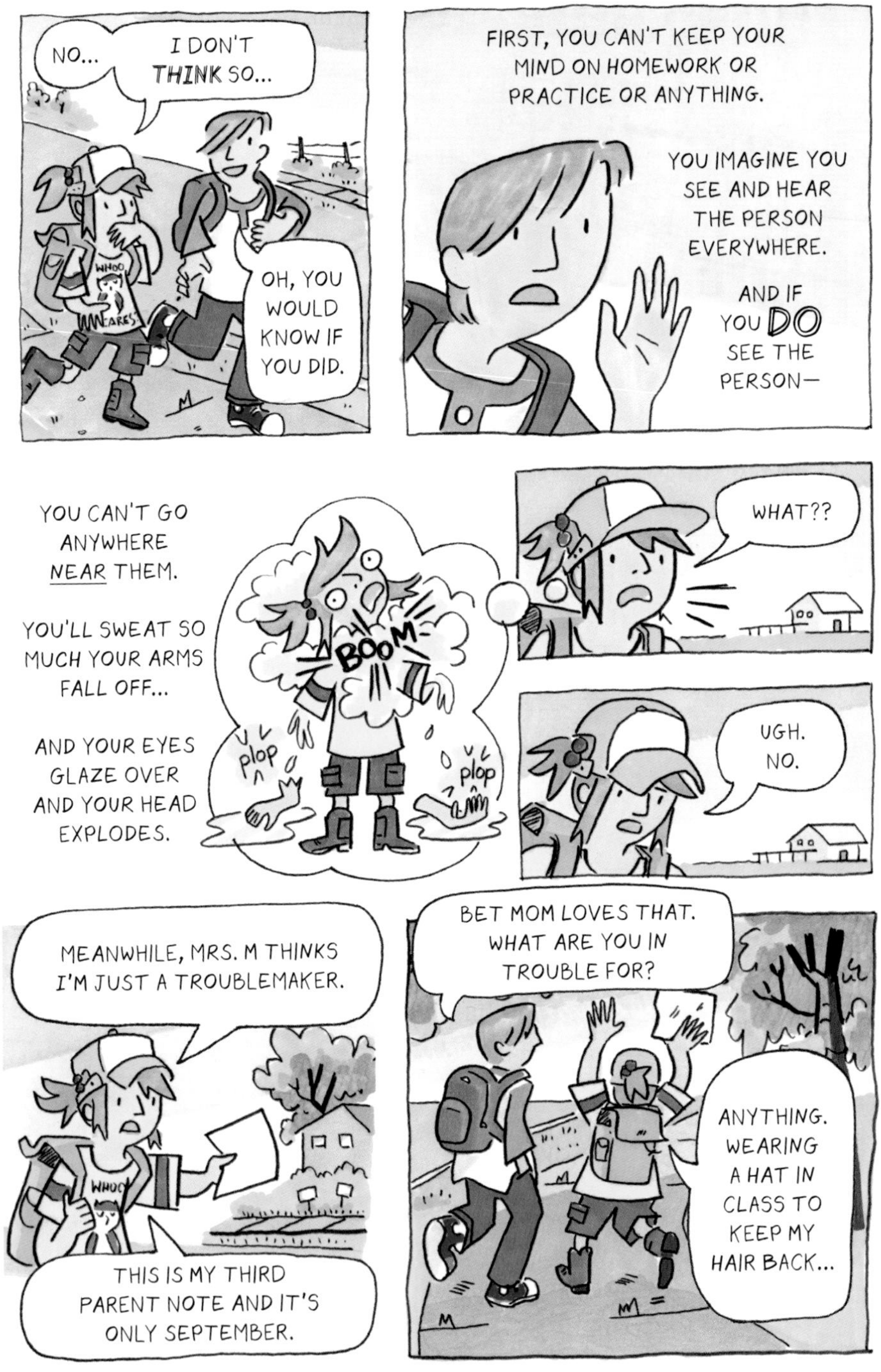
NO...
I DON'T THINK SO...
OH, YOU WOULD KNOW IF YOU DID.
FIRST, YOU CAN'T KEEP YOUR MIND ON HOMEWORK OR PRACTICE OR ANYTHING.
YOU IMAGINE YOU SEE AND HEAR THE PERSON EVERYWHERE.
AND IF YOU DO SEE THE PERSON—
YOU CAN'T GO ANYWHERE NEAR THEM.
YOU'LL SWEAT SO MUCH YOUR ARMS FALL OFF...
AND YOUR EYES GLAZE OVER AND YOUR HEAD EXPLODES.
BOOM
plop
plop
WHAT??
UGH. NO.
MEANWHILE, MRS. M THINKS I'M JUST A TROUBLEMAKER.
THIS IS MY THIRD PARENT NOTE AND IT'S ONLY SEPTEMBER.
BET MOM LOVES THAT. WHAT ARE YOU IN TROUBLE FOR?
ANYTHING. WEARING A HAT IN CLASS TO KEEP MY HAIR BACK...

DOODLING JOY POWERS ON MY WORKSHEETS.

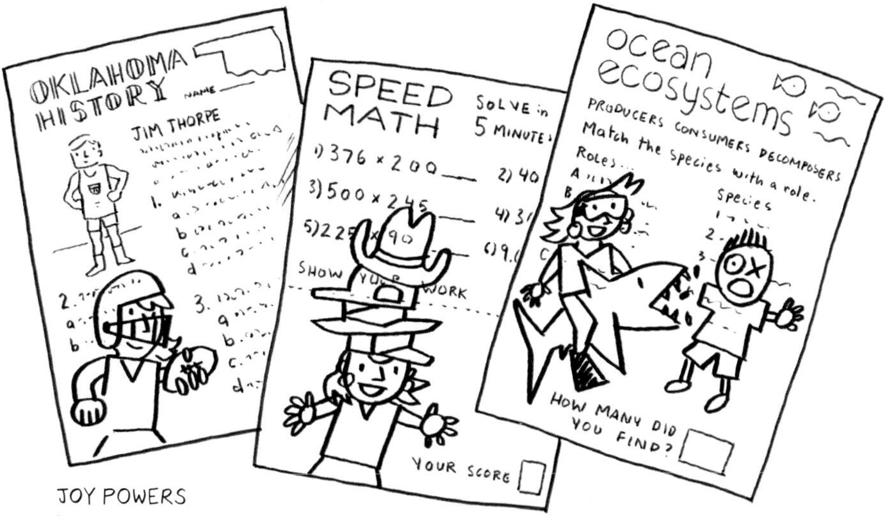
OKLAHOMA HISTORY
NAME
JIM THORPE
SPEED MATH
SOLVE in 5 MINUTES
1) 376 × 200
3) 500 × 245
SHOW YOUR WORK
YOUR SCORE
ocean ecosystems
PRODUCERS CONSUMERS DECOMPOSERS
Match the species with a role.
Roles
Species
HOW MANY DID YOU FIND?

JOY POWERS PLAYING FOOTBALL...

JOY POWERS WEARING FOUR HATS...

JOY POWERS RIDING A SHARK THAT EATS WADE.

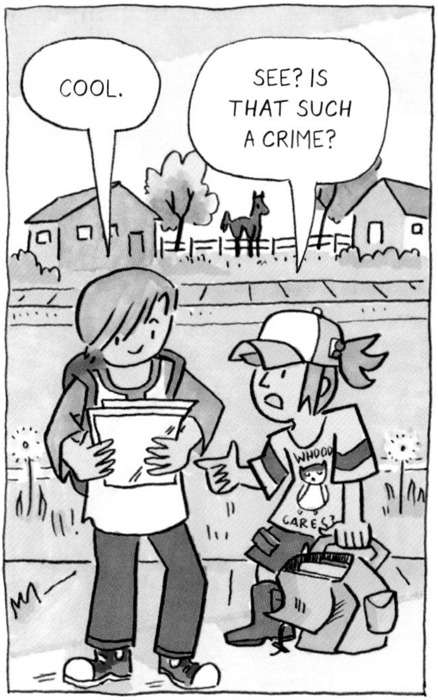
COOL.
SEE? IS THAT SUCH A CRIME?
WHOOO CARES?

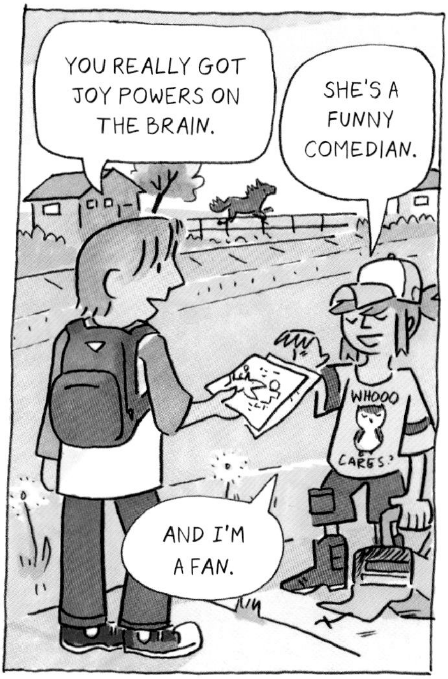
YOU REALLY GOT JOY POWERS ON THE BRAIN.
SHE'S A FUNNY COMEDIAN.
AND I'M A FAN.
WHOOO CARES?

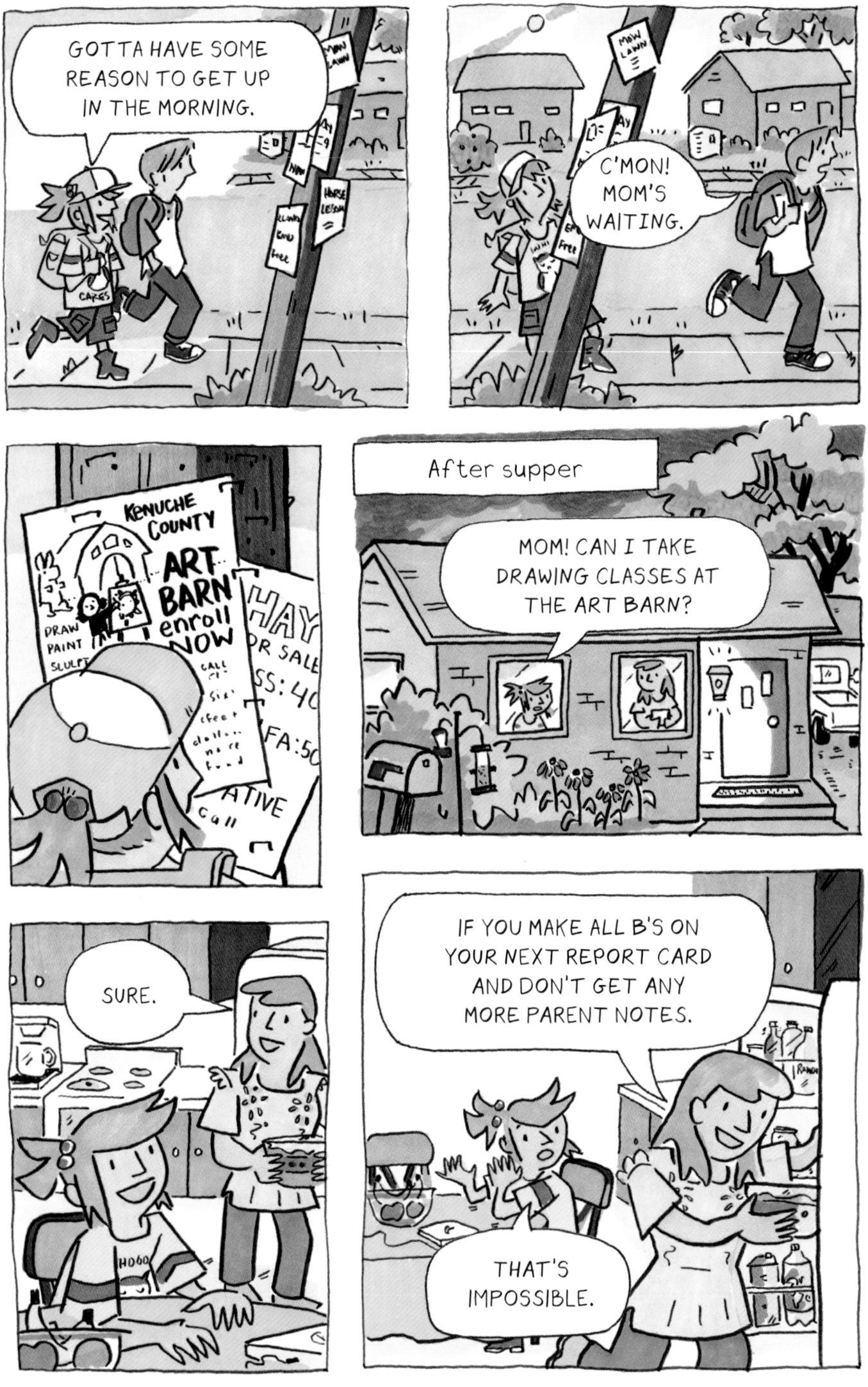
GOTTA HAVE SOME REASON TO GET UP IN THE MORNING.
C'MON! MOM'S WAITING.
KENUCHE COUNTY
ART BARN enroll NOW
DRAW
PAINT
After supper
MOM! CAN I TAKE DRAWING CLASSES AT THE ART BARN?
SURE.
IF YOU MAKE ALL B'S ON YOUR NEXT REPORT CARD AND DON'T GET ANY MORE PARENT NOTES.
THAT'S IMPOSSIBLE.

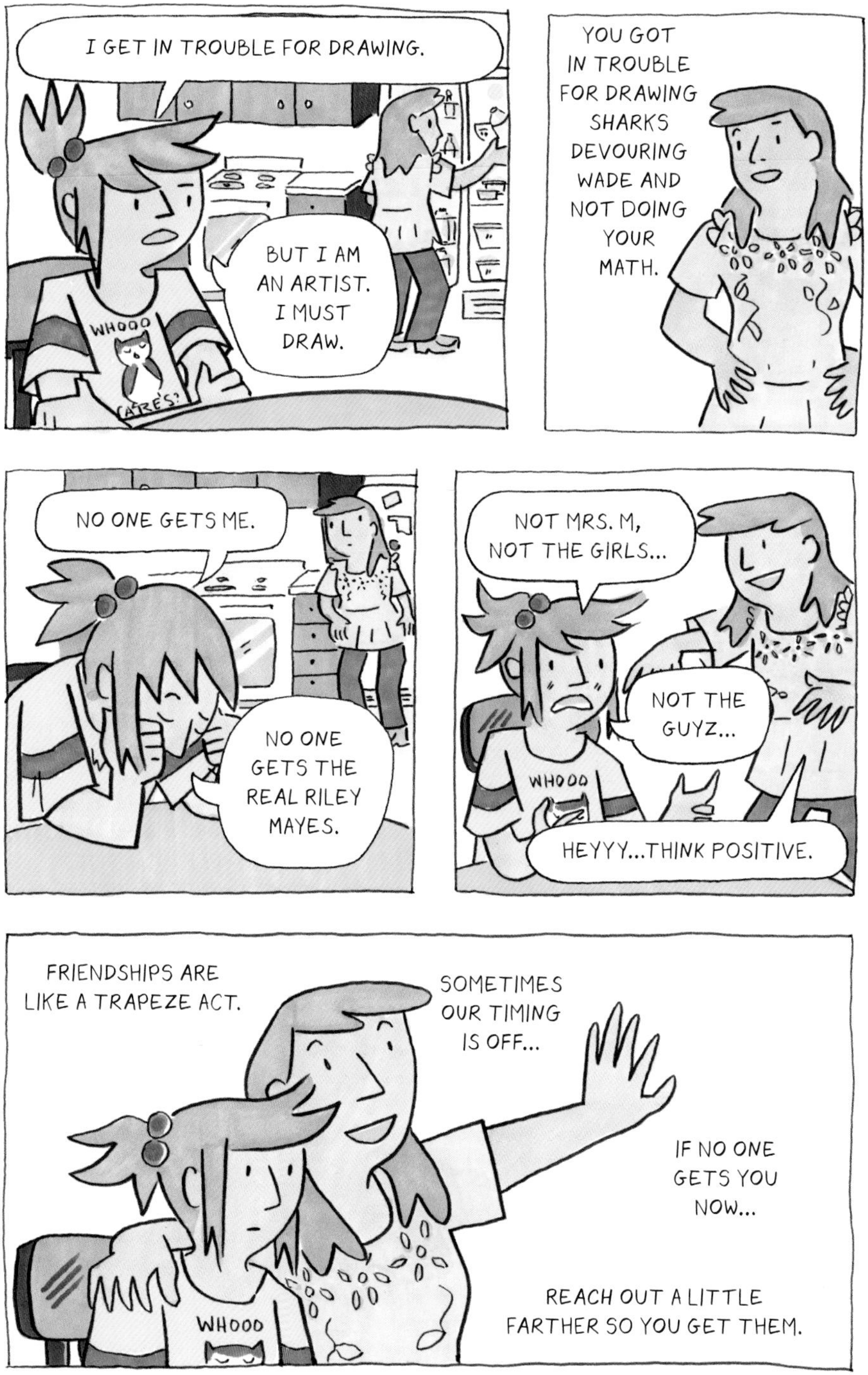
I GET IN TROUBLE FOR DRAWING.
BUT I AM AN ARTIST. I MUST DRAW.
WHOOO CARES?
YOU GOT IN TROUBLE FOR DRAWING SHARKS DEVOURING WADE AND NOT DOING YOUR MATH.
NO ONE GETS ME.
NO ONE GETS THE REAL RILEY MAYES.
NOT MRS. M, NOT THE GIRLS...
NOT THE GUYZ...
WHOOO
HEYYY...THINK POSITIVE.
FRIENDSHIPS ARE LIKE A TRAPEZE ACT.
SOMETIMES OUR TIMING IS OFF...
IF NO ONE GETS YOU NOW...
REACH OUT A LITTLE FARTHER SO YOU GET THEM.
WHOOO

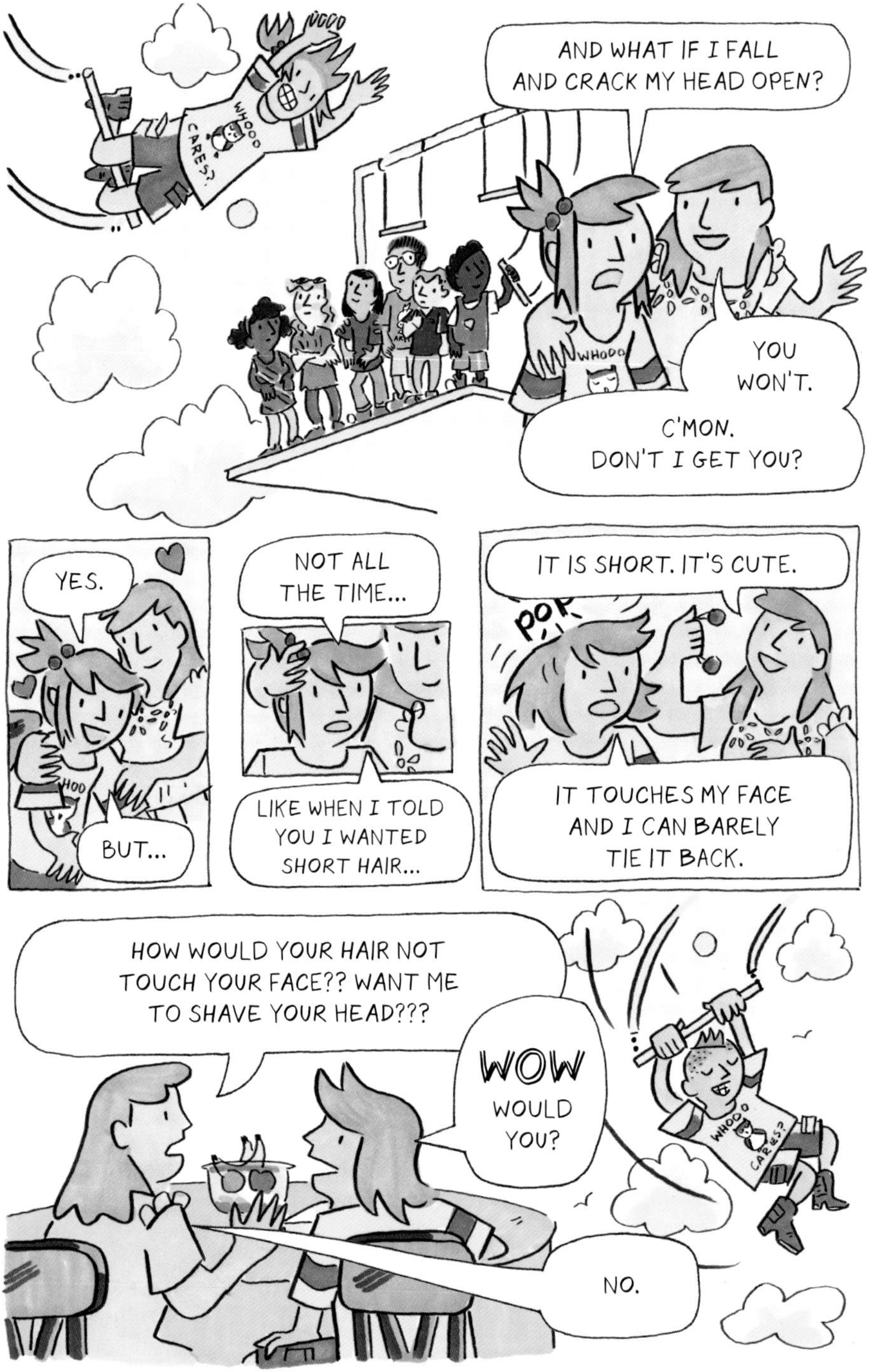
WOOO
WHOOO CARES?
AND WHAT IF I FALL AND CRACK MY HEAD OPEN?
YOU WON'T.
C'MON. DON'T I GET YOU?
YES.
BUT...
NOT ALL THE TIME...
LIKE WHEN I TOLD YOU I WANTED SHORT HAIR...
IT IS SHORT. IT'S CUTE.
POP
IT TOUCHES MY FACE AND I CAN BARELY TIE IT BACK.
HOW WOULD YOUR HAIR NOT TOUCH YOUR FACE?? WANT ME TO SHAVE YOUR HEAD???
WOW
WOULD YOU?
NO.

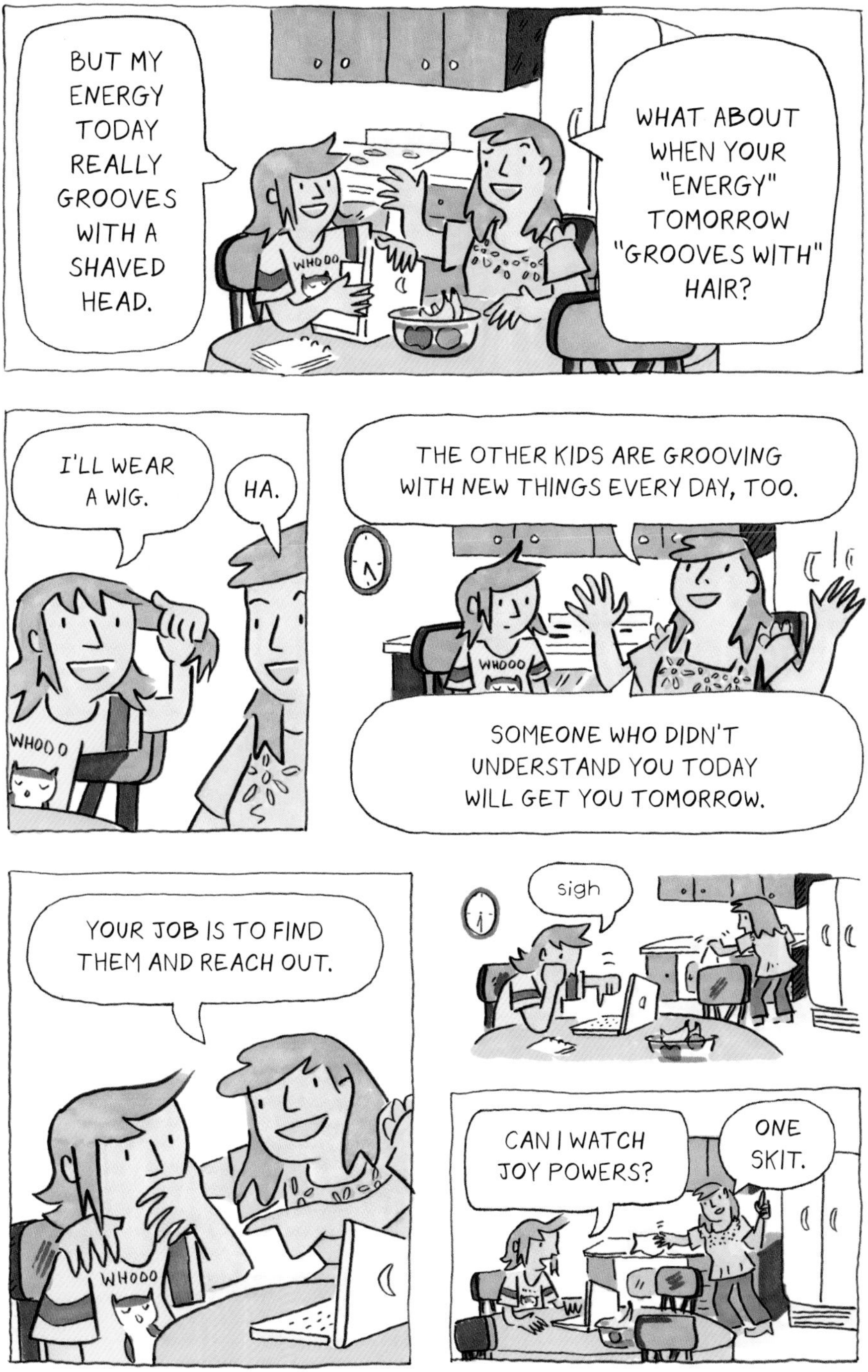
BUT MY ENERGY TODAY REALLY GROOVES WITH A SHAVED HEAD.
WHAT ABOUT WHEN YOUR "ENERGY" TOMORROW "GROOVES WITH" HAIR?
WHOOO
I'LL WEAR A WIG.
HA.
THE OTHER KIDS ARE GROOVING WITH NEW THINGS EVERY DAY, TOO.
SOMEONE WHO DIDN'T UNDERSTAND YOU TODAY WILL GET YOU TOMORROW.
YOUR JOB IS TO FIND THEM AND REACH OUT.
sigh
CAN I WATCH JOY POWERS?
ONE SKIT.

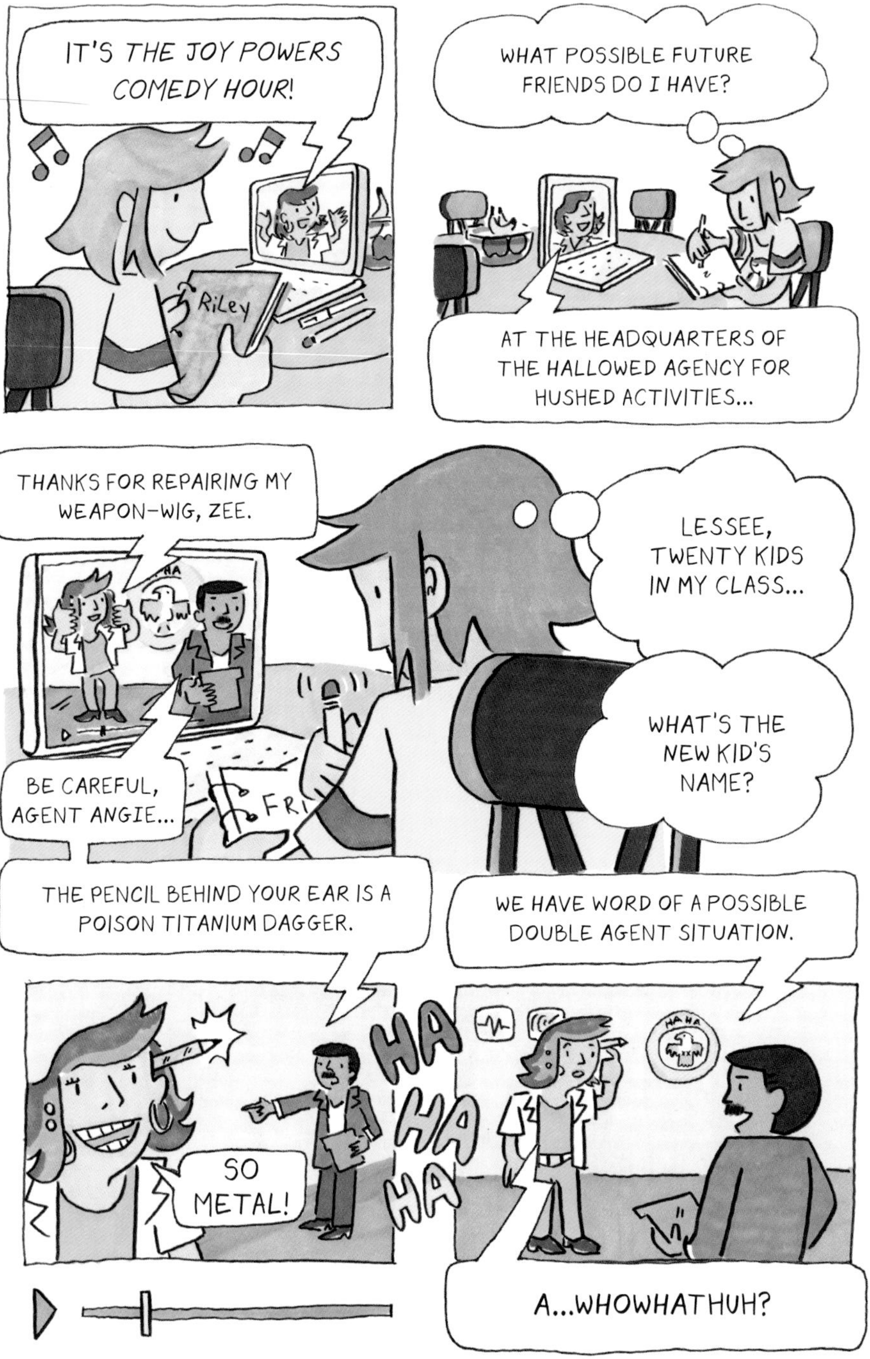
IT'S THE JOY POWERS COMEDY HOUR!
RiLey
WHAT POSSIBLE FUTURE FRIENDS DO I HAVE?
AT THE HEADQUARTERS OF THE HALLOWED AGENCY FOR HUSHED ACTIVITIES...
THANKS FOR REPAIRING MY WEAPON-WIG, ZEE.
LESSEE, TWENTY KIDS IN MY CLASS...
WHAT'S THE NEW KID'S NAME?
BE CAREFUL, AGENT ANGIE...
FRI
THE PENCIL BEHIND YOUR EAR IS A POISON TITANIUM DAGGER.
WE HAVE WORD OF A POSSIBLE DOUBLE AGENT SITUATION.
SO METAL!
HA HA HA
A...WHOWHATHUH?

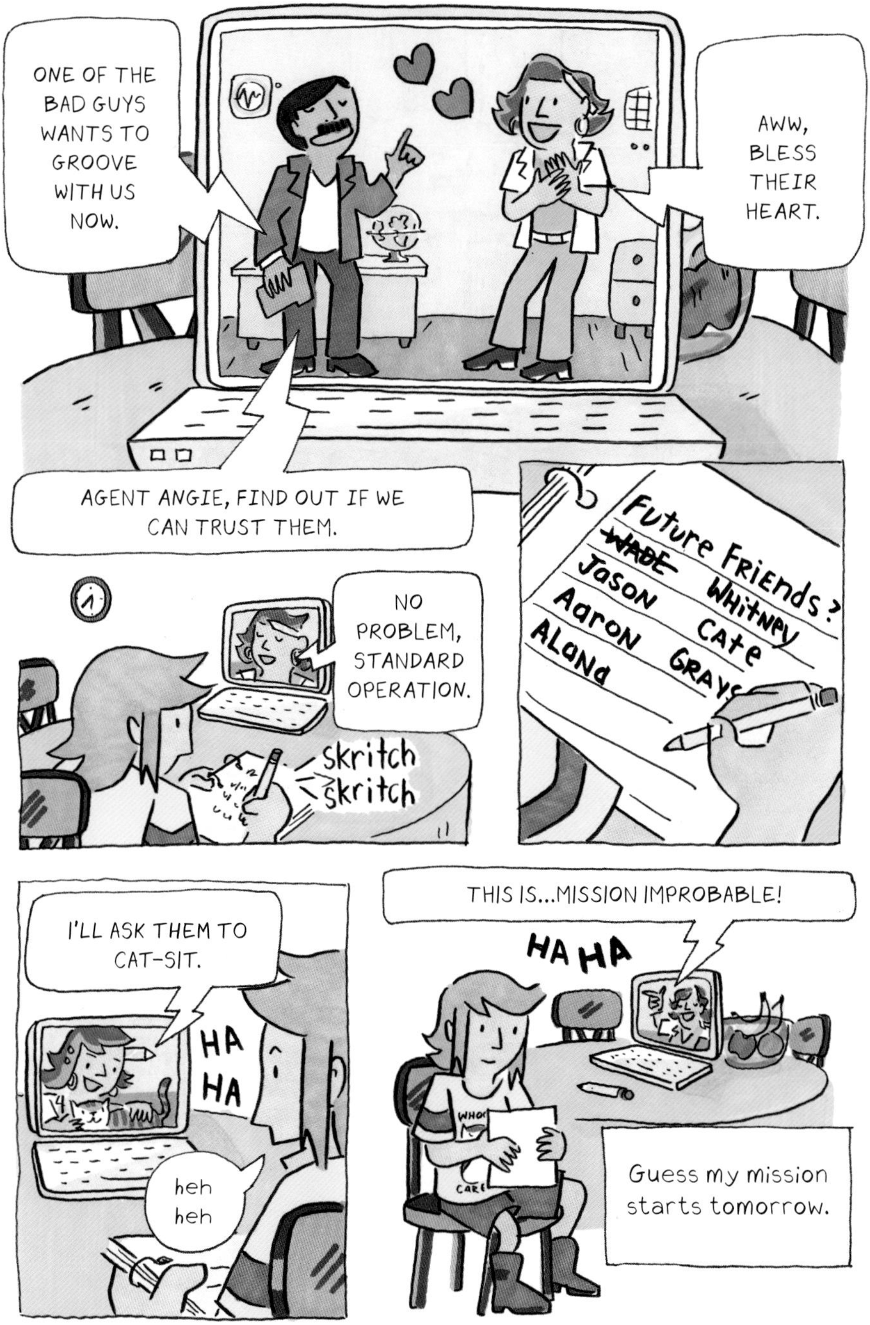
ONE OF THE BAD GUYS WANTS TO GROOVE WITH US NOW.
AWW, BLESS THEIR HEART.
AGENT ANGIE, FIND OUT IF WE CAN TRUST THEM.
NO PROBLEM, STANDARD OPERATION.
skritch
skritch
Future Friends?
WADE
Jason
Whitney
Aaron
Cate
ALand
GRAYS
I'LL ASK THEM TO CAT-SIT.
HA HA
heh heh
THIS IS...MISSION IMPROBABLE!
HA HA
Guess my mission starts tomorrow.

CHAPTER 2

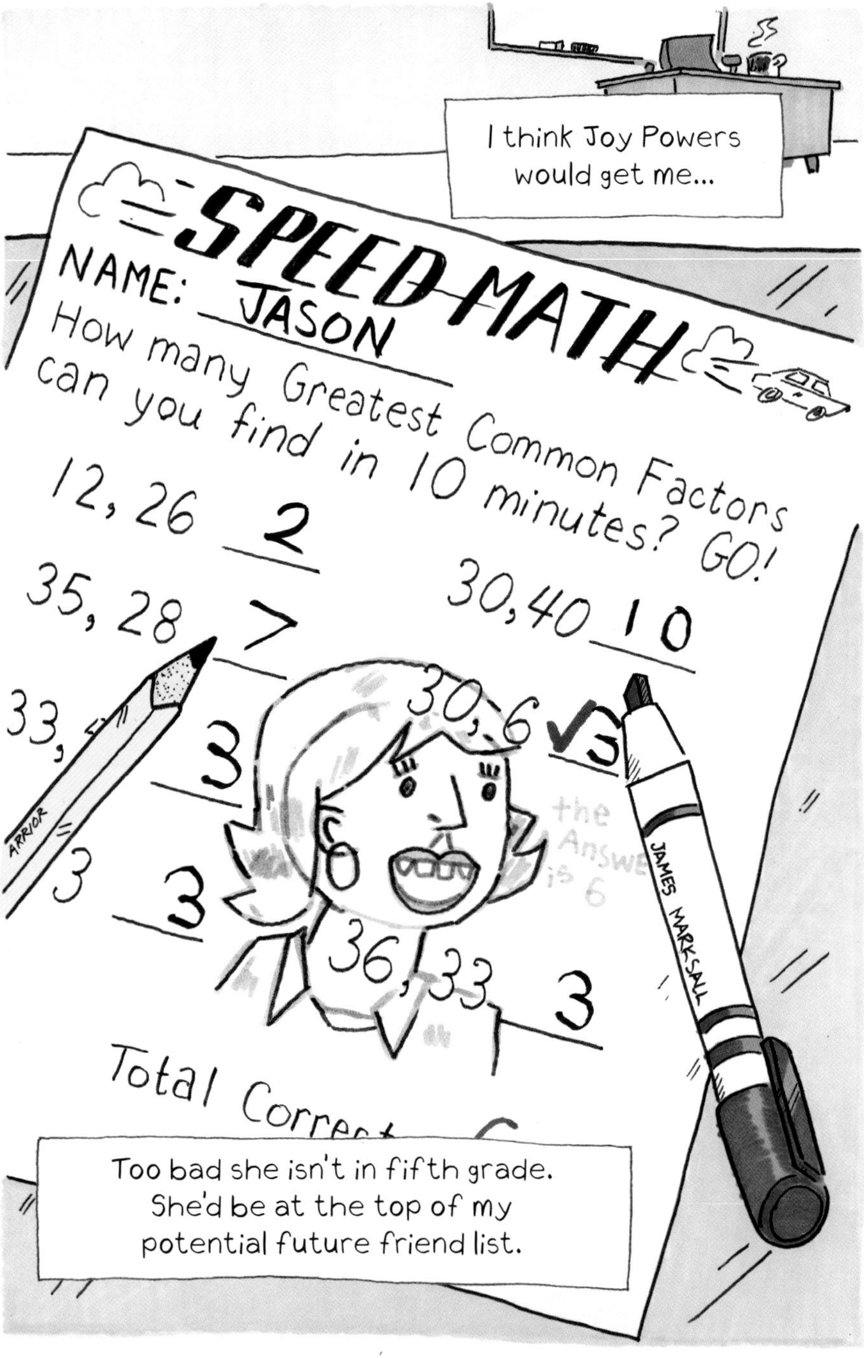
I think Joy Powers would get me...
SPEED MATH
NAME: JASON
How many Greatest Common Factors can you find in 10 minutes? GO!
12, 26 2
35, 28 7
30, 40 10
30, 6 3
the Answer is 6
36, 33 3
Total Correct
JAMES MARKSALL
Too bad she isn't in fifth grade. She'd be at the top of my potential future friend list.

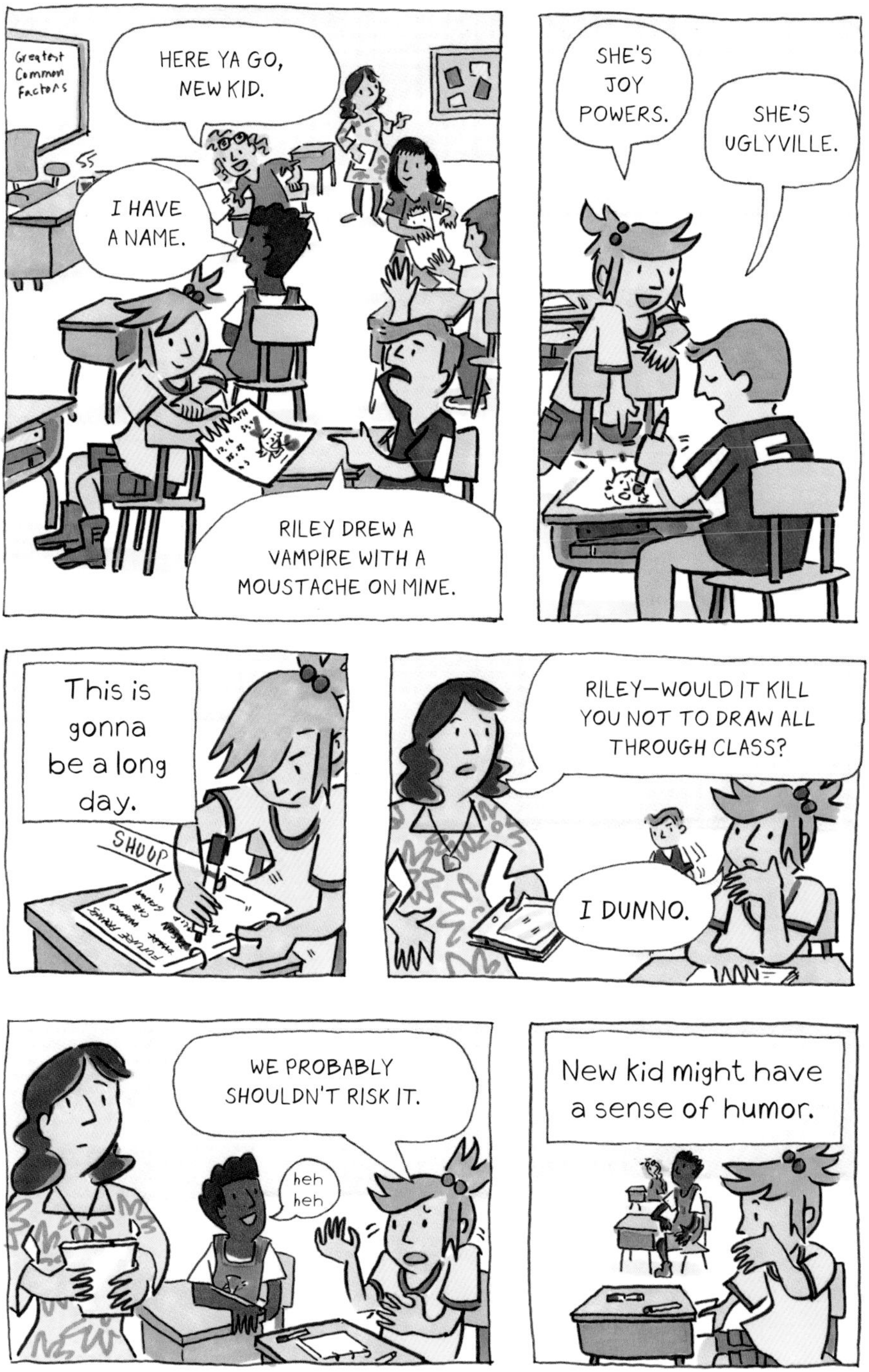
Greatest Common Factors
HERE YA GO, NEW KID.
I HAVE A NAME.
RILEY DREW A VAMPIRE WITH A MOUSTACHE ON MINE.
SHE'S JOY POWERS.
SHE'S UGLYVILLE.
This is gonna be a long day.
SHOOP
RILEY—WOULD IT KILL YOU NOT TO DRAW ALL THROUGH CLASS?
I DUNNO.
WE PROBABLY SHOULDN'T RISK IT.
heh heh
New kid might have a sense of humor.

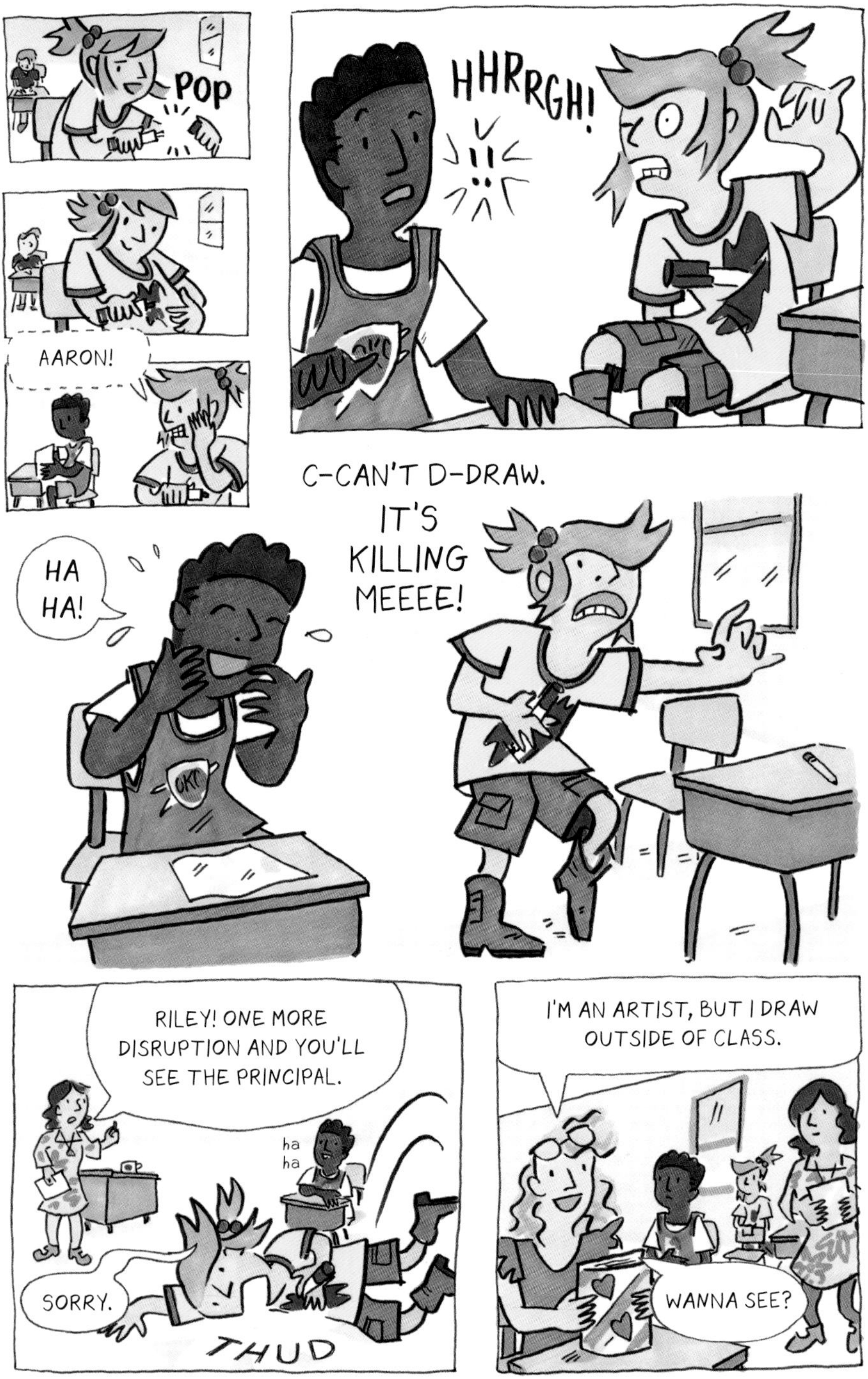
POP
AARON!
HHRRGH!
C-CAN'T D-DRAW.
IT'S KILLING MEEEE!
HA HA!
RILEY! ONE MORE DISRUPTION AND YOU'LL SEE THE PRINCIPAL.
ha ha
SORRY.
THUD
I'M AN ARTIST, BUT I DRAW OUTSIDE OF CLASS.
WANNA SEE?

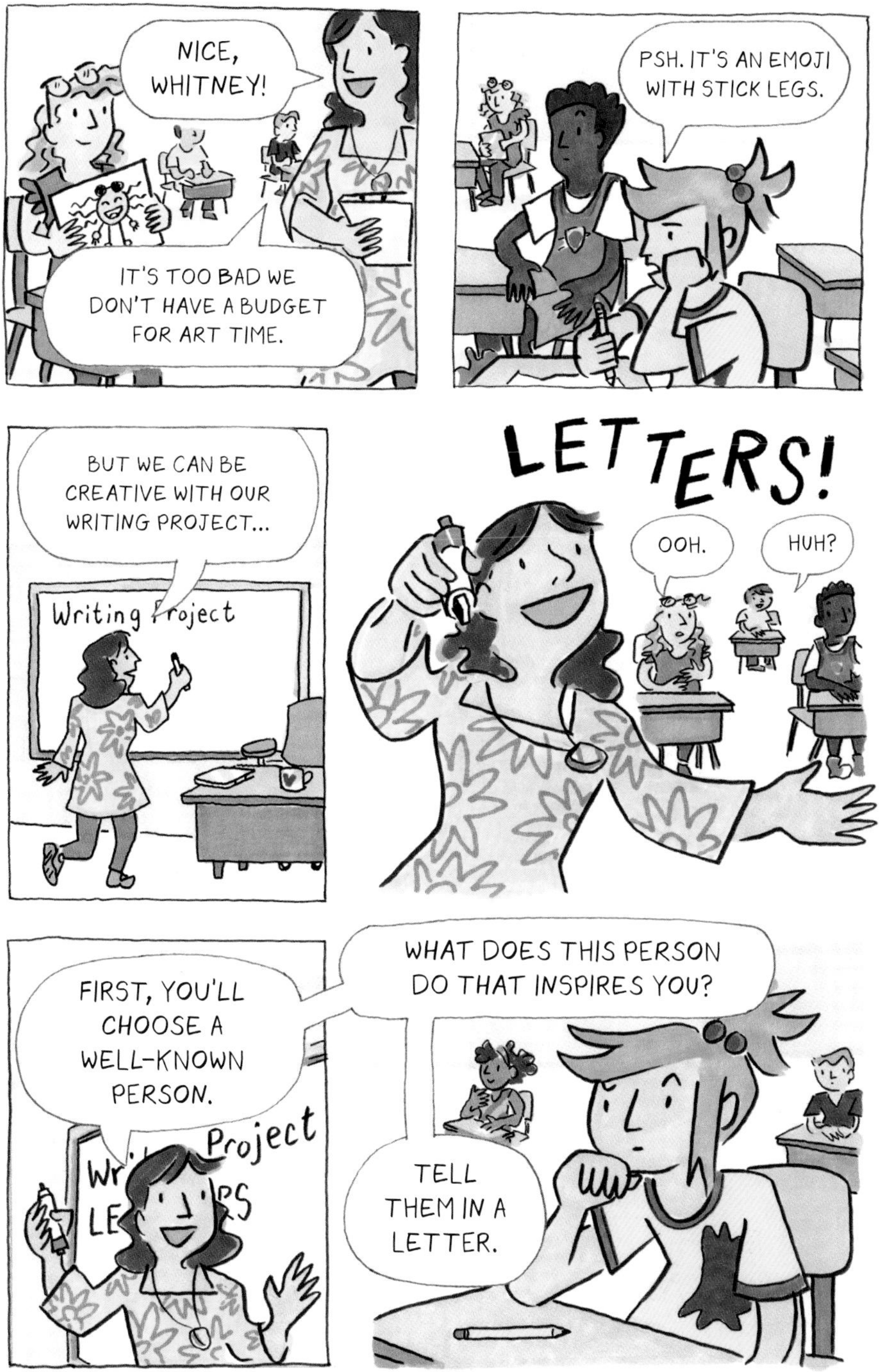
NICE, WHITNEY!
IT'S TOO BAD WE DON'T HAVE A BUDGET FOR ART TIME.
PSH. IT'S AN EMOJI WITH STICK LEGS.
BUT WE CAN BE CREATIVE WITH OUR WRITING PROJECT...
Writing Project
LETTERS!
OOH.
HUH?
FIRST, YOU'LL CHOOSE A WELL-KNOWN PERSON.
Project
WHAT DOES THIS PERSON DO THAT INSPIRES YOU?
TELL THEM IN A LETTER.

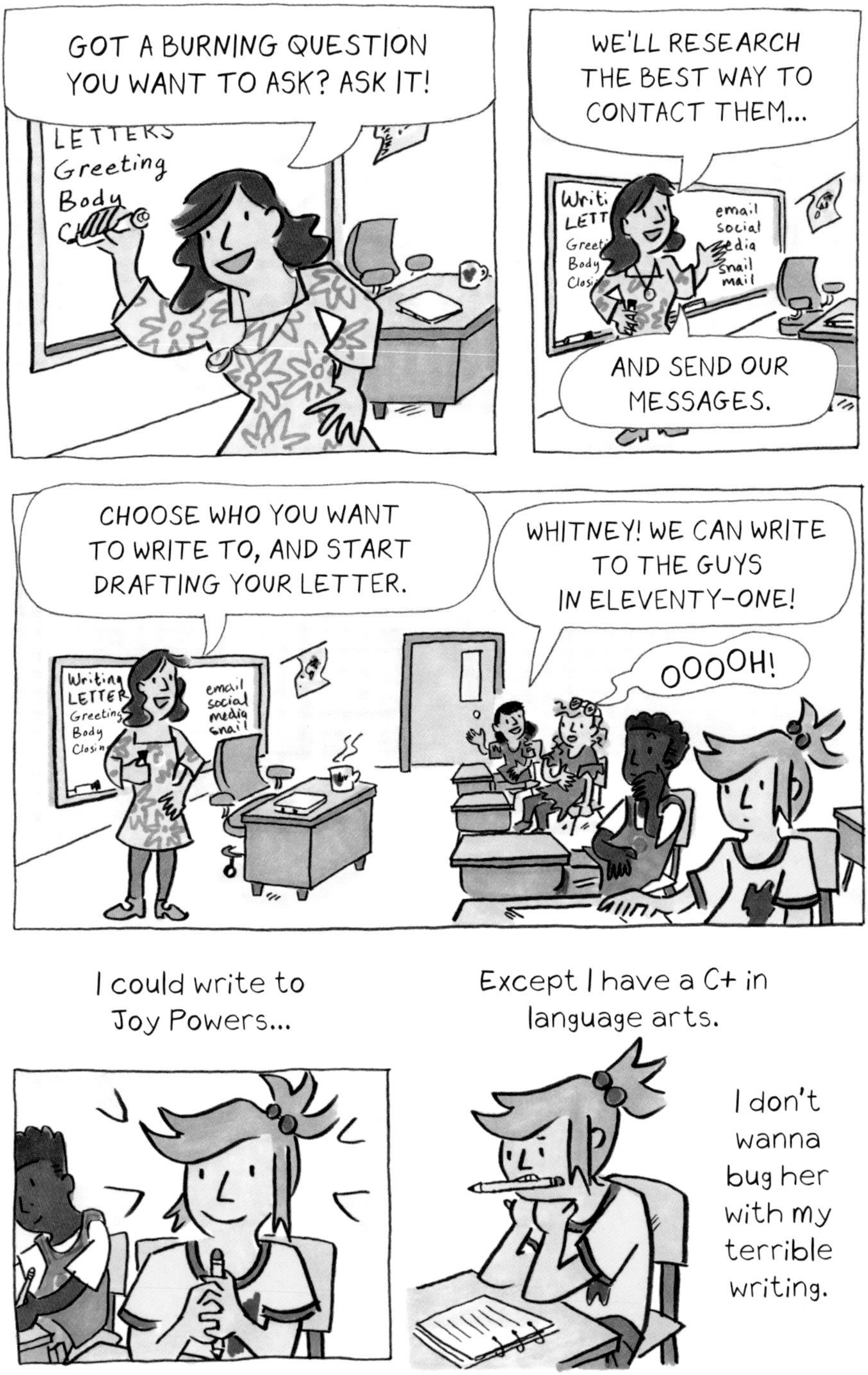
GOT A BURNING QUESTION YOU WANT TO ASK? ASK IT!
Greeting
Body
WE'LL RESEARCH THE BEST WAY TO CONTACT THEM...
email
social
media
snail
mail
AND SEND OUR MESSAGES.
CHOOSE WHO YOU WANT TO WRITE TO, AND START DRAFTING YOUR LETTER.
WHITNEY! WE CAN WRITE TO THE GUYS IN ELEVENTY-ONE!
OOOOH!
I could write to Joy Powers...
Except I have a C+ in language arts.
I don't wanna bug her with my terrible writing.

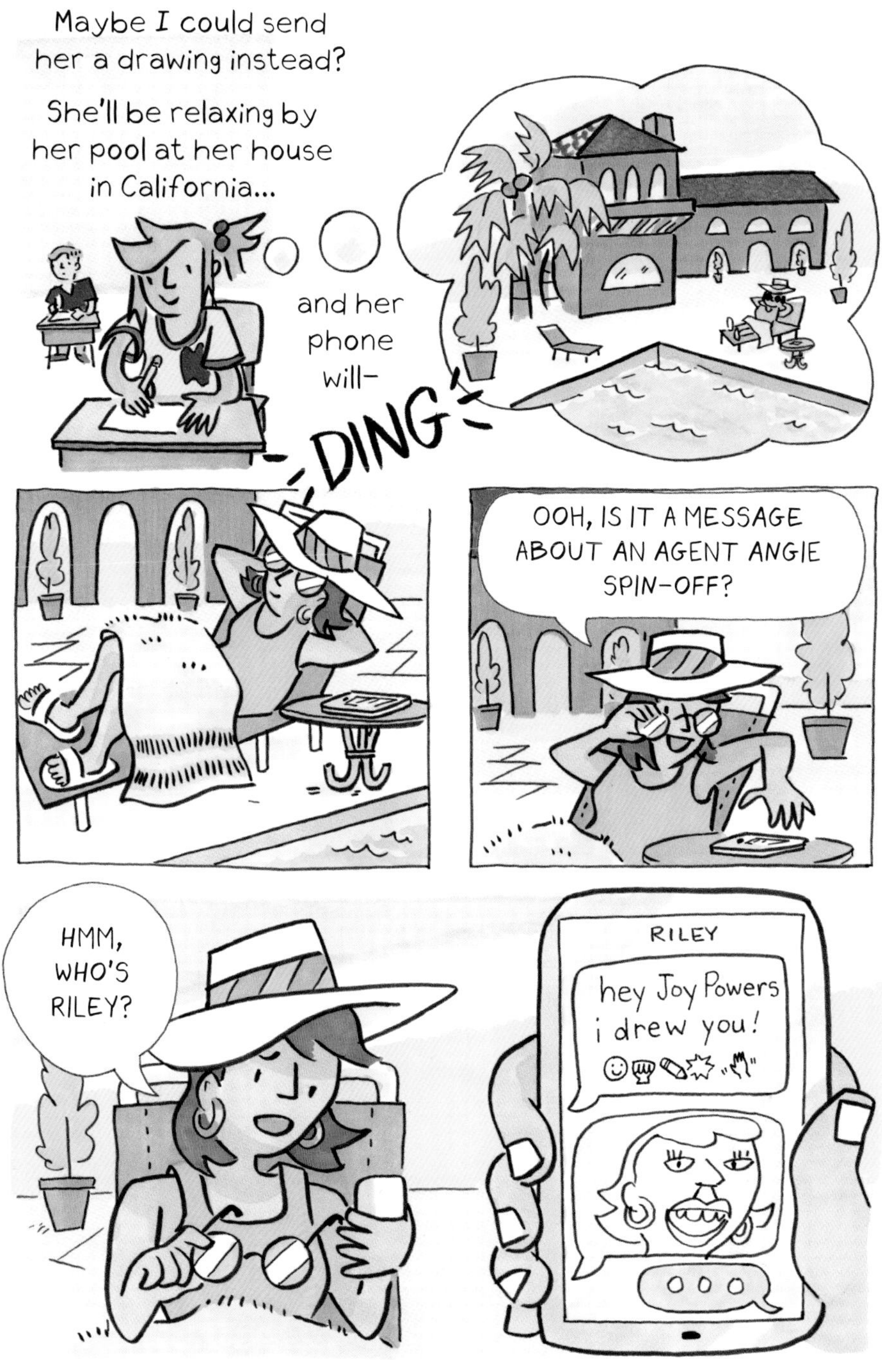
Maybe I could send her a drawing instead?
She'll be relaxing by her pool at her house in California...
and her phone will–
DING
OOH, IS IT A MESSAGE ABOUT AN AGENT ANGIE SPIN-OFF?
HMM, WHO'S RILEY?
RILEY
hey Joy Powers i drew you!

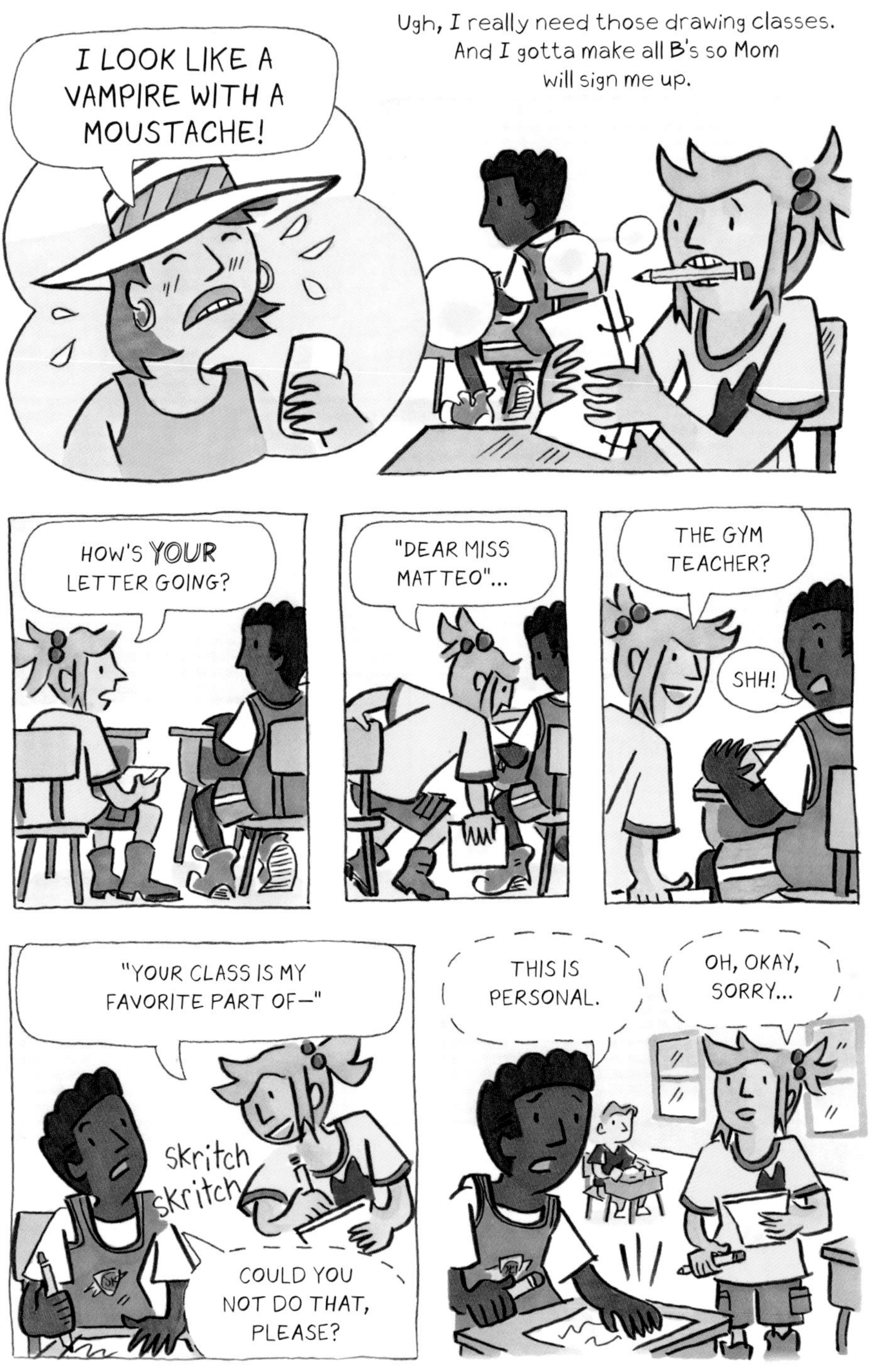
I LOOK LIKE A VAMPIRE WITH A MOUSTACHE!
Ugh, I really need those drawing classes. And I gotta make all B's so Mom will sign me up.
HOW'S YOUR LETTER GOING?
"DEAR MISS MATTEO"...
THE GYM TEACHER?
SHH!
"YOUR CLASS IS MY FAVORITE PART OF—"
skritch skritch
COULD YOU NOT DO THAT, PLEASE?
THIS IS PERSONAL.
OH, OKAY, SORRY...

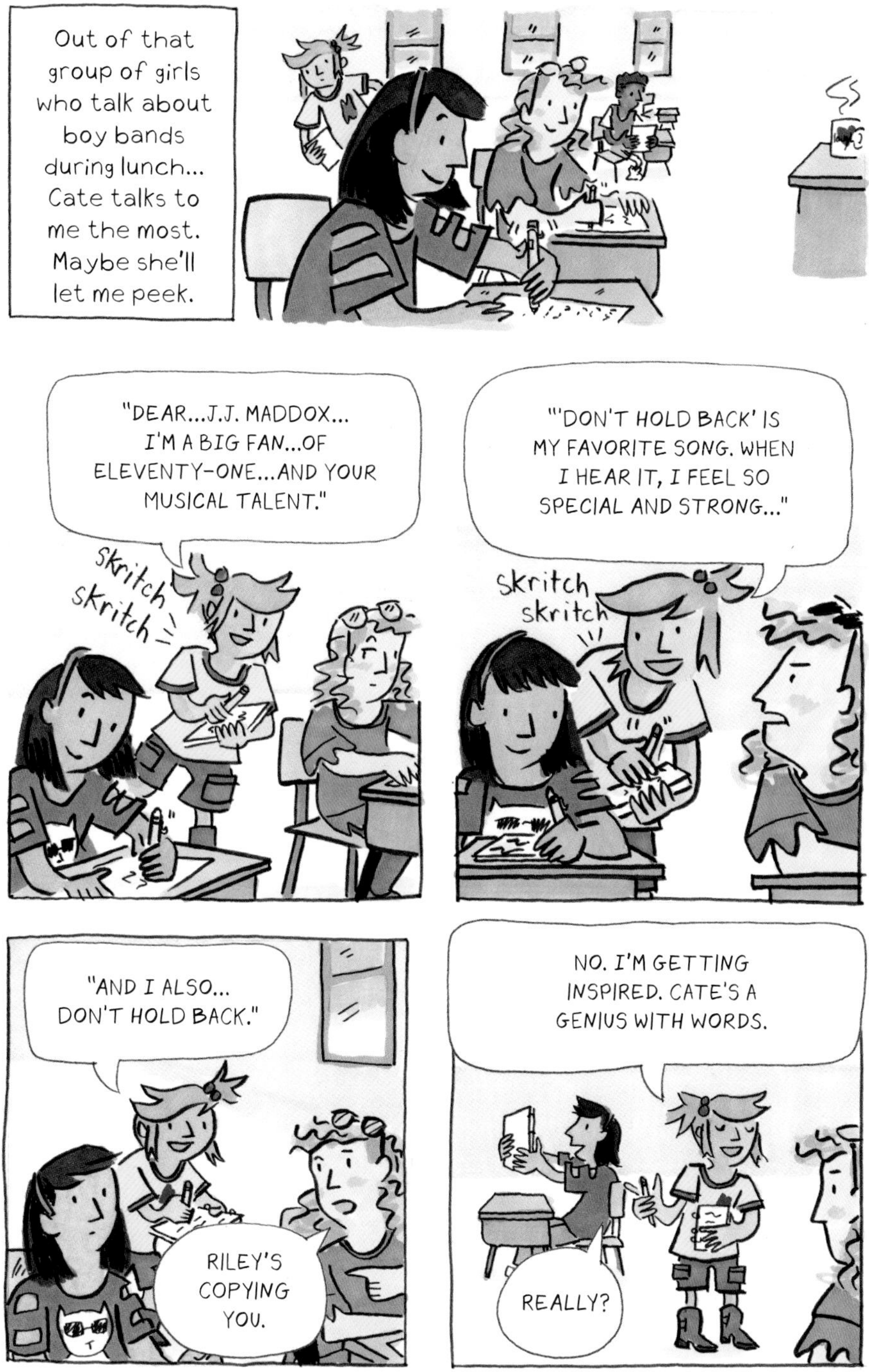
Out of that group of girls who talk about boy bands during lunch... Cate talks to me the most. Maybe she'll let me peek.
"DEAR...J.J. MADDOX... I'M A BIG FAN...OF ELEVENTY-ONE...AND YOUR MUSICAL TALENT."
Skritch skritch
"'DON'T HOLD BACK' IS MY FAVORITE SONG. WHEN I HEAR IT, I FEEL SO SPECIAL AND STRONG..."
skritch skritch
"AND I ALSO... DON'T HOLD BACK."
RILEY'S ALSO COPYING YOU.
NO. I'M GETTING INSPIRED. CATE'S A GENIUS WITH WORDS.
REALLY?

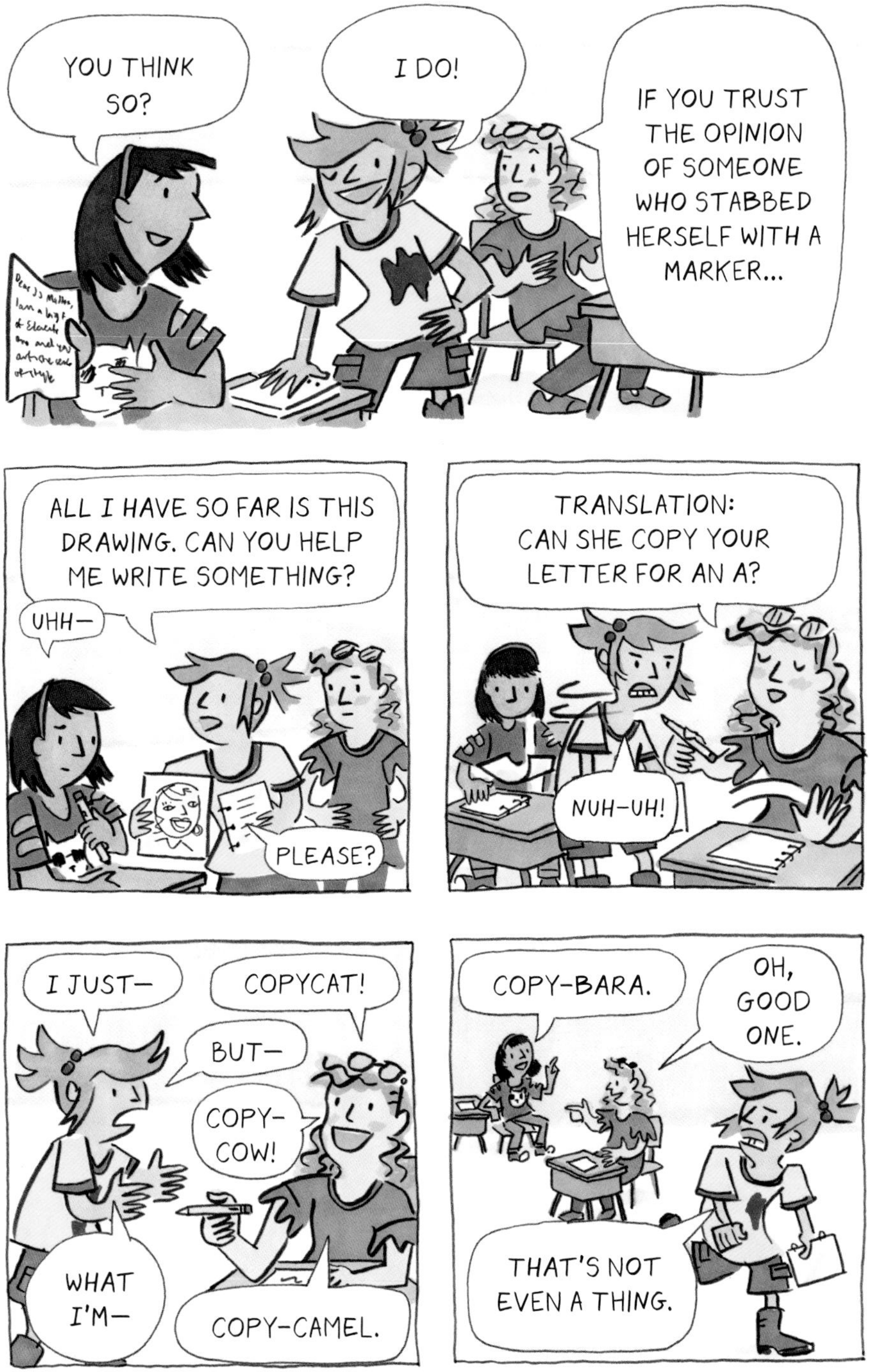
YOU THINK SO?
I DO!
IF YOU TRUST THE OPINION OF SOMEONE WHO STABBED HERSELF WITH A MARKER...
ALL I HAVE SO FAR IS THIS DRAWING. CAN YOU HELP ME WRITE SOMETHING?
UHH—
PLEASE?
TRANSLATION: CAN SHE COPY YOUR LETTER FOR AN A?
NUH-UH!
I JUST—
COPYCAT!
BUT—
COPY-COW!
WHAT I'M—
COPY-CAMEL.
COPY-BARA.
OH, GOOD ONE.
THAT'S NOT EVEN A THING.

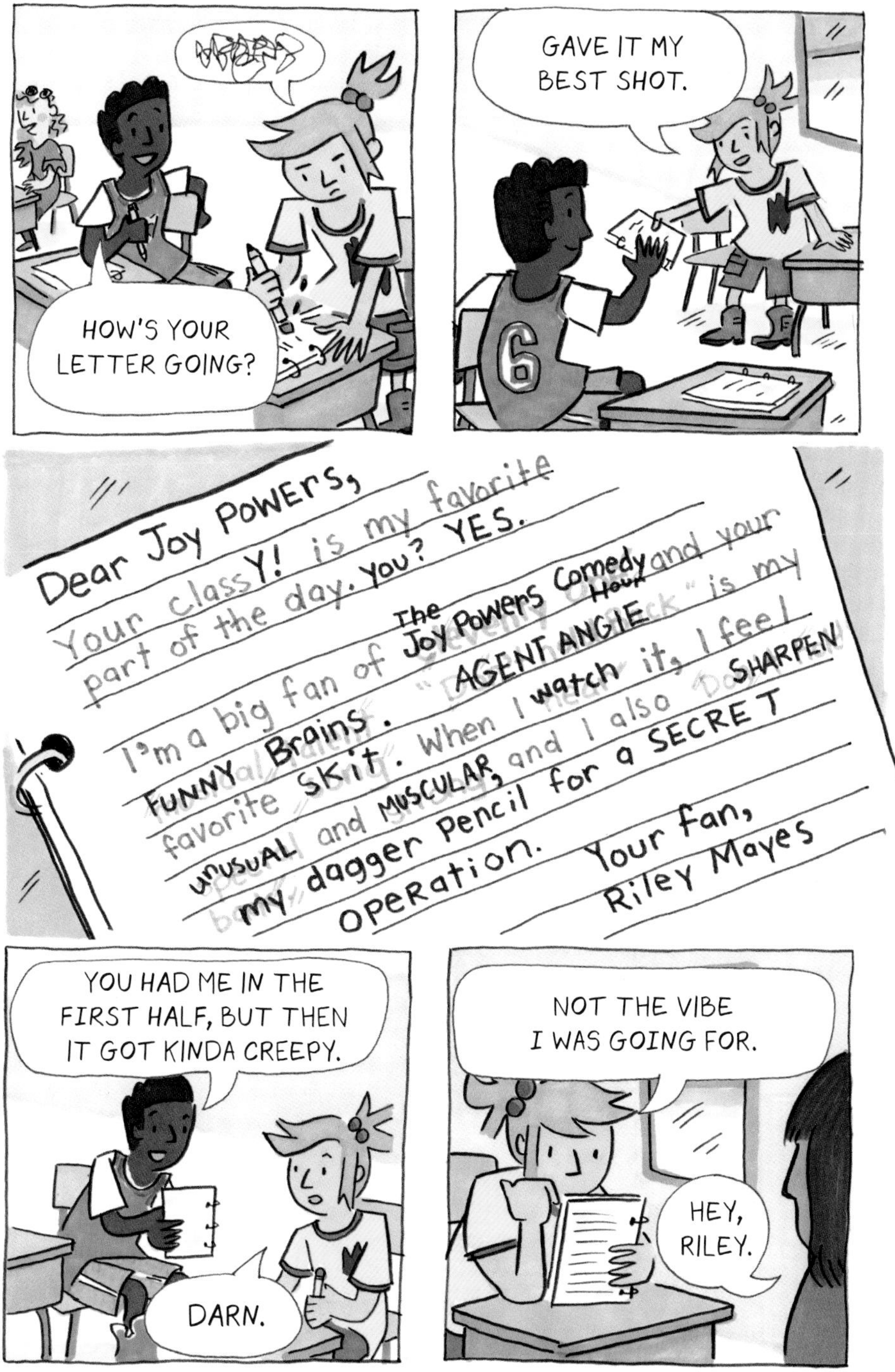
HOW'S YOUR LETTER GOING?
GAVE IT MY BEST SHOT.
Dear Joy Powers,
Your classY! is my favorite
part of the day. You? YES.
I'm a big fan of The Joy Powers Comedy Hour and your
FUNNY Brains. AGENT ANGIE is my
favorite SKIT. When I watch it, I feel
UNUSUAL and MUSCULAR, and I also SHARPEN
my dagger pencil for a SECRET
OPERATION.
Your fan,
Riley Mayes
YOU HAD ME IN THE FIRST HALF, BUT THEN IT GOT KINDA CREEPY.
DARN.
NOT THE VIBE I WAS GOING FOR.
HEY, RILEY.

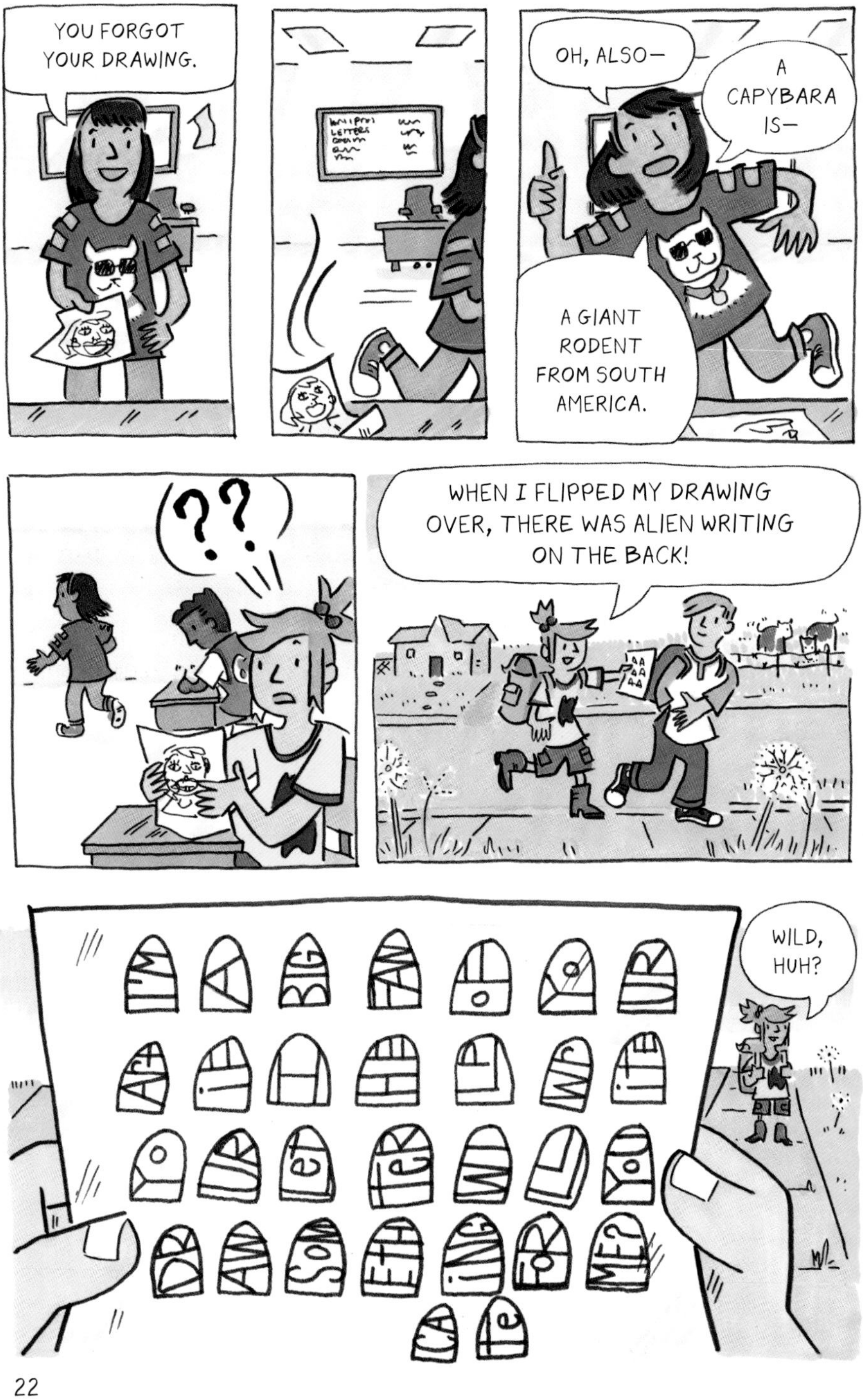
YOU FORGOT YOUR DRAWING.
OH, ALSO—
A CAPYBARA IS—
A GIANT RODENT FROM SOUTH AMERICA.
??
WHEN I FLIPPED MY DRAWING OVER, THERE WAS ALIEN WRITING ON THE BACK!
WILD, HUH?

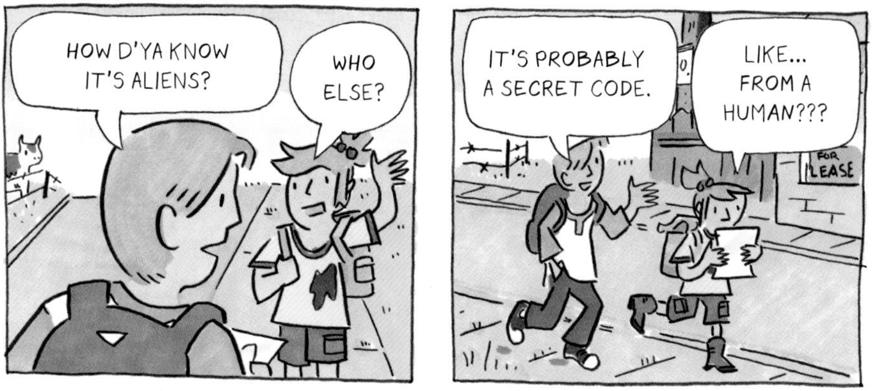
HOW D'YA KNOW IT'S ALIENS?
WHO ELSE?
IT'S PROBABLY A SECRET CODE.
LIKE... FROM A HUMAN???
FOR LEASE

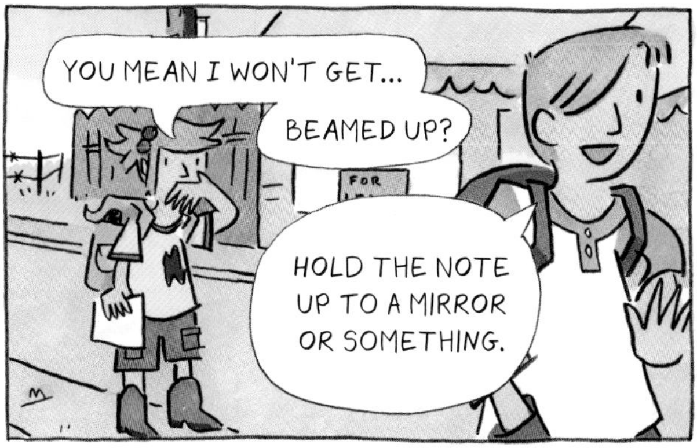
YOU MEAN I WON'T GET...
BEAMED UP?
HOLD THE NOTE UP TO A MIRROR OR SOMETHING.

Who had the time to write a code on my drawing?

What if it says something mean?

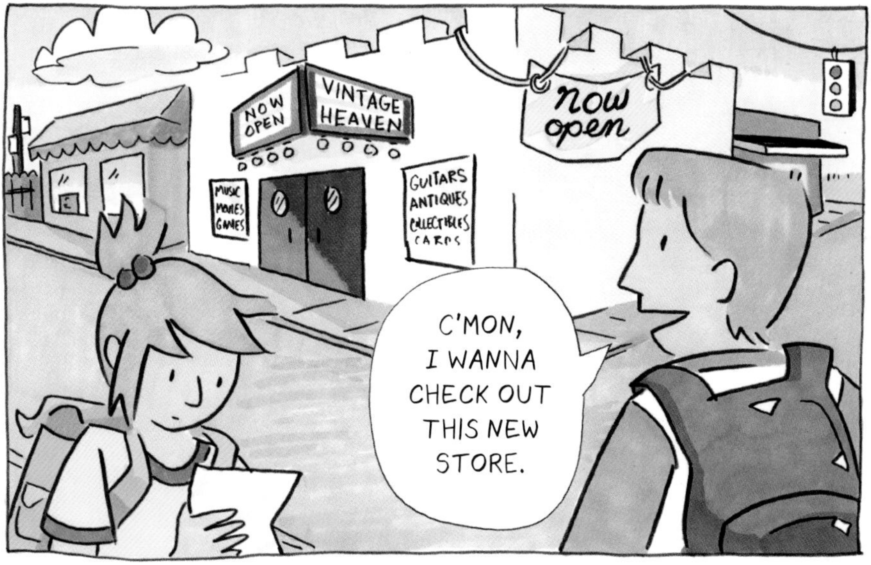
NOW OPEN
VINTAGE HEAVEN
MUSIC MOVIES GAMES
GUITARS ANTIQUES COLLECTIBLES CARDS
now open
C'MON, I WANNA CHECK OUT THIS NEW STORE.

CHAPTER 3

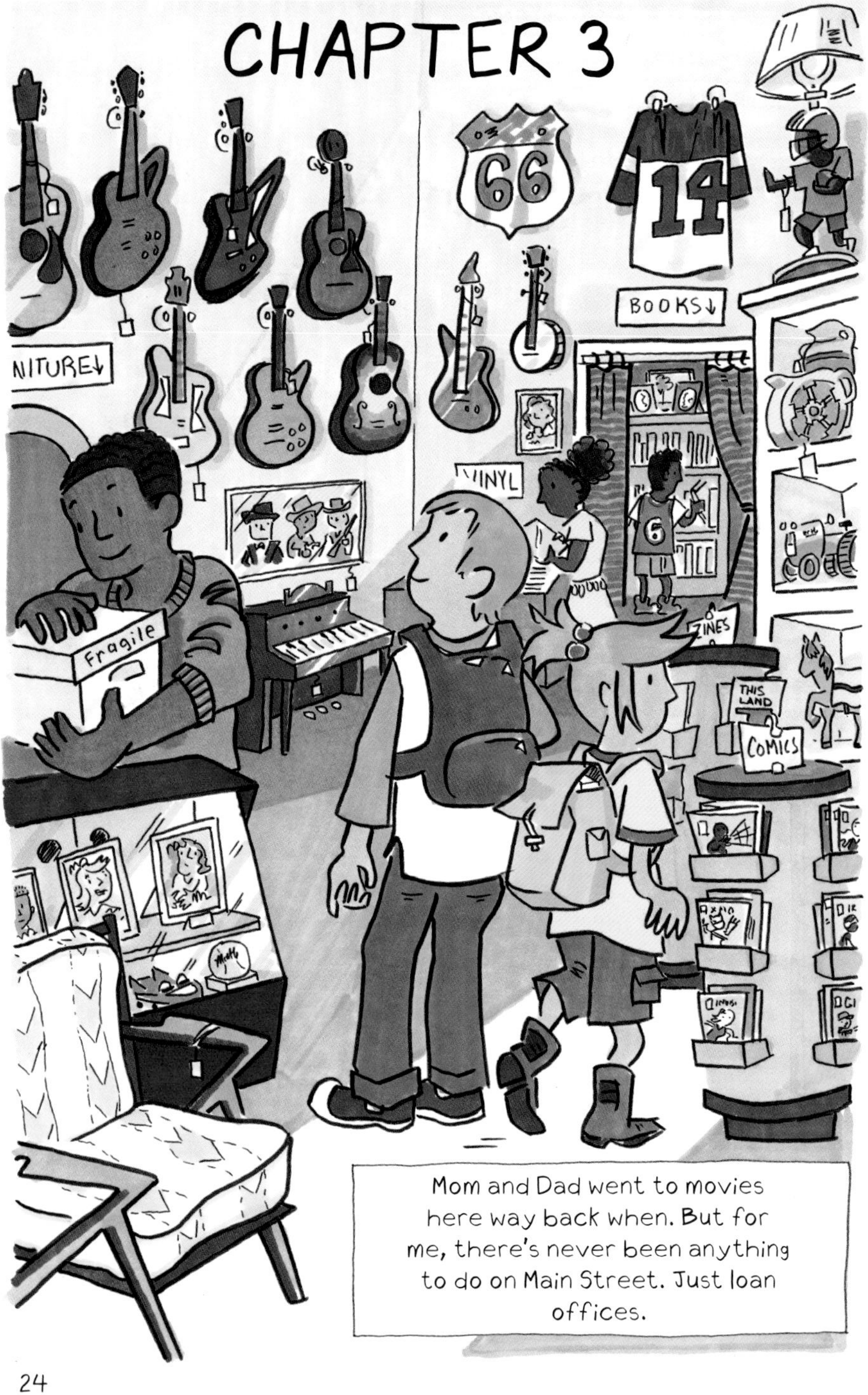
66
14
NITURE↓
BOOKS↓
VINYL
6
Fragile
ZINES
THIS LAND
COMICS
Mom and Dad went to movies here way back when. But for me, there's never been anything to do on Main Street. Just loan offices.

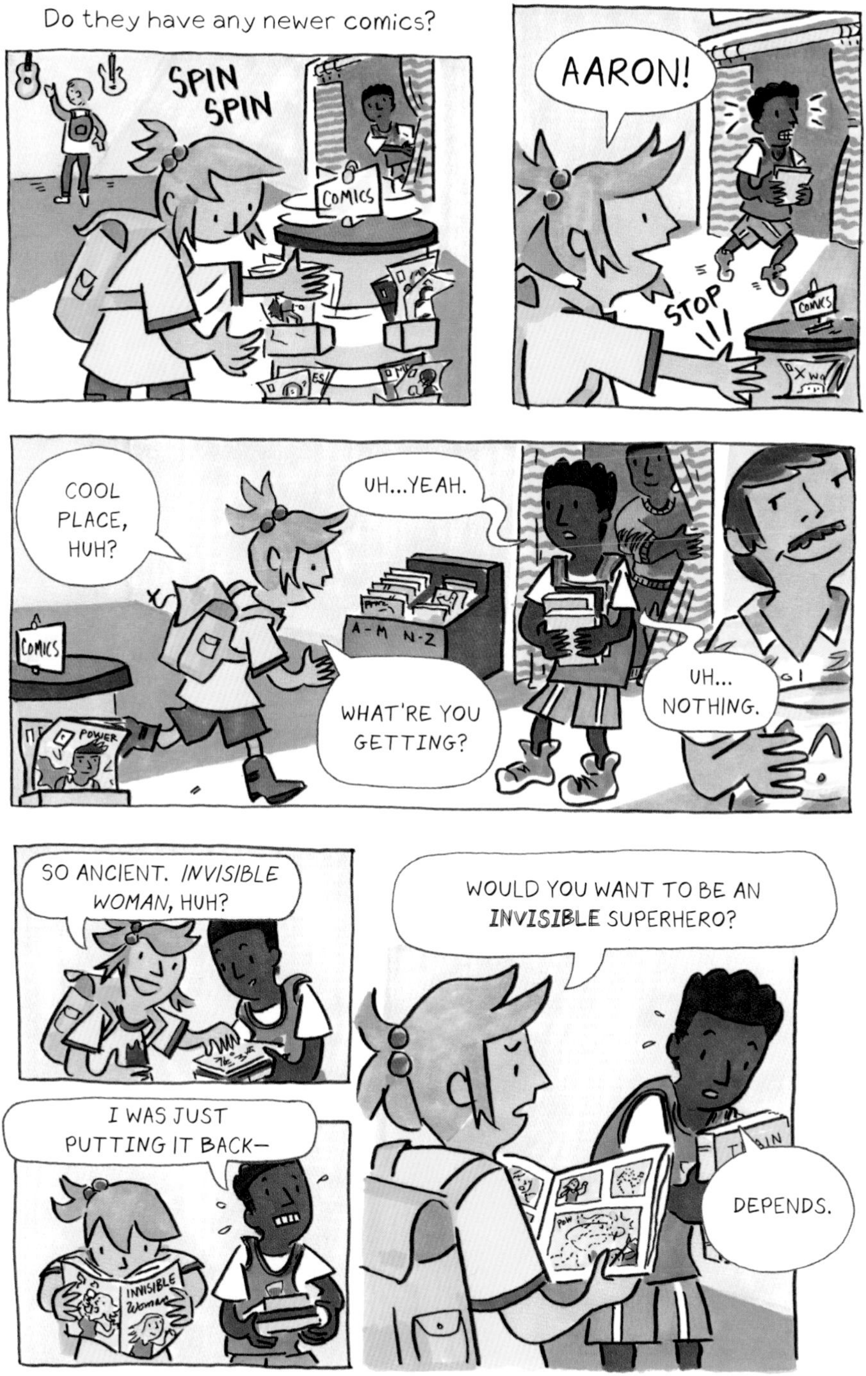
Do they have any newer comics?
SPIN SPIN
COMICS
AARON!
STOP
COMICS
COOL PLACE, HUH?
UH...YEAH.
COMICS
A-M N-Z
POWER
WHAT'RE YOU GETTING?
UH... NOTHING.
SO ANCIENT. *INVISIBLE WOMAN*, HUH?
I WAS JUST PUTTING IT BACK—
INVISIBLE Woman
WOULD YOU WANT TO BE AN INVISIBLE SUPERHERO?
POW
DEPENDS.

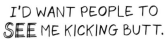

I'D WANT PEOPLE TO **SEE** ME KICKING BUTT.

POW

WHO'S YOUR FRIEND, AARON?

UHRR

OOH, INTRODUCE US, PLEASE!

INVISIBLE Worm

FRIEND?

THIS IS RILEY. SHE SITS NEXT TO ME AT SCHOOL.

HI, RILEY! I'M TREY, AARON'S DAD.

AND I'M AARON'S OTHER DAD, JOE.

HOPE YOU LIKE OUR STORE.

'SCUSE ME— HOW MUCH?

SEE YA, RILEY...

YOUR DADS ARE **GAY.**

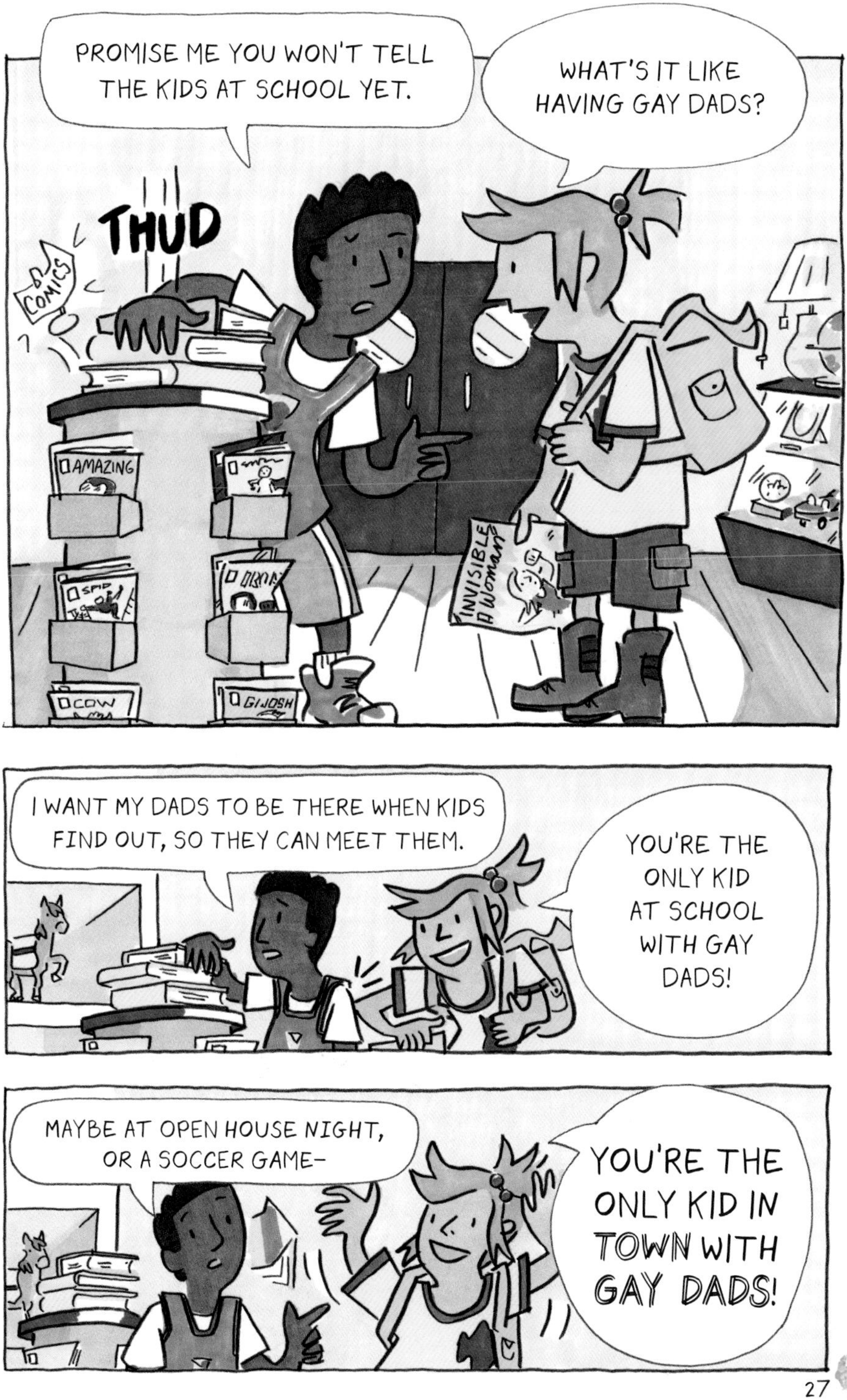
PROMISE ME YOU WON'T TELL THE KIDS AT SCHOOL YET.
WHAT'S IT LIKE HAVING GAY DADS?
THUD
COMICS
AMAZING
SPID
GIJOSH
COW
INVISIBLE WOMAN
I WANT MY DADS TO BE THERE WHEN KIDS FIND OUT, SO THEY CAN MEET THEM.
YOU'RE THE ONLY KID AT SCHOOL WITH GAY DADS!
MAYBE AT OPEN HOUSE NIGHT, OR A SOCCER GAME–
YOU'RE THE ONLY KID IN TOWN WITH GAY DADS!

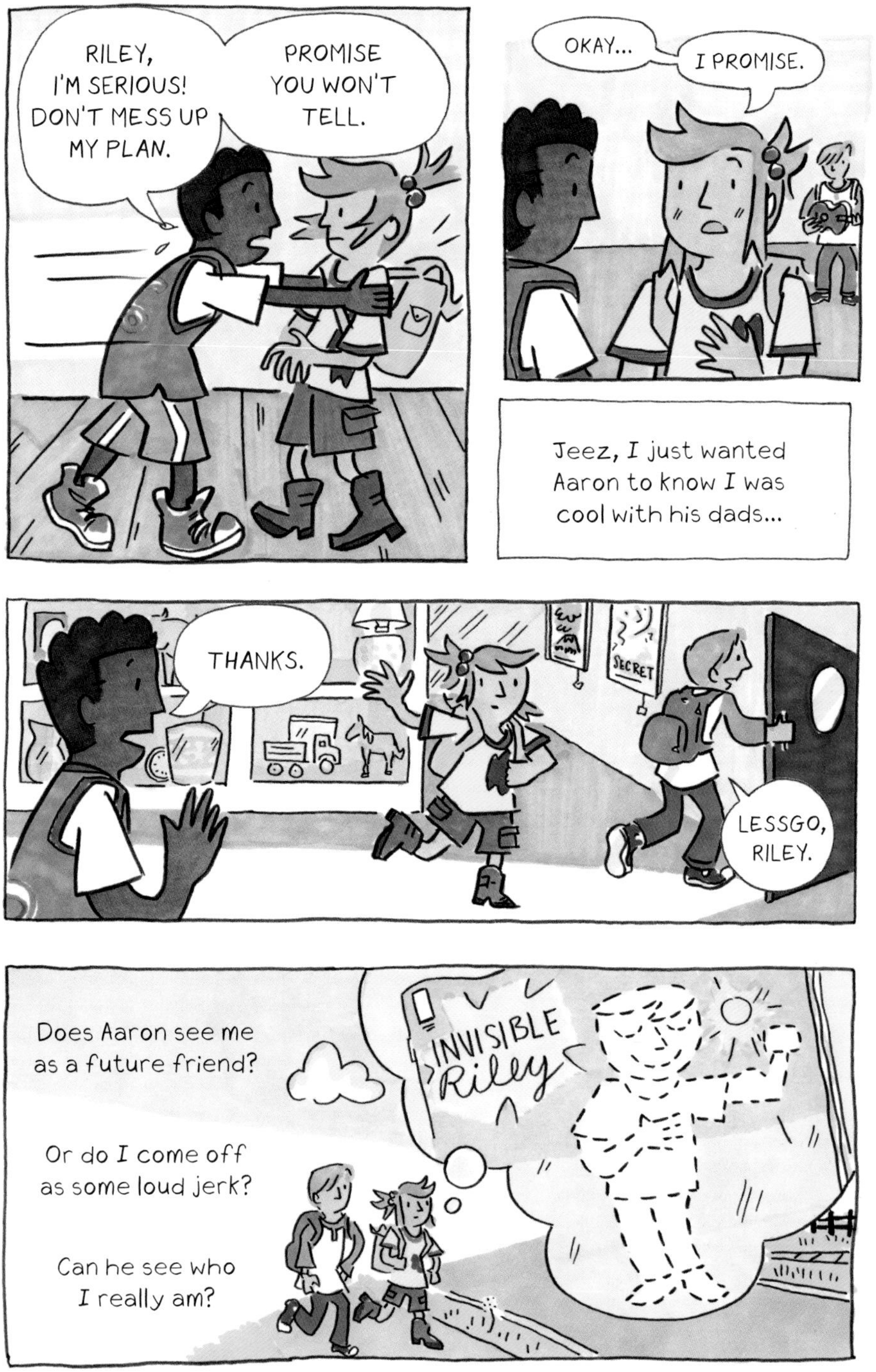
RILEY,
I'M SERIOUS!
DON'T MESS UP
MY PLAN.
PROMISE
YOU WON'T
TELL.
OKAY...
I PROMISE.
Jeez, I just wanted
Aaron to know I was
cool with his dads...
THANKS.
SECRET
LESSGO,
RILEY.
Does Aaron see me
as a future friend?
INVISIBLE
Riley
Or do I come off
as some loud jerk?
Can he see who
I really am?

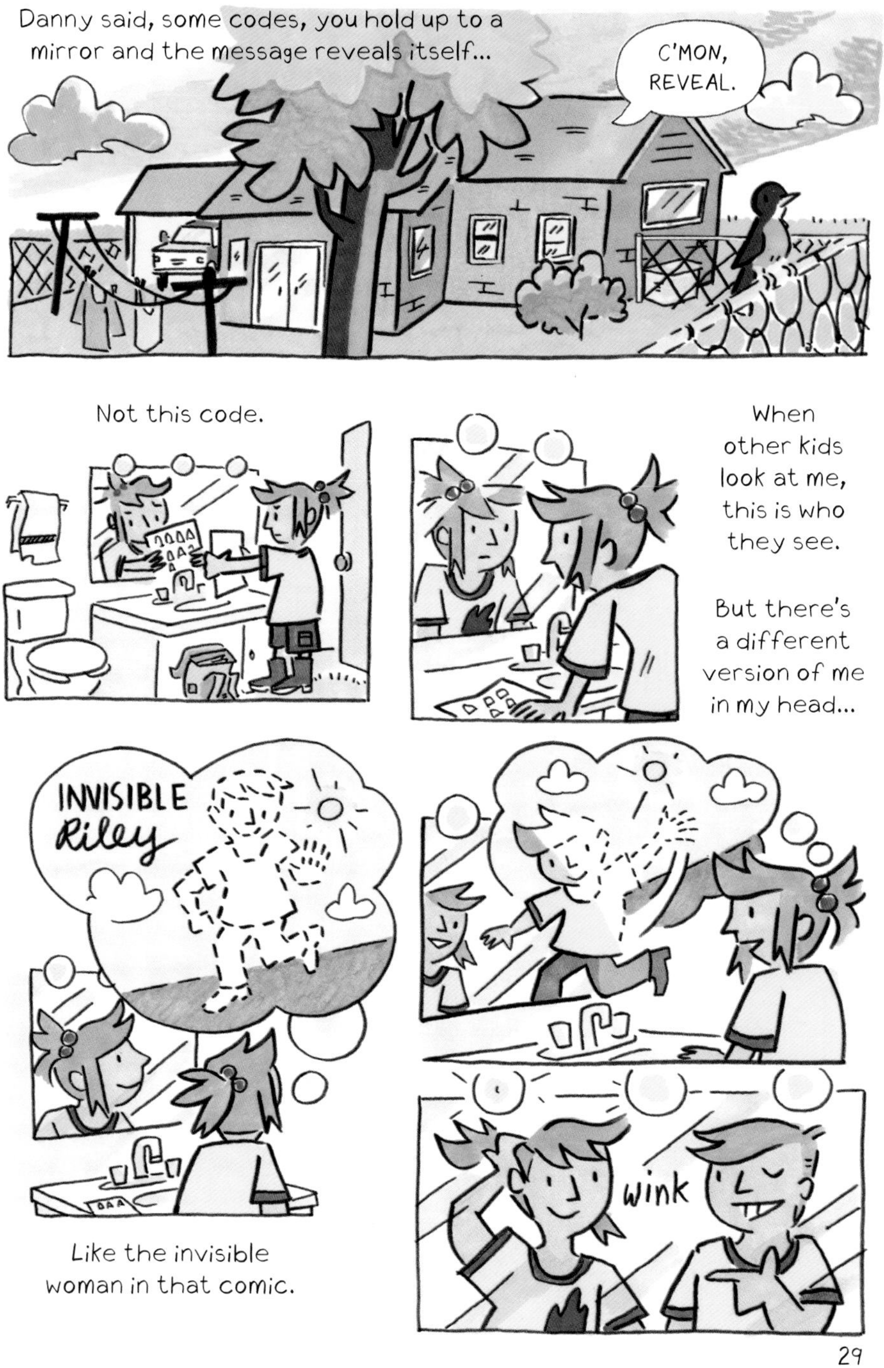

Danny said, some codes, you hold up to a mirror and the message reveals itself...
C'MON, REVEAL.
Not this code.
When other kids look at me, this is who they see.
But there's a different version of me in my head...
INVISIBLE Riley
Like the invisible woman in that comic.
wink

I see her all day, but no one else does.

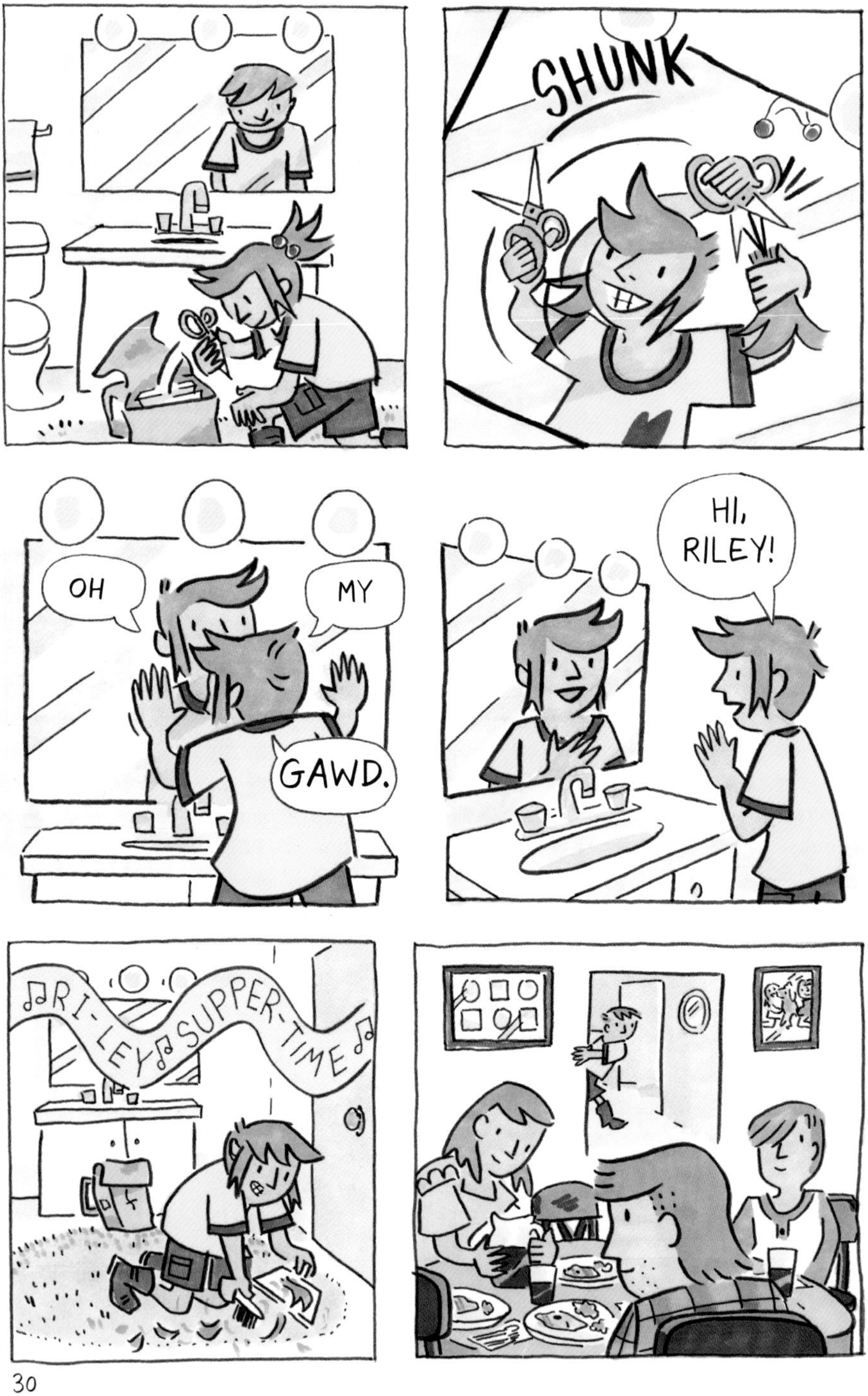
SHUNK
OH
MY
GAWD.
HI, RILEY!
RI-LEY SUPPER-TIME

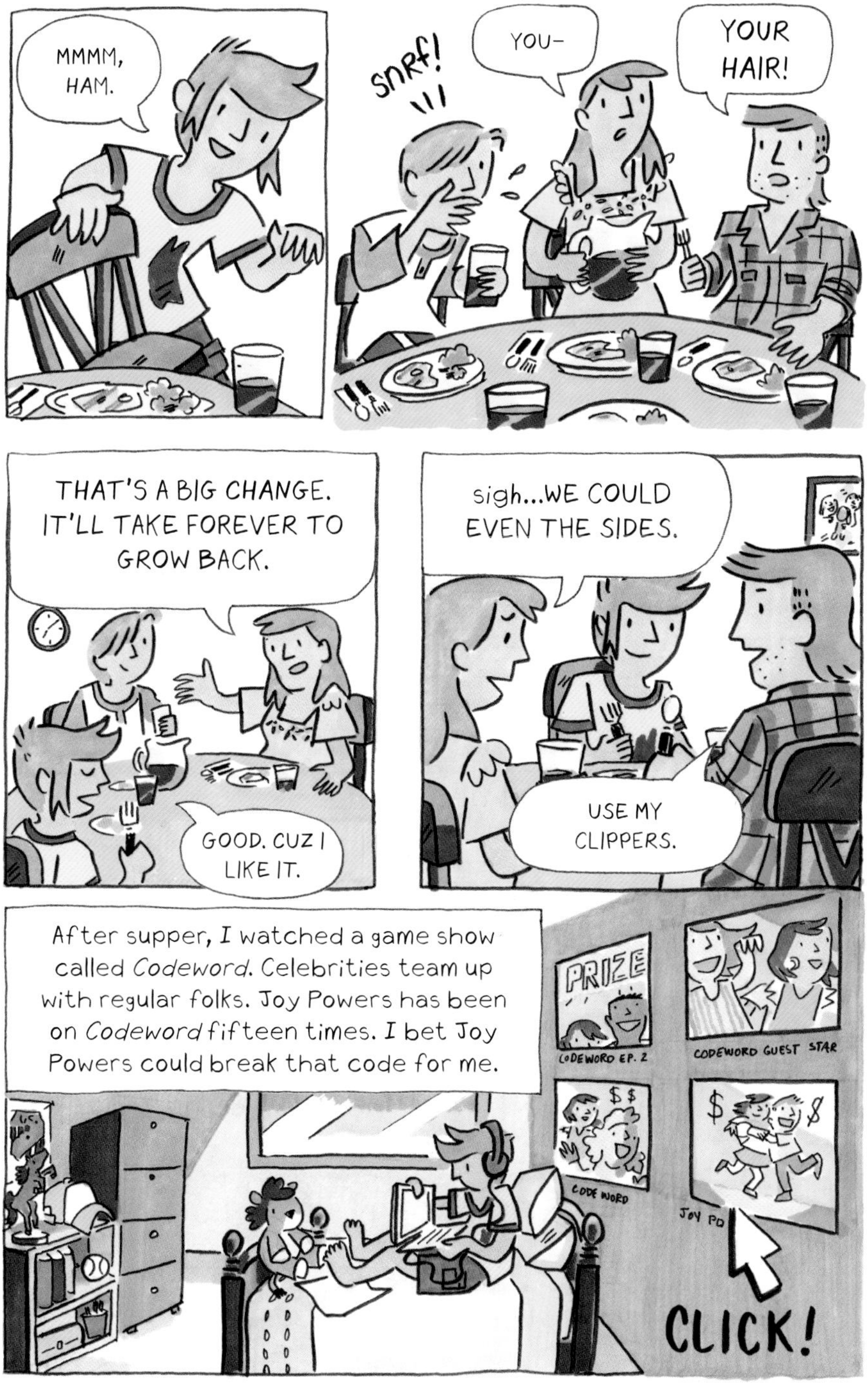
MMMM, HAM.
snrf!
YOU-
YOUR HAIR!
THAT'S A BIG CHANGE. IT'LL TAKE FOREVER TO GROW BACK.
GOOD. CUZ I LIKE IT.
sigh...WE COULD EVEN THE SIDES.
USE MY CLIPPERS.
After supper, I watched a game show called *Codeword*. Celebrities team up with regular folks. Joy Powers has been on *Codeword* fifteen times. I bet Joy Powers could break that code for me.
PRIZE
CODEWORD EP. 2
CODEWORD GUEST STAR
CODE WORD
JOY PO
CLICK!

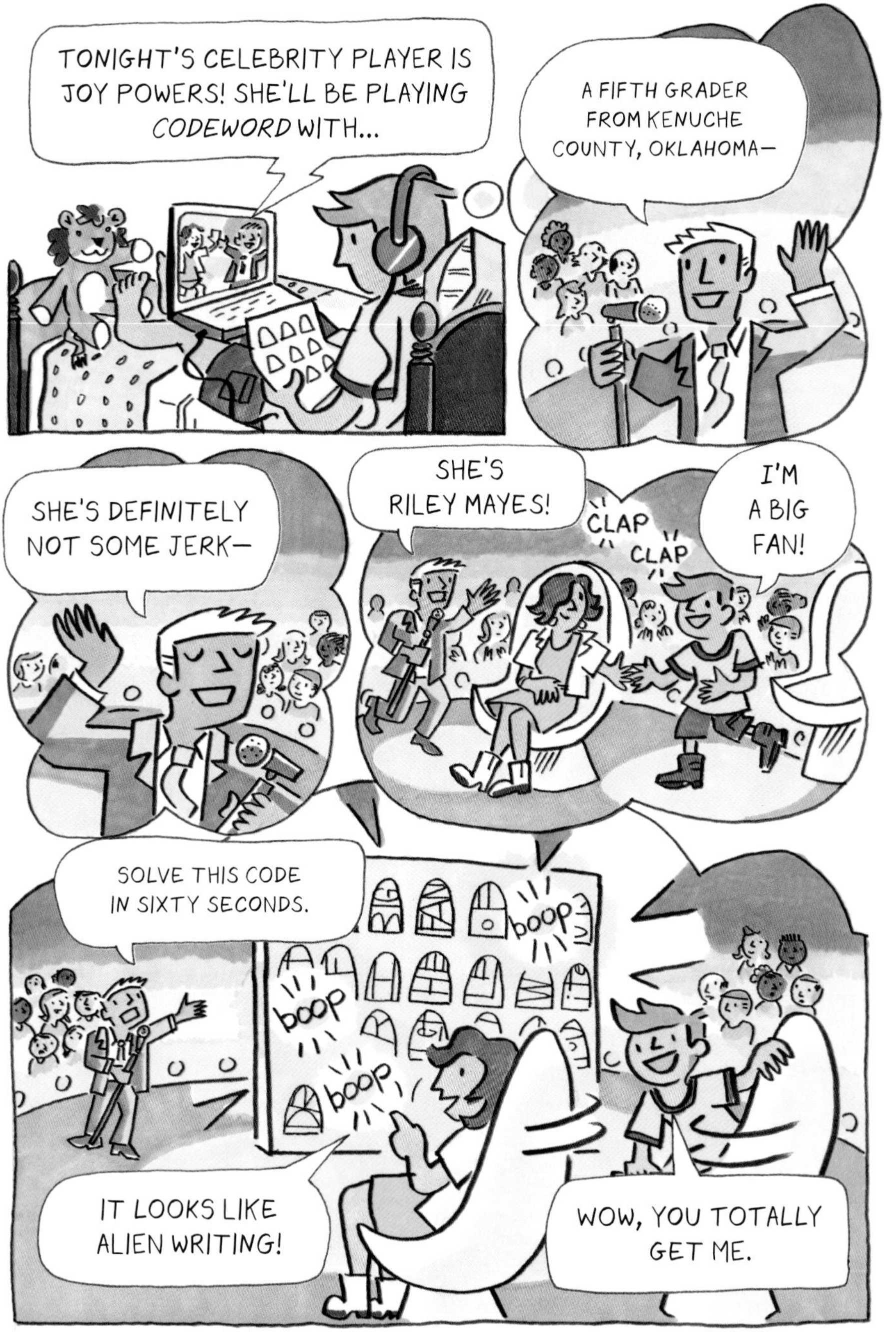
TONIGHT'S CELEBRITY PLAYER IS JOY POWERS! SHE'LL BE PLAYING *CODEWORD* WITH...
A FIFTH GRADER FROM KENUCHE COUNTY, OKLAHOMA—
SHE'S DEFINITELY NOT SOME JERK—
SHE'S RILEY MAYES!
CLAP
CLAP
I'M A BIG FAN!
SOLVE THIS CODE IN SIXTY SECONDS.
boop
boop
boop
IT LOOKS LIKE ALIEN WRITING!
WOW, YOU TOTALLY GET ME.

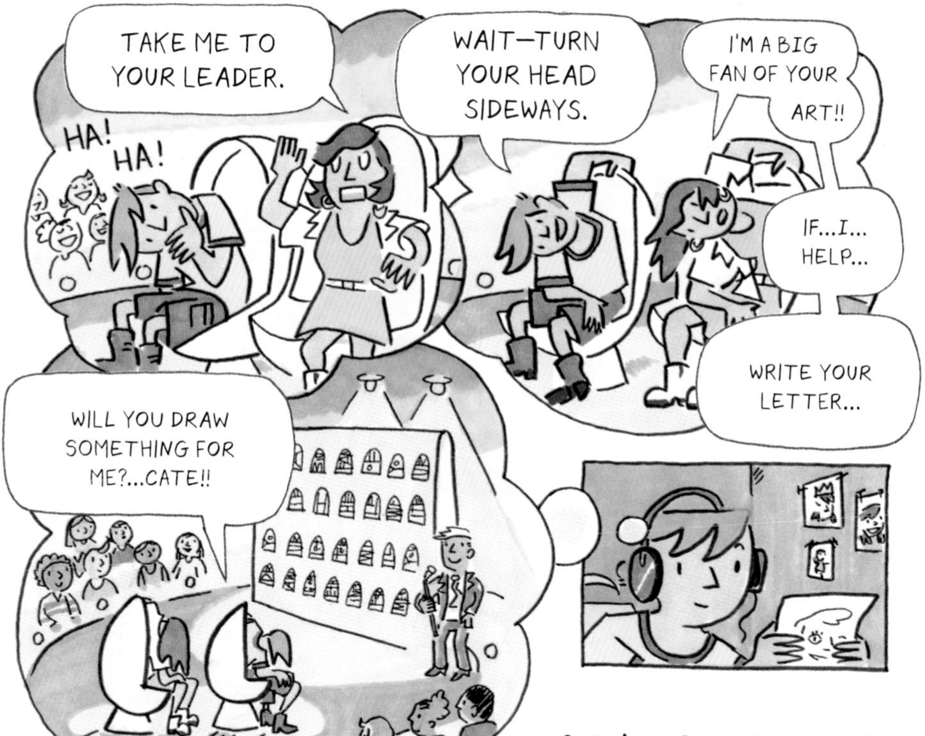

TAKE ME TO YOUR LEADER.
HA! HA!
WAIT—TURN YOUR HEAD SIDEWAYS.
I'M A BIG FAN OF YOUR ART!!
IF...I... HELP...
WRITE YOUR LETTER...
WILL YOU DRAW SOMETHING FOR ME?...CATE!!

Cate's a fan of my art?

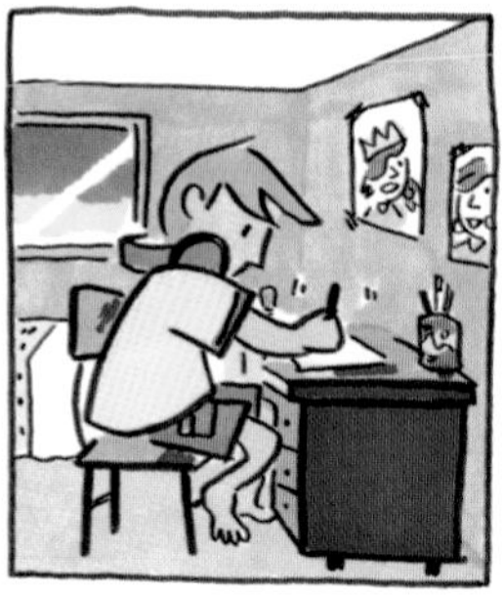

I wonder what she wants me to draw?

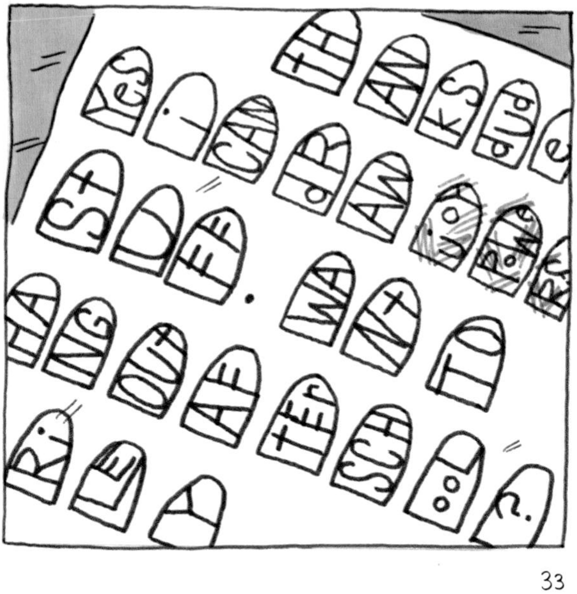

CHAPTER 4

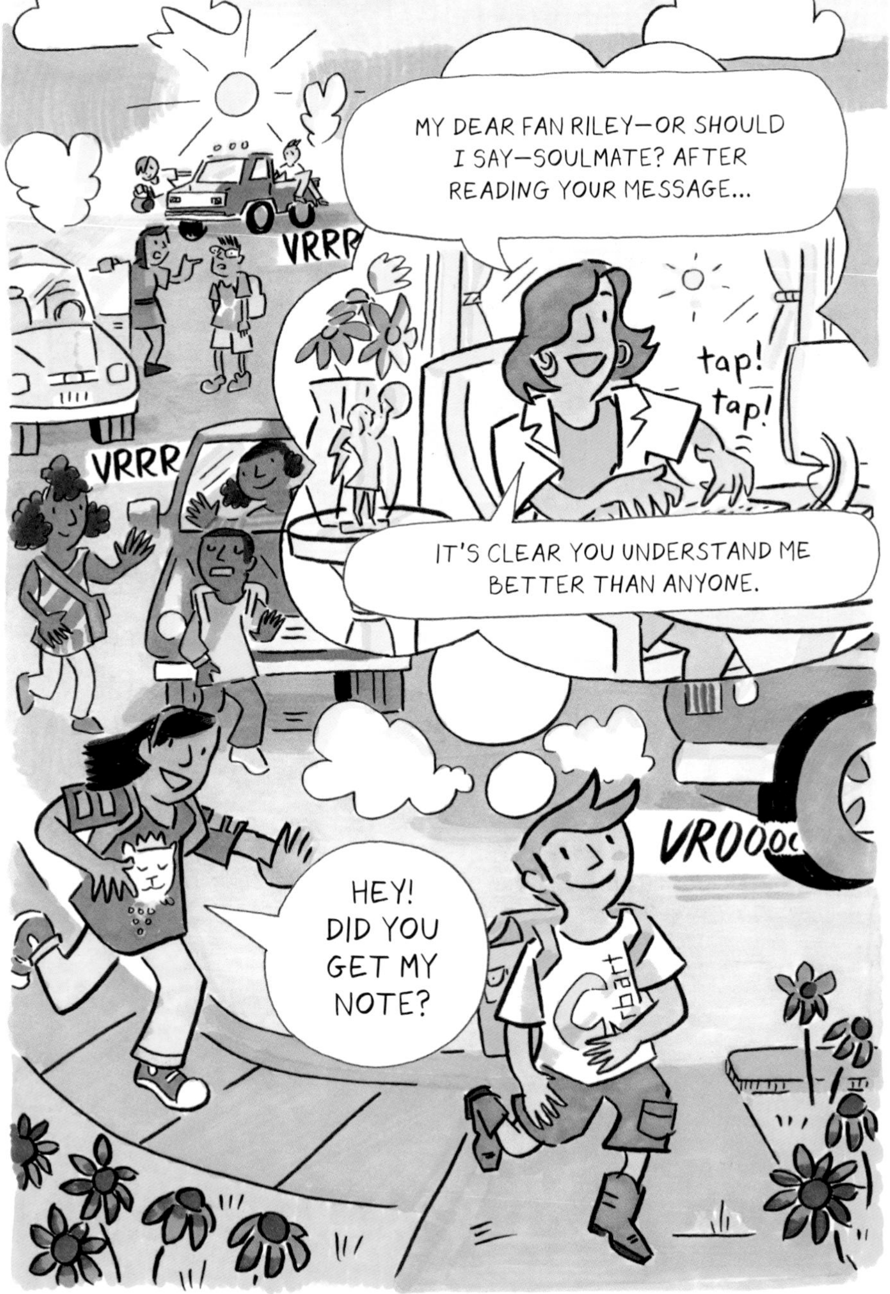
VRRR
VRRR
MY DEAR FAN RILEY—OR SHOULD I SAY—SOULMATE? AFTER READING YOUR MESSAGE...
tap! tap!
IT'S CLEAR YOU UNDERSTAND ME BETTER THAN ANYONE.
VROOO
HEY! DID YOU GET MY NOTE?

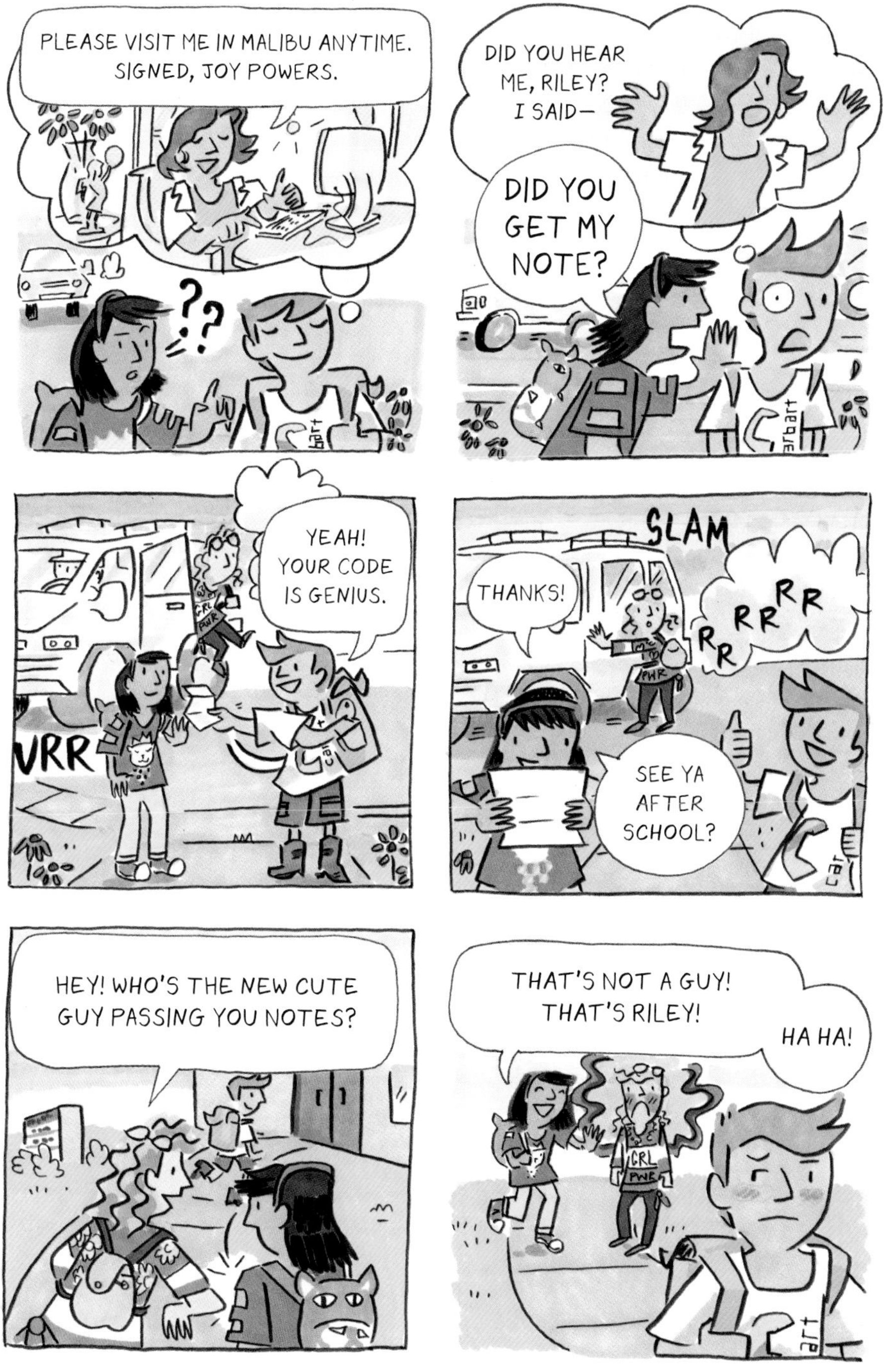
PLEASE VISIT ME IN MALIBU ANYTIME. SIGNED, JOY POWERS.
DID YOU HEAR ME, RILEY? I SAID—
DID YOU GET MY NOTE?
YEAH! YOUR CODE IS GENIUS.
VRR
SLAM
THANKS!
RRRRRR
SEE YA AFTER SCHOOL?
HEY! WHO'S THE NEW CUTE GUY PASSING YOU NOTES?
THAT'S NOT A GUY! THAT'S RILEY!
HA HA!

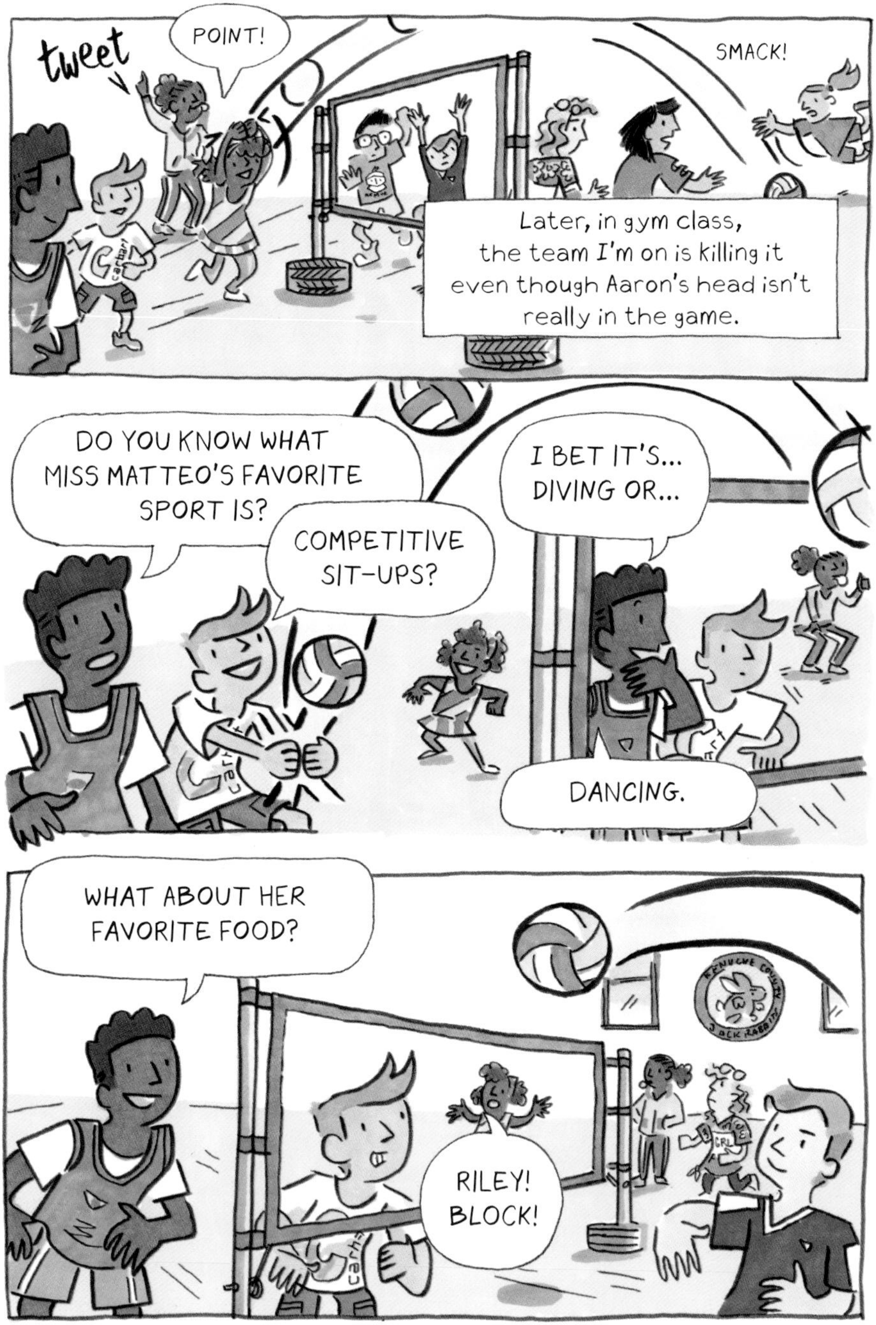
tweet
POINT!
SMACK!
Later, in gym class, the team I'm on is killing it even though Aaron's head isn't really in the game.
DO YOU KNOW WHAT MISS MATTEO'S FAVORITE SPORT IS?
COMPETITIVE SIT-UPS?
I BET IT'S... DIVING OR...
DANCING.
WHAT ABOUT HER FAVORITE FOOD?
RILEY! BLOCK!

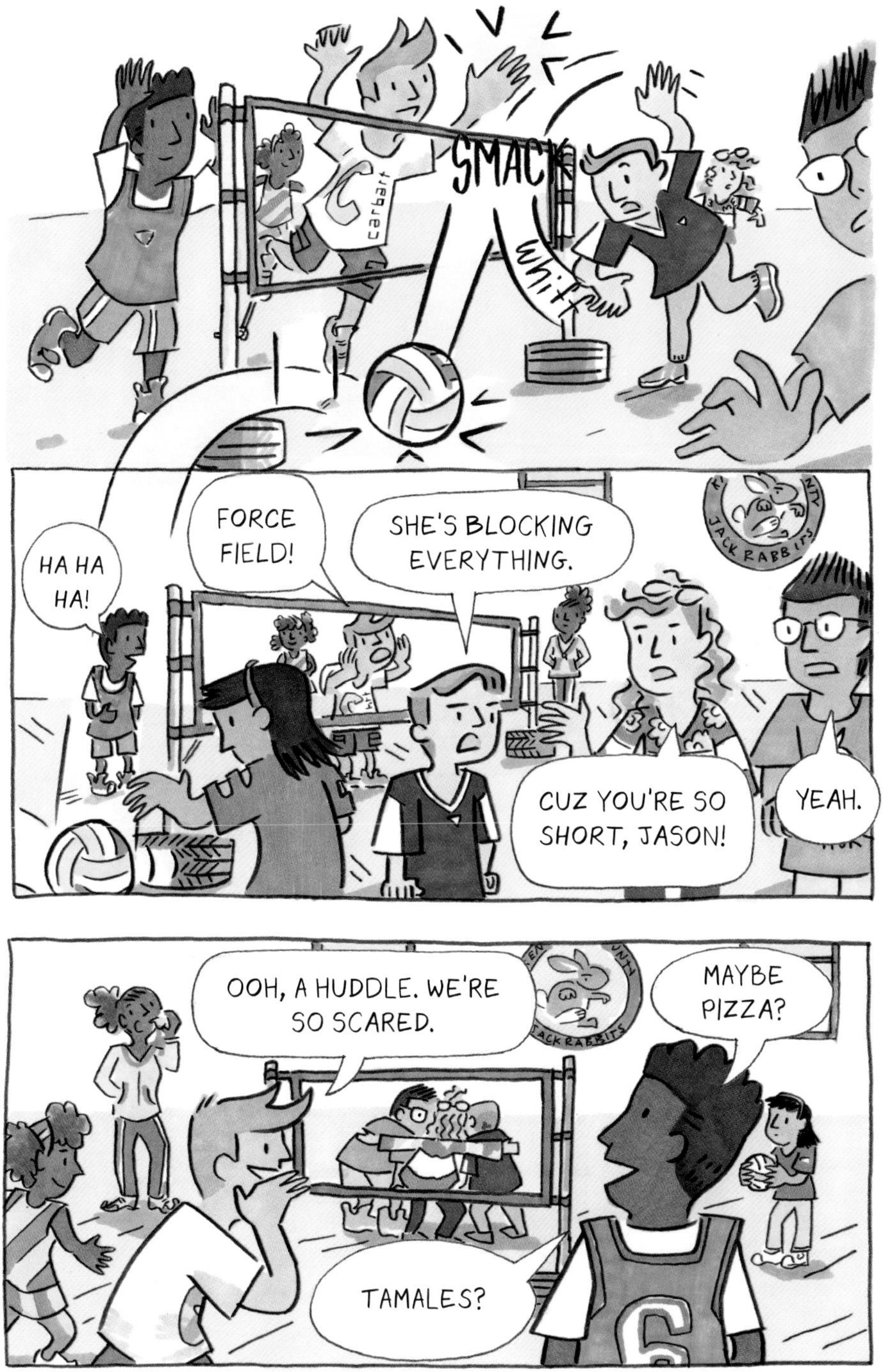
SMACK
whiff
HA HA HA!
FORCE FIELD!
SHE'S BLOCKING EVERYTHING.
CUZ YOU'RE SO SHORT, JASON!
YEAH.
OOH, A HUDDLE. WE'RE SO SCARED.
MAYBE PIZZA?
TAMALES?

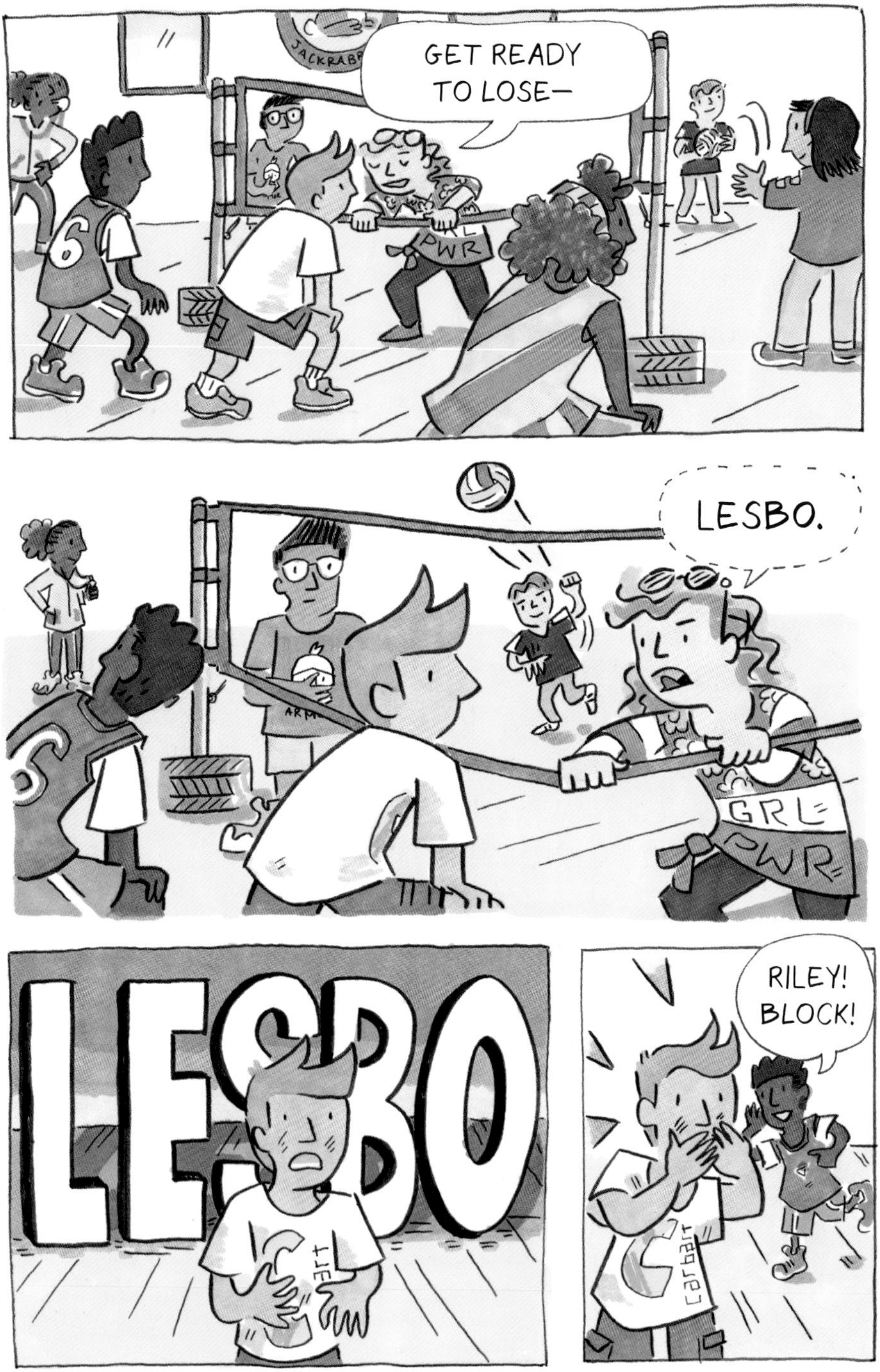
GET READY TO LOSE—
PWR
LESBO.
GRL PWR
LESBO
RILEY! BLOCK!

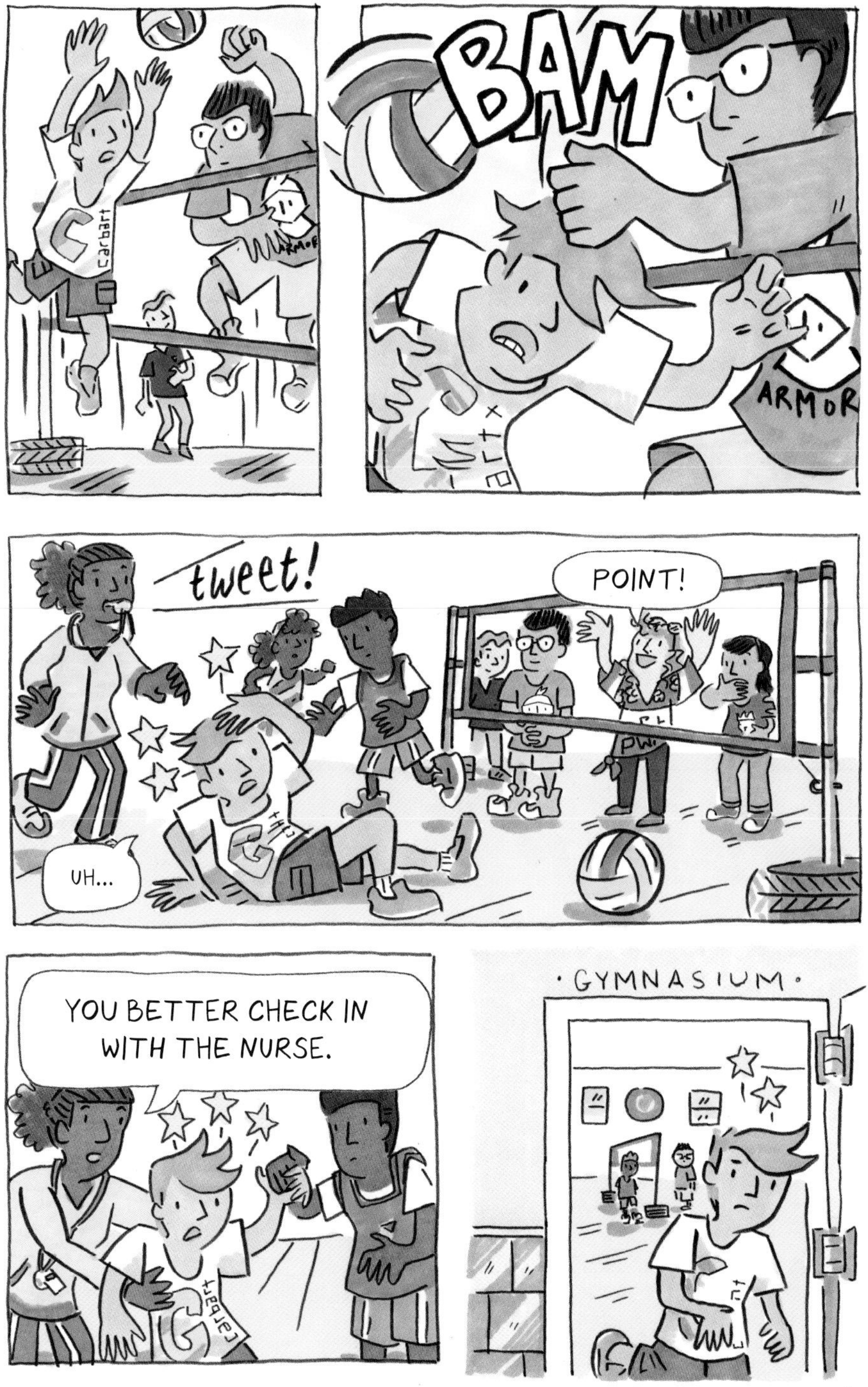

Carbart
ARMOR
BAM
ARMOR
tweet!
POINT!
UH...
YOU BETTER CHECK IN WITH THE NURSE.
Carbart
·GYMNASIUM·

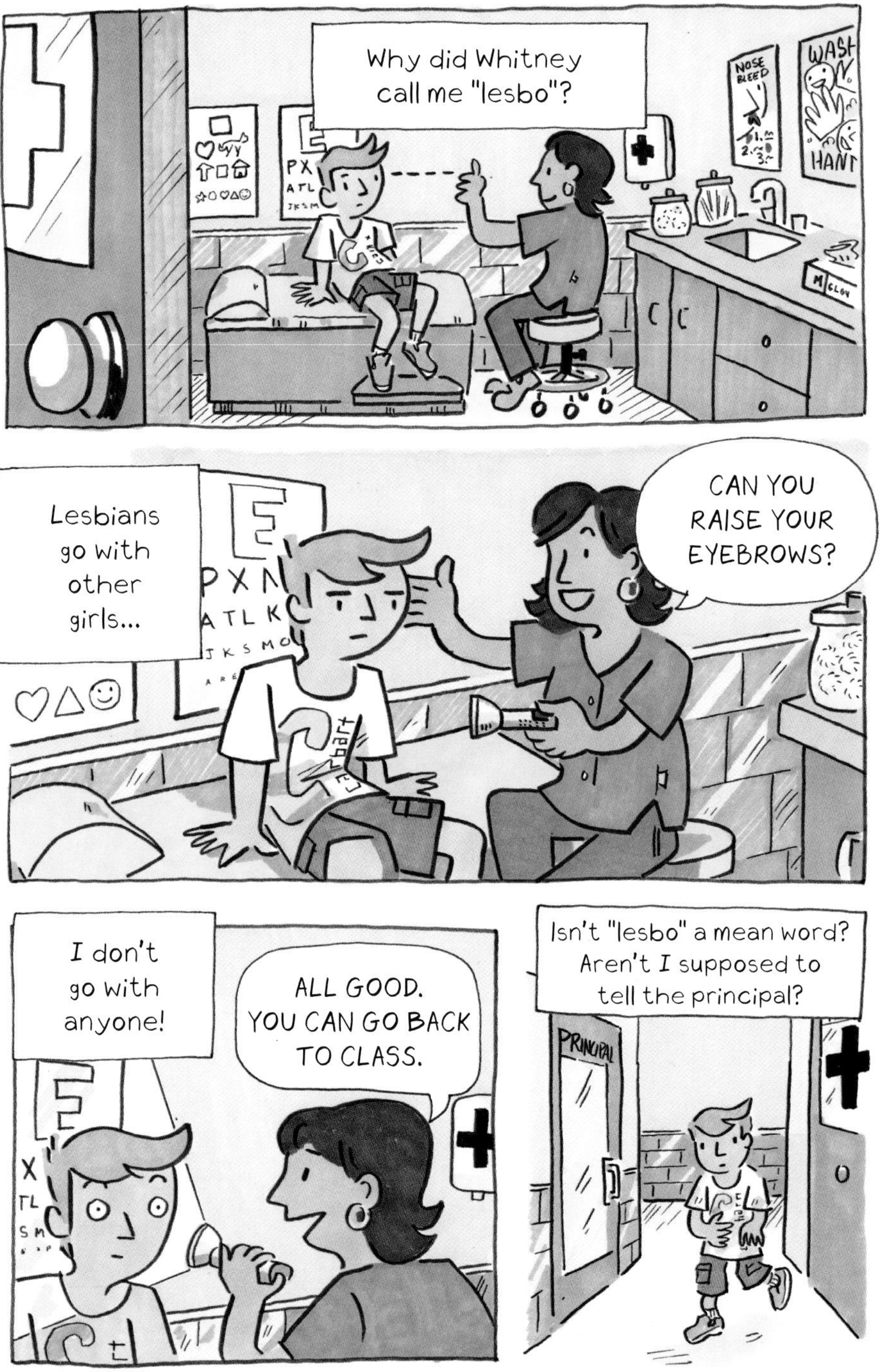

Why did Whitney call me "lesbo"?
NOSE BLEED
WASH
Lesbians go with other girls...
CAN YOU RAISE YOUR EYEBROWS?
I don't go with anyone!
ALL GOOD. YOU CAN GO BACK TO CLASS.
Isn't "lesbo" a mean word? Aren't I supposed to tell the principal?
PRINCIPAL

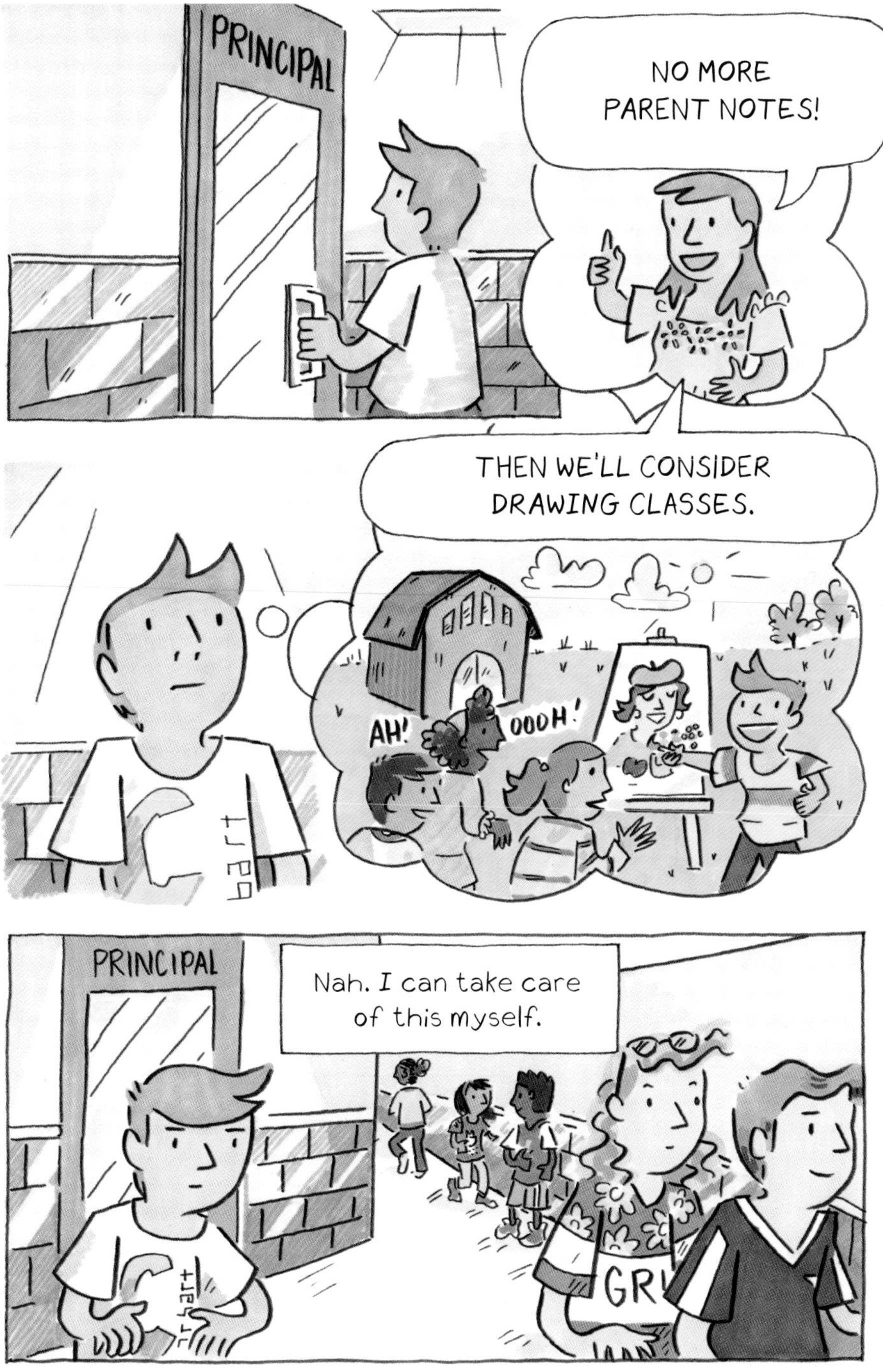
PRINCIPAL
NO MORE PARENT NOTES!
THEN WE'LL CONSIDER DRAWING CLASSES.
AH!
OOOH!
PRINCIPAL
Nah. I can take care of this myself.

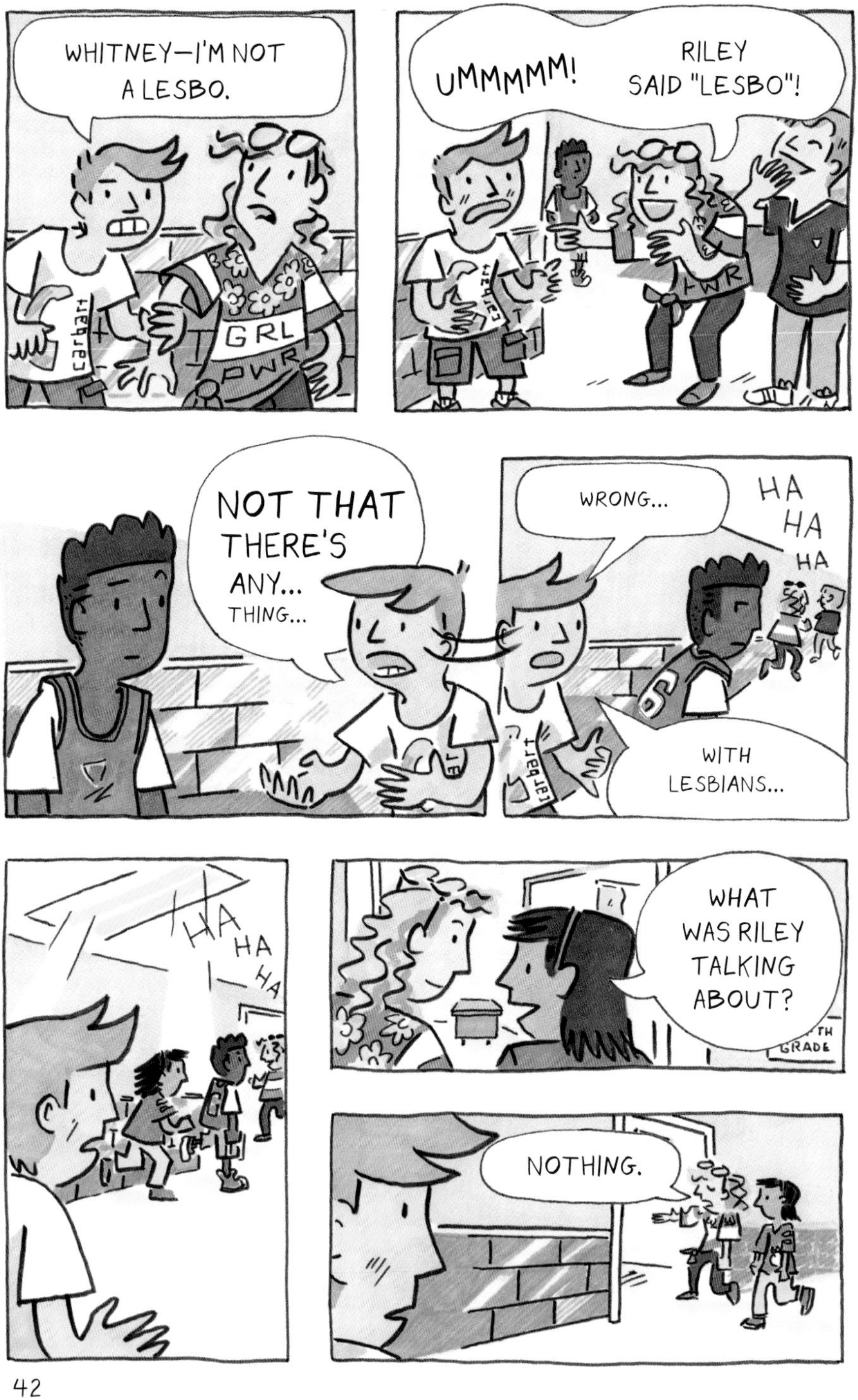
WHITNEY—I'M NOT A LESBO.
UMMMMM!
RILEY SAID "LESBO"!
GRL PWR
NOT THAT THERE'S ANY... THING...
WRONG...
HA HA HA
WITH LESBIANS...
HA HA HA
WHAT WAS RILEY TALKING ABOUT?
NOTHING.

CHAPTER 5

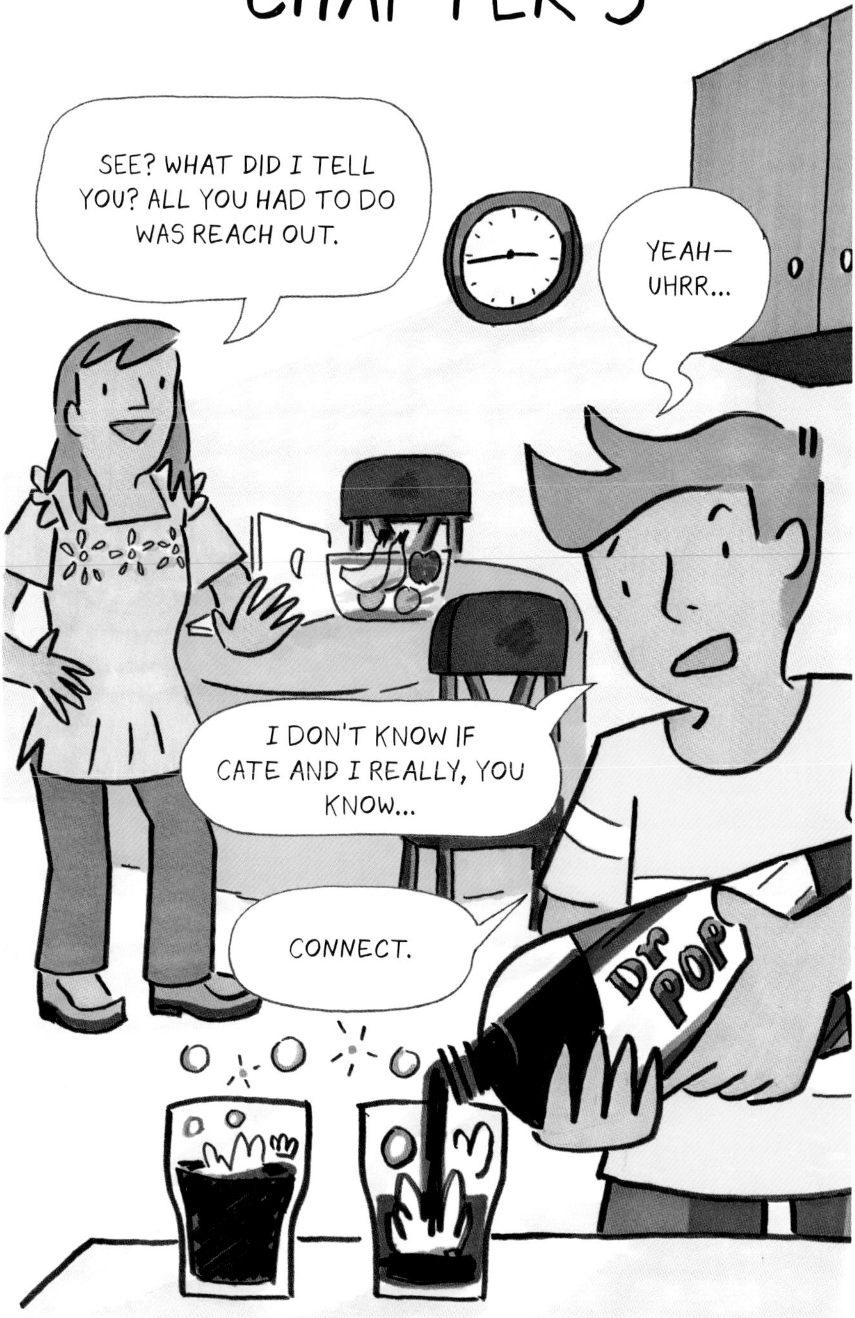
SEE? WHAT DID I TELL YOU? ALL YOU HAD TO DO WAS REACH OUT.
YEAH— UHRR...
I DON'T KNOW IF CATE AND I REALLY, YOU KNOW...
CONNECT.
Dr POP

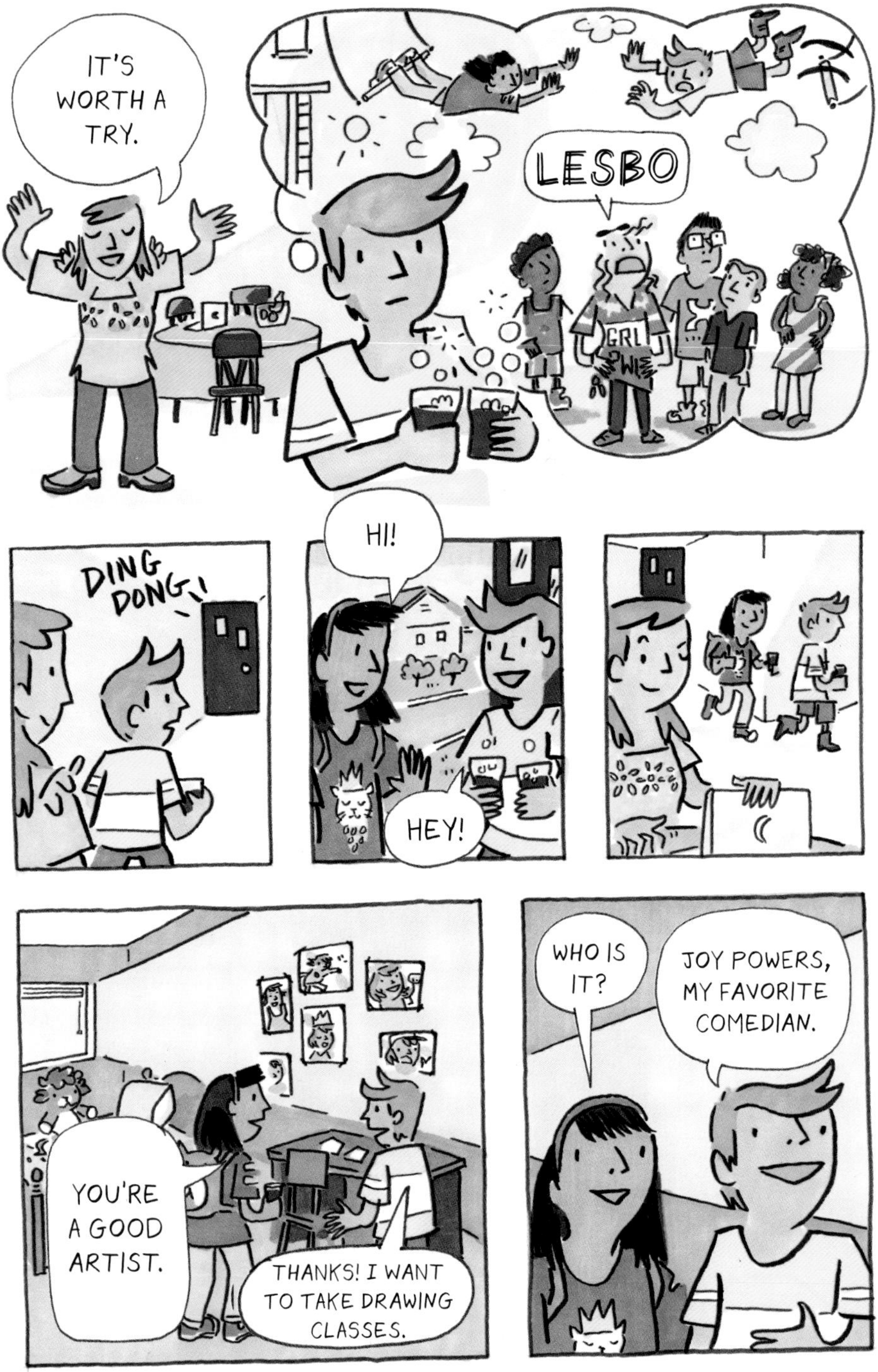
IT'S WORTH A TRY.
LESBO
GRL PWR
DING DONG
HI!
HEY!
YOU'RE A GOOD ARTIST.
THANKS! I WANT TO TAKE DRAWING CLASSES.
WHO IS IT?
JOY POWERS, MY FAVORITE COMEDIAN.

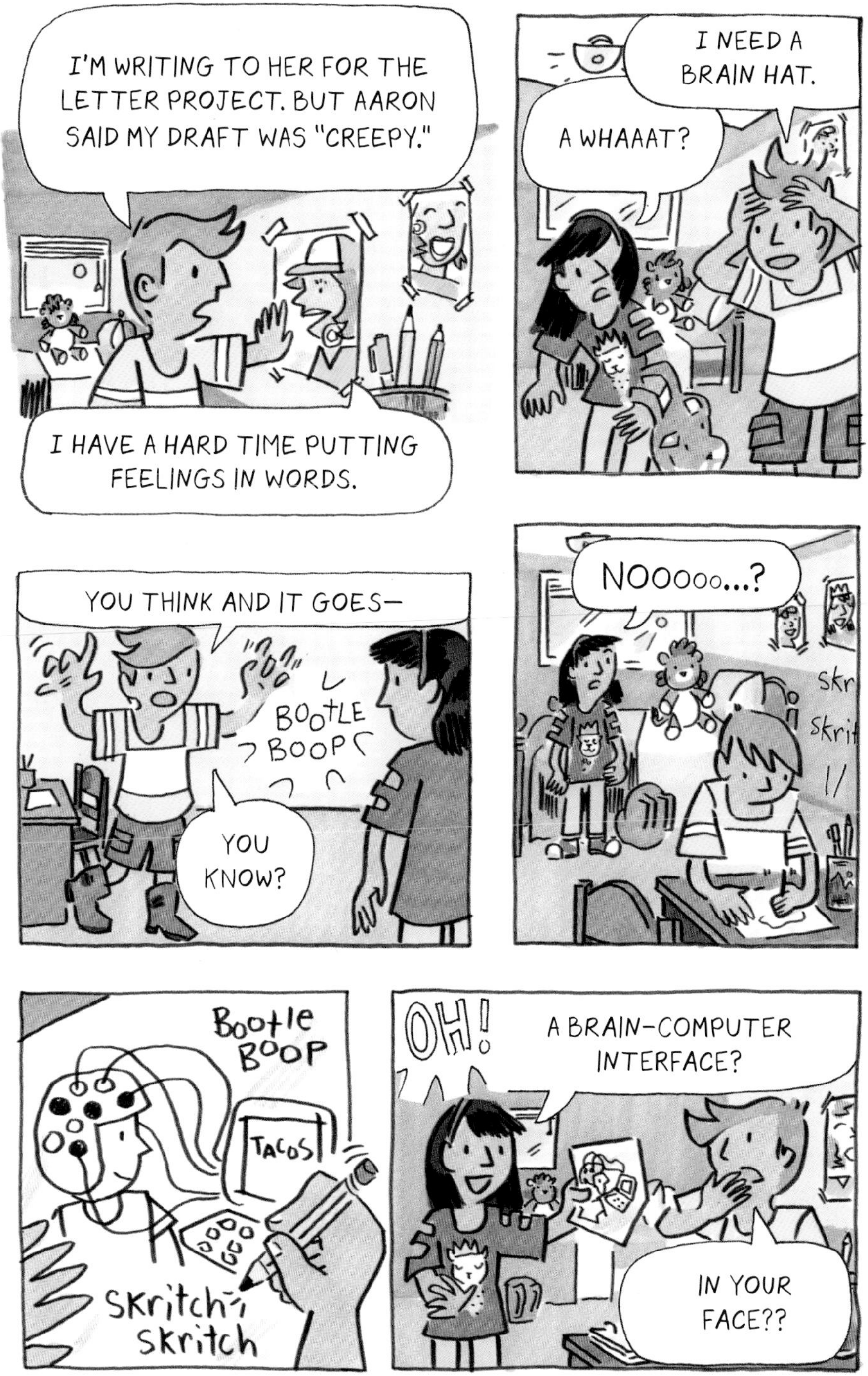
I'M WRITING TO HER FOR THE LETTER PROJECT. BUT AARON SAID MY DRAFT WAS "CREEPY."
I HAVE A HARD TIME PUTTING FEELINGS IN WORDS.
I NEED A BRAIN HAT.
A WHAAAT?
YOU THINK AND IT GOES—
BOOTLE BOOP
YOU KNOW?
NOOooo...?
Skr
Skrit
Bootle BOOP
TACOS
Skritch Skritch
OH!
A BRAIN-COMPUTER INTERFACE?
IN YOUR FACE??

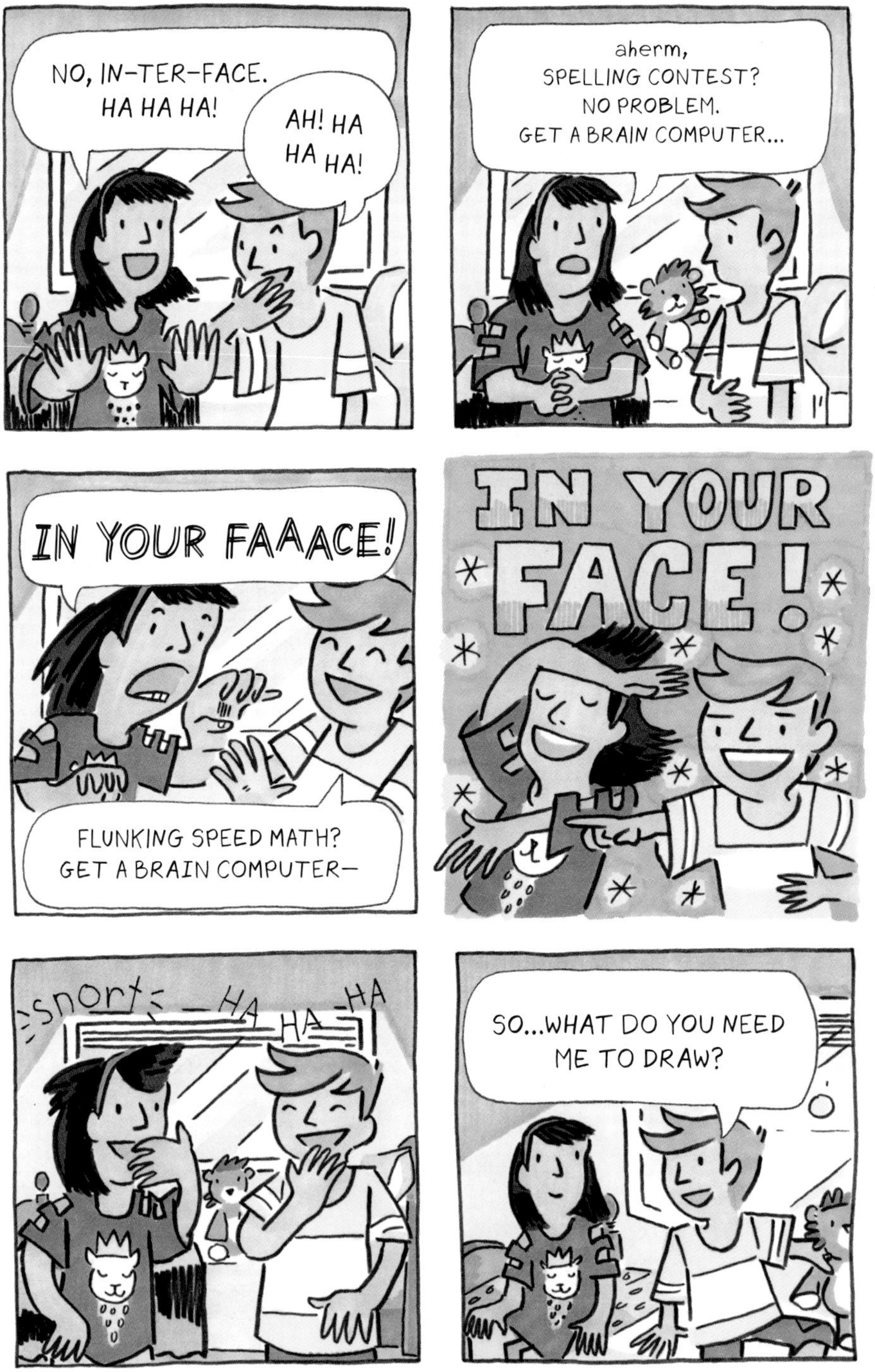
NO, IN-TER-FACE.
HA HA HA!
AH! HA
HA HA!
aherm,
SPELLING CONTEST?
NO PROBLEM.
GET A BRAIN COMPUTER...
IN YOUR FAAACE!
FLUNKING SPEED MATH?
GET A BRAIN COMPUTER–
IN YOUR FACE!
snort
HA HA HA
SO...WHAT DO YOU NEED
ME TO DRAW?

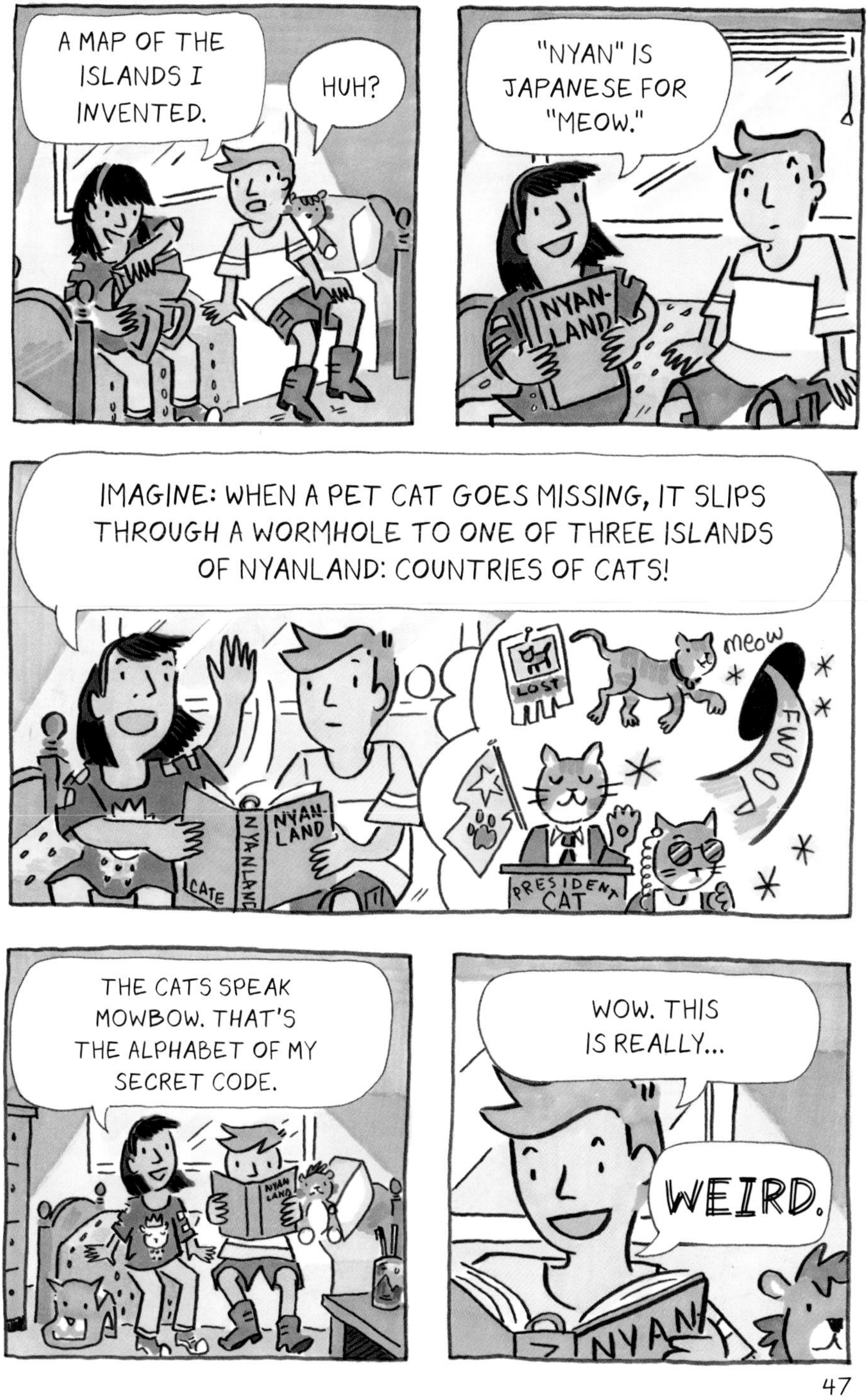
A MAP OF THE ISLANDS I INVENTED.
HUH?
"NYAN" IS JAPANESE FOR "MEOW."
NYAN-LAND
IMAGINE: WHEN A PET CAT GOES MISSING, IT SLIPS THROUGH A WORMHOLE TO ONE OF THREE ISLANDS OF NYANLAND: COUNTRIES OF CATS!
NYAN-LAND
NYANLAND
CATE
LOST
meow
FWOOP
PRESIDENT CAT
THE CATS SPEAK MOWBOW. THAT'S THE ALPHABET OF MY SECRET CODE.
WOW. THIS IS REALLY...
WEIRD.
NYAN

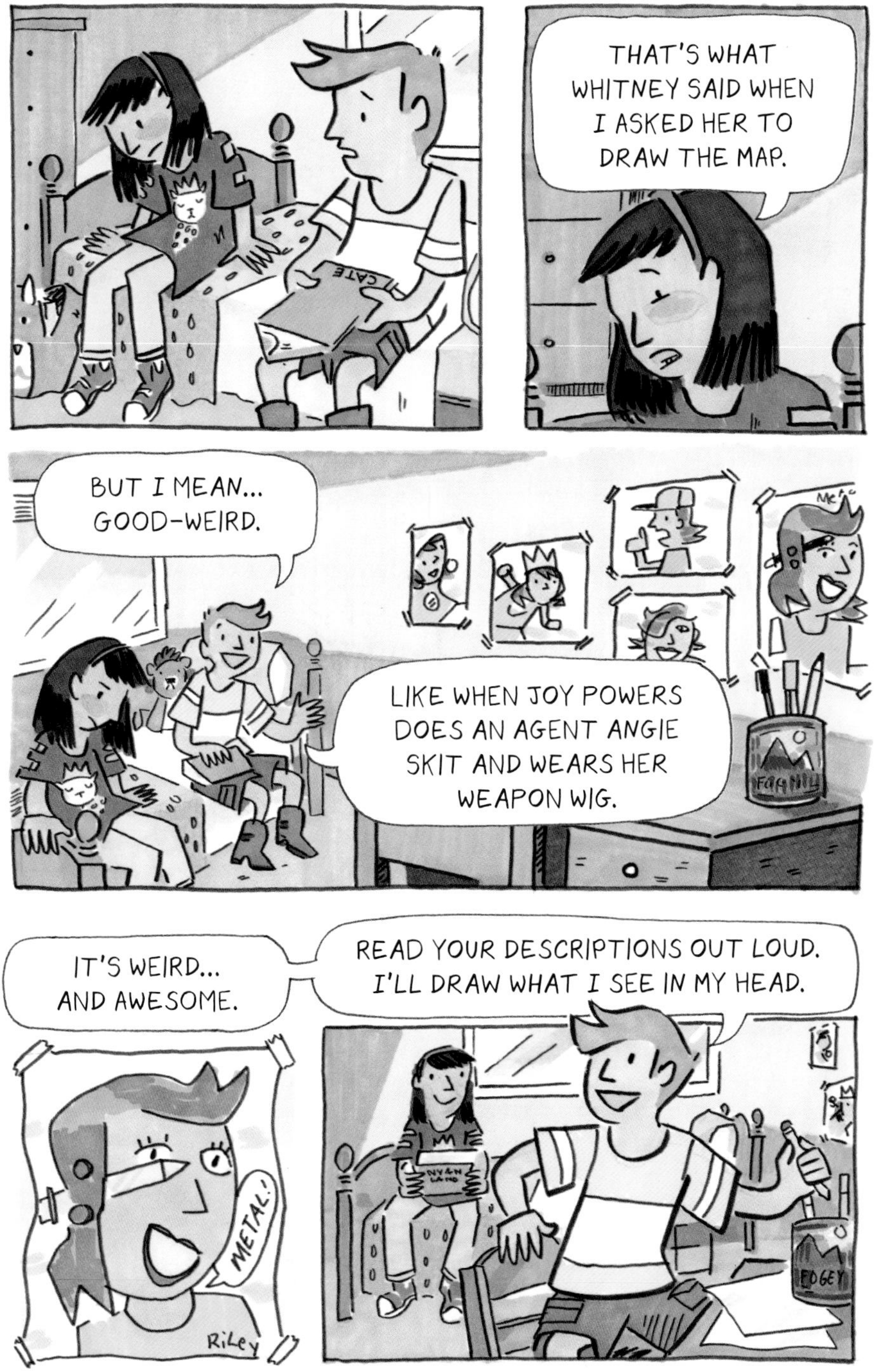
CATE
THAT'S WHAT WHITNEY SAID WHEN I ASKED HER TO DRAW THE MAP.
BUT I MEAN... GOOD-WEIRD.
LIKE WHEN JOY POWERS DOES AN AGENT ANGIE SKIT AND WEARS HER WEAPON WIG.
IT'S WEIRD... AND AWESOME.
READ YOUR DESCRIPTIONS OUT LOUD. I'LL DRAW WHAT I SEE IN MY HEAD.
METAL!
Riley
FOGEY

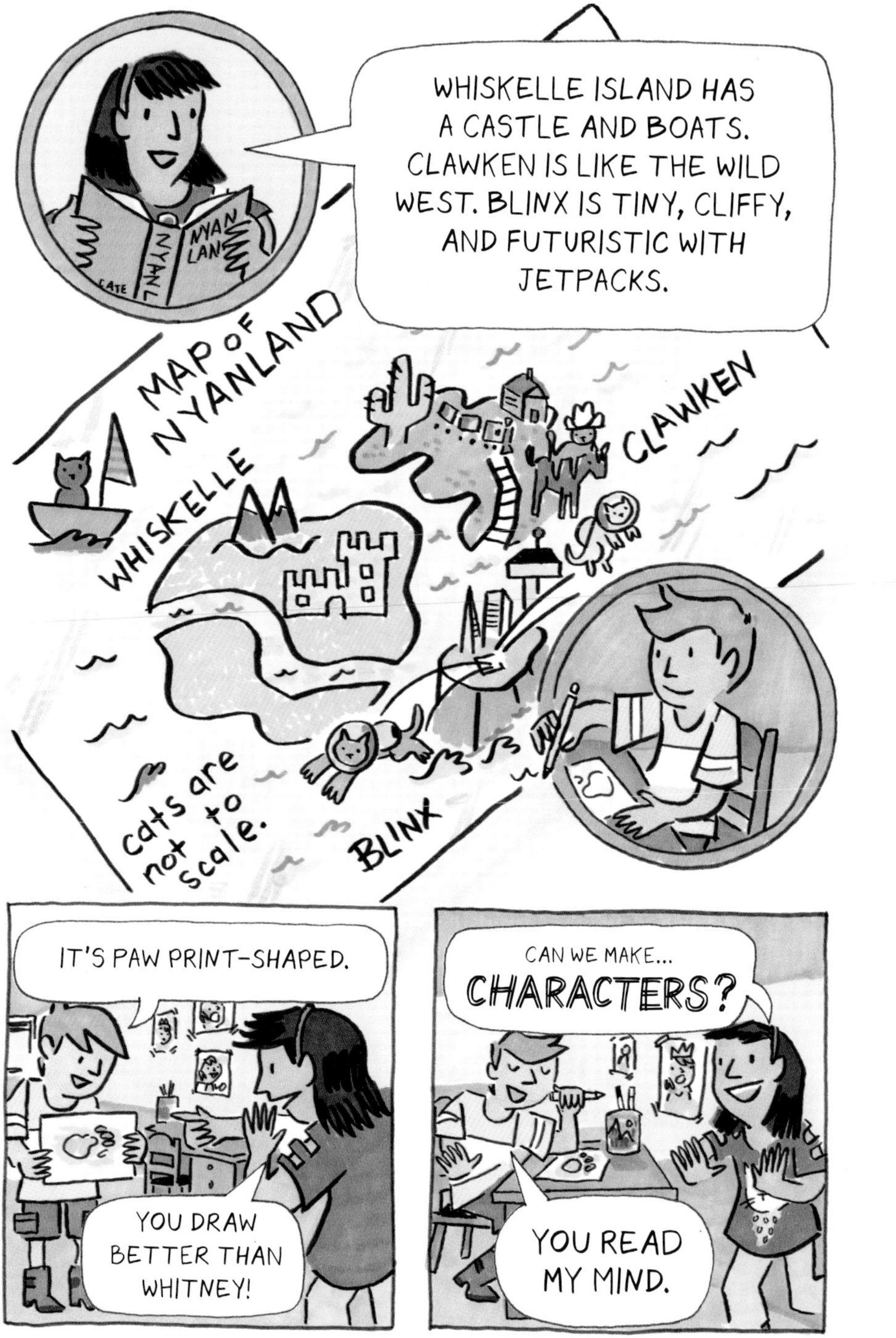
WHISKELLE ISLAND HAS A CASTLE AND BOATS. CLAWKEN IS LIKE THE WILD WEST. BLINX IS TINY, CLIFFY, AND FUTURISTIC WITH JETPACKS.
NYANLAND
NYAN LAND
CATE
MAP OF NYANLAND
WHISKELLE
CLAWKEN
BLINX
cats are not to scale.
IT'S PAW PRINT-SHAPED.
YOU DRAW BETTER THAN WHITNEY!
CAN WE MAKE... CHARACTERS?
YOU READ MY MIND.

Cate's imagination is nonstop.
I draw a hat on a cat, and she invents a whole story.
It's fun to draw someone else's thoughts for a change.

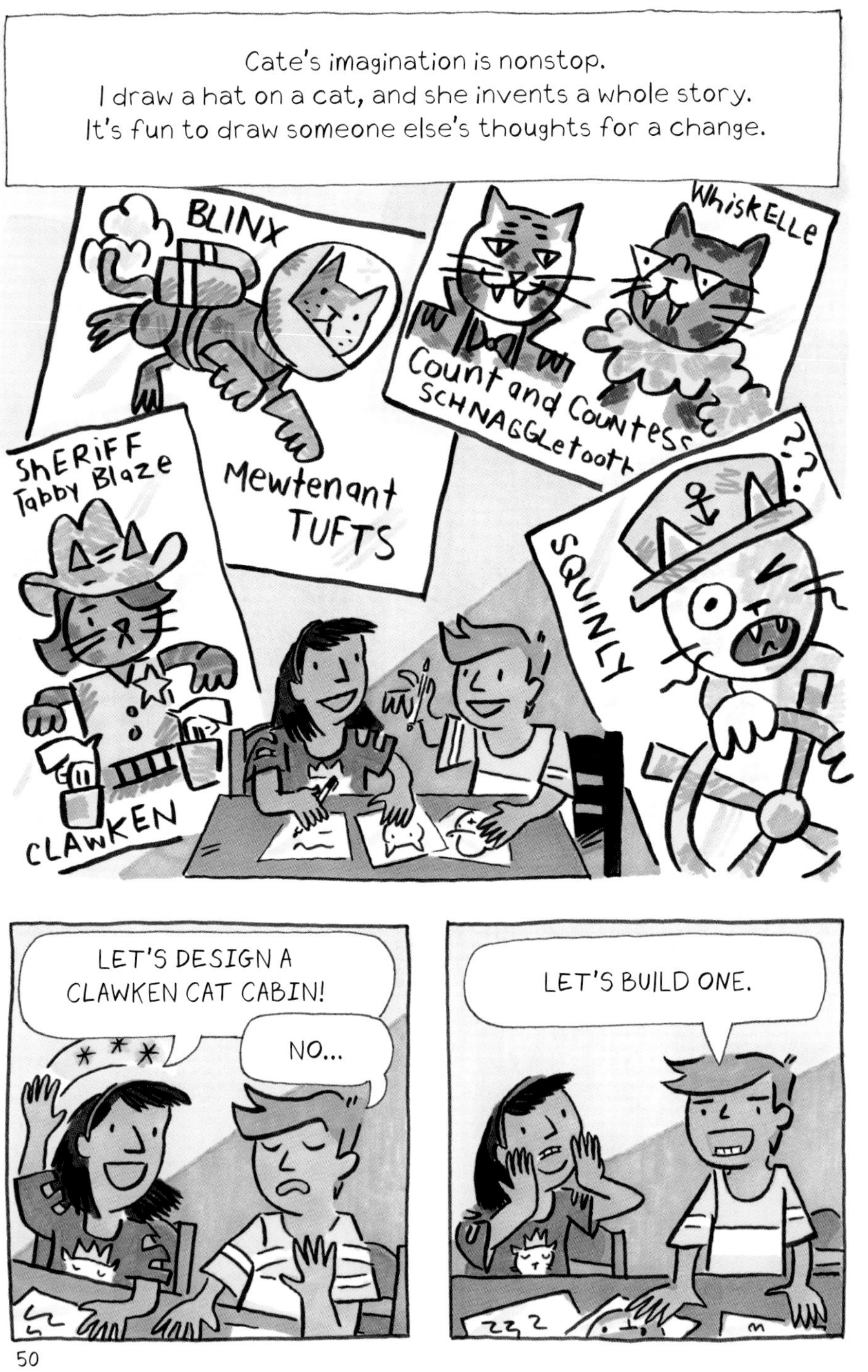
BLINX
WhisKELLE
Count and Countess SCHNAGGLetooth
SHERIFF Tabby Blaze
Mewtenant TUFTS
SQUINLY
CLAWKEN
LET'S DESIGN A CLAWKEN CAT CABIN!
NO...
LET'S BUILD ONE.

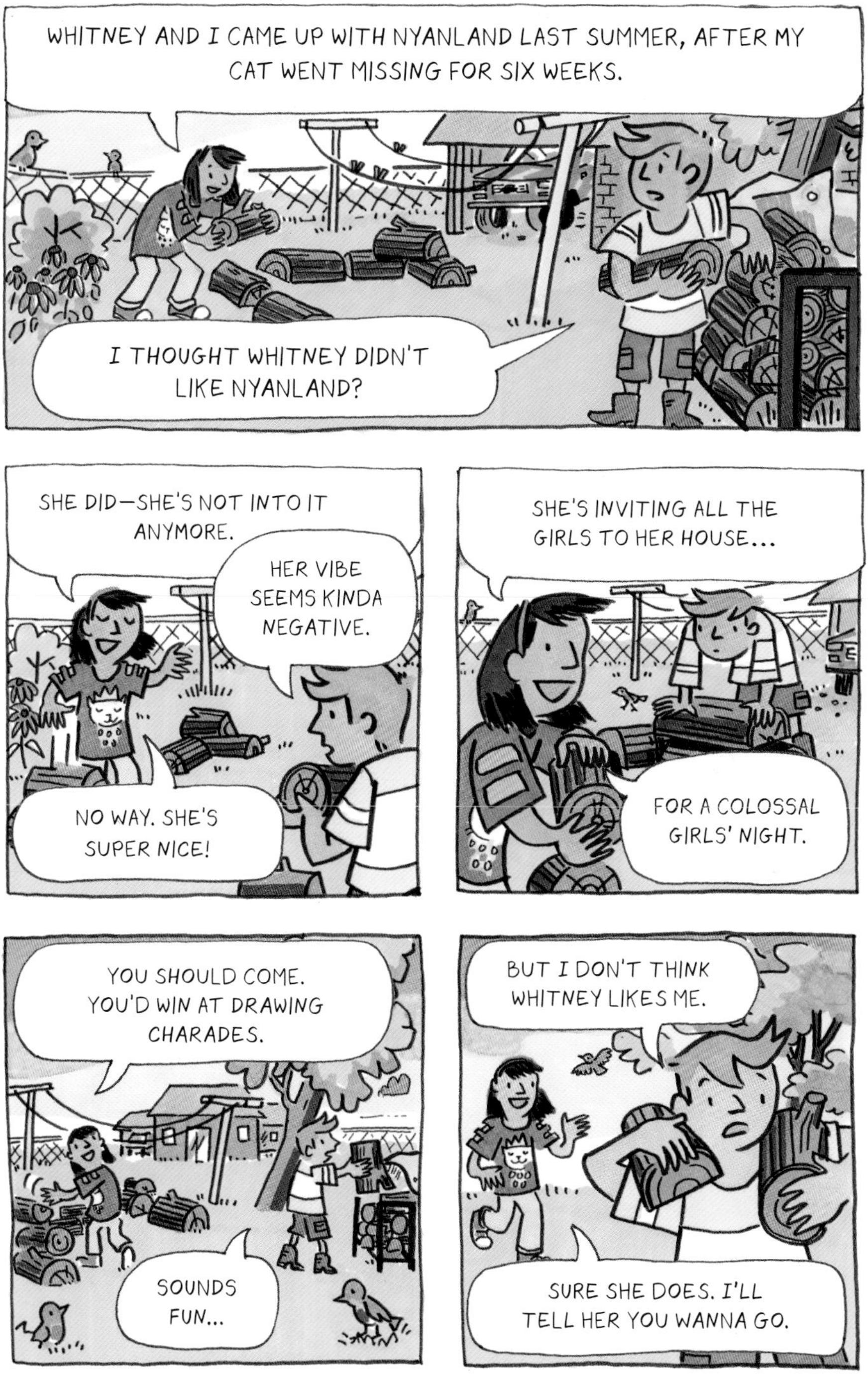
WHITNEY AND I CAME UP WITH NYANLAND LAST SUMMER, AFTER MY CAT WENT MISSING FOR SIX WEEKS.
I THOUGHT WHITNEY DIDN'T LIKE NYANLAND?
SHE DID—SHE'S NOT INTO IT ANYMORE.
HER VIBE SEEMS KINDA NEGATIVE.
NO WAY. SHE'S SUPER NICE!
SHE'S INVITING ALL THE GIRLS TO HER HOUSE...
FOR A COLOSSAL GIRLS' NIGHT.
YOU SHOULD COME. YOU'D WIN AT DRAWING CHARADES.
SOUNDS FUN...
BUT I DON'T THINK WHITNEY LIKES ME.
SURE SHE DOES. I'LL TELL HER YOU WANNA GO.

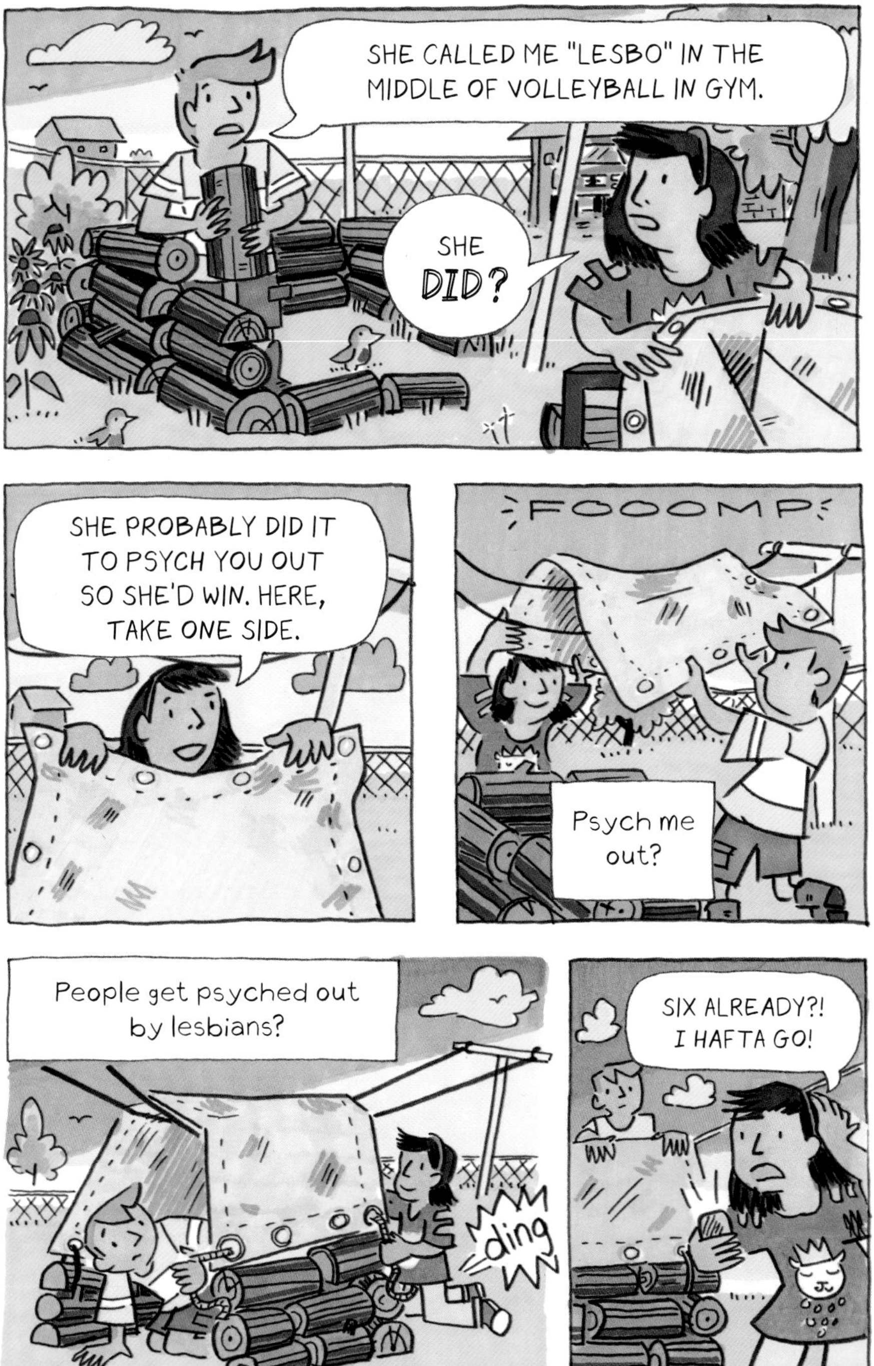
SHE CALLED ME "LESBO" IN THE MIDDLE OF VOLLEYBALL IN GYM.
SHE DID?
SHE PROBABLY DID IT TO PSYCH YOU OUT SO SHE'D WIN. HERE, TAKE ONE SIDE.
FOOOMP
Psych me out?
People get psyched out by lesbians?
ding
SIX ALREADY?! I HAFTA GO!

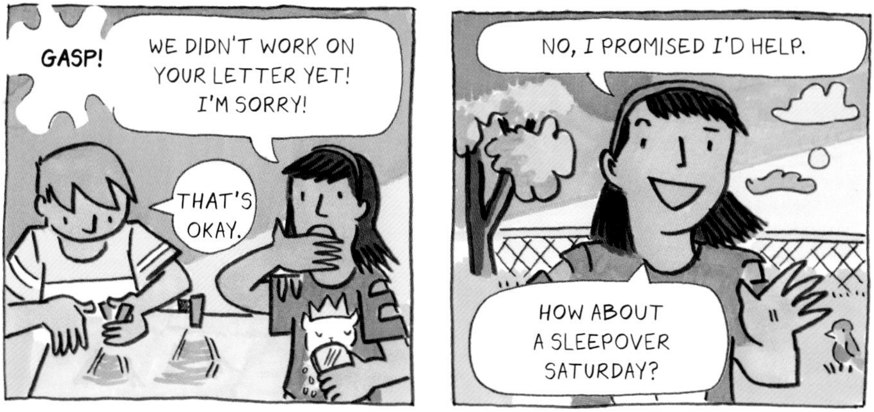
GASP!
WE DIDN'T WORK ON YOUR LETTER YET! I'M SORRY!
THAT'S OKAY.
NO, I PROMISED I'D HELP.
HOW ABOUT A SLEEPOVER SATURDAY?

If Mom is right and friendship is like a trapeze act—

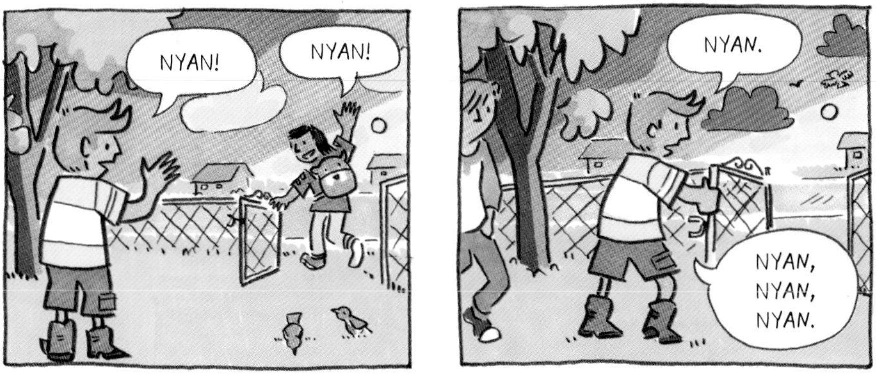
NYAN!
NYAN!
NYAN.
NYAN, NYAN, NYAN.

I'm starting to think Cate gets me.

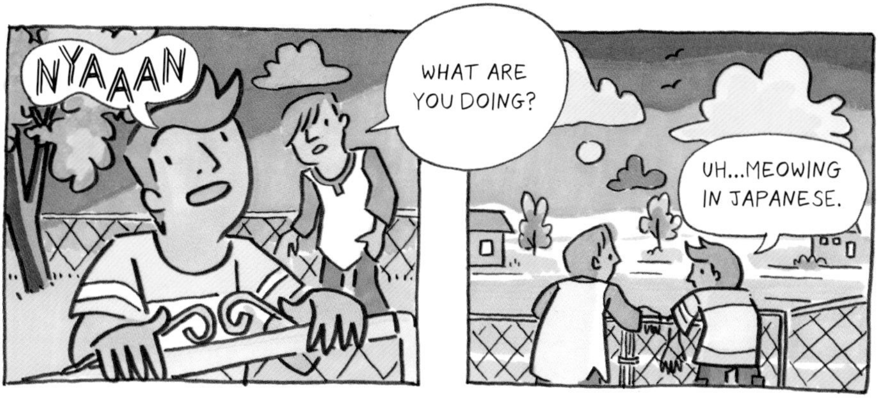
NYAAAN
WHAT ARE YOU DOING?
UH...MEOWING IN JAPANESE.

But I also kinda wish I had a safety net.

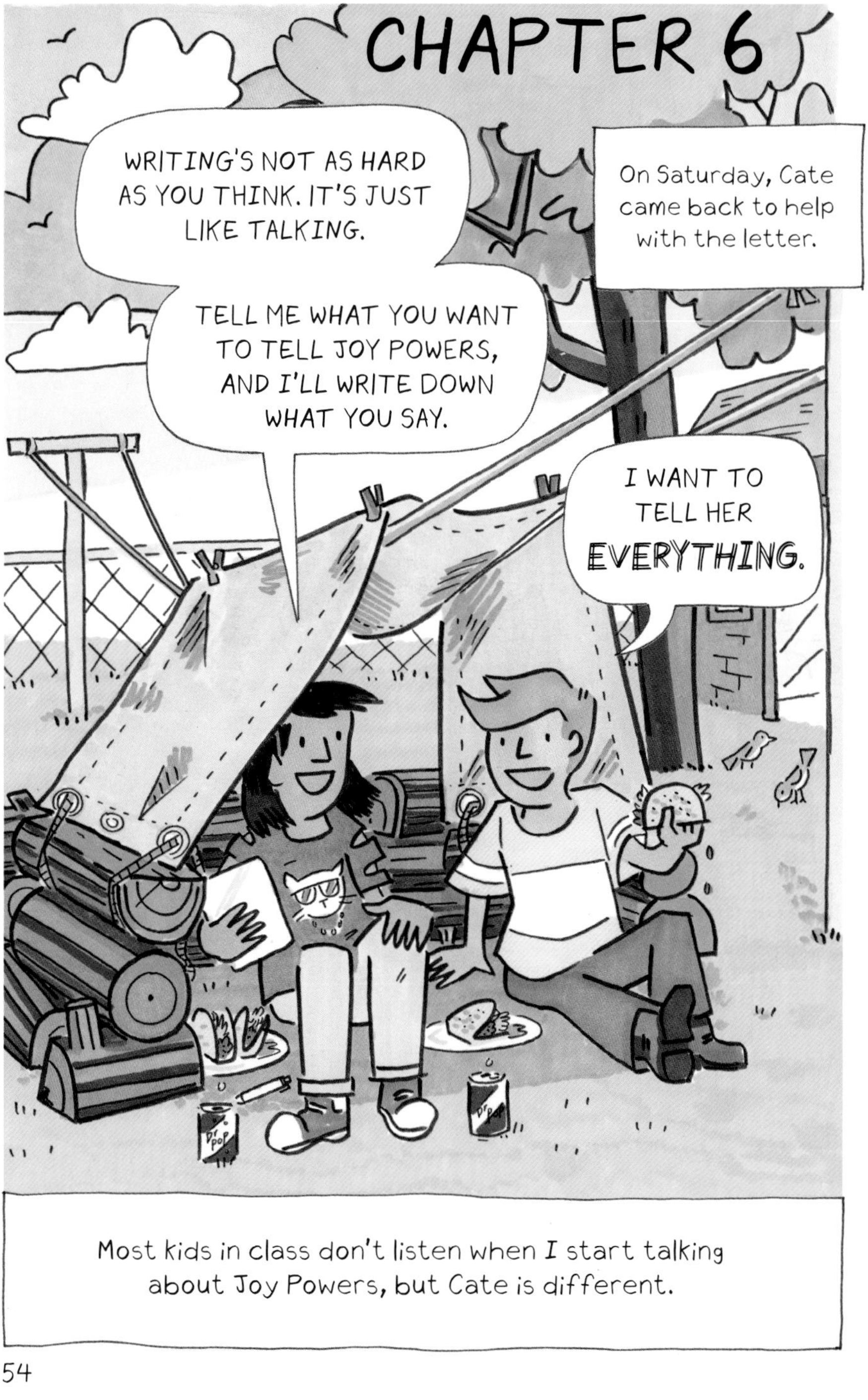
CHAPTER 6
On Saturday, Cate came back to help with the letter.
WRITING'S NOT AS HARD AS YOU THINK. IT'S JUST LIKE TALKING.
TELL ME WHAT YOU WANT TO TELL JOY POWERS, AND I'LL WRITE DOWN WHAT YOU SAY.
I WANT TO TELL HER EVERYTHING.
Most kids in class don't listen when I start talking about Joy Powers, but Cate is different.

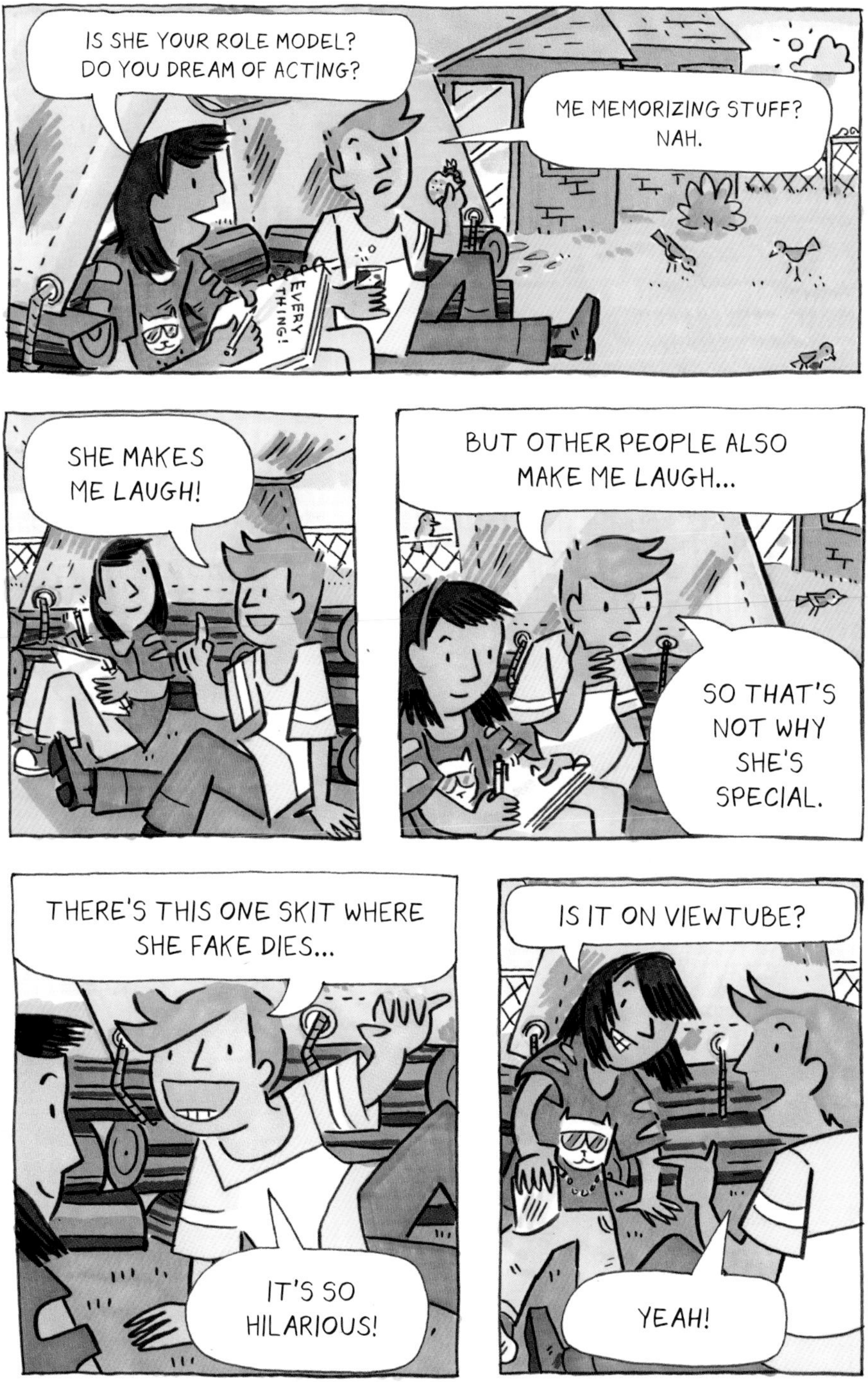
IS SHE YOUR ROLE MODEL? DO YOU DREAM OF ACTING?
ME MEMORIZING STUFF? NAH.
EVERYTHING!
SHE MAKES ME LAUGH!
BUT OTHER PEOPLE ALSO MAKE ME LAUGH...
SO THAT'S NOT WHY SHE'S SPECIAL.
THERE'S THIS ONE SKIT WHERE SHE FAKE DIES...
IT'S SO HILARIOUS!
IS IT ON VIEWTUBE?
YEAH!

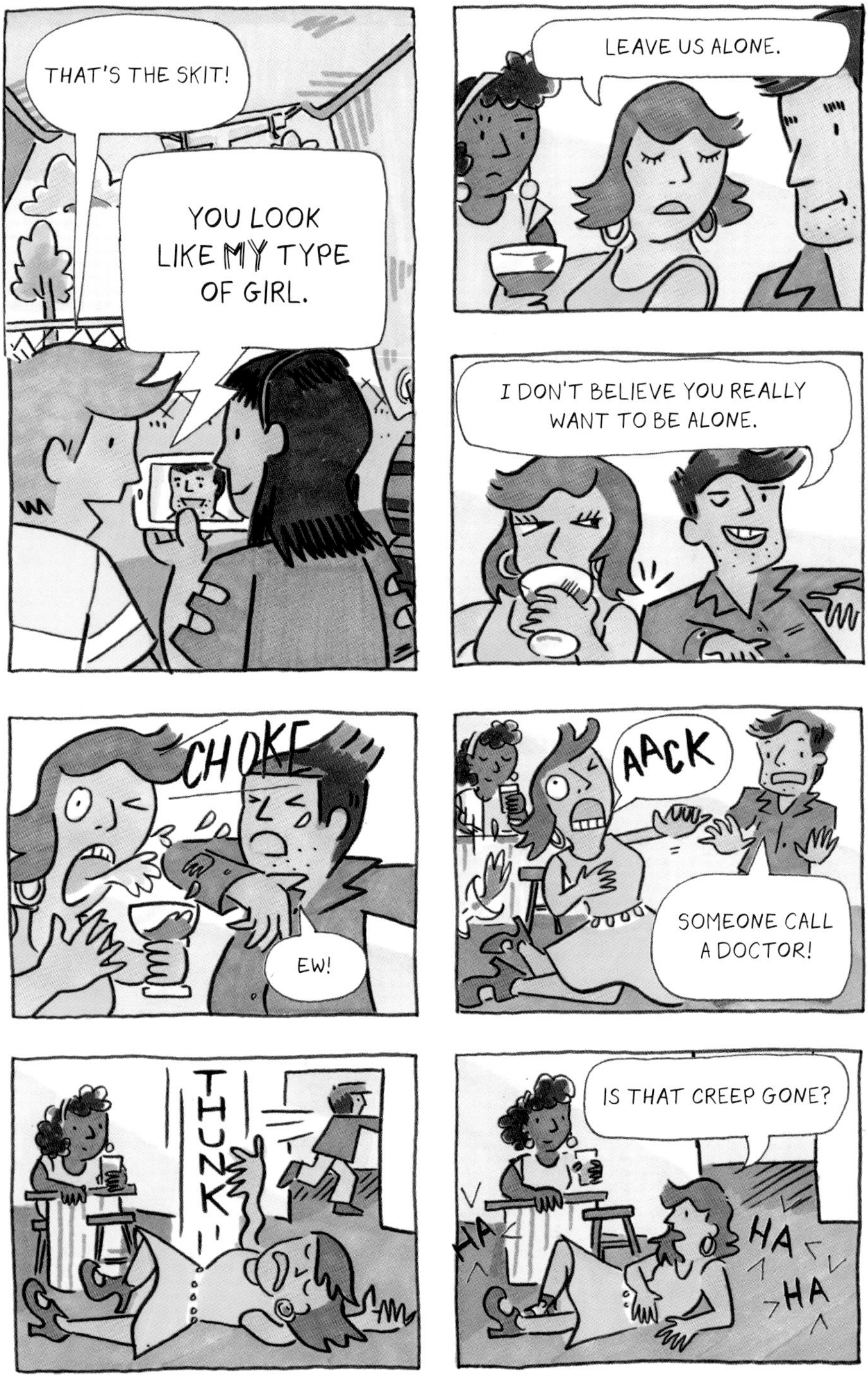
THAT'S THE SKIT!
YOU LOOK LIKE MY TYPE OF GIRL.
LEAVE US ALONE.
I DON'T BELIEVE YOU REALLY WANT TO BE ALONE.
CHOKE
EW!
AACK
SOMEONE CALL A DOCTOR!
THUNK
IS THAT CREEP GONE?
HA
HA
HA

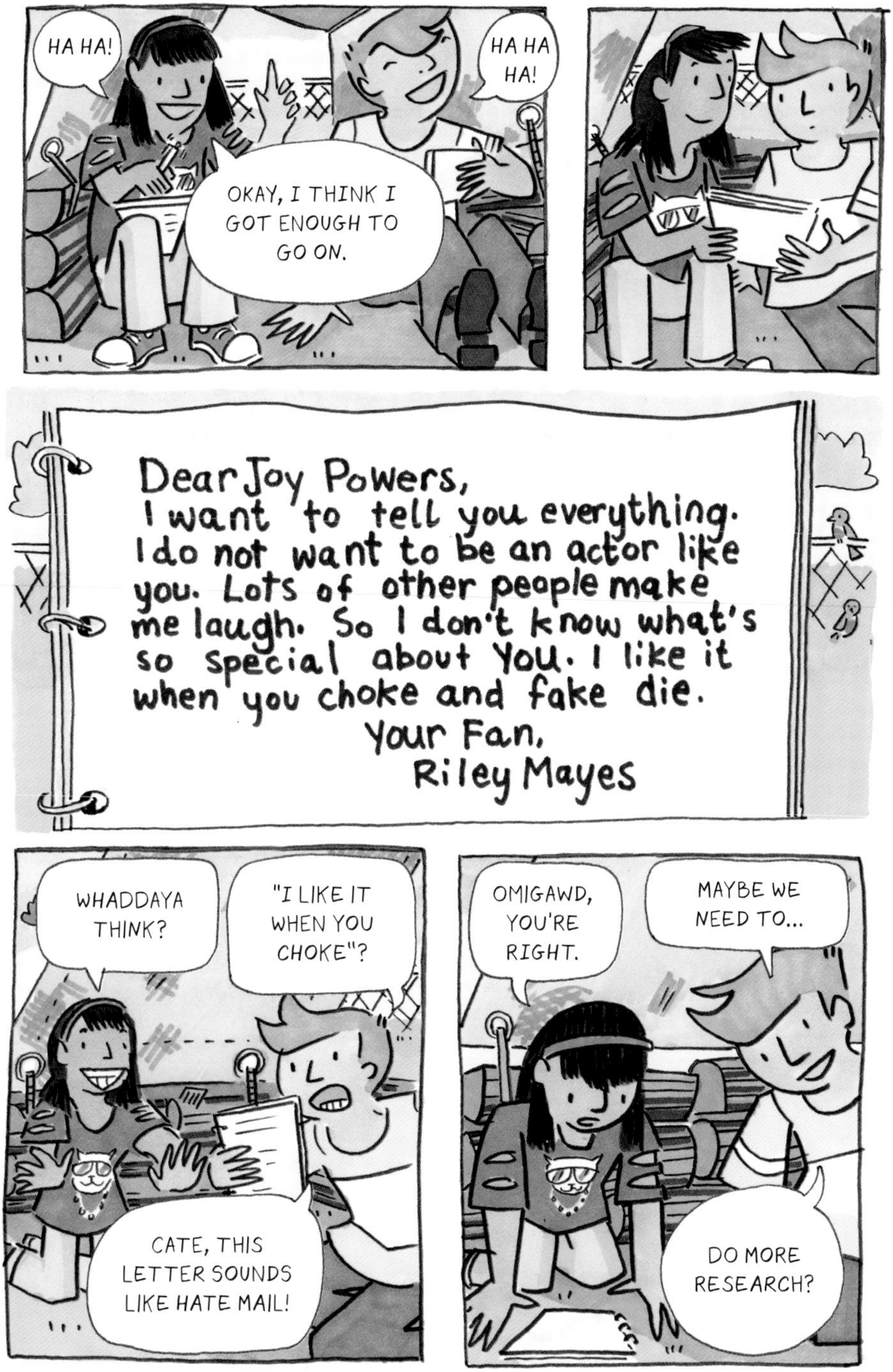
HA HA!
HA HA HA!
OKAY, I THINK I GOT ENOUGH TO GO ON.
Dear Joy Powers,
I want to tell you everything. I do not want to be an actor like you. Lots of other people make me laugh. So I don't know what's so special about You. I like it when you choke and fake die.
Your Fan,
Riley Mayes
WHADDAYA THINK?
"I LIKE IT WHEN YOU CHOKE"?
CATE, THIS LETTER SOUNDS LIKE HATE MAIL!
OMIGAWD, YOU'RE RIGHT.
MAYBE WE NEED TO...
DO MORE RESEARCH?

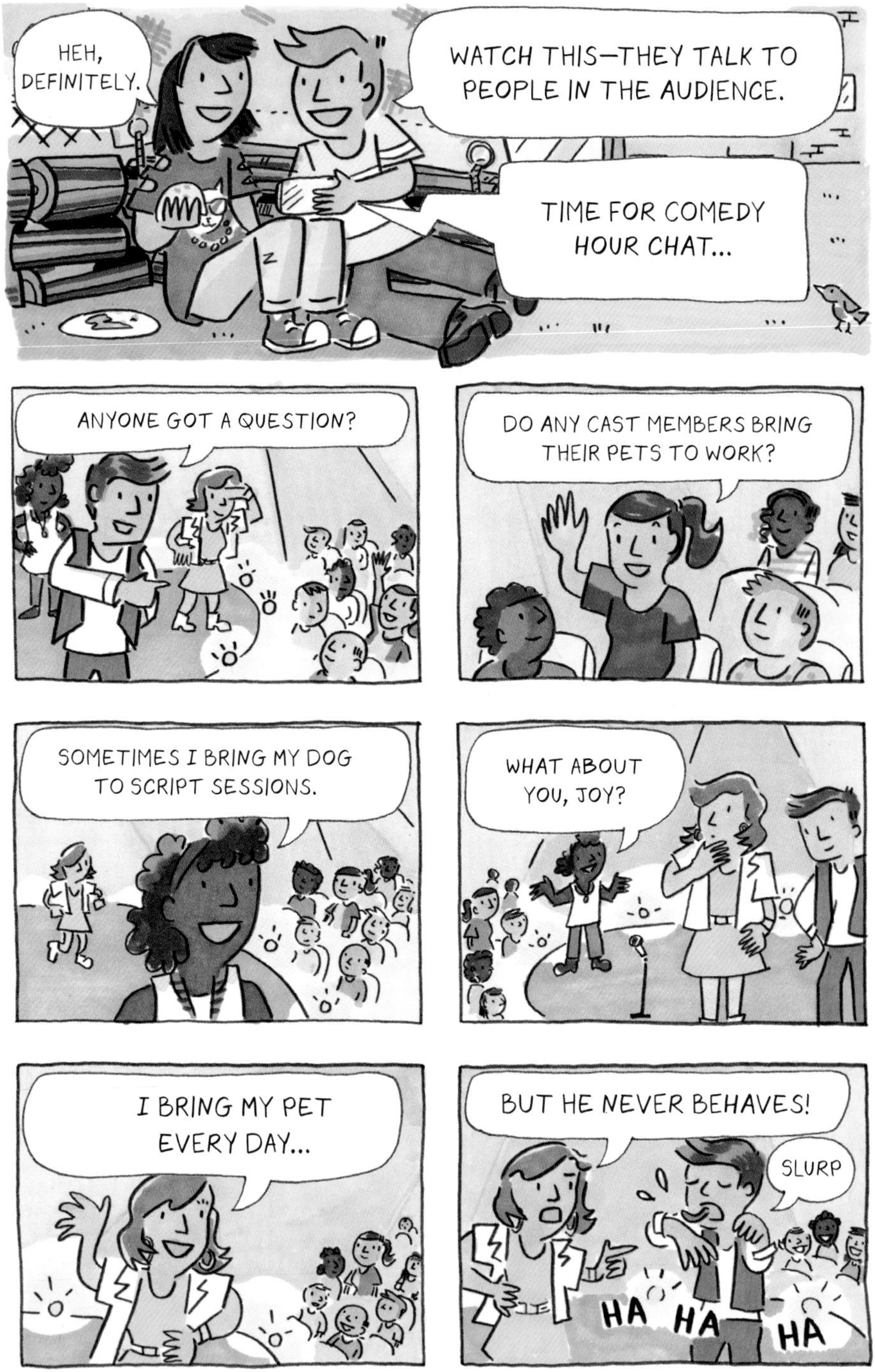
HEH, DEFINITELY.
WATCH THIS—THEY TALK TO PEOPLE IN THE AUDIENCE.
TIME FOR COMEDY HOUR CHAT...
ANYONE GOT A QUESTION?
DO ANY CAST MEMBERS BRING THEIR PETS TO WORK?
SOMETIMES I BRING MY DOG TO SCRIPT SESSIONS.
WHAT ABOUT YOU, JOY?
I BRING MY PET EVERY DAY...
BUT HE NEVER BEHAVES!
SLURP
HA
HA
HA

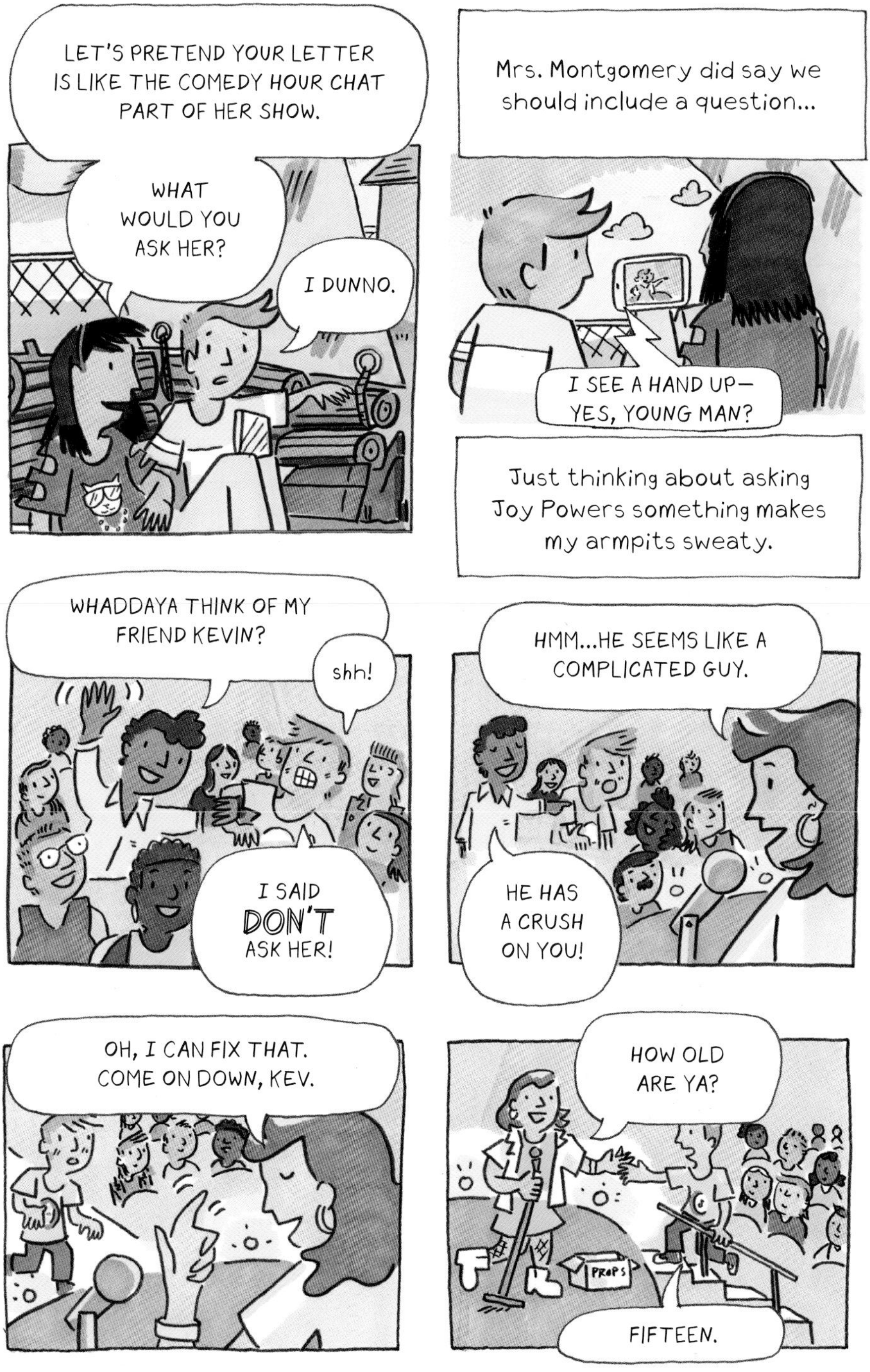
LET'S PRETEND YOUR LETTER IS LIKE THE COMEDY HOUR CHAT PART OF HER SHOW.
WHAT WOULD YOU ASK HER?
I DUNNO.
Mrs. Montgomery did say we should include a question...
I SEE A HAND UP— YES, YOUNG MAN?
Just thinking about asking Joy Powers something makes my armpits sweaty.
WHADDAYA THINK OF MY FRIEND KEVIN?
shh!
I SAID DON'T ASK HER!
HMM...HE SEEMS LIKE A COMPLICATED GUY.
HE HAS A CRUSH ON YOU!
OH, I CAN FIX THAT. COME ON DOWN, KEV.
HOW OLD ARE YA?
PROPS
FIFTEEN.

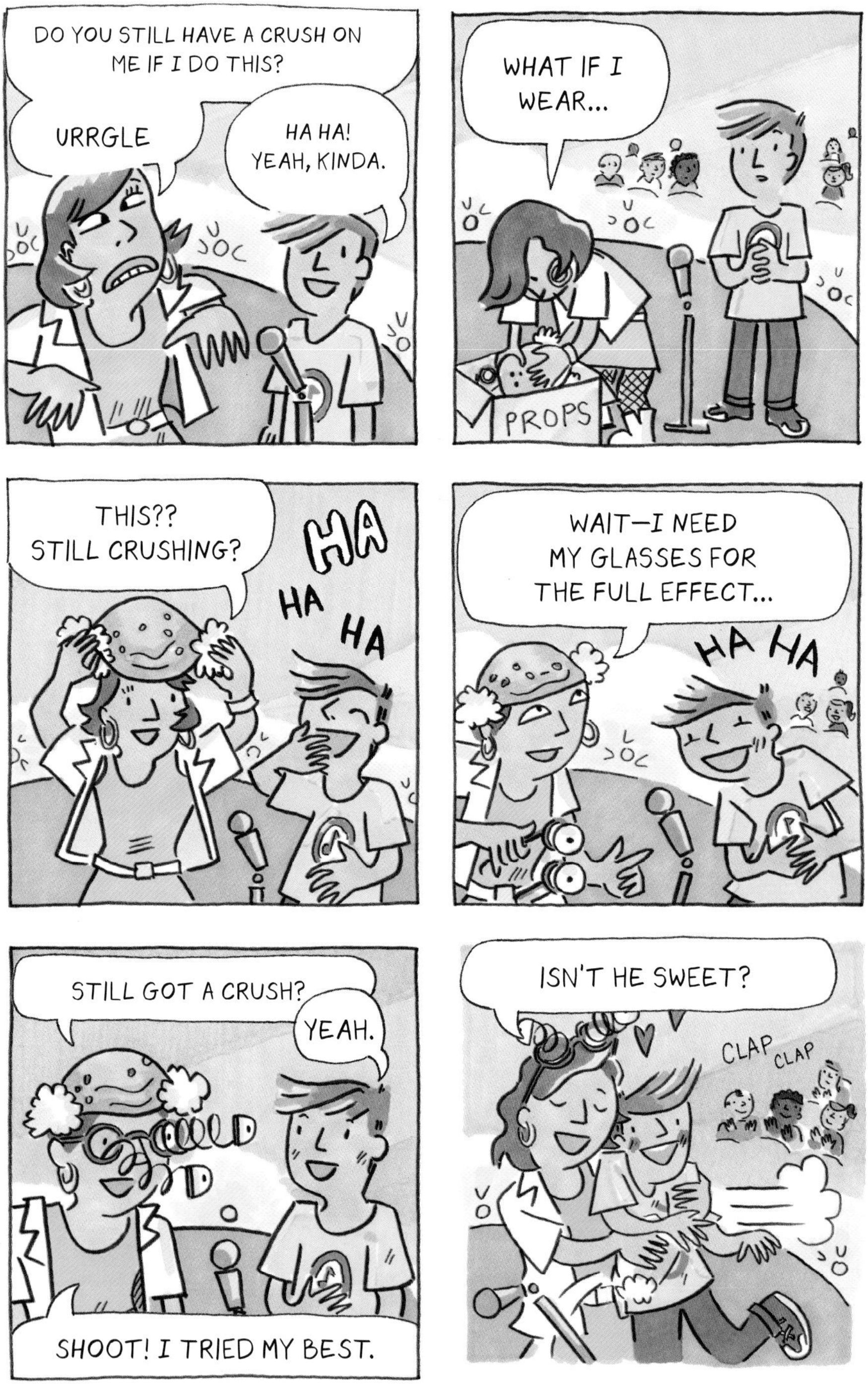
DO YOU STILL HAVE A CRUSH ON ME IF I DO THIS?
URRGLE
HA HA! YEAH, KINDA.
WHAT IF I WEAR...
PROPS
THIS?? STILL CRUSHING?
HA
HA
HA
WAIT—I NEED MY GLASSES FOR THE FULL EFFECT...
HA HA
STILL GOT A CRUSH?
YEAH.
SHOOT! I TRIED MY BEST.
ISN'T HE SWEET?
CLAP CLAP

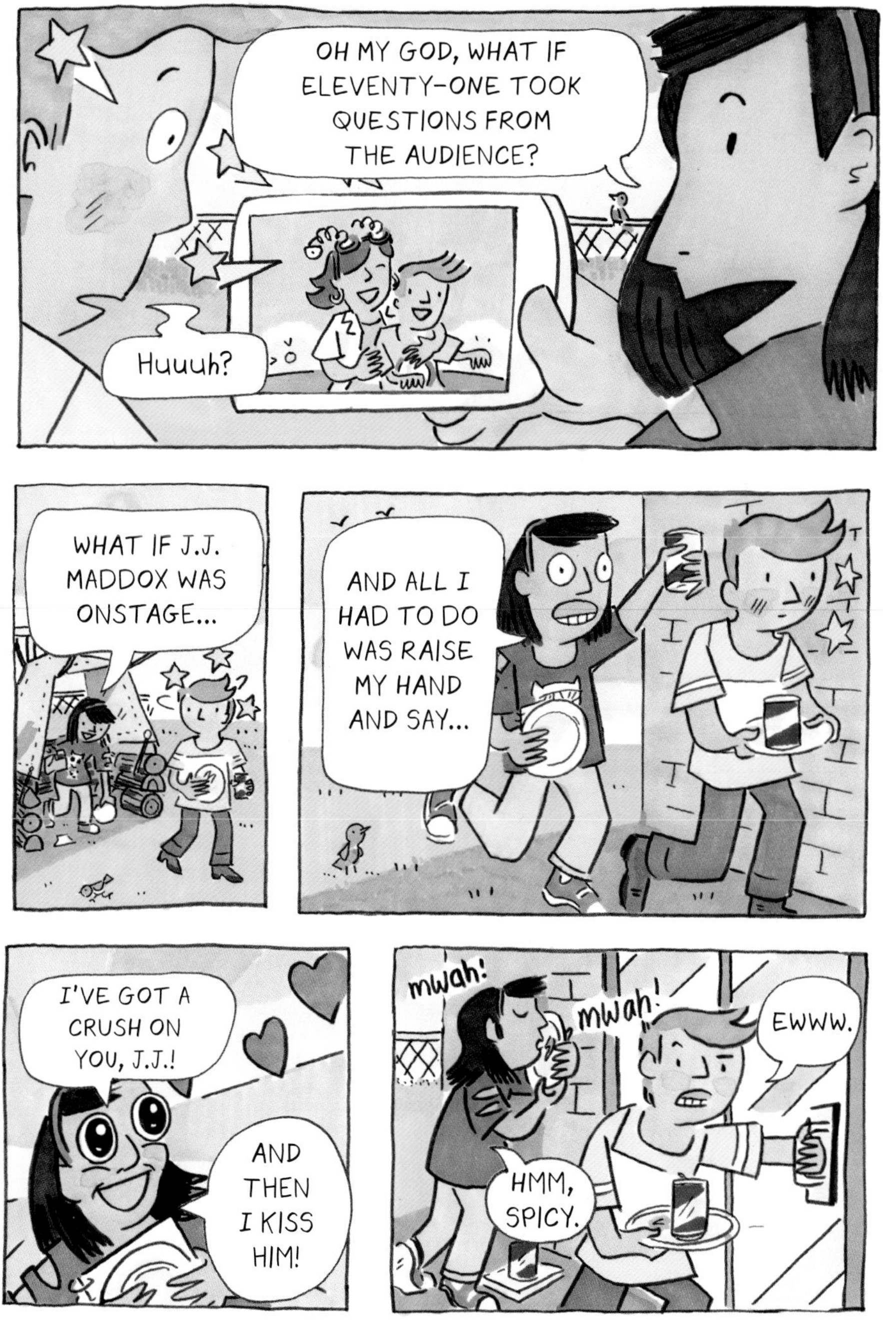
OH MY GOD, WHAT IF ELEVENTY-ONE TOOK QUESTIONS FROM THE AUDIENCE?
Huuuh?
WHAT IF J.J. MADDOX WAS ONSTAGE...
AND ALL I HAD TO DO WAS RAISE MY HAND AND SAY...
I'VE GOT A CRUSH ON YOU, J.J.!
AND THEN I KISS HIM!
mwah!
mwah!
EWWW.
HMM, SPICY.

I don't get Cate's crush on a boy band dude.

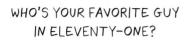
Later that night...

WHO'S YOUR FAVORITE GUY IN ELEVENTY-ONE?

I'M NOT A FAN, REALLY.

WOULD YOU KISS J.J.? THE GUY IN THE JACKET?

GI-IRL

ICK.

WHAT ABOUT THE OTHER GUYS?

YEAH!

GI-IRL!

...SO?

THAT'S IT?

I THOUGHT THERE WERE ELEVENTY-ONE OF THEM.

HA HA! LIKE A MARCHING BOY BAND.

GI-IRL YE-AH

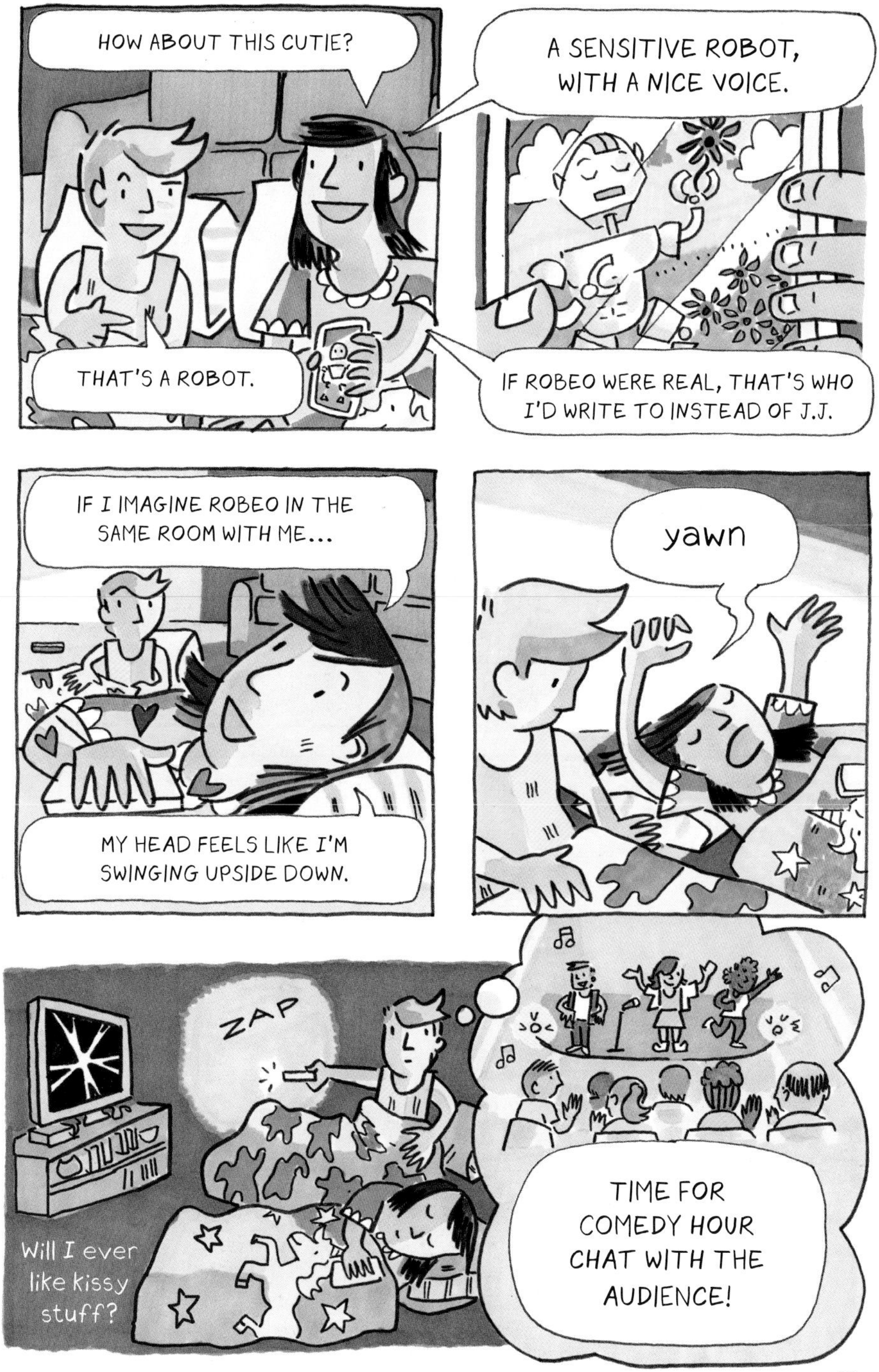
HOW ABOUT THIS CUTIE?
THAT'S A ROBOT.
A SENSITIVE ROBOT, WITH A NICE VOICE.
IF ROBEO WERE REAL, THAT'S WHO I'D WRITE TO INSTEAD OF J.J.
IF I IMAGINE ROBEO IN THE SAME ROOM WITH ME...
MY HEAD FEELS LIKE I'M SWINGING UPSIDE DOWN.
yawn
ZAP
TIME FOR COMEDY HOUR CHAT WITH THE AUDIENCE!
Will I ever like kissy stuff?

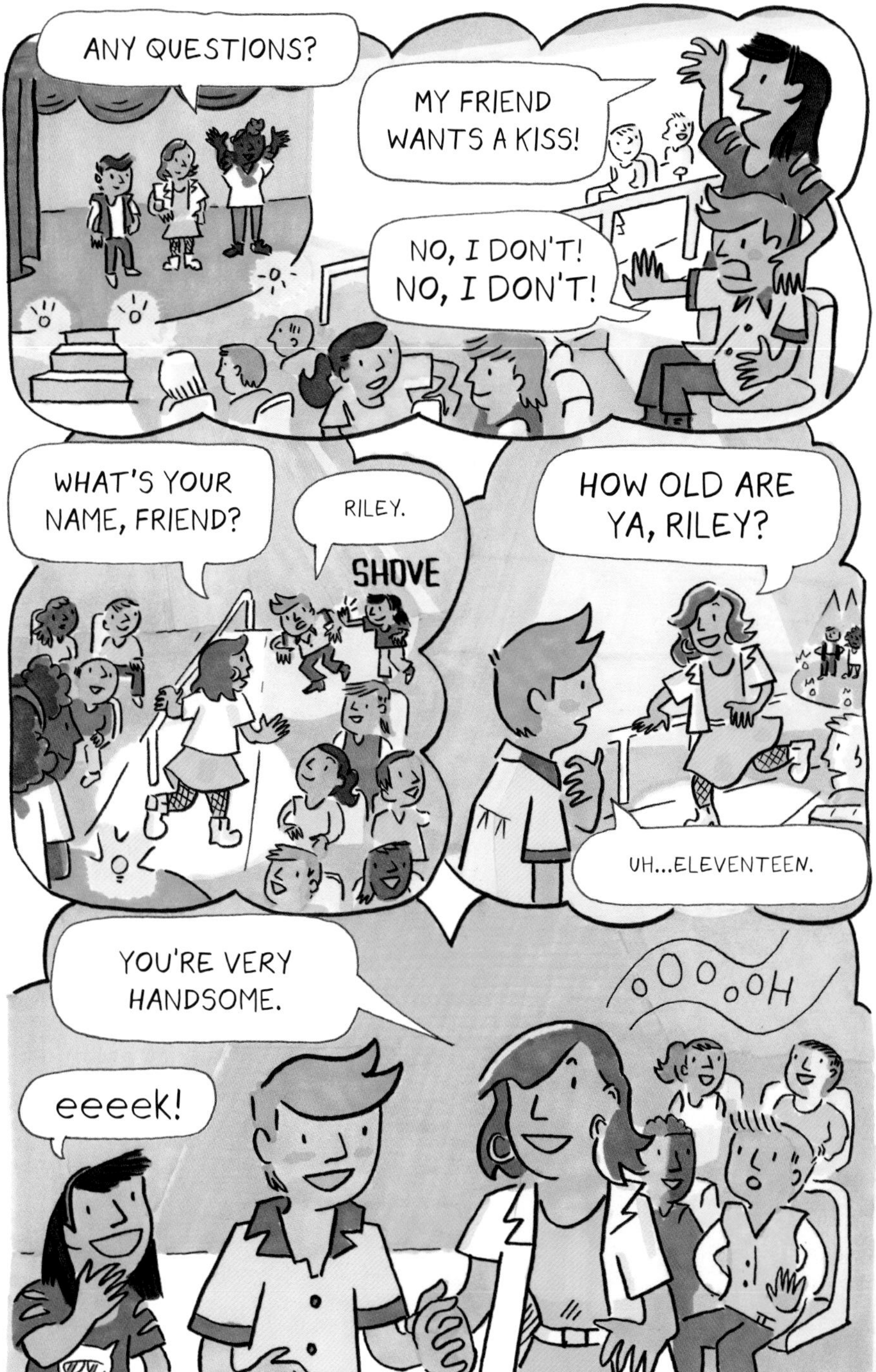
ANY QUESTIONS?
MY FRIEND WANTS A KISS!
NO, I DON'T! NO, I DON'T!
WHAT'S YOUR NAME, FRIEND?
RILEY.
SHOVE
HOW OLD ARE YA, RILEY?
UH...ELEVENTEEN.
YOU'RE VERY HANDSOME.
oOOooOH
eeeek!

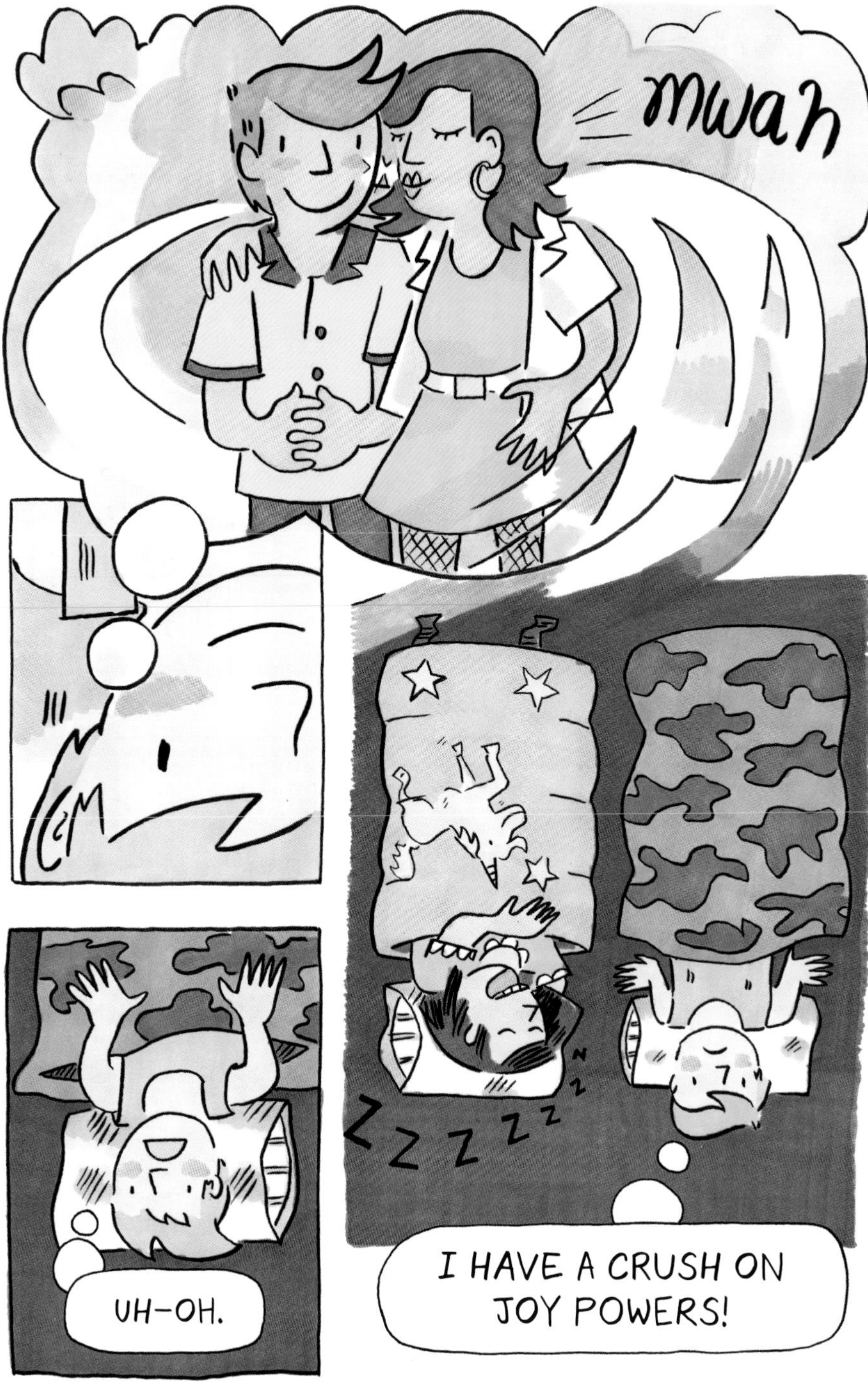
mwah
ZZZZZZ
UH-OH.
I HAVE A CRUSH ON JOY POWERS!

CHAPTER 7

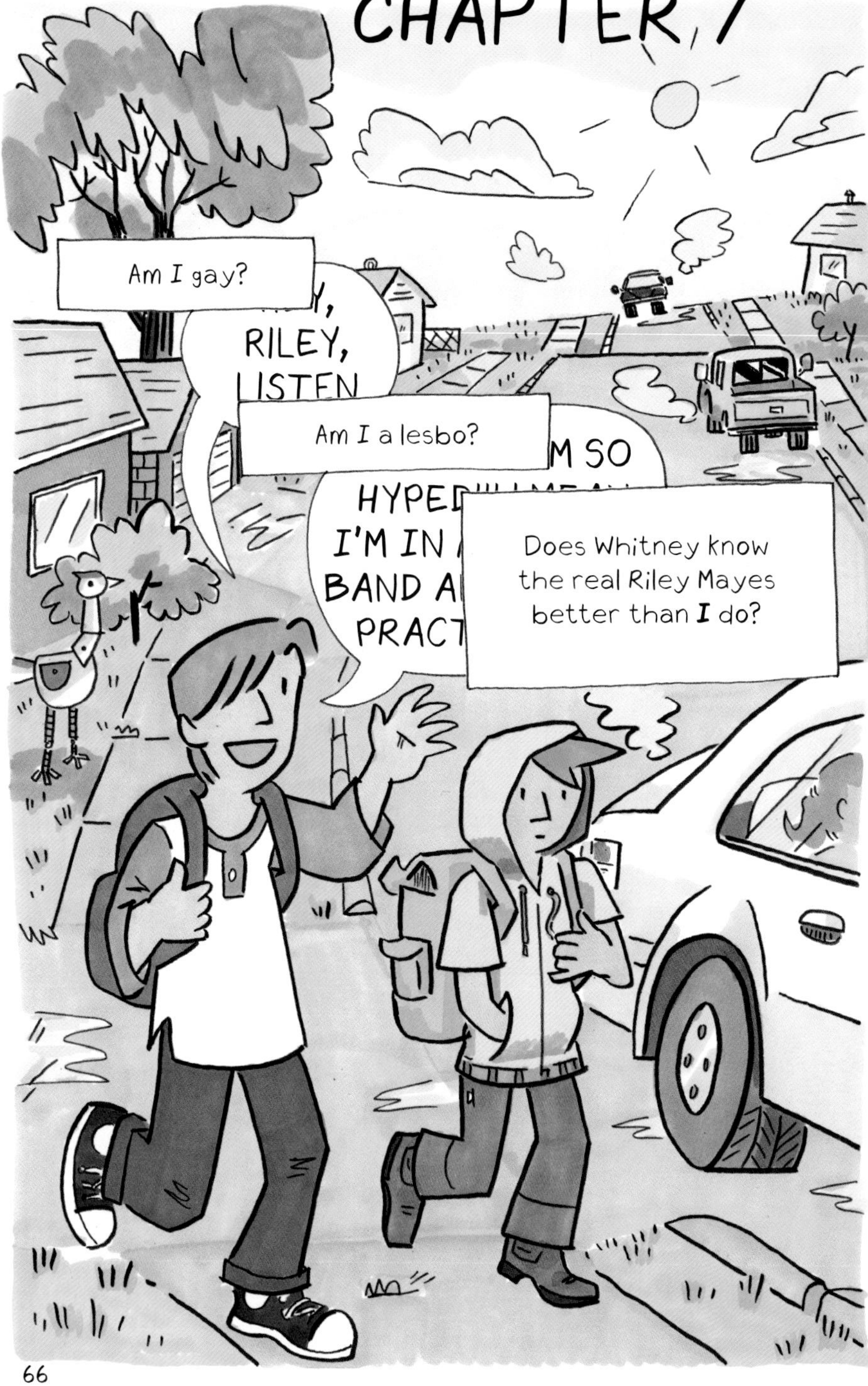
Am I gay?
RILEY, LISTEN
Am I a lesbo?
Does Whitney know the real Riley Mayes better than I do?

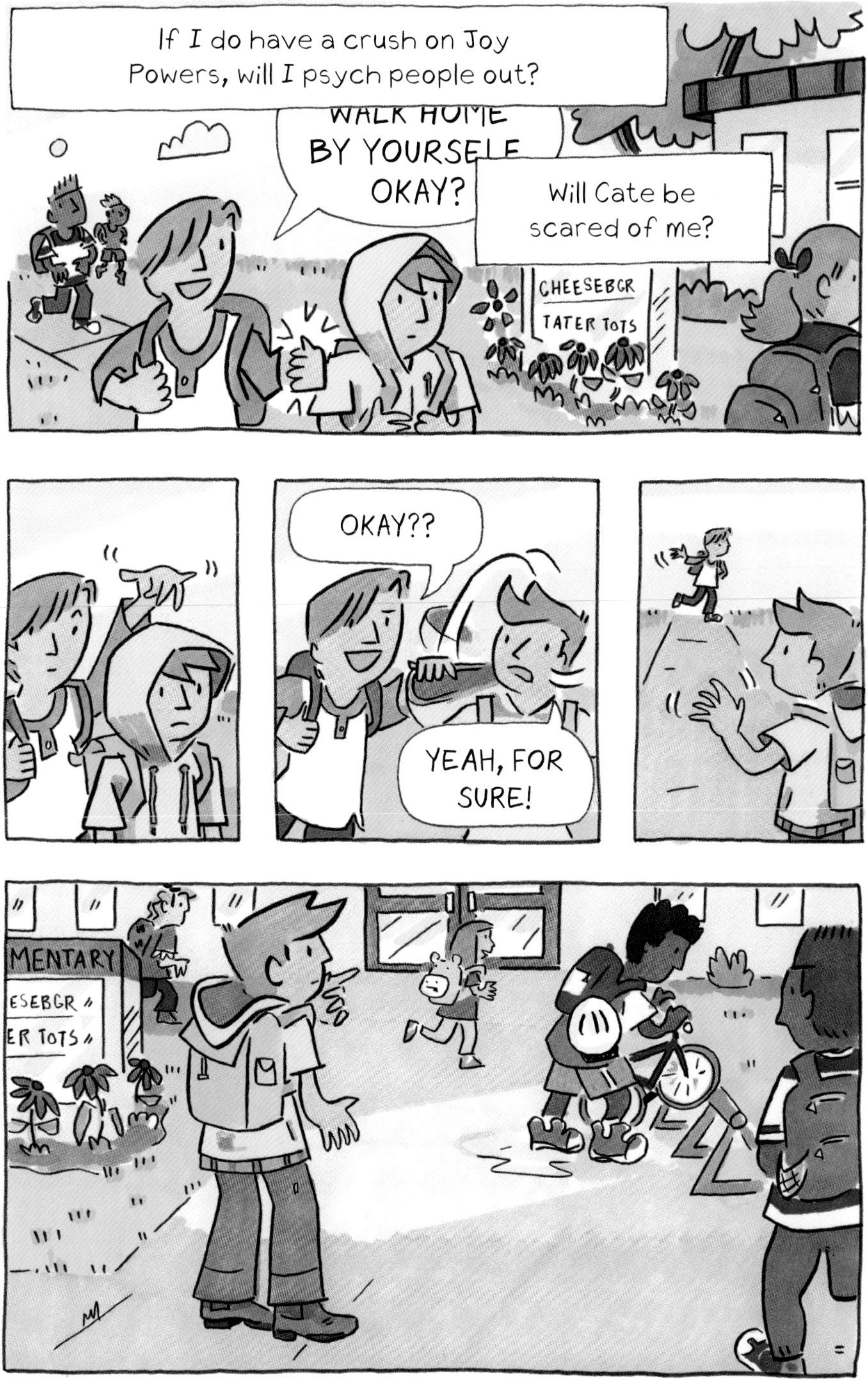
If I do have a crush on Joy Powers, will I psych people out?
WALK HOME BY YOURSELF OKAY?
Will Cate be scared of me?
CHEESEBGR
TATER TOTS
OKAY??
YEAH, FOR SURE!
MENTARY
ESEBGR
ER TOTS

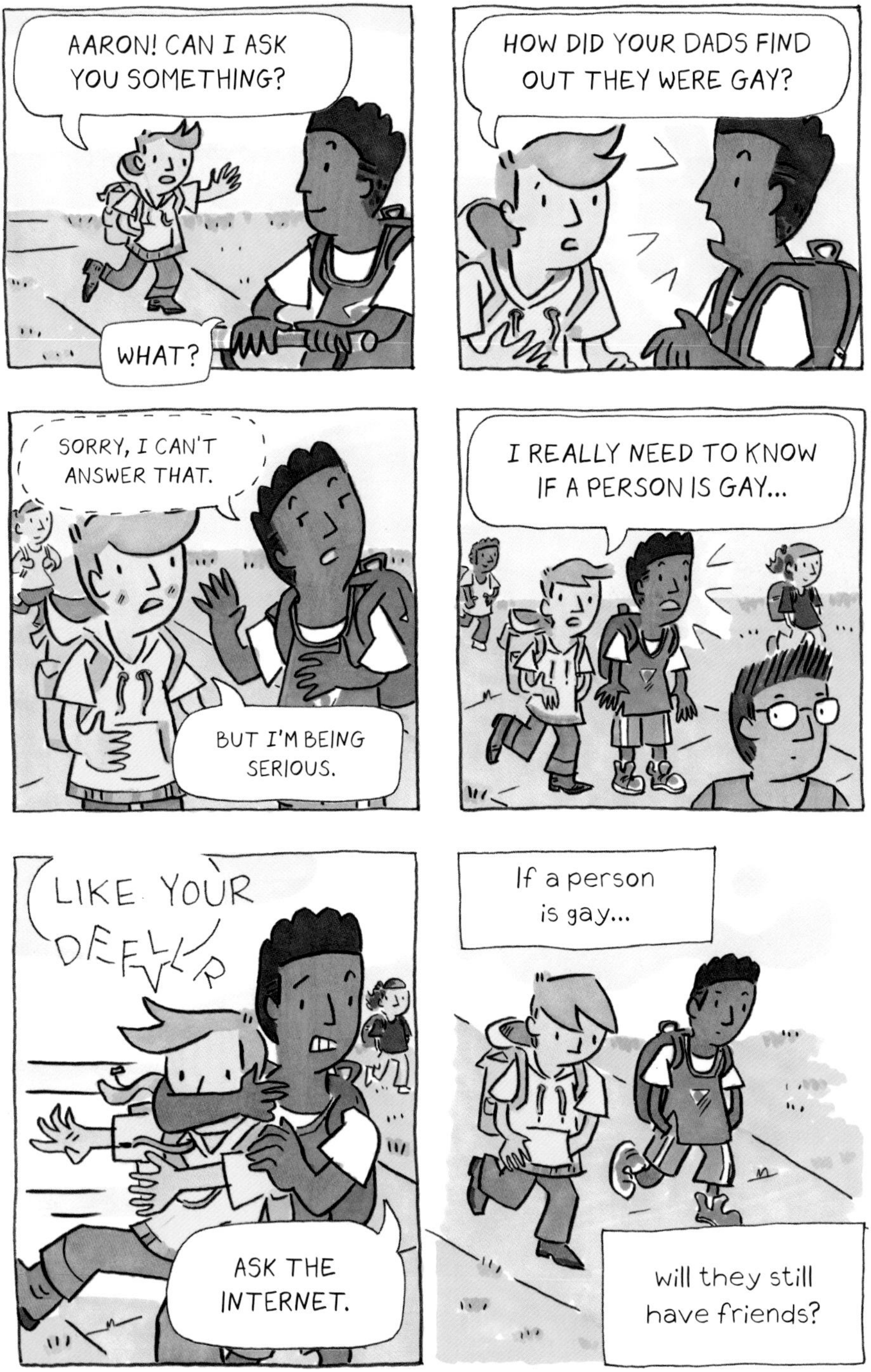
AARON! CAN I ASK YOU SOMETHING?
WHAT?
HOW DID YOUR DADS FIND OUT THEY WERE GAY?
SORRY, I CAN'T ANSWER THAT.
BUT I'M BEING SERIOUS.
I REALLY NEED TO KNOW IF A PERSON IS GAY...
LIKE YOUR
ASK THE INTERNET.
If a person is gay...
will they still have friends?

Mrs. M sent the whole class to the library.
I'm supposed to find a way to contact Joy Powers.

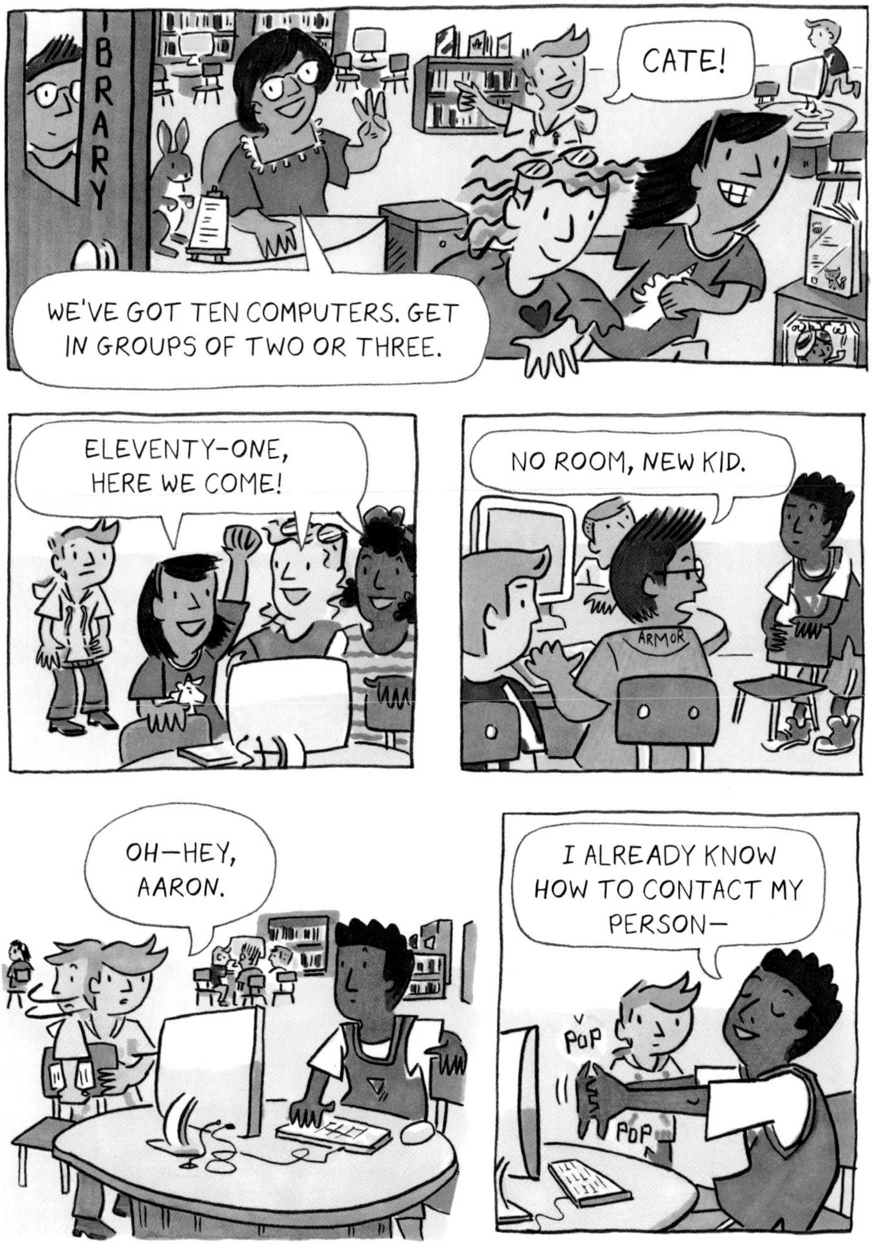
LIBRARY
CATE!
WE'VE GOT TEN COMPUTERS. GET IN GROUPS OF TWO OR THREE.
ELEVENTY-ONE, HERE WE COME!
NO ROOM, NEW KID.
ARMOR
OH—HEY, AARON.
I ALREADY KNOW HOW TO CONTACT MY PERSON—
POP
POP

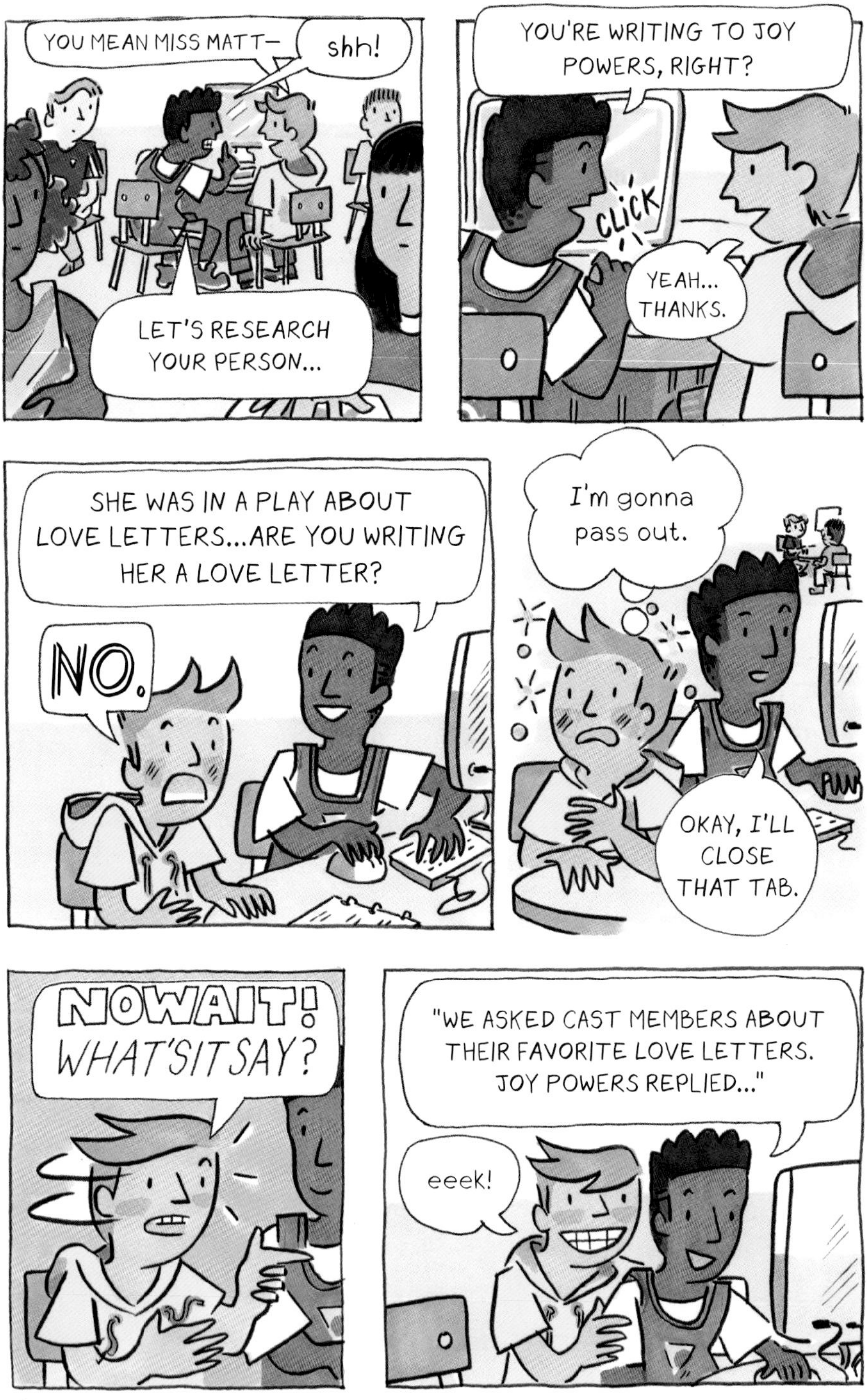
YOU MEAN MISS MATT—
shh!
LET'S RESEARCH YOUR PERSON...
YOU'RE WRITING TO JOY POWERS, RIGHT?
CLICK
YEAH... THANKS.
SHE WAS IN A PLAY ABOUT LOVE LETTERS...ARE YOU WRITING HER A LOVE LETTER?
NO.
I'm gonna pass out.
OKAY, I'LL CLOSE THAT TAB.
NO WAIT! WHAT'S IT SAY?
"WE ASKED CAST MEMBERS ABOUT THEIR FAVORITE LOVE LETTERS. JOY POWERS REPLIED..."
eeek!

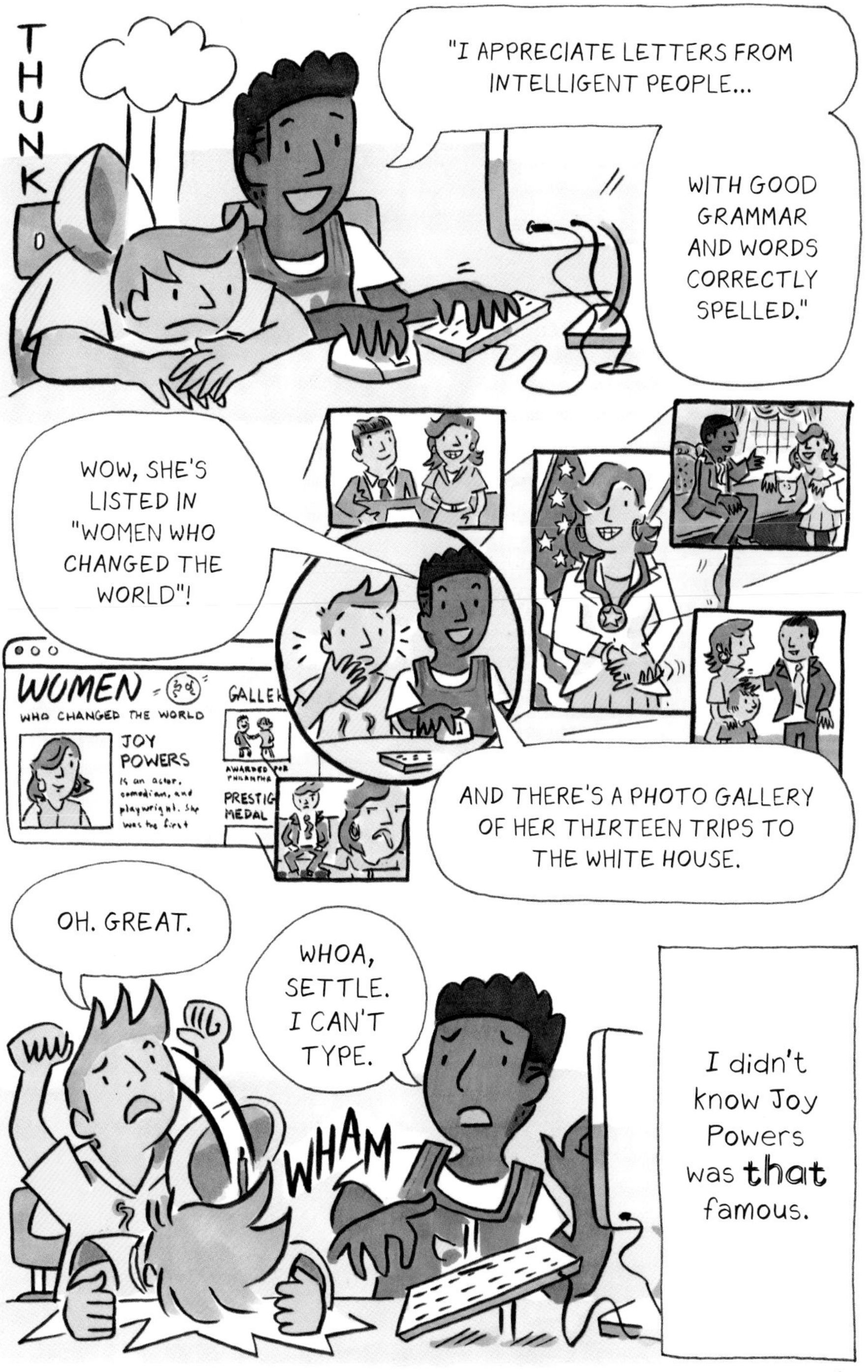
THUNK
"I APPRECIATE LETTERS FROM INTELLIGENT PEOPLE...
WITH GOOD GRAMMAR AND WORDS CORRECTLY SPELLED."
WOW, SHE'S LISTED IN "WOMEN WHO CHANGED THE WORLD"!
WOMEN
WHO CHANGED THE WORLD
JOY POWERS
is an actor, comedian, and playwright. She was the first
MEDAL
AND THERE'S A PHOTO GALLERY OF HER THIRTEEN TRIPS TO THE WHITE HOUSE.
OH. GREAT.
WHOA, SETTLE. I CAN'T TYPE.
WHAM
I didn't know Joy Powers was **that** famous.

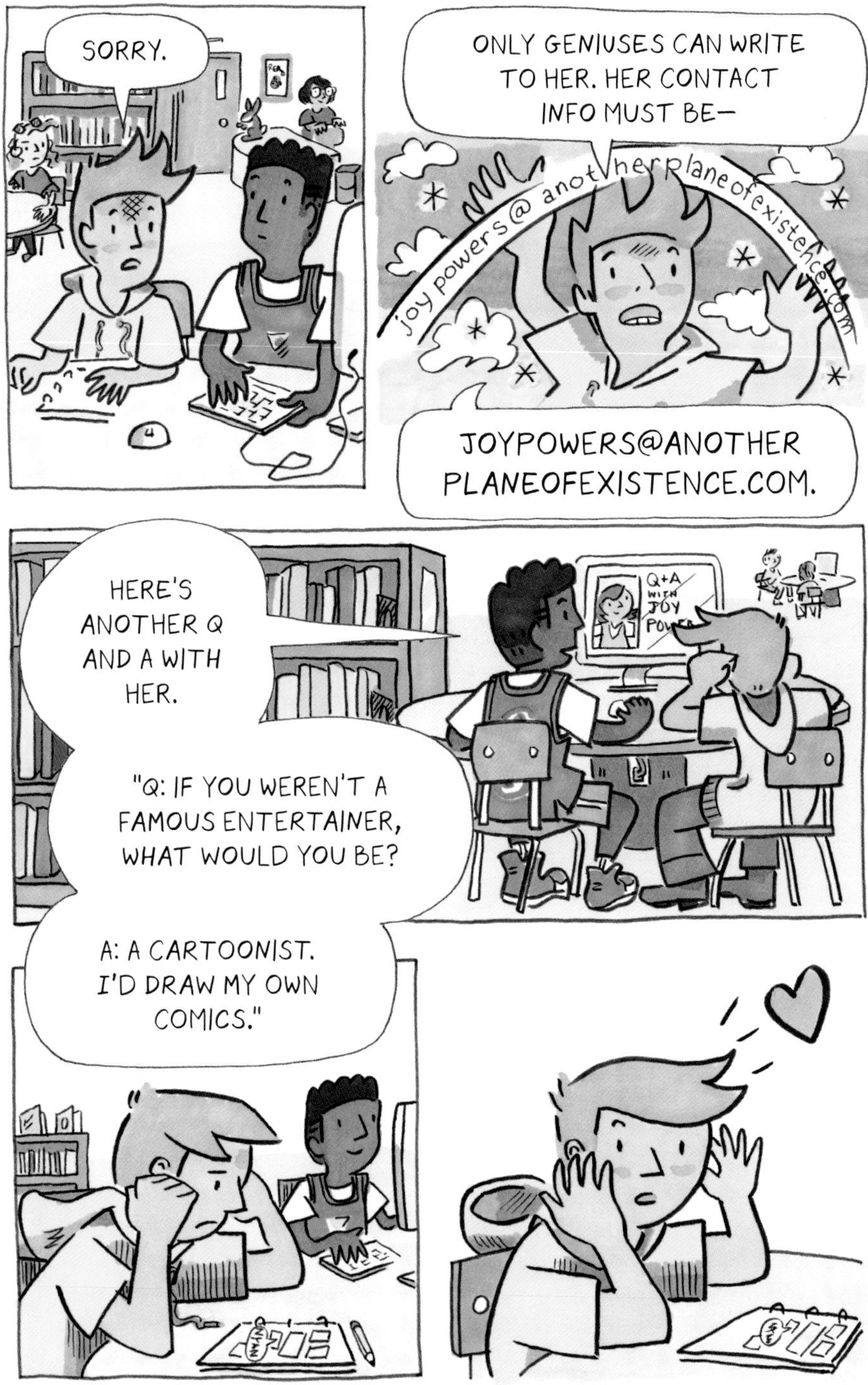
SORRY.
ONLY GENIUSES CAN WRITE TO HER. HER CONTACT INFO MUST BE—
joy powers@anotherplaneofexistence.com
JOYPOWERS@ANOTHER PLANEOFEXISTENCE.COM.
HERE'S ANOTHER Q AND A WITH HER.
Q+A WITH JOY POWERS
"Q: IF YOU WEREN'T A FAMOUS ENTERTAINER, WHAT WOULD YOU BE?
A: A CARTOONIST. I'D DRAW MY OWN COMICS."

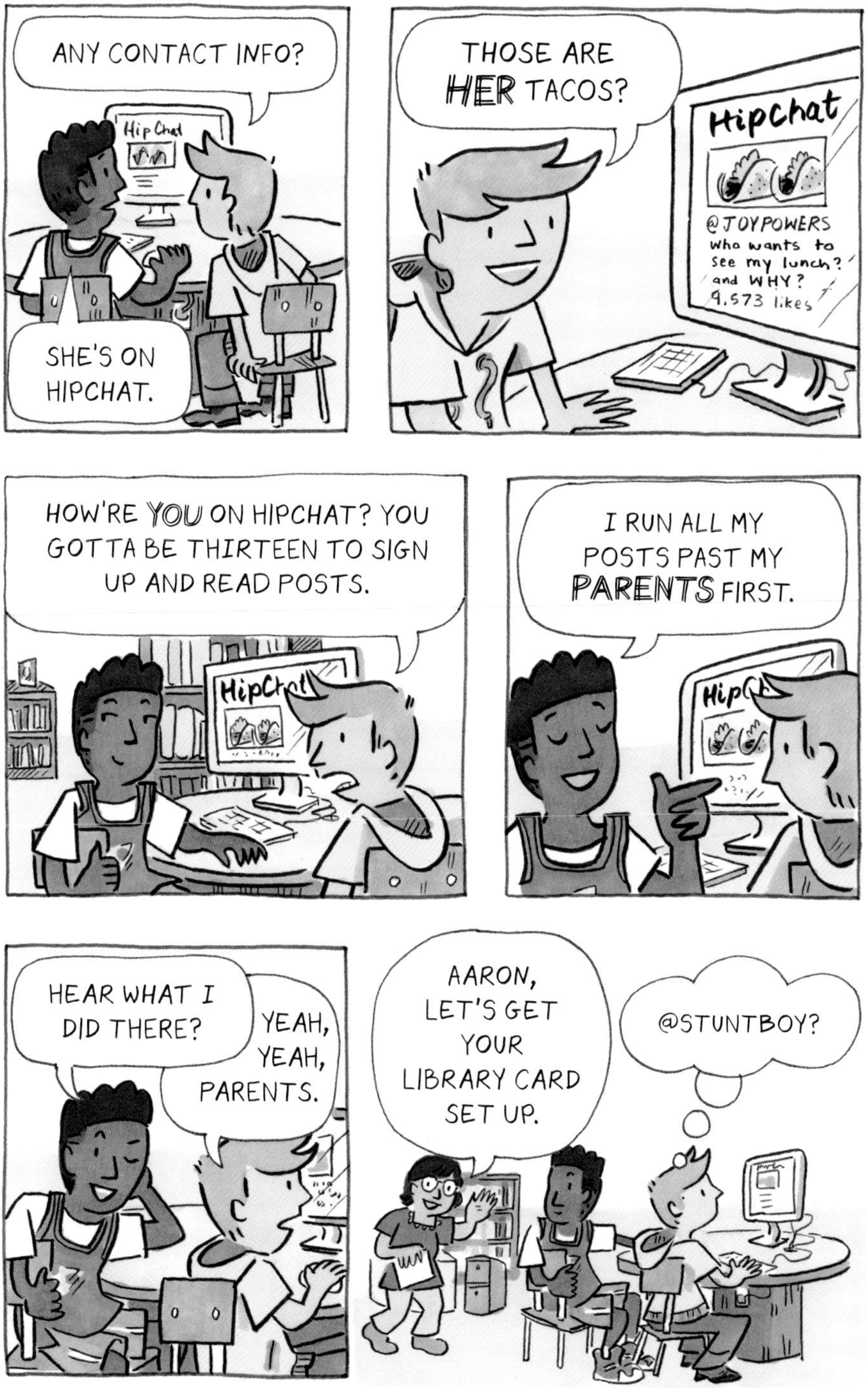
ANY CONTACT INFO?
Hip Chat
SHE'S ON HIPCHAT.
THOSE ARE HER TACOS?
Hipchat
@JOYPOWERS
who wants to see my lunch? and WHY?
4,573 likes
HOW'RE YOU ON HIPCHAT? YOU GOTTA BE THIRTEEN TO SIGN UP AND READ POSTS.
HipChat
I RUN ALL MY POSTS PAST MY PARENTS FIRST.
HEAR WHAT I DID THERE?
YEAH, YEAH, PARENTS.
AARON, LET'S GET YOUR LIBRARY CARD SET UP.
@STUNTBOY?

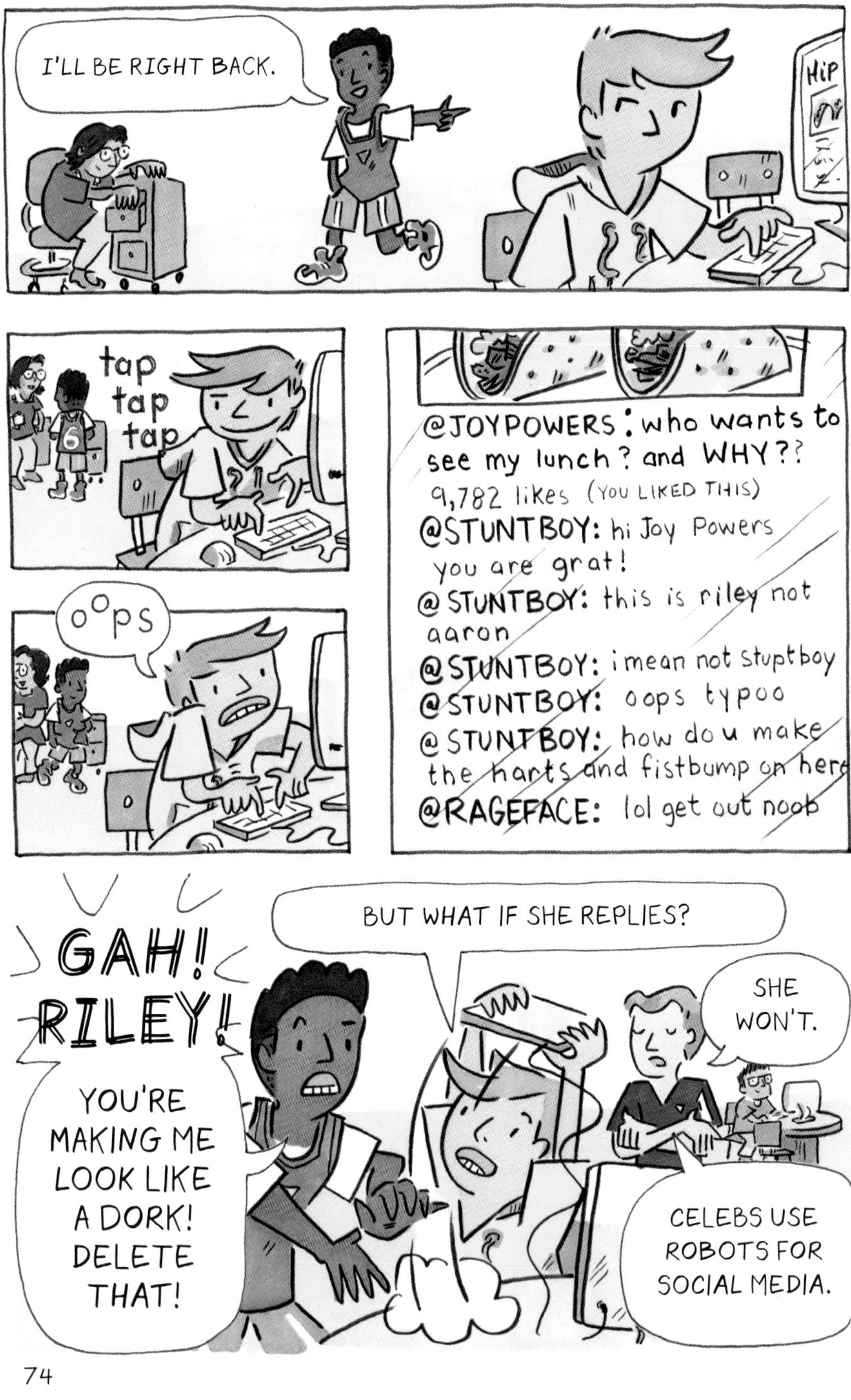
I'LL BE RIGHT BACK.
tap tap tap
oops
@JOYPOWERS: who wants to see my lunch? and WHY??
9,782 likes (YOU LIKED THIS)
@STUNTBOY: hi Joy Powers you are grat!
@STUNTBOY: this is riley not aaron
@STUNTBOY: i mean not stuptboy
@STUNTBOY: oops typoo
@STUNTBOY: how do u make the harts and fistbump on here
@RAGEFACE: lol get out noob
GAH! RILEY!
YOU'RE MAKING ME LOOK LIKE A DORK! DELETE THAT!
BUT WHAT IF SHE REPLIES?
SHE WON'T.
CELEBS USE ROBOTS FOR SOCIAL MEDIA.

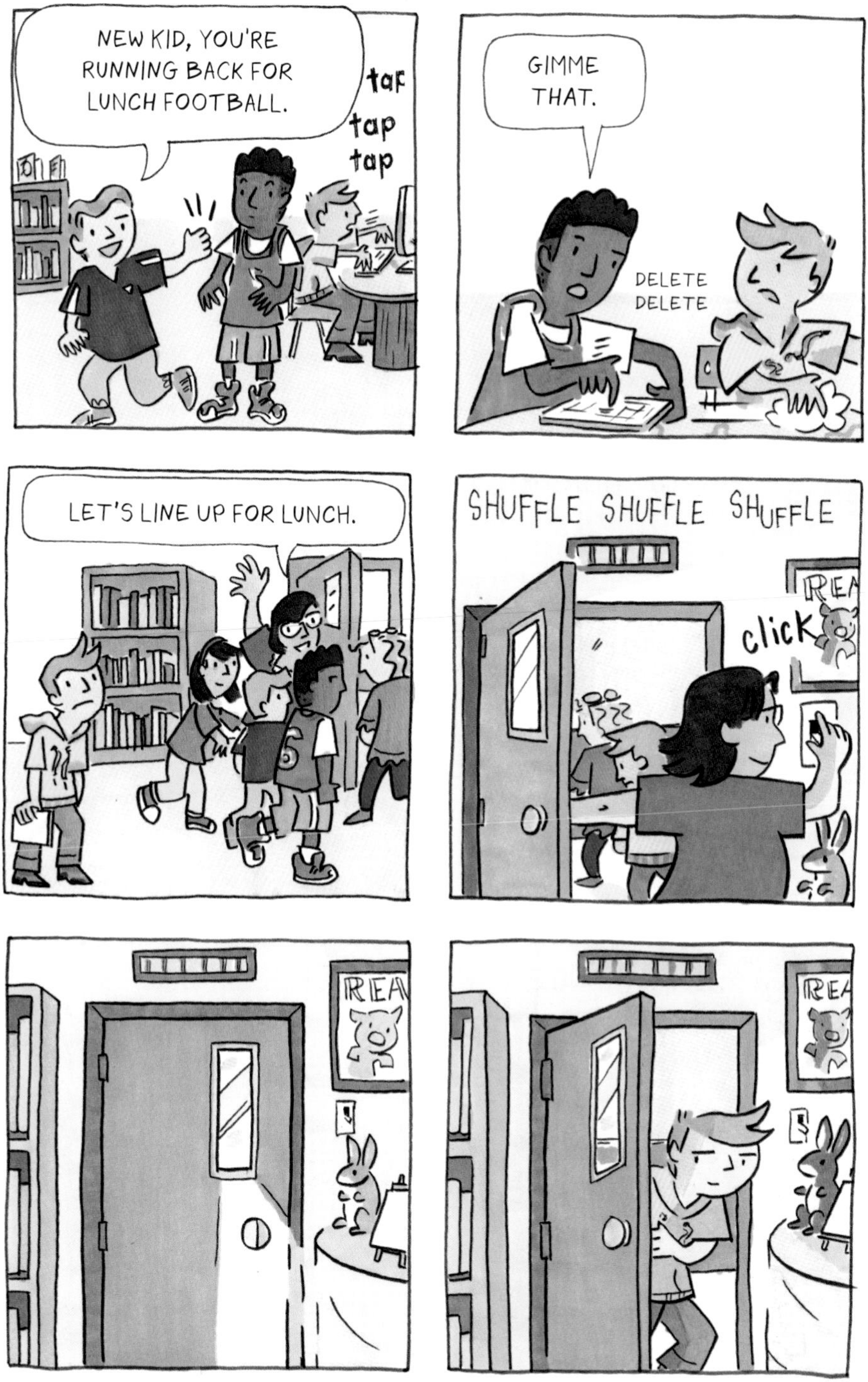
NEW KID, YOU'RE RUNNING BACK FOR LUNCH FOOTBALL.
tap
tap
tap
GIMME THAT.
DELETE
DELETE
LET'S LINE UP FOR LUNCH.
SHUFFLE SHUFFLE SHUFFLE
REA
click
REA
REA

CHAPTER 8

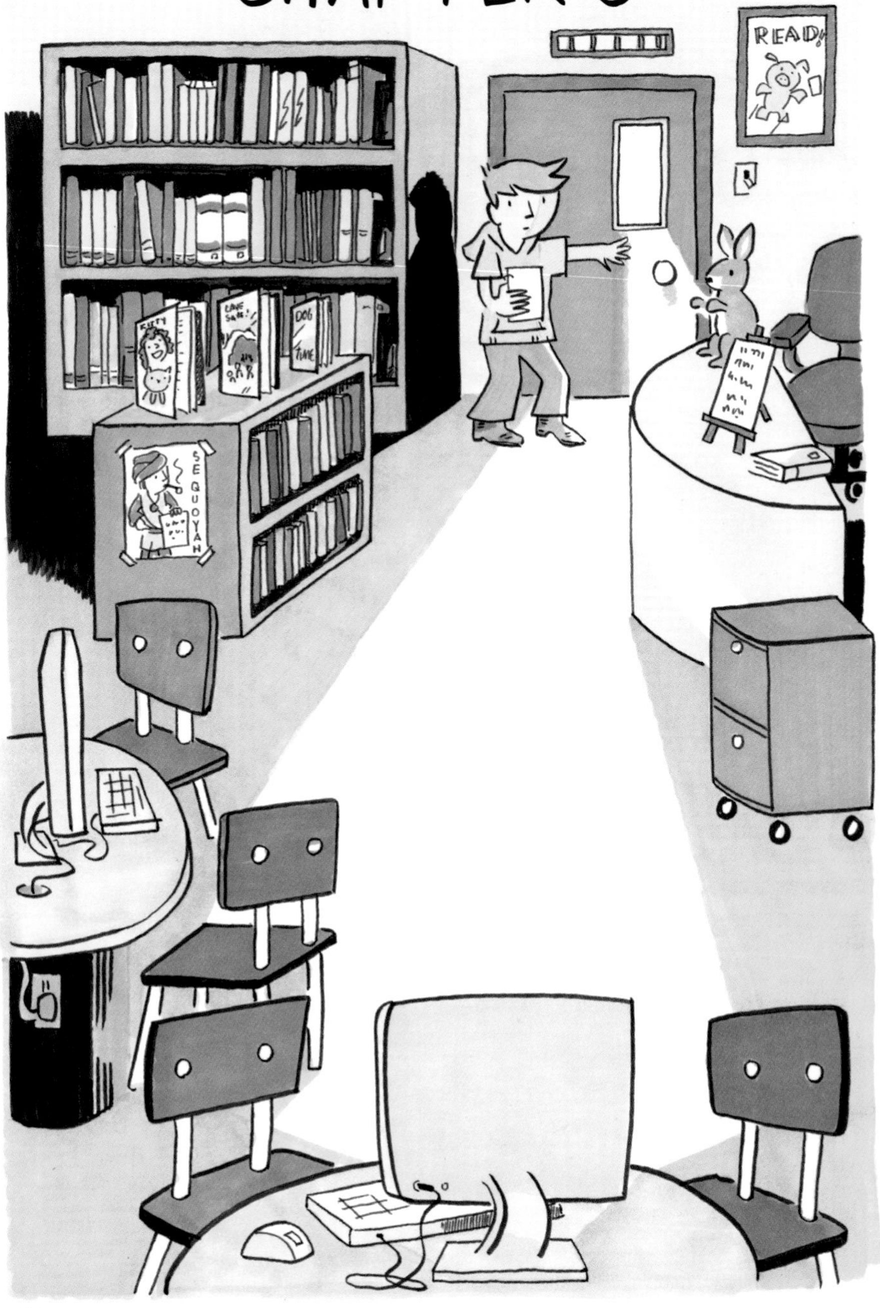
READ!
KITTY
CAVE SAFE!
DOG TIME
SEQUOYAH

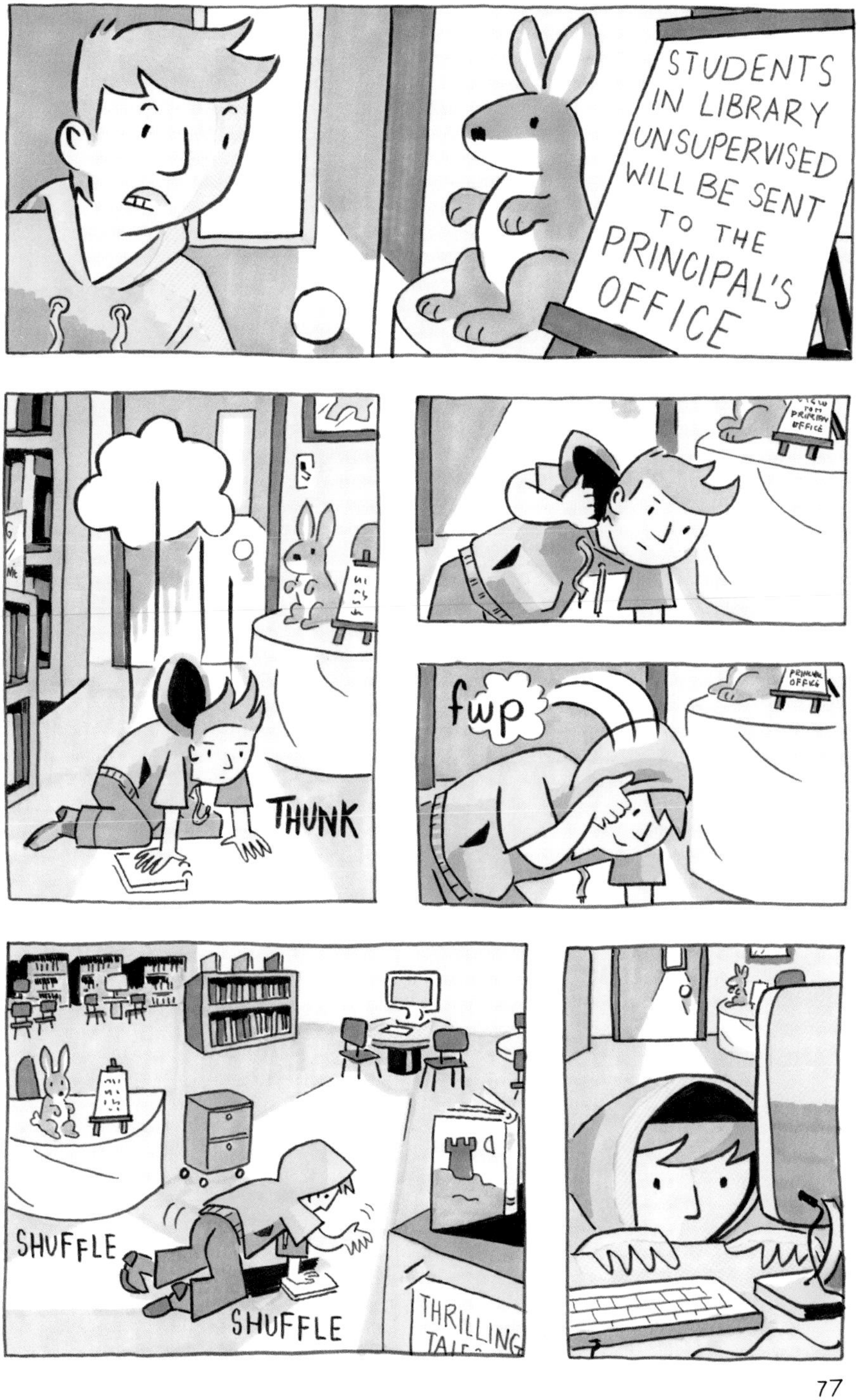
STUDENTS IN LIBRARY UNSUPERVISED WILL BE SENT TO THE PRINCIPAL'S OFFICE
THUNK
fwp
SHUFFLE
SHUFFLE
THRILLING

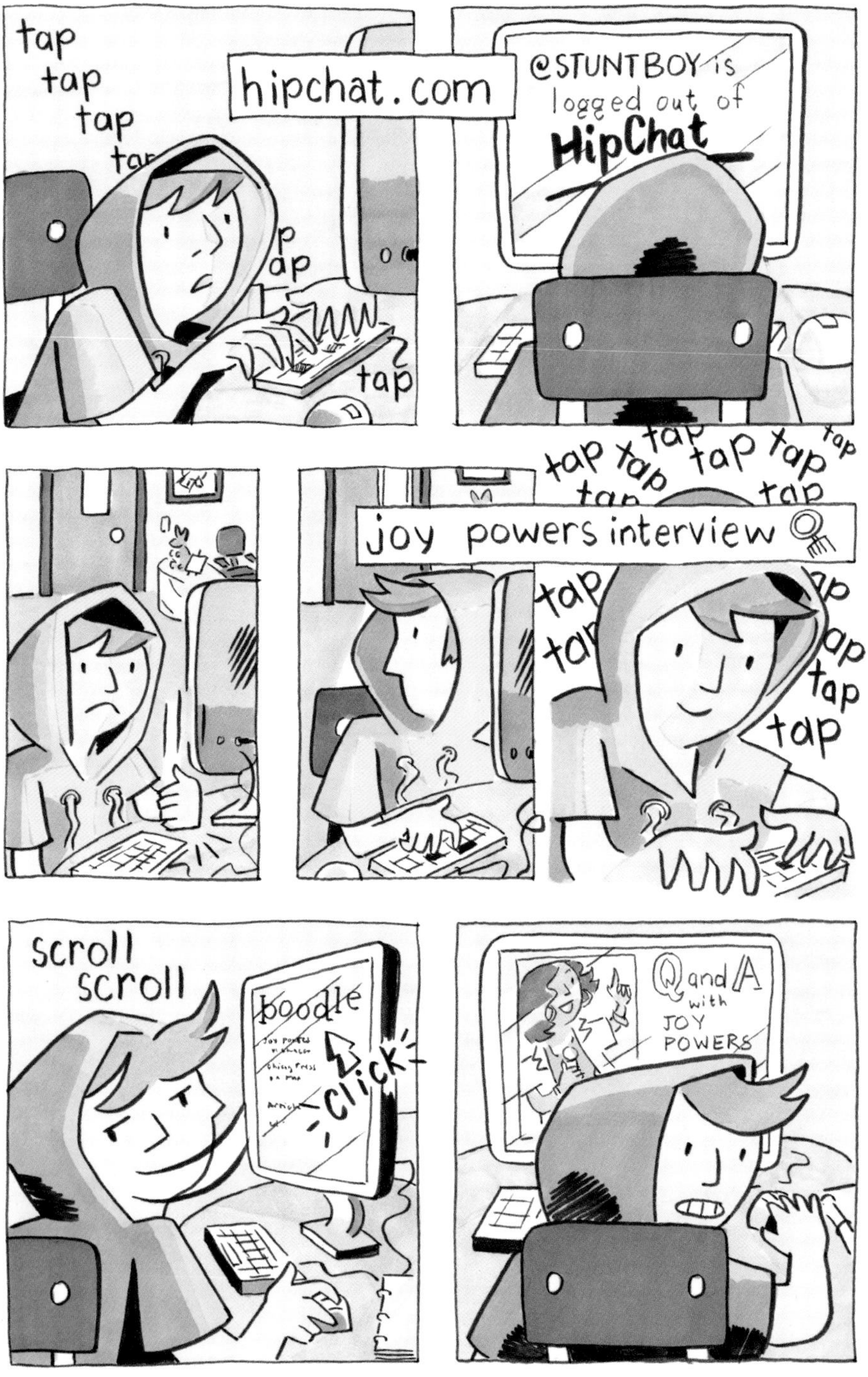
tap
tap
tap
hipchat.com
tap
@STUNTBOY is
logged out of
HipChat
joy powers interview
tap
tap
tap
scroll
scroll
boodle
CLICK
Q and A
with
JOY
POWERS

Q
JO
PO
Ever
you
kno
your

Scroll
scroll

(Q) and (A)
with
JOY
POWERS
Everything you want
to know about your
favorite comedian!

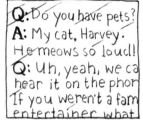

Q: Do you have pets?
A: My cat, Harvey.
He meows so loud!
Q: Uh, yeah, we ca
hear it on the phor
If you weren't a fam
entertainer what

Scroll
scroll
s

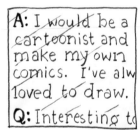

A: I would be a
cartoonist and
make my own
comics. I've alw
loved to draw.
Q: Interesting to

Q: Describe your
ideal Sunday.
A: Hmm...Swimming
roller-skating, or d
quiet evening of
solving crosswor
puzzles

Q: Name somethin
you can't do that
you wish you coulc
A: I'd like to go to
the moon and
look back at the
earth.

79

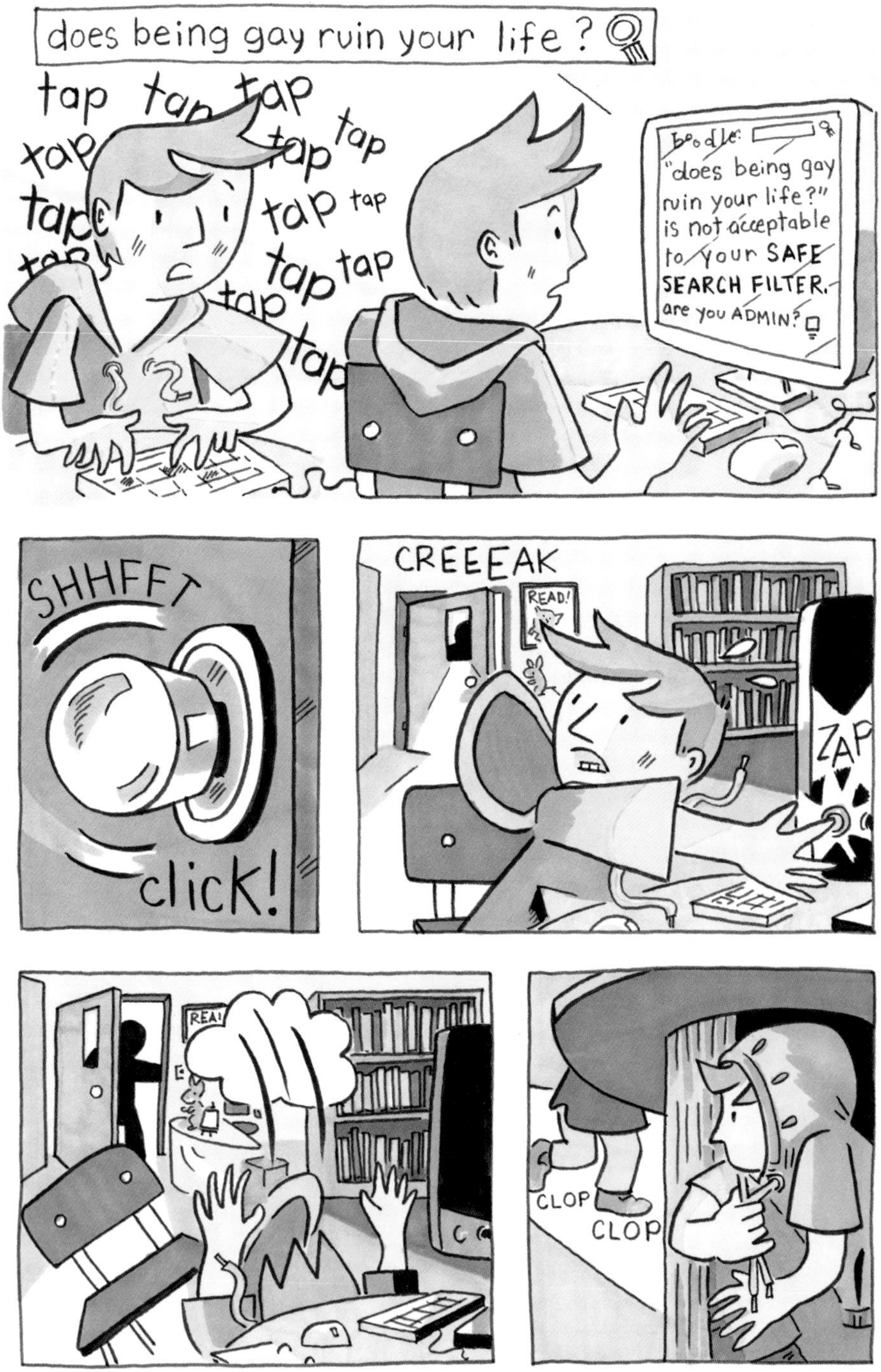
does being gay ruin your life?
tap tap tap tap tap tap tap tap tap tap tap tap tap tap
boodle:
"does being gay ruin your life?" is not acceptable to your SAFE SEARCH FILTER.
are you ADMIN?
SHHFFT
click!
CREEEAK
READ!
ZAP
CLOP
CLOP

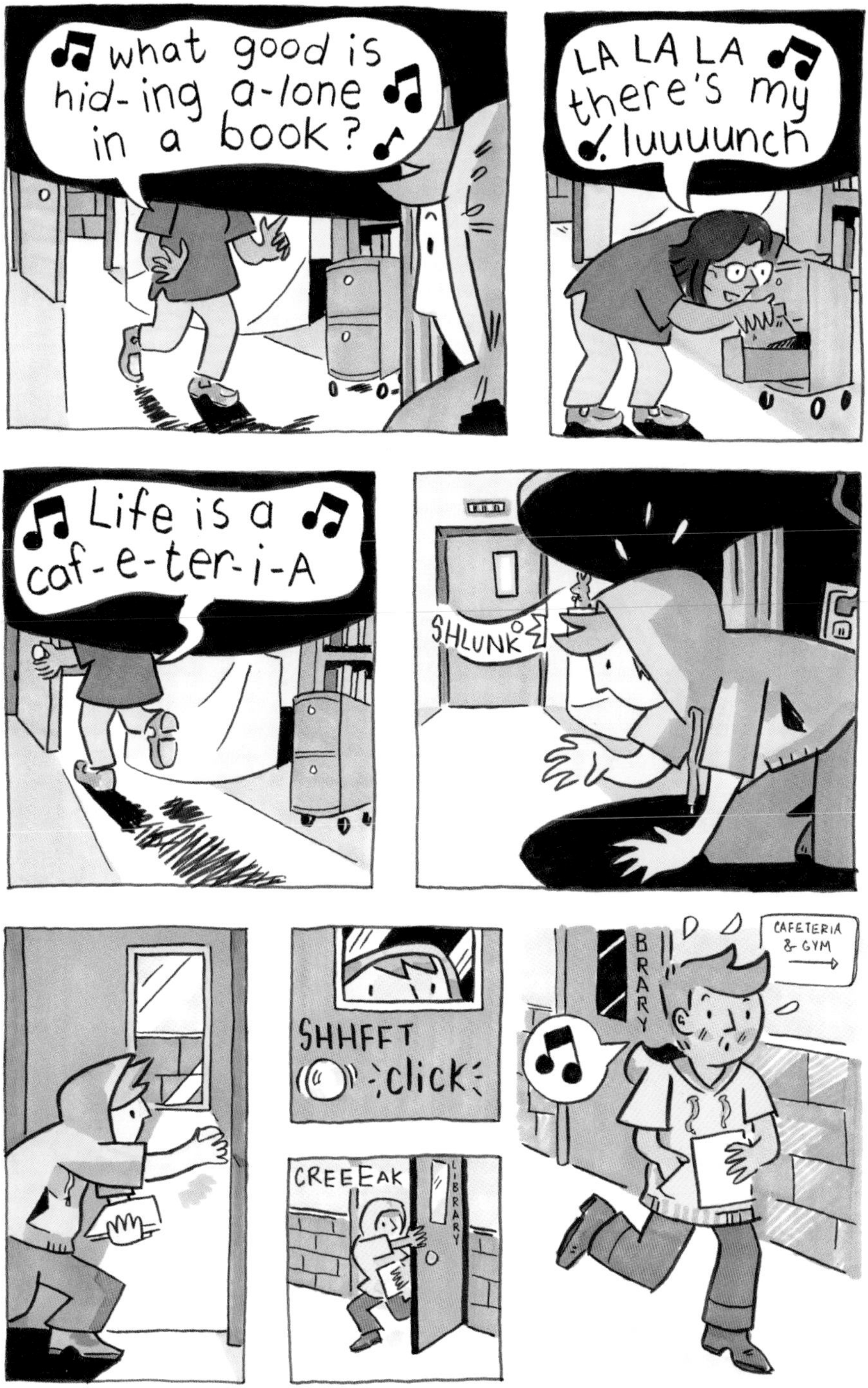
what good is hid-ing a-lone in a book?
LA LA LA there's my luuuunch
Life is a caf-e-ter-i-A
SHLUNK
SHHFFT
click
CREEEAK
LIBRARY
BRARY
CAFETERIA & GYM

CHAPTER 9

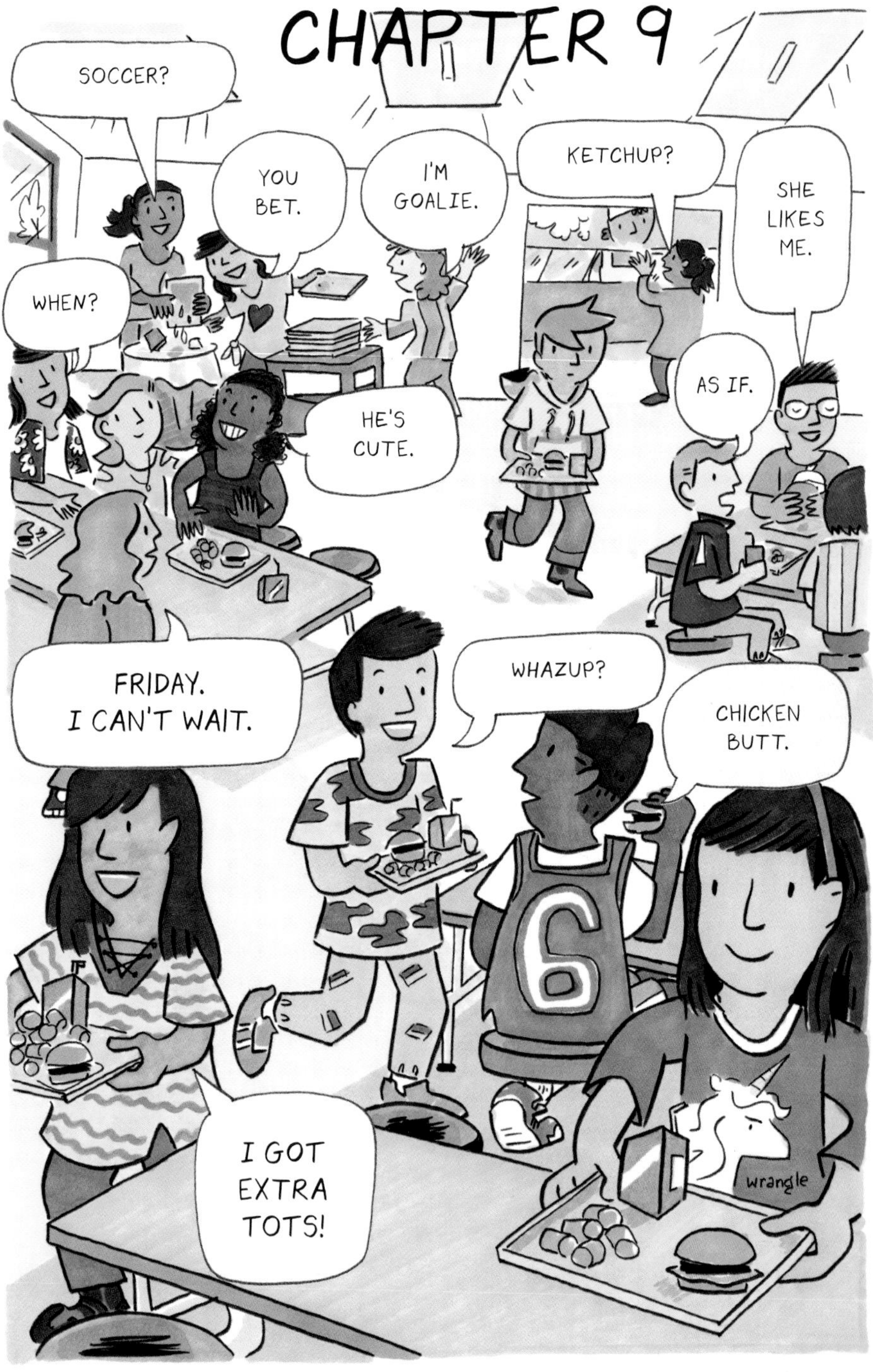
SOCCER?
YOU BET.
I'M GOALIE.
KETCHUP?
SHE LIKES ME.
WHEN?
HE'S CUTE.
AS IF.
FRIDAY. I CAN'T WAIT.
WHAZUP?
CHICKEN BUTT.
I GOT EXTRA TOTS!
wrangle

I've been having lunch with Cate the past few days.

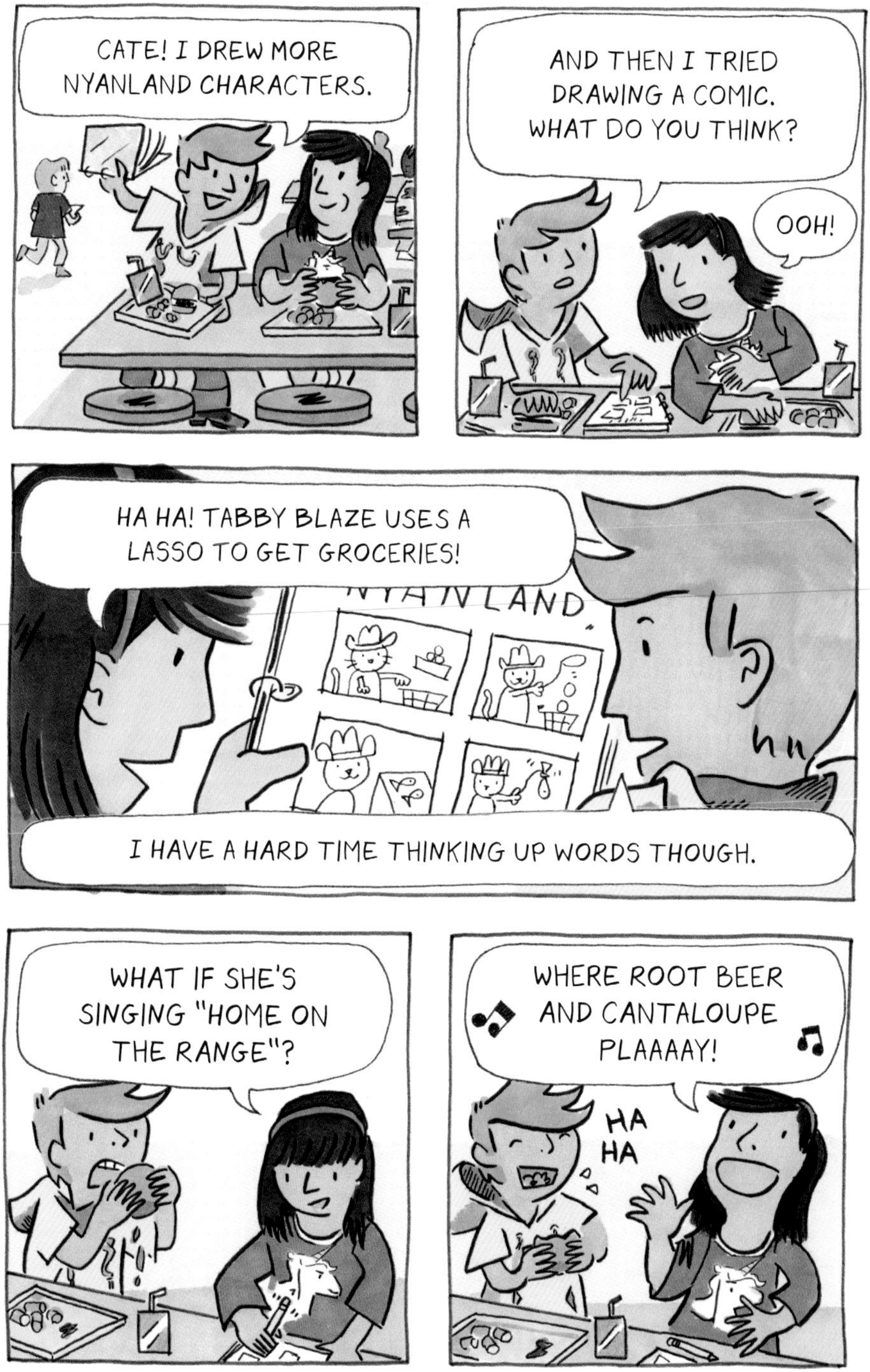
CATE! I DREW MORE NYANLAND CHARACTERS.
AND THEN I TRIED DRAWING A COMIC. WHAT DO YOU THINK?
OOH!
HA HA! TABBY BLAZE USES A LASSO TO GET GROCERIES!
NYANLAND
I HAVE A HARD TIME THINKING UP WORDS THOUGH.
WHAT IF SHE'S SINGING "HOME ON THE RANGE"?
WHERE ROOT BEER AND CANTALOUPE PLAAAAY!
HA HA

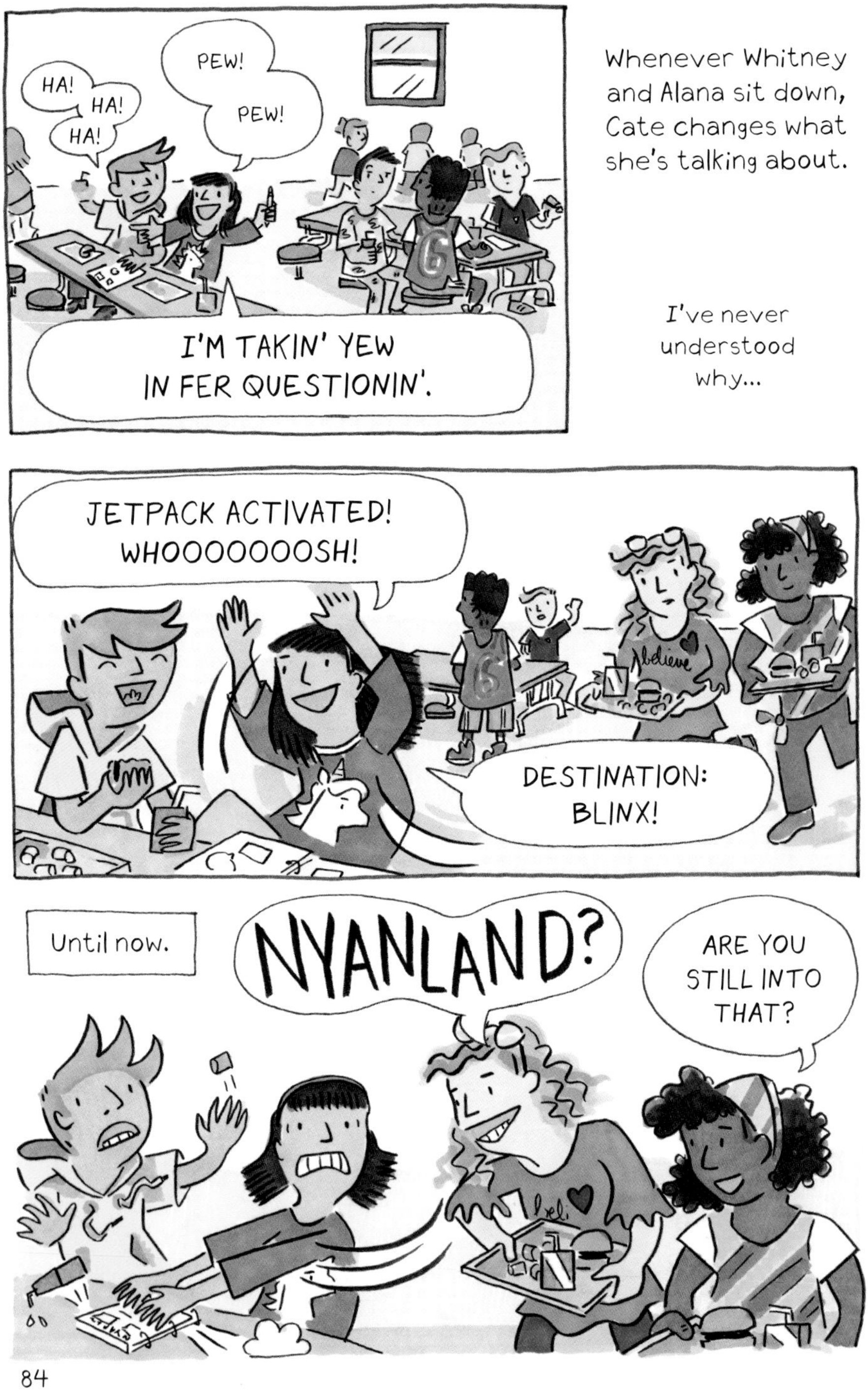

HA! HA! HA!
PEW! PEW!
I'M TAKIN' YEW IN FER QUESTIONIN'.
Whenever Whitney and Alana sit down, Cate changes what she's talking about.
I've never understood why...
JETPACK ACTIVATED! WHOOOOOOOSH!
DESTINATION: BLINX!
Until now.
NYANLAND?
ARE YOU STILL INTO THAT?

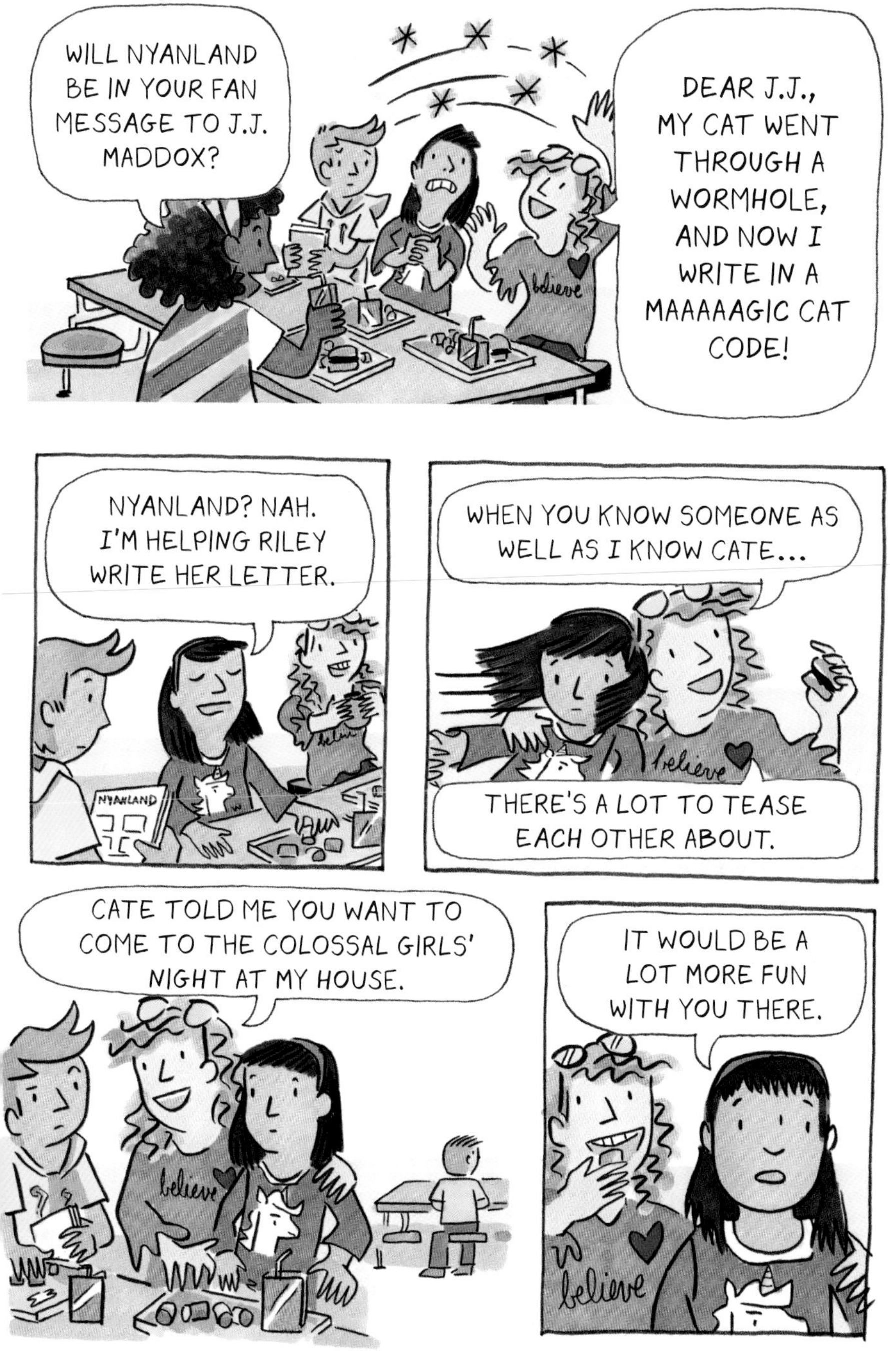
WILL NYANLAND BE IN YOUR FAN MESSAGE TO J.J. MADDOX?
DEAR J.J., MY CAT WENT THROUGH A WORMHOLE, AND NOW I WRITE IN A MAAAAAGIC CAT CODE!
believe
NYANLAND? NAH. I'M HELPING RILEY WRITE HER LETTER.
NYANLAND
WHEN YOU KNOW SOMEONE AS WELL AS I KNOW CATE...
THERE'S A LOT TO TEASE EACH OTHER ABOUT.
CATE TOLD ME YOU WANT TO COME TO THE COLOSSAL GIRLS' NIGHT AT MY HOUSE.
IT WOULD BE A LOT MORE FUN WITH YOU THERE.

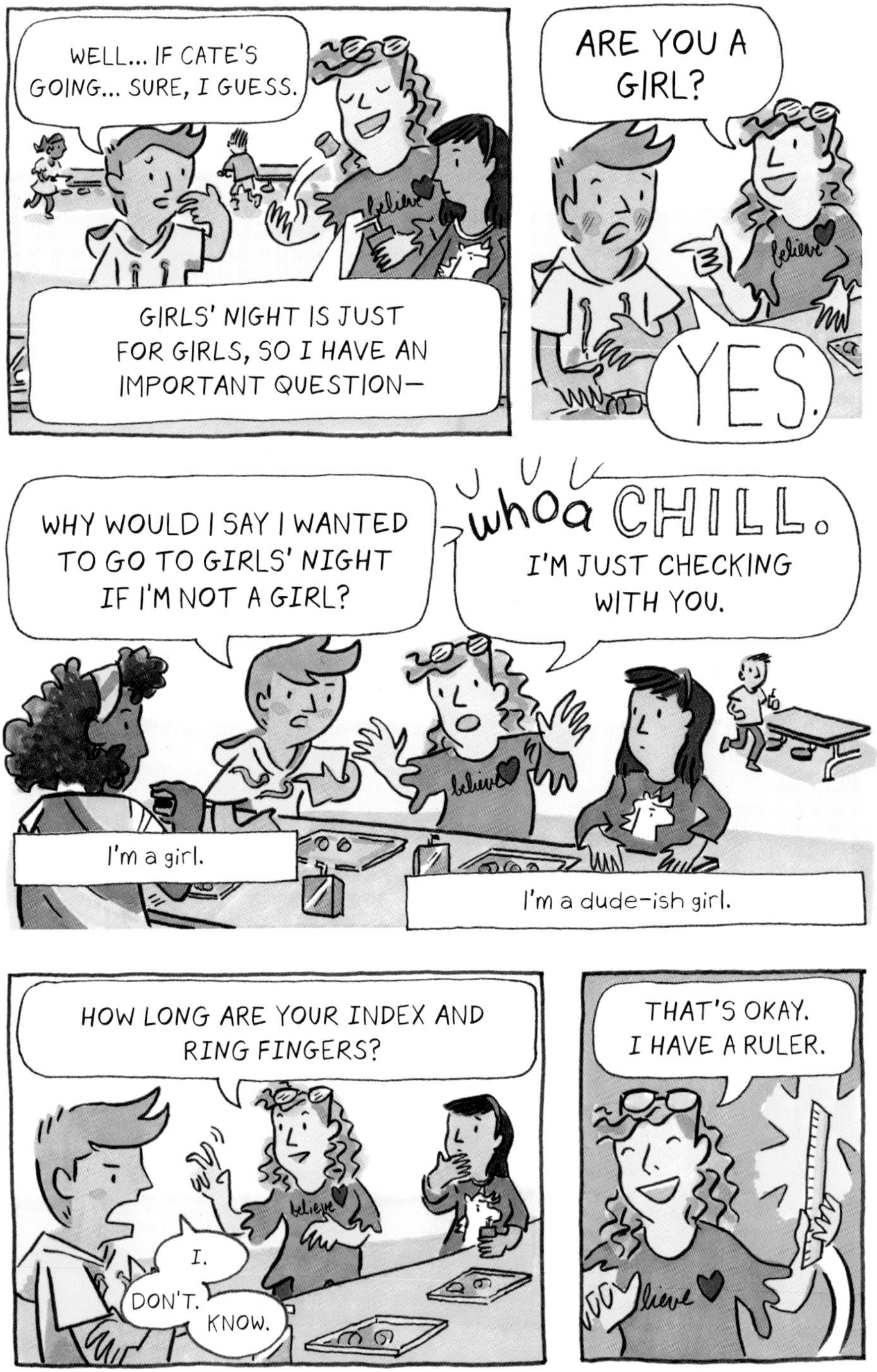
WELL... IF CATE'S GOING... SURE, I GUESS.
GIRLS' NIGHT IS JUST FOR GIRLS, SO I HAVE AN IMPORTANT QUESTION—
ARE YOU A GIRL?
YES.
WHY WOULD I SAY I WANTED TO GO TO GIRLS' NIGHT IF I'M NOT A GIRL?
whoa CHILL.
I'M JUST CHECKING WITH YOU.
I'm a girl.
I'm a dude-ish girl.
HOW LONG ARE YOUR INDEX AND RING FINGERS?
I.
DON'T.
KNOW.
THAT'S OKAY. I HAVE A RULER.

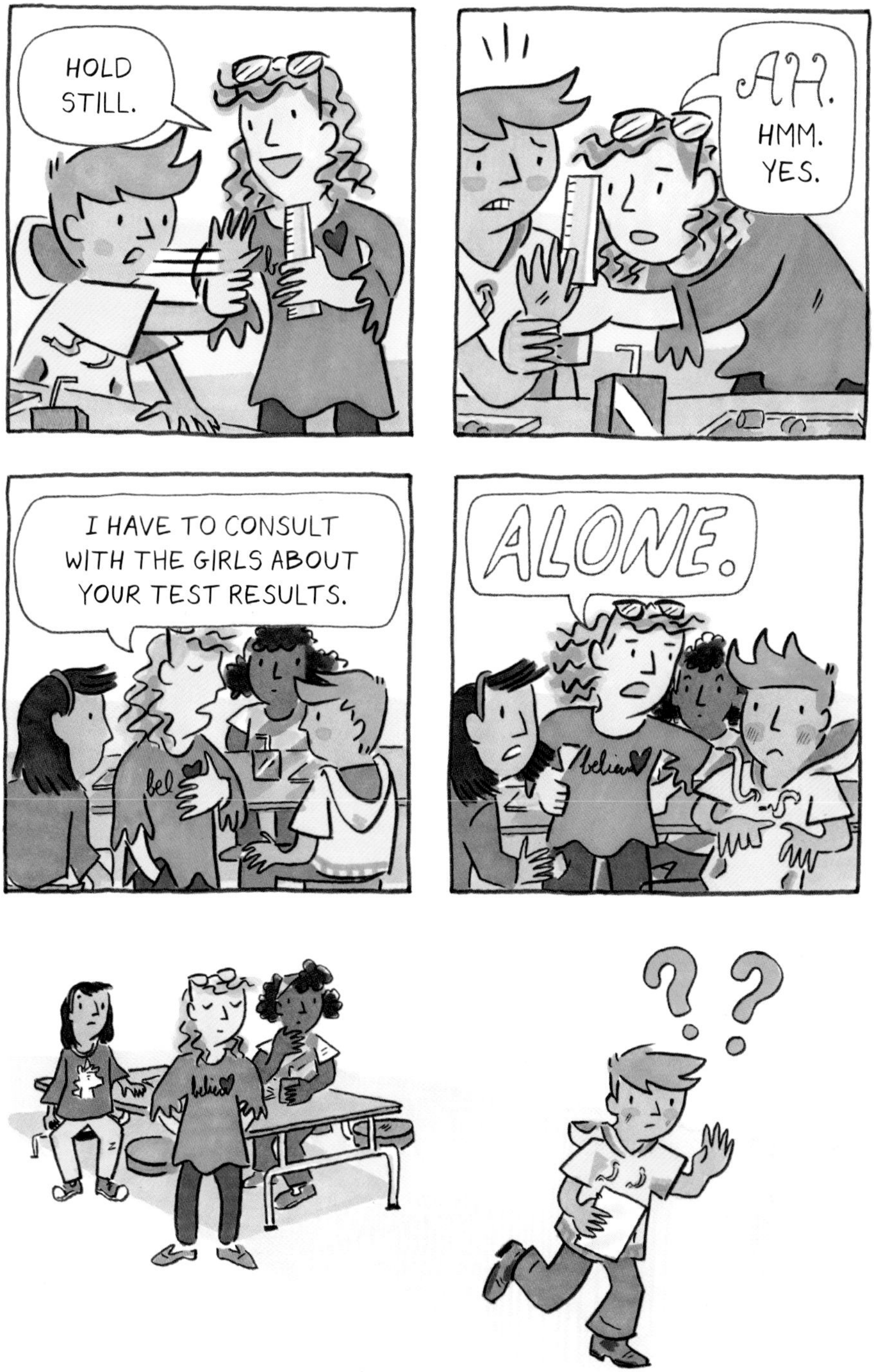
HOLD STILL.
AH. HMM. YES.
I HAVE TO CONSULT WITH THE GIRLS ABOUT YOUR TEST RESULTS.
ALONE.
??

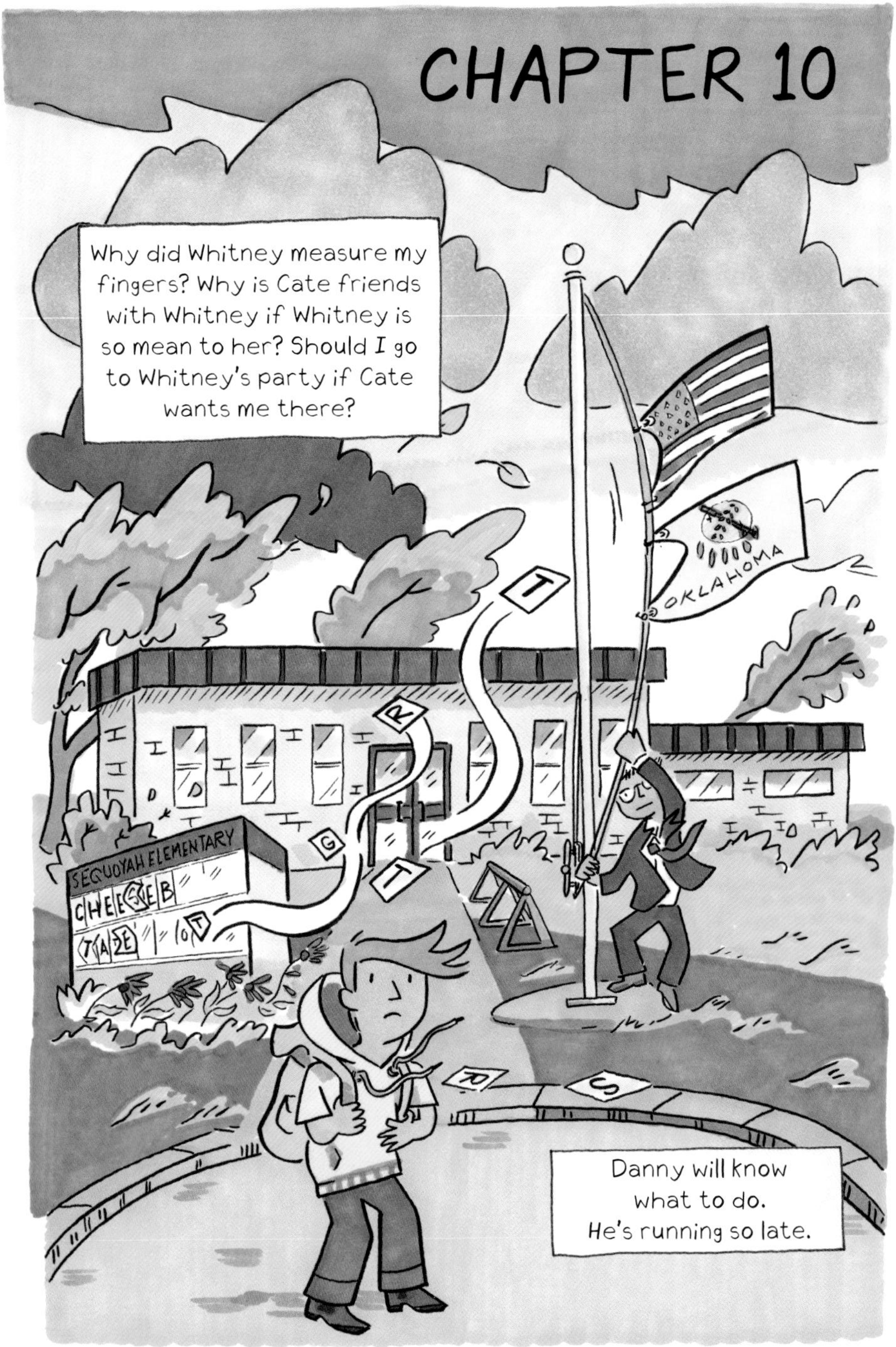
CHAPTER 10
Why did Whitney measure my fingers? Why is Cate friends with Whitney if Whitney is so mean to her? Should I go to Whitney's party if Cate wants me there?
OKLAHOMA
SEQUOYAH ELEMENTARY
Danny will know what to do. He's running so late.

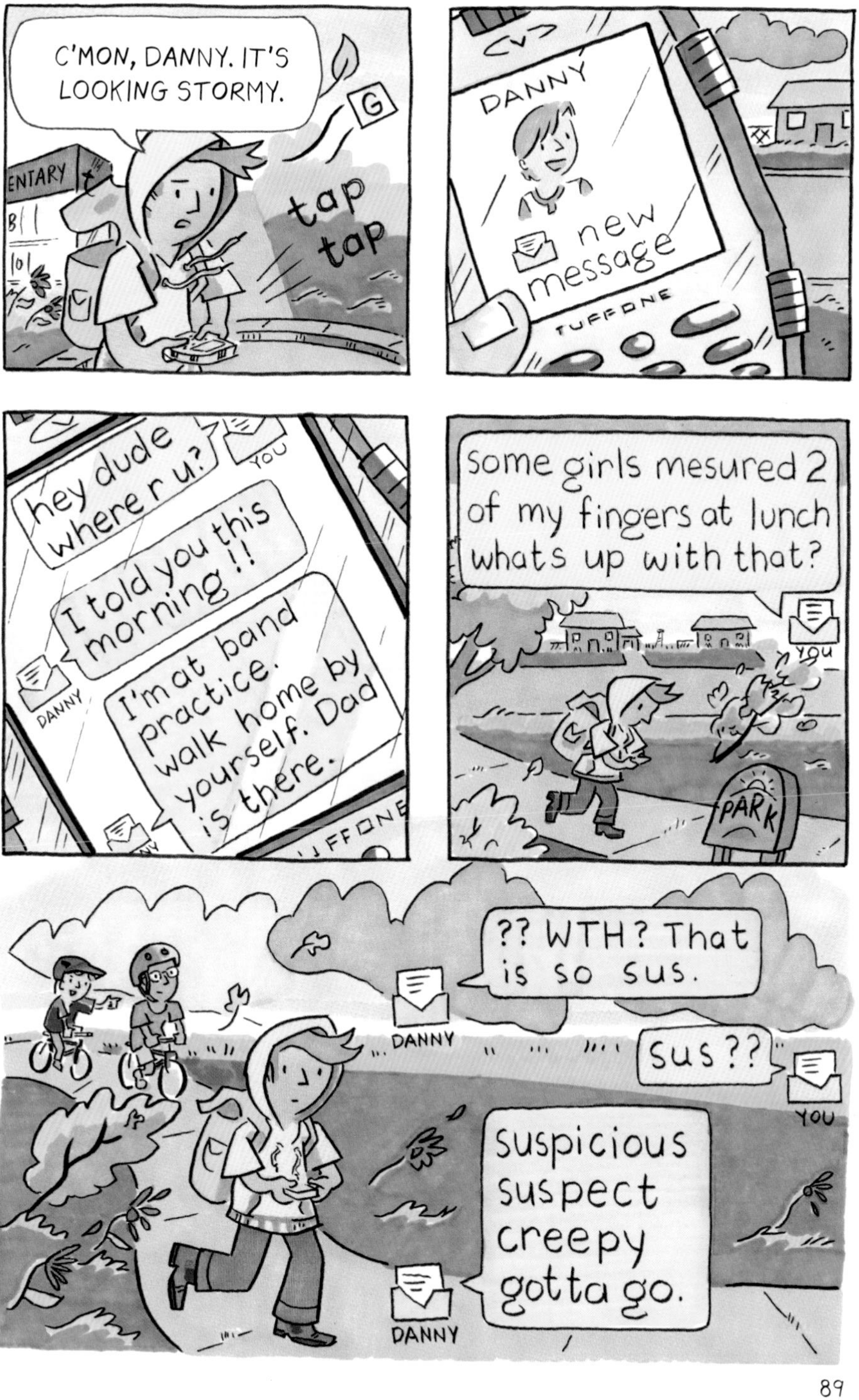
C'MON, DANNY. IT'S LOOKING STORMY.
tap tap
DANNY
new message
TUFFONE
hey dude where r u?
YOU
I told you this morning!!
DANNY
I'm at band practice. walk home by yourself. Dad is there.
Some girls mesured 2 of my fingers at lunch whats up with that?
YOU
PARK
?? WTH? That is so sus.
DANNY
Sus??
YOU
suspicious suspect creepy gotta go.
DANNY

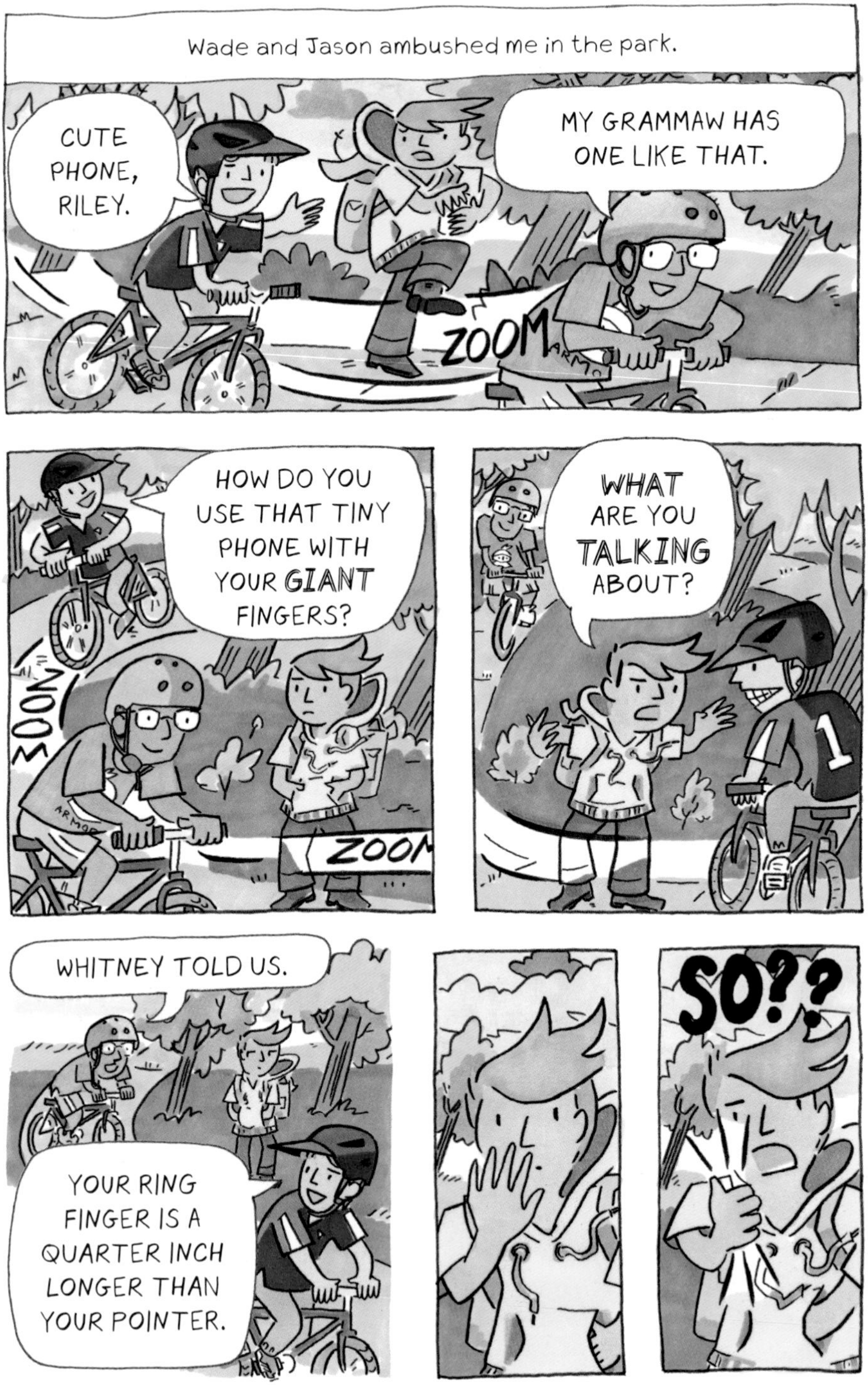
Wade and Jason ambushed me in the park.
CUTE PHONE, RILEY.
MY GRAMMAW HAS ONE LIKE THAT.
ZOOM
HOW DO YOU USE THAT TINY PHONE WITH YOUR GIANT FINGERS?
ZOOM
ZOOM
WHAT ARE YOU TALKING ABOUT?
WHITNEY TOLD US.
YOUR RING FINGER IS A QUARTER INCH LONGER THAN YOUR POINTER.
SO??

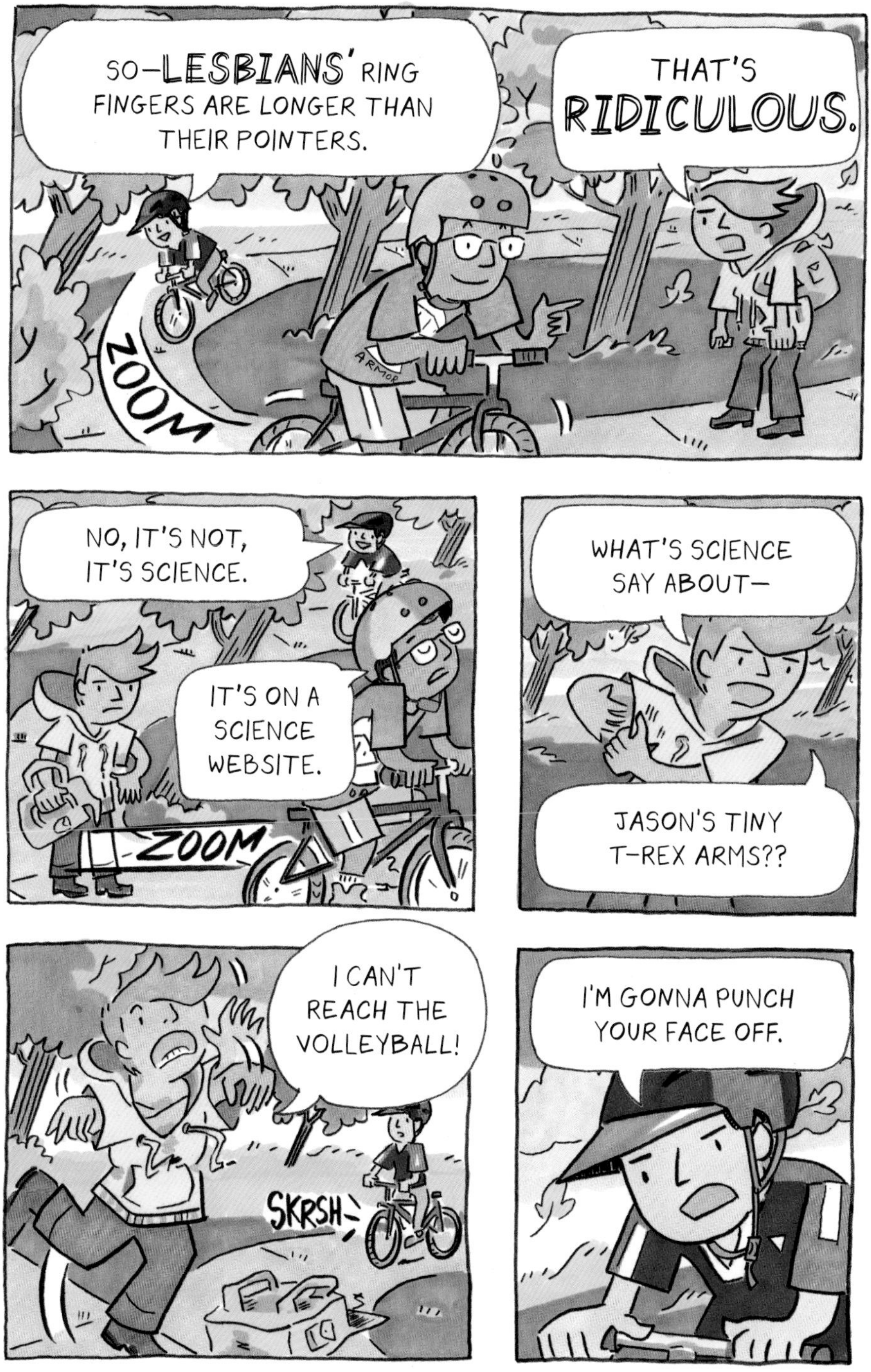
SO—LESBIANS' RING FINGERS ARE LONGER THAN THEIR POINTERS.
THAT'S RIDICULOUS.
ZOOM
ARMOR
NO, IT'S NOT, IT'S SCIENCE.
IT'S ON A SCIENCE WEBSITE.
ZOOM
WHAT'S SCIENCE SAY ABOUT—
JASON'S TINY T-REX ARMS??
I CAN'T REACH THE VOLLEYBALL!
SKRSH
I'M GONNA PUNCH YOUR FACE OFF.

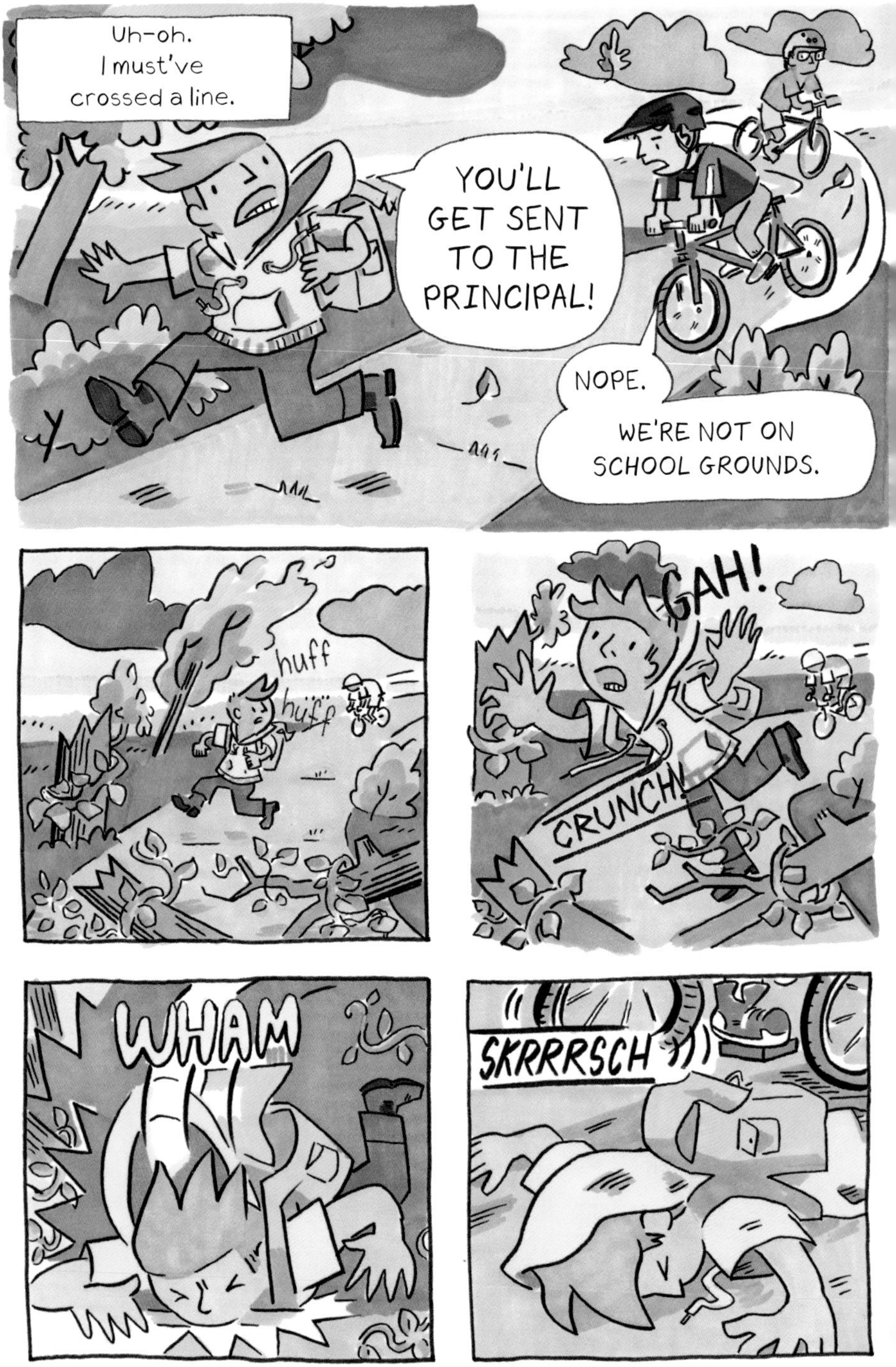
Uh-oh.
I must've crossed a line.
YOU'LL GET SENT TO THE PRINCIPAL!
NOPE.
WE'RE NOT ON SCHOOL GROUNDS.
huff
huff
GAH!
CRUNCH
WHAM
SKRRRSCH

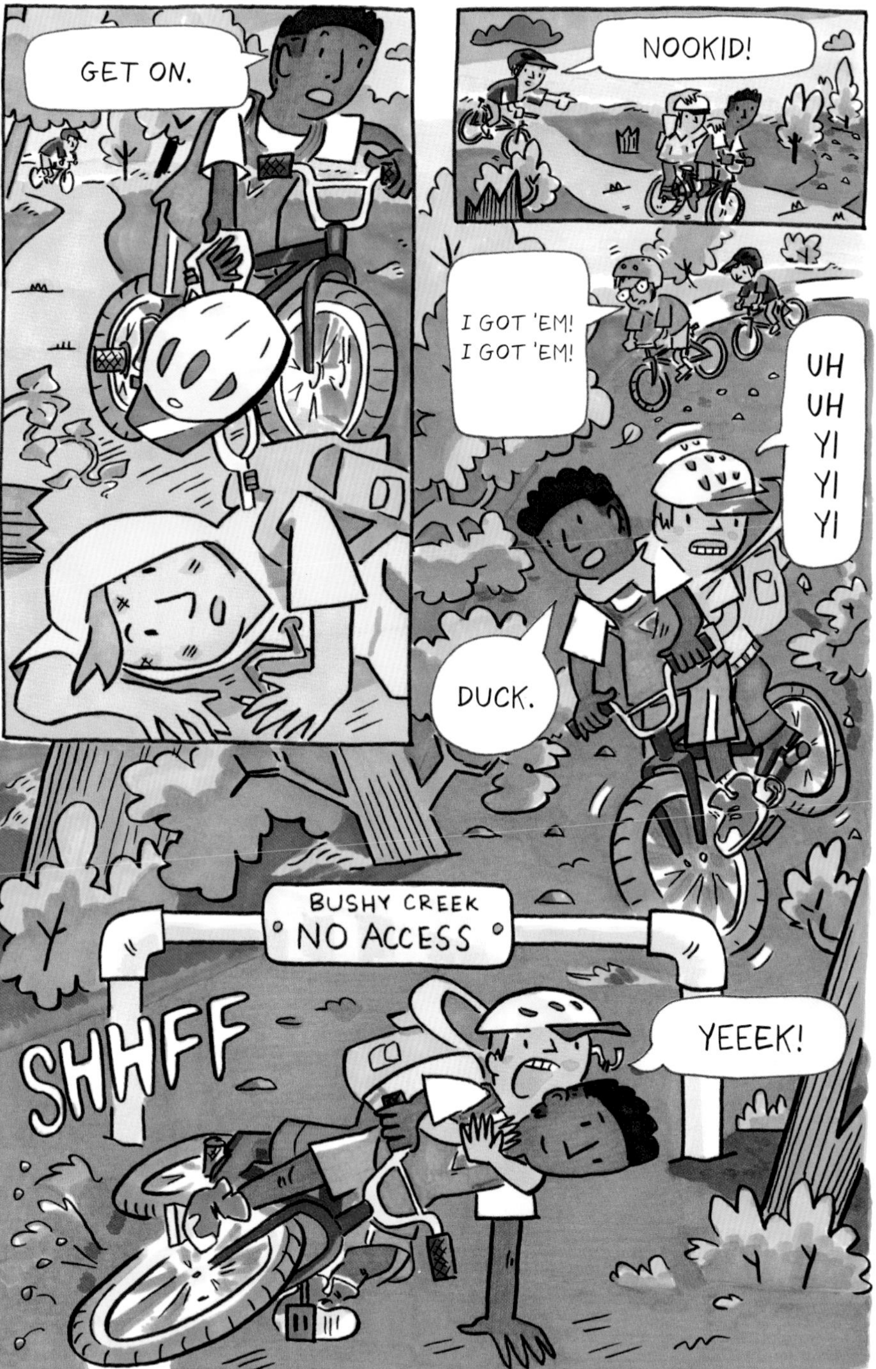
GET ON.
NOOKID!
I GOT 'EM! I GOT 'EM!
UH UH YI YI YI
DUCK.
BUSHY CREEK NO ACCESS
SHHFF
YEEEK!

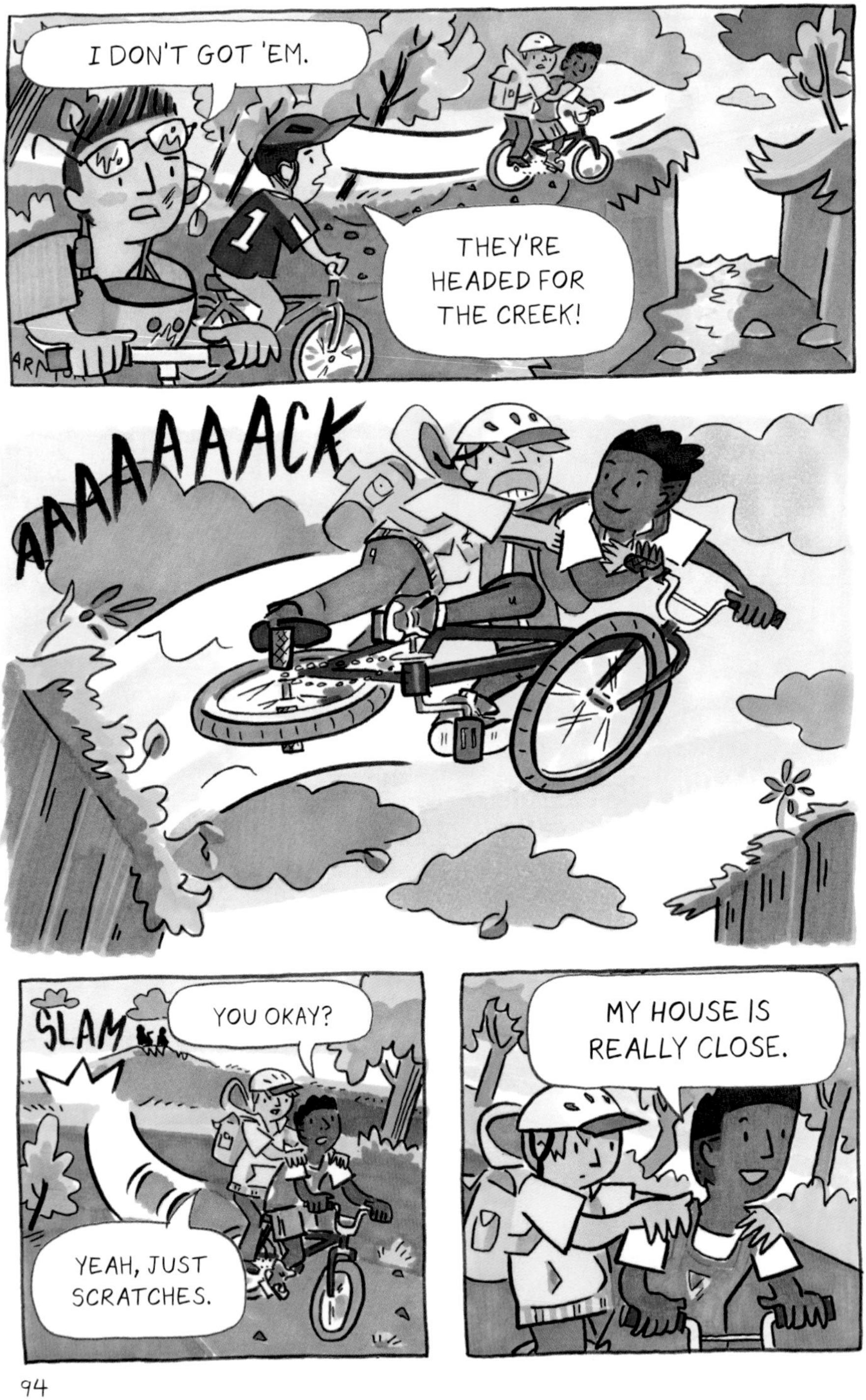
I DON'T GOT 'EM.
THEY'RE HEADED FOR THE CREEK!
AAAAAAACK
SLAM
YOU OKAY?
YEAH, JUST SCRATCHES.
MY HOUSE IS REALLY CLOSE.

WHY ARE WADE AND JASON CHASING YOU?

SCIENCE FINGERS LE
LESBIAN SCIENCE F
NGERS SCIE

uh-

I MADE FUN OF JASON'S TINY ARMS.

RILEY!

SOMETIMES YOU GOTTA STOP AND THINK BEFORE CRACKING JOKES.

bump

bump

SOMETHING FUNNY TO YOU MIGHT SEEM MEAN TO SOMEONE ELSE.

YEAH. I KNOW.

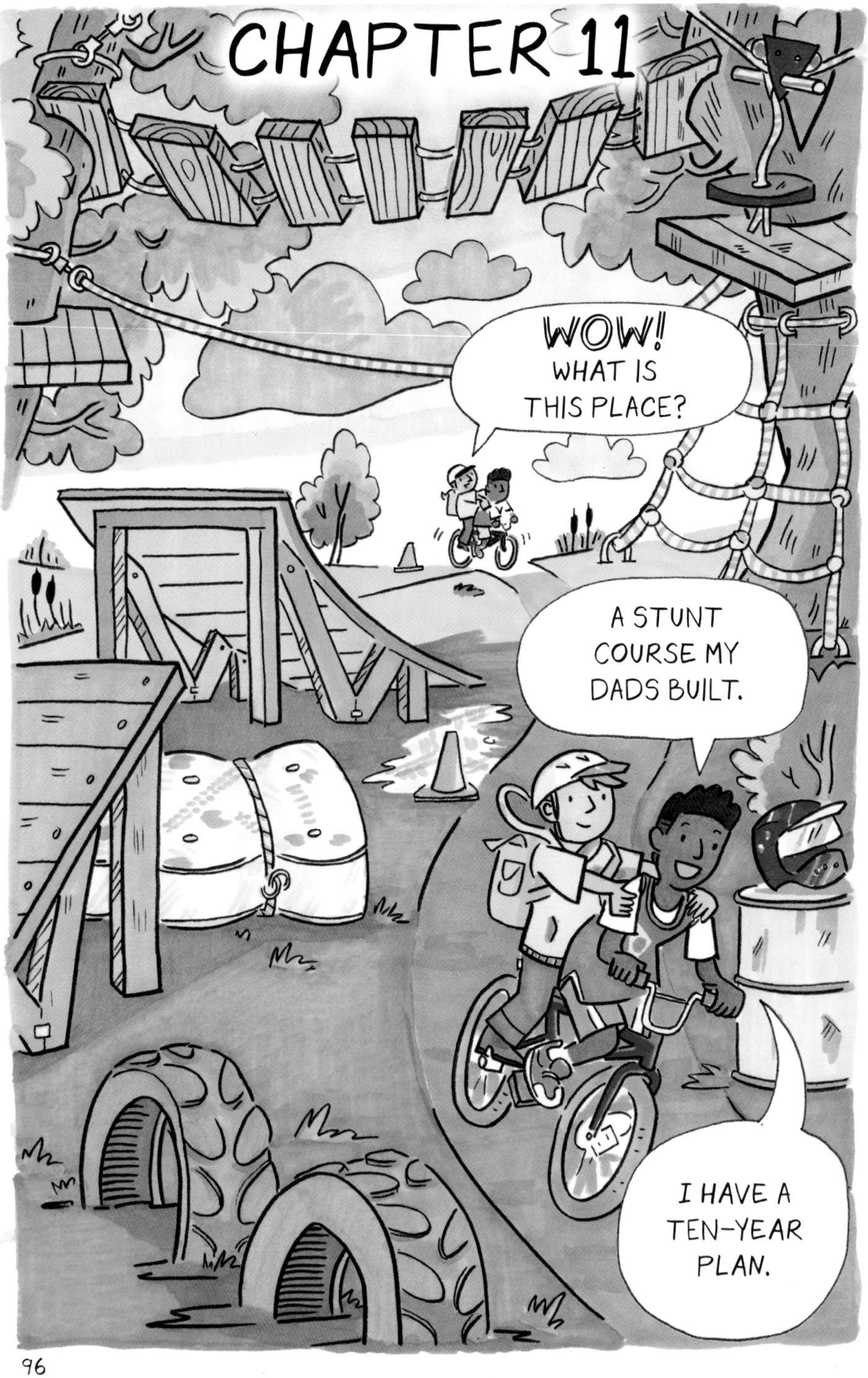
CHAPTER 11
WOW! WHAT IS THIS PLACE?
A STUNT COURSE MY DADS BUILT.
I HAVE A TEN-YEAR PLAN.

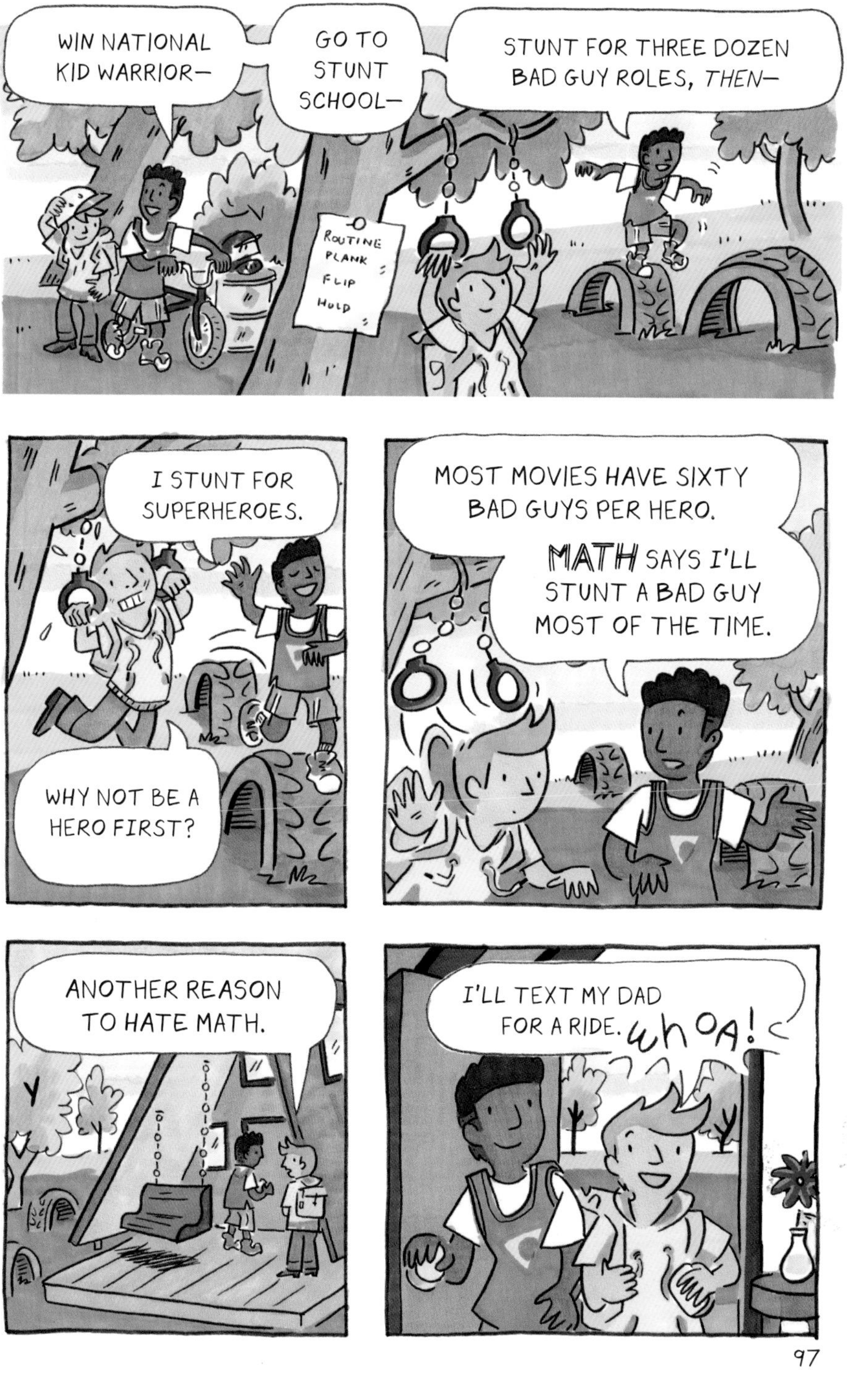
WIN NATIONAL KID WARRIOR—
GO TO STUNT SCHOOL—
STUNT FOR THREE DOZEN BAD GUY ROLES, *THEN*—
ROUTINE
PLANK
FLIP
HOLD
I STUNT FOR SUPERHEROES.
WHY NOT BE A HERO FIRST?
MOST MOVIES HAVE SIXTY BAD GUYS PER HERO.
MATH SAYS I'LL STUNT A BAD GUY MOST OF THE TIME.
ANOTHER REASON TO HATE MATH.
I'LL TEXT MY DAD FOR A RIDE.
WHOA!

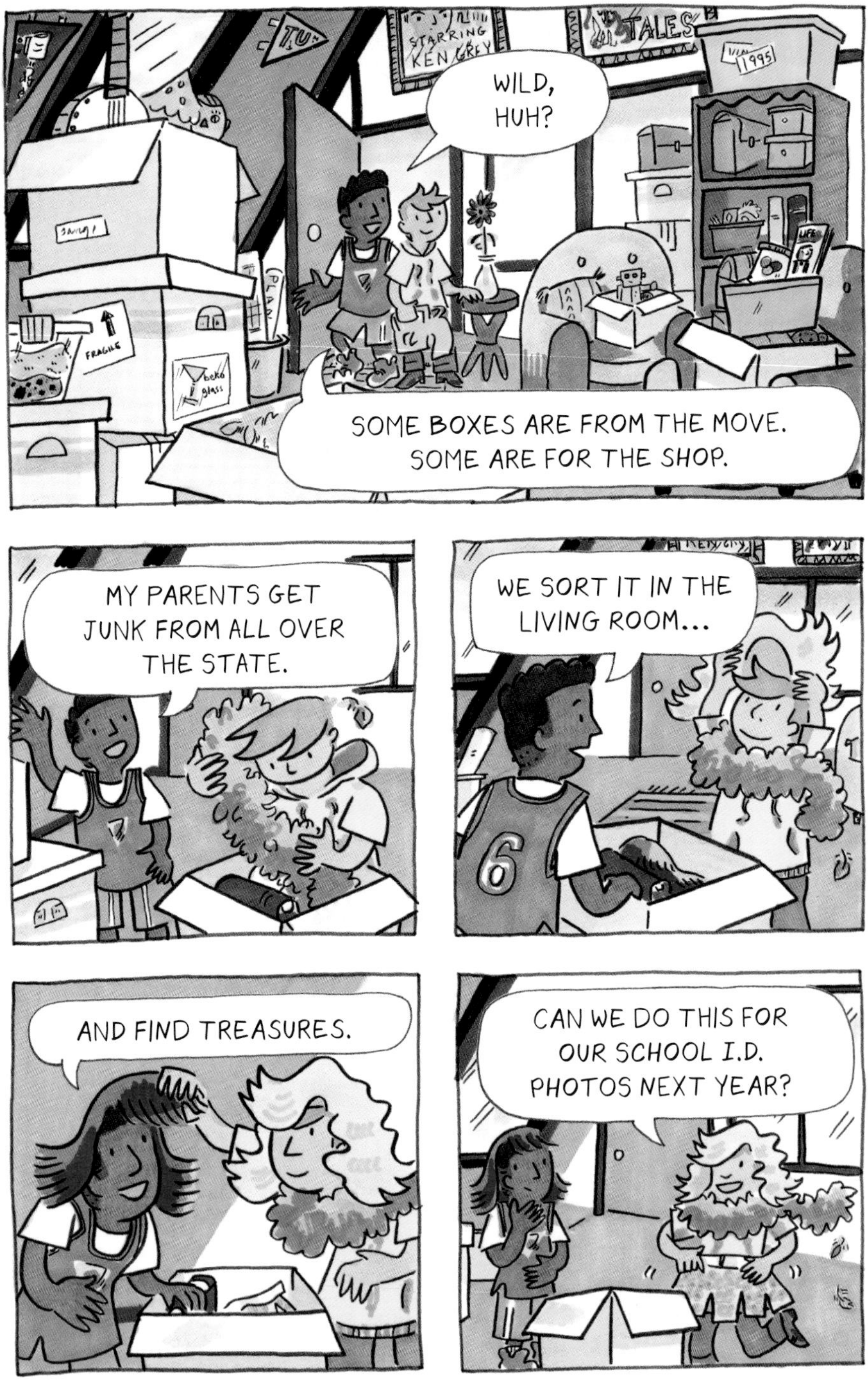
STARRING KEN GREY
TALES
1995
WILD, HUH?
SOME BOXES ARE FROM THE MOVE. SOME ARE FOR THE SHOP.
FRAGILE
MY PARENTS GET JUNK FROM ALL OVER THE STATE.
WE SORT IT IN THE LIVING ROOM...
6
AND FIND TREASURES.
CAN WE DO THIS FOR OUR SCHOOL I.D. PHOTOS NEXT YEAR?

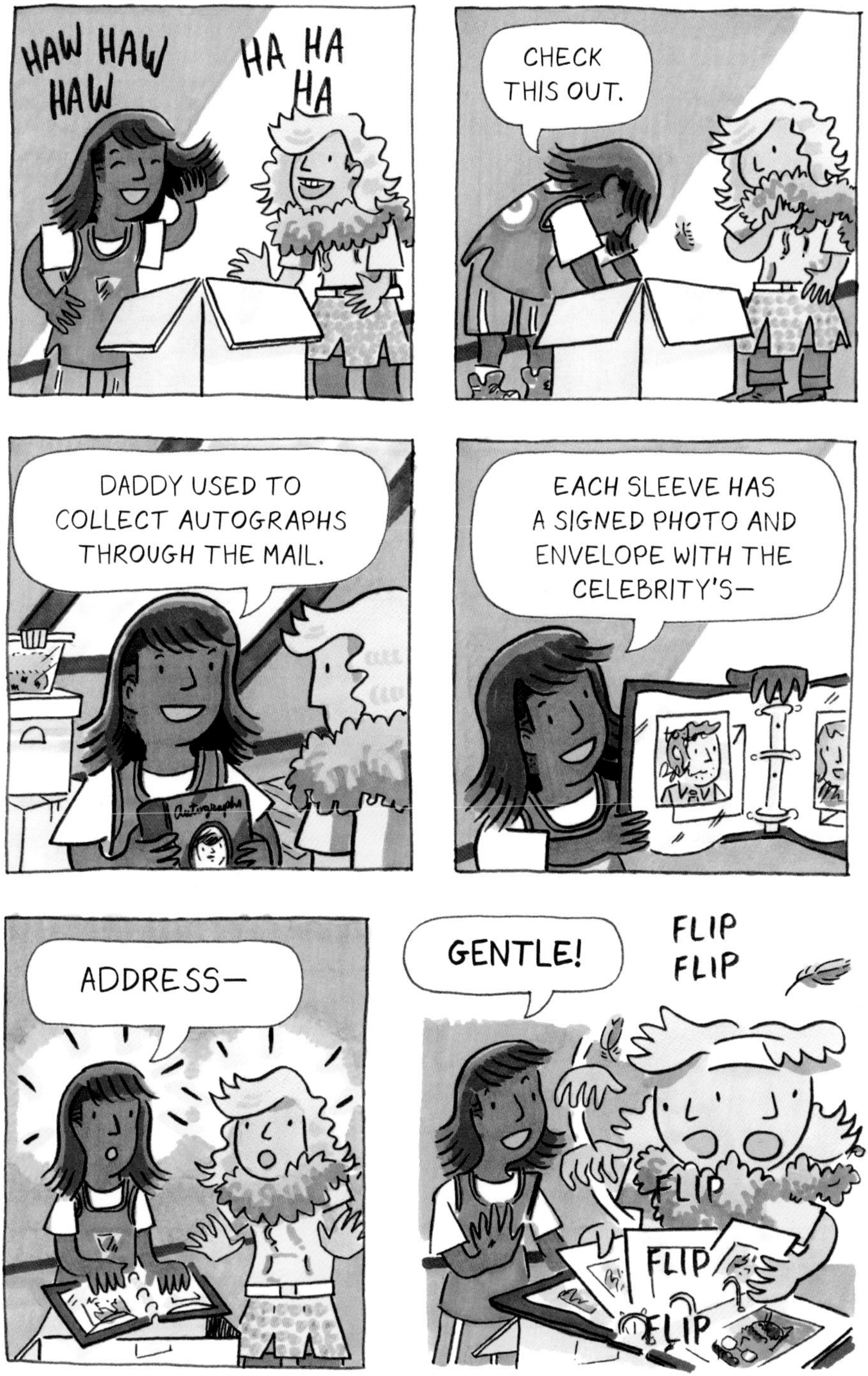
HAW HAW HAW
HA HA HA
CHECK THIS OUT.
DADDY USED TO COLLECT AUTOGRAPHS THROUGH THE MAIL.
EACH SLEEVE HAS A SIGNED PHOTO AND ENVELOPE WITH THE CELEBRITY'S—
ADDRESS—
GENTLE!
FLIP FLIP
FLIP
FLIP
FLIP

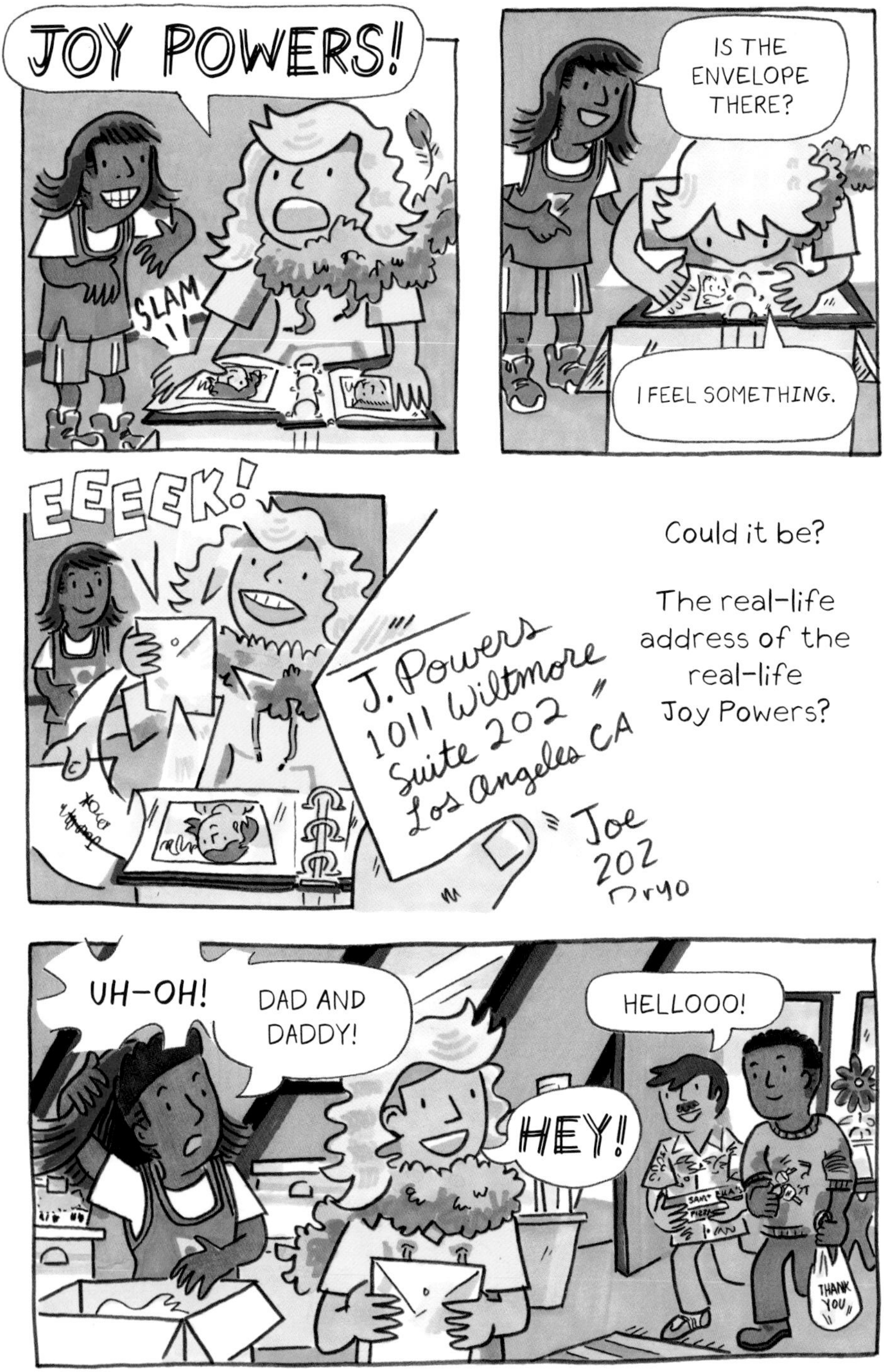
JOY POWERS!
SLAM
IS THE ENVELOPE THERE?
I FEEL SOMETHING.
EEEEK!
J. Powers
1011 Wiltmore
Suite 202
Los Angeles CA
Joe
202
Could it be?
The real-life address of the real-life Joy Powers?
UH-OH!
DAD AND DADDY!
HEY!
HELLOOO!
THANK YOU

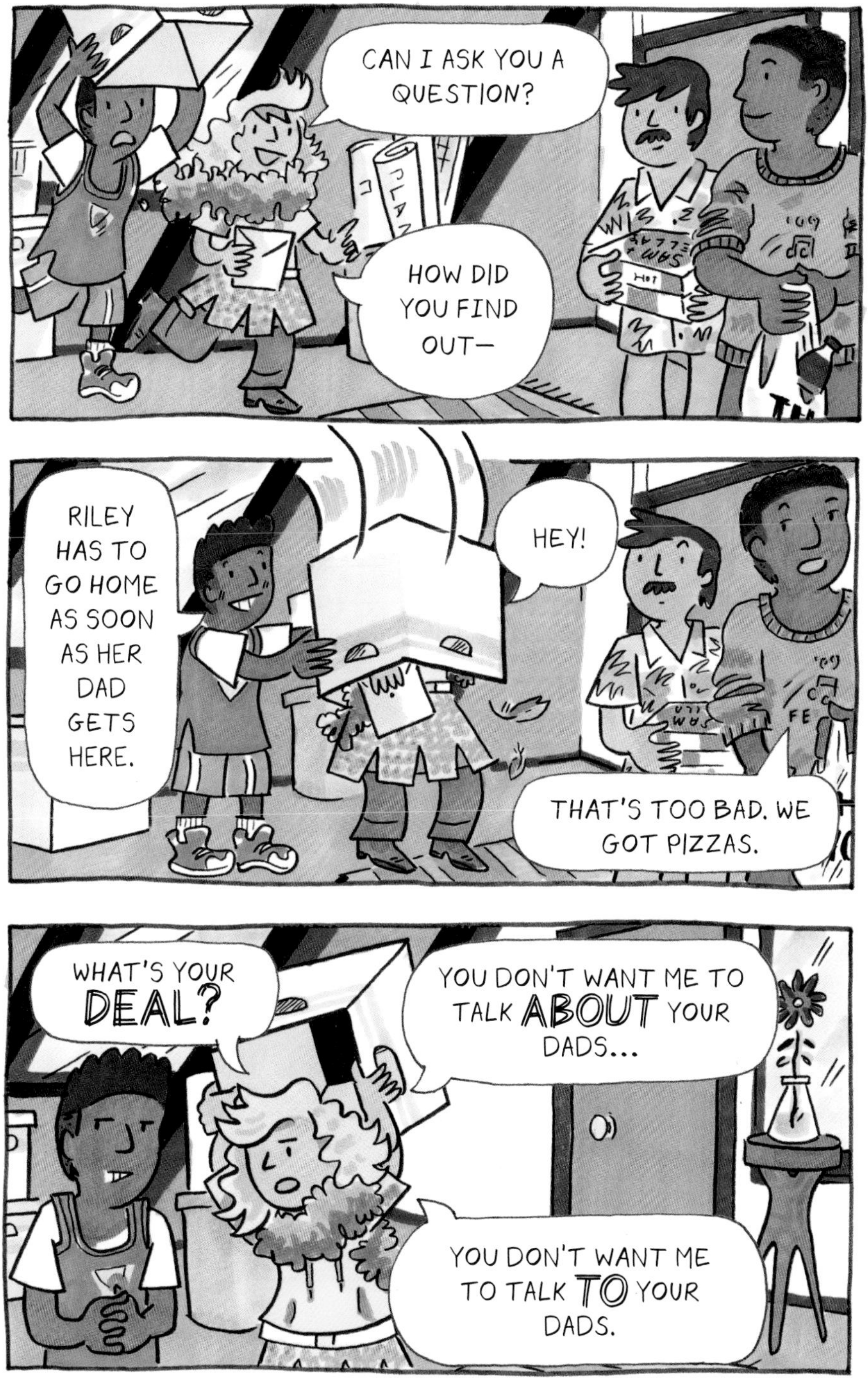
CAN I ASK YOU A QUESTION?
HOW DID YOU FIND OUT—
RILEY HAS TO GO HOME AS SOON AS HER DAD GETS HERE.
HEY!
THAT'S TOO BAD. WE GOT PIZZAS.
WHAT'S YOUR DEAL?
YOU DON'T WANT ME TO TALK ABOUT YOUR DADS...
YOU DON'T WANT ME TO TALK TO YOUR DADS.

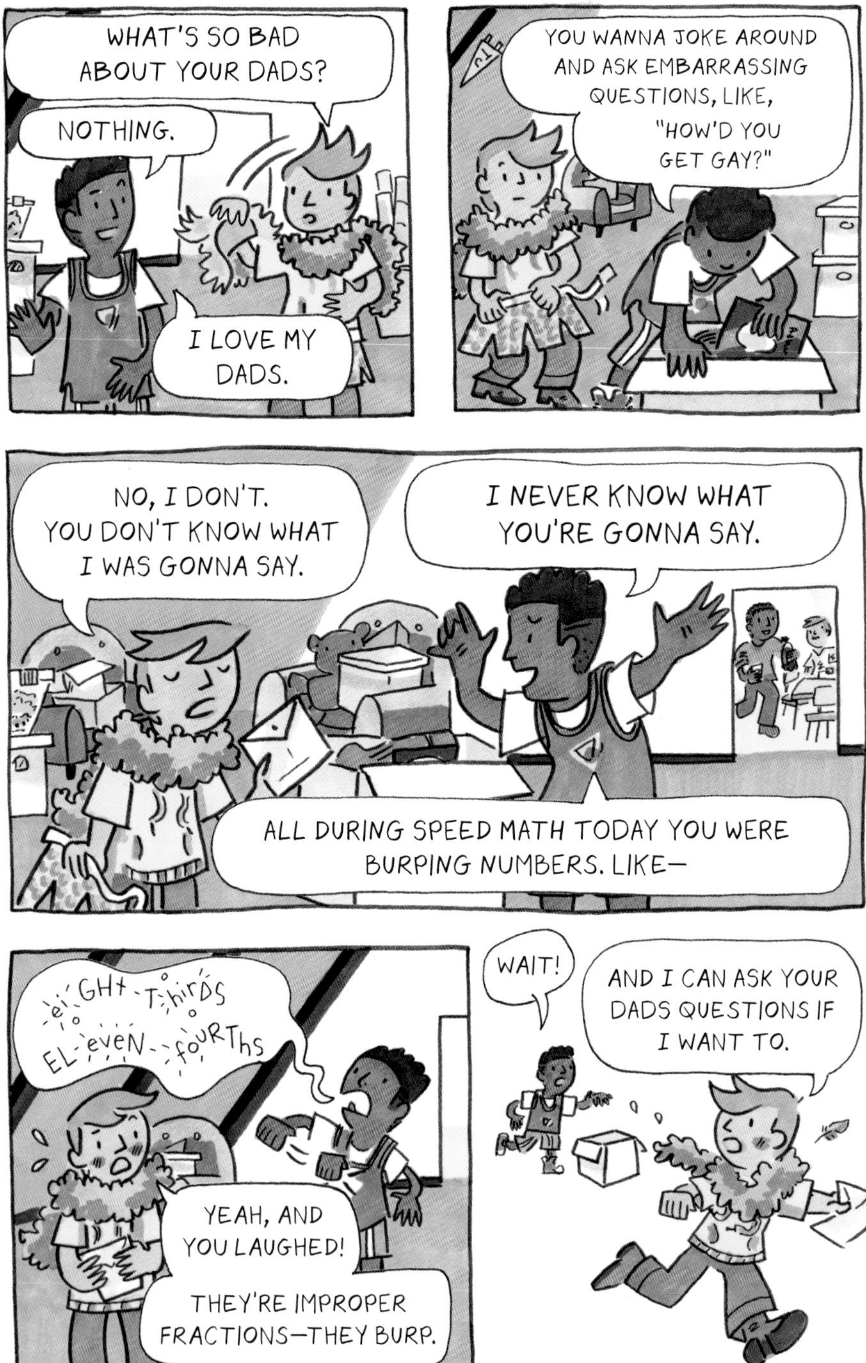
WHAT'S SO BAD ABOUT YOUR DADS?
NOTHING.
I LOVE MY DADS.
YOU WANNA JOKE AROUND AND ASK EMBARRASSING QUESTIONS, LIKE, "HOW'D YOU GET GAY?"
NO, I DON'T. YOU DON'T KNOW WHAT I WAS GONNA SAY.
I NEVER KNOW WHAT YOU'RE GONNA SAY.
ALL DURING SPEED MATH TODAY YOU WERE BURPING NUMBERS. LIKE—
eiGHt-Thirds
ELeven-fouRThs
YEAH, AND YOU LAUGHED!
THEY'RE IMPROPER FRACTIONS—THEY BURP.
WAIT!
AND I CAN ASK YOUR DADS QUESTIONS IF I WANT TO.

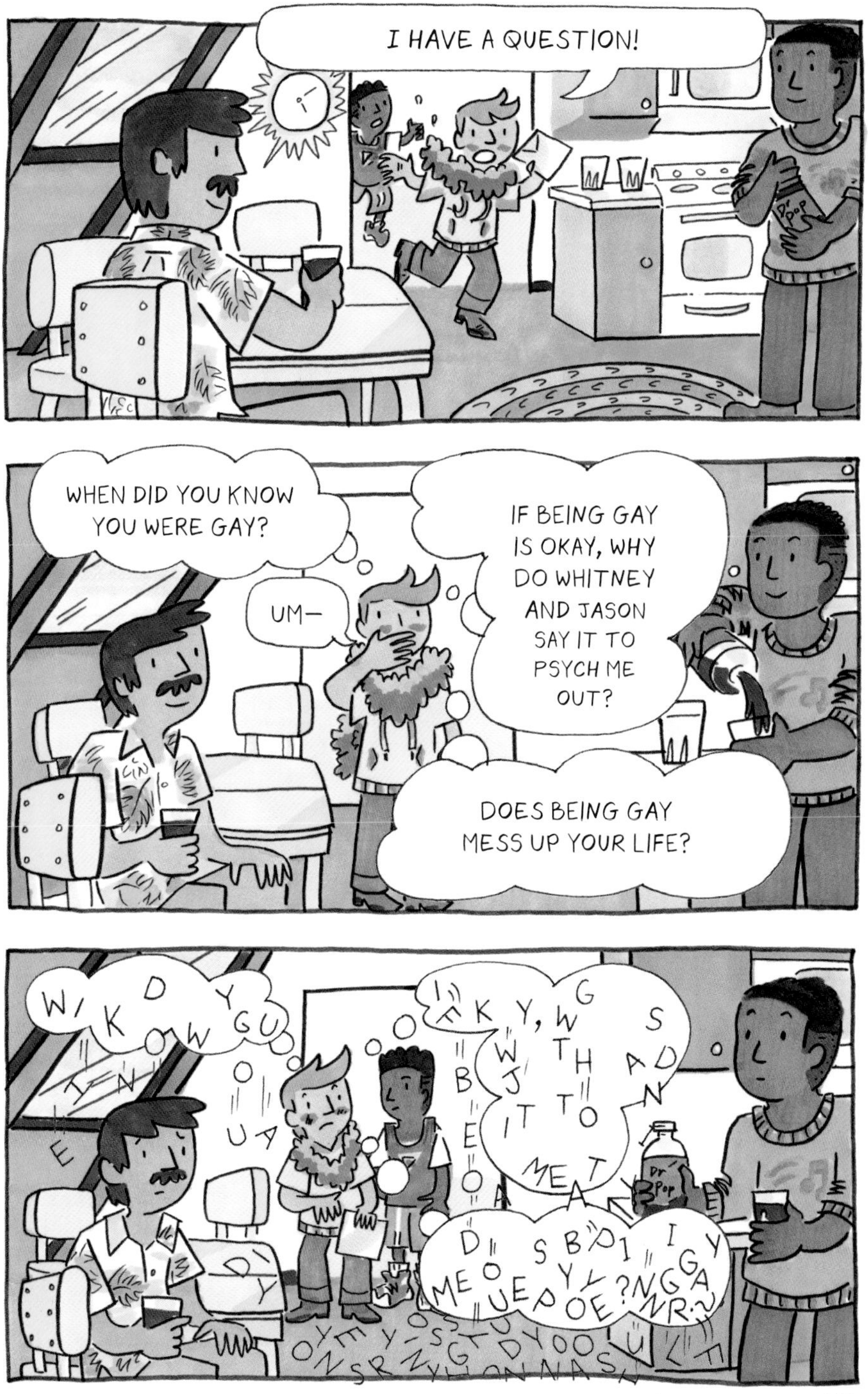
I HAVE A QUESTION!
WHEN DID YOU KNOW YOU WERE GAY?
UM—
IF BEING GAY IS OKAY, WHY DO WHITNEY AND JASON SAY IT TO PSYCH ME OUT?
DOES BEING GAY MESS UP YOUR LIFE?

IS THIS JOY POWERS'S ADDRESS? CAN I BORROW IT?

Joy Powers
Wittman
Apt 202
Los angeles, CA

SURE! BUT IT MIGHT BE OUTDATED. BEEN YEARS SINCE I SENT FAN MAIL.

SHOW DADDY YOUR DRAWINGS.

OH, WOW! IT'S AGENT ANGIE!

YEAH! YOU KNOW HER?

ONE OF MY FAVORITE SKITS.

THIS!

IS!

DING DONG

MISSION IMPROBABLE!

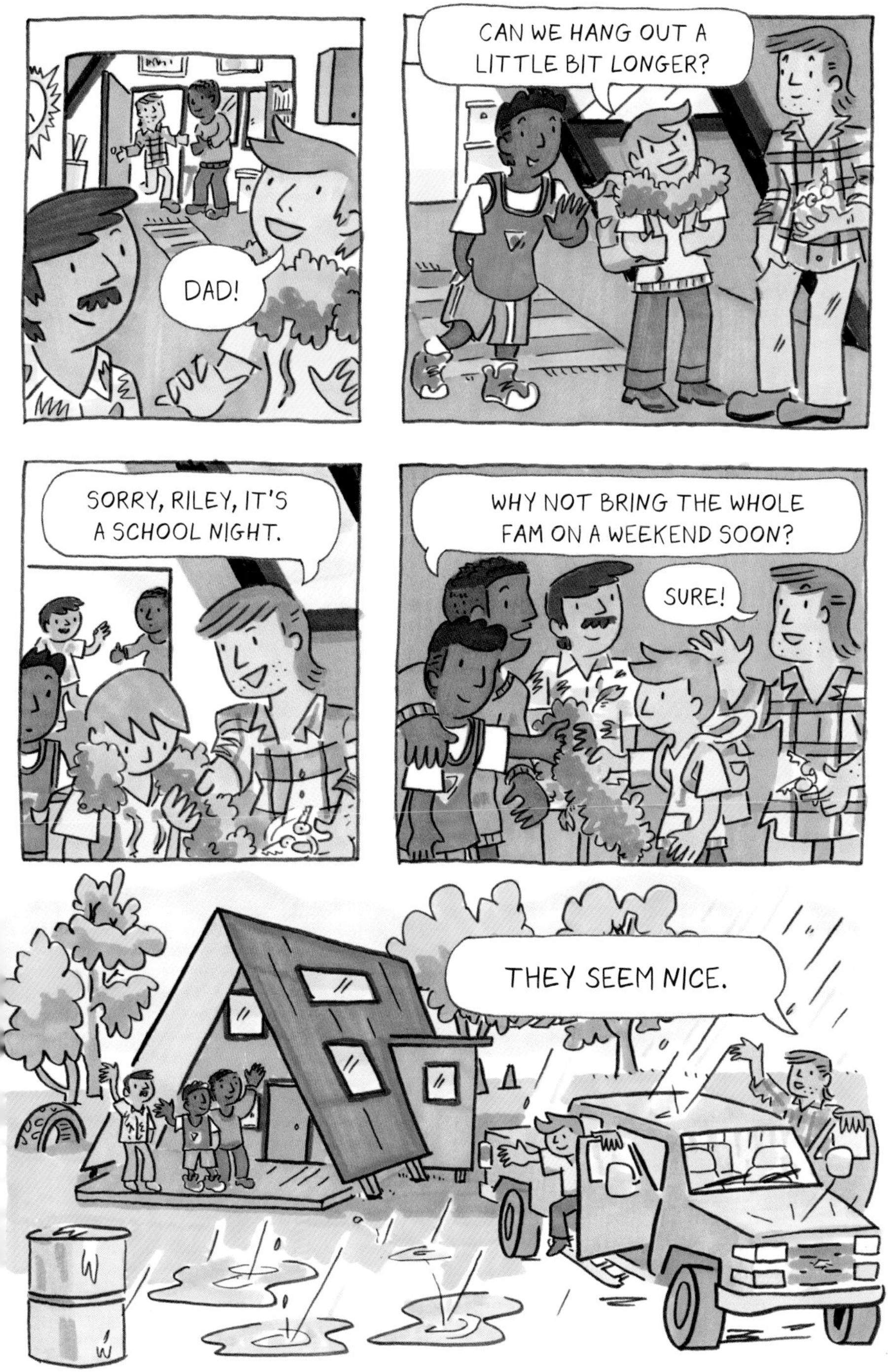
DAD!
CAN WE HANG OUT A LITTLE BIT LONGER?
SORRY, RILEY, IT'S A SCHOOL NIGHT.
WHY NOT BRING THE WHOLE FAM ON A WEEKEND SOON?
SURE!
THEY SEEM NICE.

YOU DON'T MIND THAT THEY'RE GAY?

OF COURSE NOT.

DO *YOU*?

PSH. **NO.**

LOVE IS LOVE.

RIGHT! LOVE IS LOVE.

I KNOW IT'S TRUE...

WHAT DOES IT MEAN?

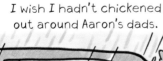

I wish I hadn't chickened out around Aaron's dads.

I wish I knew some right way to talk to them.

I have a lot of questions.

CHAPTER 12

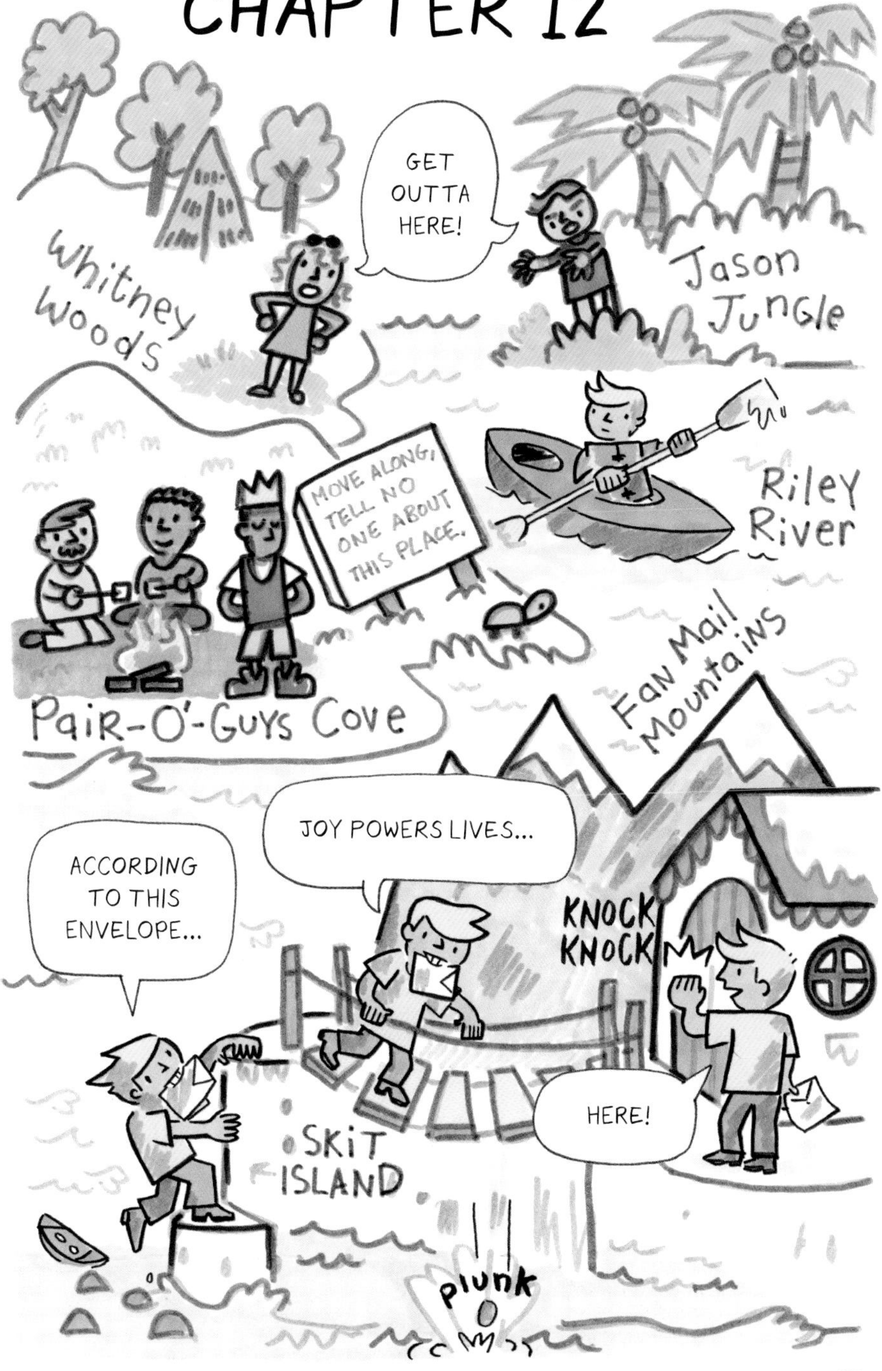
Whitney Woods
GET OUTTA HERE!
Jason Jungle
Riley River
MOVE ALONG. TELL NO ONE ABOUT THIS PLACE.
Pair-O'-Guys Cove
Fan Mail Mountains
ACCORDING TO THIS ENVELOPE...
JOY POWERS LIVES...
KNOCK KNOCK
HERE!
SKIT ISLAND
plunk

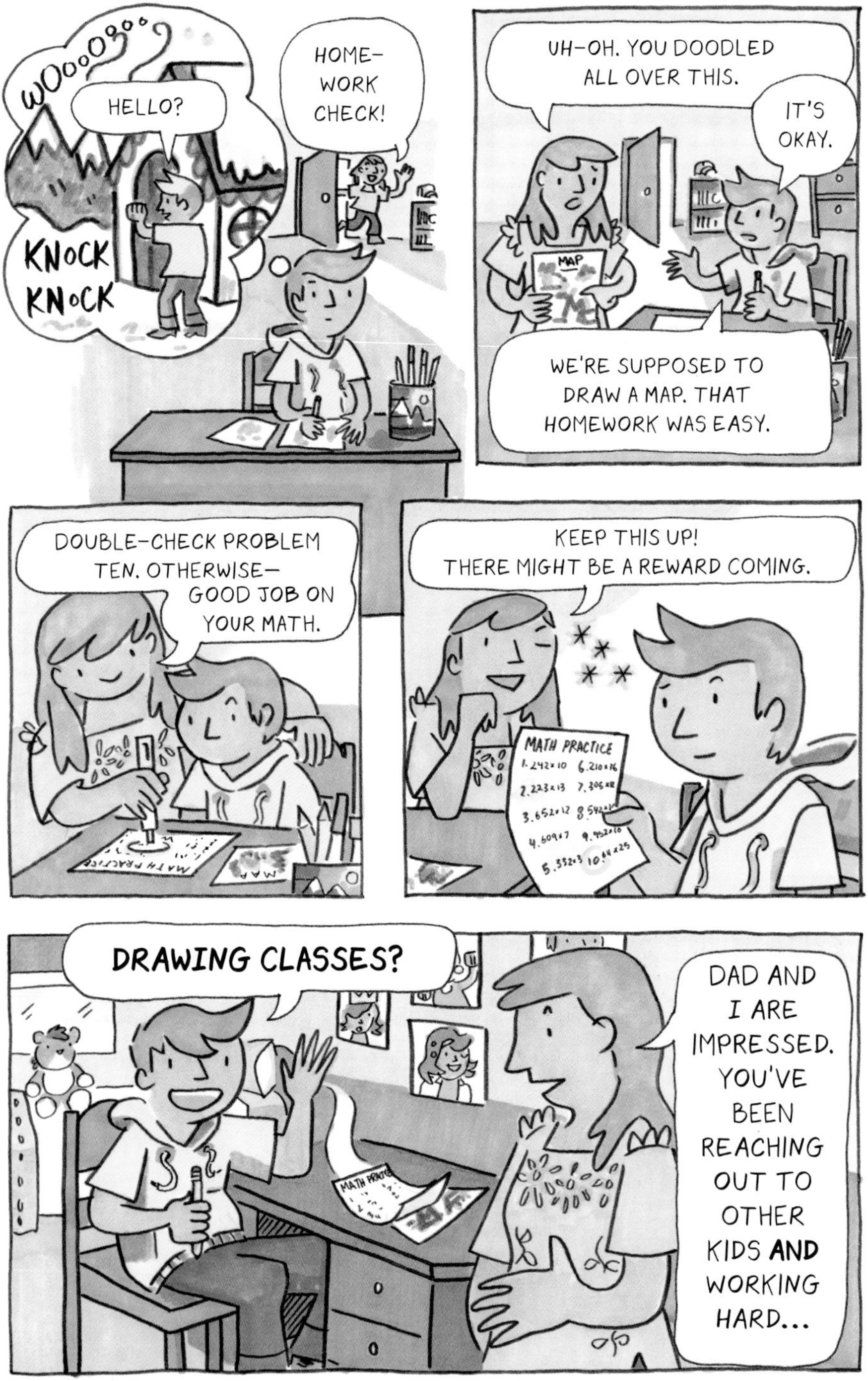
WOOoOOoo
HELLO?
KNOCK KNOCK
HOME-WORK CHECK!
UH-OH. YOU DOODLED ALL OVER THIS.
IT'S OKAY.
MAP
WE'RE SUPPOSED TO DRAW A MAP. THAT HOMEWORK WAS EASY.
DOUBLE-CHECK PROBLEM TEN. OTHERWISE—GOOD JOB ON YOUR MATH.
MATH PRACTICE
KEEP THIS UP! THERE MIGHT BE A REWARD COMING.
MATH PRACTICE
DRAWING CLASSES?
DAD AND I ARE IMPRESSED. YOU'VE BEEN REACHING OUT TO OTHER KIDS **AND** WORKING HARD...

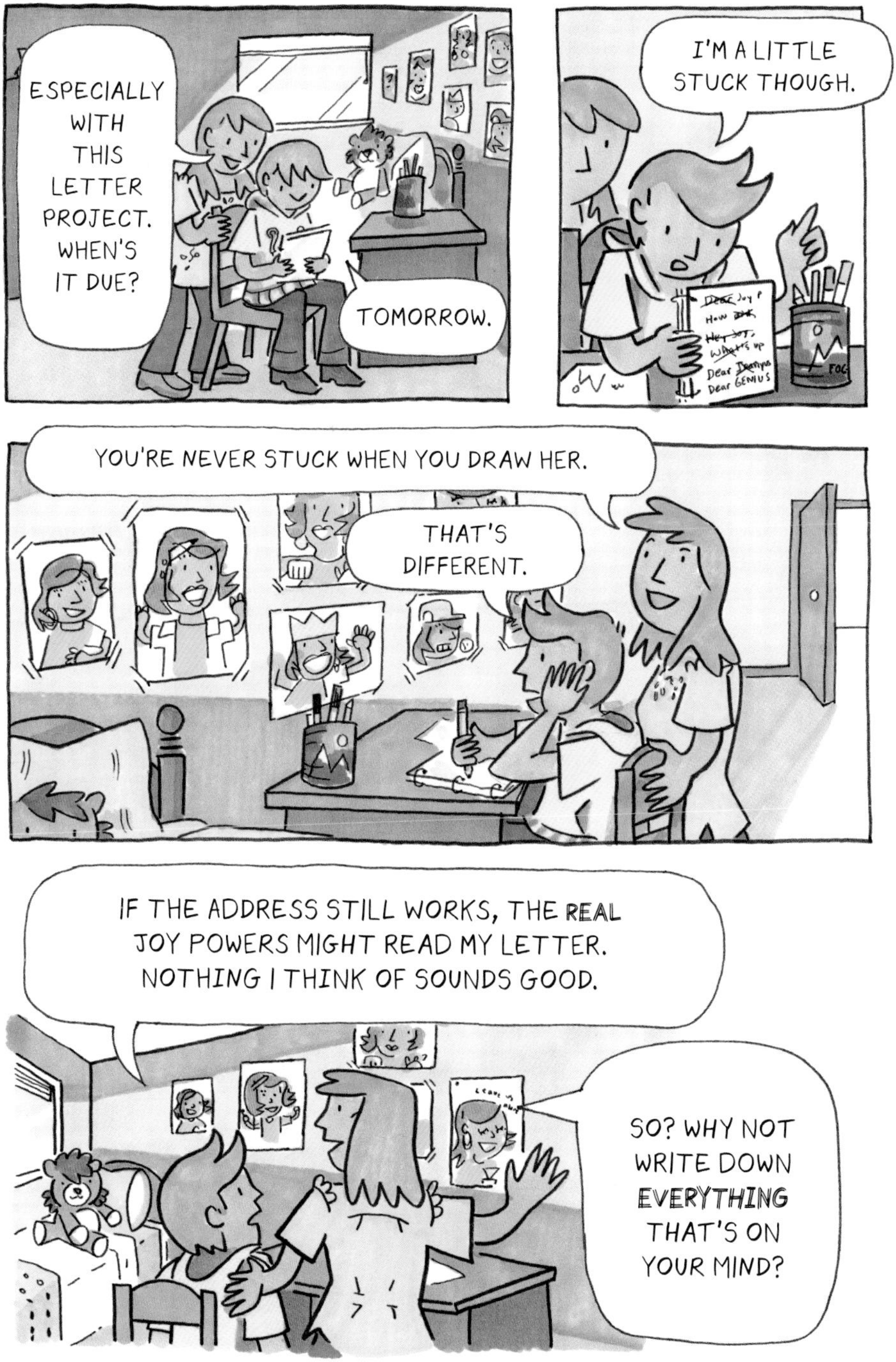
ESPECIALLY WITH THIS LETTER PROJECT. WHEN'S IT DUE?
TOMORROW.
I'M A LITTLE STUCK THOUGH.
YOU'RE NEVER STUCK WHEN YOU DRAW HER.
THAT'S DIFFERENT.
IF THE ADDRESS STILL WORKS, THE REAL JOY POWERS MIGHT READ MY LETTER. NOTHING I THINK OF SOUNDS GOOD.
SO? WHY NOT WRITE DOWN EVERYTHING THAT'S ON YOUR MIND?

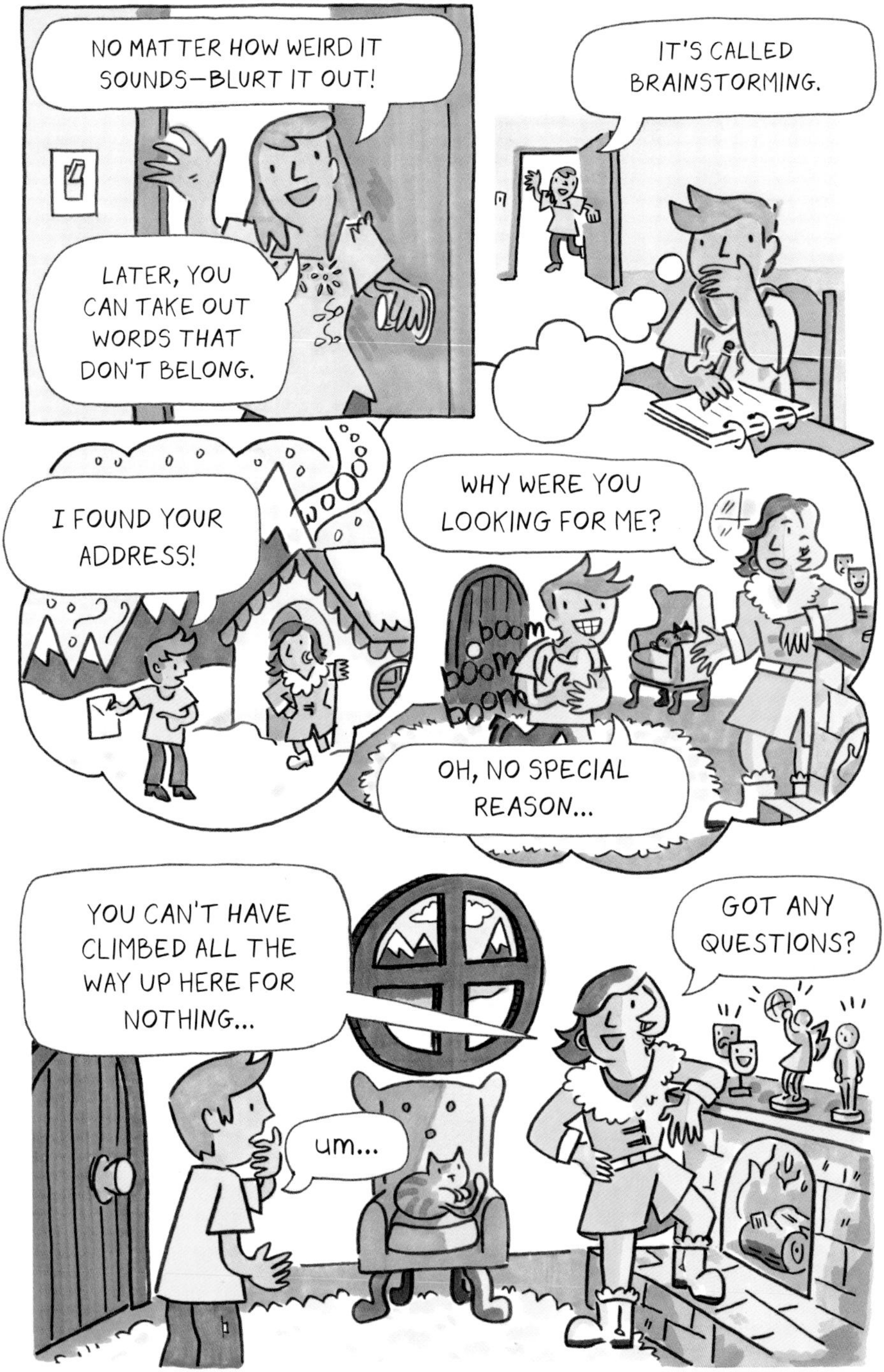
NO MATTER HOW WEIRD IT SOUNDS—BLURT IT OUT!
LATER, YOU CAN TAKE OUT WORDS THAT DON'T BELONG.
IT'S CALLED BRAINSTORMING.
I FOUND YOUR ADDRESS!
WHY WERE YOU LOOKING FOR ME?
boom boom boom
OH, NO SPECIAL REASON...
YOU CAN'T HAVE CLIMBED ALL THE WAY UP HERE FOR NOTHING...
GOT ANY QUESTIONS?
um...

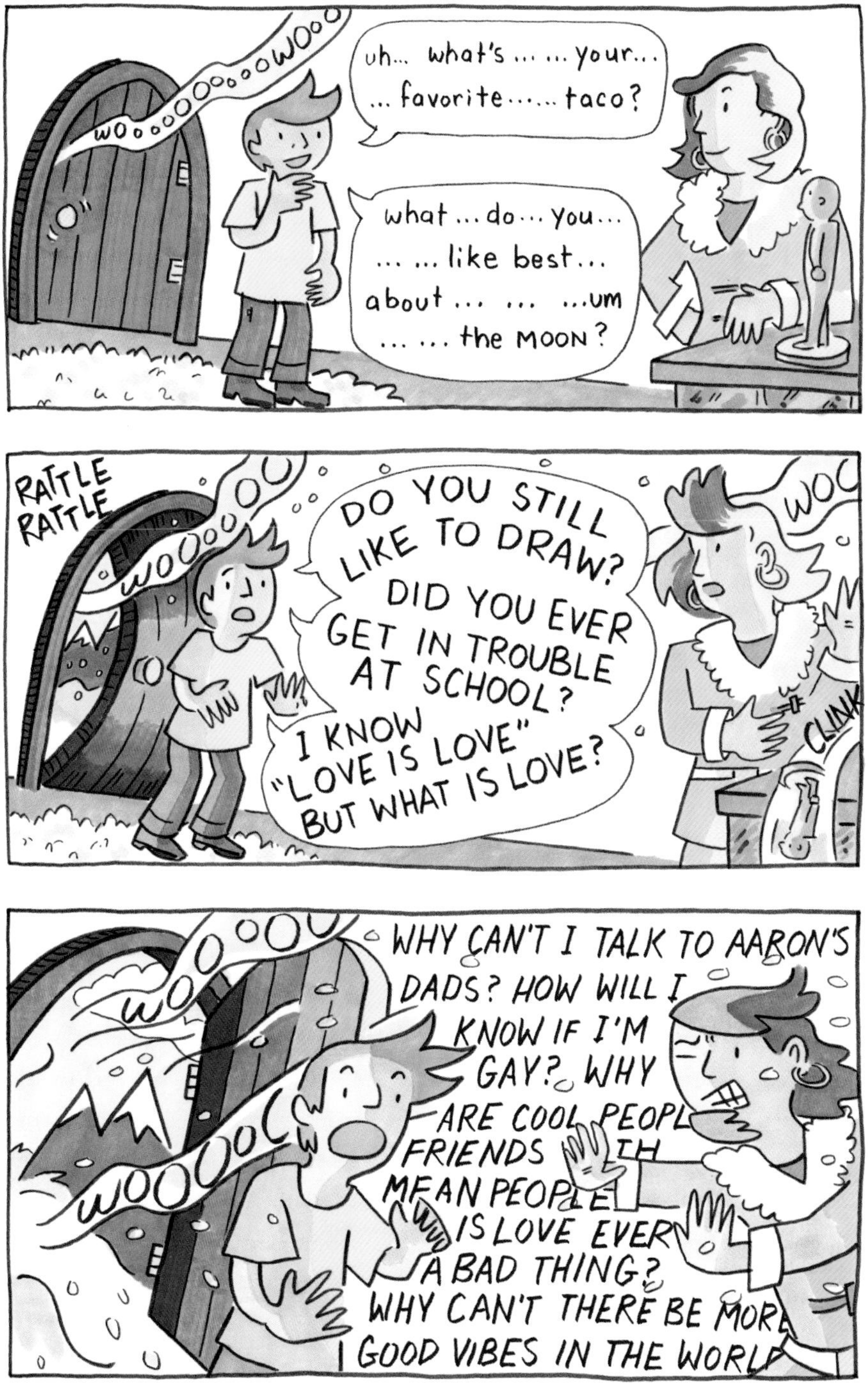
uh... what's ... ... your... ... favorite...... taco?
what ... do ... you ... ... like best ... about ... ...um ... ... the MOON?
RATTLE RATTLE
DO YOU STILL LIKE TO DRAW?
DID YOU EVER GET IN TROUBLE AT SCHOOL?
I KNOW "LOVE IS LOVE" BUT WHAT IS LOVE?
CLINK
WHY CAN'T I TALK TO AARON'S DADS? HOW WILL I KNOW IF I'M GAY? WHY ARE COOL PEOPL FRIENDS TH MEAN PEOPLE IS LOVE EVER A BAD THING? WHY CAN'T THERE BE MORE GOOD VIBES IN THE WORL

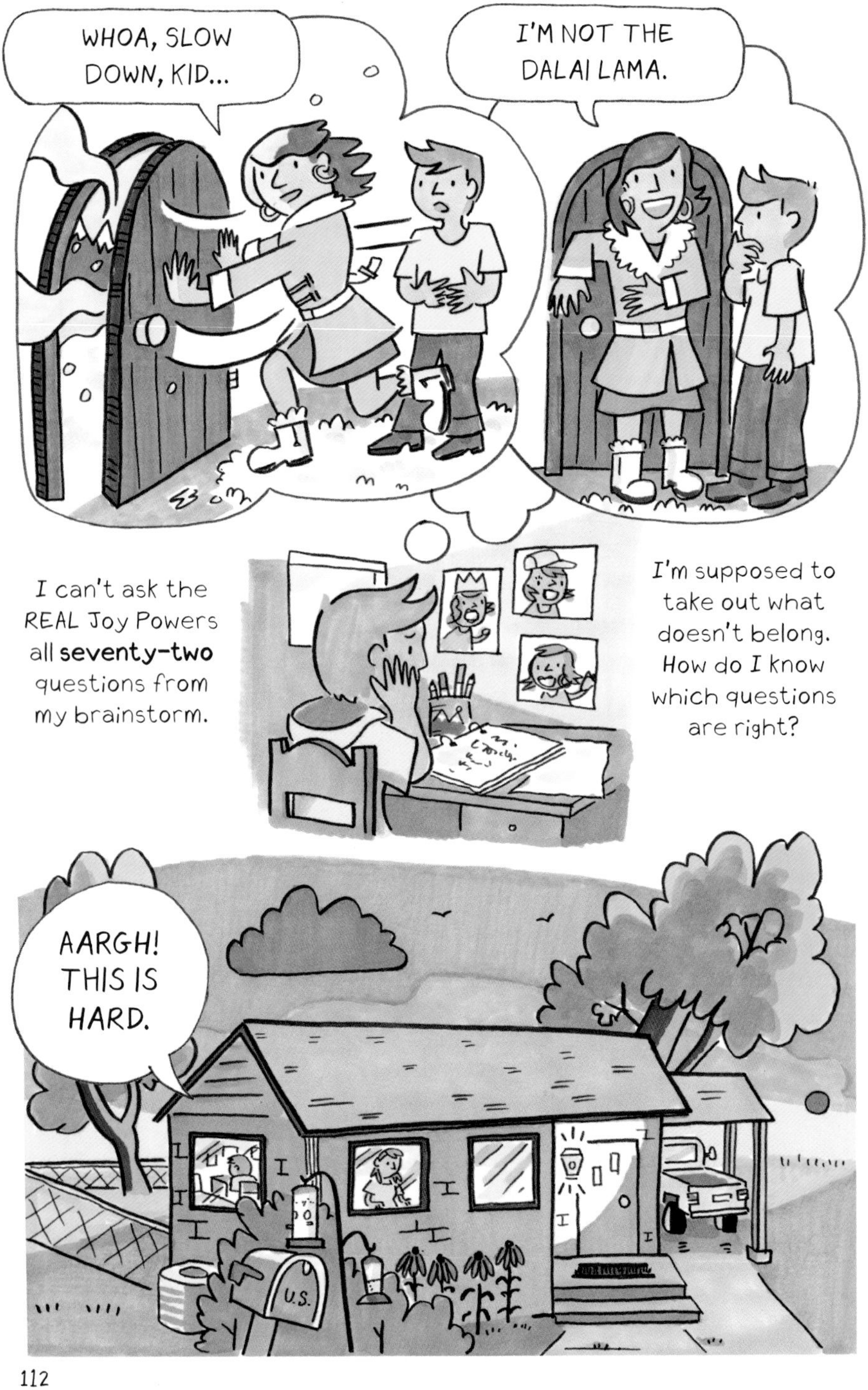
WHOA, SLOW DOWN, KID...
I'M NOT THE DALAI LAMA.
I can't ask the REAL Joy Powers all **seventy-two** questions from my brainstorm.
I'm supposed to take out what doesn't belong. How do I know which questions are right?
AARGH! THIS IS HARD.
U.S.

The next morning, I ask Danny about the Whitney situation.

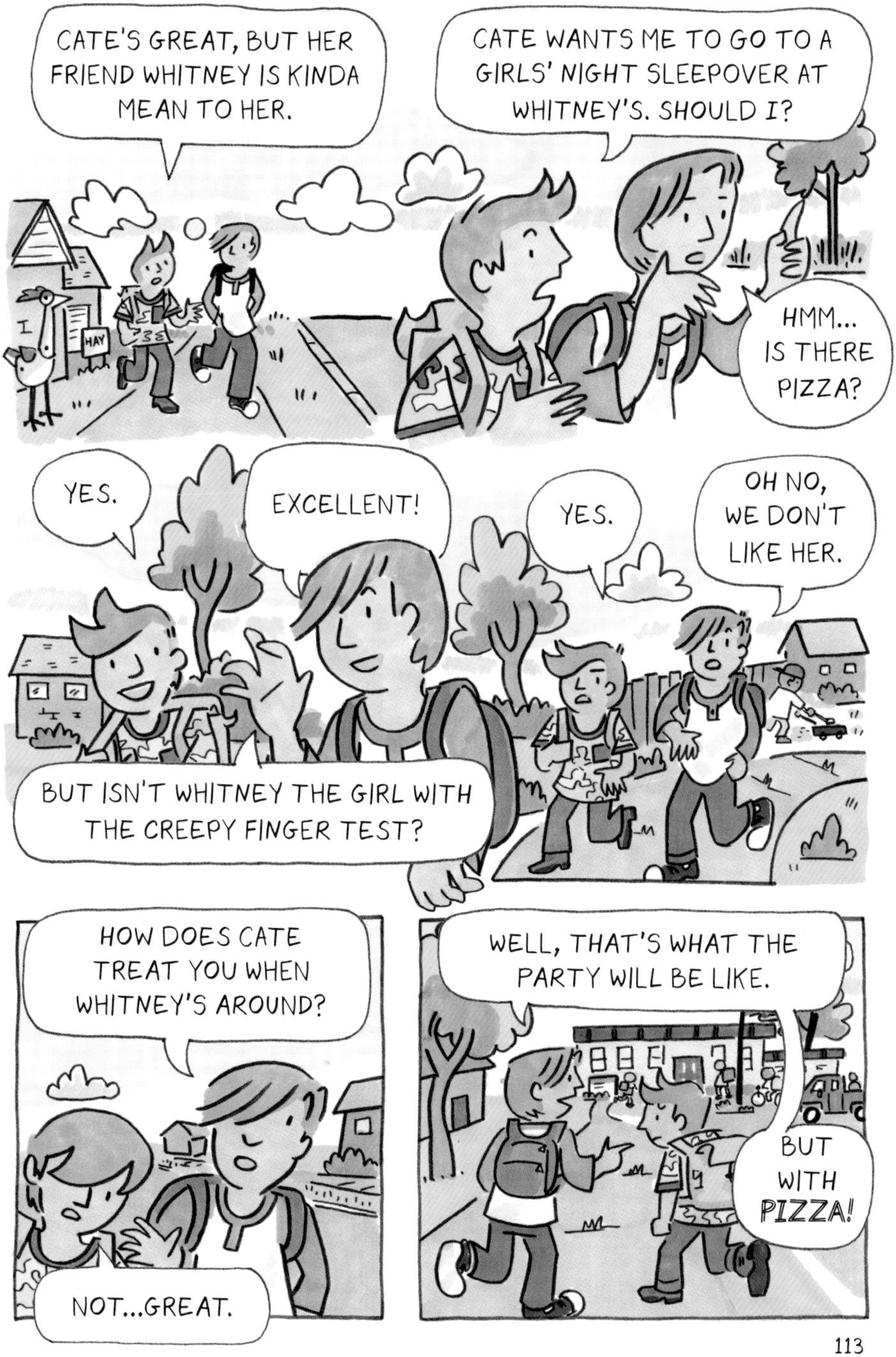
CATE'S GREAT, BUT HER FRIEND WHITNEY IS KINDA MEAN TO HER.
CATE WANTS ME TO GO TO A GIRLS' NIGHT SLEEPOVER AT WHITNEY'S. SHOULD I?
HMM... IS THERE PIZZA?
HAY
YES.
EXCELLENT!
YES.
OH NO, WE DON'T LIKE HER.
BUT ISN'T WHITNEY THE GIRL WITH THE CREEPY FINGER TEST?
HOW DOES CATE TREAT YOU WHEN WHITNEY'S AROUND?
NOT...GREAT.
WELL, THAT'S WHAT THE PARTY WILL BE LIKE.
BUT WITH PIZZA!

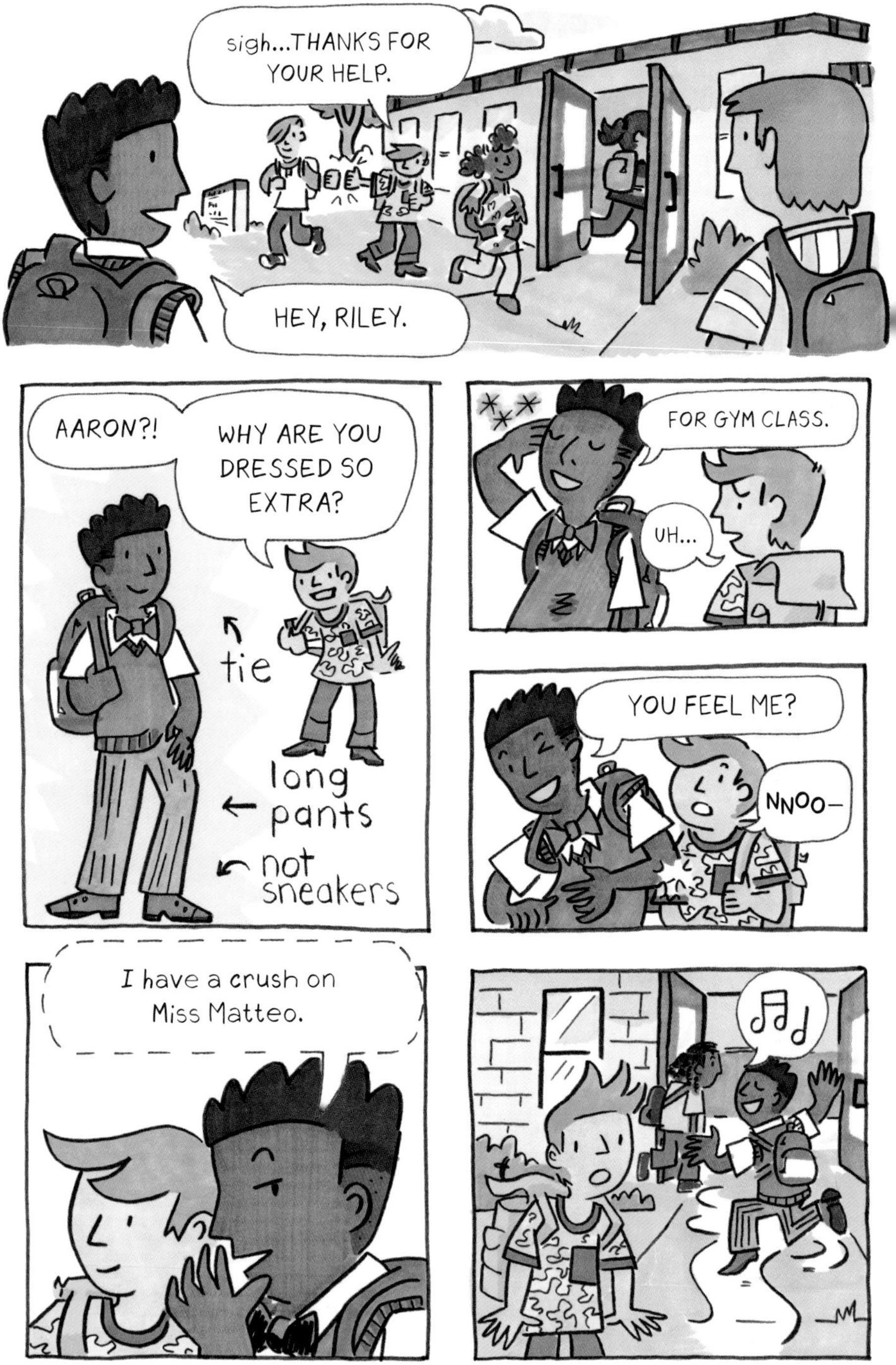
sigh...THANKS FOR YOUR HELP.
HEY, RILEY.
AARON?!
WHY ARE YOU DRESSED SO EXTRA?
tie
long pants
not sneakers
FOR GYM CLASS.
UH...
YOU FEEL ME?
NNOO—
I have a crush on Miss Matteo.

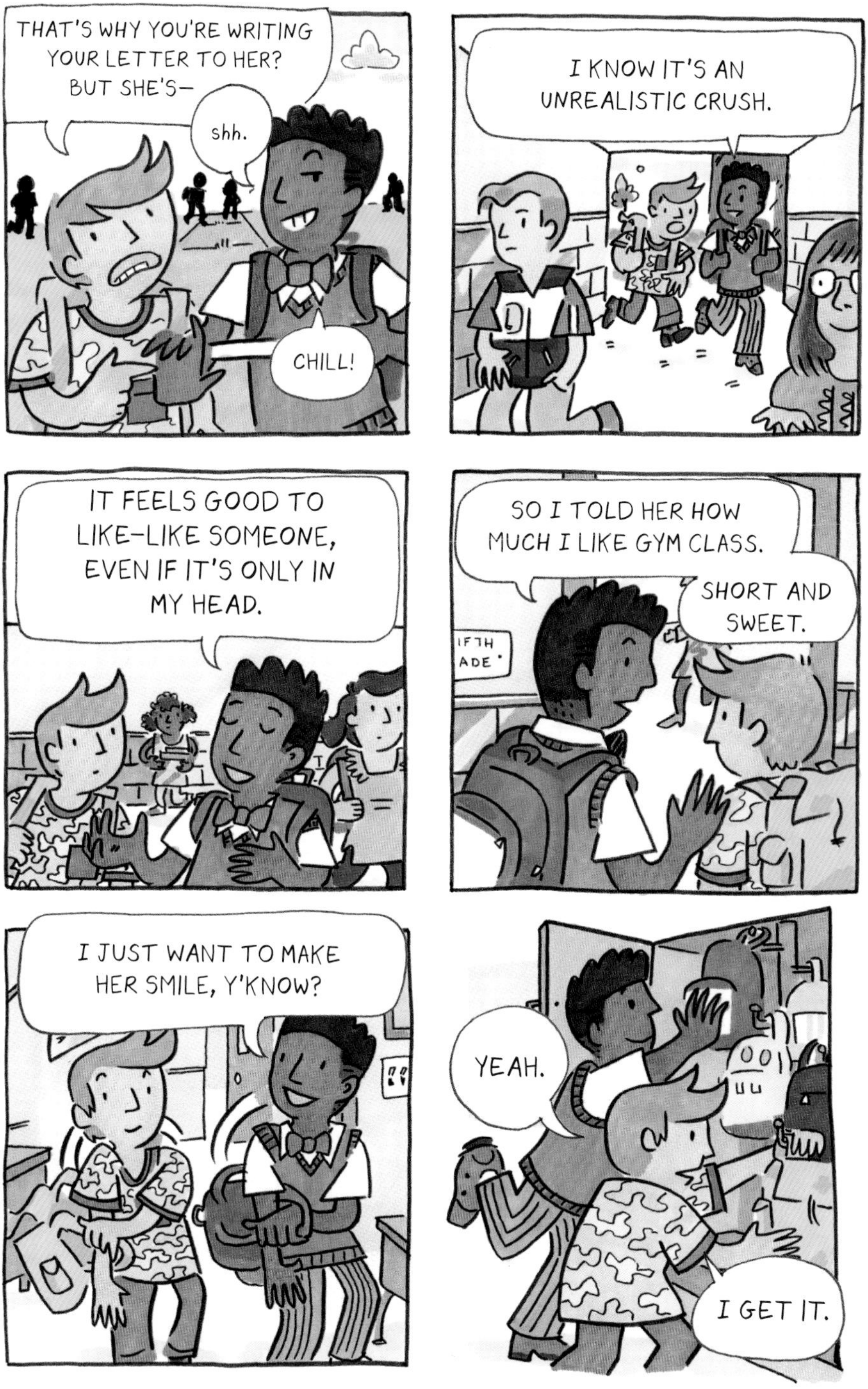
THAT'S WHY YOU'RE WRITING YOUR LETTER TO HER? BUT SHE'S—
shh.
CHILL!
I KNOW IT'S AN UNREALISTIC CRUSH.
IT FEELS GOOD TO LIKE-LIKE SOMEONE, EVEN IF IT'S ONLY IN MY HEAD.
SO I TOLD HER HOW MUCH I LIKE GYM CLASS.
SHORT AND SWEET.
I JUST WANT TO MAKE HER SMILE, Y'KNOW?
YEAH.
I GET IT.

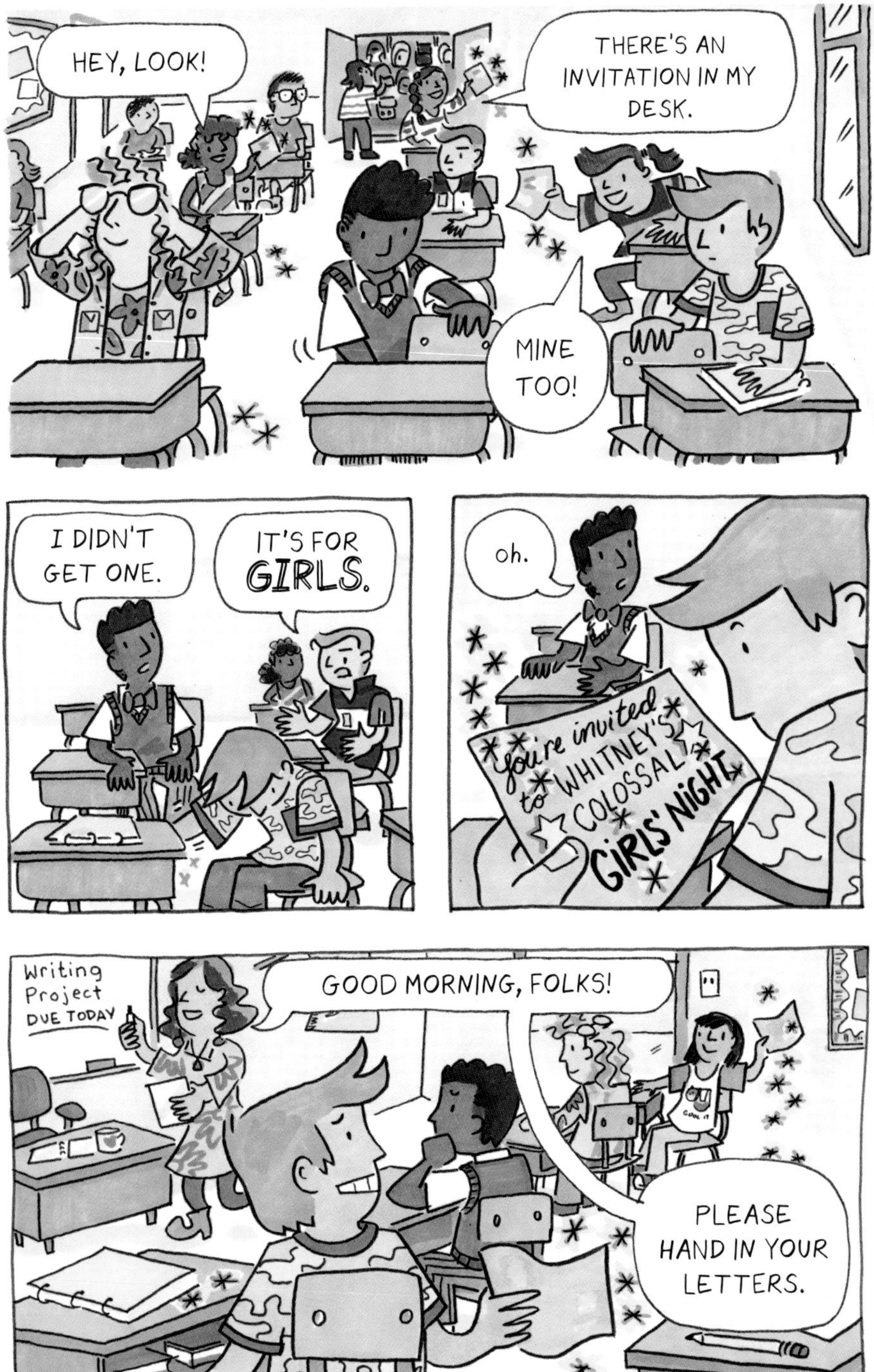
HEY, LOOK!
THERE'S AN INVITATION IN MY DESK.
MINE TOO!
I DIDN'T GET ONE.
IT'S FOR GIRLS.
oh.
You're invited to WHITNEY'S COLOSSAL GIRLS' NIGHT
Writing Project DUE TODAY
GOOD MORNING, FOLKS!
PLEASE HAND IN YOUR LETTERS.

CHAPTER 13

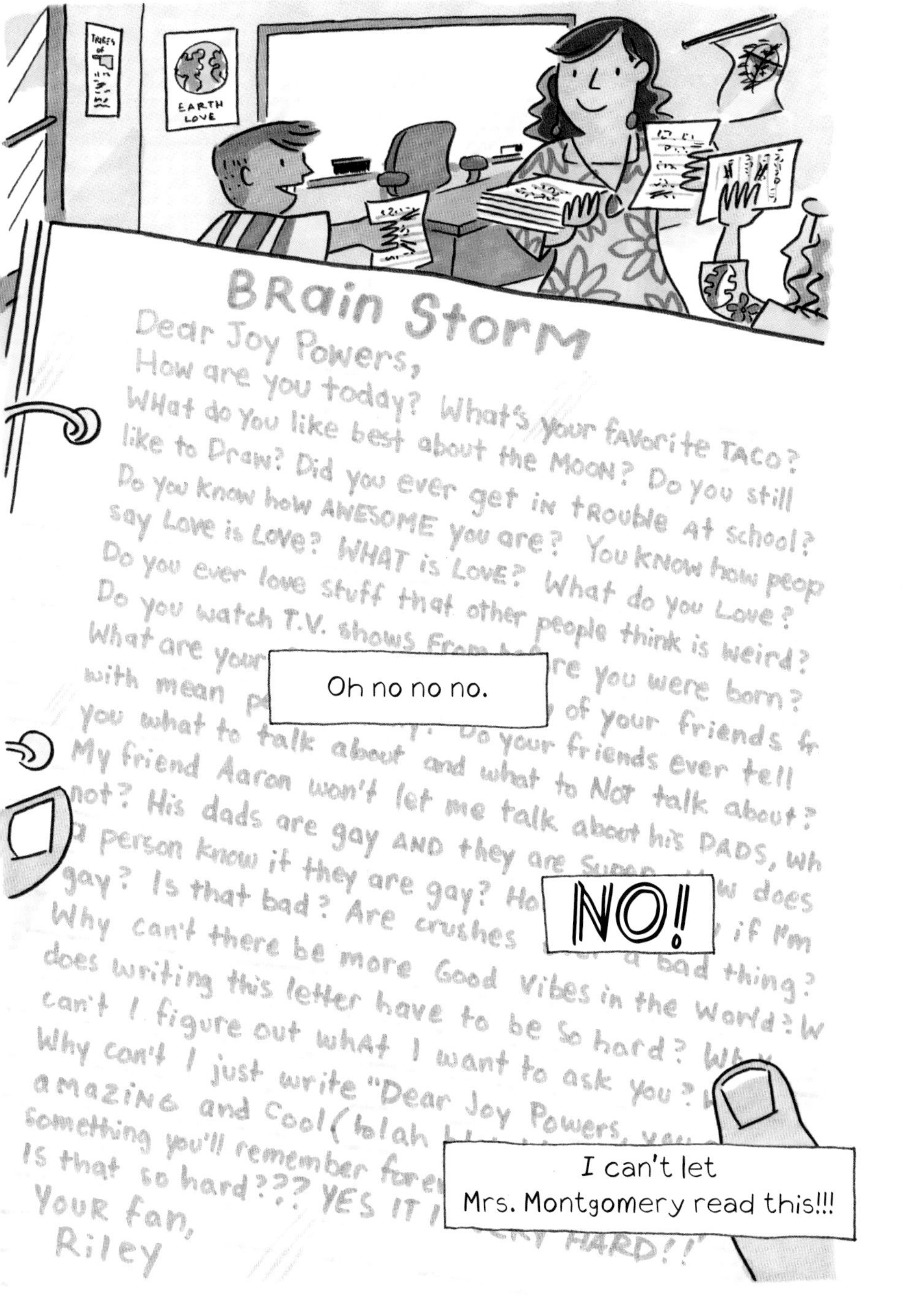
EARTH LOVE
Brain Storm
Dear Joy Powers,
How are you today? What's your favorite TACO?
WHat do You like best about the MOON? Do you still
like to Draw? Did you ever get in trouble at school?
Do you know how AWESOME you are? You know how peop
say Love is Love? WHAT is Love? What do you Love?
Do you ever love stuff that other people think is weird?
Do you watch T.V. shows
re you were born?
What are your
of your friends fr
with mean
Do your friends ever tell
you what to talk about and what to Not talk about?
My friend Aaron won't let me talk about his DADS, wh
not? His dads are gay AND they are
w does
a person know if they are gay?
if I'm
gay? Is that bad? Are crushes
a bad thing?
Why can't there be more Good Vibes in the World? W
does writing this letter have to be so hard?
can't I figure out what I want to ask you?
Why can't I just write "Dear Joy Powers,
amazing and Cool (blah
something you'll remember
Is that so hard??? YES IT
HARD!!
Your fan,
Riley
Oh no no no.
NO!
I can't let Mrs. Montgomery read this!!!

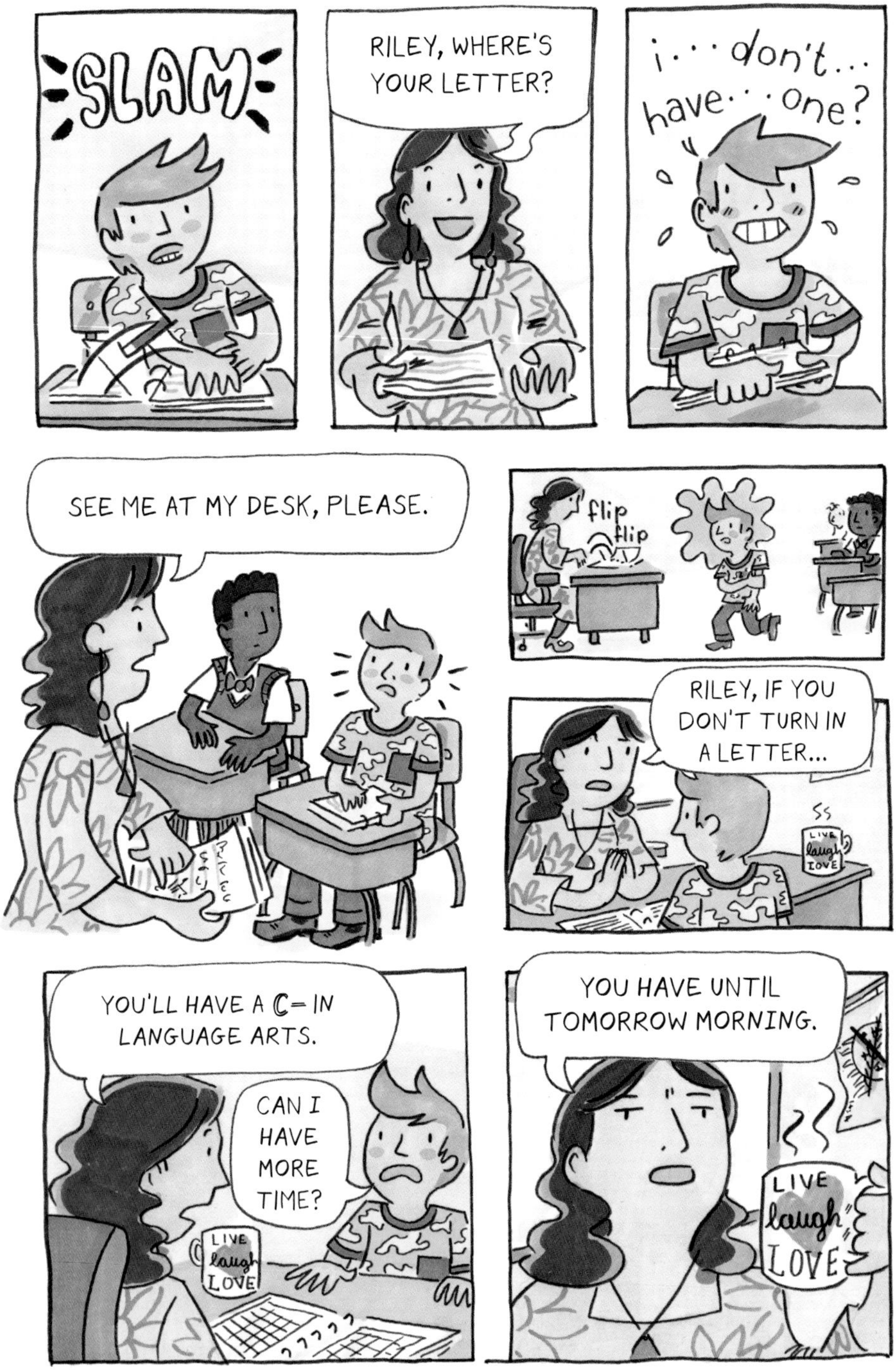
SLAM
RILEY, WHERE'S YOUR LETTER?
i... don't... have... one?
SEE ME AT MY DESK, PLEASE.
flip flip
RILEY, IF YOU DON'T TURN IN A LETTER...
LIVE laugh LOVE
YOU'LL HAVE A C- IN LANGUAGE ARTS.
CAN I HAVE MORE TIME?
LIVE laugh LOVE
YOU HAVE UNTIL TOMORROW MORNING.
LIVE laugh LOVE

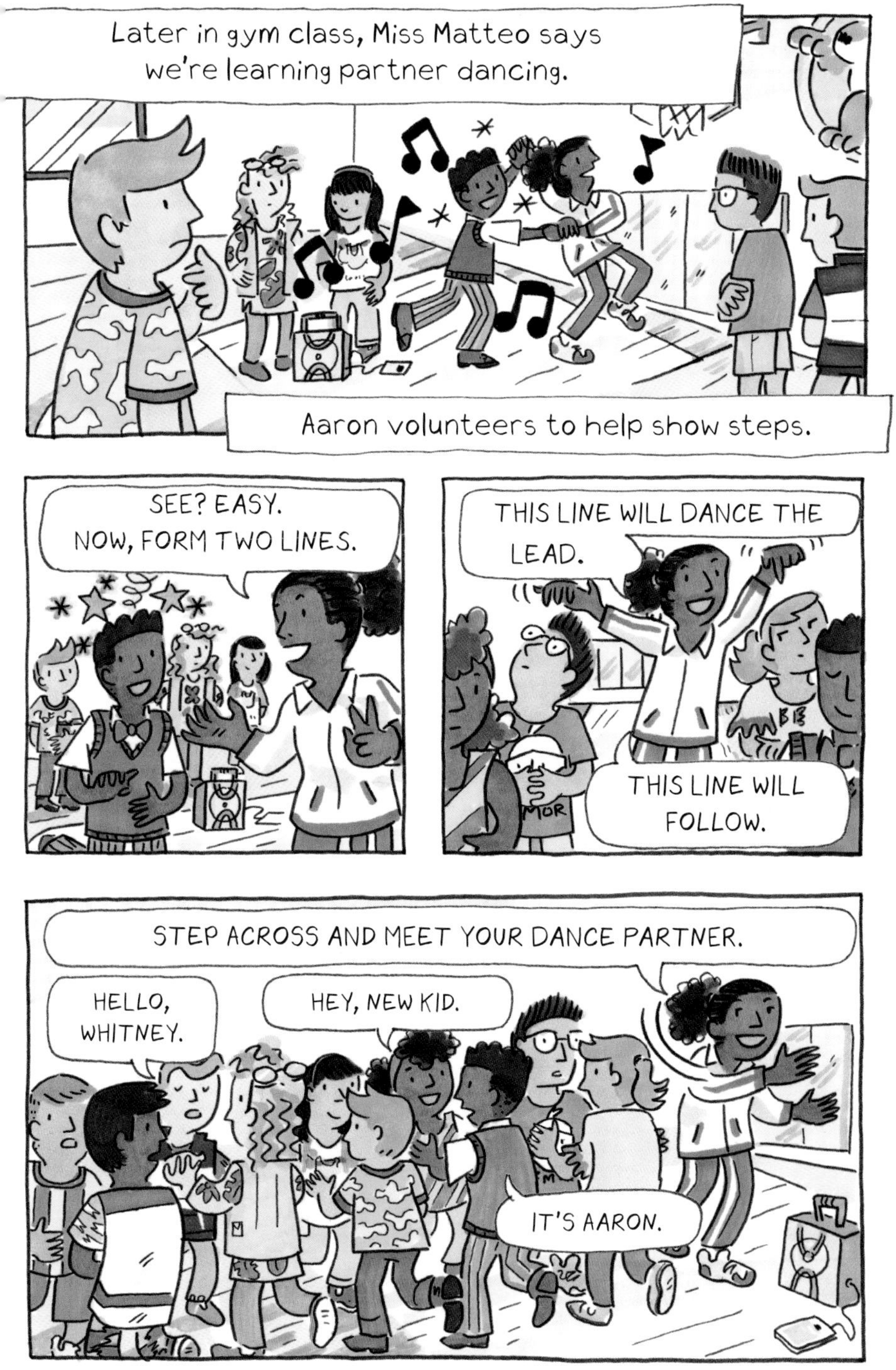
Later in gym class, Miss Matteo says we're learning partner dancing.
Aaron volunteers to help show steps.
SEE? EASY. NOW, FORM TWO LINES.
THIS LINE WILL DANCE THE LEAD.
THIS LINE WILL FOLLOW.
STEP ACROSS AND MEET YOUR DANCE PARTNER.
HELLO, WHITNEY.
HEY, NEW KID.
IT'S AARON.

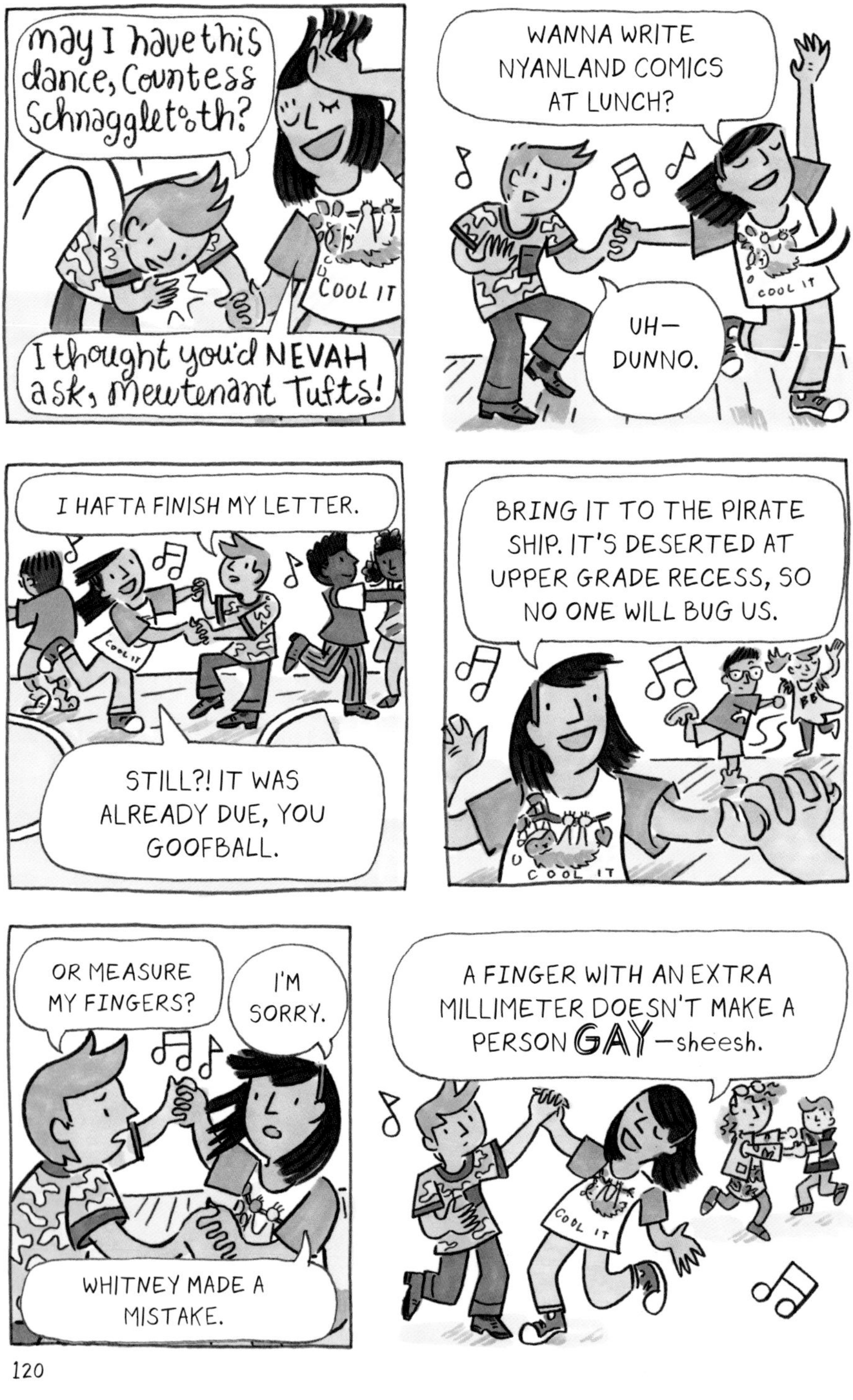
May I have this dance, Countess Schnaggletooth?
I thought you'd NEVAH ask, Mewtenant Tufts!
COOL IT
WANNA WRITE NYANLAND COMICS AT LUNCH?
UH— DUNNO.
I HAFTA FINISH MY LETTER.
STILL?! IT WAS ALREADY DUE, YOU GOOFBALL.
BRING IT TO THE PIRATE SHIP. IT'S DESERTED AT UPPER GRADE RECESS, SO NO ONE WILL BUG US.
OR MEASURE MY FINGERS?
I'M SORRY.
WHITNEY MADE A MISTAKE.
A FINGER WITH AN EXTRA MILLIMETER DOESN'T MAKE A PERSON GAY—sheesh.

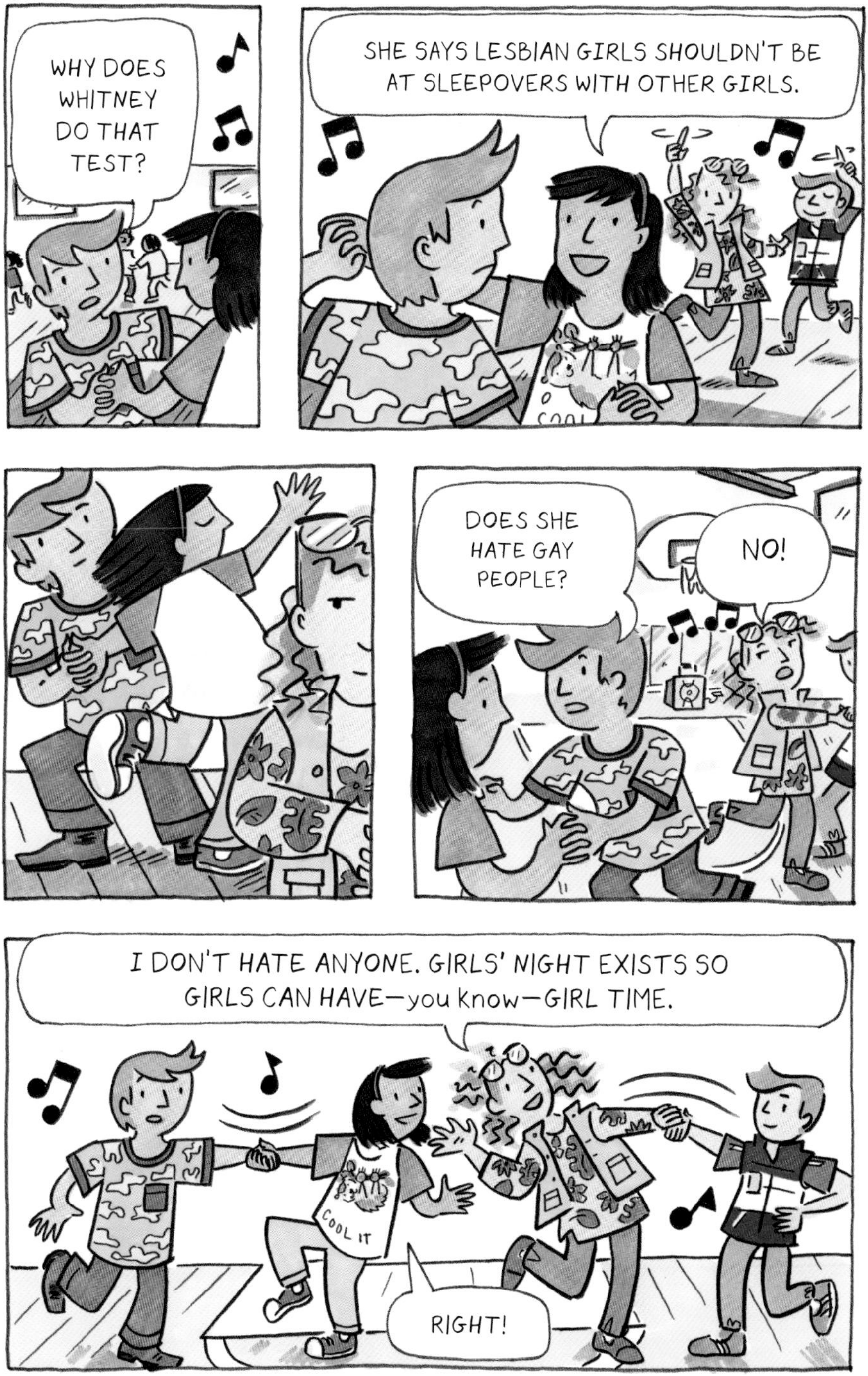
WHY DOES WHITNEY DO THAT TEST?
SHE SAYS LESBIAN GIRLS SHOULDN'T BE AT SLEEPOVERS WITH OTHER GIRLS.
COOL
DOES SHE HATE GAY PEOPLE?
NO!
I DON'T HATE ANYONE. GIRLS' NIGHT EXISTS SO GIRLS CAN HAVE—you know—GIRL TIME.
COOL IT
RIGHT!

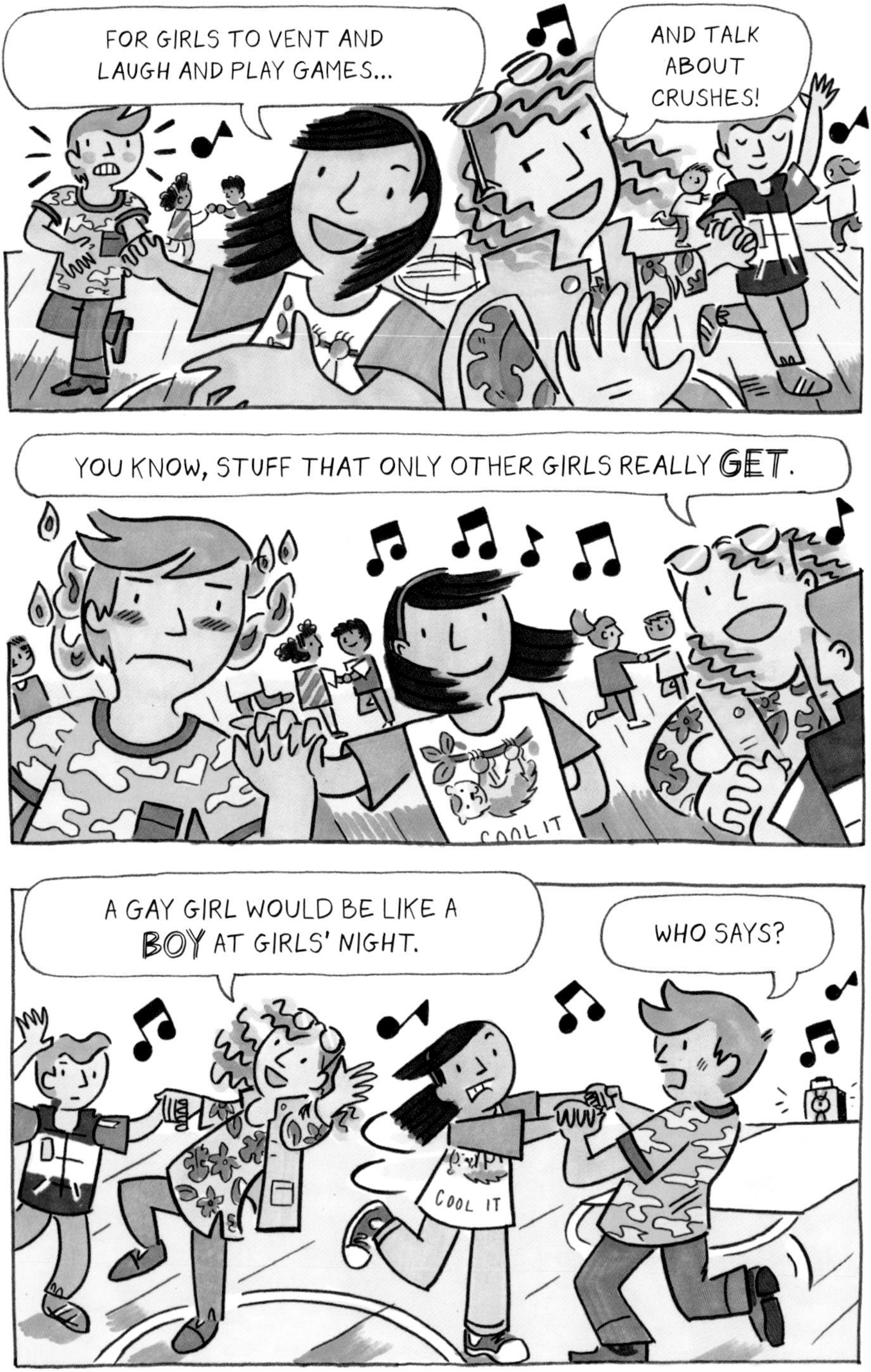
FOR GIRLS TO VENT AND LAUGH AND PLAY GAMES...
AND TALK ABOUT CRUSHES!
YOU KNOW, STUFF THAT ONLY OTHER GIRLS REALLY GET.
COOL IT
A GAY GIRL WOULD BE LIKE A BOY AT GIRLS' NIGHT.
WHO SAYS?
COOL IT

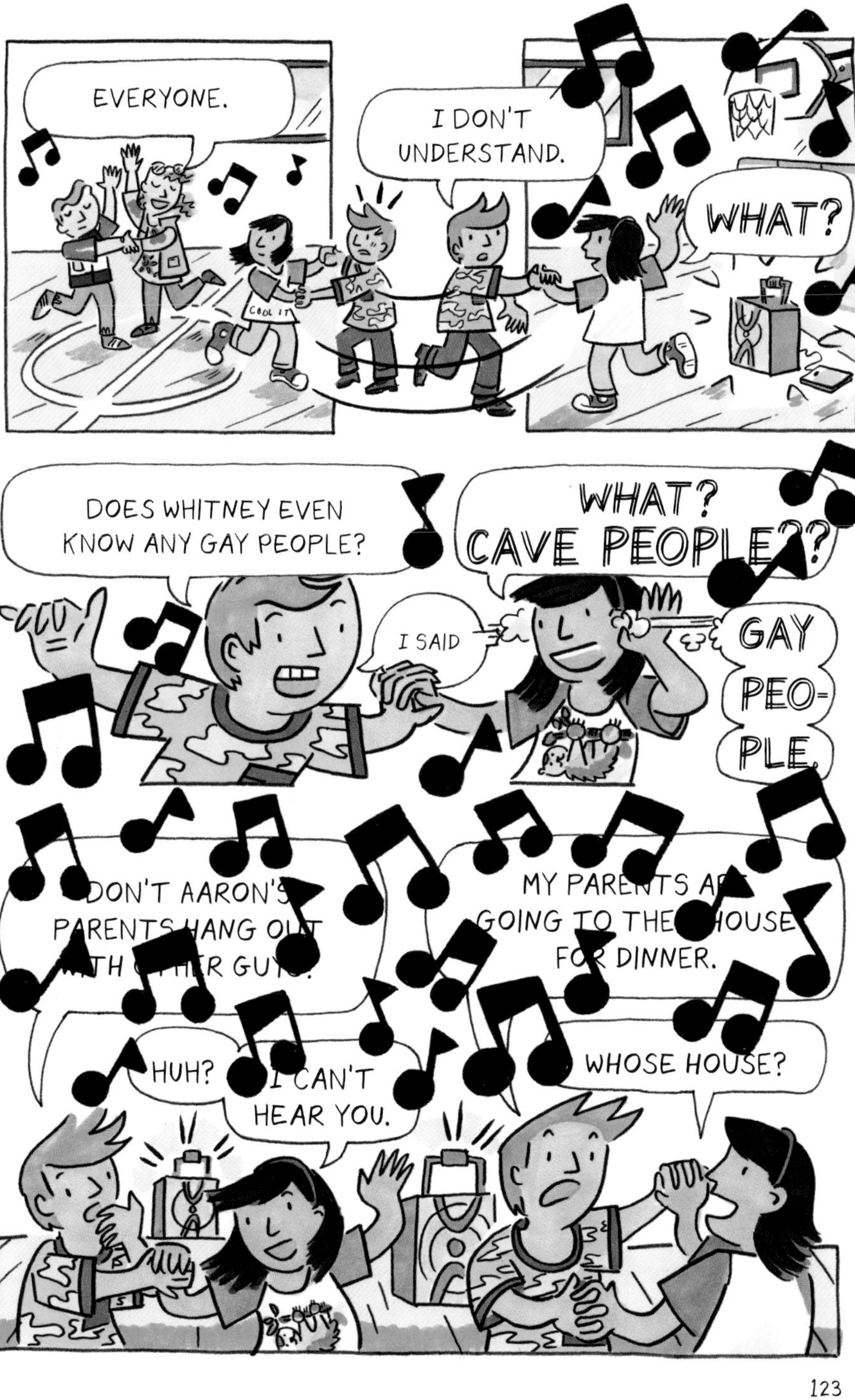
EVERYONE.
I DON'T UNDERSTAND.
WHAT?
DOES WHITNEY EVEN KNOW ANY GAY PEOPLE?
WHAT? CAVE PEOPLE??
I SAID
GAY PEO- PLE.
DON'T AARON'S PARENTS HANG
MY PARENTS
GOING TO THE HOUSE
FOR DINNER.
HUH?
I CAN'T HEAR YOU.
WHOSE HOUSE?
COOL IT

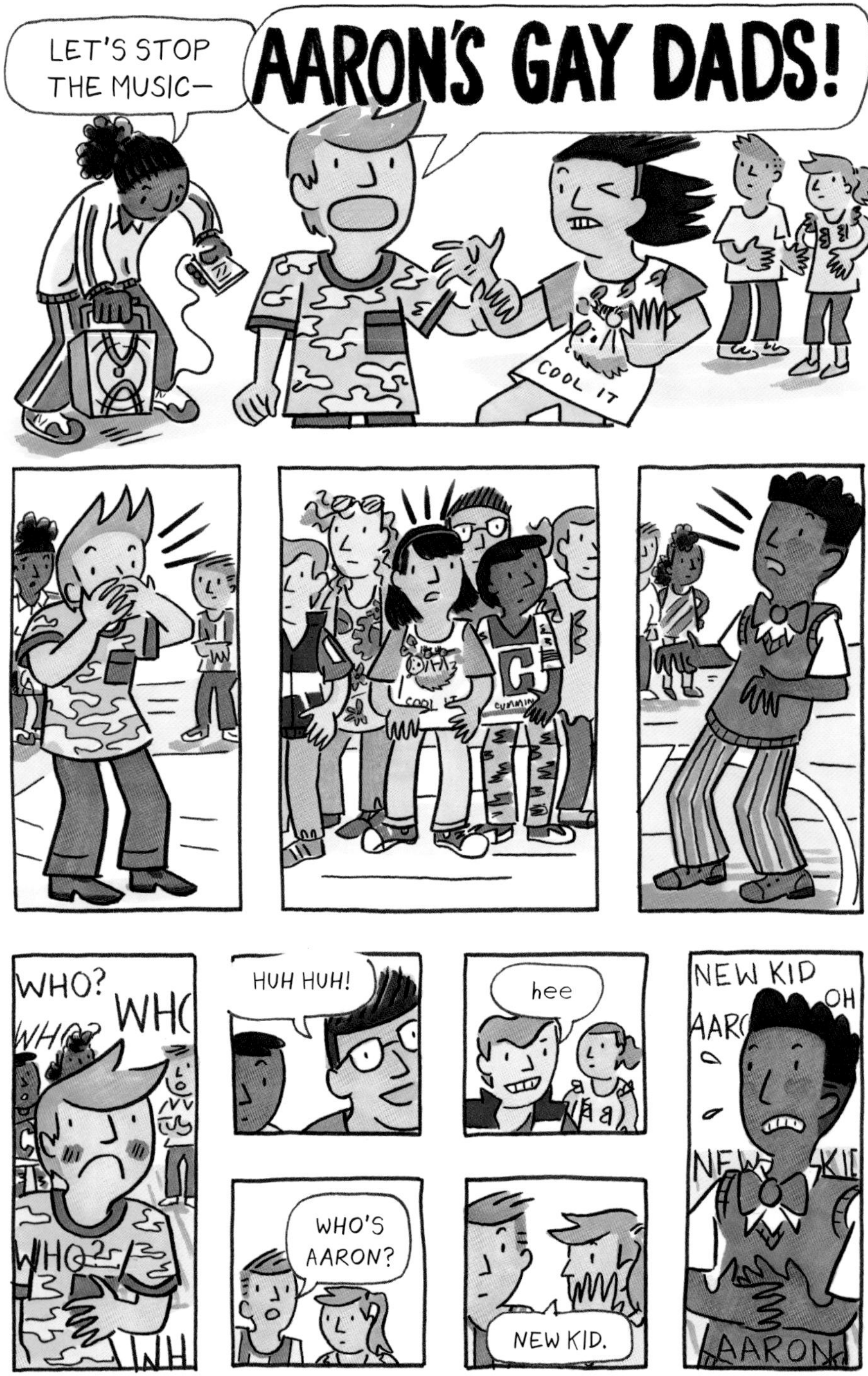

LET'S STOP THE MUSIC—
AARON'S GAY DADS!
COOL IT
WHO?
WHO
HUH HUH!
hee
NEW KID
OH
WHO'S AARON?
NEW KID.
AARON

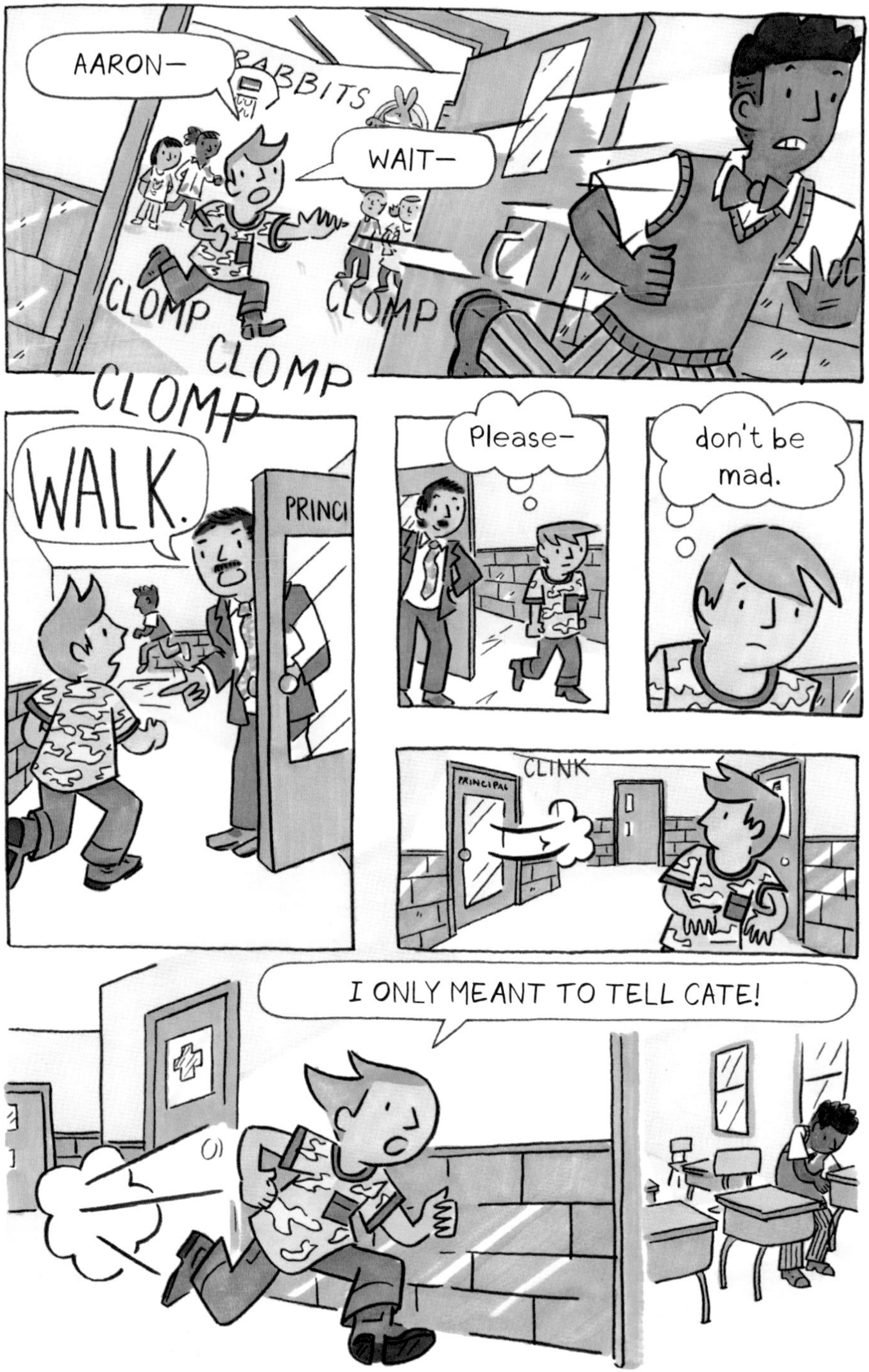
AARON—
RABBITS
WAIT—
CLOMP
CLOMP
CLOMP
CLOMP
WALK.
PRINCI
Please-
don't be
mad.
PRINCIPAL
CLINK
I ONLY MEANT TO TELL CATE!

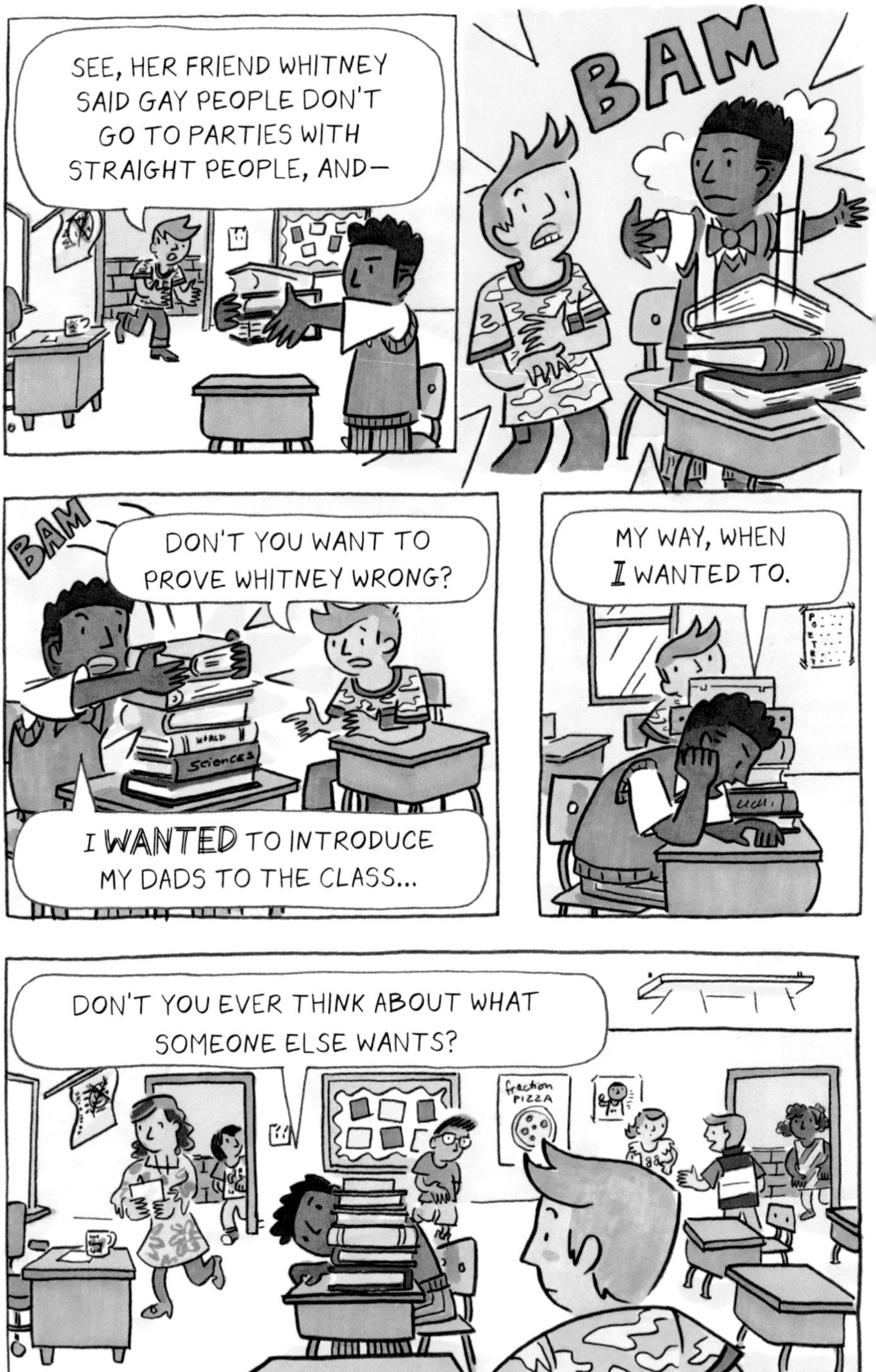
SEE, HER FRIEND WHITNEY SAID GAY PEOPLE DON'T GO TO PARTIES WITH STRAIGHT PEOPLE, AND—
BAM
BAM
DON'T YOU WANT TO PROVE WHITNEY WRONG?
I WANTED TO INTRODUCE MY DADS TO THE CLASS...
MY WAY, WHEN I WANTED TO.
DON'T YOU EVER THINK ABOUT WHAT SOMEONE ELSE WANTS?
fraction PIZZA

CHAPTER 14

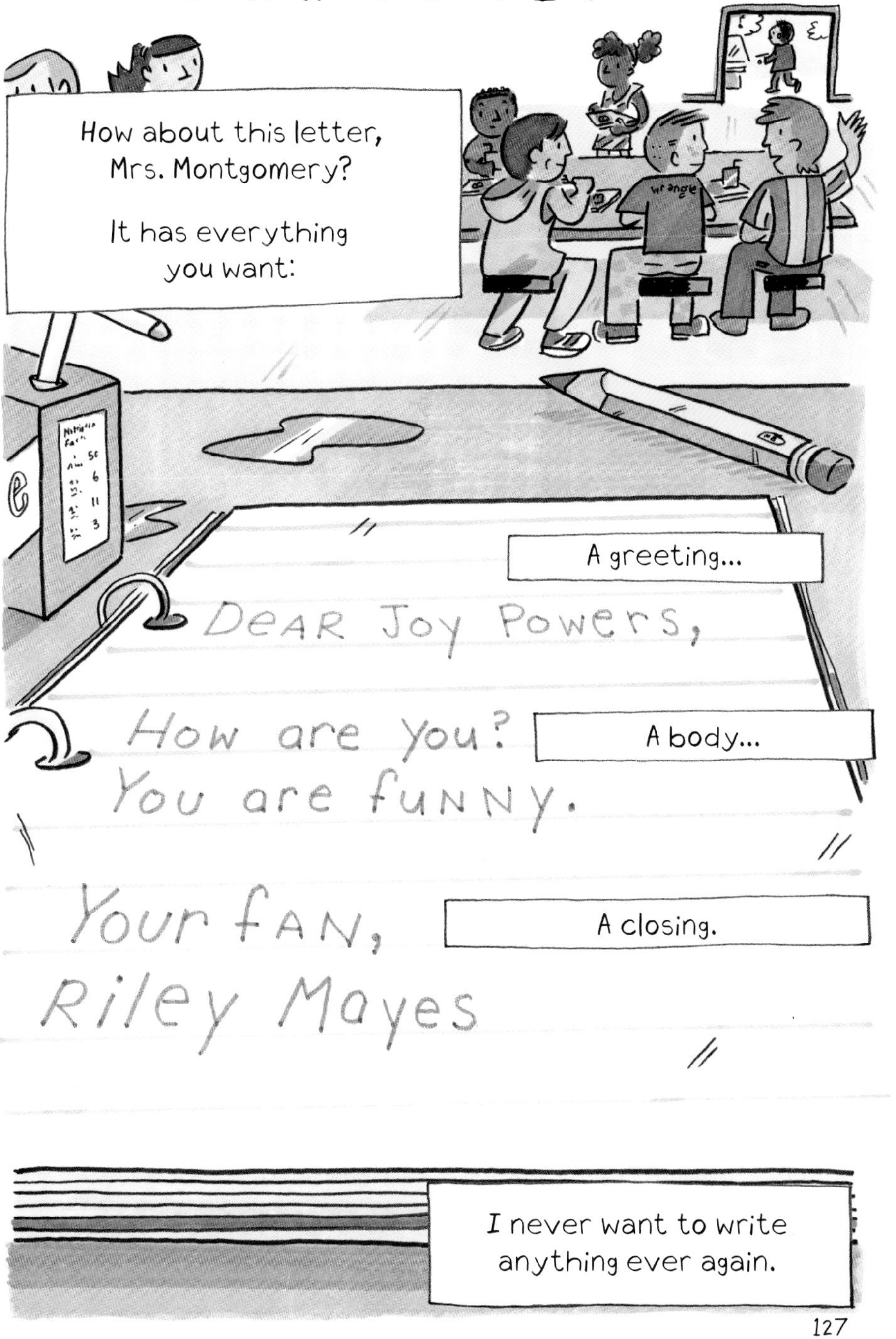
How about this letter, Mrs. Montgomery?
It has everything you want:
A greeting...
Dear Joy Powers,
How are you? You are funny.
A body...
Your fan, Riley Mayes
A closing.
I never want to write anything ever again.

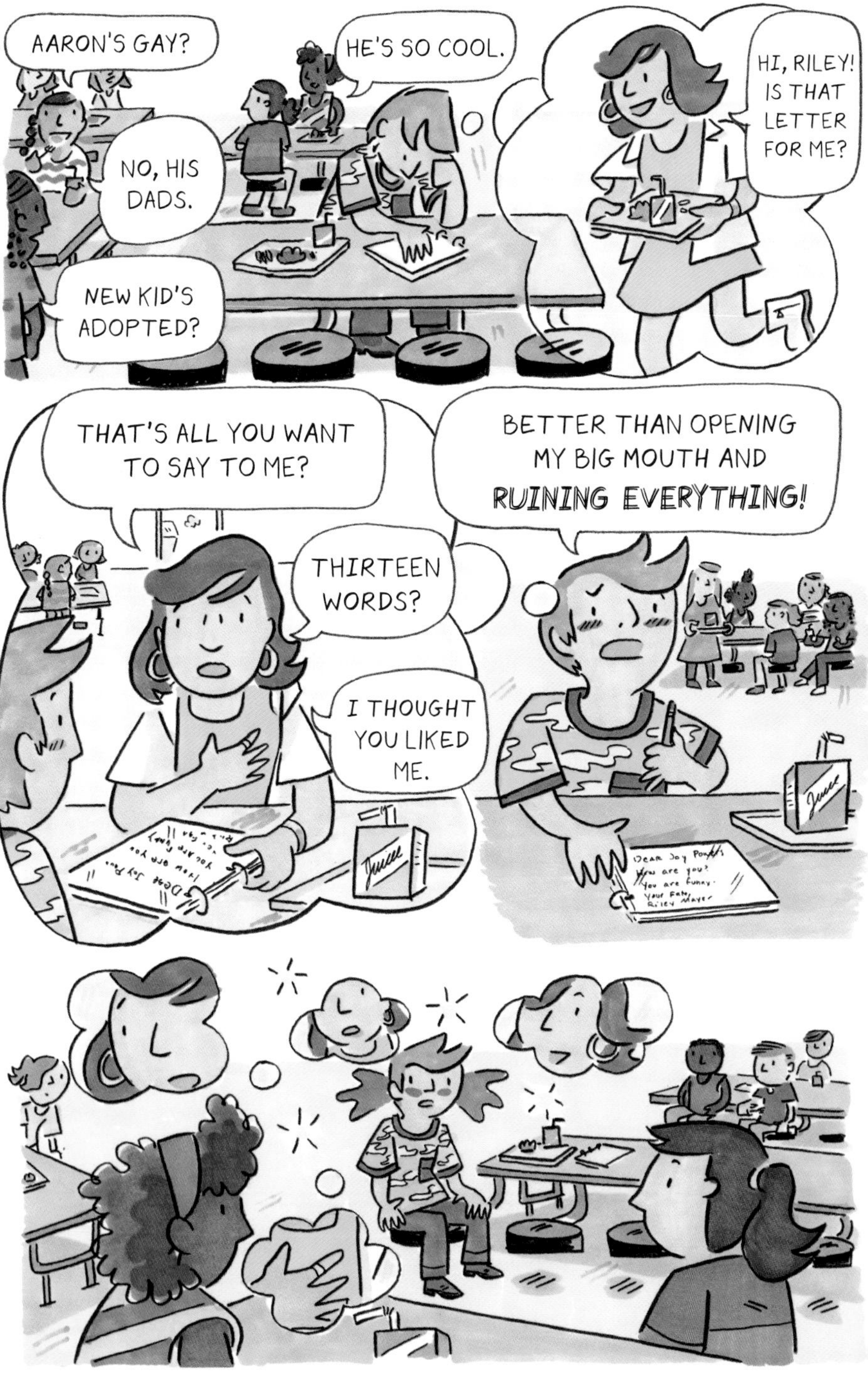
AARON'S GAY?
NO, HIS DADS.
NEW KID'S ADOPTED?
HE'S SO COOL.
HI, RILEY! IS THAT LETTER FOR ME?
THAT'S ALL YOU WANT TO SAY TO ME?
THIRTEEN WORDS?
I THOUGHT YOU LIKED ME.
BETTER THAN OPENING MY BIG MOUTH AND RUINING EVERYTHING!

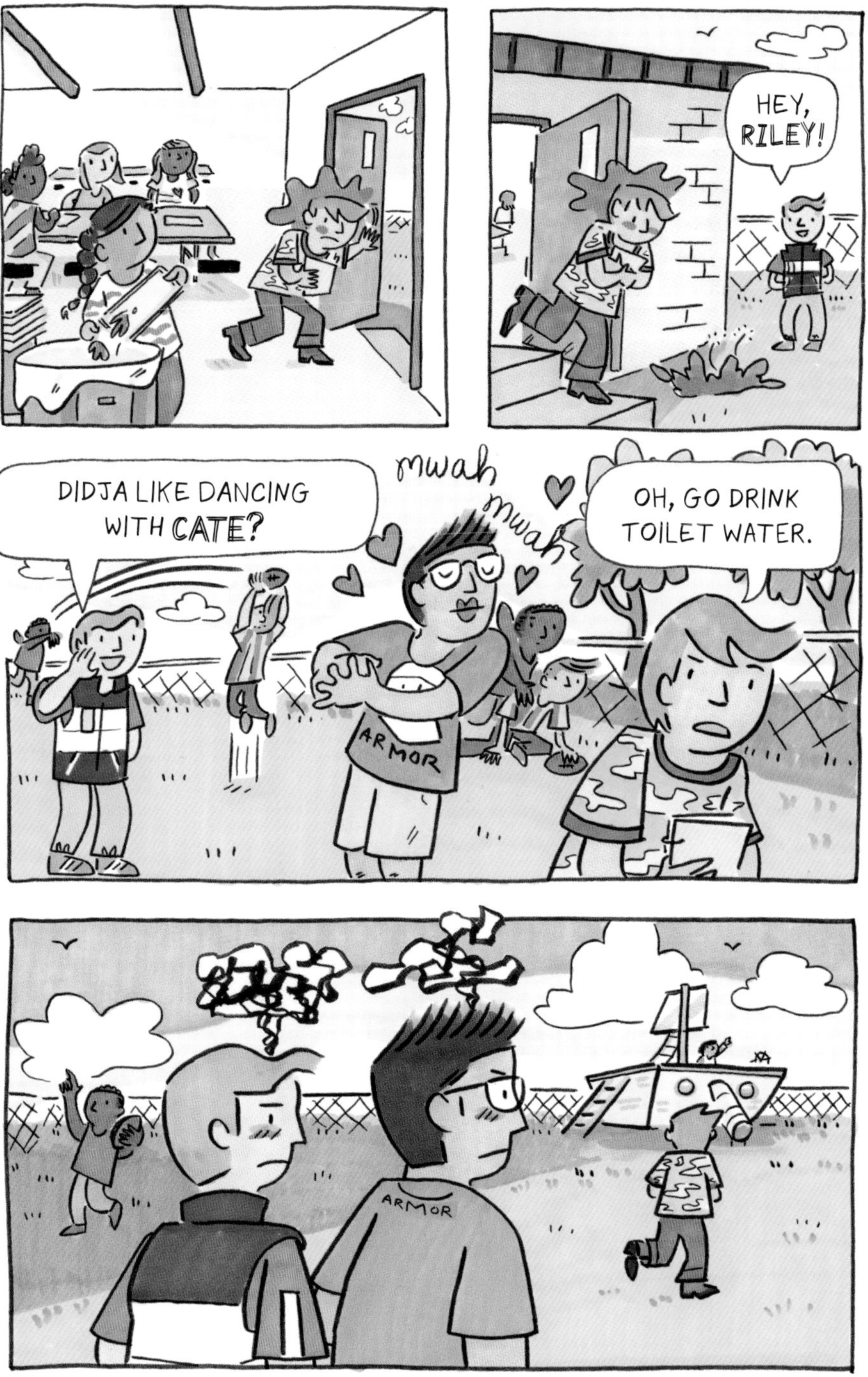
HEY, RILEY!
DIDJA LIKE DANCING WITH CATE?
mwah
mwah
OH, GO DRINK TOILET WATER.
ARMOR
ARMOR

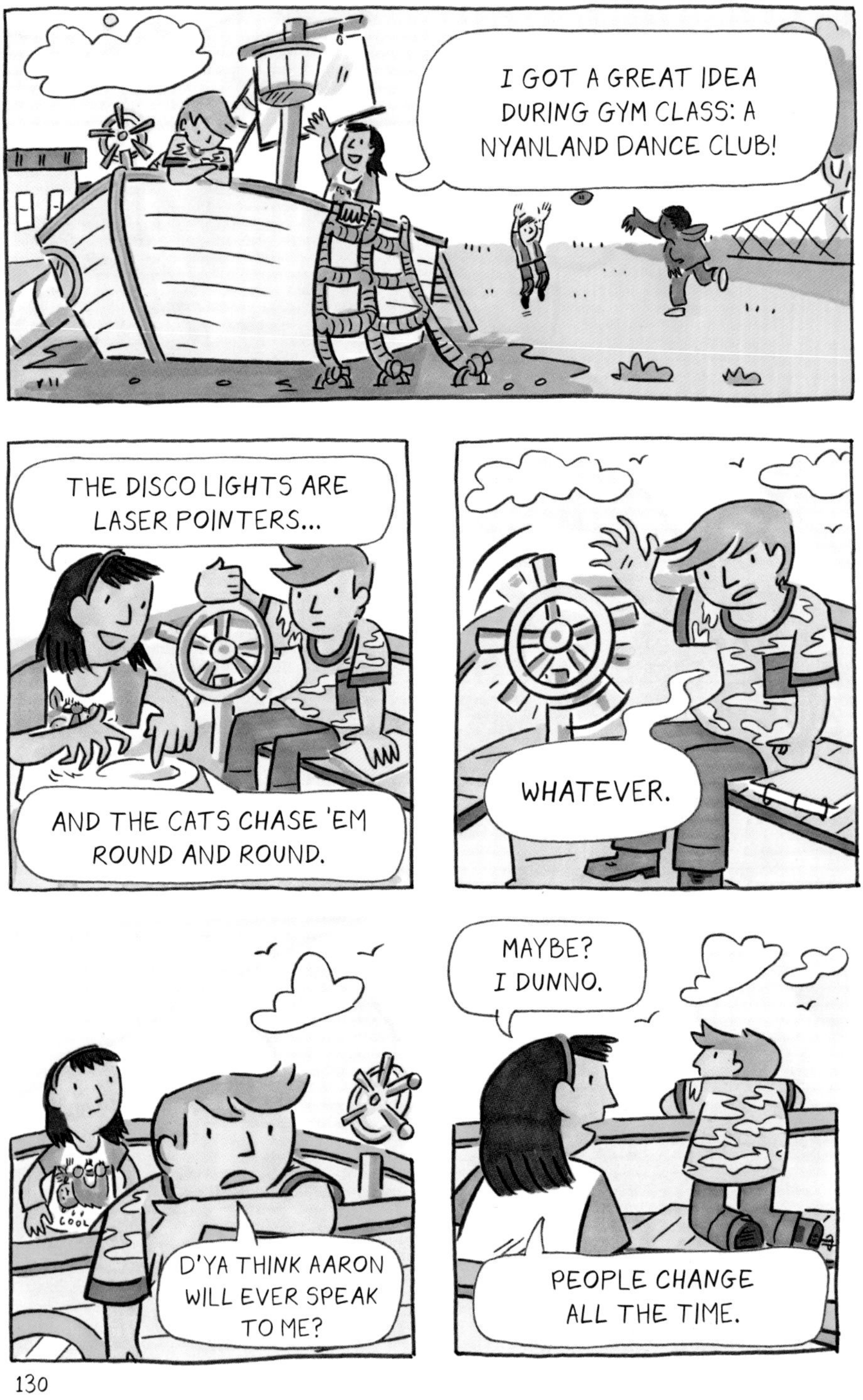
I GOT A GREAT IDEA DURING GYM CLASS: A NYANLAND DANCE CLUB!
THE DISCO LIGHTS ARE LASER POINTERS...
AND THE CATS CHASE 'EM ROUND AND ROUND.
WHATEVER.
COOL
D'YA THINK AARON WILL EVER SPEAK TO ME?
MAYBE? I DUNNO.
PEOPLE CHANGE ALL THE TIME.

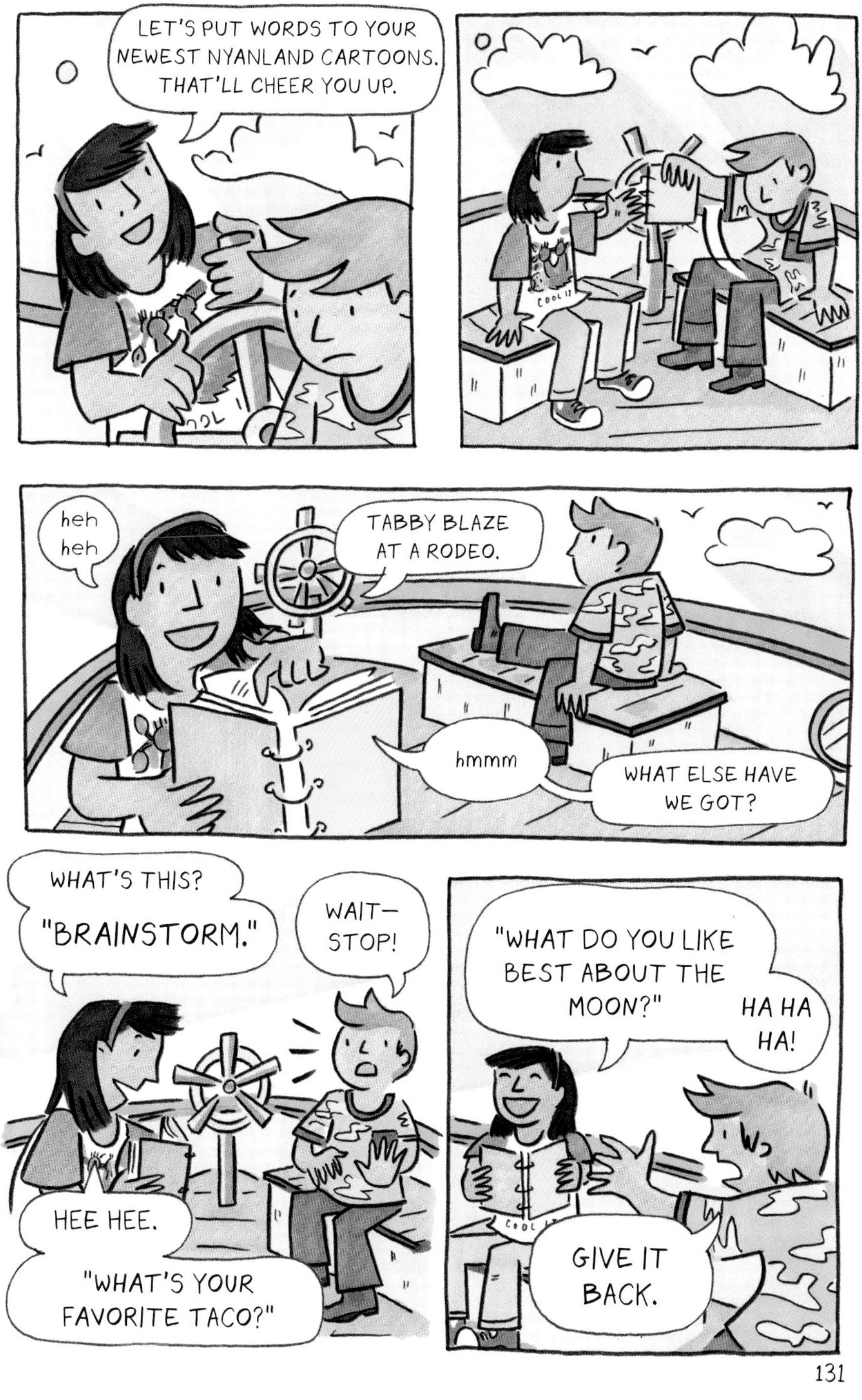
LET'S PUT WORDS TO YOUR NEWEST NYANLAND CARTOONS. THAT'LL CHEER YOU UP.
heh heh
TABBY BLAZE AT A RODEO.
hmmm
WHAT ELSE HAVE WE GOT?
WHAT'S THIS?
"BRAINSTORM."
WAIT— STOP!
HEE HEE.
"WHAT'S YOUR FAVORITE TACO?"
"WHAT DO YOU LIKE BEST ABOUT THE MOON?"
HA HA HA!
GIVE IT BACK.

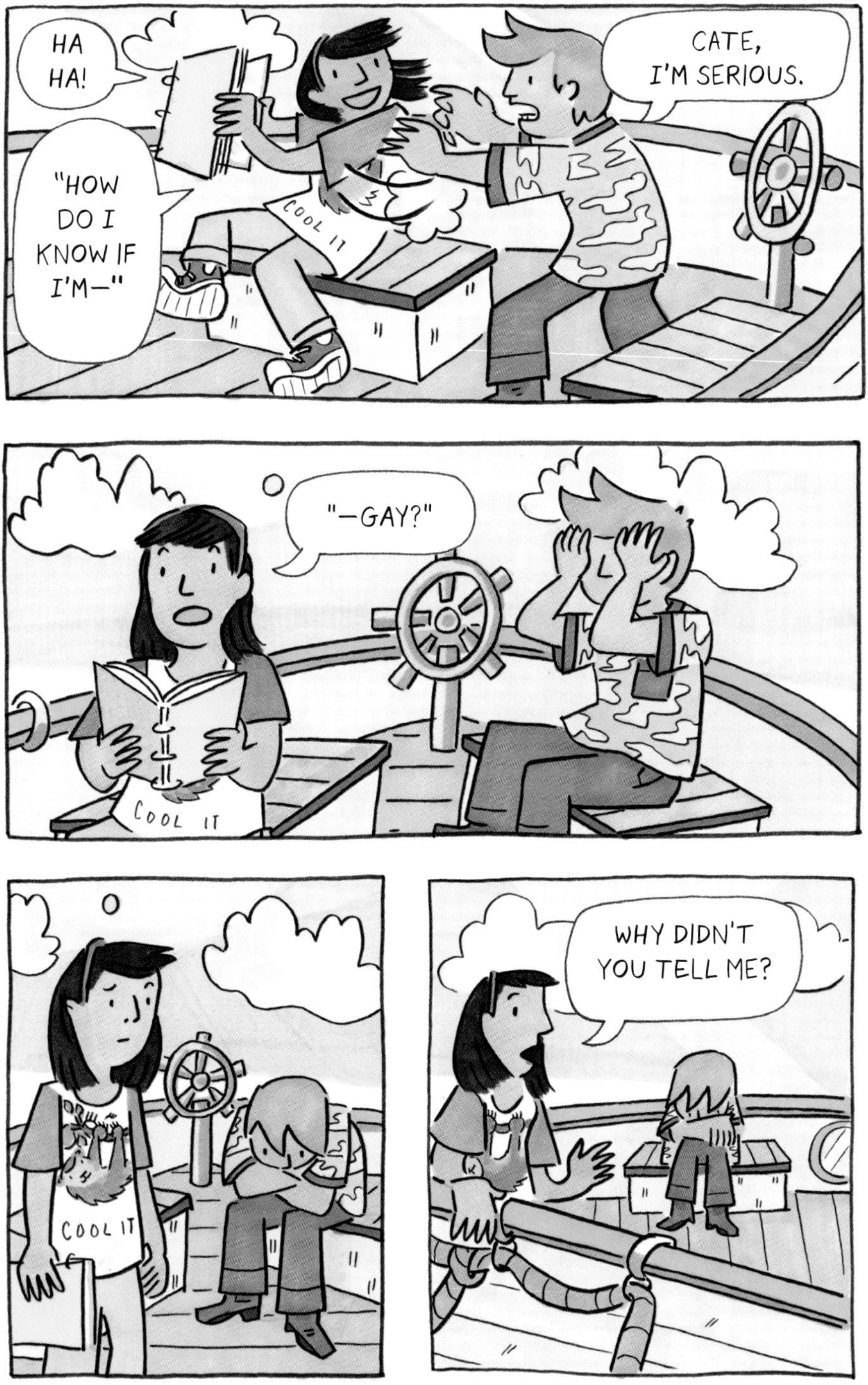
HA HA!
"HOW DO I KNOW IF I'M—"
CATE, I'M SERIOUS.
COOL IT
"—GAY?"
COOL IT
COOL IT
WHY DIDN'T YOU TELL ME?

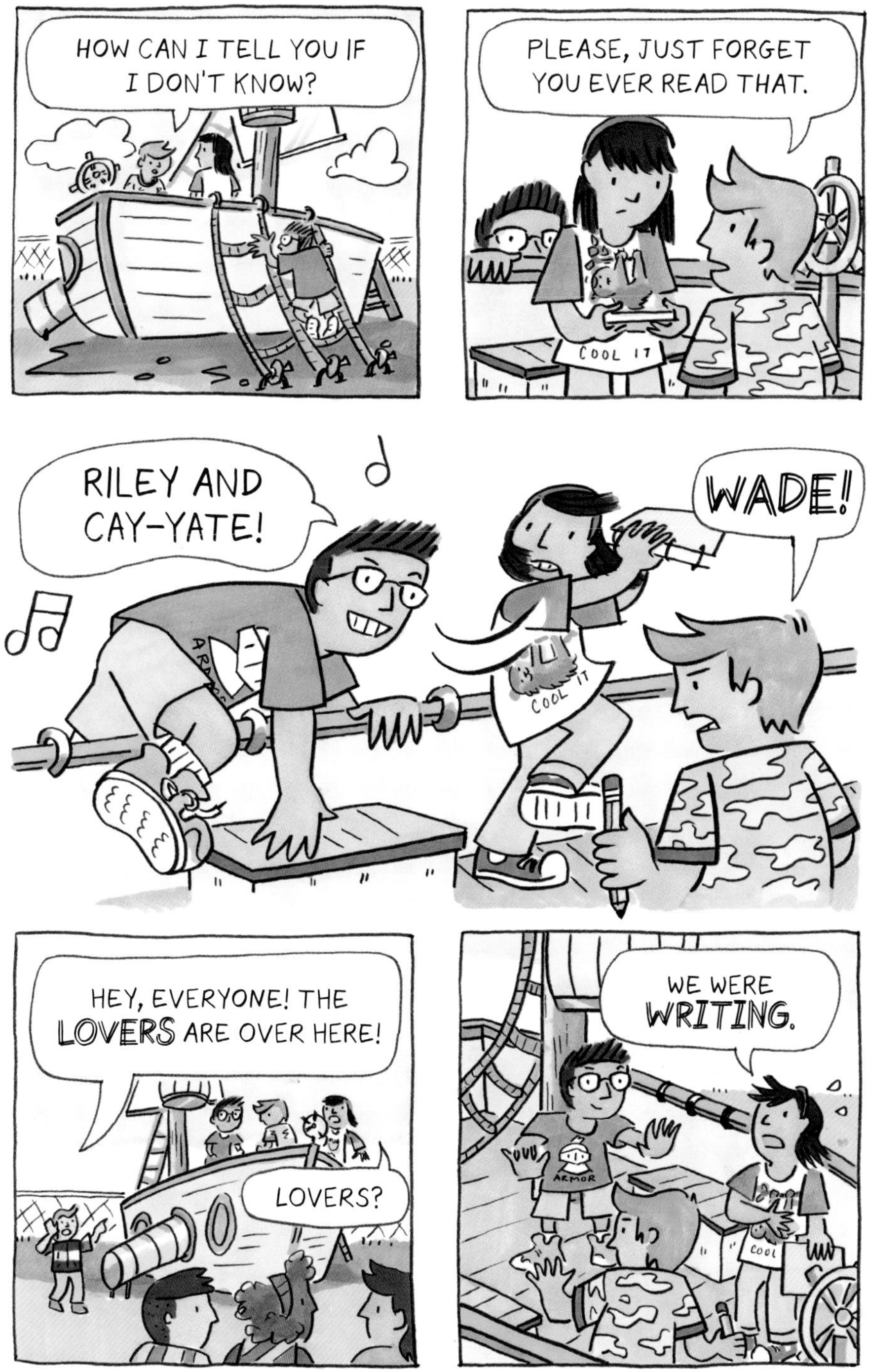
HOW CAN I TELL YOU IF I DON'T KNOW?
PLEASE, JUST FORGET YOU EVER READ THAT.
COOL IT
RILEY AND CAY-YATE!
WADE!
COOL IT
HEY, EVERYONE! THE LOVERS ARE OVER HERE!
LOVERS?
WE WERE WRITING.
ARMOR
COOL

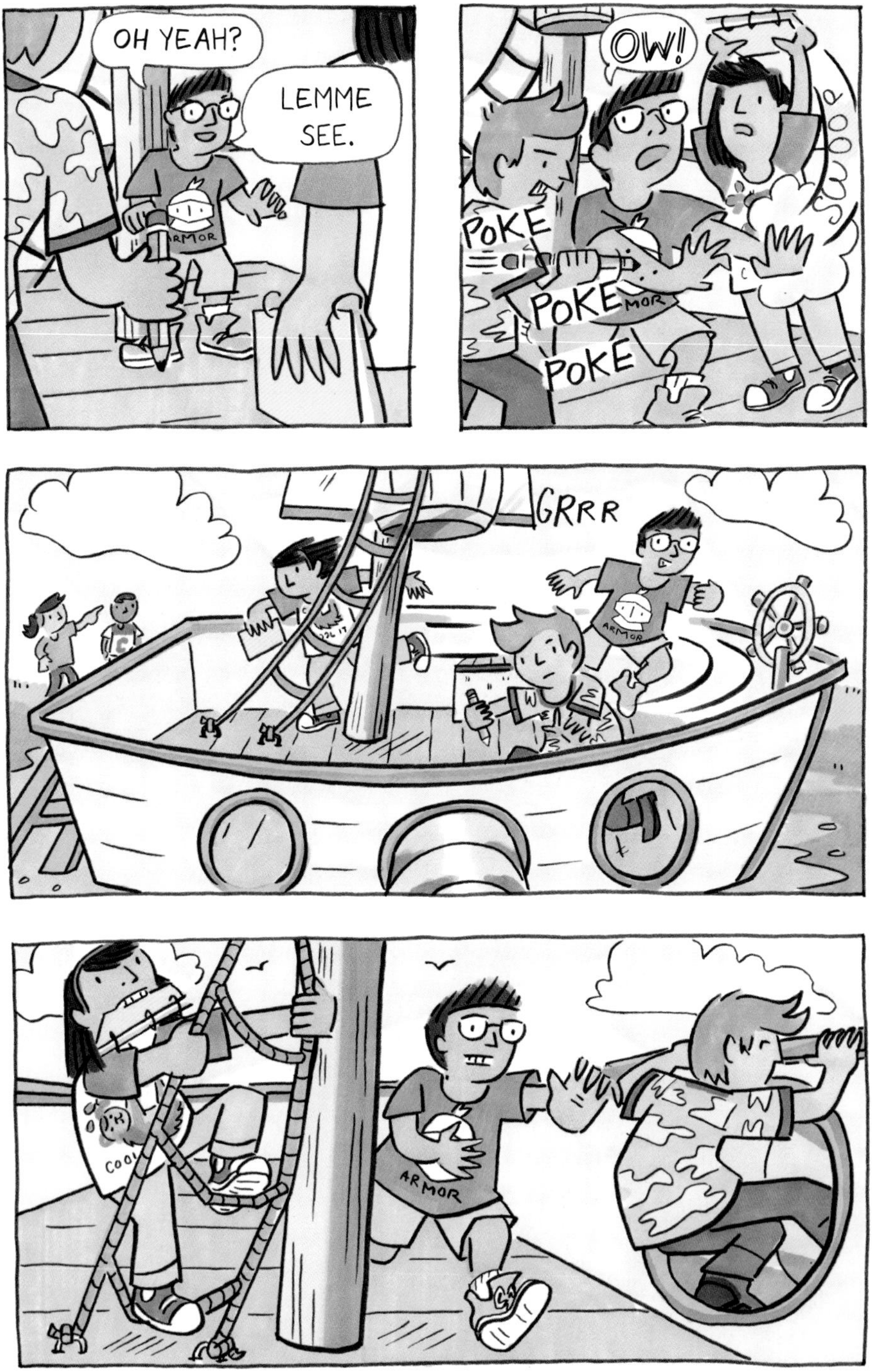
OH YEAH?
LEMME SEE.
OW!
POKE
POKE
POKE
GRRR

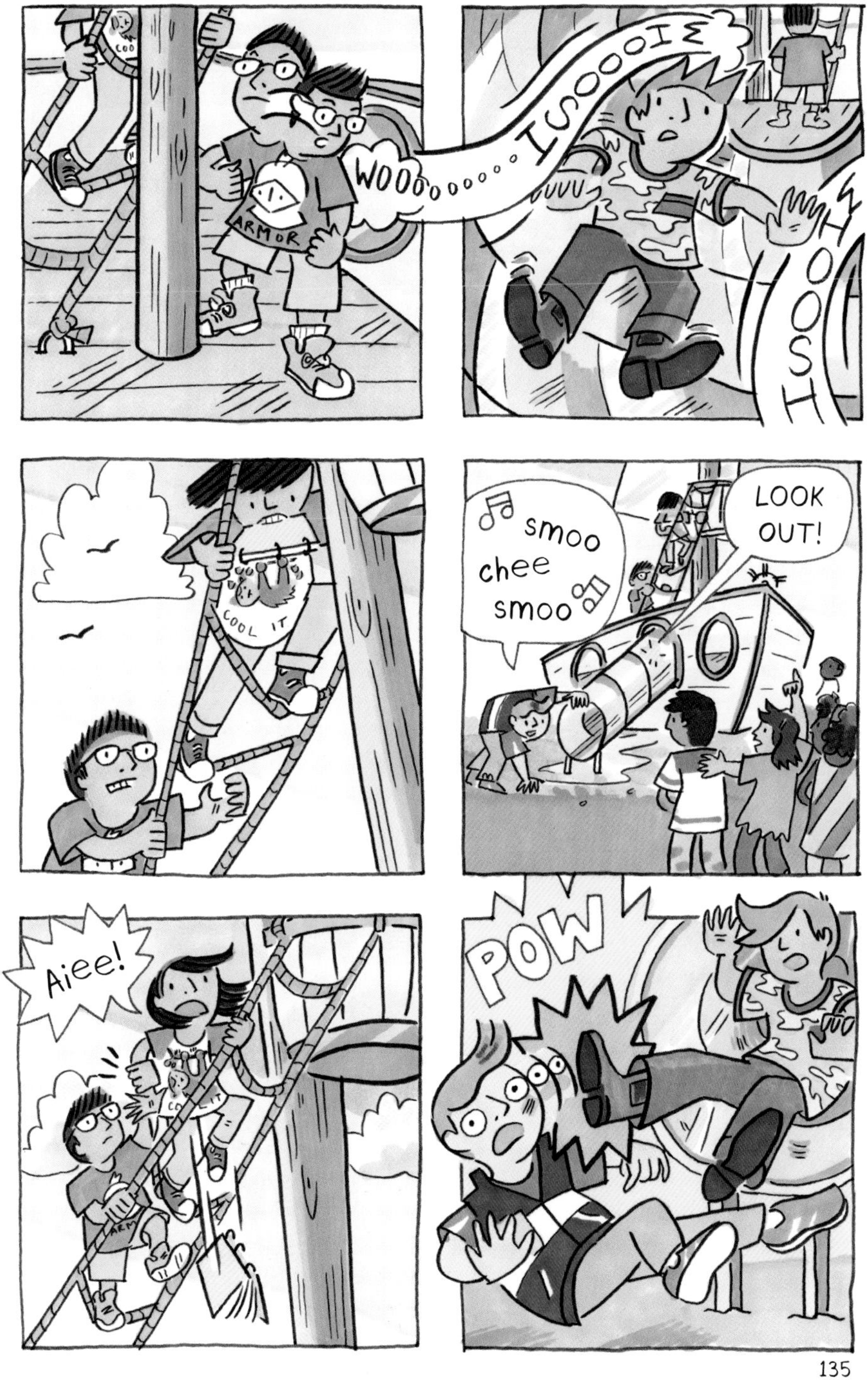
ARMOR
WOOoooooooo
WHOOSH
COOL IT
smoo chee smoo
LOOK OUT!
Aiee!
POW

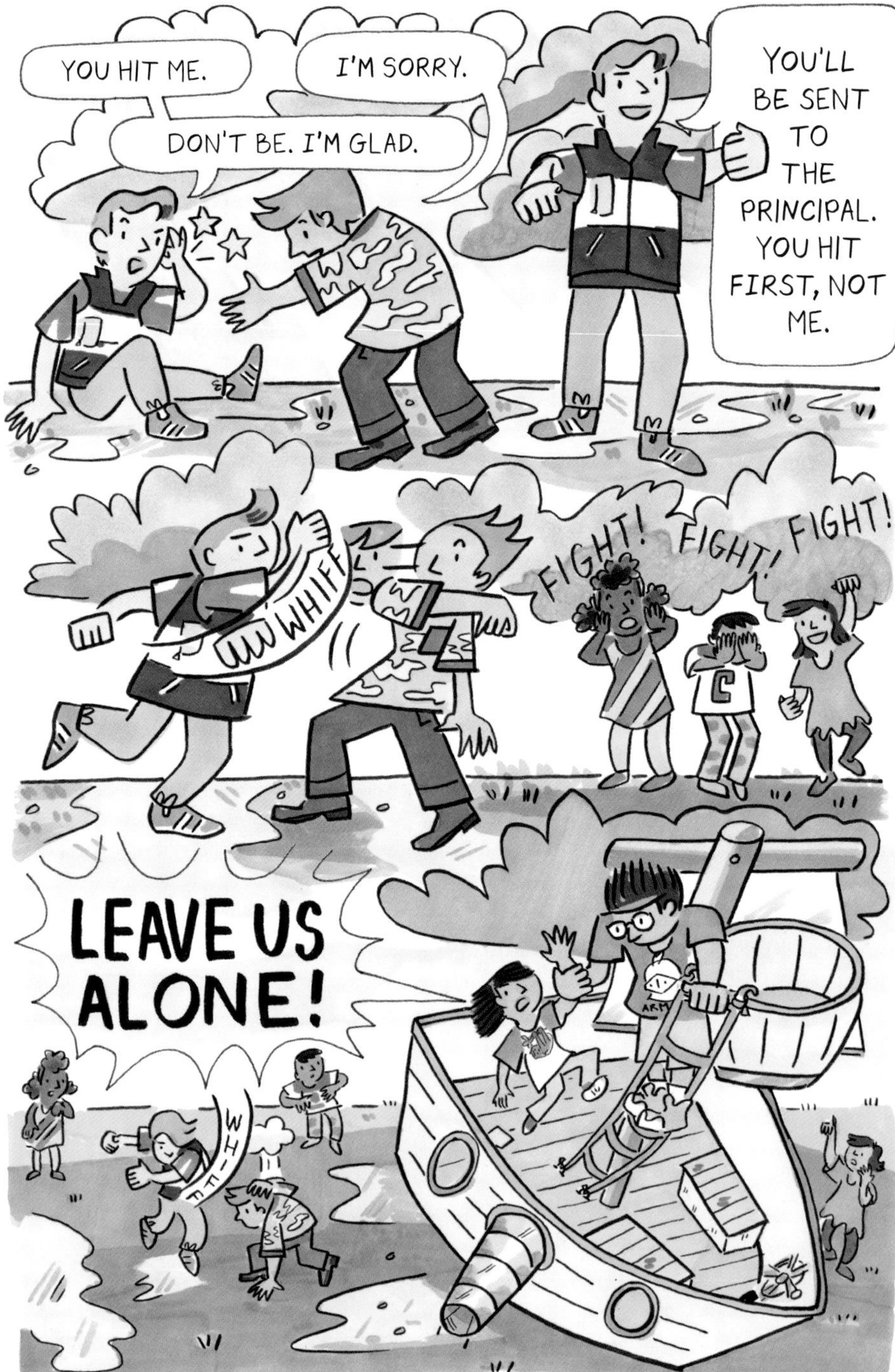
YOU HIT ME.
I'M SORRY.
DON'T BE. I'M GLAD.
YOU'LL BE SENT TO THE PRINCIPAL. YOU HIT FIRST, NOT ME.
WHIFF
FIGHT! FIGHT! FIGHT!
C
LEAVE US ALONE!
WHIFF

CHAPTER 15

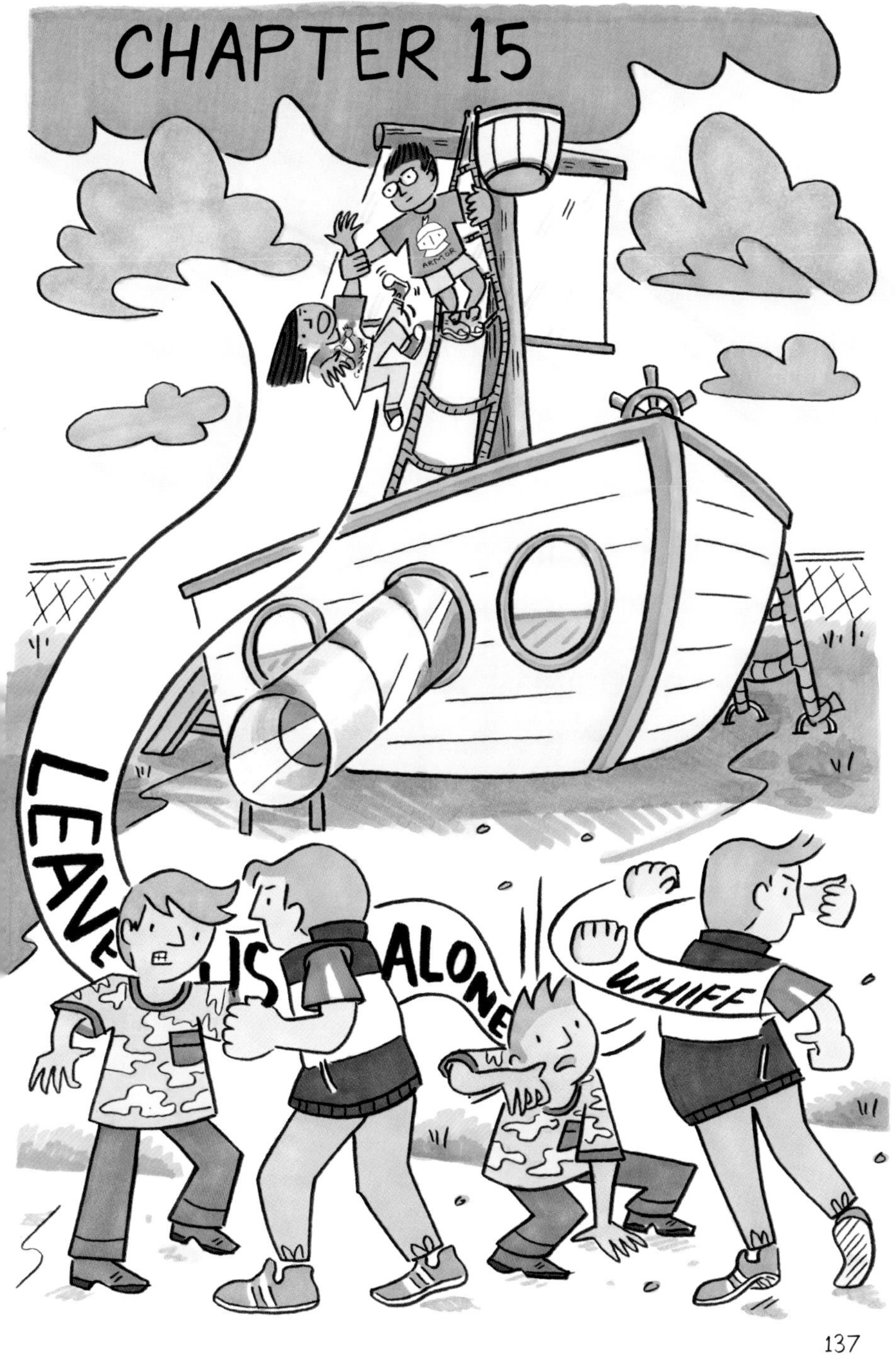
LEAVE US ALONE
WHIFF

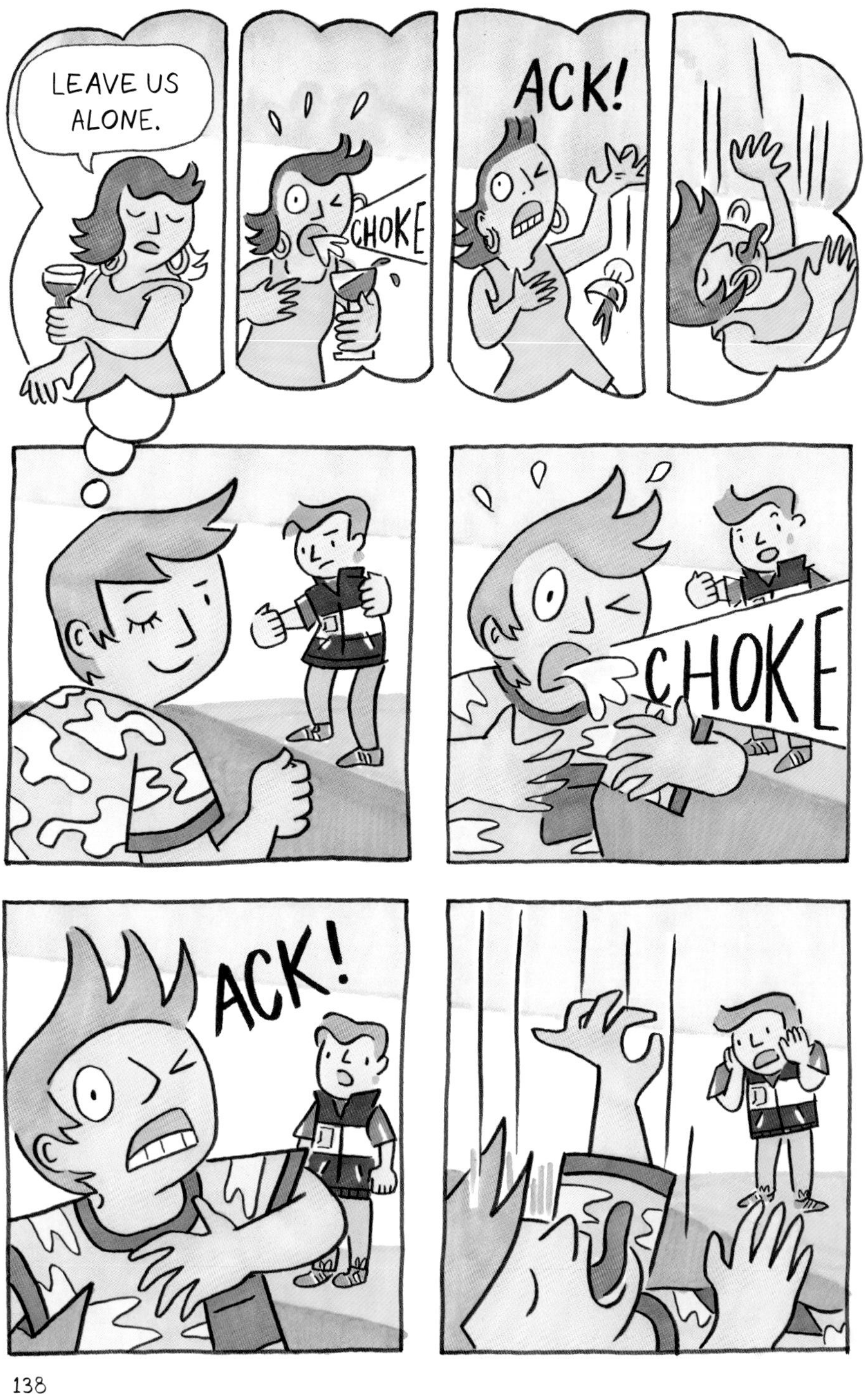
LEAVE US ALONE.
CHOKE
ACK!
CHOKE
ACK!

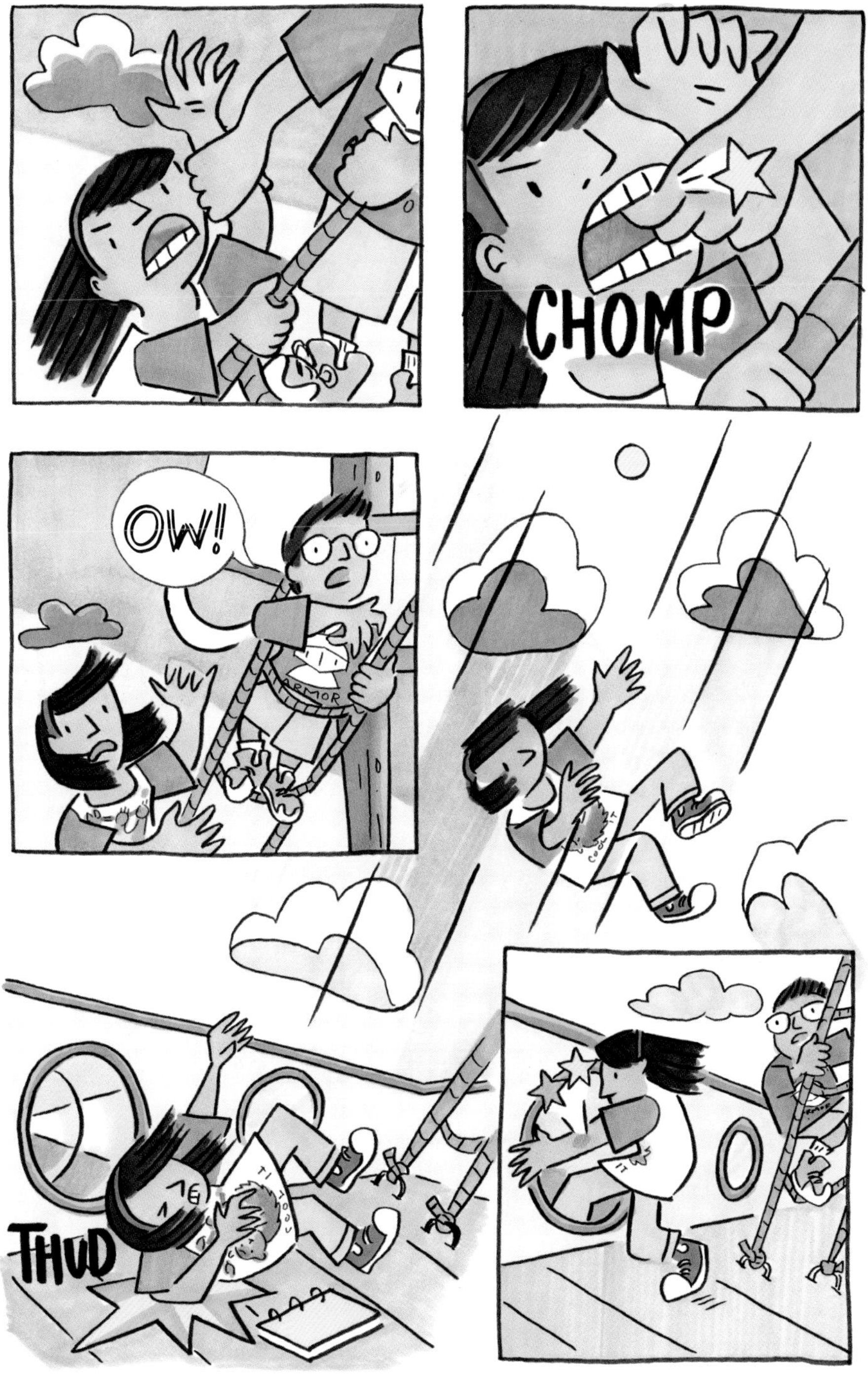
CHOMP
OW!
ARMOR
THUD

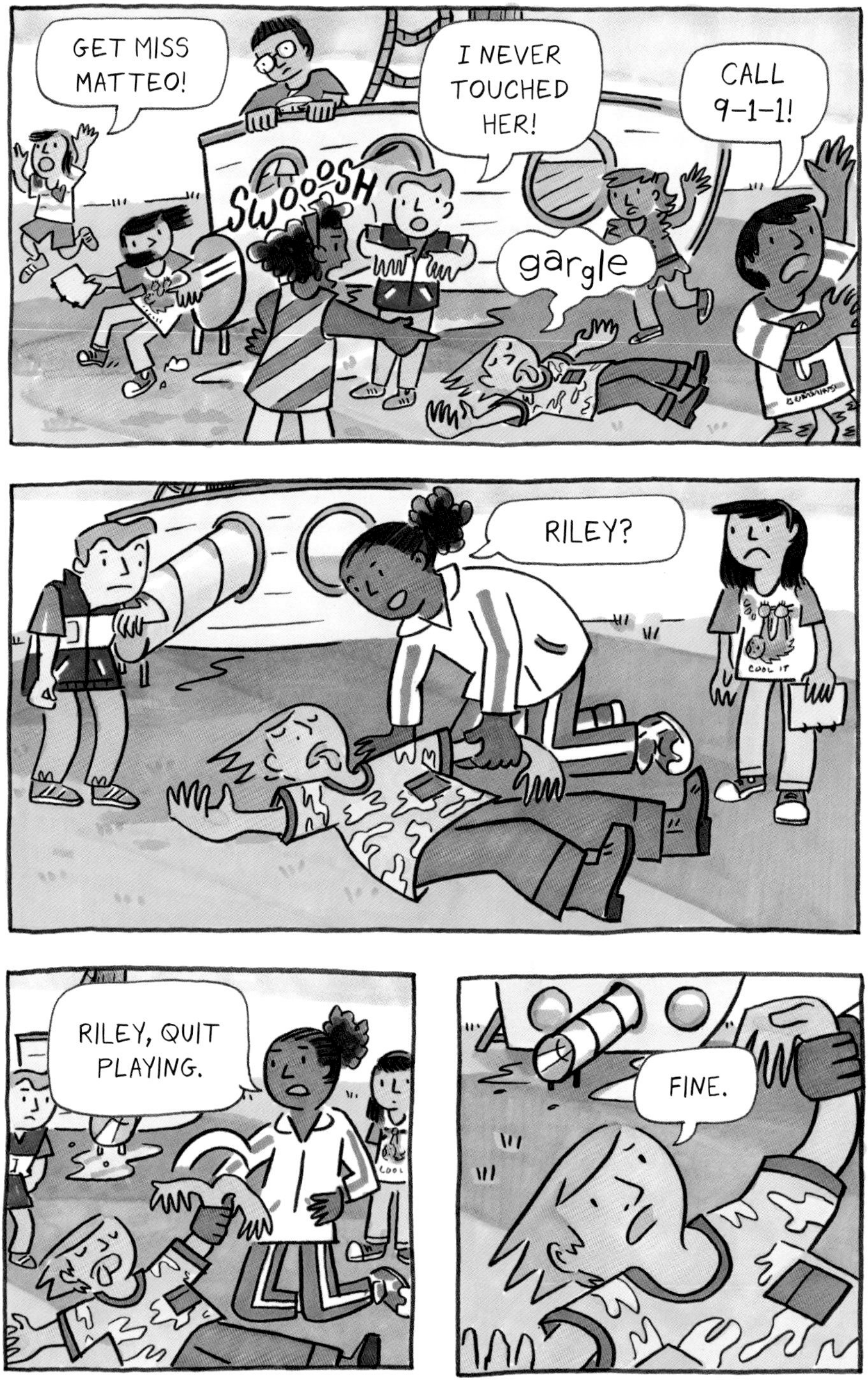
GET MISS MATTEO!
I NEVER TOUCHED HER!
CALL 9-1-1!
SWOOOOSH
gargle
RILEY?
RILEY, QUIT PLAYING.
FINE.

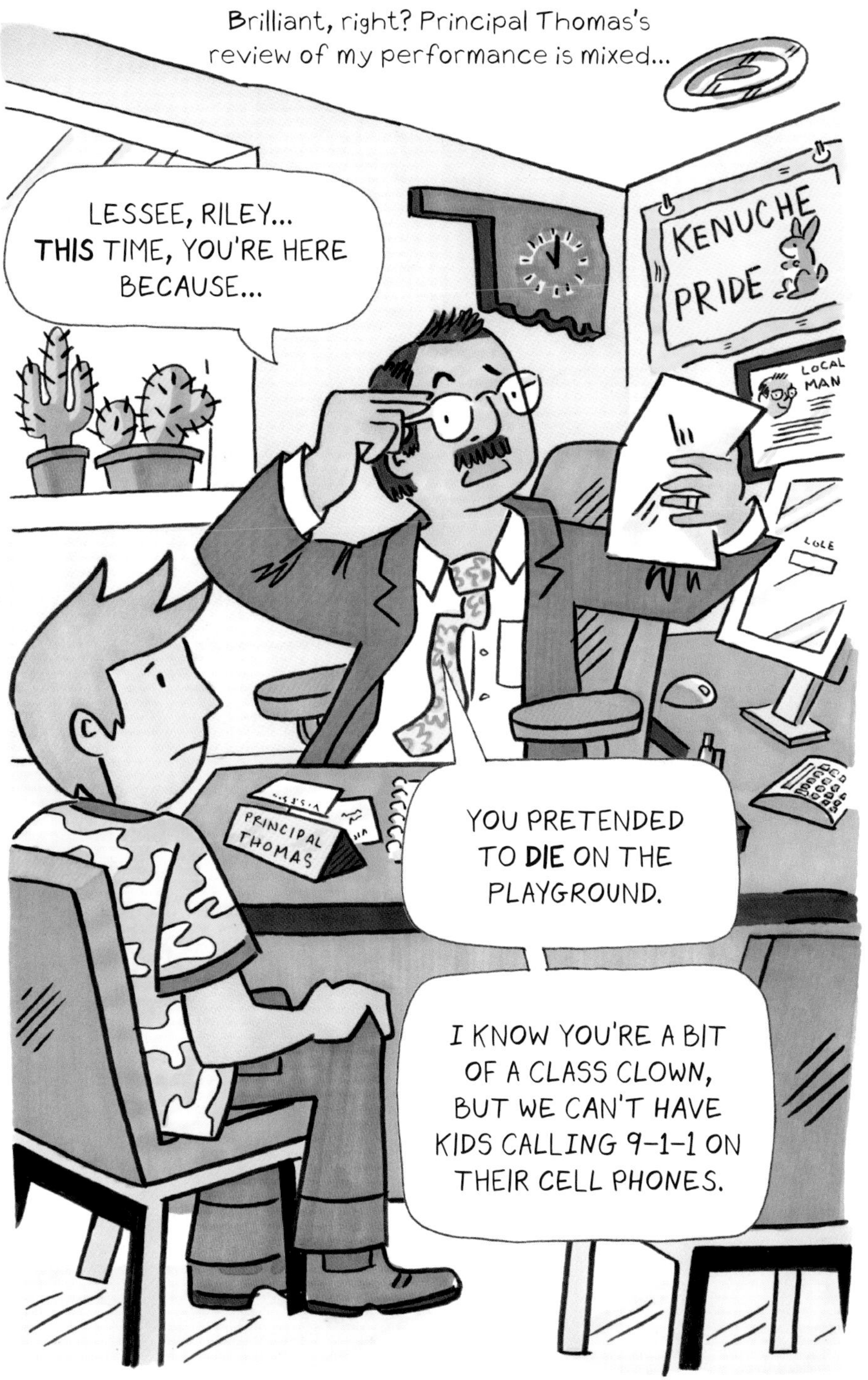
Brilliant, right? Principal Thomas's review of my performance is mixed...
LESSEE, RILEY... **THIS** TIME, YOU'RE HERE BECAUSE...
KENUCHE PRIDE
LOCAL MAN
PRINCIPAL THOMAS
YOU PRETENDED TO **DIE** ON THE PLAYGROUND.
I KNOW YOU'RE A BIT OF A CLASS CLOWN, BUT WE CAN'T HAVE KIDS CALLING 9-1-1 ON THEIR CELL PHONES.

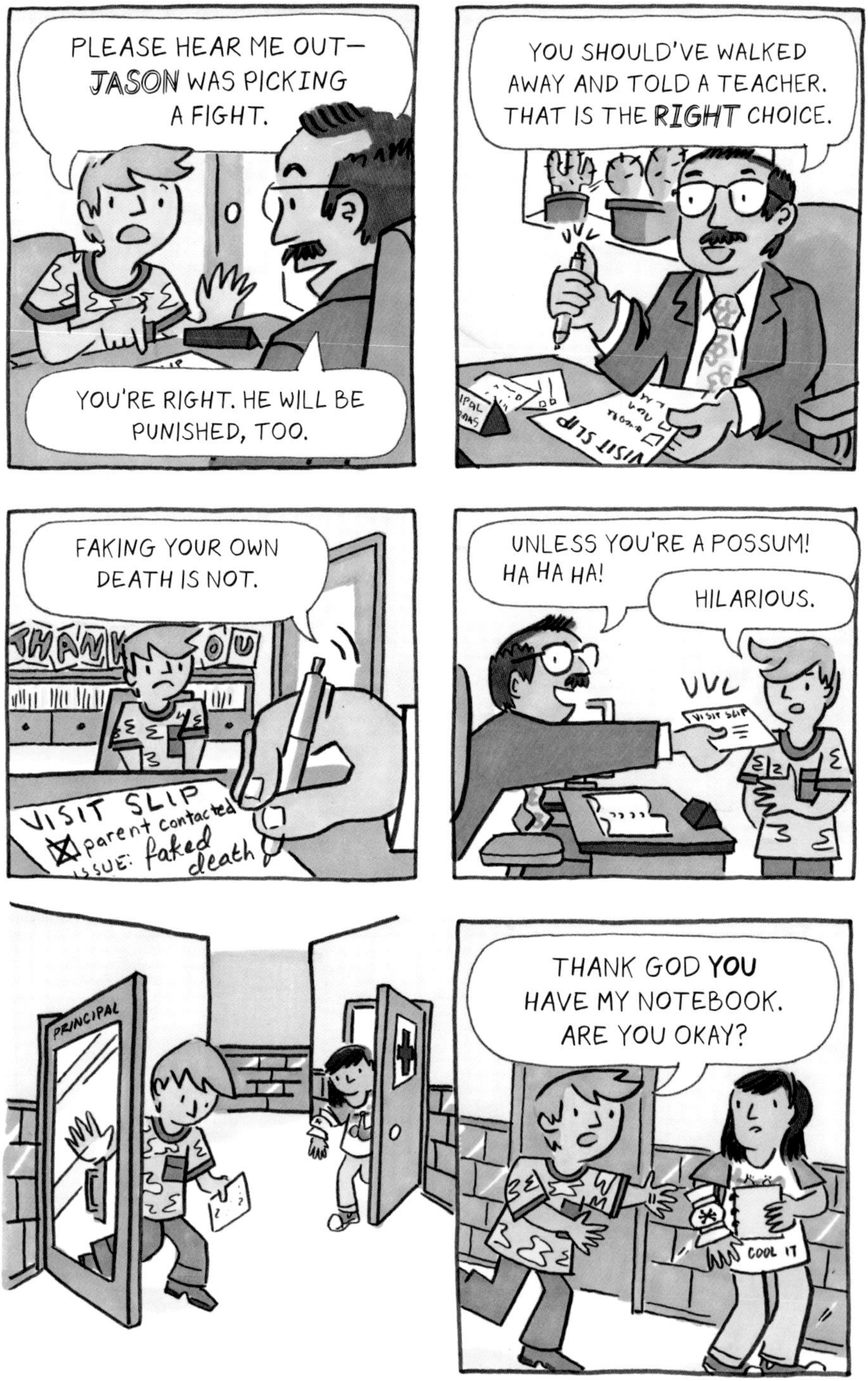
PLEASE HEAR ME OUT—JASON WAS PICKING A FIGHT.
YOU'RE RIGHT. HE WILL BE PUNISHED, TOO.
YOU SHOULD'VE WALKED AWAY AND TOLD A TEACHER. THAT IS THE RIGHT CHOICE.
VISIT SLIP
FAKING YOUR OWN DEATH IS NOT.
THANK YOU
VISIT SLIP
parent contacted
ISSUE: faked death
UNLESS YOU'RE A POSSUM! HA HA HA!
HILARIOUS.
VISIT SLIP
PRINCIPAL
THANK GOD YOU HAVE MY NOTEBOOK. ARE YOU OKAY?
COOL IT

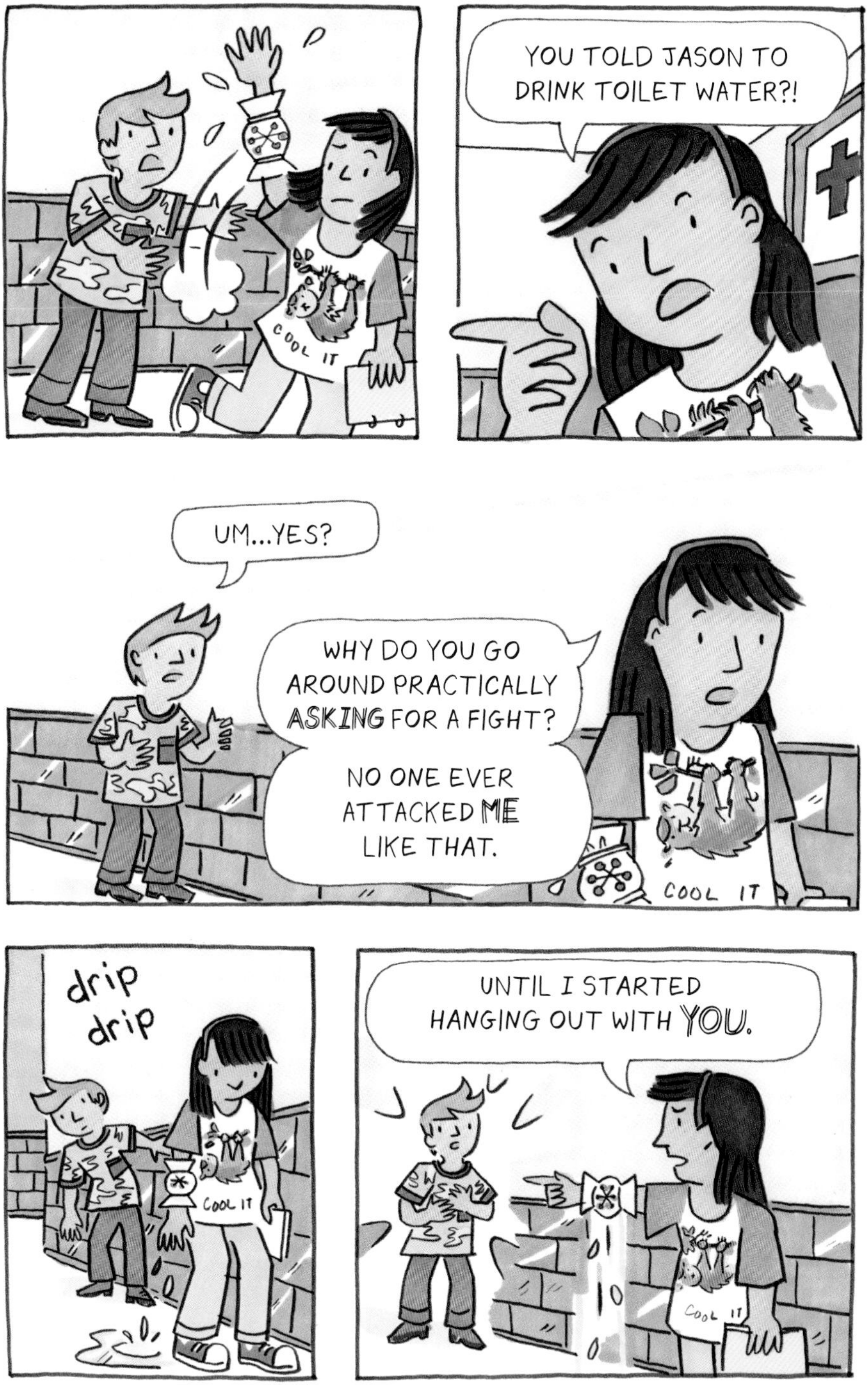
YOU TOLD JASON TO DRINK TOILET WATER?!
COOL IT
UM...YES?
WHY DO YOU GO AROUND PRACTICALLY ASKING FOR A FIGHT?
NO ONE EVER ATTACKED ME LIKE THAT.
COOL IT
drip drip
COOL IT
UNTIL I STARTED HANGING OUT WITH YOU.
COOL IT

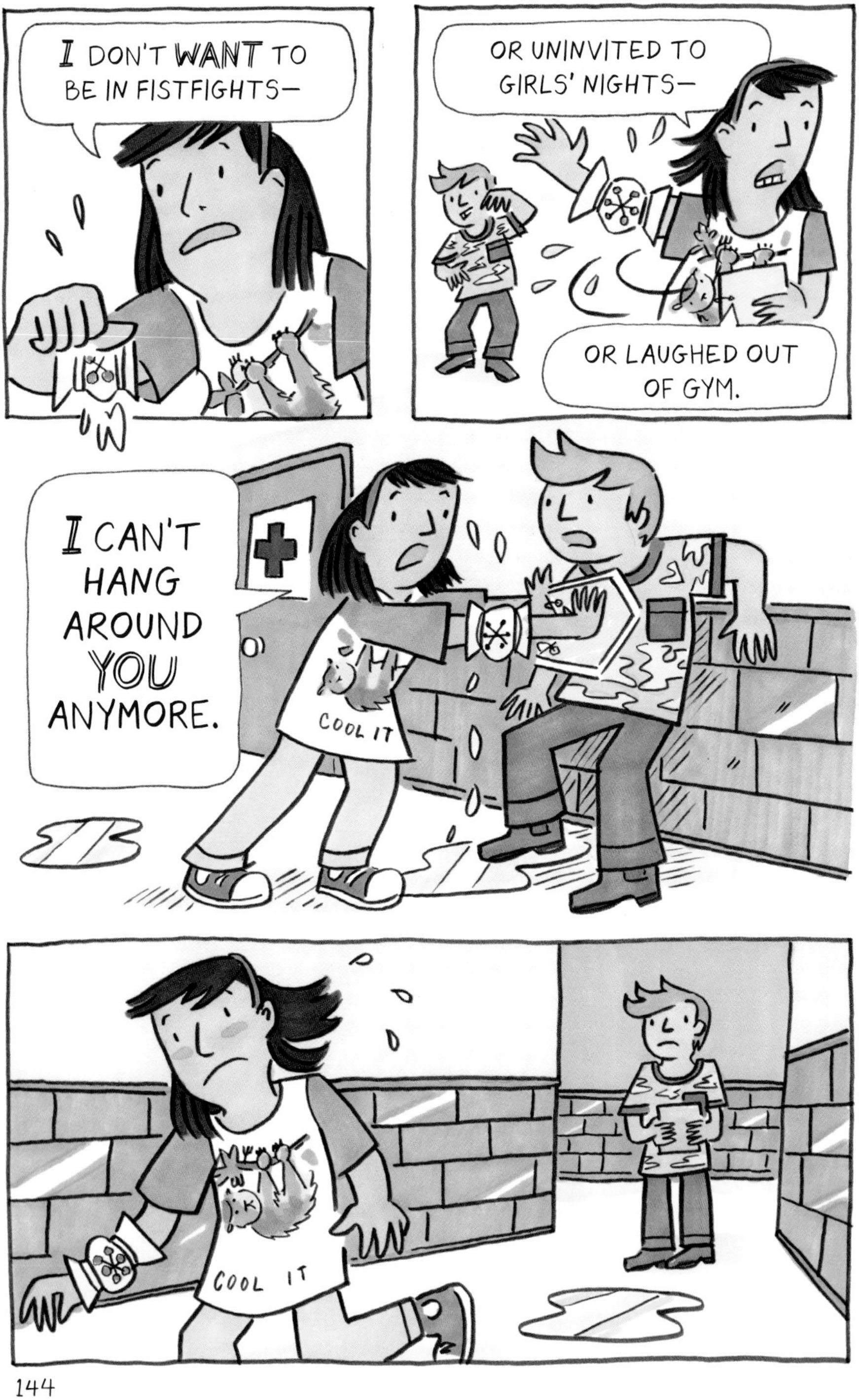
I DON'T WANT TO BE IN FISTFIGHTS—
OR UNINVITED TO GIRLS' NIGHTS—
OR LAUGHED OUT OF GYM.
I CAN'T HANG AROUND YOU ANYMORE.
COOL IT
COOL IT

CHAPTER 16

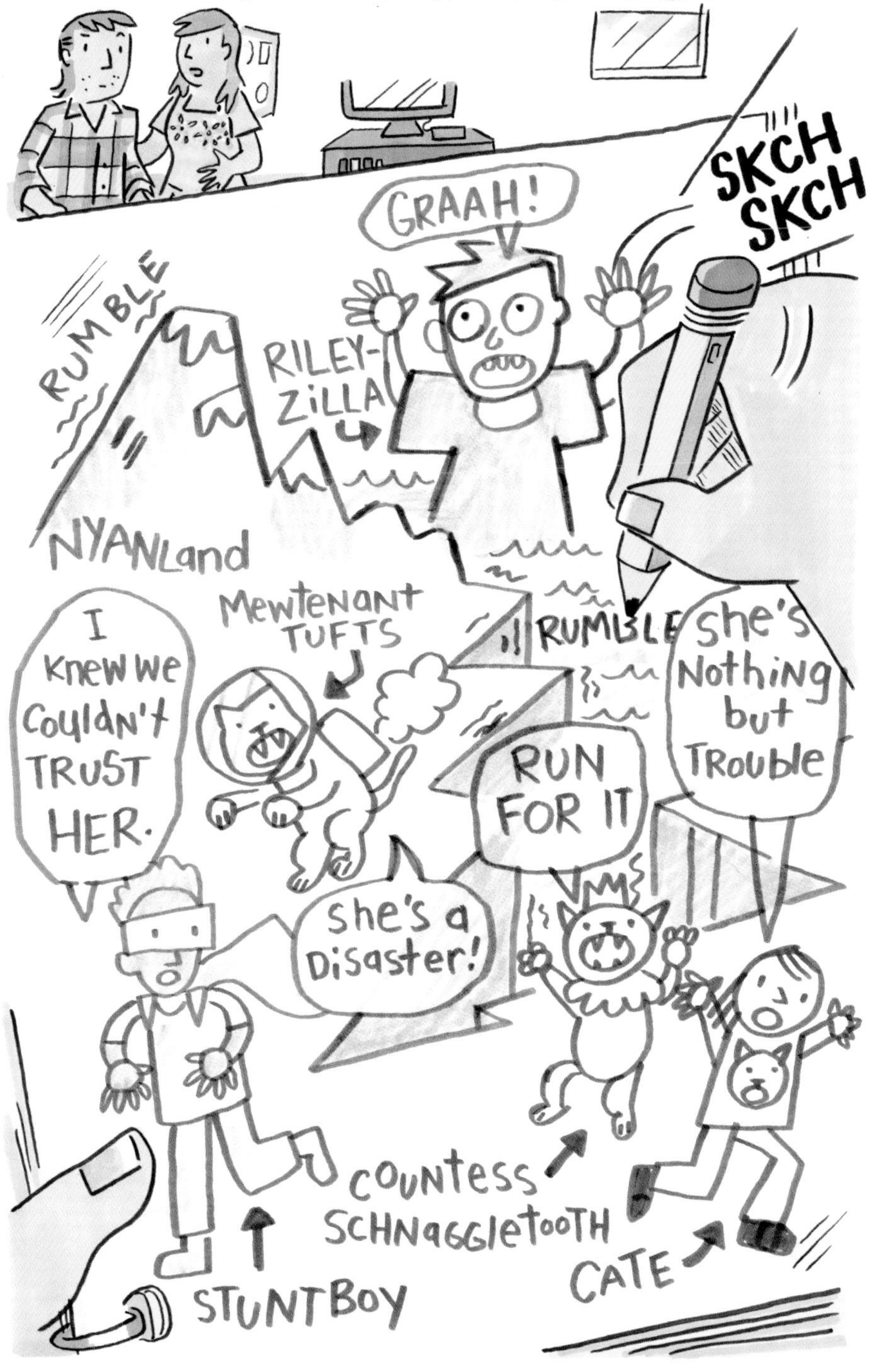
SKCH
SKCH
GRAAH!
RUMBLE
RILEY-ZILLA
NYANLand
Mewtenant TUFTS
RUMBLE
I knew we couldn't TRUST HER.
She's Nothing but Trouble
RUN FOR IT
She's a Disaster!
COUNTESS SCHNAGGLETOOTH
STUNTBOY
CATE

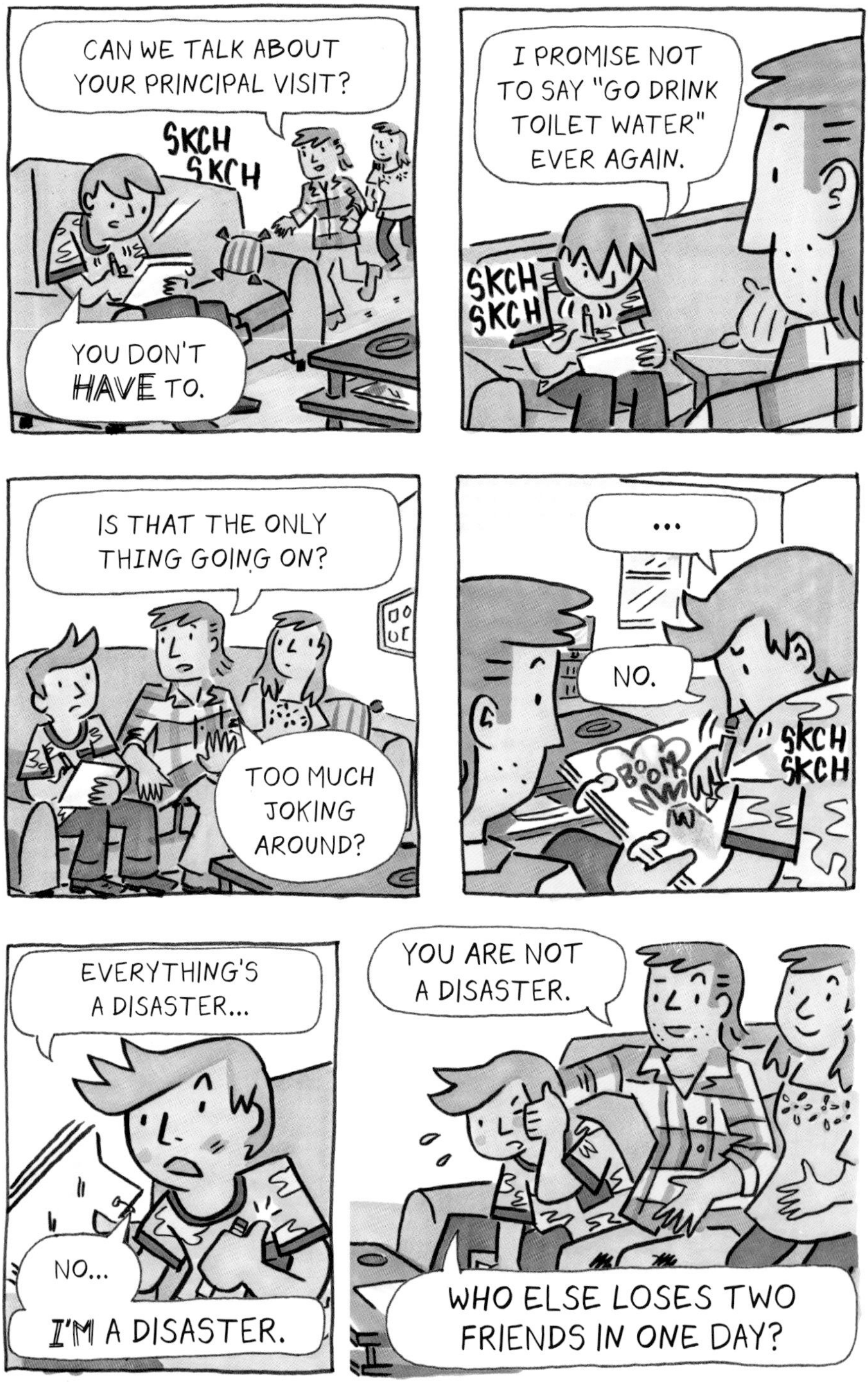
CAN WE TALK ABOUT YOUR PRINCIPAL VISIT?
SKCH SKCH
YOU DON'T HAVE TO.
I PROMISE NOT TO SAY "GO DRINK TOILET WATER" EVER AGAIN.
SKCH SKCH
IS THAT THE ONLY THING GOING ON?
TOO MUCH JOKING AROUND?
...
NO.
SKCH SKCH
BOOM
EVERYTHING'S A DISASTER...
NO...
I'M A DISASTER.
YOU ARE NOT A DISASTER.
WHO ELSE LOSES TWO FRIENDS IN ONE DAY?

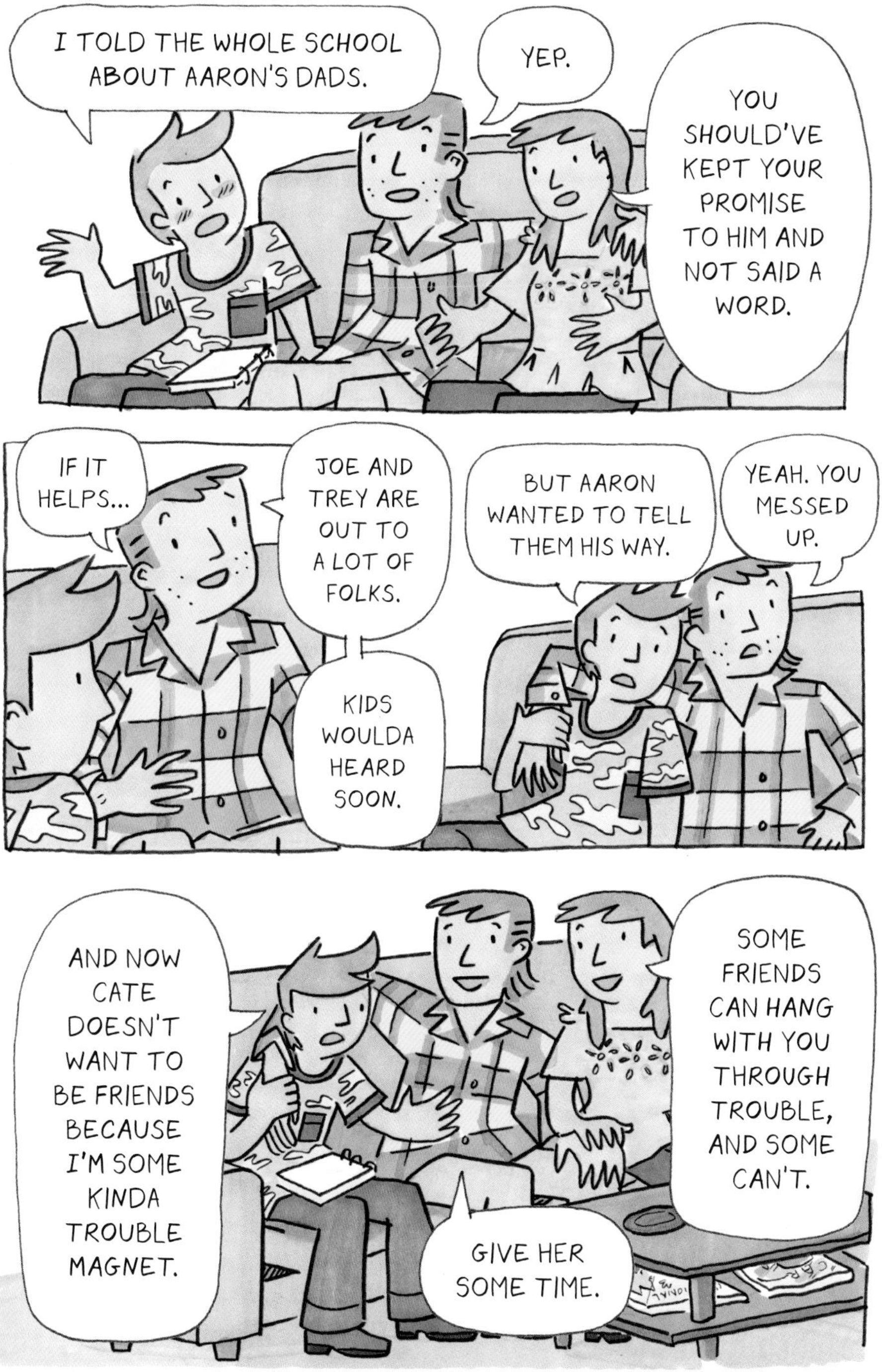
I TOLD THE WHOLE SCHOOL ABOUT AARON'S DADS.
YEP.
YOU SHOULD'VE KEPT YOUR PROMISE TO HIM AND NOT SAID A WORD.
IF IT HELPS...
JOE AND TREY ARE OUT TO A LOT OF FOLKS.
KIDS WOULDA HEARD SOON.
BUT AARON WANTED TO TELL THEM HIS WAY.
YEAH. YOU MESSED UP.
AND NOW CATE DOESN'T WANT TO BE FRIENDS BECAUSE I'M SOME KINDA TROUBLE MAGNET.
SOME FRIENDS CAN HANG WITH YOU THROUGH TROUBLE, AND SOME CAN'T.
GIVE HER SOME TIME.

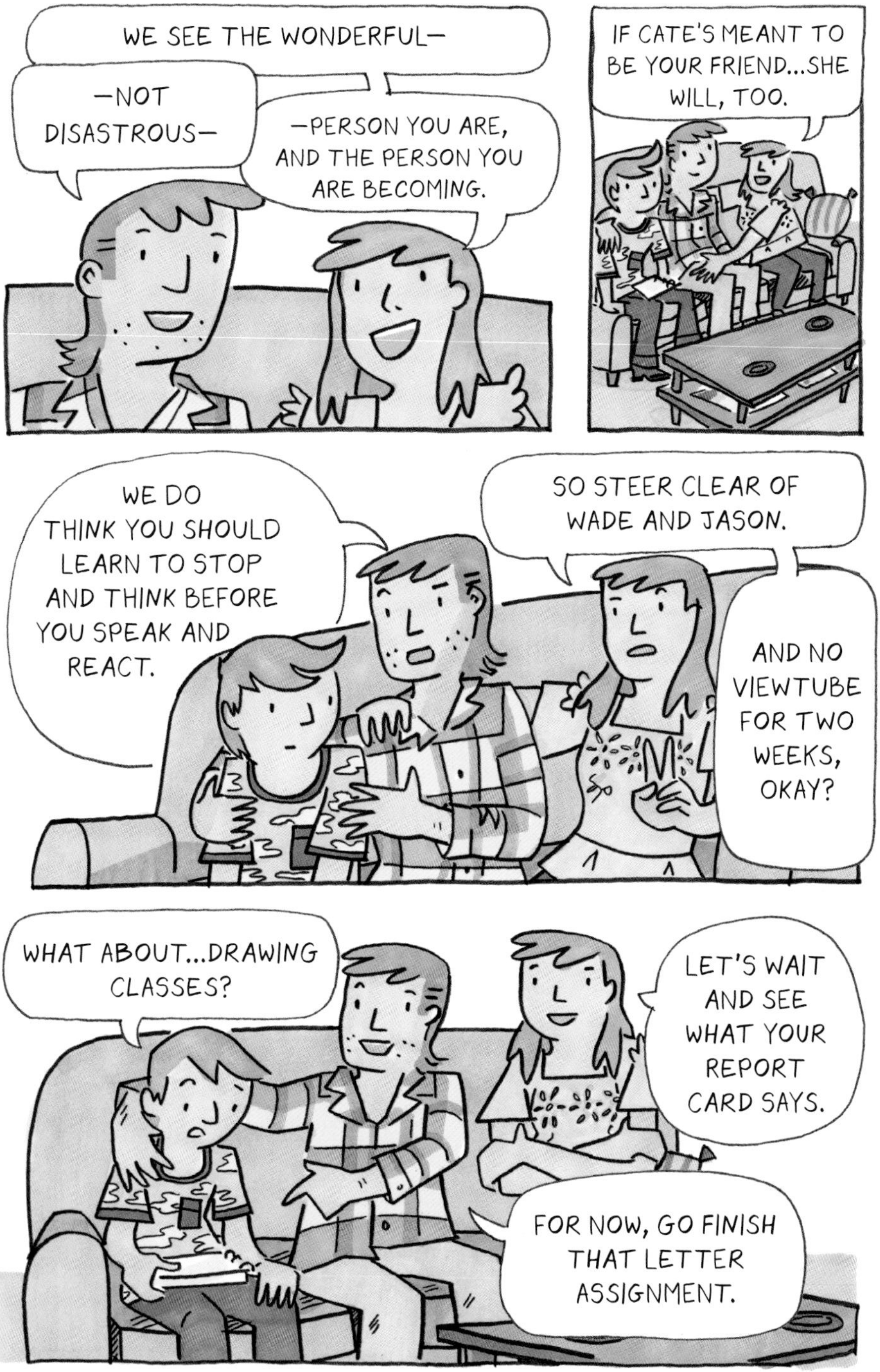
WE SEE THE WONDERFUL—
—NOT DISASTROUS—
—PERSON YOU ARE, AND THE PERSON YOU ARE BECOMING.
IF CATE'S MEANT TO BE YOUR FRIEND...SHE WILL, TOO.
WE DO THINK YOU SHOULD LEARN TO STOP AND THINK BEFORE YOU SPEAK AND REACT.
SO STEER CLEAR OF WADE AND JASON.
AND NO VIEWTUBE FOR TWO WEEKS, OKAY?
WHAT ABOUT...DRAWING CLASSES?
LET'S WAIT AND SEE WHAT YOUR REPORT CARD SAYS.
FOR NOW, GO FINISH THAT LETTER ASSIGNMENT.

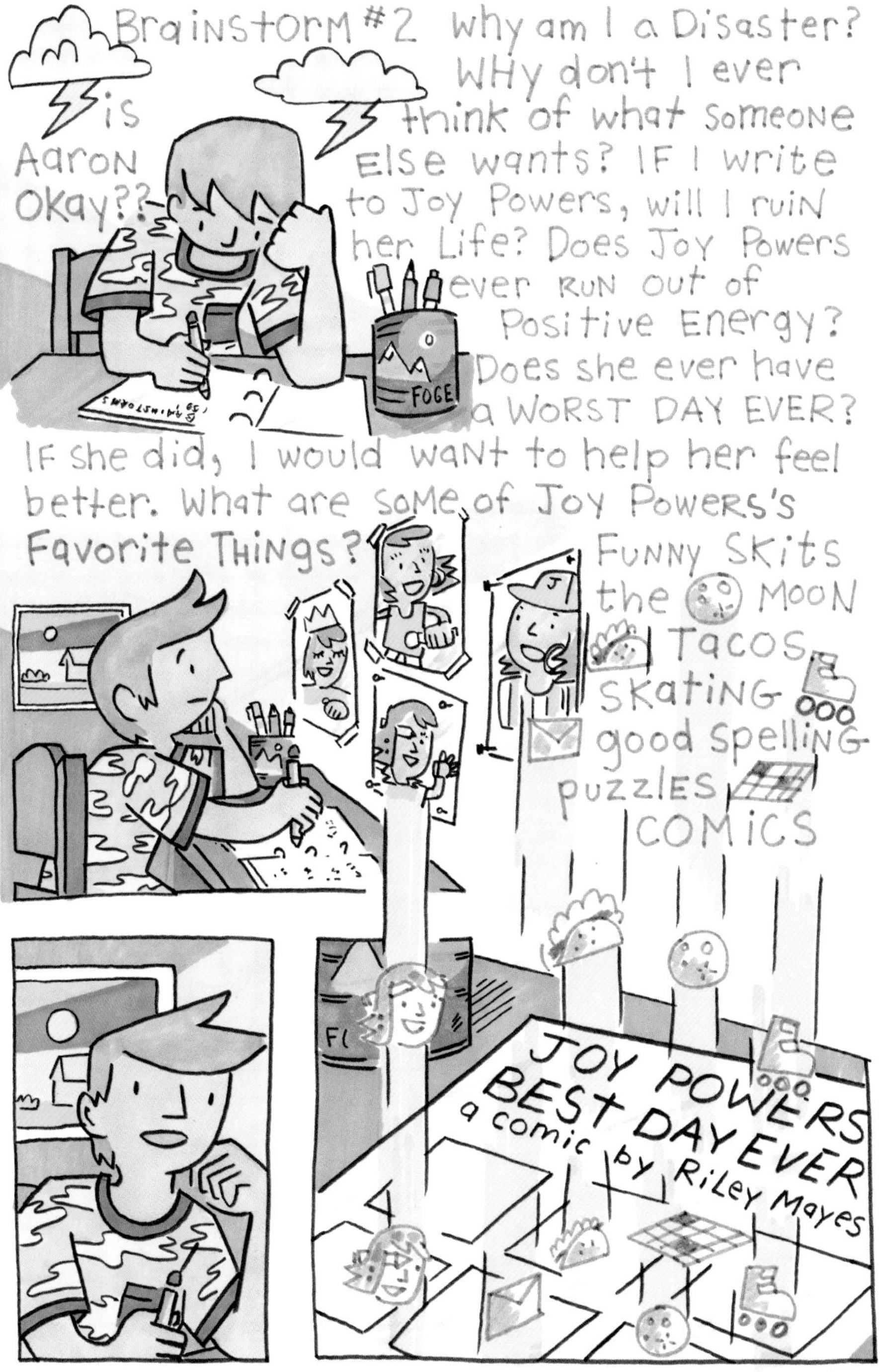
Brainstorm #2 Why am I a Disaster?
is Aaron Okay??
WHY don't I ever think of what someone else wants? If I write to Joy Powers, will I ruin her Life? Does Joy Powers ever run out of Positive Energy? Does she ever have a WORST DAY EVER?
FOGE
If she did, I would want to help her feel better. What are some of Joy Powers's Favorite Things?
Funny Skits
the MOON
Tacos
Skating
good spelling
puzzles
COMICS
JOY POWERS BEST DAY EVER
a comic by Riley Mayes

JOY POWERS'S BEST DAY EVER

a comic by: Riley Mayes

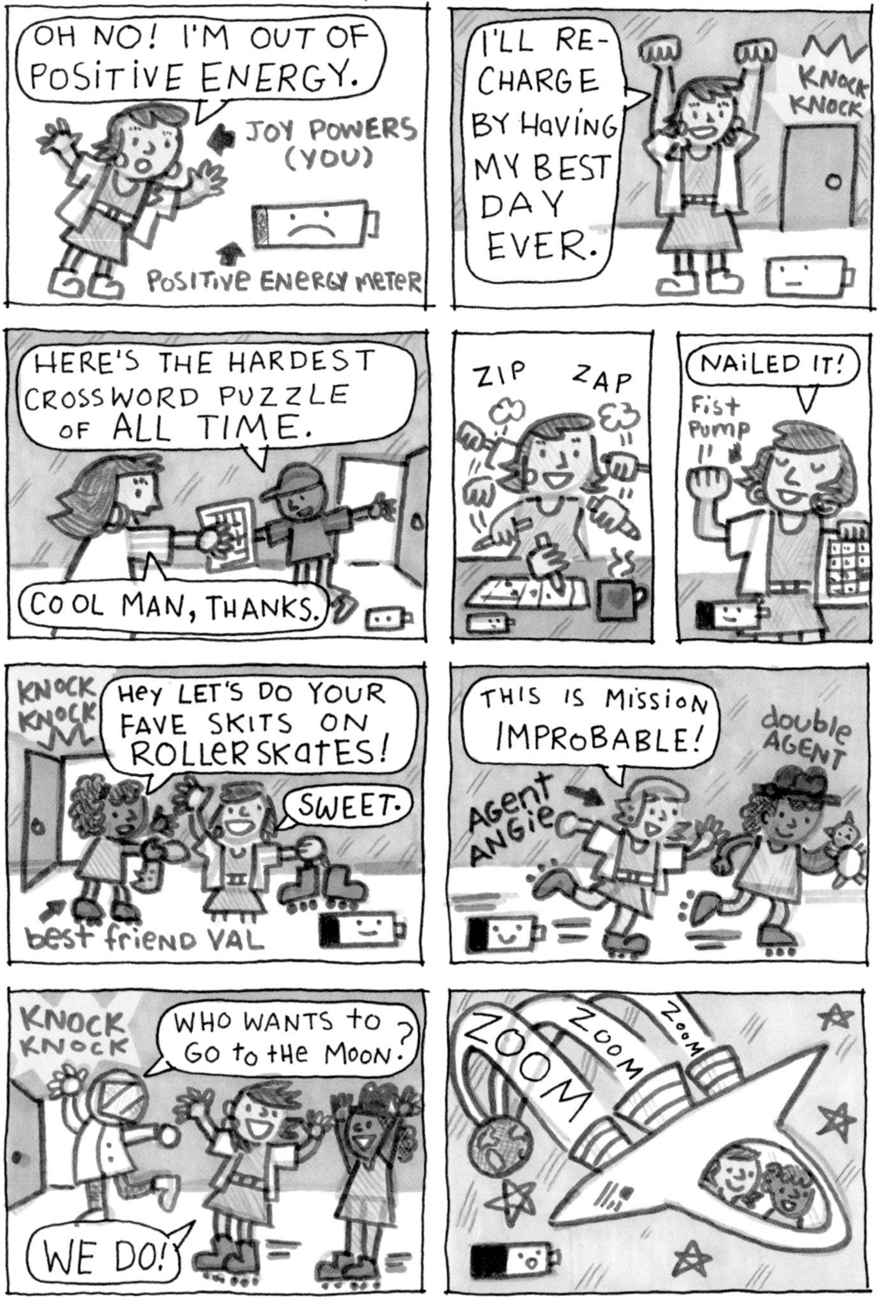

OH NO! I'M OUT OF POSITIVE ENERGY.
JOY POWERS (YOU)
POSITIVE ENERGY METER
I'LL RE-CHARGE BY HAVING MY BEST DAY EVER.
KNOCK KNOCK
HERE'S THE HARDEST CROSSWORD PUZZLE OF ALL TIME.
COOL MAN, THANKS.
ZIP
ZAP
NAILED IT!
Fist Pump
KNOCK KNOCK
Hey LET'S DO YOUR FAVE SKITS ON ROLLERSKATES!
SWEET.
best friend VAL
THIS IS MISSION IMPROBABLE!
Agent ANGIE
double AGENT
KNOCK KNOCK
WHO WANTS to GO to tHE MOON?
WE DO!
ZOOM
ZOOM
ZOOM

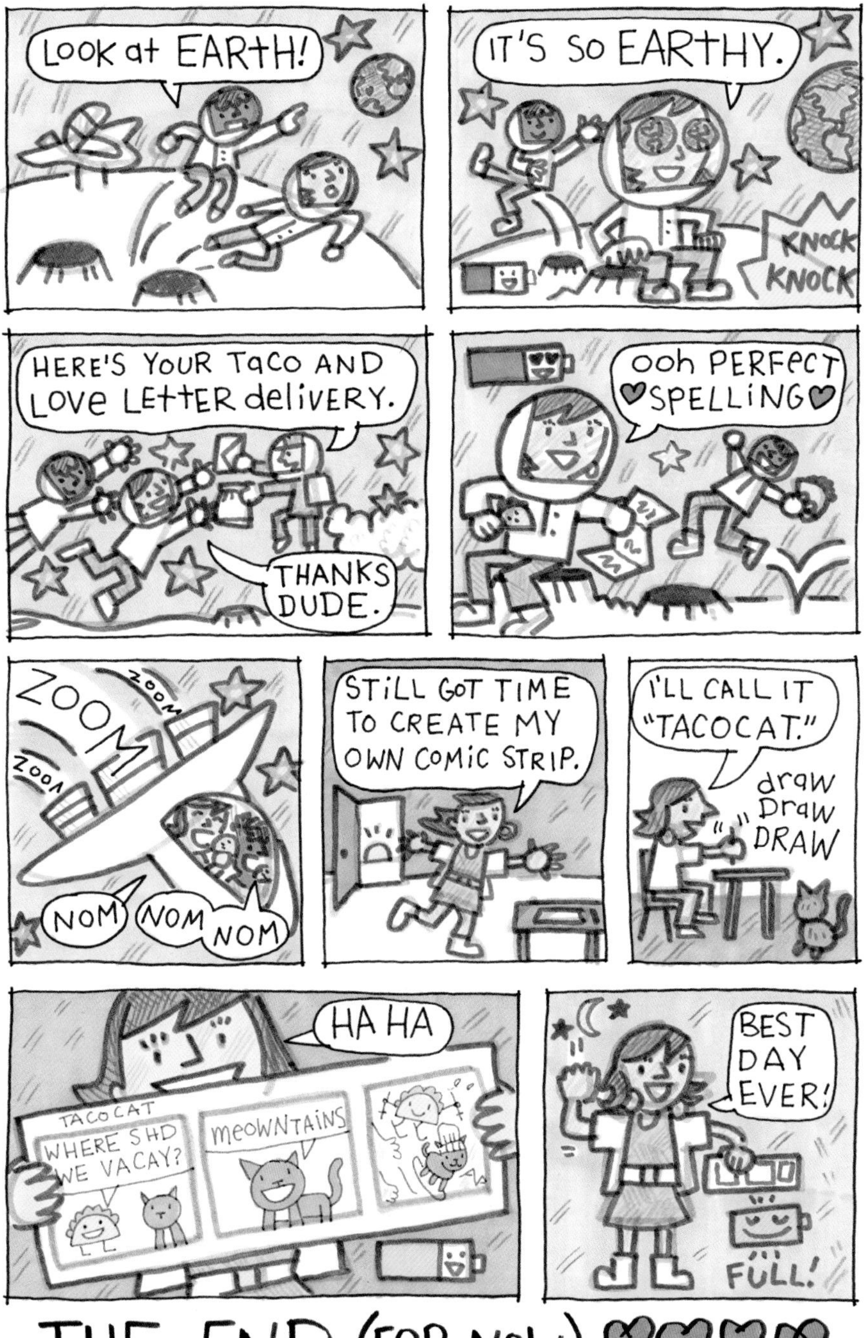
LOOK at EARTH!
IT'S SO EARTHY.
KNOCK KNOCK
HERE'S YOUR TaCO AND LOVE LETTER delivERY.
THANKS DUDE.
ooh PERFECT SPELLING
ZOOM
ZOOM
ZOOM
NOM NOM NOM
STILL GOT TIME TO CREATE MY OWN COMIC STRIP.
I'LL CALL IT "TACOCAT."
draw Draw DRAW
HA HA
TACOCAT
WHERE SHD WE VACAY?
meOWNTAINS
BEST DAY EVER!
FULL!

THE END (FOR NOW)

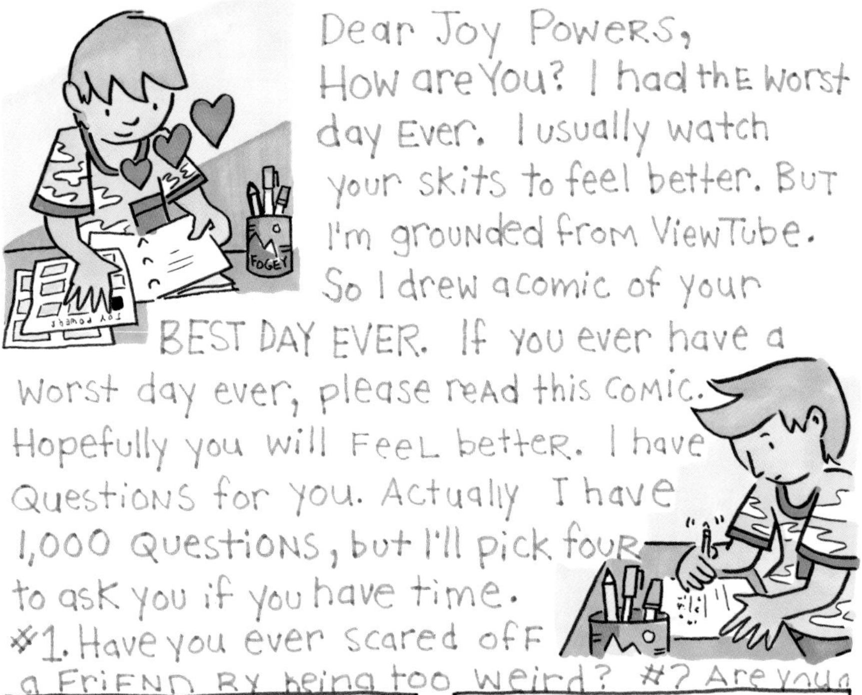
Dear Joy Powers,
How are You? I had the worst day Ever. I usually watch your skits to feel better. But I'm grounded from ViewTube. So I drew a comic of your BEST DAY EVER. If you ever have a worst day ever, please read this comic. Hopefully you will feel better. I have Questions for you. Actually I have 1,000 Questions, but I'll pick four to ask you if you have time.
#1. Have you ever scared off a Friend by being too weird? #2 Are you
FOGEY

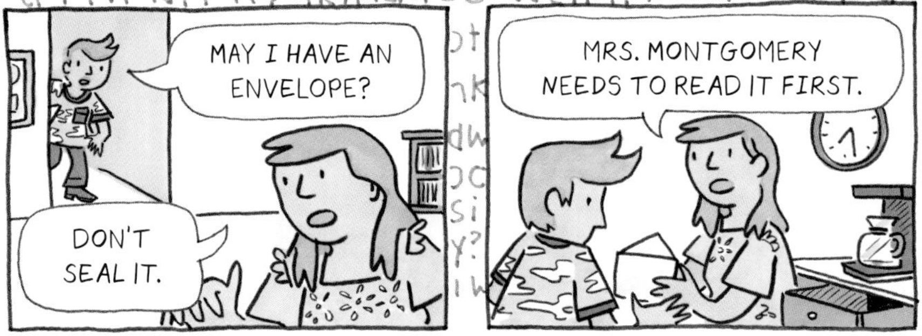
MAY I HAVE AN ENVELOPE?
DON'T SEAL IT.
MRS. MONTGOMERY NEEDS TO READ IT FIRST.

I don't want Mrs. M to read it.
This letter is between Joy Powers and me.

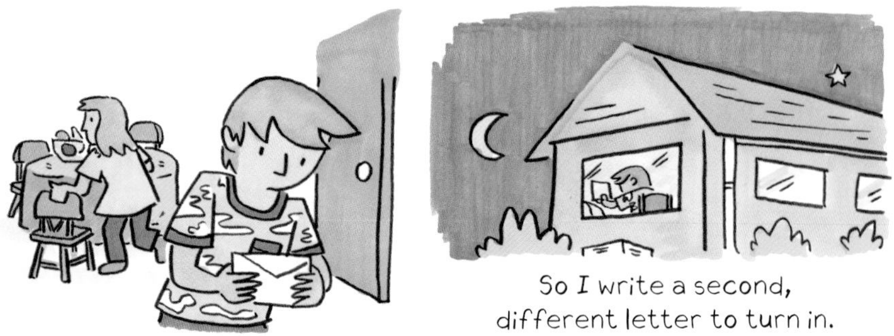

So I write a second,
different letter to turn in.

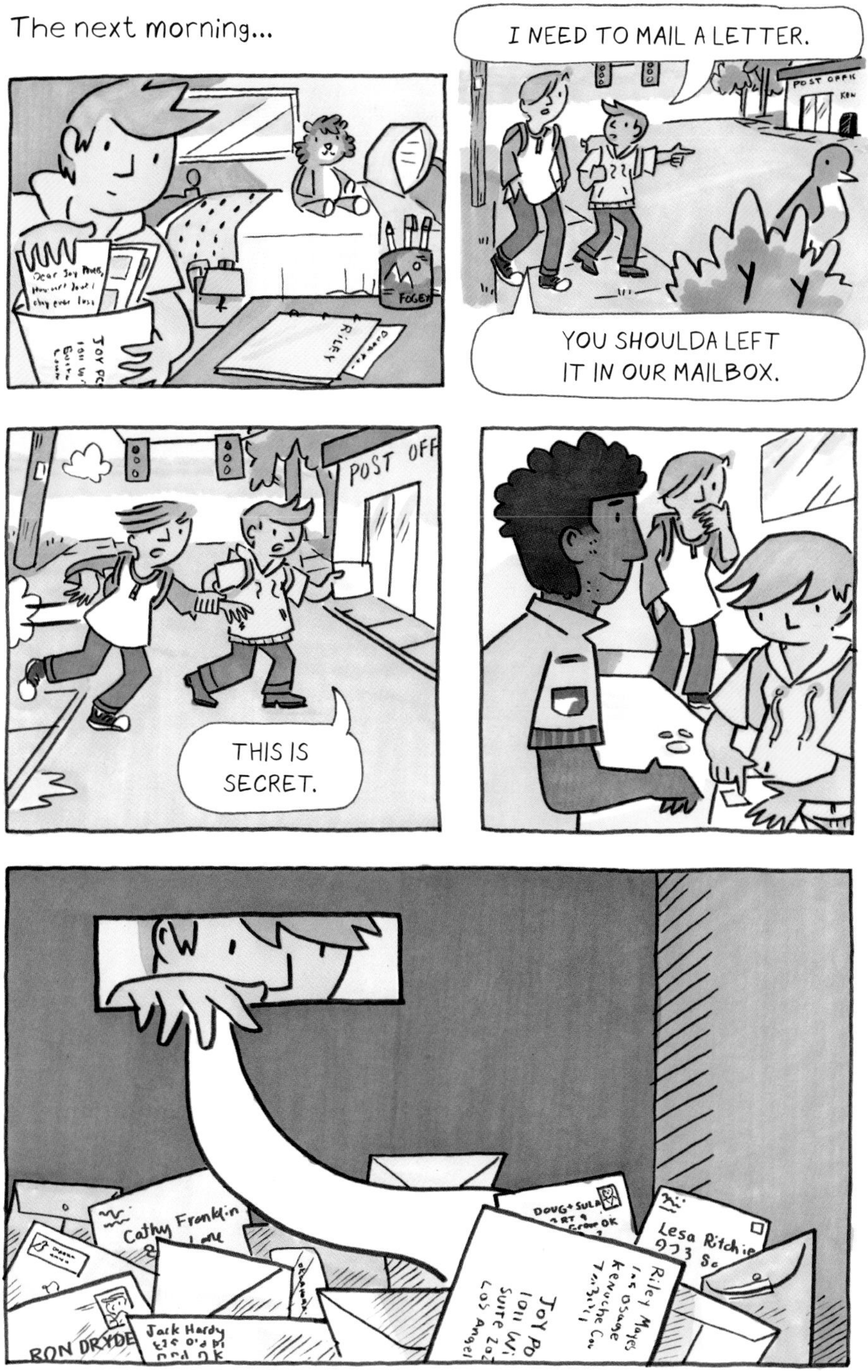
The next morning...
I NEED TO MAIL A LETTER.
YOU SHOULDA LEFT IT IN OUR MAILBOX.
POST OFF
THIS IS SECRET.
Cathy Franklin
Lesa Ritchie
Riley Mayes
JOY PO
Jack Hardy
RON DRYDE

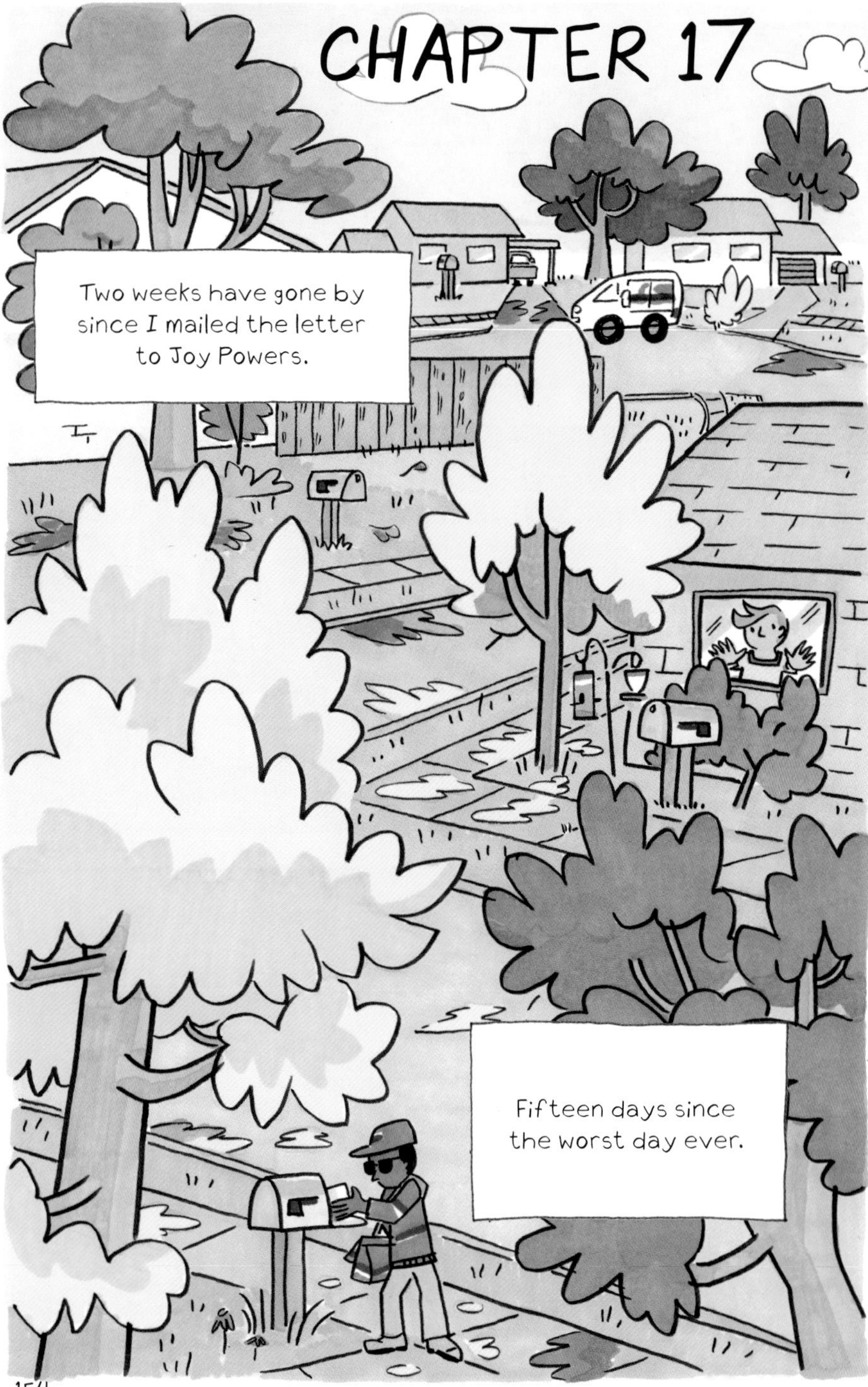
CHAPTER 17
Two weeks have gone by since I mailed the letter to Joy Powers.
Fifteen days since the worst day ever.

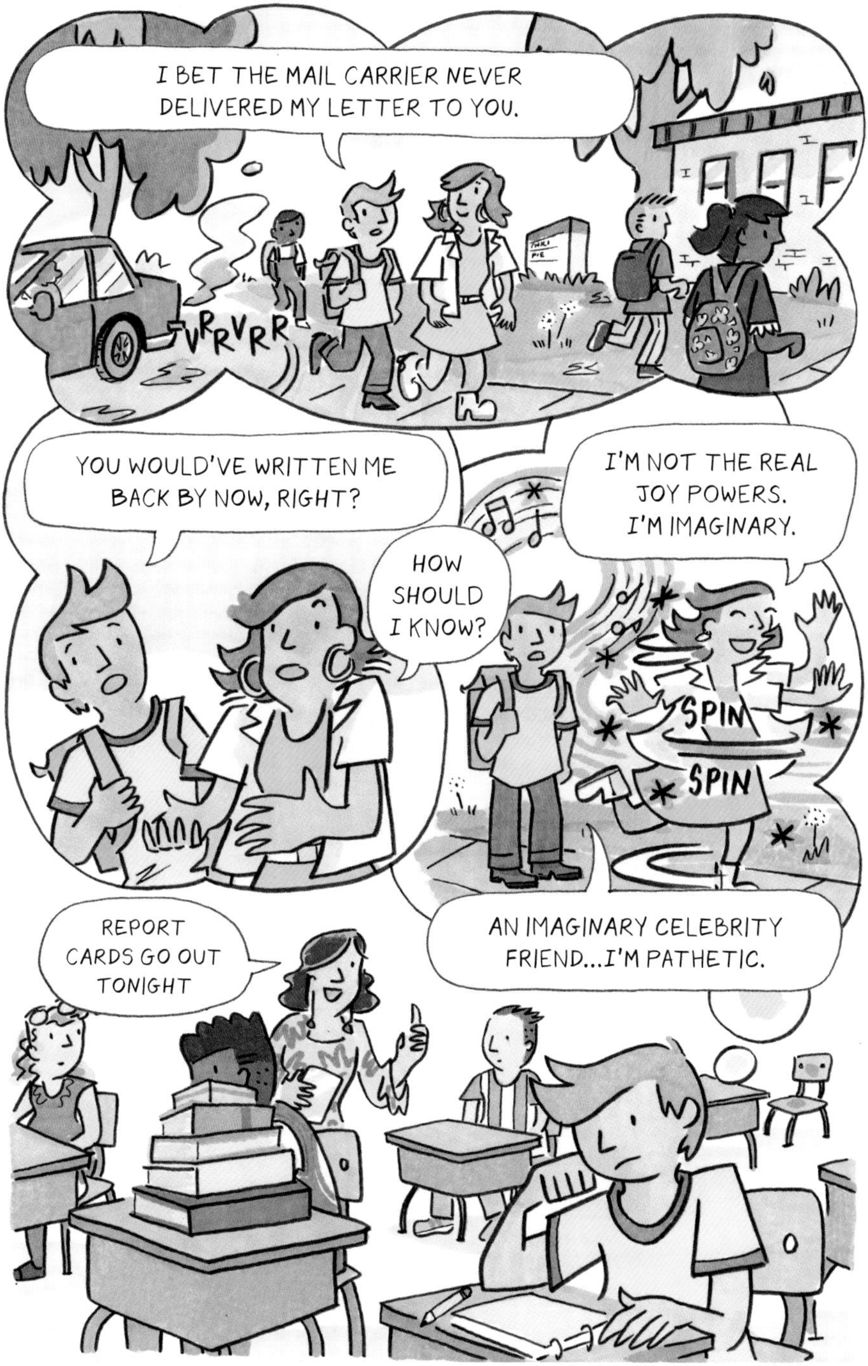
I BET THE MAIL CARRIER NEVER DELIVERED MY LETTER TO YOU.
VRRVRR
YOU WOULD'VE WRITTEN ME BACK BY NOW, RIGHT?
HOW SHOULD I KNOW?
I'M NOT THE REAL JOY POWERS. I'M IMAGINARY.
SPIN
SPIN
AN IMAGINARY CELEBRITY FRIEND...I'M PATHETIC.
REPORT CARDS GO OUT TONIGHT

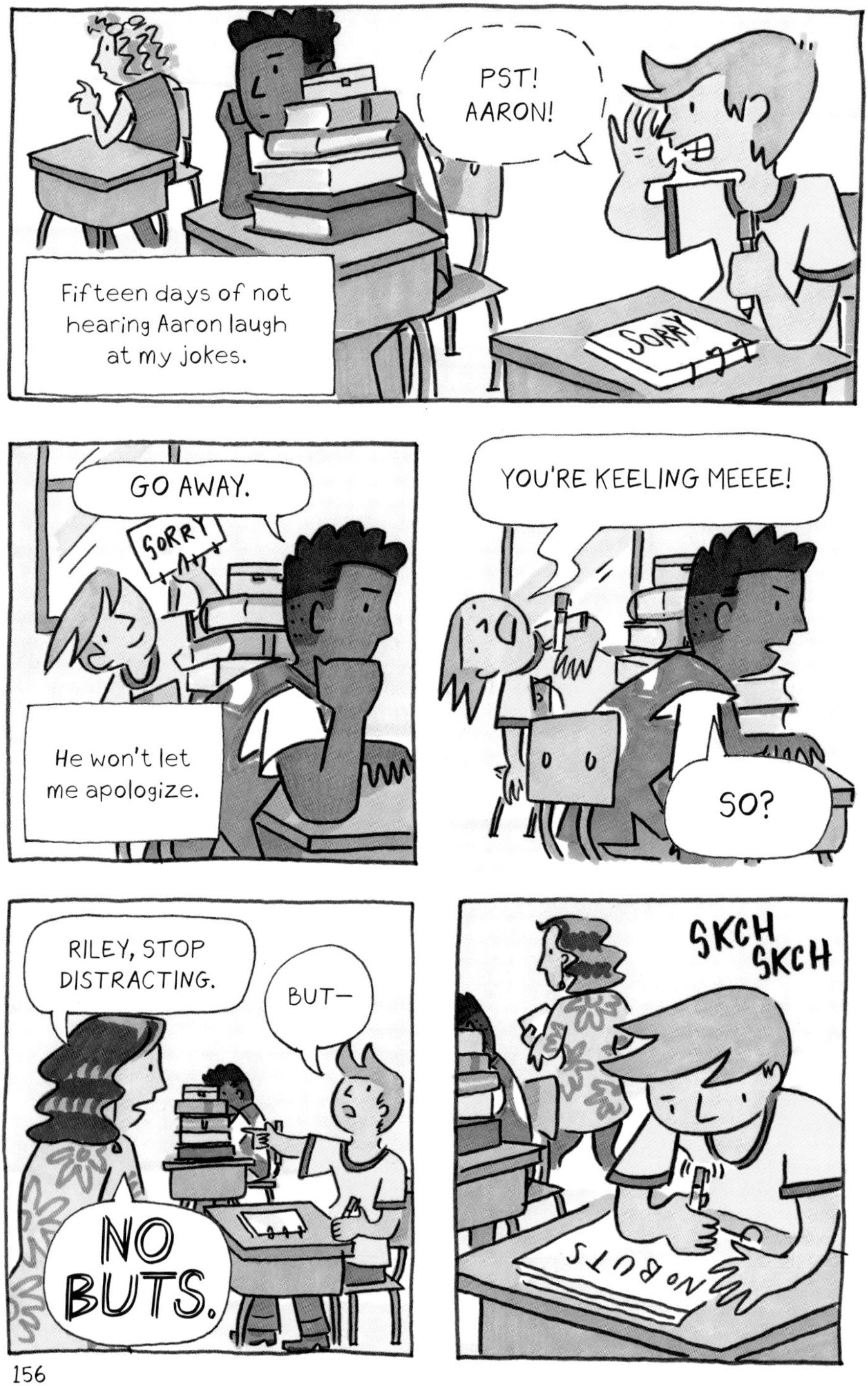
PST! AARON!
SORRY
Fifteen days of not hearing Aaron laugh at my jokes.
GO AWAY.
SORRY
He won't let me apologize.
YOU'RE KEELING MEEEE!
SO?
RILEY, STOP DISTRACTING.
BUT—
NO BUTS.
SKCH SKCH
NO BUTS

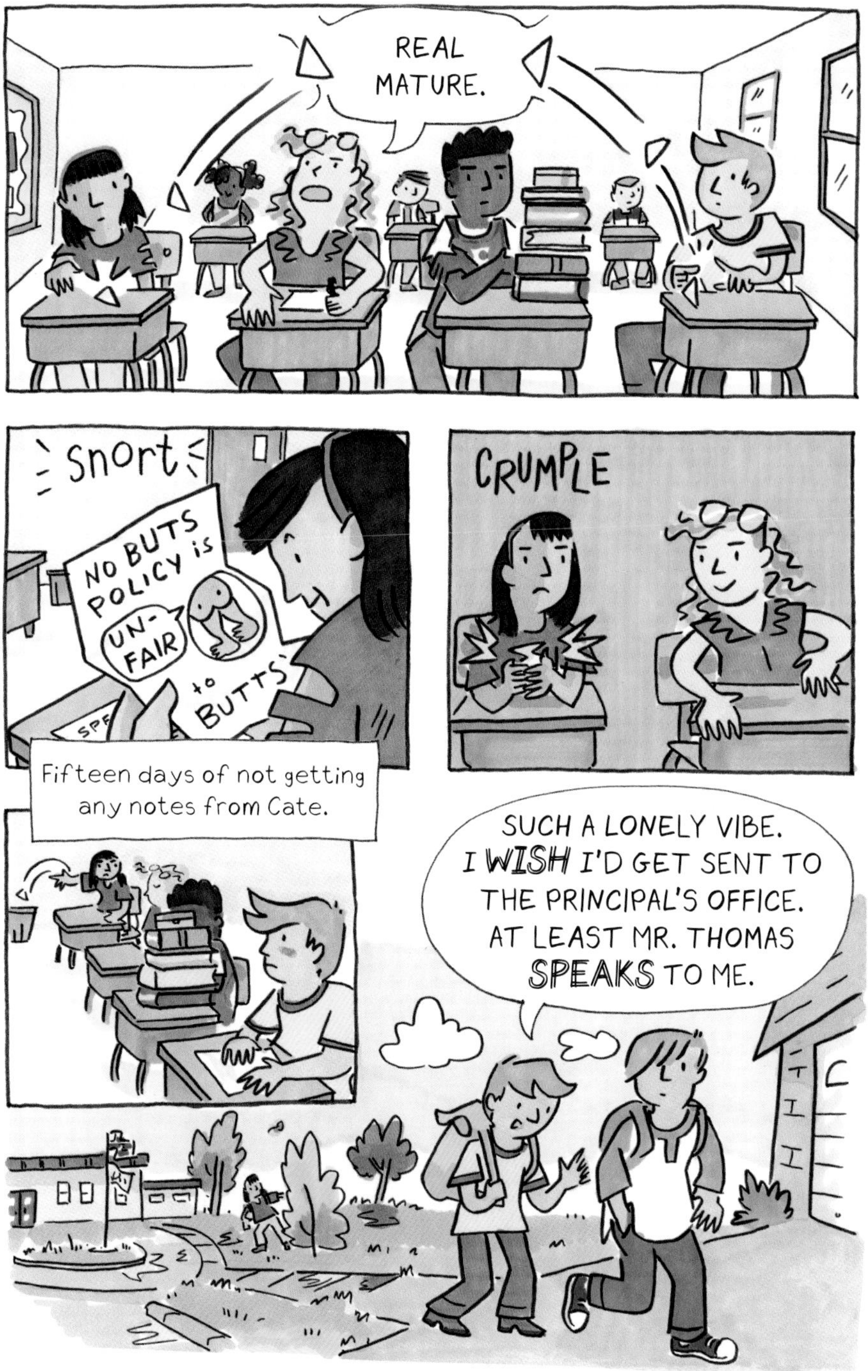
REAL MATURE.
Snort
NO BUTS POLICY IS UN-FAIR to BUTTS
CRUMPLE
Fifteen days of not getting any notes from Cate.
SUCH A LONELY VIBE. I WISH I'D GET SENT TO THE PRINCIPAL'S OFFICE. AT LEAST MR. THOMAS SPEAKS TO ME.

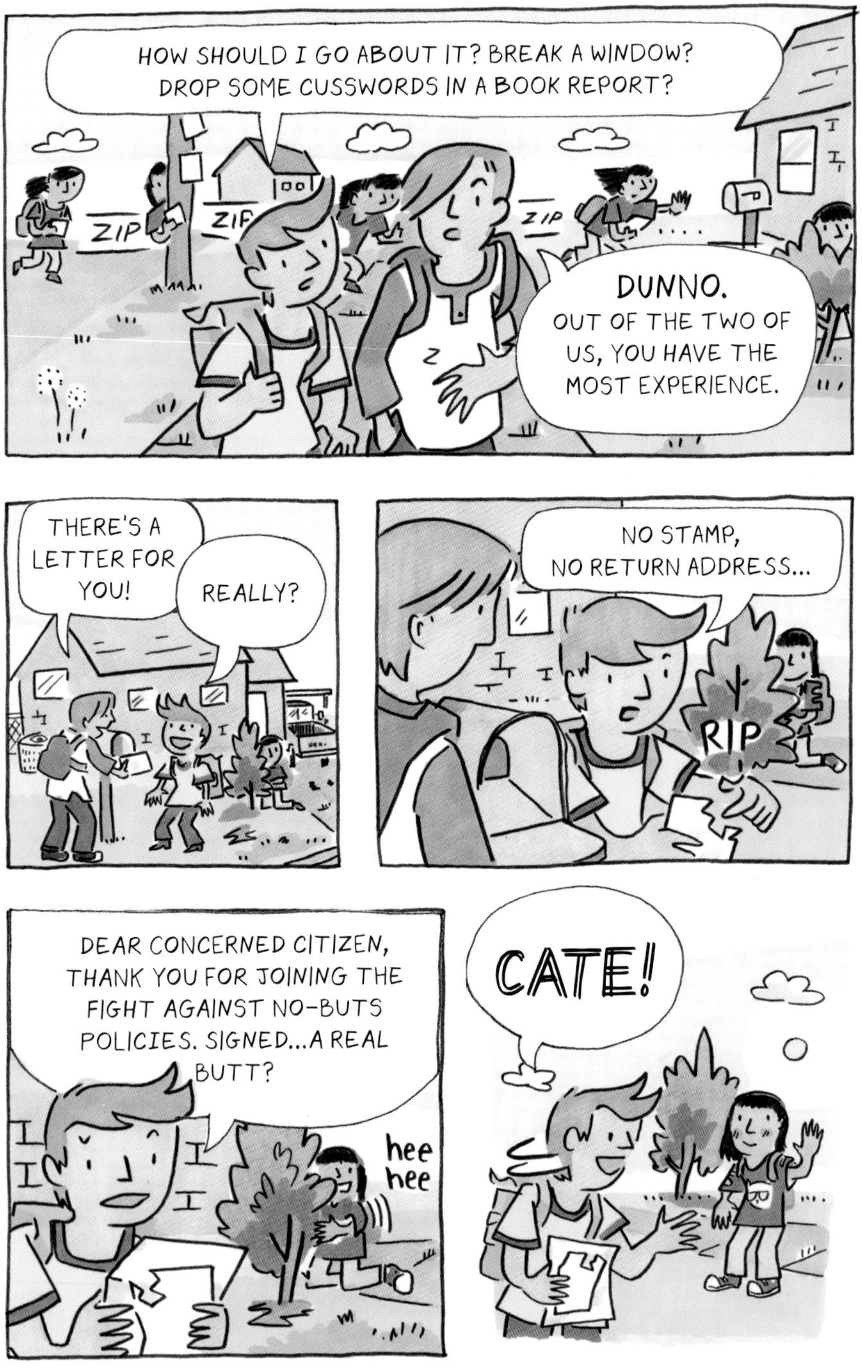
HOW SHOULD I GO ABOUT IT? BREAK A WINDOW? DROP SOME CUSSWORDS IN A BOOK REPORT?
ZIP
ZIP
ZIP
DUNNO. OUT OF THE TWO OF US, YOU HAVE THE MOST EXPERIENCE.
THERE'S A LETTER FOR YOU!
REALLY?
NO STAMP, NO RETURN ADDRESS...
RIP
DEAR CONCERNED CITIZEN, THANK YOU FOR JOINING THE FIGHT AGAINST NO-BUTS POLICIES. SIGNED...A REAL BUTT?
hee hee
CATE!

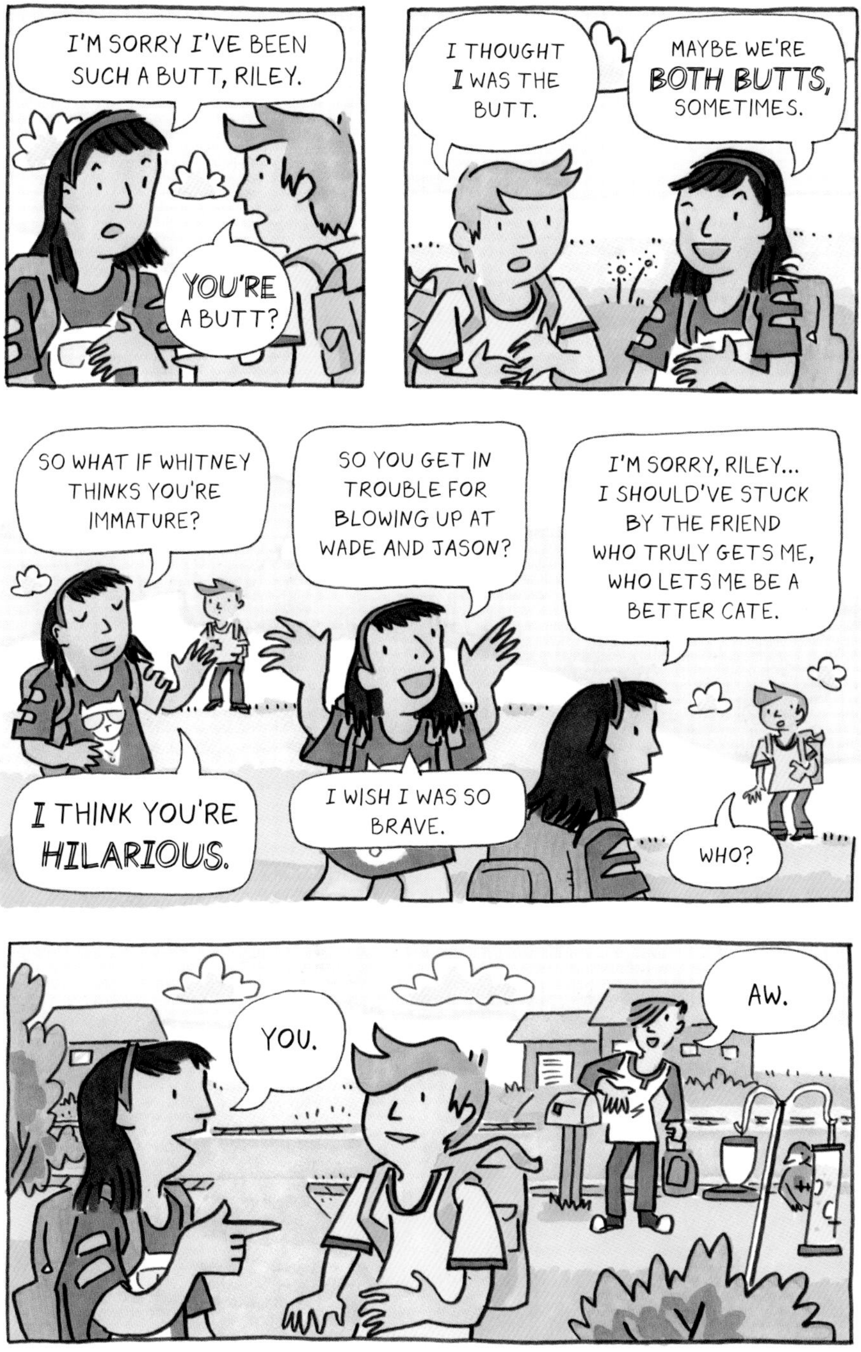

I'M SORRY I'VE BEEN SUCH A BUTT, RILEY.
YOU'RE A BUTT?
I THOUGHT I WAS THE BUTT.
MAYBE WE'RE BOTH BUTTS, SOMETIMES.
SO WHAT IF WHITNEY THINKS YOU'RE IMMATURE?
I THINK YOU'RE HILARIOUS.
SO YOU GET IN TROUBLE FOR BLOWING UP AT WADE AND JASON?
I WISH I WAS SO BRAVE.
I'M SORRY, RILEY... I SHOULD'VE STUCK BY THE FRIEND WHO TRULY GETS ME, WHO LETS ME BE A BETTER CATE.
WHO?
YOU.
AW.

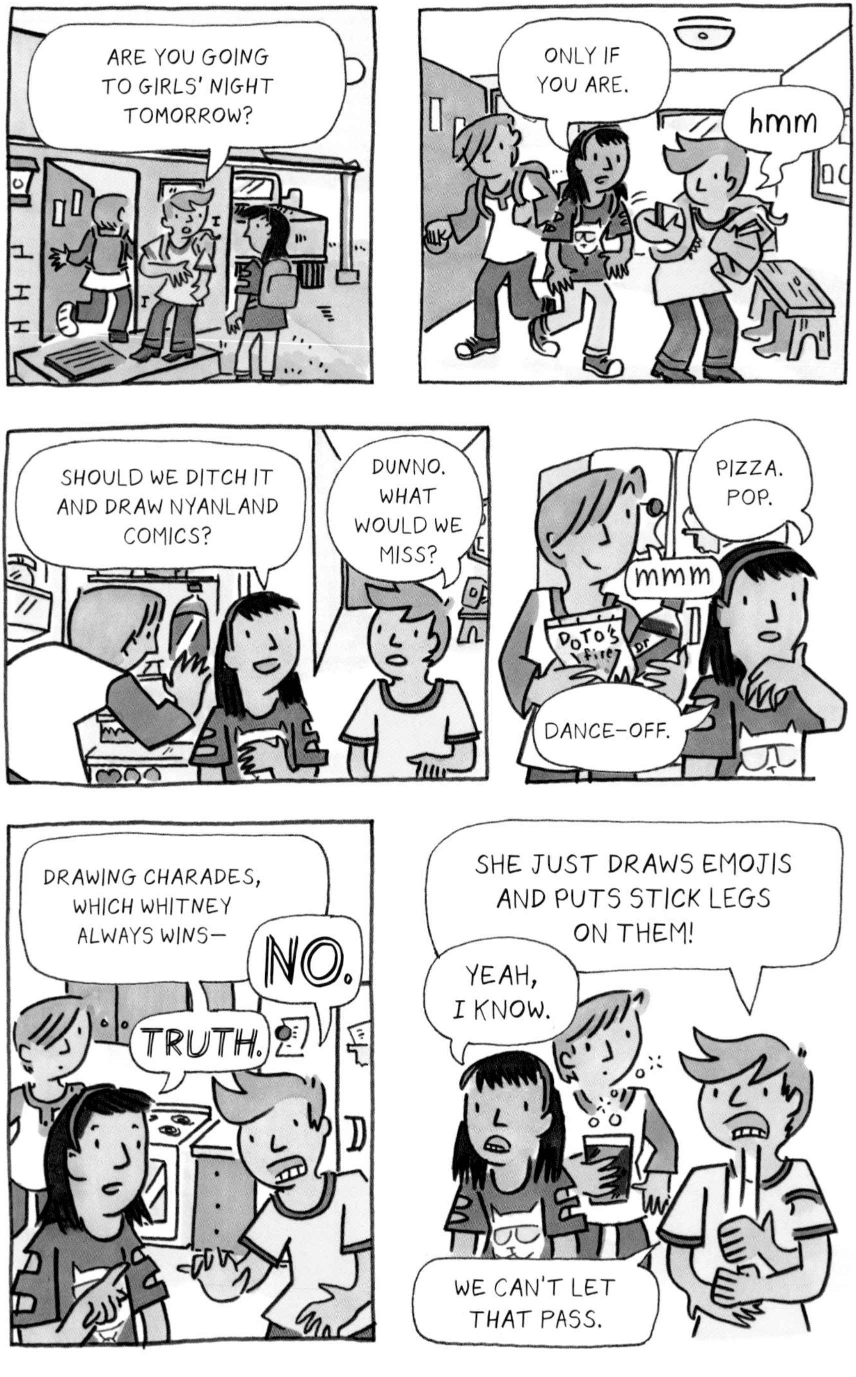
ARE YOU GOING TO GIRLS' NIGHT TOMORROW?
ONLY IF YOU ARE.
hmm
SHOULD WE DITCH IT AND DRAW NYANLAND COMICS?
DUNNO. WHAT WOULD WE MISS?
PIZZA. POP.
mmm
DANCE-OFF.
DRAWING CHARADES, WHICH WHITNEY ALWAYS WINS—
NO.
TRUTH.
SHE JUST DRAWS EMOJIS AND PUTS STICK LEGS ON THEM!
YEAH, I KNOW.
WE CAN'T LET THAT PASS.

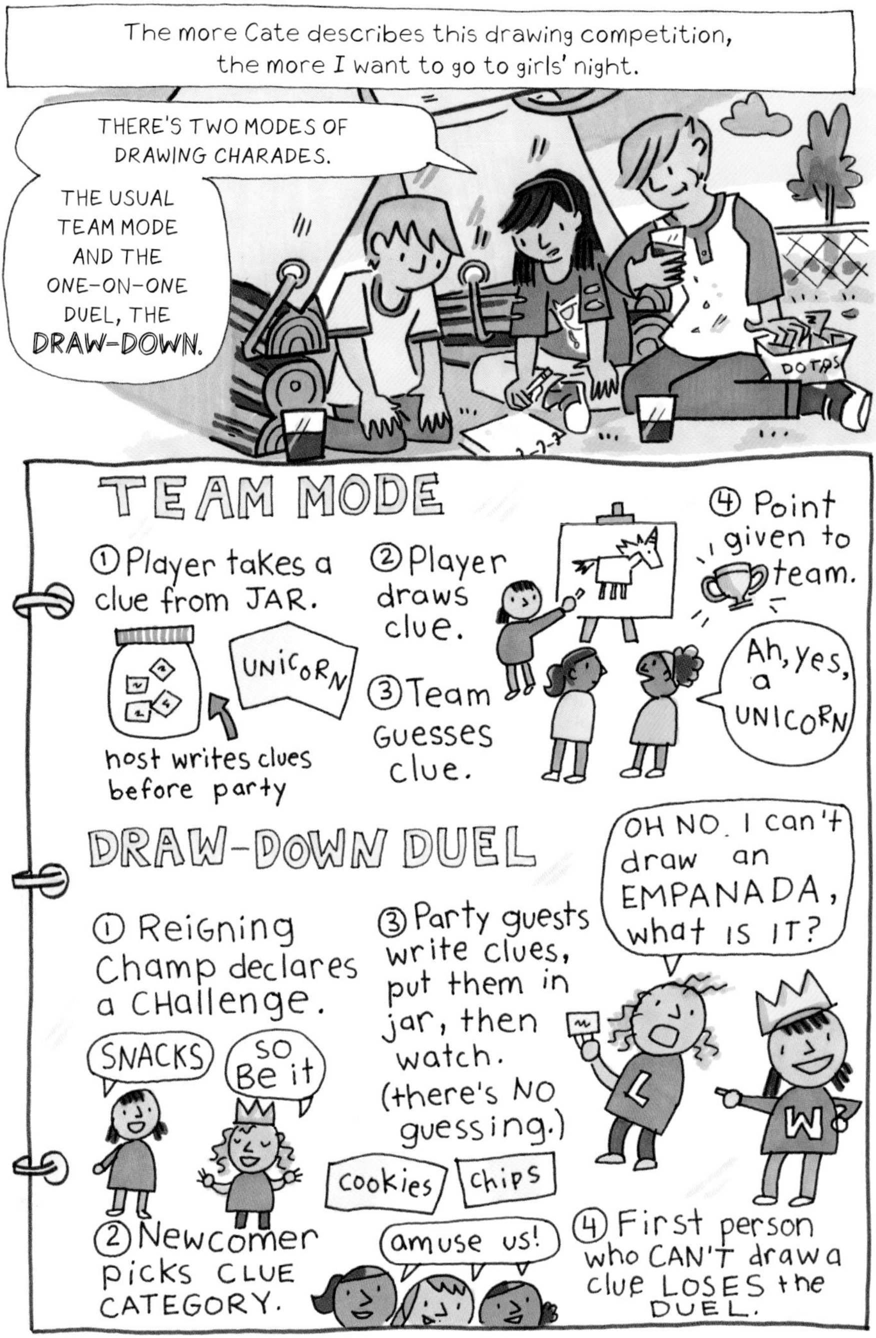
The more Cate describes this drawing competition, the more I want to go to girls' night.
THERE'S TWO MODES OF DRAWING CHARADES.
THE USUAL TEAM MODE AND THE ONE-ON-ONE DUEL, THE DRAW-DOWN.
TEAM MODE
① Player takes a clue from JAR.
UNICORN
host writes clues before party
② Player draws clue.
③ Team Guesses clue.
④ Point given to team.
Ah, yes, a UNICORN
DRAW-DOWN DUEL
① Reigning Champ declares a Challenge.
SNACKS
So Be it
② Newcomer picks CLUE CATEGORY.
③ Party guests write clues, put them in jar, then watch. (there's NO guessing.)
cookies
chips
amuse us!
OH NO. I can't draw an EMPANADA, what is IT?
L
W
④ First person who CAN'T draw a clue LOSES the DUEL.

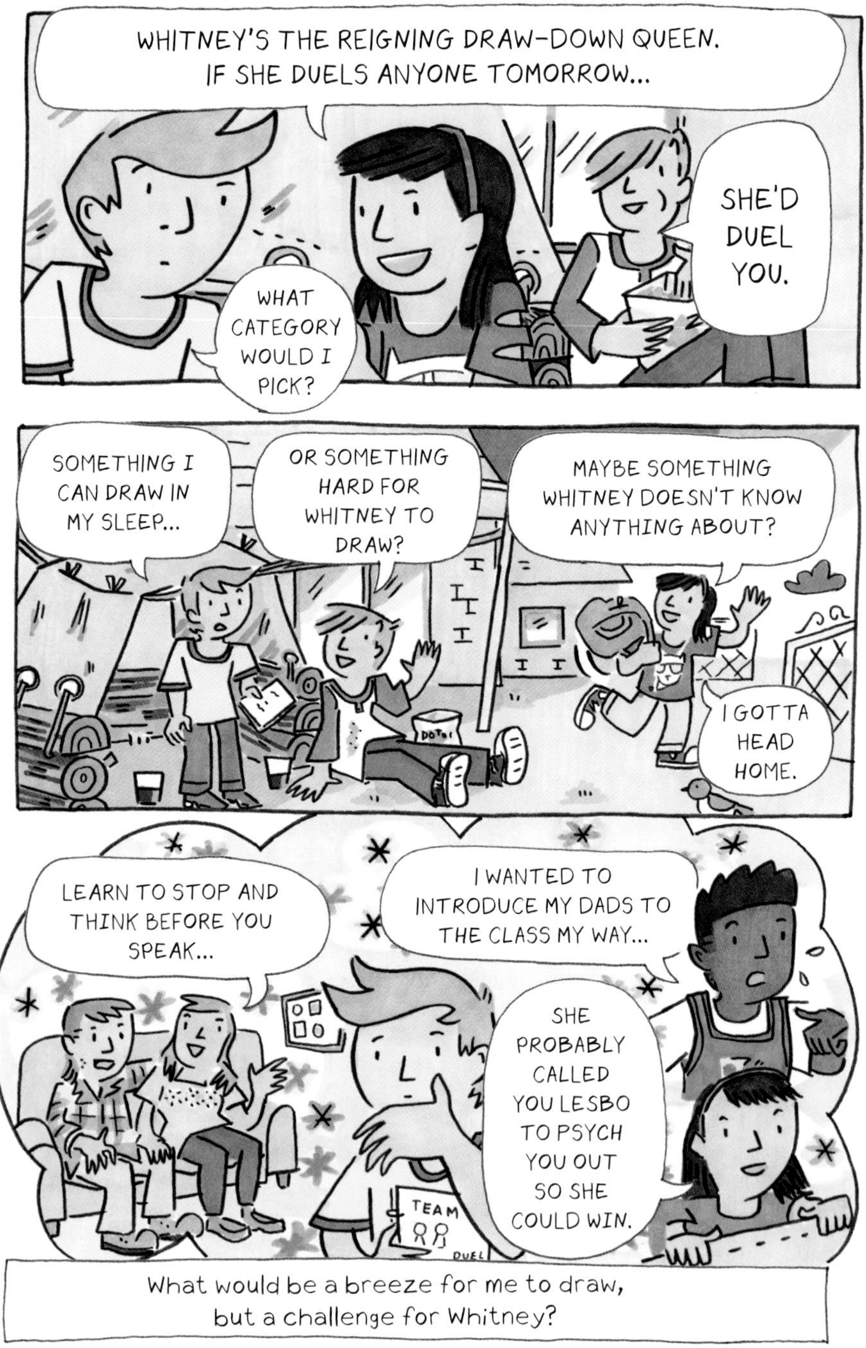
WHITNEY'S THE REIGNING DRAW-DOWN QUEEN. IF SHE DUELS ANYONE TOMORROW...
SHE'D DUEL YOU.
WHAT CATEGORY WOULD I PICK?
SOMETHING I CAN DRAW IN MY SLEEP...
OR SOMETHING HARD FOR WHITNEY TO DRAW?
MAYBE SOMETHING WHITNEY DOESN'T KNOW ANYTHING ABOUT?
I GOTTA HEAD HOME.
LEARN TO STOP AND THINK BEFORE YOU SPEAK...
I WANTED TO INTRODUCE MY DADS TO THE CLASS MY WAY...
SHE PROBABLY CALLED YOU LESBO TO PSYCH YOU OUT SO SHE COULD WIN.
TEAM
DUEL
What would be a breeze for me to draw, but a challenge for Whitney?

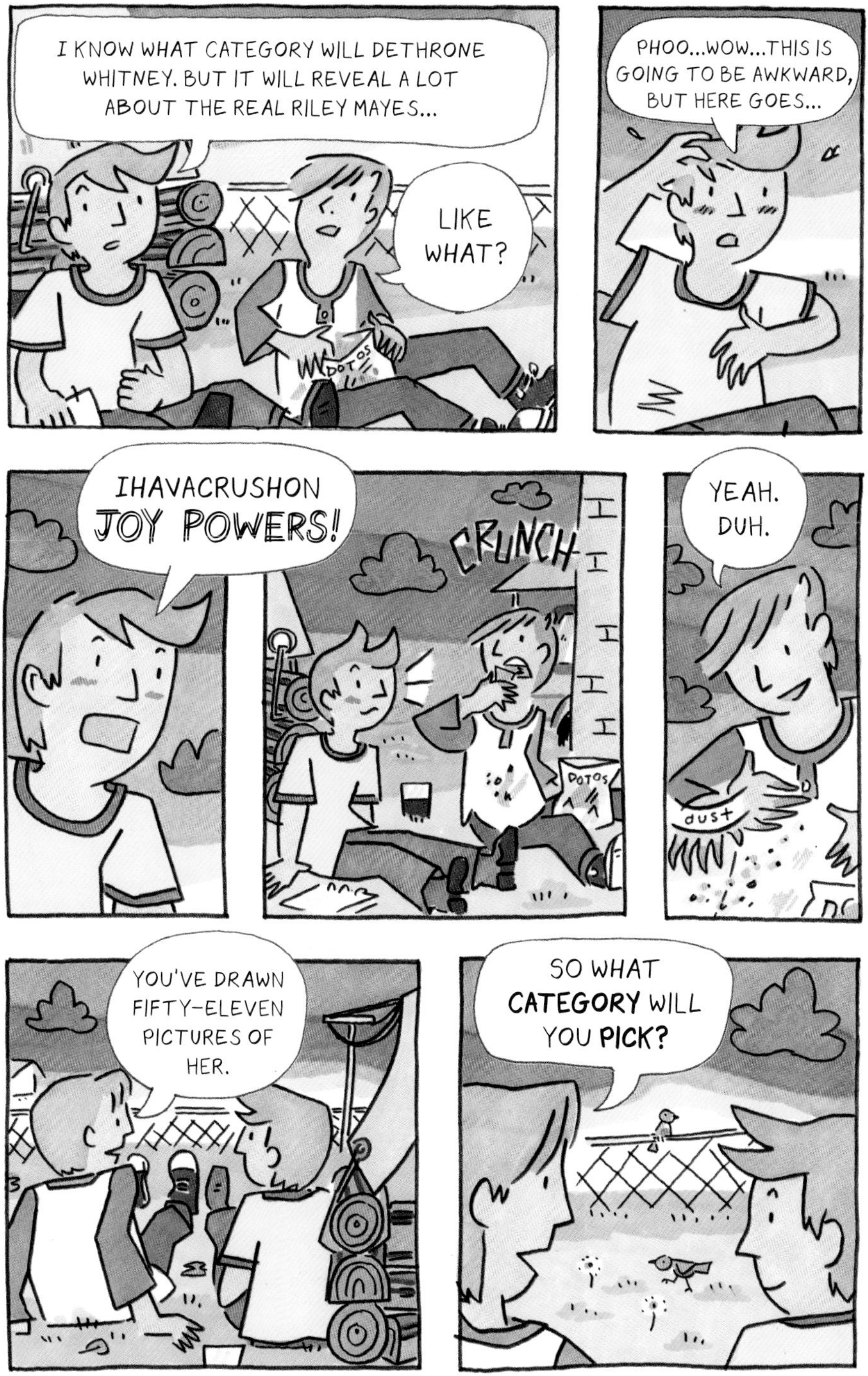

I KNOW WHAT CATEGORY WILL DETHRONE WHITNEY. BUT IT WILL REVEAL A LOT ABOUT THE REAL RILEY MAYES...
LIKE WHAT?
DOTOS
PHOO...WOW...THIS IS GOING TO BE AWKWARD, BUT HERE GOES...
IHAVACRUSHON JOY POWERS!
CRUNCH
DOTOS
YEAH. DUH.
dust
YOU'VE DRAWN FIFTY-ELEVEN PICTURES OF HER.
SO WHAT CATEGORY WILL YOU PICK?

CHAPTER 18

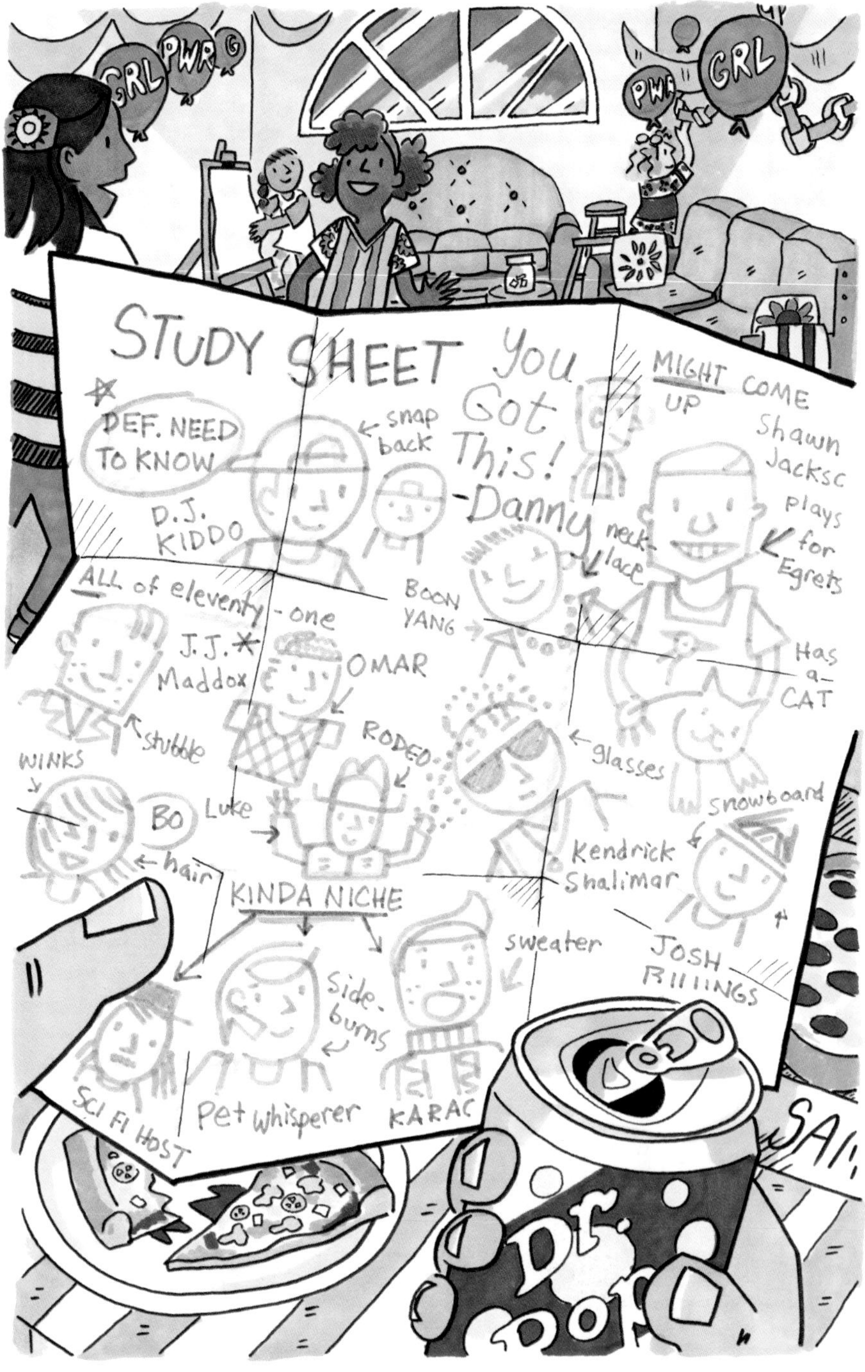

GRL PWR G
PWR GRL UP
STUDY SHEET
You Got This! -Danny
DEF. NEED TO KNOW
snap back
D.J. KIDDO
MIGHT COME UP
Shawn Jacksc
plays for Egrets
neck-lace
ALL of eleventy-one
BOON YANG
J.J. Maddox
OMAR
stubble
Has a CAT
RODEO
glasses
WINKS
BO
Luke
hair
snowboard
Kendrick Shalimar
KINDA NICHE
sweater
JOSH BILLINGS
Side-burns
SCI FI HOST
Pet whisperer
KARAC
Dr. Pop

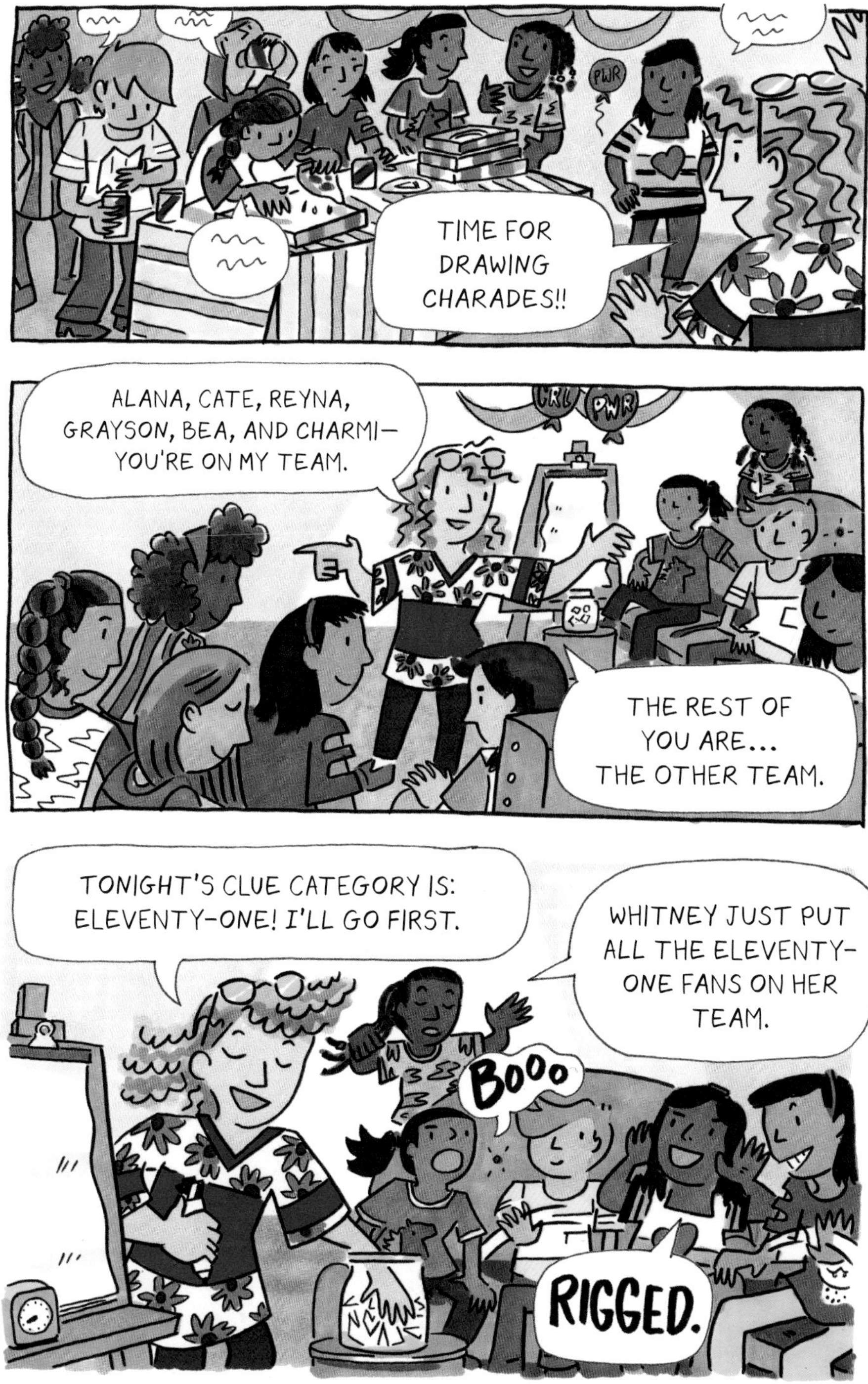

PWR
TIME FOR DRAWING CHARADES!!
CRL
PWR
ALANA, CATE, REYNA, GRAYSON, BEA, AND CHARMI— YOU'RE ON MY TEAM.
THE REST OF YOU ARE... THE OTHER TEAM.
TONIGHT'S CLUE CATEGORY IS: ELEVENTY-ONE! I'LL GO FIRST.
WHITNEY JUST PUT ALL THE ELEVENTY-ONE FANS ON HER TEAM.
BOOO
RIGGED.

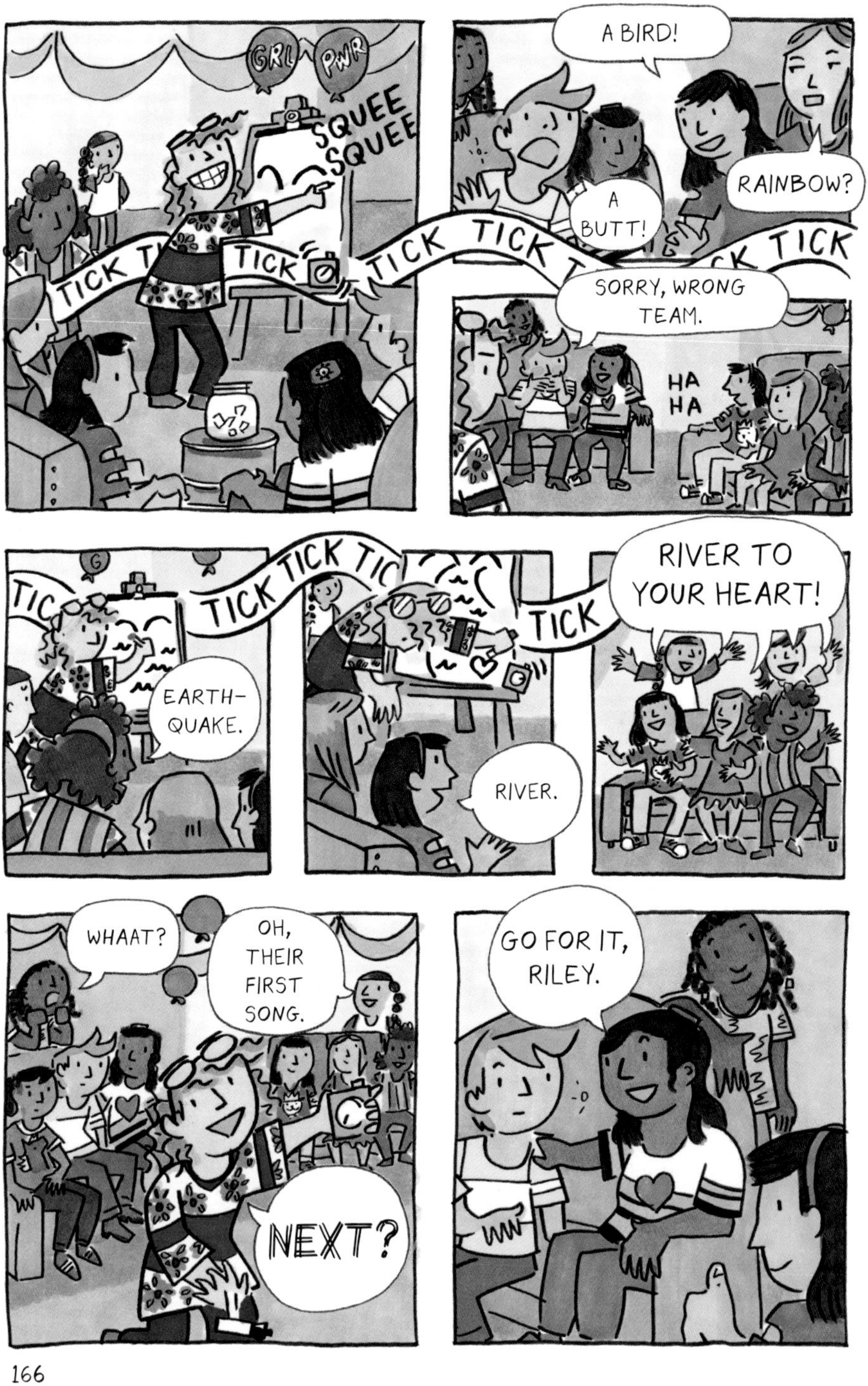
GRL
PWR
SQUEE
SQUEE
TICK TICK TICK TICK TICK TICK TICK
A BIRD!
A BUTT!
RAINBOW?
SORRY, WRONG TEAM.
HA HA
TICK TICK TICK TICK
EARTH-QUAKE.
RIVER.
RIVER TO YOUR HEART!
WHAAT?
OH, THEIR FIRST SONG.
NEXT?
GO FOR IT, RILEY.

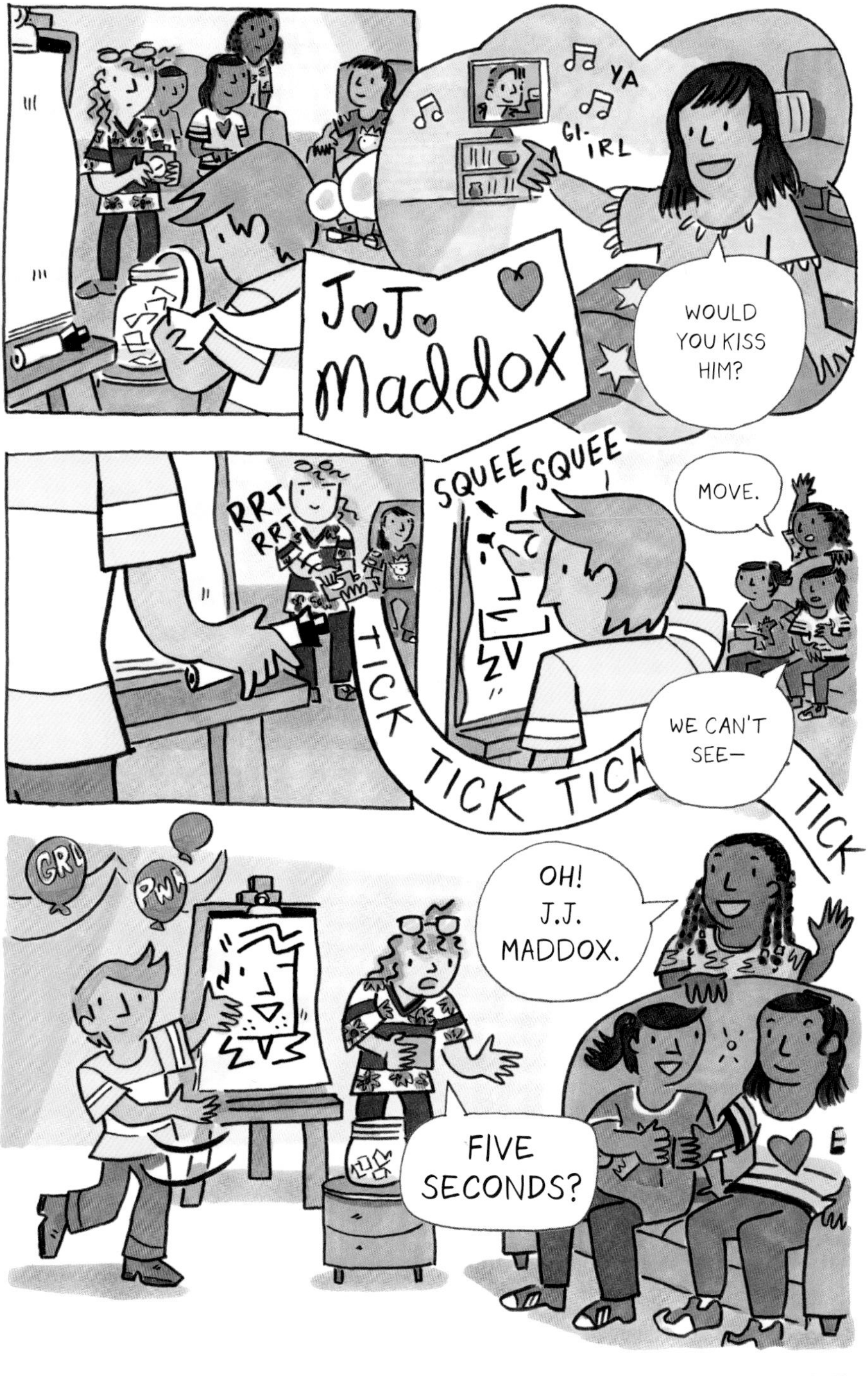
YA
GI-IRL
J J MADDOX
WOULD YOU KISS HIM?
RRT RRT
SQUEE SQUEE
MOVE.
TICK TICK TICK TICK
WE CAN'T SEE—
GRL
PWR
OH! J.J. MADDOX.
FIVE SECONDS?

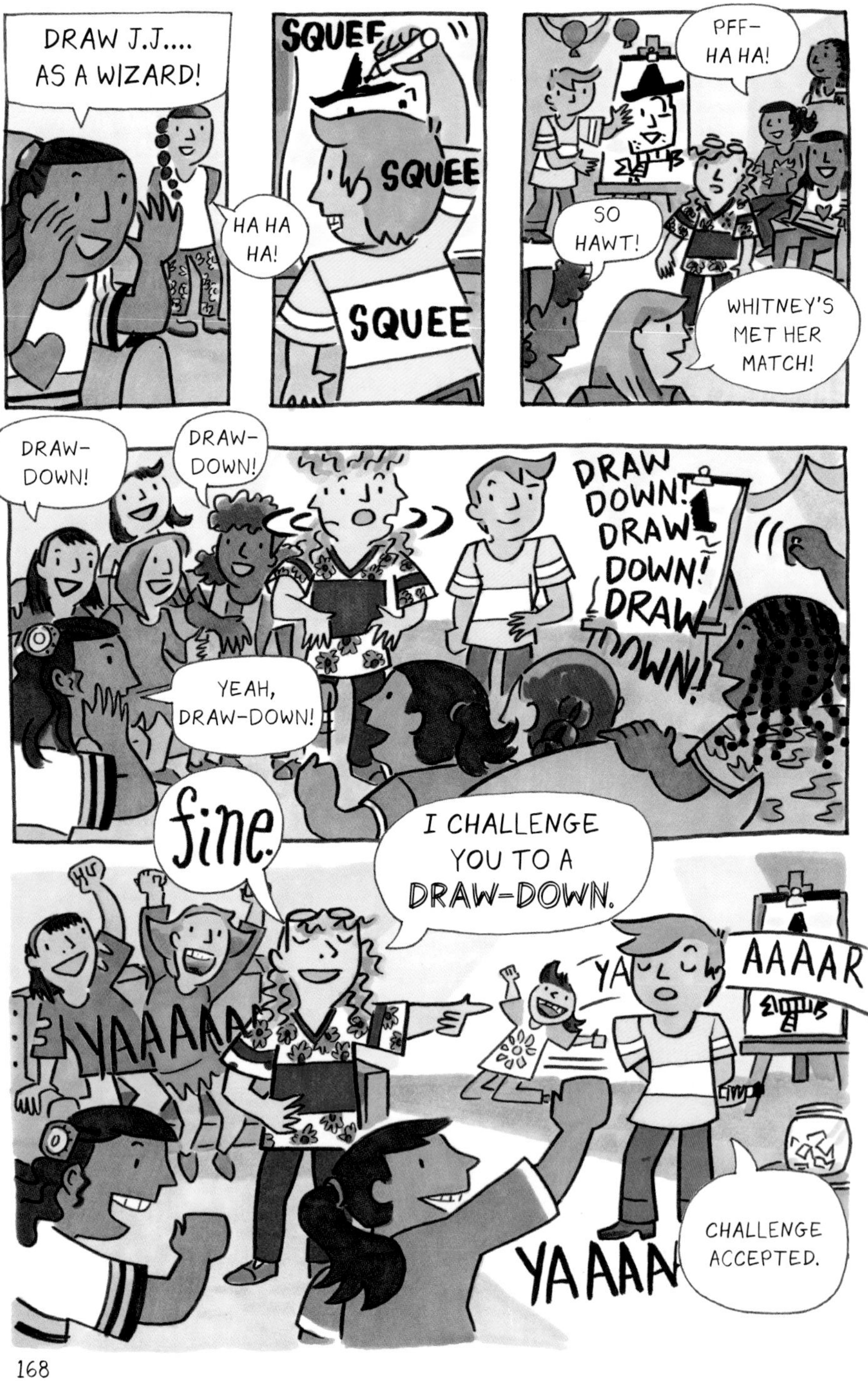
DRAW J.J.... AS A WIZARD!
HA HA HA!
SQUEE
SQUEE
SQUEE
PFF— HA HA!
SO HAWT!
WHITNEY'S MET HER MATCH!
DRAW-DOWN!
DRAW-DOWN!
DRAW DOWN! DRAW DOWN! DRAW DOWN!
YEAH, DRAW-DOWN!
fine.
I CHALLENGE YOU TO A DRAW-DOWN.
YAAAAA
YA
AAAAR
YAAAA
CHALLENGE ACCEPTED.

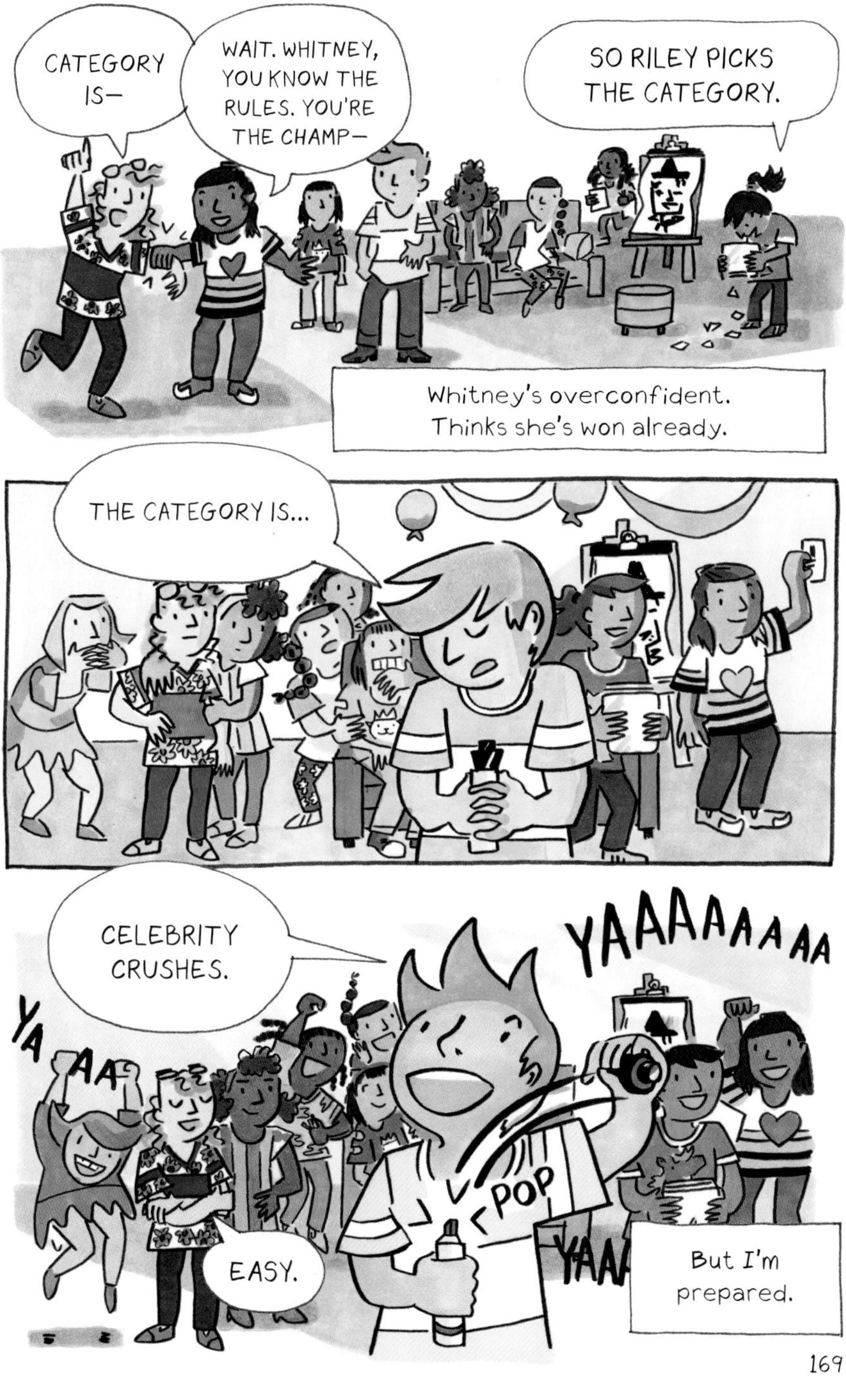
CATEGORY IS—
WAIT. WHITNEY, YOU KNOW THE RULES. YOU'RE THE CHAMP—
SO RILEY PICKS THE CATEGORY.
Whitney's overconfident. Thinks she's won already.
THE CATEGORY IS...
CELEBRITY CRUSHES.
YAAAAAAAAA
YA AA
POP
EASY.
YAA
But I'm prepared.

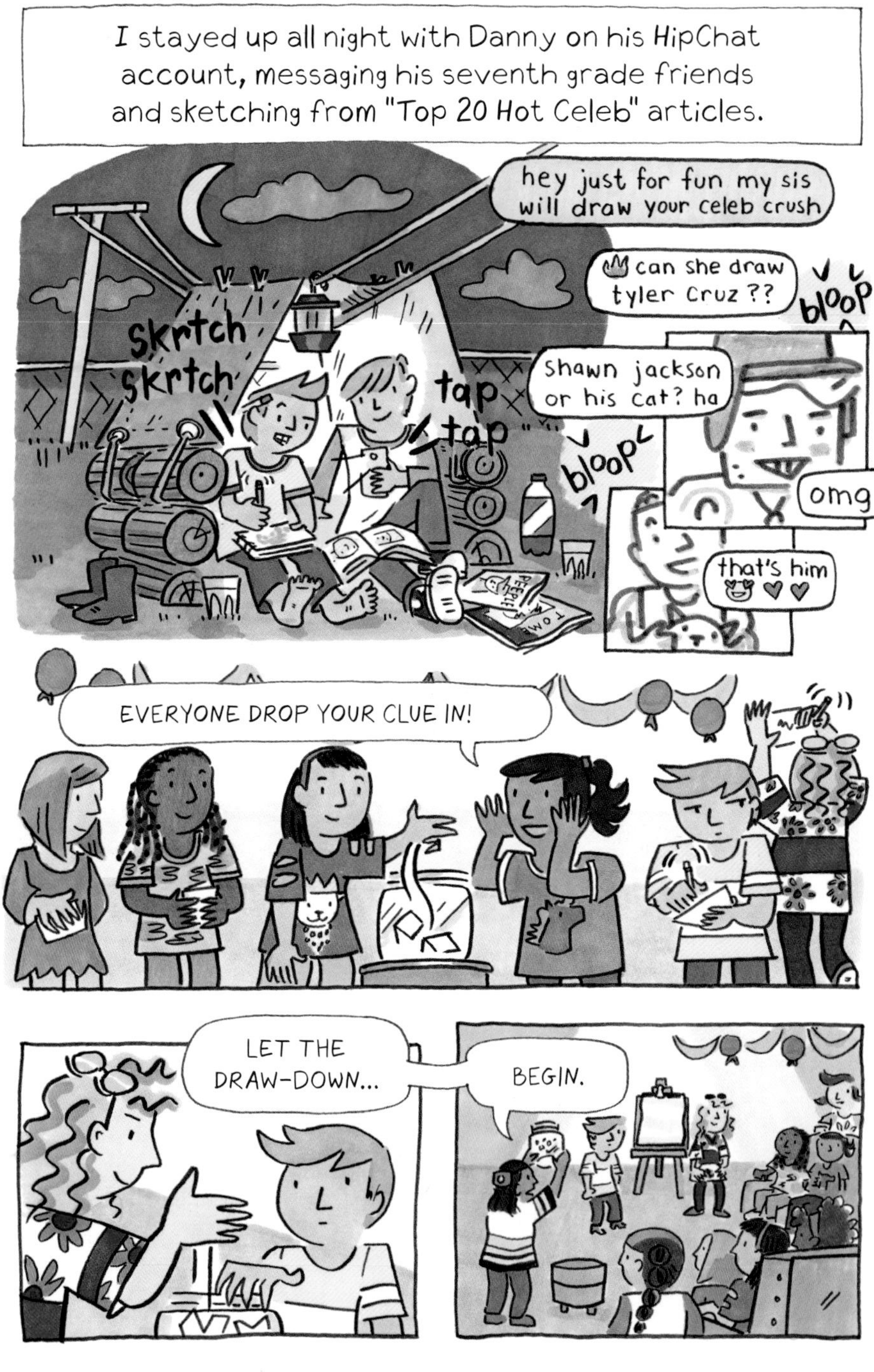

I stayed up all night with Danny on his HipChat account, messaging his seventh grade friends and sketching from "Top 20 Hot Celeb" articles.
skrtch skrtch
tap tap
hey just for fun my sis will draw your celeb crush
can she draw tyler cruz ??
bloop
shawn jackson or his cat? ha
bloop
omg
that's him
EVERYONE DROP YOUR CLUE IN!
LET THE DRAW-DOWN...
BEGIN.

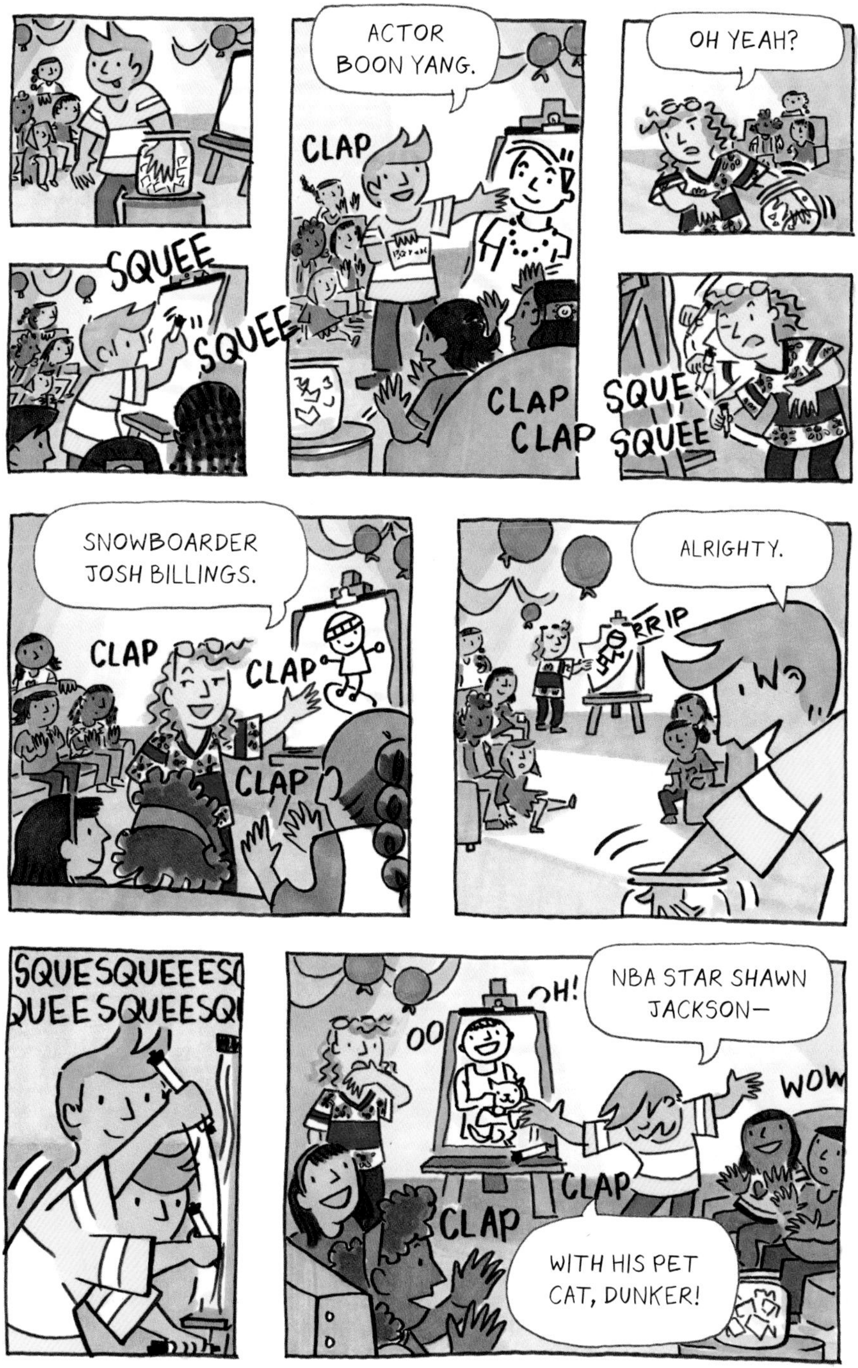

ACTOR BOON YANG.
CLAP
OH YEAH?
SQUEE
SQUEE
CLAP
CLAP
SQUE
SQUEE
SNOWBOARDER JOSH BILLINGS.
CLAP
CLAP
CLAP
ALRIGHTY.
RRIP
SQUESQUEEESQ
QUEESQUEESQ
OH!
OO
NBA STAR SHAWN JACKSON—
WOW
CLAP
CLAP
WITH HIS PET CAT, DUNKER!

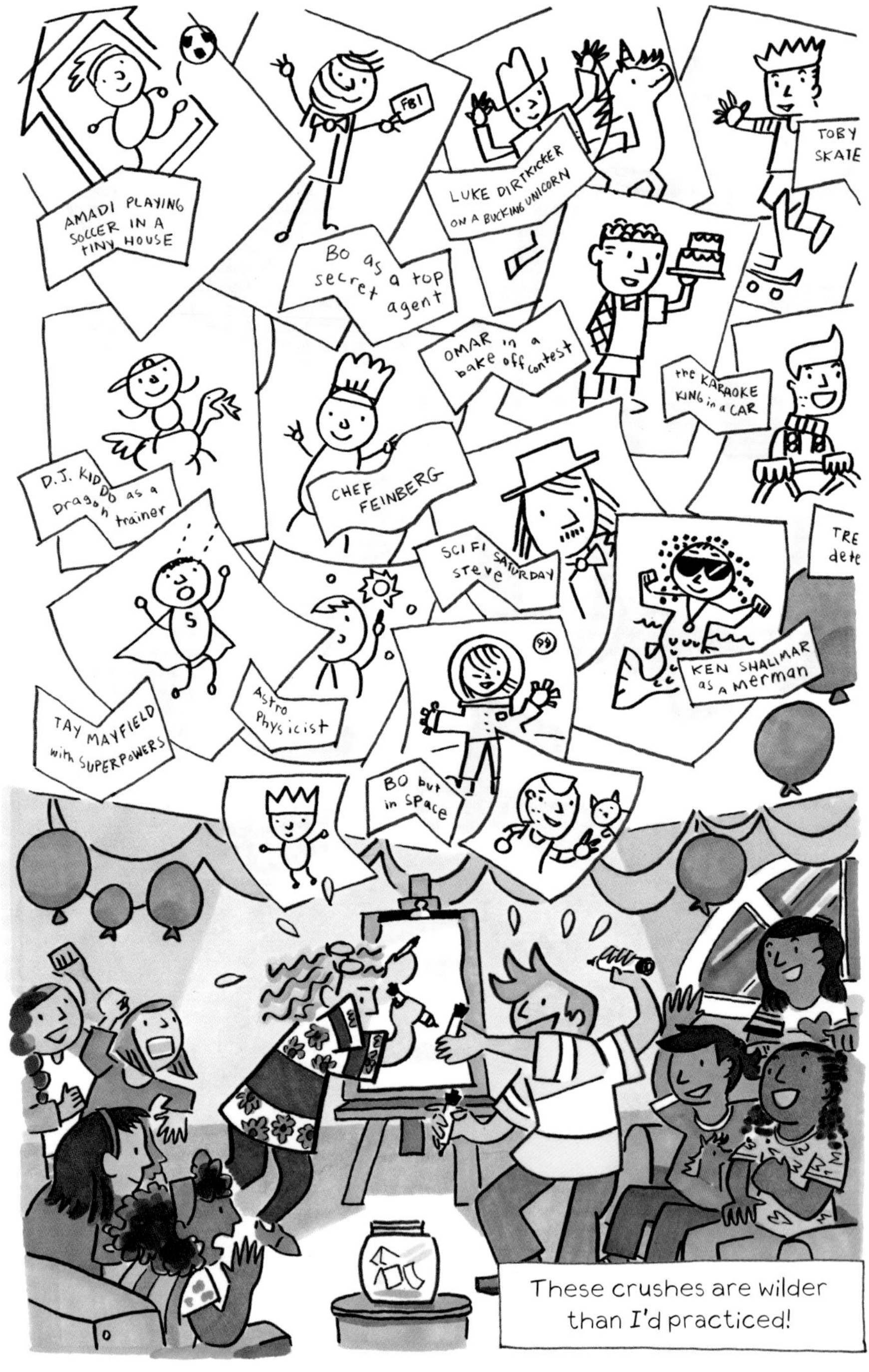
AMADI PLAYING SOCCER IN A TINY HOUSE
FBI
Bo as a top secret agent
LUKE DIRTKICKER ON A BUCKING UNICORN
TOBY SKATE
OMAR in a bake off contest
the KARAOKE KING in a CAR
D.J. KIDDO as a Dragon trainer
CHEF FEINBERG
SCI FI SATURDAY STEVE
KEN SHALIMAR as a merman
S
Astro Physicist
TAY MAYFIELD with SUPERPOWERS
BO but in Space
These crushes are wilder than I'd practiced!

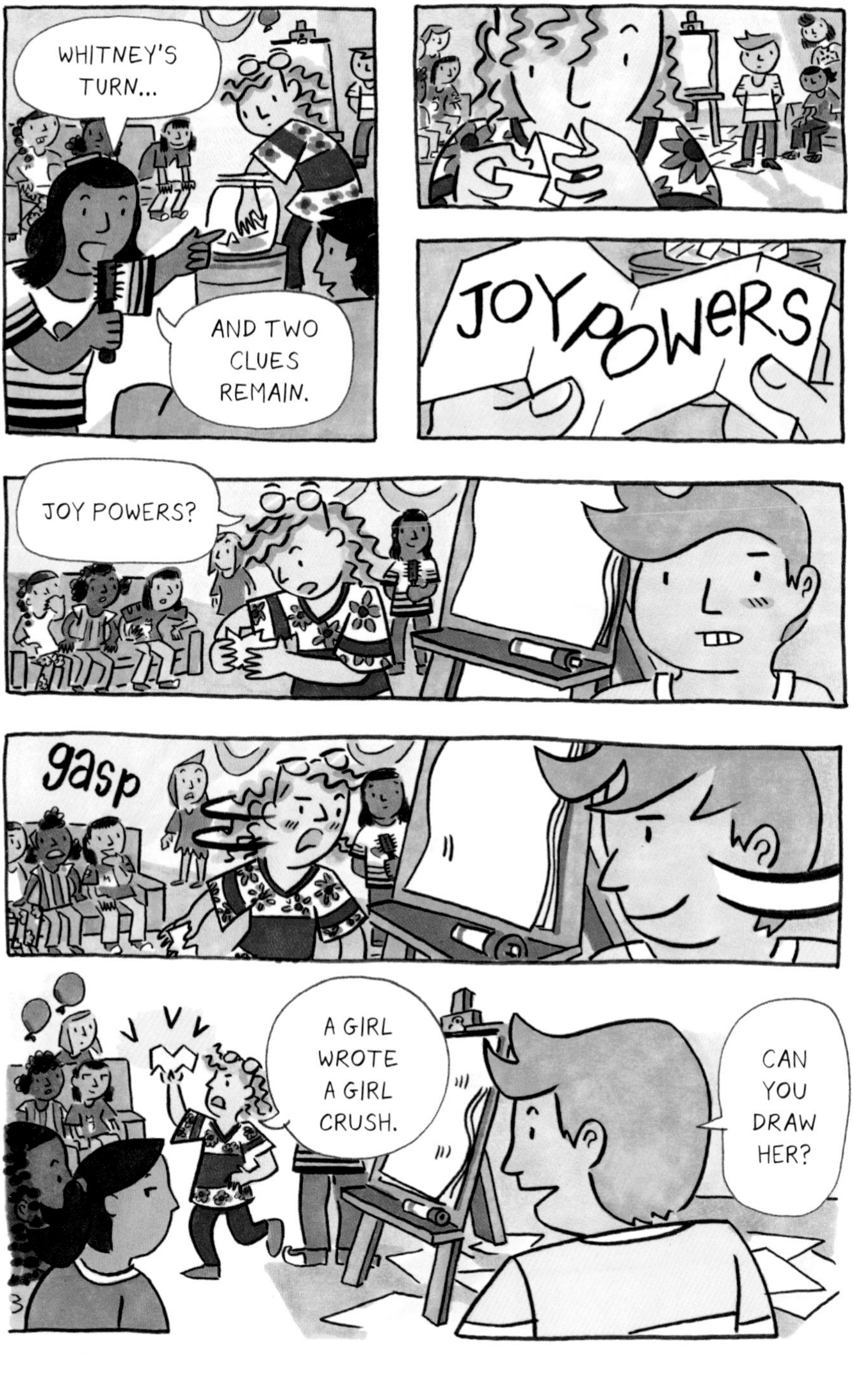
WHITNEY'S TURN...
AND TWO CLUES REMAIN.
JOY POWERS
JOY POWERS?
gasp
A GIRL WROTE A GIRL CRUSH.
CAN YOU DRAW HER?

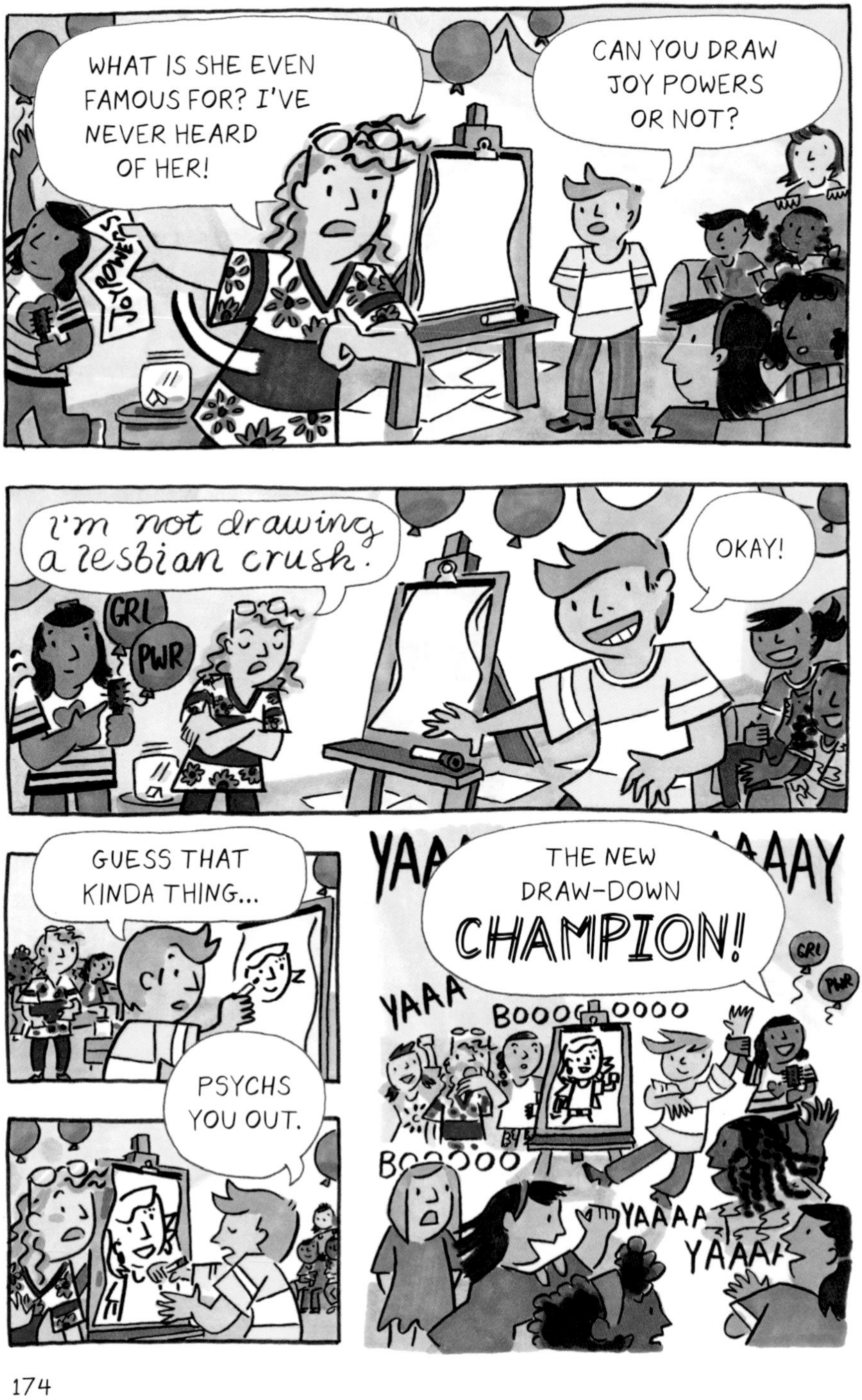
WHAT IS SHE EVEN FAMOUS FOR? I'VE NEVER HEARD OF HER!
JOY POWERS
CAN YOU DRAW JOY POWERS OR NOT?
i'm not drawing a lesbian crush.
GRL
PWR
OKAY!
GUESS THAT KINDA THING...
PSYCHS YOU OUT.
YAAAAAAAAAAY
THE NEW DRAW-DOWN CHAMPION!
GRL
PWR
YAAA
BOOOOOOOO
BOOOOOO
YAAAA
YAAAA

CHAPTER 19

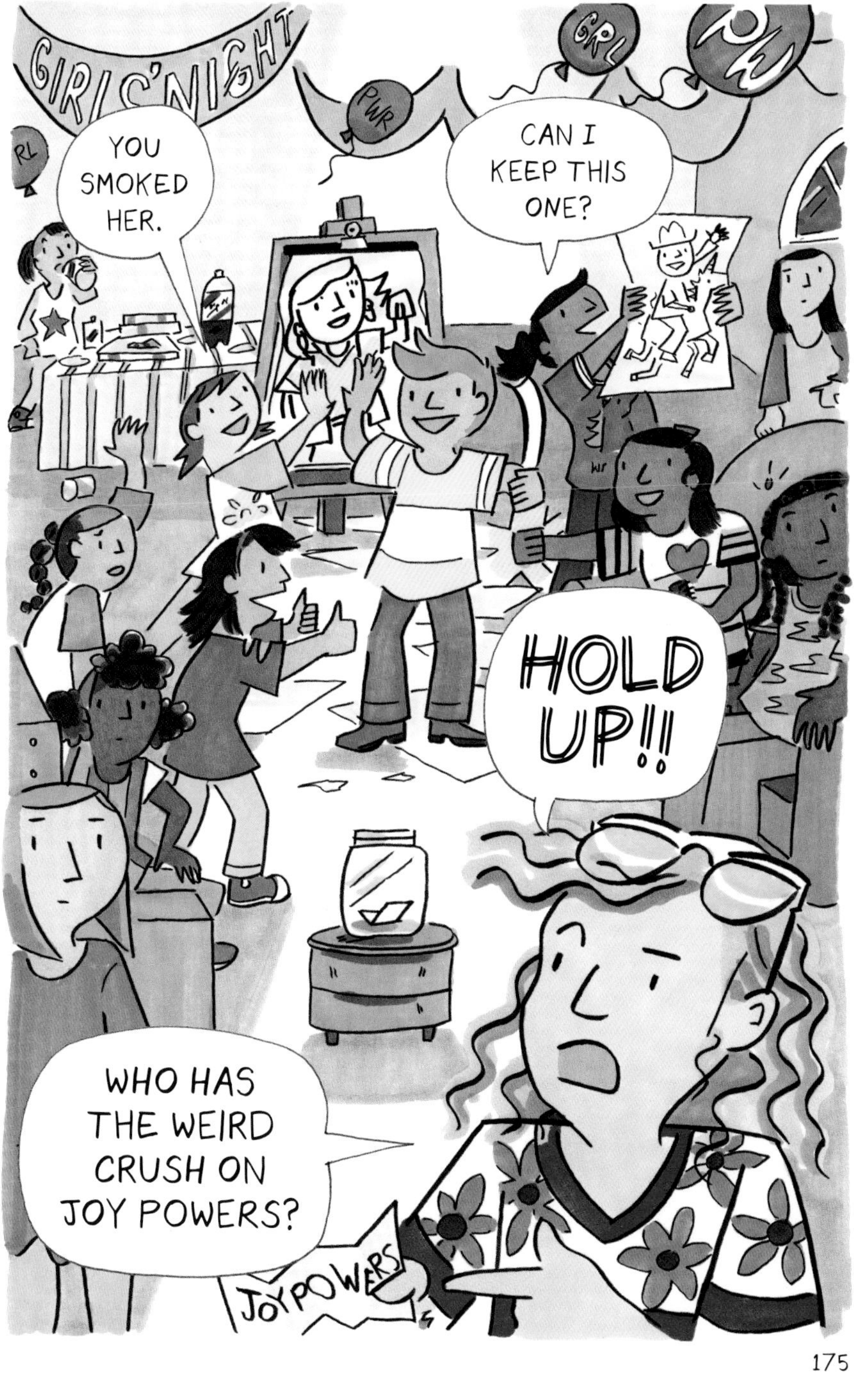
GIRLS' NIGHT
GRL
PWR
YOU SMOKED HER.
CAN I KEEP THIS ONE?
HOLD UP!!
WHO HAS THE WEIRD CRUSH ON JOY POWERS?
JOY POWERS

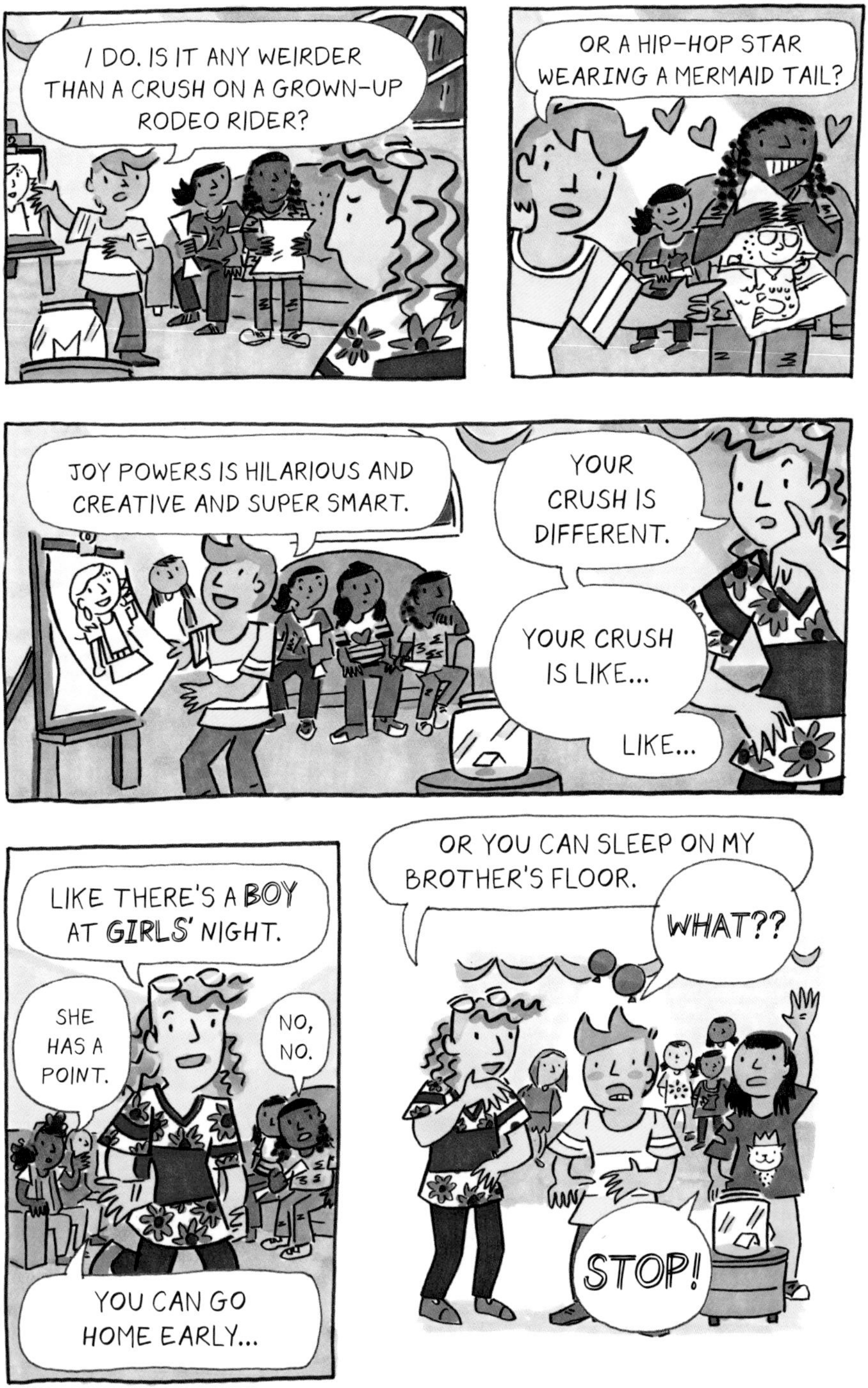
I DO. IS IT ANY WEIRDER THAN A CRUSH ON A GROWN-UP RODEO RIDER?
OR A HIP-HOP STAR WEARING A MERMAID TAIL?
JOY POWERS IS HILARIOUS AND CREATIVE AND SUPER SMART.
YOUR CRUSH IS DIFFERENT.
YOUR CRUSH IS LIKE...
LIKE...
LIKE THERE'S A BOY AT GIRLS' NIGHT.
SHE HAS A POINT.
NO, NO.
YOU CAN GO HOME EARLY...
OR YOU CAN SLEEP ON MY BROTHER'S FLOOR.
WHAT??
STOP!

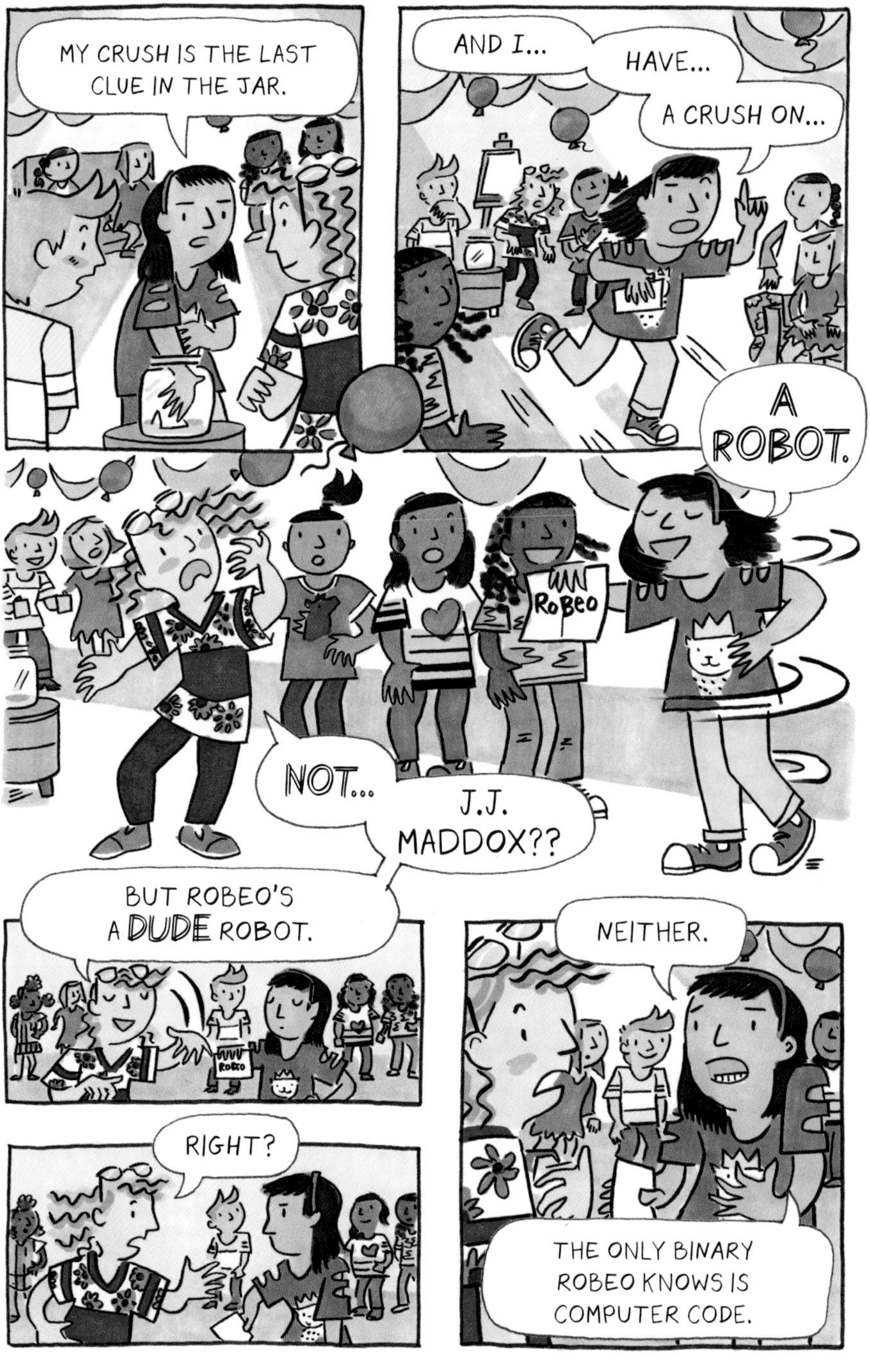
MY CRUSH IS THE LAST CLUE IN THE JAR.
AND I...
HAVE...
A CRUSH ON...
A ROBOT.
RoBeo
NOT...
J.J. MADDOX??
BUT ROBEO'S A DUDE ROBOT.
ROBEO
RIGHT?
NEITHER.
THE ONLY BINARY ROBEO KNOWS IS COMPUTER CODE.

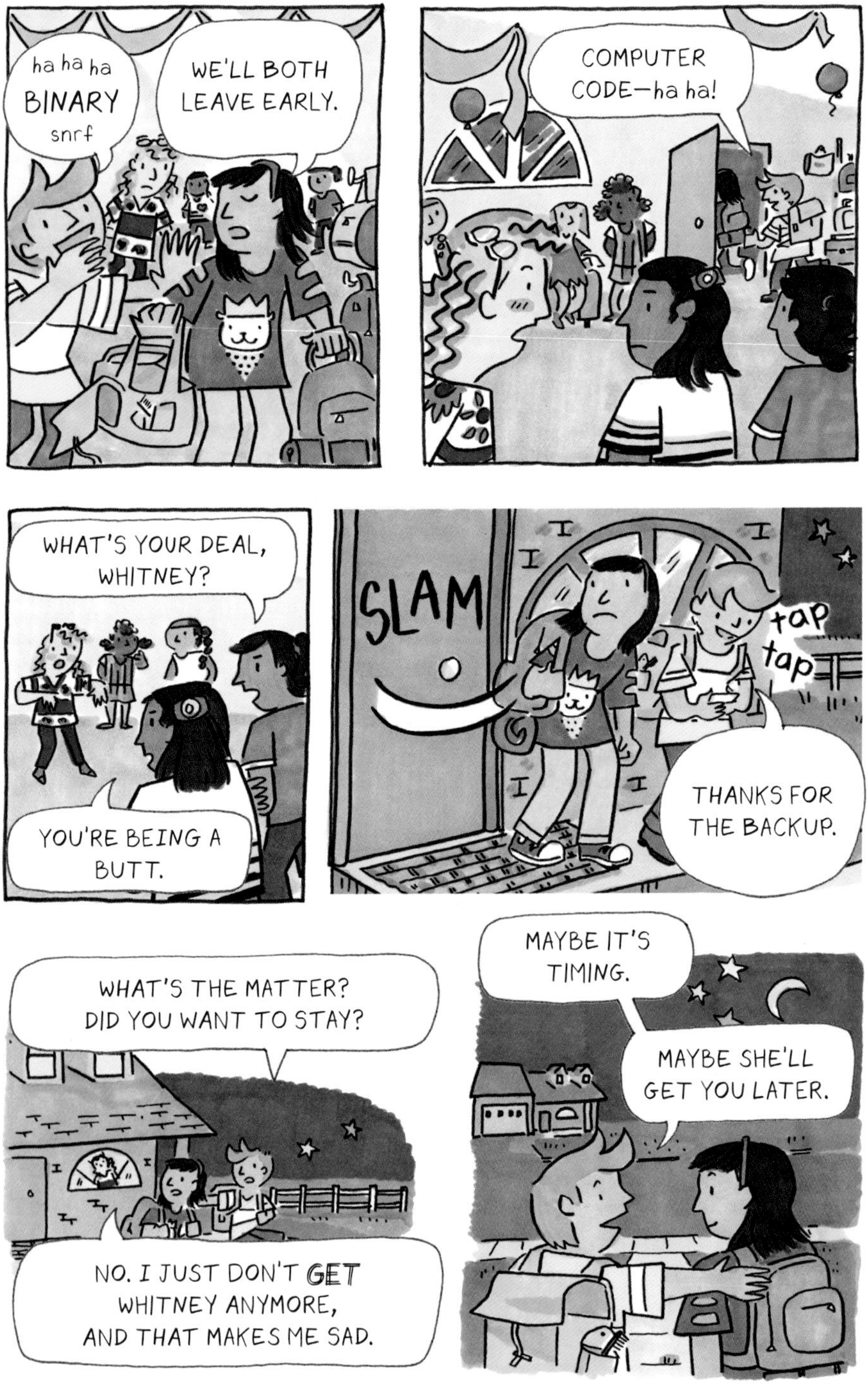
ha ha ha BINARY snrf
WE'LL BOTH LEAVE EARLY.
COMPUTER CODE—ha ha!
WHAT'S YOUR DEAL, WHITNEY?
YOU'RE BEING A BUTT.
SLAM
tap tap
THANKS FOR THE BACKUP.
WHAT'S THE MATTER? DID YOU WANT TO STAY?
NO. I JUST DON'T GET WHITNEY ANYMORE, AND THAT MAKES ME SAD.
MAYBE IT'S TIMING.
MAYBE SHE'LL GET YOU LATER.

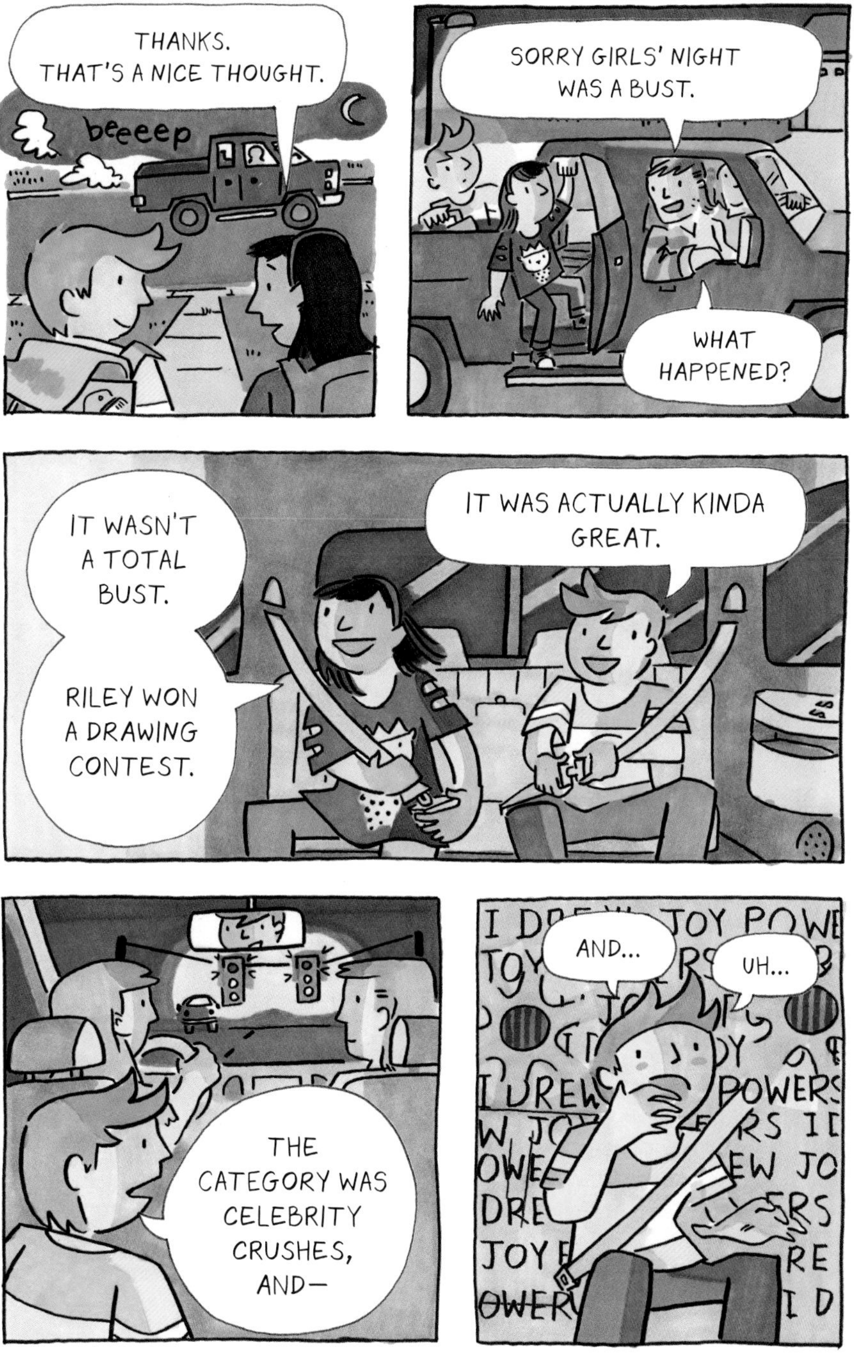
THANKS. THAT'S A NICE THOUGHT.
beeeep
SORRY GIRLS' NIGHT WAS A BUST.
WHAT HAPPENED?
IT WASN'T A TOTAL BUST.
RILEY WON A DRAWING CONTEST.
IT WAS ACTUALLY KINDA GREAT.
THE CATEGORY WAS CELEBRITY CRUSHES, AND—
AND...
UH...

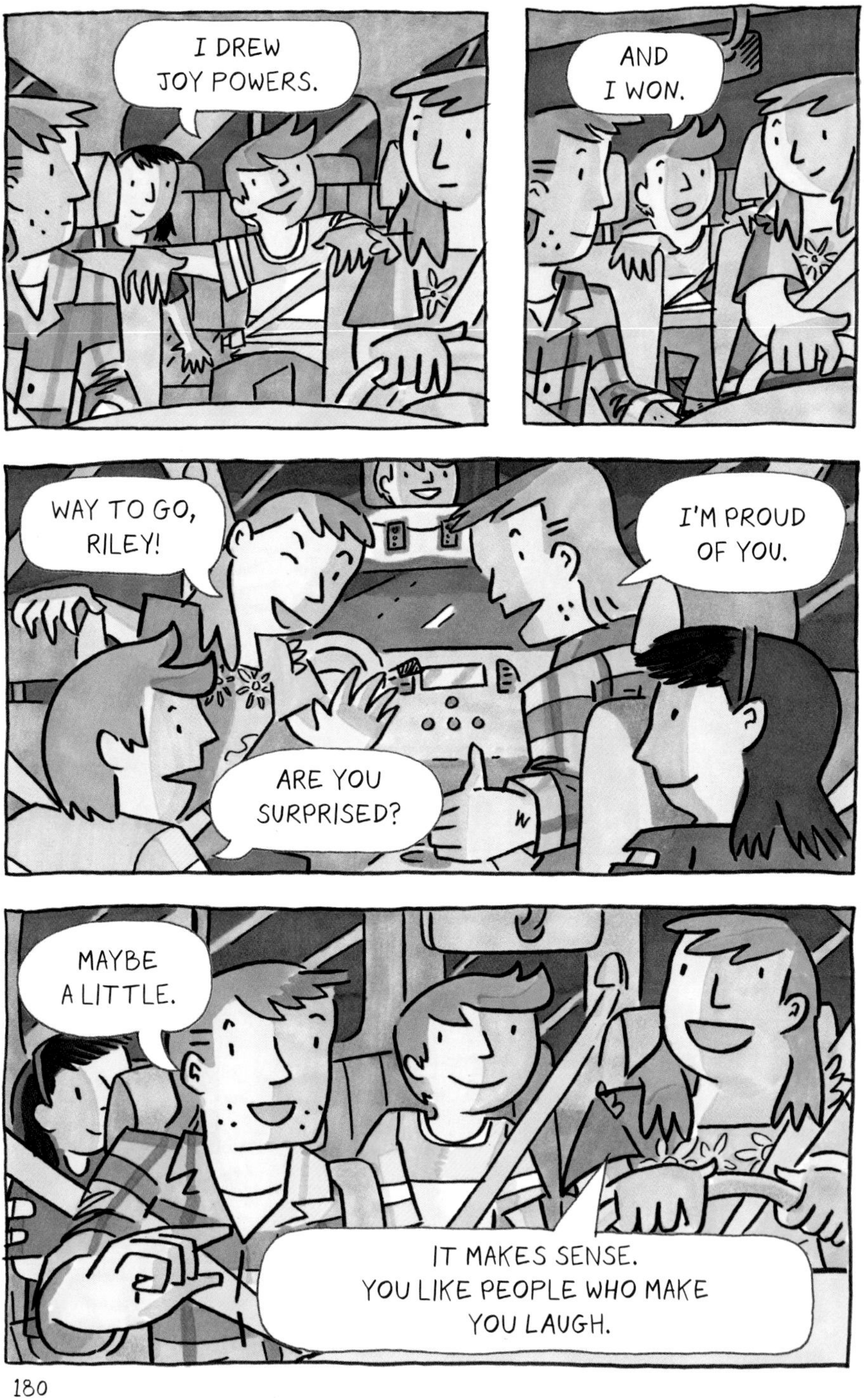
I DREW JOY POWERS.
AND I WON.
WAY TO GO, RILEY!
I'M PROUD OF YOU.
ARE YOU SURPRISED?
MAYBE A LITTLE.
IT MAKES SENSE. YOU LIKE PEOPLE WHO MAKE YOU LAUGH.

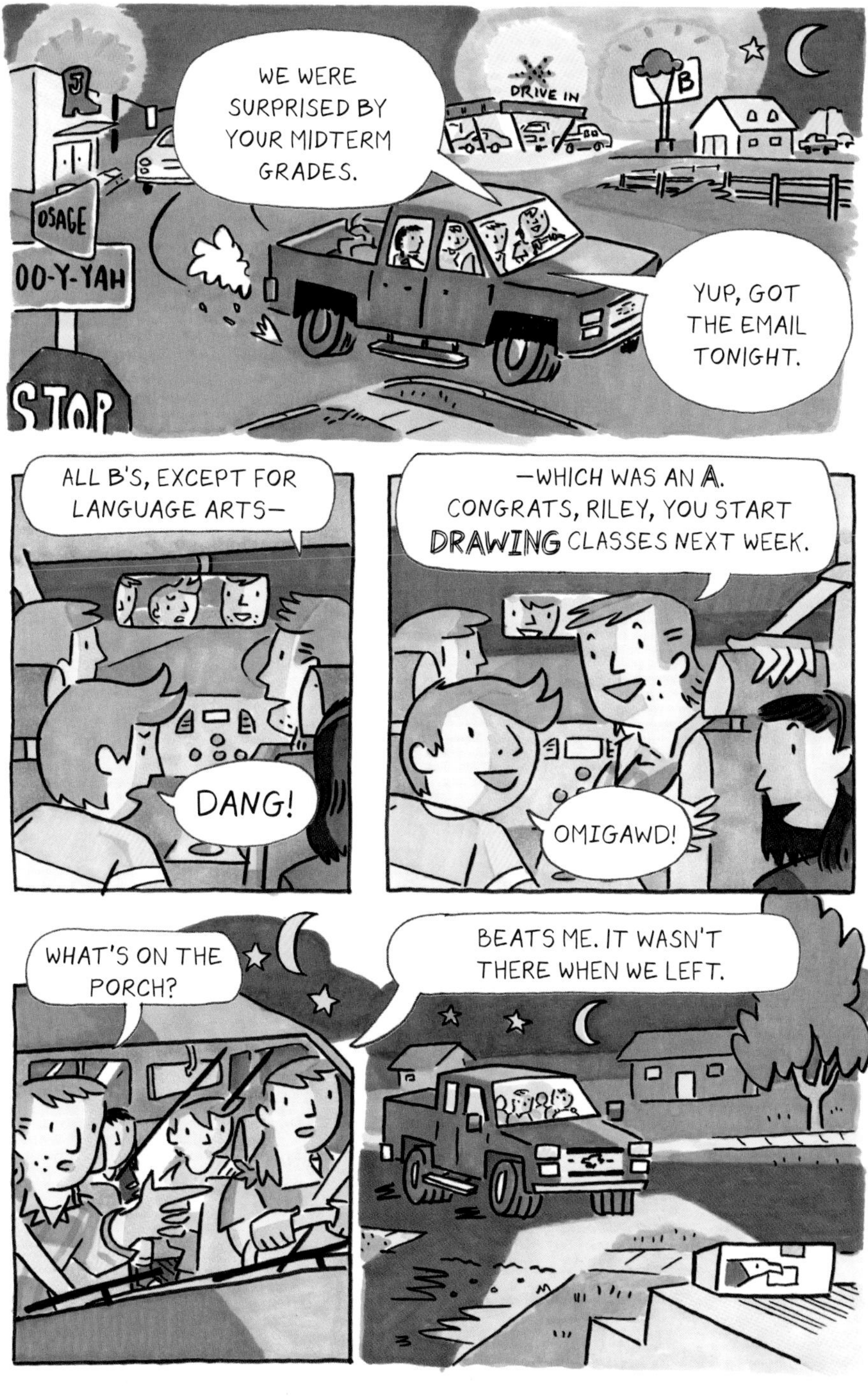
J
OSAGE
OO-Y-YAH
STOP
DRIVE IN
B
WE WERE SURPRISED BY YOUR MIDTERM GRADES.
YUP, GOT THE EMAIL TONIGHT.
ALL B'S, EXCEPT FOR LANGUAGE ARTS—
DANG!
—WHICH WAS AN A. CONGRATS, RILEY, YOU START DRAWING CLASSES NEXT WEEK.
OMIGAWD!
WHAT'S ON THE PORCH?
BEATS ME. IT WASN'T THERE WHEN WE LEFT.

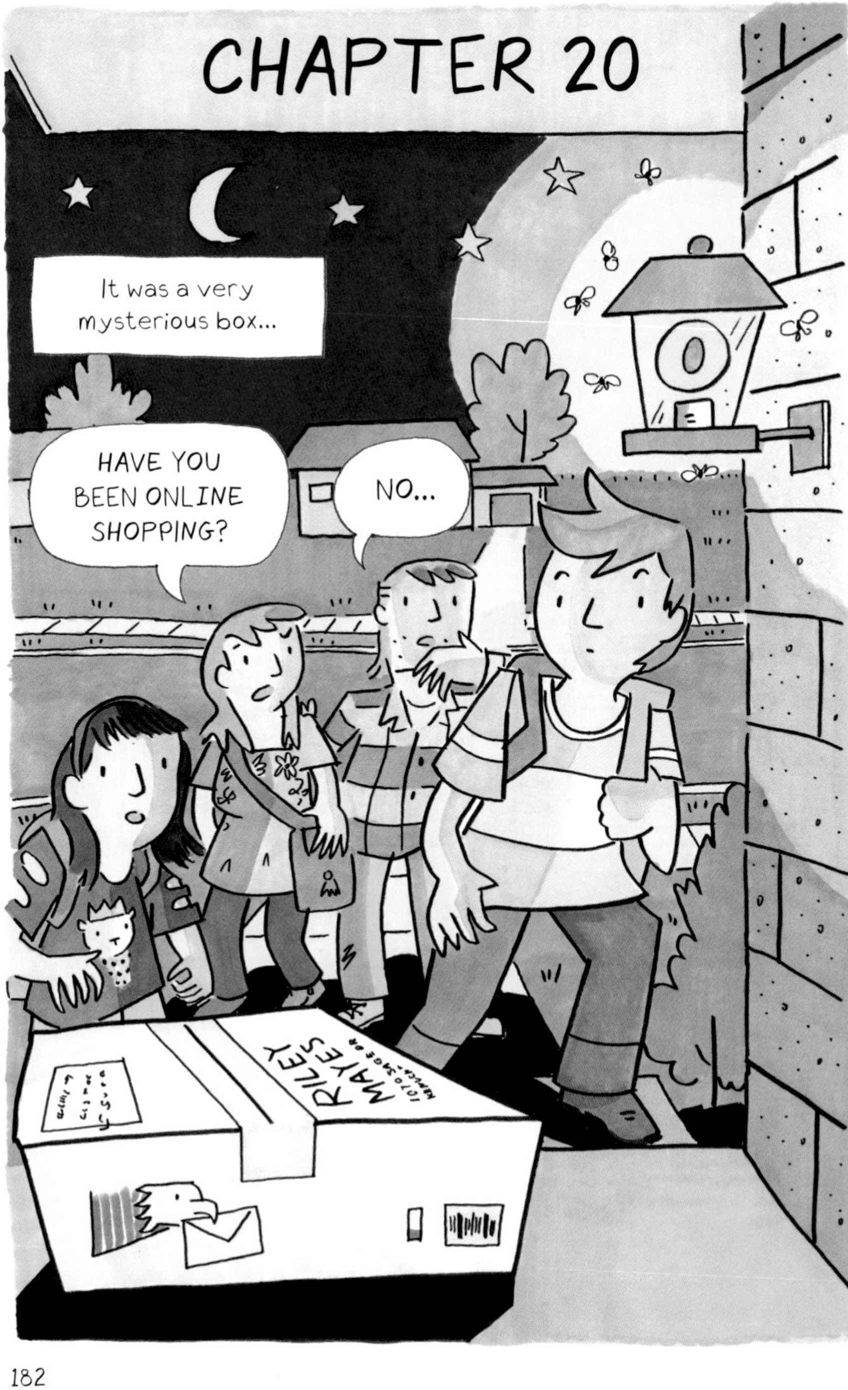
CHAPTER 20
It was a very mysterious box...
HAVE YOU BEEN ONLINE SHOPPING?
NO...
RILEY MAYES

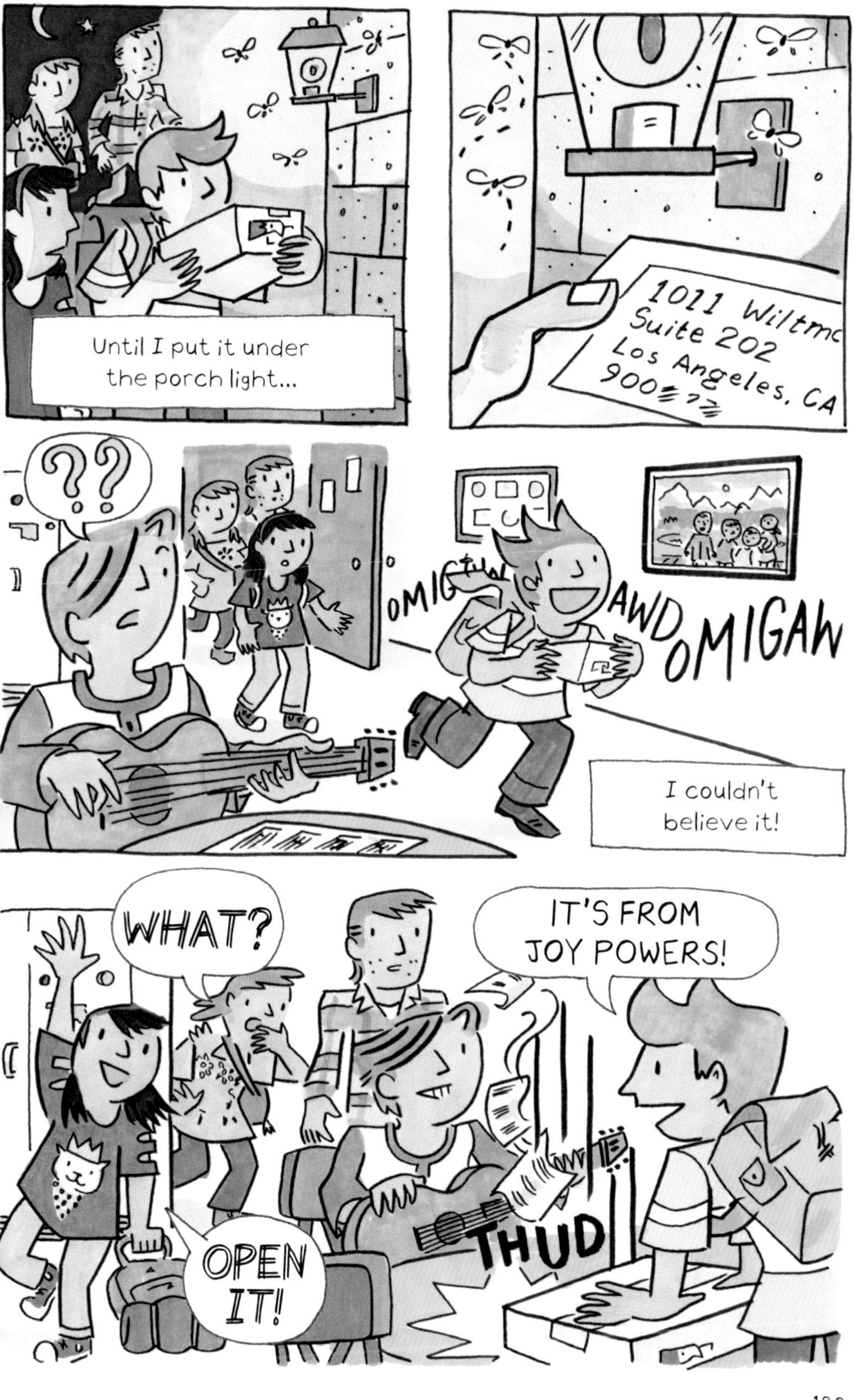
Until I put it under the porch light...
1011 Wiltmo
Suite 202
Los Angeles, CA
??
OMIGAWD OMIGAW
I couldn't believe it!
WHAT?
IT'S FROM JOY POWERS!
OPEN IT!
THUD

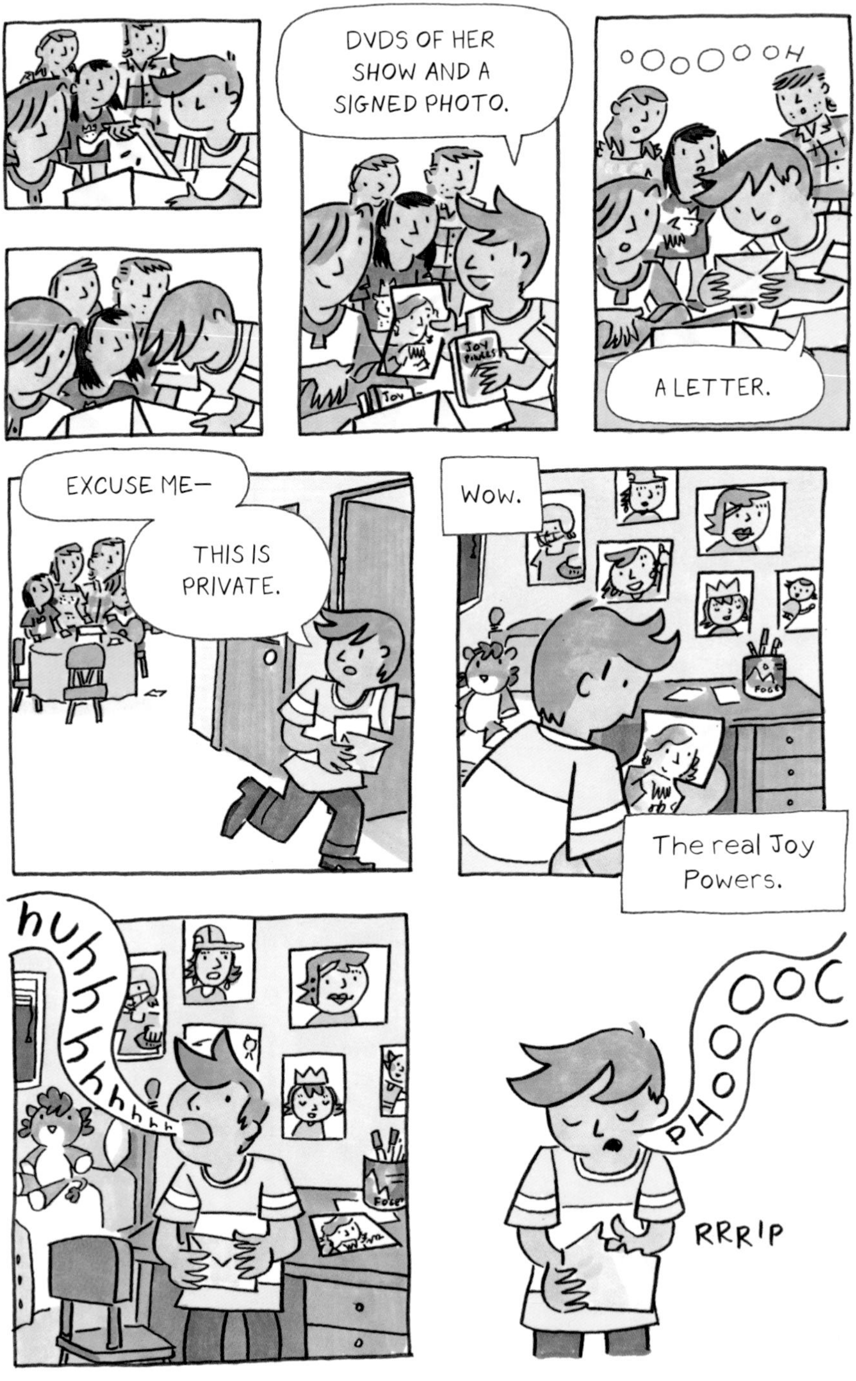
DVDS OF HER SHOW AND A SIGNED PHOTO.
JOY POWERS
JOY
OOOOOOH
A LETTER.
EXCUSE ME—
THIS IS PRIVATE.
Wow.
FOGE
The real Joy Powers.
huhhhhhhhh
FOGE
PHOOOOC
RRRIP

#2

JOY POWERS

Dear Riley,

When I got your comic, I'd truly had one of my WORST days ever. Thank you for sending me a BEST DAY EVER! I'm so sorry to hear about your worst day. Hopefully you'll get some positive energy from these DVDs, no View Tube required.

In answer to your questions:

① "WILL YOU DRAW SOMETHING SO I KNOW YOU ARE JOY POWERS AND NOT A ROBOT?"

Okay, here:

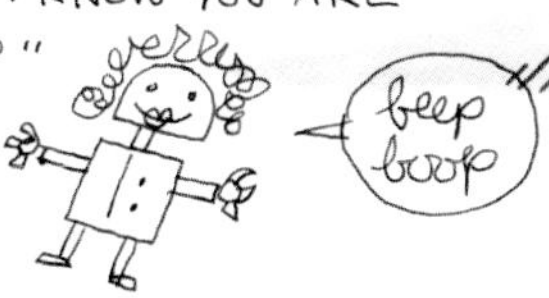
beep boop

② "DO YOU KNOW HOW AWESOME I THINK YOU ARE?" Stop.

You'll give me a big head and I'll need to buy new wigs.

③ "HAVE YOU EVER BEEN SO WEIRD YOU SCARED OFF A FRIEND?"

What do you mean by "weird"? If you mean absurd and silly, my friends all love that. Maybe you mean something else. Friends know me really well. People are scared of UNFAMILIAR things. So a friend wouldn't be scared of me. If I make a WEIRD MISTAKE I'll apologize. But if I'm being myself and someone thinks I'm "strange," they need time to get to know me better.

④ "WHAT DO YOU DO IF YOU RUN OUT OF POSITIVE ENERGY?" Well, I don't go to the MOON but I do talk to friends, write, sing songs, or do something nice for someone else. We have to get off our butts and MAKE more positive energy— Like you did for me by drawing a comic.

Riley, I can't wait to see the positive energy you make next!

Your Fan,
Joy Powers

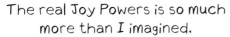
The real Joy Powers is so much more than I imagined.

KNOCK KNOCK

I get her.

I get what she said about friends.

IT'S ME!

SO? WHAT'D SHE SAY?

LOTSA STUFF.

SHE SAYS WE GOTTA MAKE POSITIVE ENERGY.

HUH?

LIKE ART AND MUSIC AND STORIES.

I KEEP READING IT OVER AND OVER.
I WISH IT DIDN'T HAVE AN END.

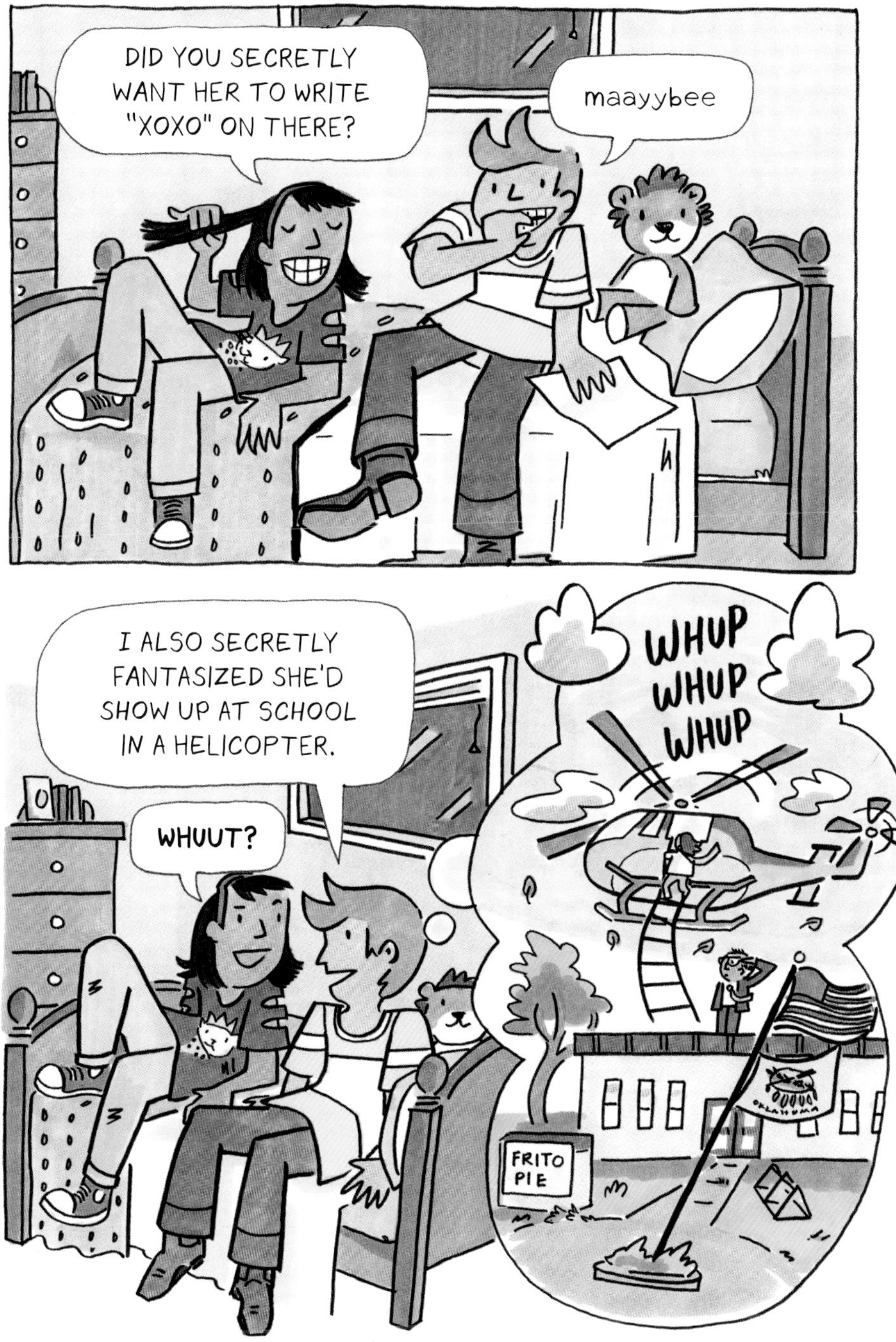
DID YOU SECRETLY WANT HER TO WRITE "XOXO" ON THERE?
maaayybee
I ALSO SECRETLY FANTASIZED SHE'D SHOW UP AT SCHOOL IN A HELICOPTER.
WHUUT?
WHUP WHUP WHUP
FRITO PIE
OKLAHOMA

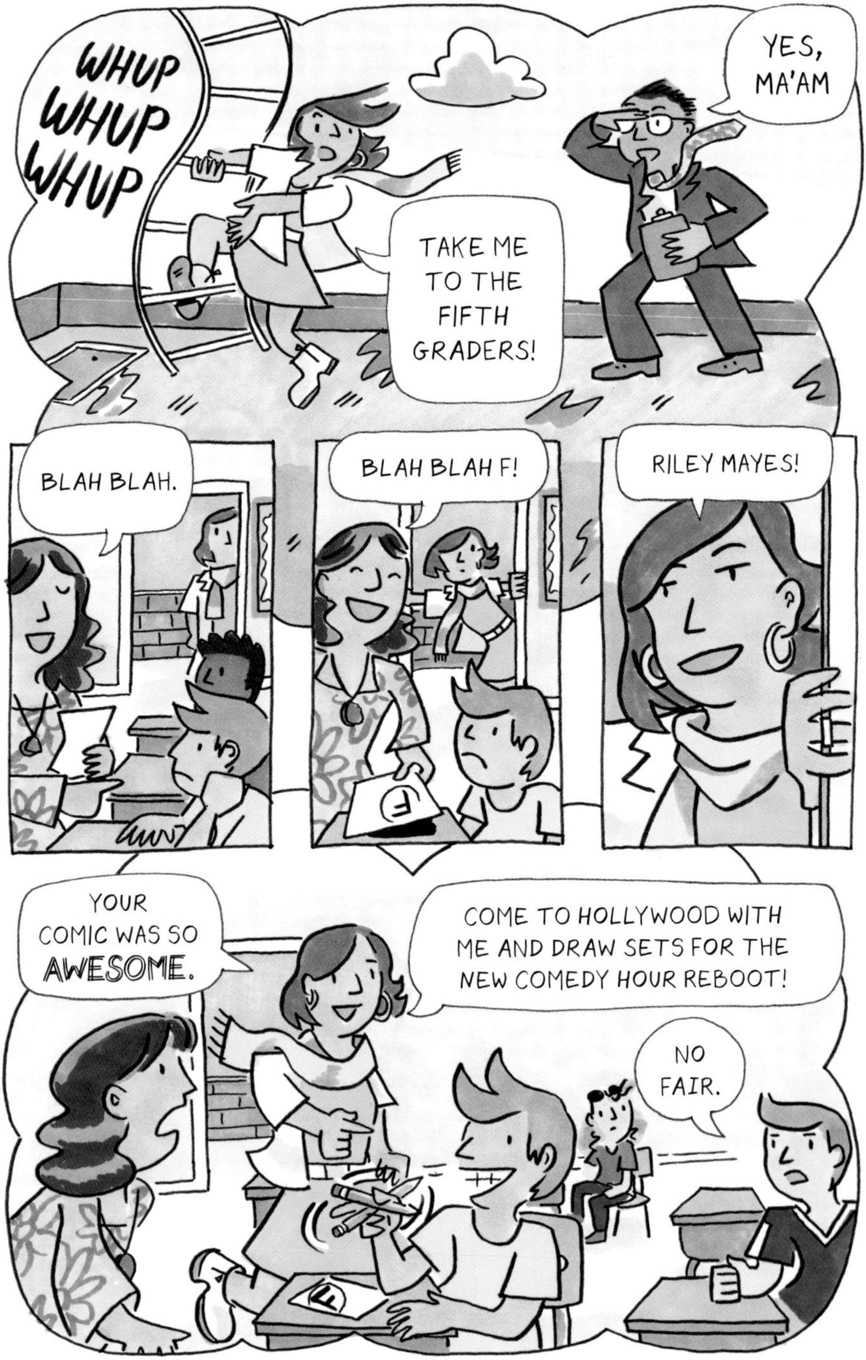
WHUP WHUP WHUP
YES, MA'AM
TAKE ME TO THE FIFTH GRADERS!
BLAH BLAH.
BLAH BLAH F!
RILEY MAYES!
YOUR COMIC WAS SO AWESOME.
COME TO HOLLYWOOD WITH ME AND DRAW SETS FOR THE NEW COMEDY HOUR REBOOT!
NO FAIR.

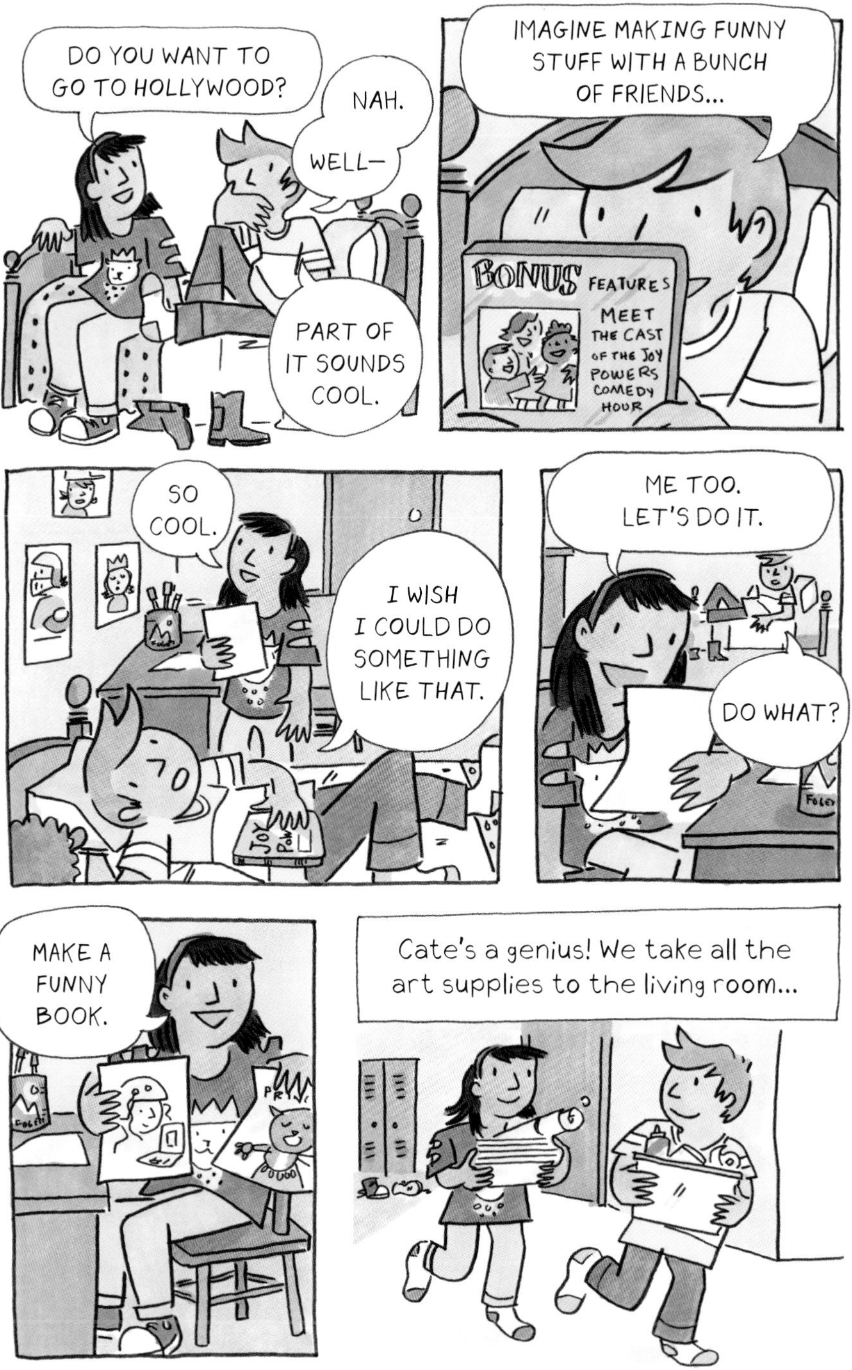
DO YOU WANT TO GO TO HOLLYWOOD?
NAH.
WELL—
PART OF IT SOUNDS COOL.
IMAGINE MAKING FUNNY STUFF WITH A BUNCH OF FRIENDS...
BONUS FEATURES
MEET THE CAST OF THE JOY POWERS COMEDY HOUR
SO COOL.
I WISH I COULD DO SOMETHING LIKE THAT.
ME TOO. LET'S DO IT.
DO WHAT?
MAKE A FUNNY BOOK.
Cate's a genius! We take all the art supplies to the living room...

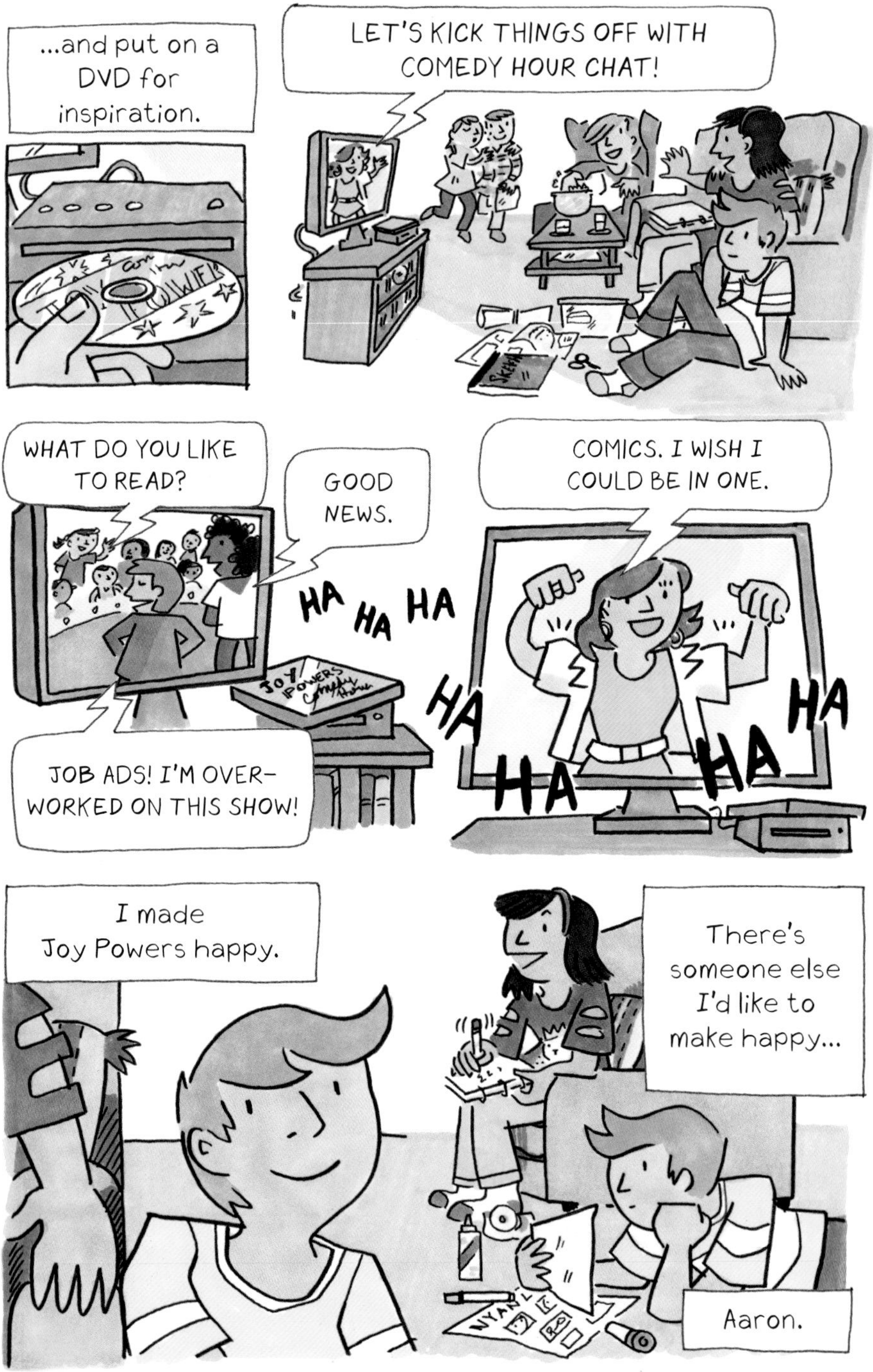
...and put on a DVD for inspiration.
LET'S KICK THINGS OFF WITH COMEDY HOUR CHAT!
WHAT DO YOU LIKE TO READ?
GOOD NEWS.
JOB ADS! I'M OVER-WORKED ON THIS SHOW!
HA HA HA
COMICS. I WISH I COULD BE IN ONE.
HA HA HA HA
I made Joy Powers happy.
There's someone else I'd like to make happy...
Aaron.

CHAPTER 21

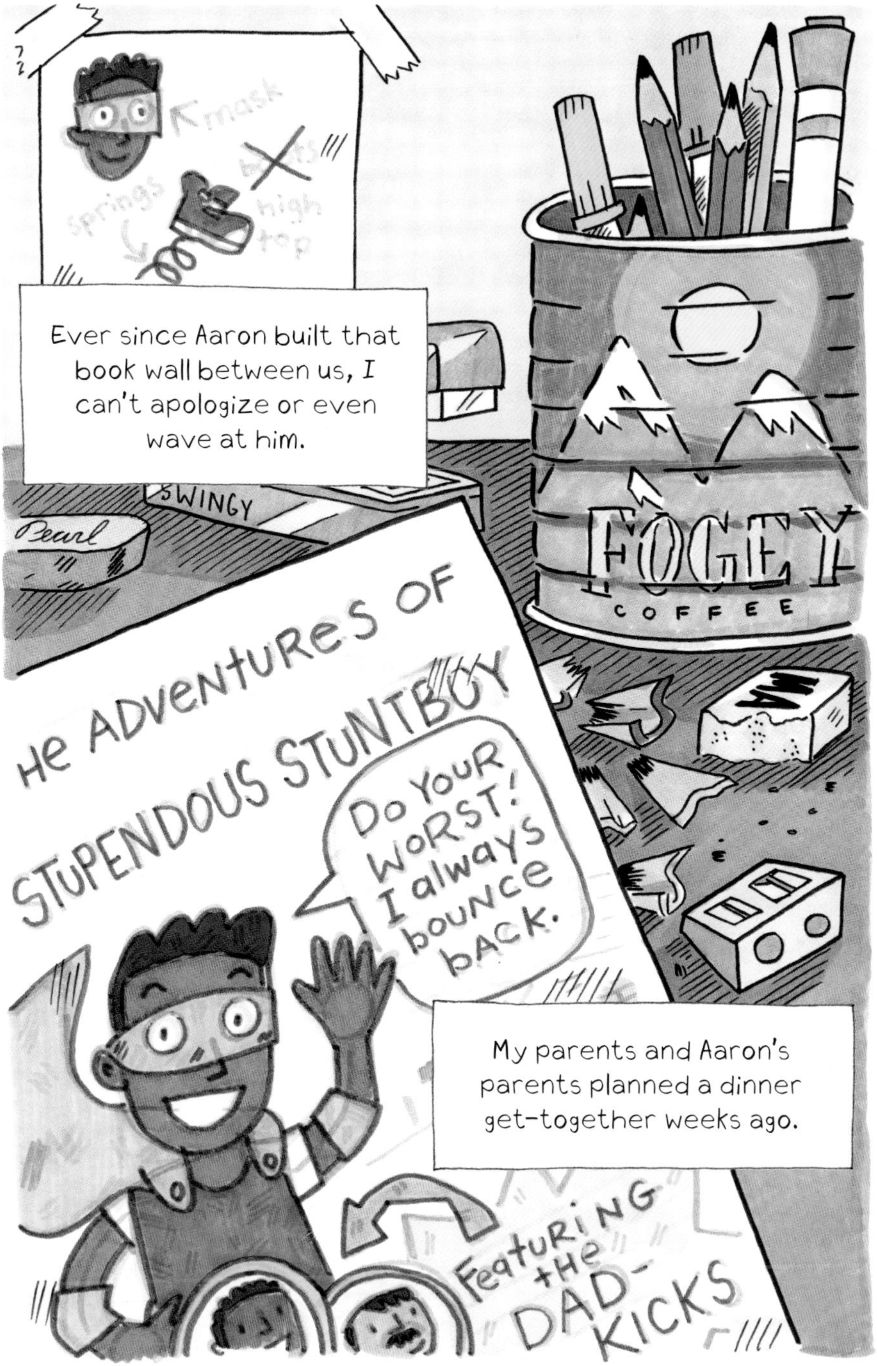

mask
springs
high top
Ever since Aaron built that book wall between us, I can't apologize or even wave at him.
SWINGY
Pearl
FOGEY
COFFEE
HE ADVENTURES OF
STUPENDOUS STUNTBOY
Do YOUR WORST! I always bounce back.
My parents and Aaron's parents planned a dinner get-together weeks ago.
Featuring the DAD-KICKS

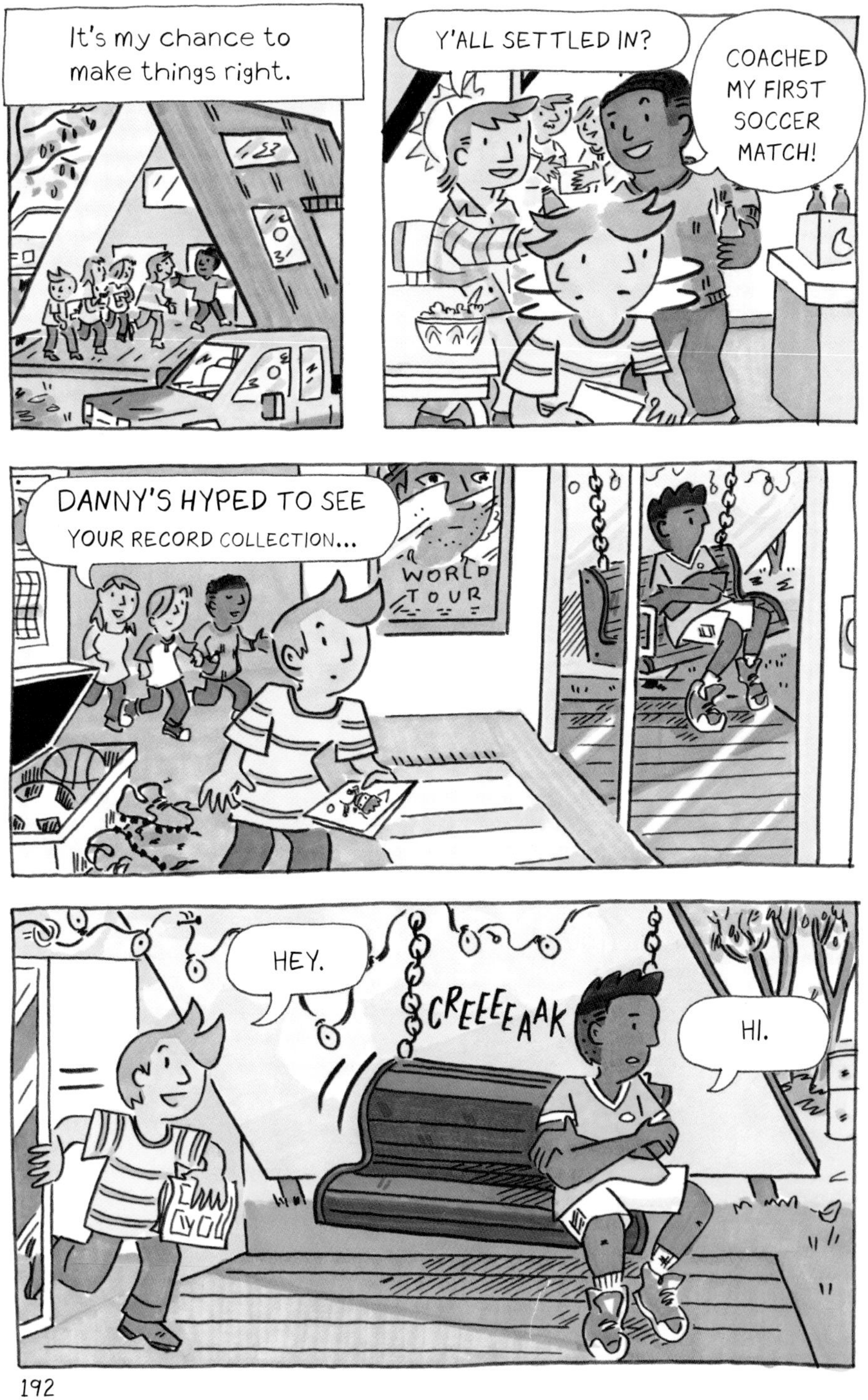
It's my chance to make things right.
Y'ALL SETTLED IN?
COACHED MY FIRST SOCCER MATCH!
DANNY'S HYPED TO SEE YOUR RECORD COLLECTION...
WORLD TOUR
HEY.
CREEEEAAK
HI.

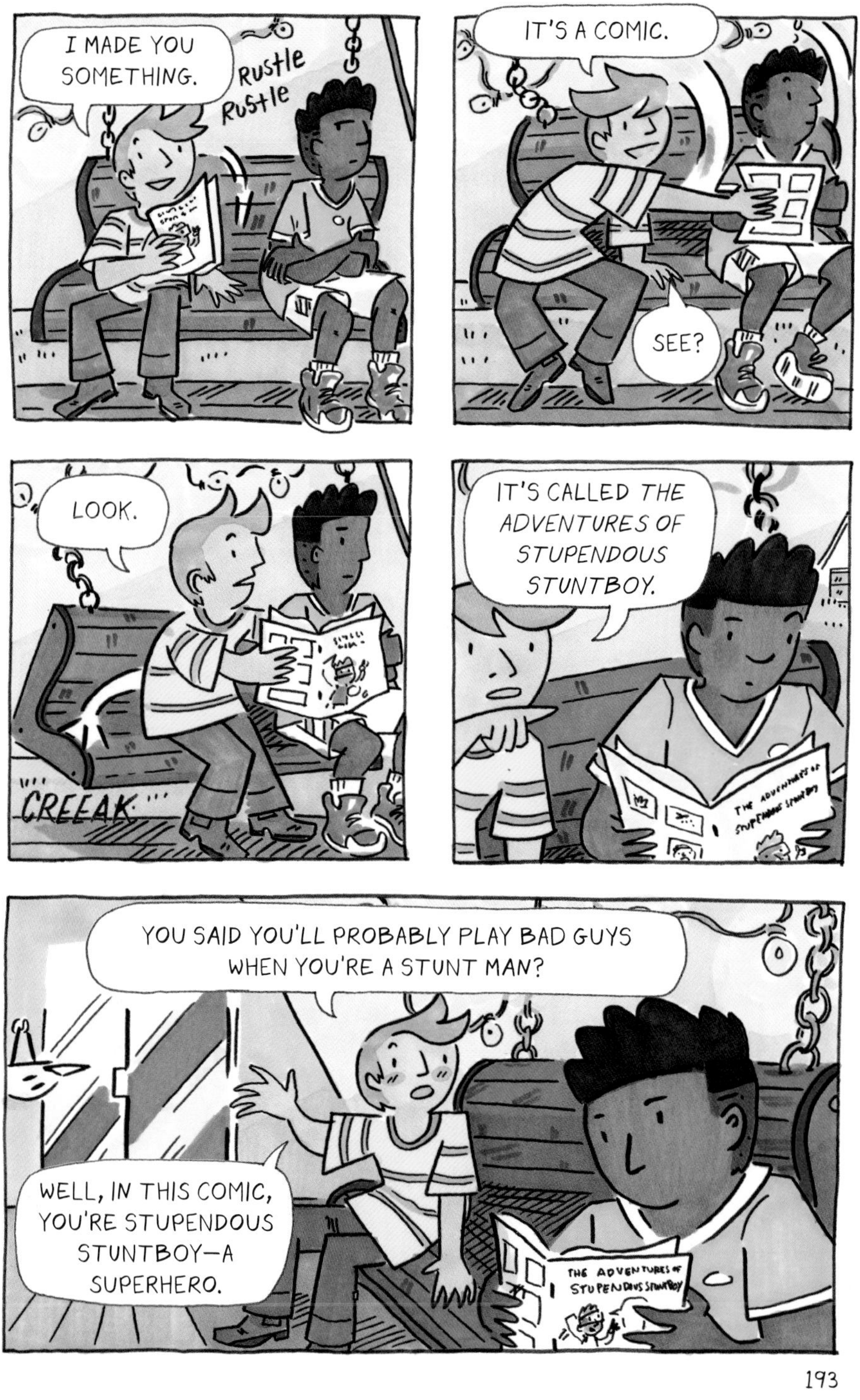
I MADE YOU SOMETHING.
Rustle Rustle
IT'S A COMIC.
SEE?
LOOK.
CREEAK
IT'S CALLED *THE ADVENTURES OF STUPENDOUS STUNTBOY.*
THE ADVENTURES OF STUPENDOUS STUNTBOY
YOU SAID YOU'LL PROBABLY PLAY BAD GUYS WHEN YOU'RE A STUNT MAN?
WELL, IN THIS COMIC, YOU'RE STUPENDOUS STUNTBOY—A SUPERHERO.
THE ADVENTURES OF STUPENDOUS STUNTBOY

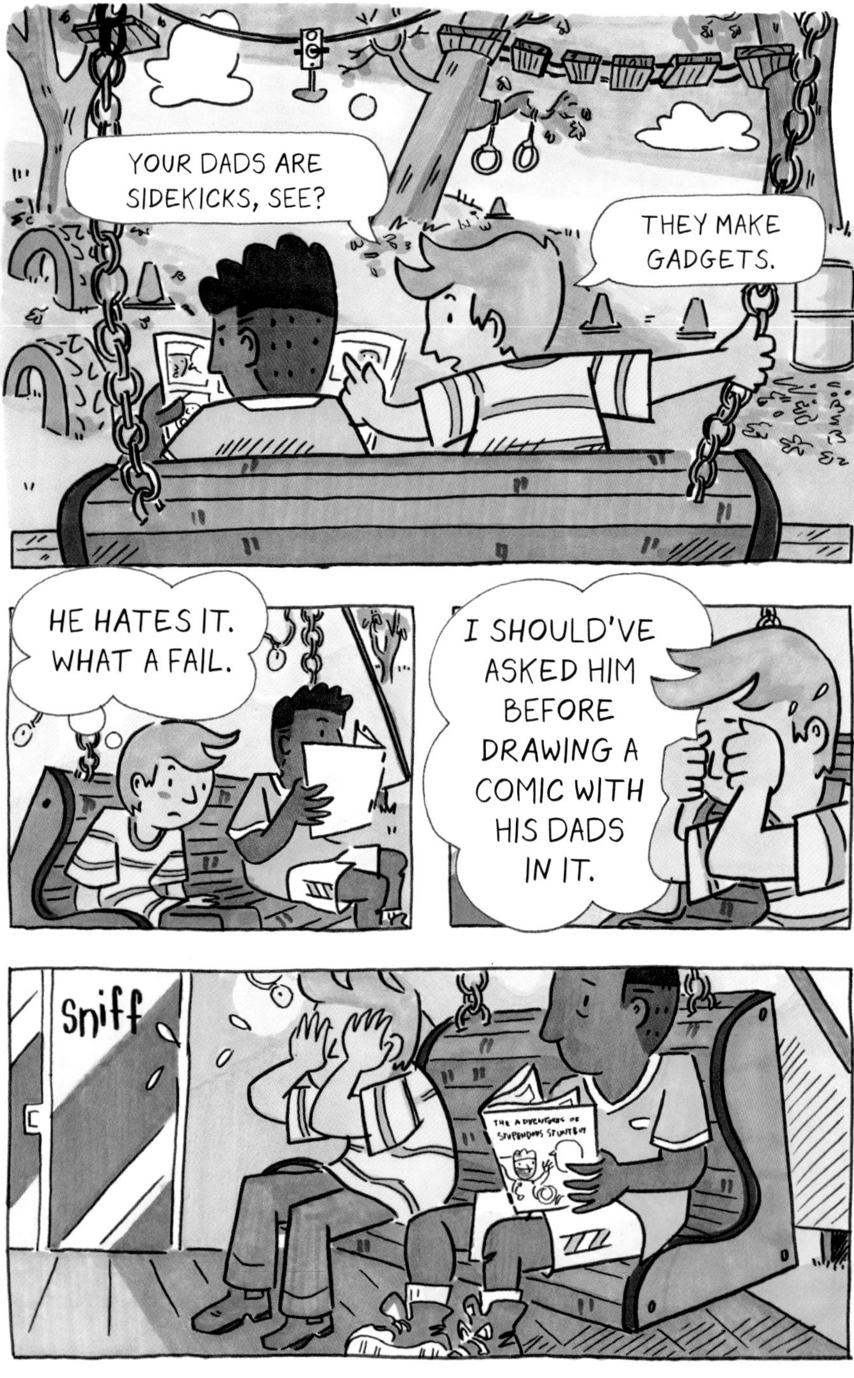
YOUR DADS ARE SIDEKICKS, SEE?
THEY MAKE GADGETS.
HE HATES IT. WHAT A FAIL.
I SHOULD'VE ASKED HIM BEFORE DRAWING A COMIC WITH HIS DADS IN IT.
Sniff
THE ADVENTURES OF STUPENDOUS STUNTBOY

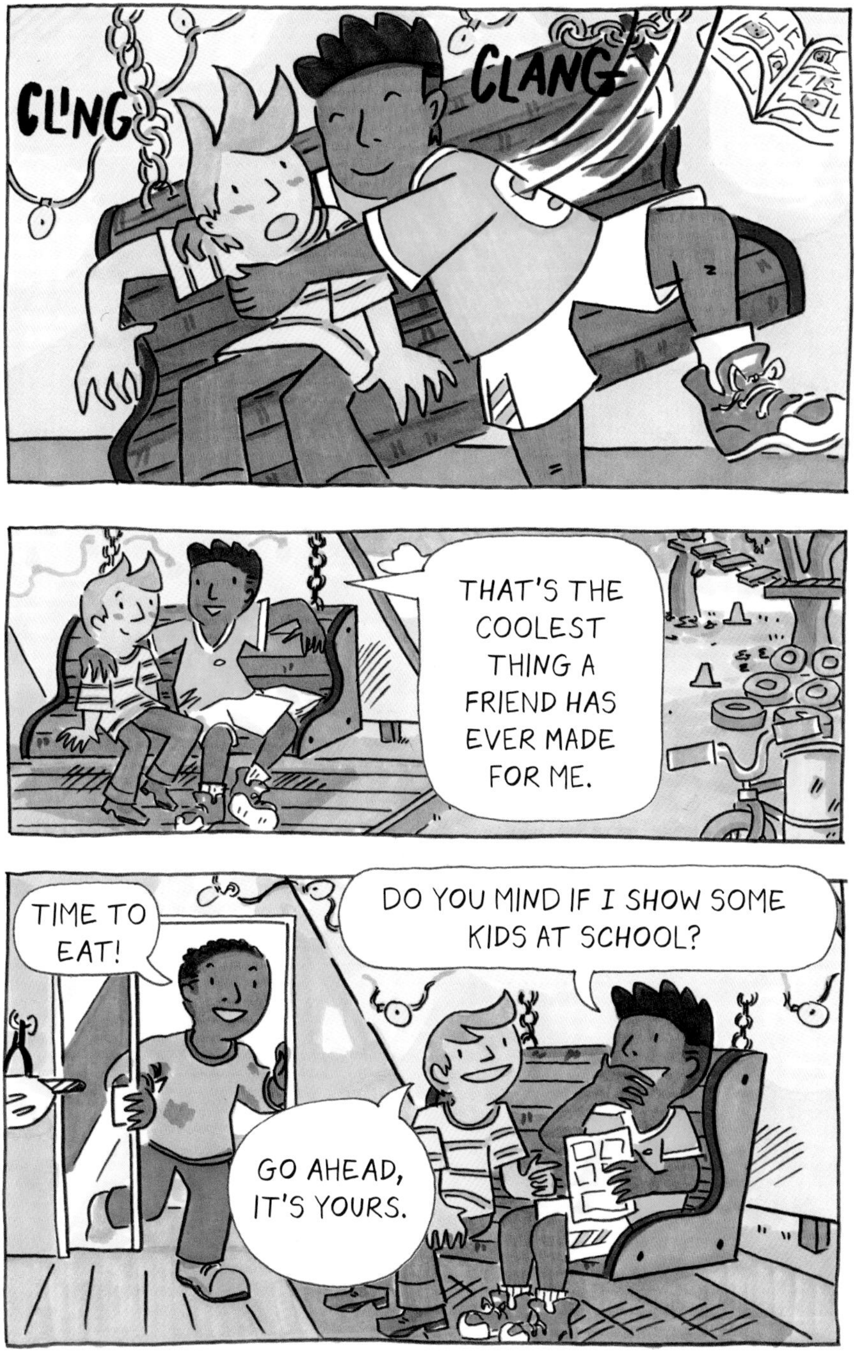
CLING
CLANG
THAT'S THE COOLEST THING A FRIEND HAS EVER MADE FOR ME.
TIME TO EAT!
DO YOU MIND IF I SHOW SOME KIDS AT SCHOOL?
GO AHEAD, IT'S YOURS.

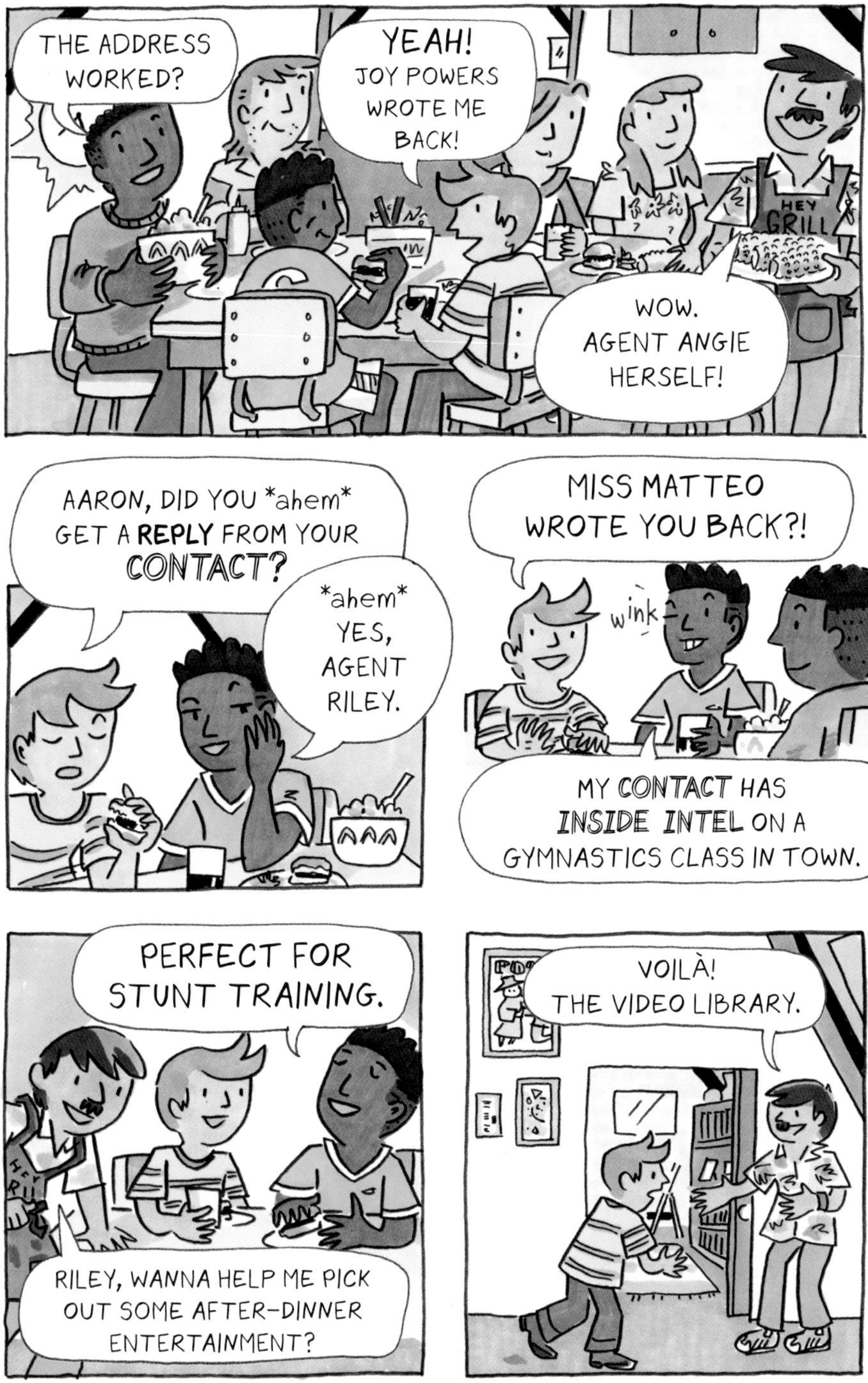
THE ADDRESS WORKED?
YEAH! JOY POWERS WROTE ME BACK!
WOW. AGENT ANGIE HERSELF!
HEY GRILL
AARON, DID YOU *ahem* GET A REPLY FROM YOUR CONTACT?
ahem YES, AGENT RILEY.
MISS MATTEO WROTE YOU BACK?!
wink
MY CONTACT HAS INSIDE INTEL ON A GYMNASTICS CLASS IN TOWN.
PERFECT FOR STUNT TRAINING.
RILEY, WANNA HELP ME PICK OUT SOME AFTER-DINNER ENTERTAINMENT?
VOILÀ! THE VIDEO LIBRARY.

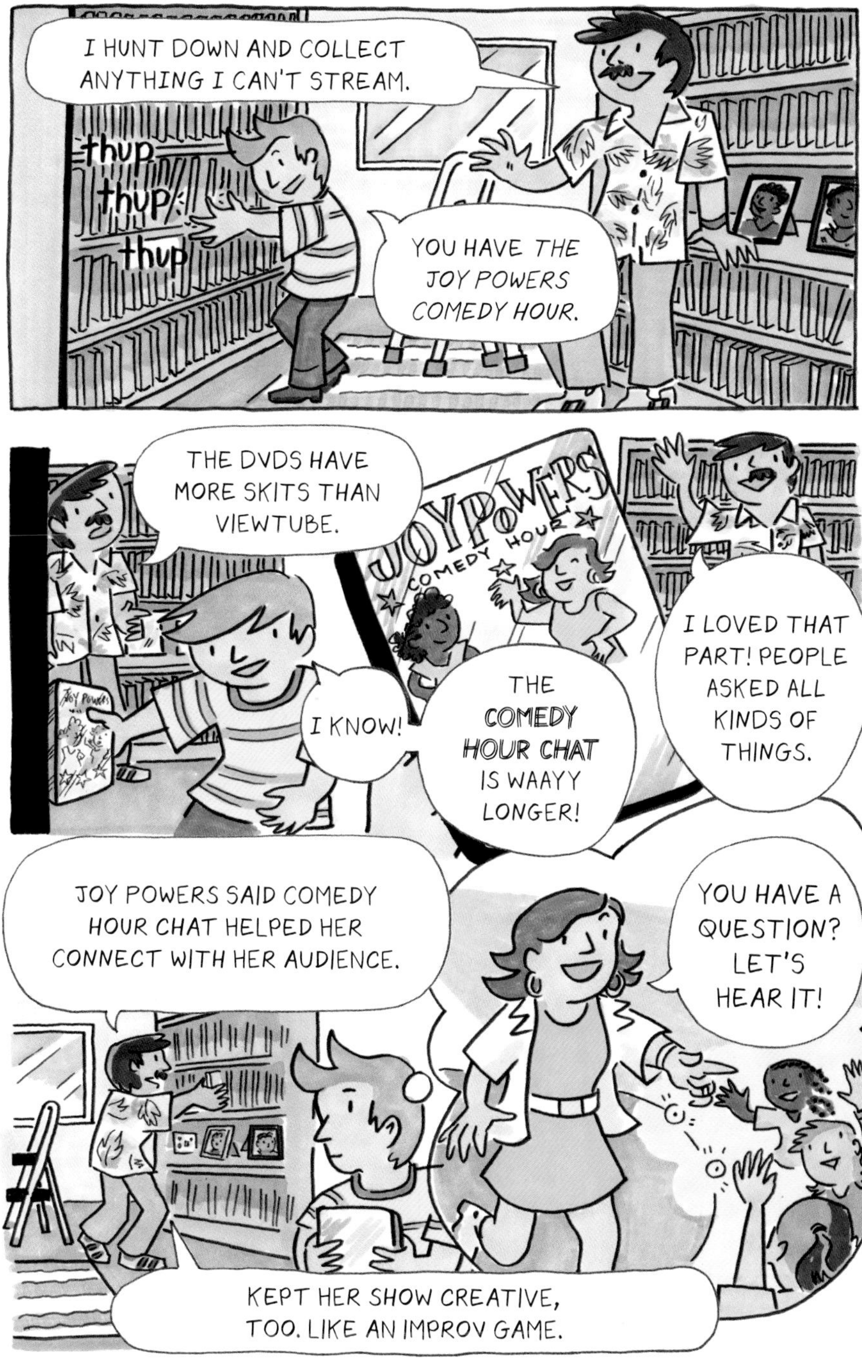
I HUNT DOWN AND COLLECT ANYTHING I CAN'T STREAM.
thup
thup
thup
YOU HAVE *THE JOY POWERS COMEDY HOUR.*
THE DVDS HAVE MORE SKITS THAN VIEWTUBE.
JOY POWERS COMEDY HOUR
I KNOW!
THE **COMEDY HOUR CHAT** IS WAAYY LONGER!
I LOVED THAT PART! PEOPLE ASKED ALL KINDS OF THINGS.
JOY POWERS SAID COMEDY HOUR CHAT HELPED HER CONNECT WITH HER AUDIENCE.
YOU HAVE A QUESTION? LET'S HEAR IT!
KEPT HER SHOW CREATIVE, TOO. LIKE AN IMPROV GAME.

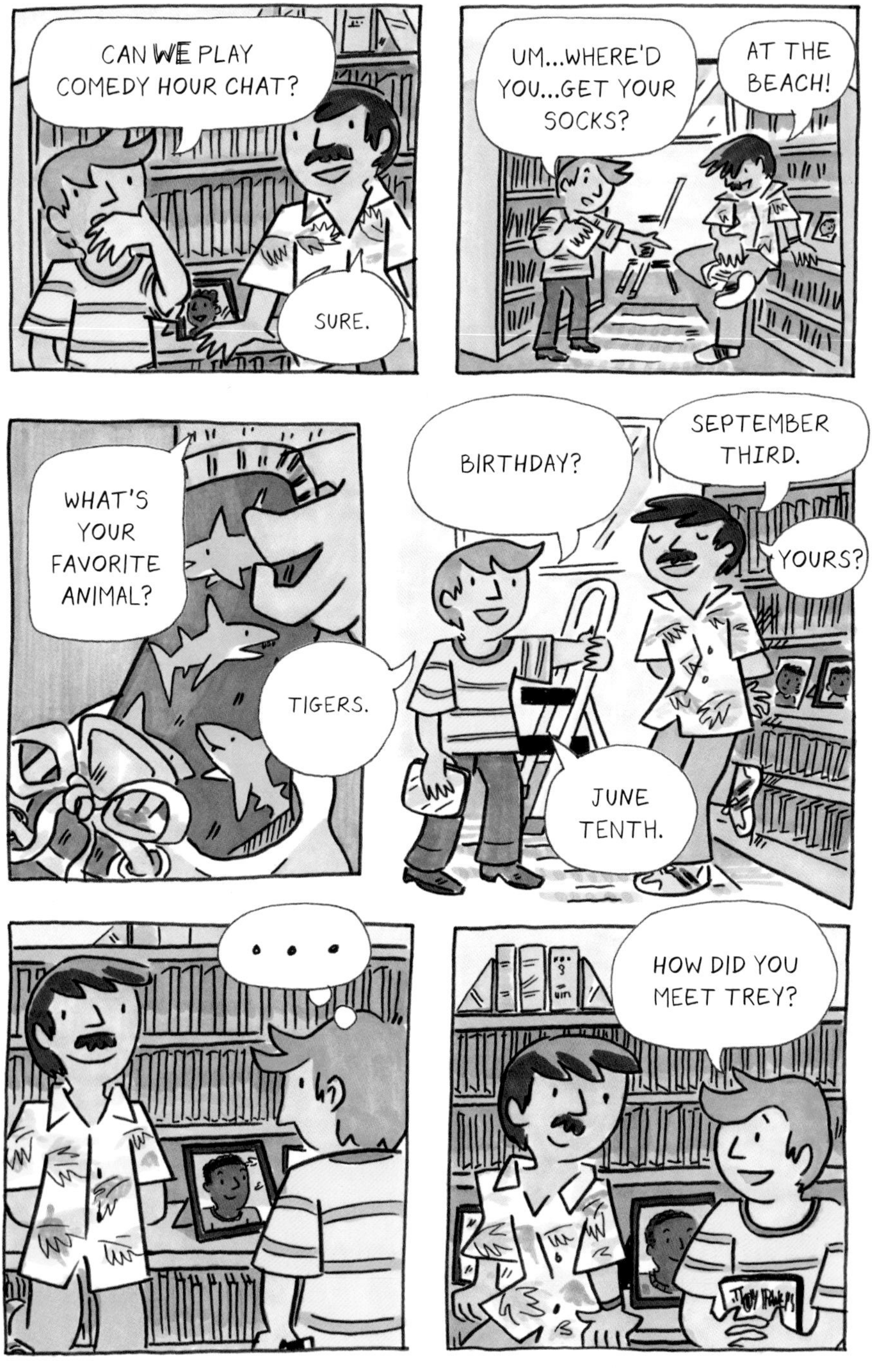
CAN WE PLAY COMEDY HOUR CHAT?
SURE.
UM...WHERE'D YOU...GET YOUR SOCKS?
AT THE BEACH!
WHAT'S YOUR FAVORITE ANIMAL?
TIGERS.
BIRTHDAY?
SEPTEMBER THIRD.
YOURS?
JUNE TENTH.
. . .
HOW DID YOU MEET TREY?

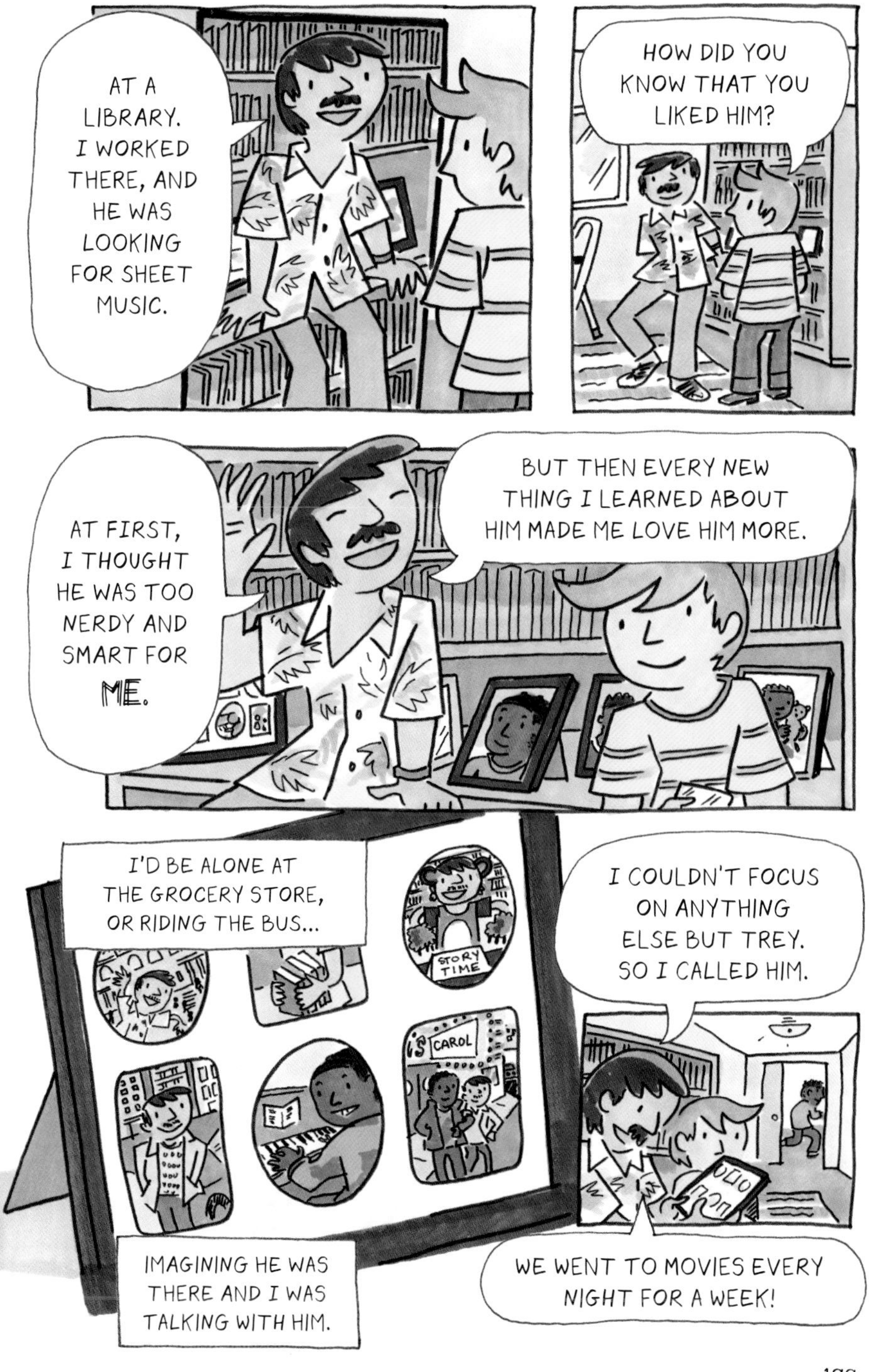
AT A LIBRARY. I WORKED THERE, AND HE WAS LOOKING FOR SHEET MUSIC.
HOW DID YOU KNOW THAT YOU LIKED HIM?
AT FIRST, I THOUGHT HE WAS TOO NERDY AND SMART FOR ME.
BUT THEN EVERY NEW THING I LEARNED ABOUT HIM MADE ME LOVE HIM MORE.
I'D BE ALONE AT THE GROCERY STORE, OR RIDING THE BUS...
STORY TIME
CAROL
IMAGINING HE WAS THERE AND I WAS TALKING WITH HIM.
I COULDN'T FOCUS ON ANYTHING ELSE BUT TREY. SO I CALLED HIM.
WE WENT TO MOVIES EVERY NIGHT FOR A WEEK!

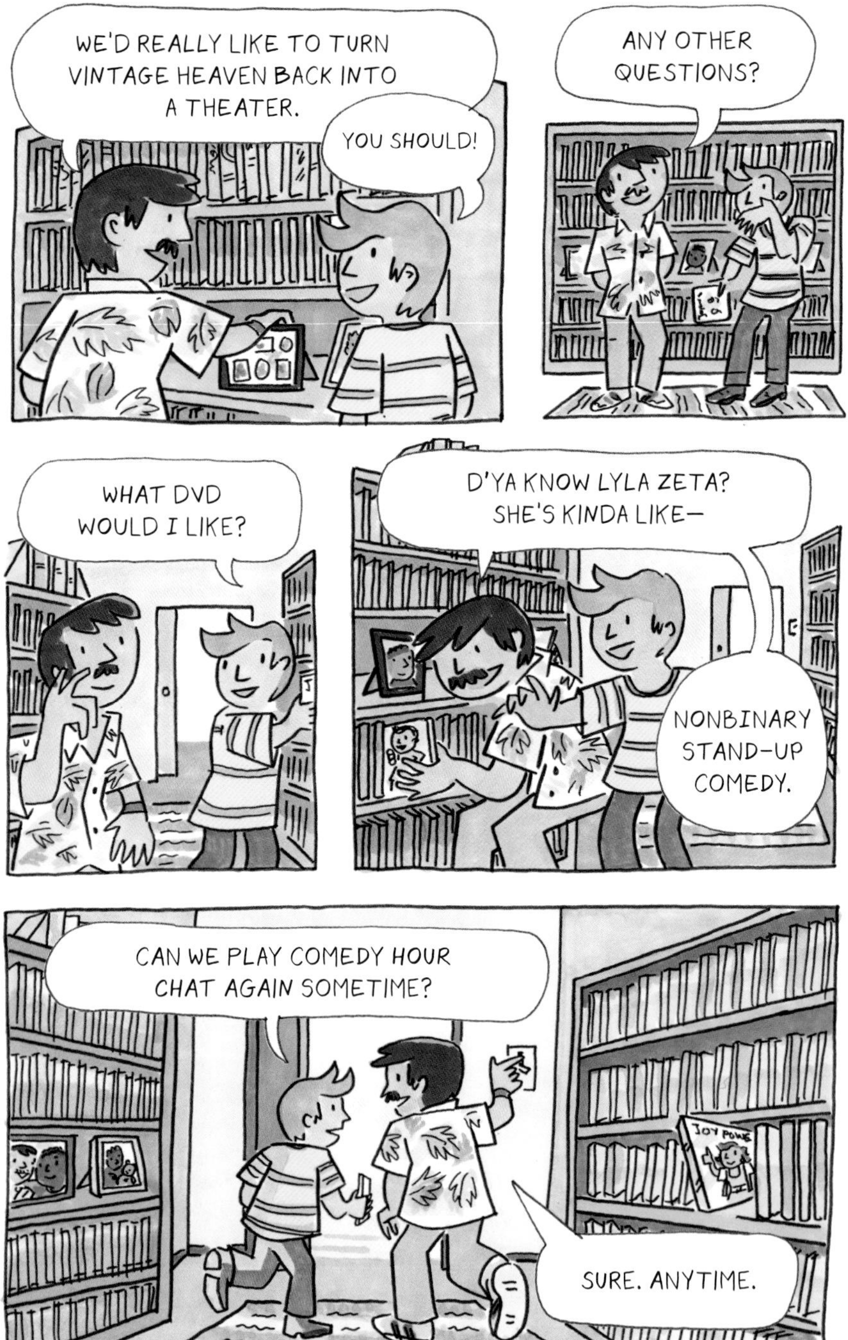
WE'D REALLY LIKE TO TURN VINTAGE HEAVEN BACK INTO A THEATER.
YOU SHOULD!
ANY OTHER QUESTIONS?
WHAT DVD WOULD I LIKE?
D'YA KNOW LYLA ZETA? SHE'S KINDA LIKE—
NONBINARY STAND-UP COMEDY.
CAN WE PLAY COMEDY HOUR CHAT AGAIN SOMETIME?
SURE. ANYTIME.

CHAPTER 22

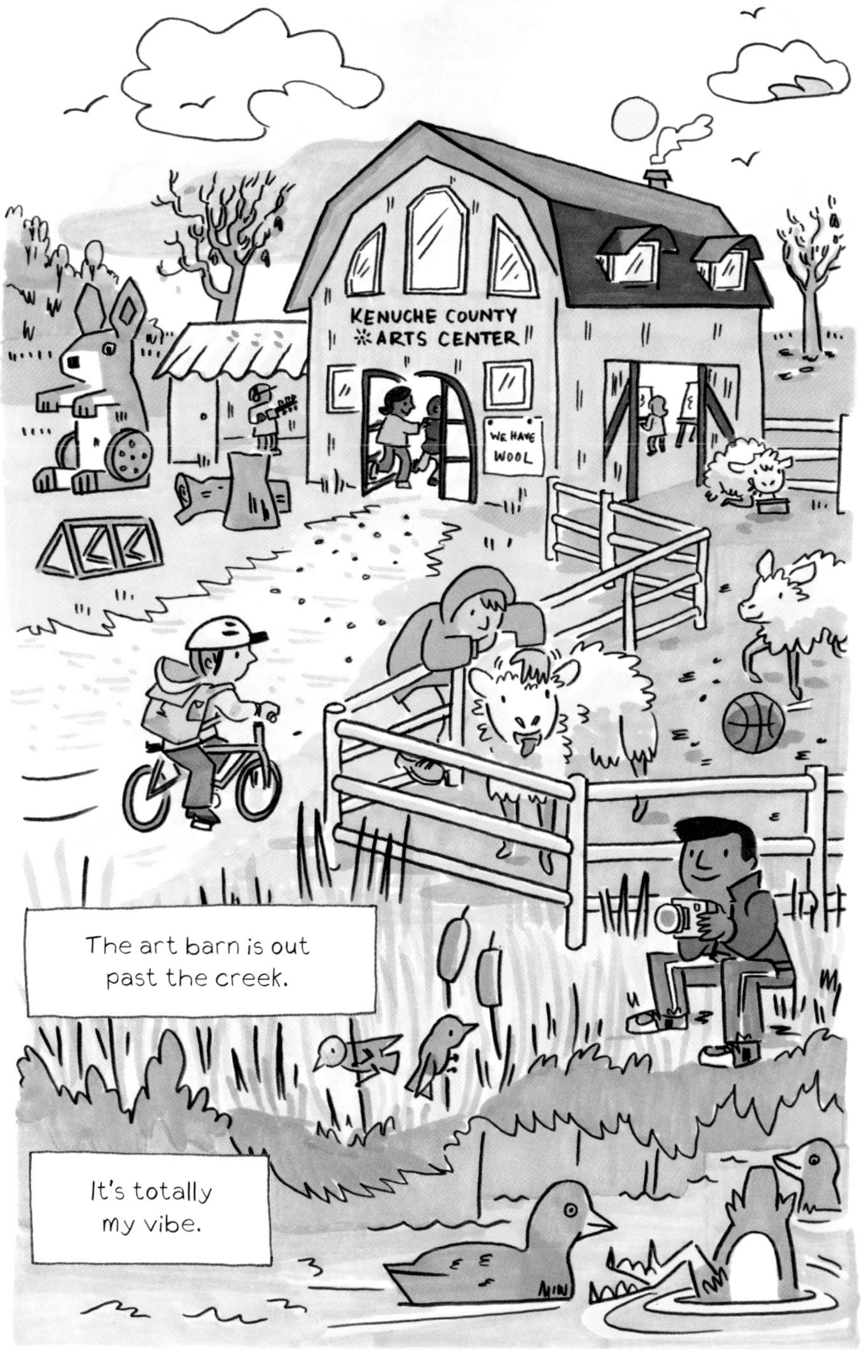

KENUCHE COUNTY
ARTS CENTER
WE HAVE WOOL
The art barn is out past the creek.
It's totally my vibe.

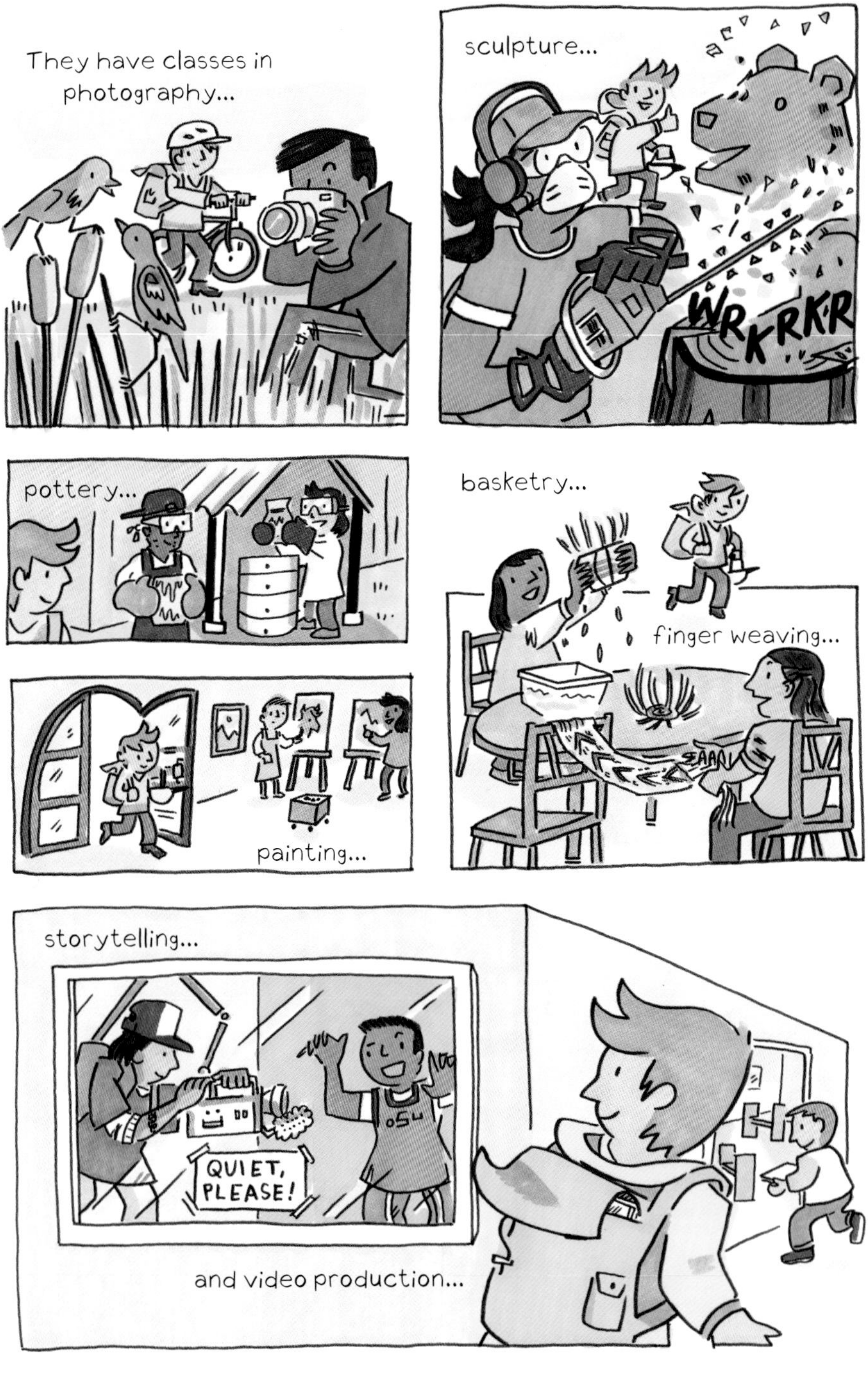
They have classes in photography...
sculpture...
WRKRKR
pottery...
basketry...
finger weaving...
painting...
storytelling...
QUIET, PLEASE!
OSU
and video production...

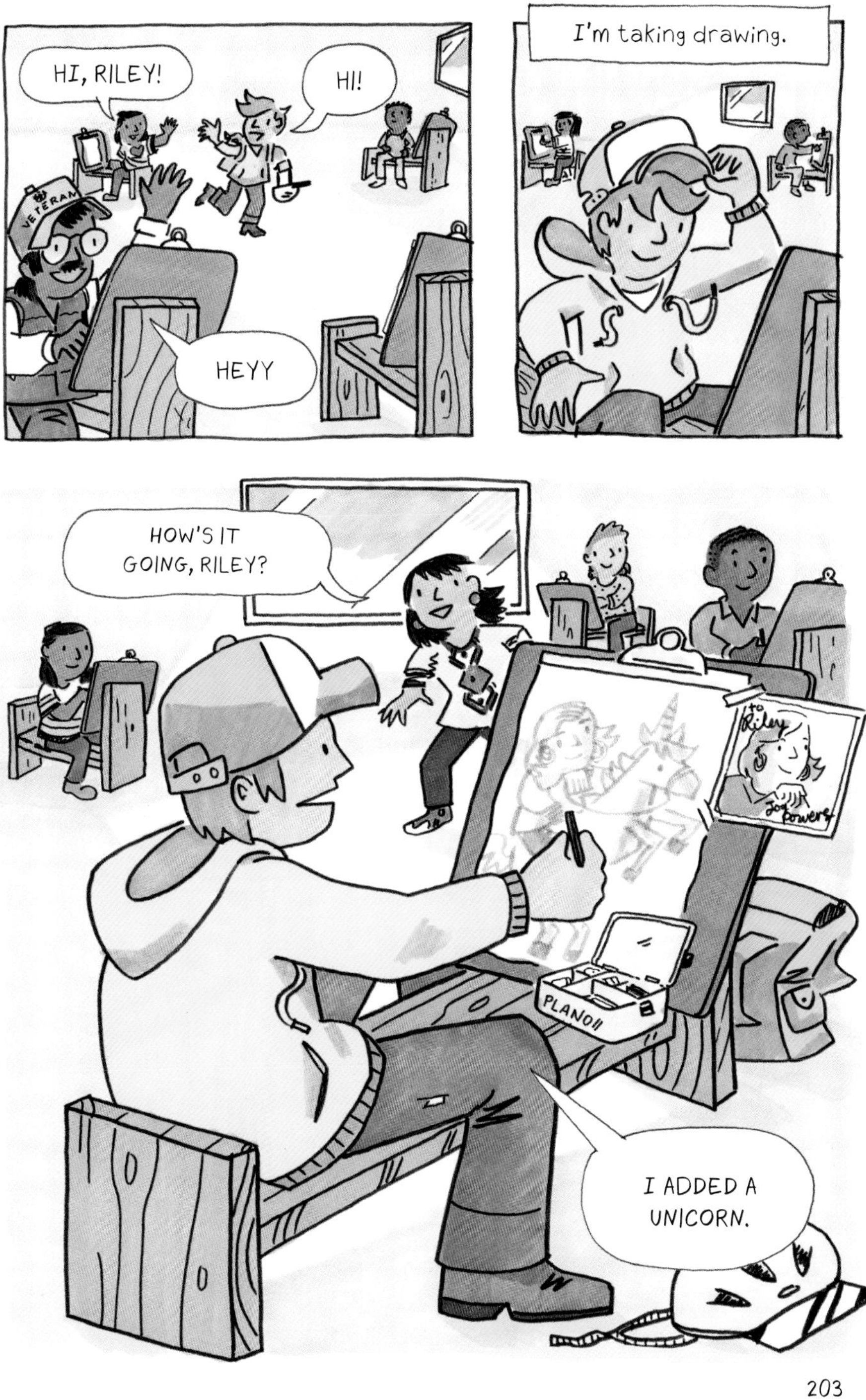
HI, RILEY!
HI!
VETERAN
HEYY
I'm taking drawing.
HOW'S IT GOING, RILEY?
to Riley
Joy Powers
PLANO
I ADDED A UNICORN.

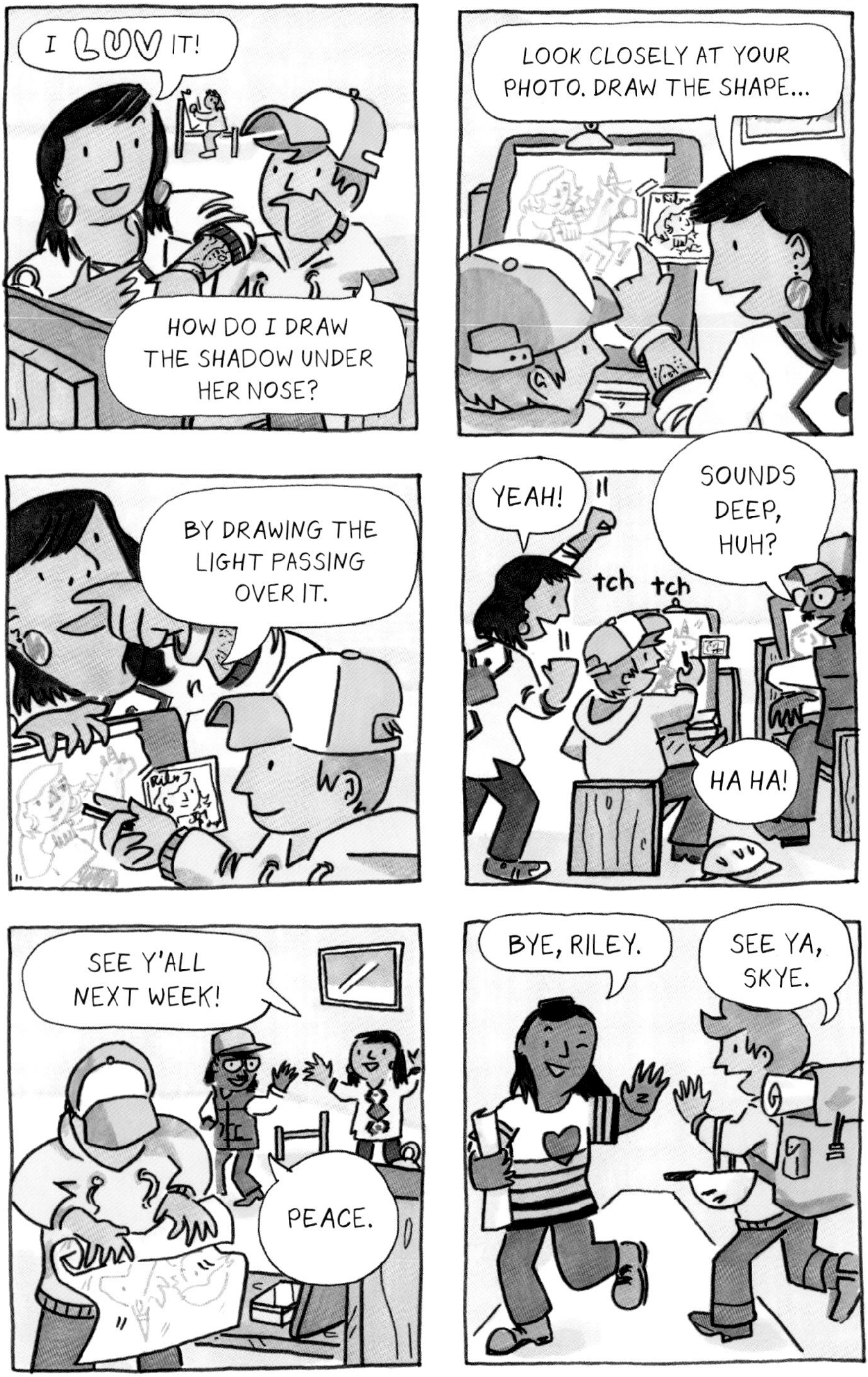
I LUV IT!
HOW DO I DRAW THE SHADOW UNDER HER NOSE?
LOOK CLOSELY AT YOUR PHOTO. DRAW THE SHAPE...
BY DRAWING THE LIGHT PASSING OVER IT.
YEAH!
SOUNDS DEEP, HUH?
tch tch
HA HA!
SEE Y'ALL NEXT WEEK!
PEACE.
BYE, RILEY.
SEE YA, SKYE.

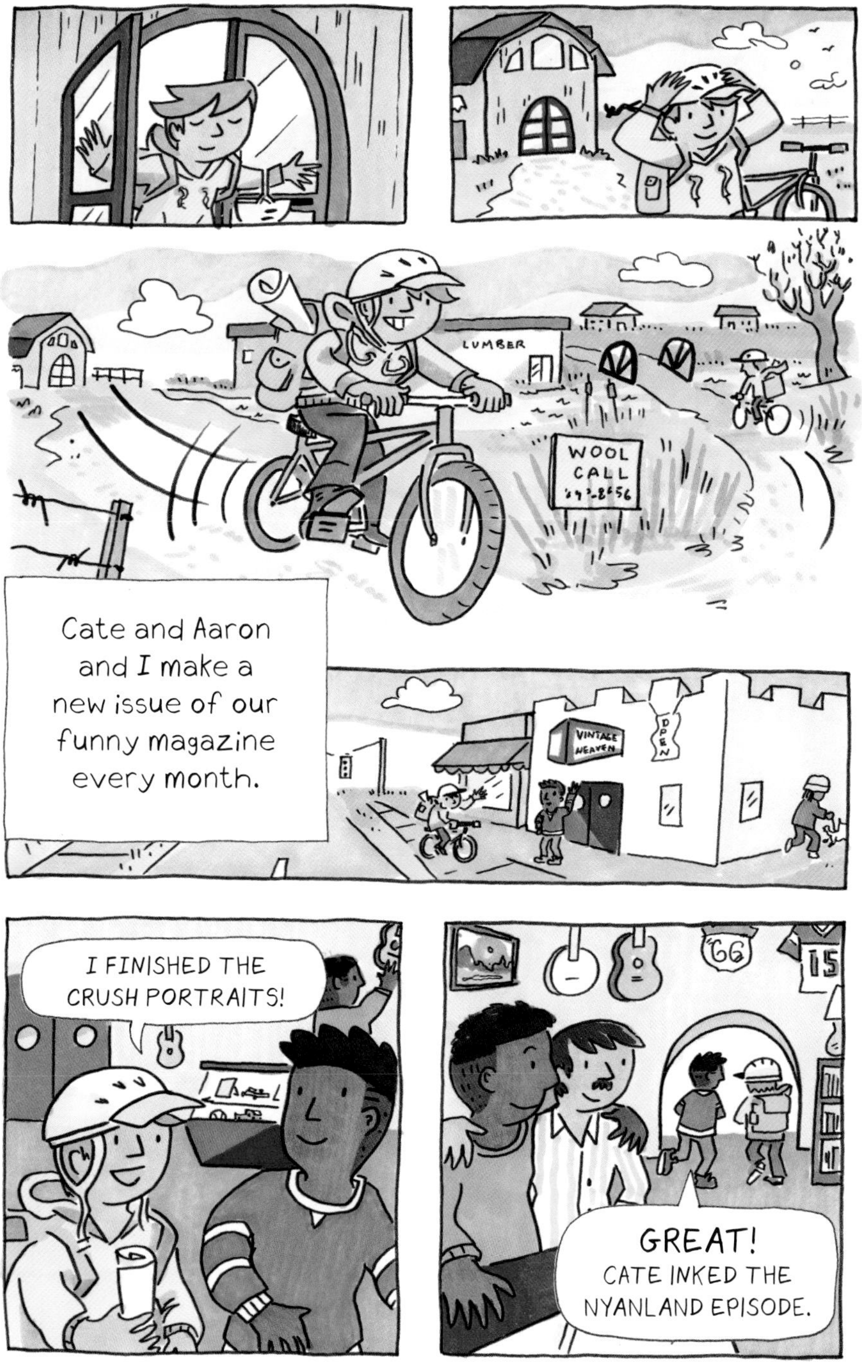
LUMBER
WOOL CALL
Cate and Aaron and I make a new issue of our funny magazine every month.
VINTAGE HEAVEN
OPEN
I FINISHED THE CRUSH PORTRAITS!
66
15
GREAT! CATE INKED THE NYANLAND EPISODE.

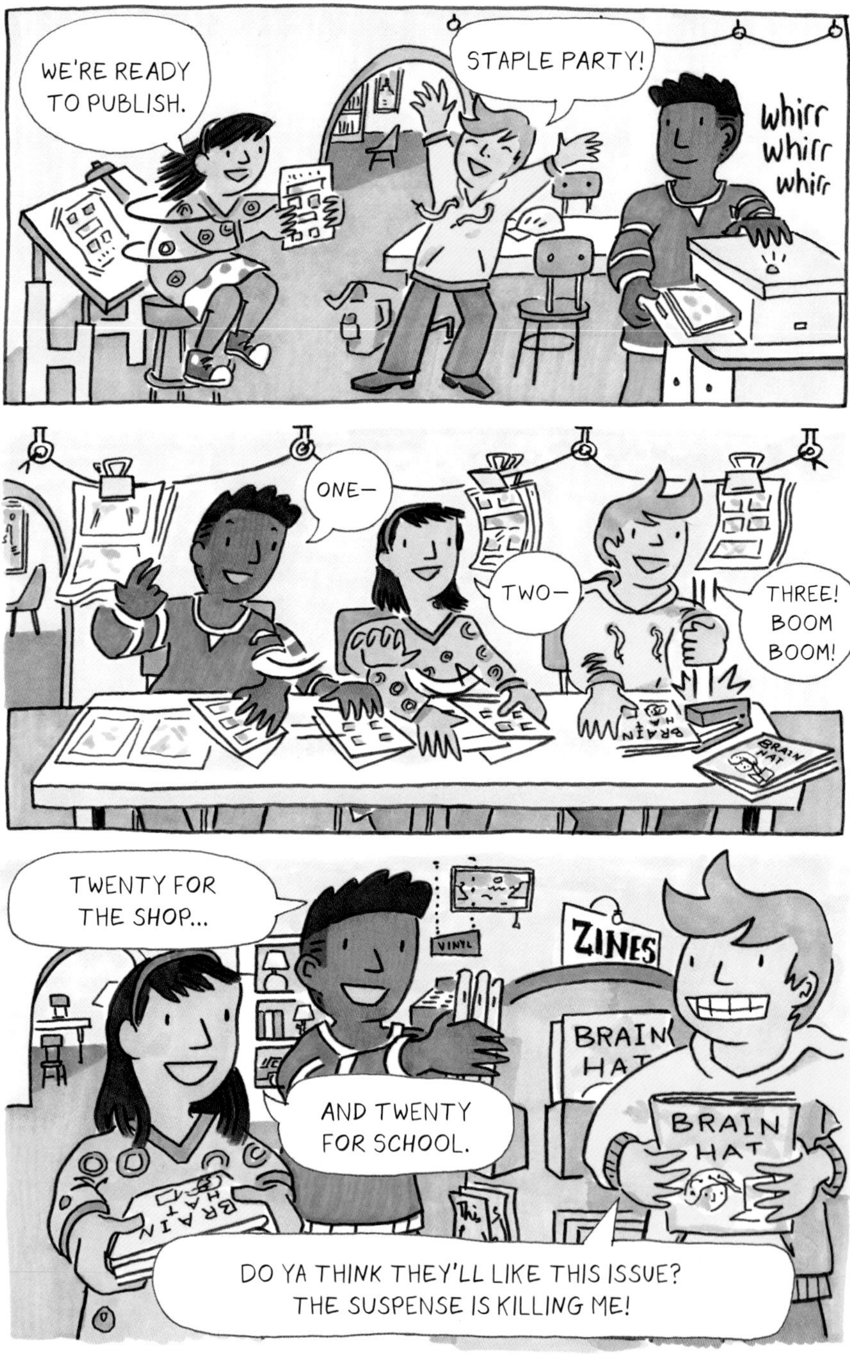
WE'RE READY TO PUBLISH.
STAPLE PARTY!
whirr whirr whirr
ONE—
TWO—
THREE! BOOM BOOM!
BRAIN HAT
TWENTY FOR THE SHOP...
VINYL
ZINES
BRAIN HAT
AND TWENTY FOR SCHOOL.
BRAIN HAT
DO YA THINK THEY'LL LIKE THIS ISSUE? THE SUSPENSE IS KILLING ME!

CHAPTER 23

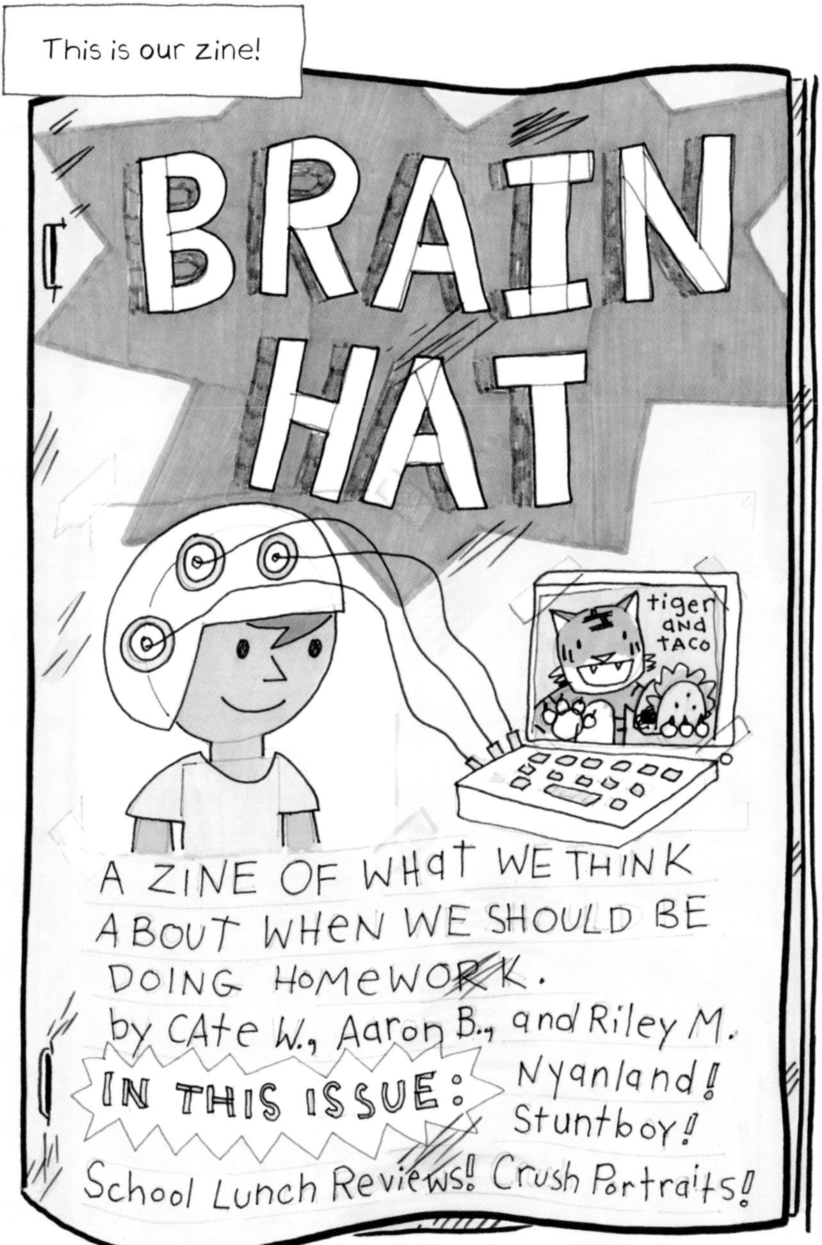
This is our zine!
BRAIN HAT
tiger and TACO
A ZINE OF WHAT WE THINK ABOUT WHEN WE SHOULD BE DOING HOMEWORK.
by CATe W., Aaron B., and Riley M.
IN THIS ISSUE: Nyanland! Stuntboy!
School Lunch Reviews! Crush Portraits!

NYANLAND: COUNTRIES OF CATS

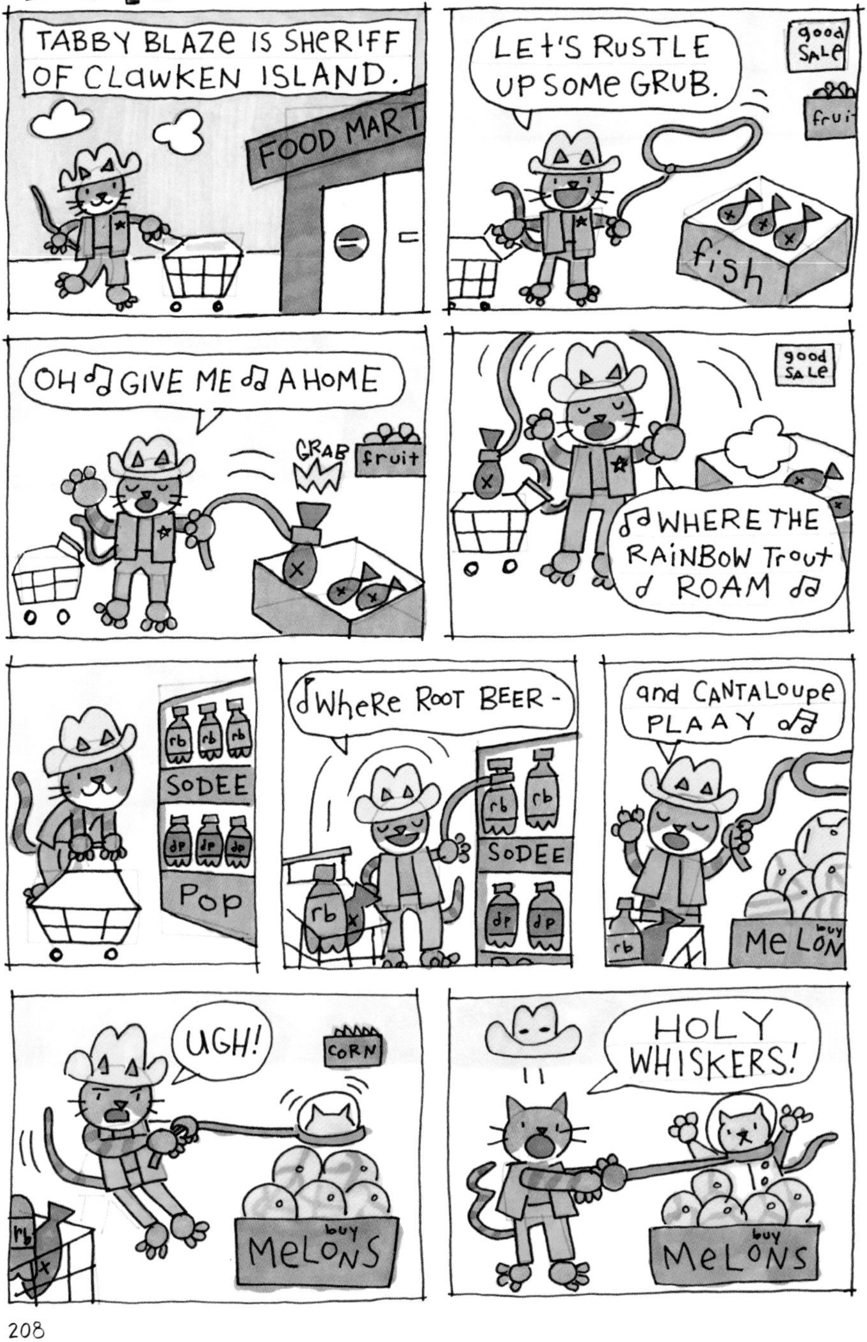
TABBY BLAZE IS SHERIFF OF CLAWKEN ISLAND.
FOOD MART
LET'S RUSTLE UP SOME GRUB.
good SALE
fruit
fish
OH ♫ GIVE ME ♫ A HOME
GRAB
fruit
good SALE
♫ WHERE THE RAINBOW Trout ♩ ROAM ♫
rb
SODEE
dp
Pop
♩ Where ROOT BEER -
rb
SODEE
dp
and CANTALOUPE PLAAY ♫
buy
MELON
UGH!
CORN
rb
buy
MELONS
HOLY WHISKERS!
buy
MELONS

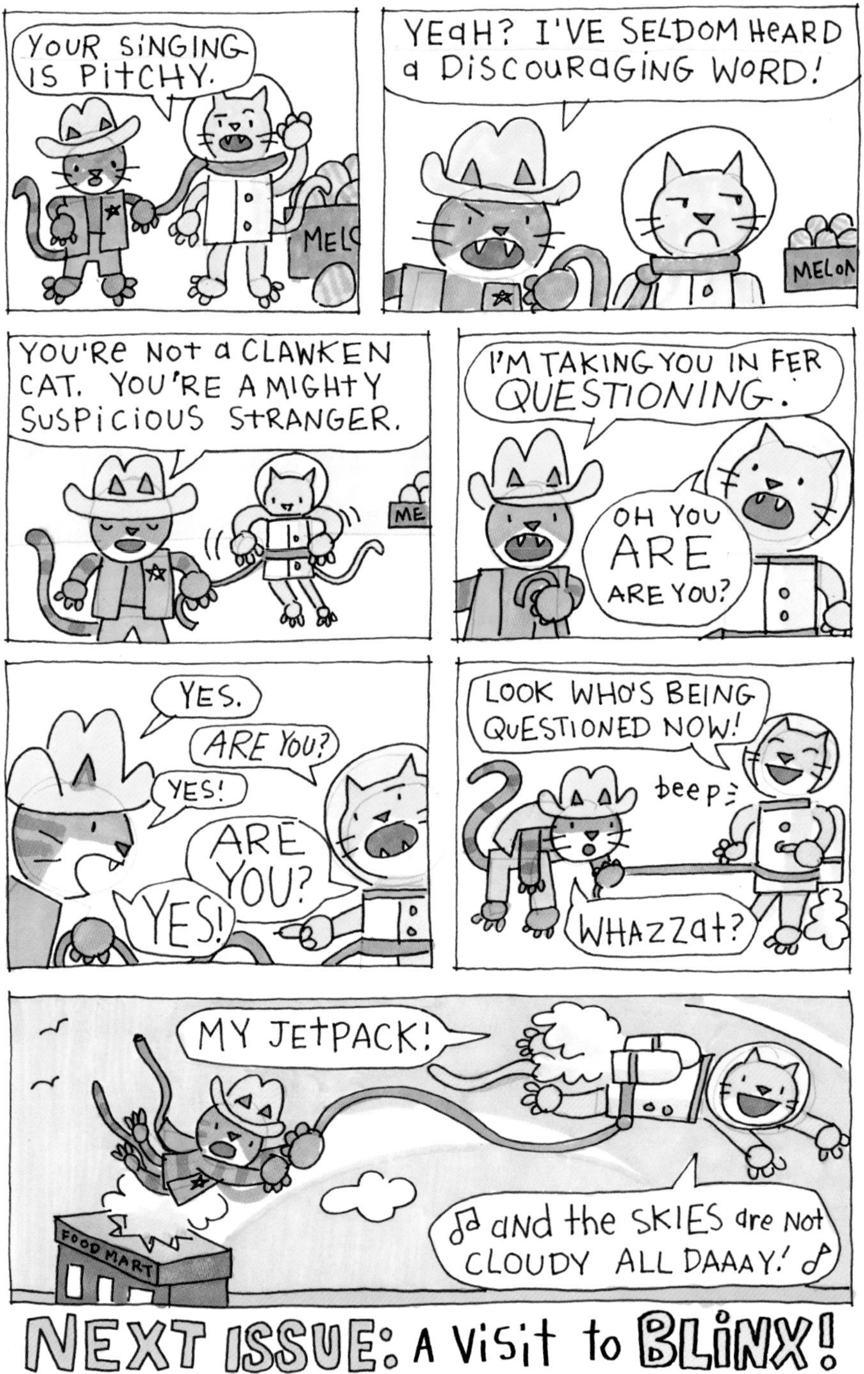
YOUR SINGING IS PITCHY.
MELO
YEAH? I'VE SELDOM HEARD A DISCOURAGING WORD!
MELON
YOU'RE NOT A CLAWKEN CAT. YOU'RE A MIGHTY SUSPICIOUS STRANGER.
ME
I'M TAKING YOU IN FER QUESTIONING.
OH YOU ARE ARE YOU?
YES.
ARE YOU?
YES!
ARE YOU?
YES!
LOOK WHO'S BEING QUESTIONED NOW!
beep
WHAZZAT?
MY JETPACK!
FOOD MART
AND THE SKIES ARE NOT CLOUDY ALL DAAAY!

NEXT ISSUE: A Visit to BLINX!

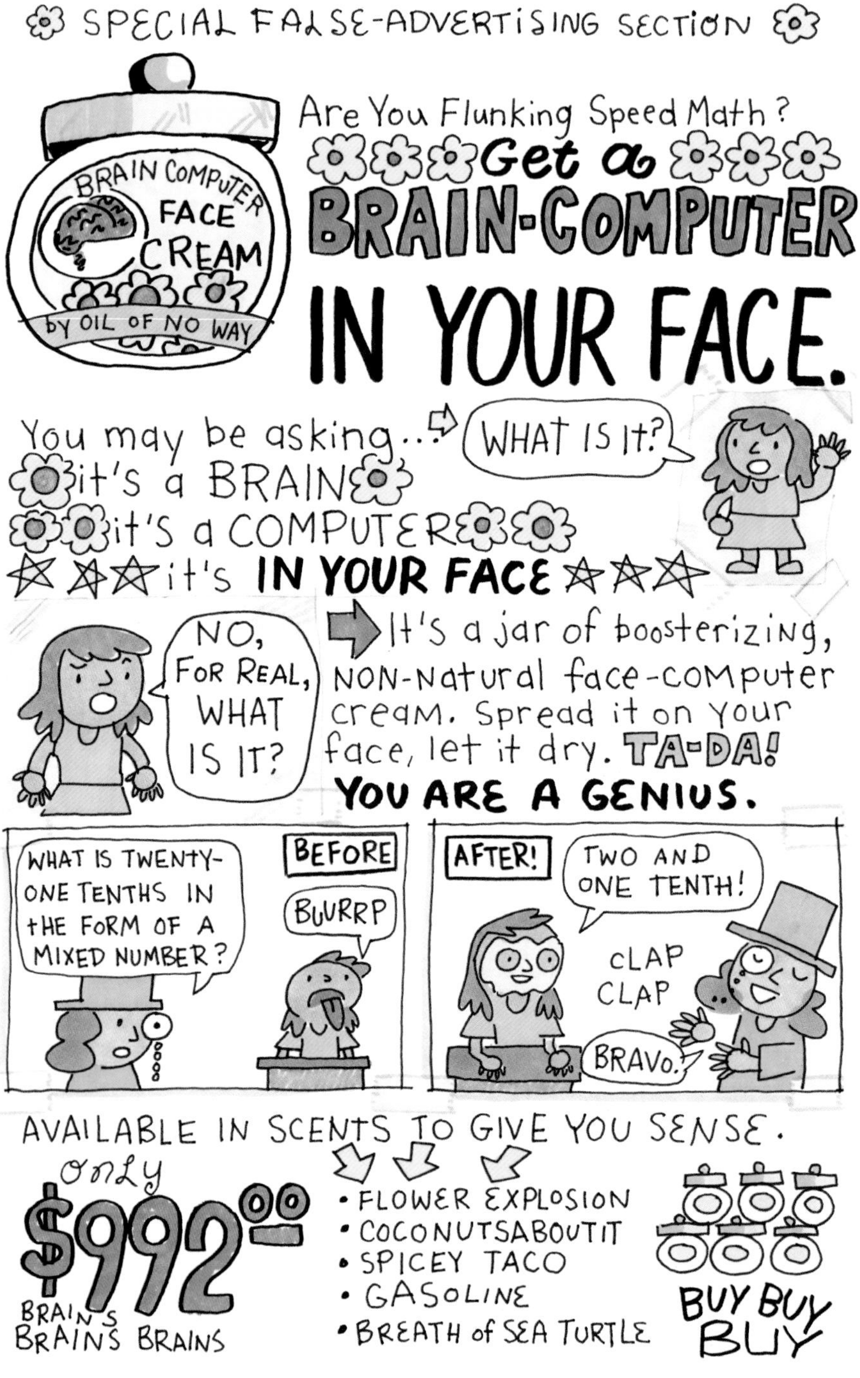
SPECIAL FALSE-ADVERTISING SECTION
BRAIN COMPUTER FACE CREAM
by OIL OF NO WAY
Are You Flunking Speed Math?
Get a BRAIN-COMPUTER IN YOUR FACE.
You may be asking...
WHAT IS IT?
it's a BRAIN
it's a COMPUTER
it's IN YOUR FACE
NO, FOR REAL, WHAT IS IT?
It's a jar of boosterizing, NON-Natural face-computer cream. Spread it on your face, let it dry. TA-DA!
YOU ARE A GENIUS.
WHAT IS TWENTY-ONE TENTHS IN THE FORM OF A MIXED NUMBER?
BEFORE
BUURRP
AFTER!
TWO AND ONE TENTH!
CLAP CLAP
BRAVO.
AVAILABLE IN SCENTS TO GIVE YOU SENSE.
only $992.00
BRAIN'S BRAINS BRAINS
• FLOWER EXPLOSION
• COCONUTSABOUTIT
• SPICEY TACO
• GASOLINE
• BREATH of SEA TURTLE
BUY BUY BUY

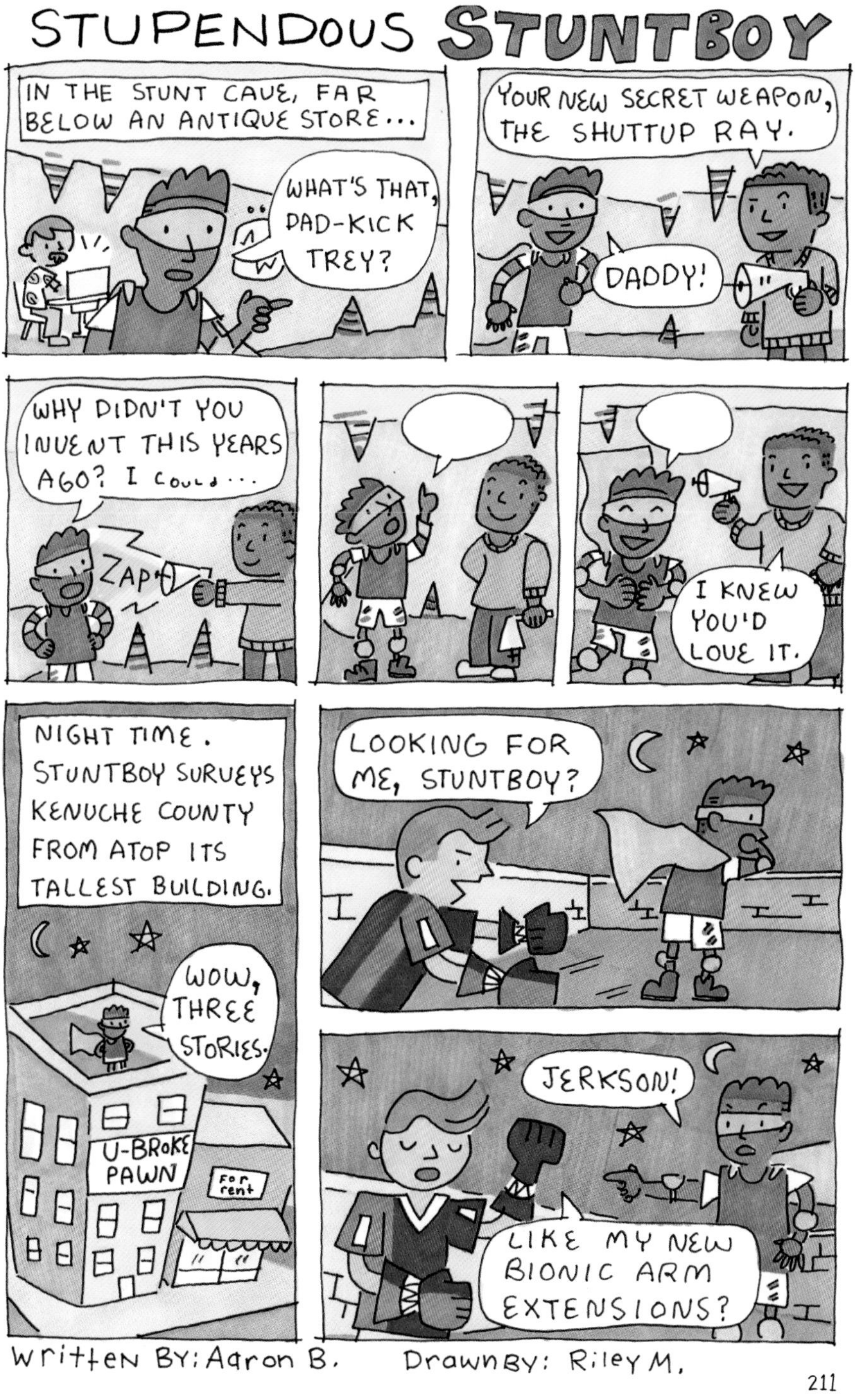
STUPENDOUS STUNTBOY
IN THE STUNT CAVE, FAR BELOW AN ANTIQUE STORE...
WHAT'S THAT, DAD-KICK TREY?
YOUR NEW SECRET WEAPON, THE SHUTTUP RAY.
DADDY!
WHY DIDN'T YOU INVENT THIS YEARS AGO? I COULD...
ZAP
I KNEW YOU'D LOVE IT.
NIGHT TIME. STUNTBOY SURVEYS KENUCHE COUNTY FROM ATOP ITS TALLEST BUILDING.
WOW, THREE STORIES.
U-BROKE PAWN
For rent
LOOKING FOR ME, STUNTBOY?
JERKSON!
LIKE MY NEW BIONIC ARM EXTENSIONS?
Written BY: Aaron B.
Drawn BY: Riley M.

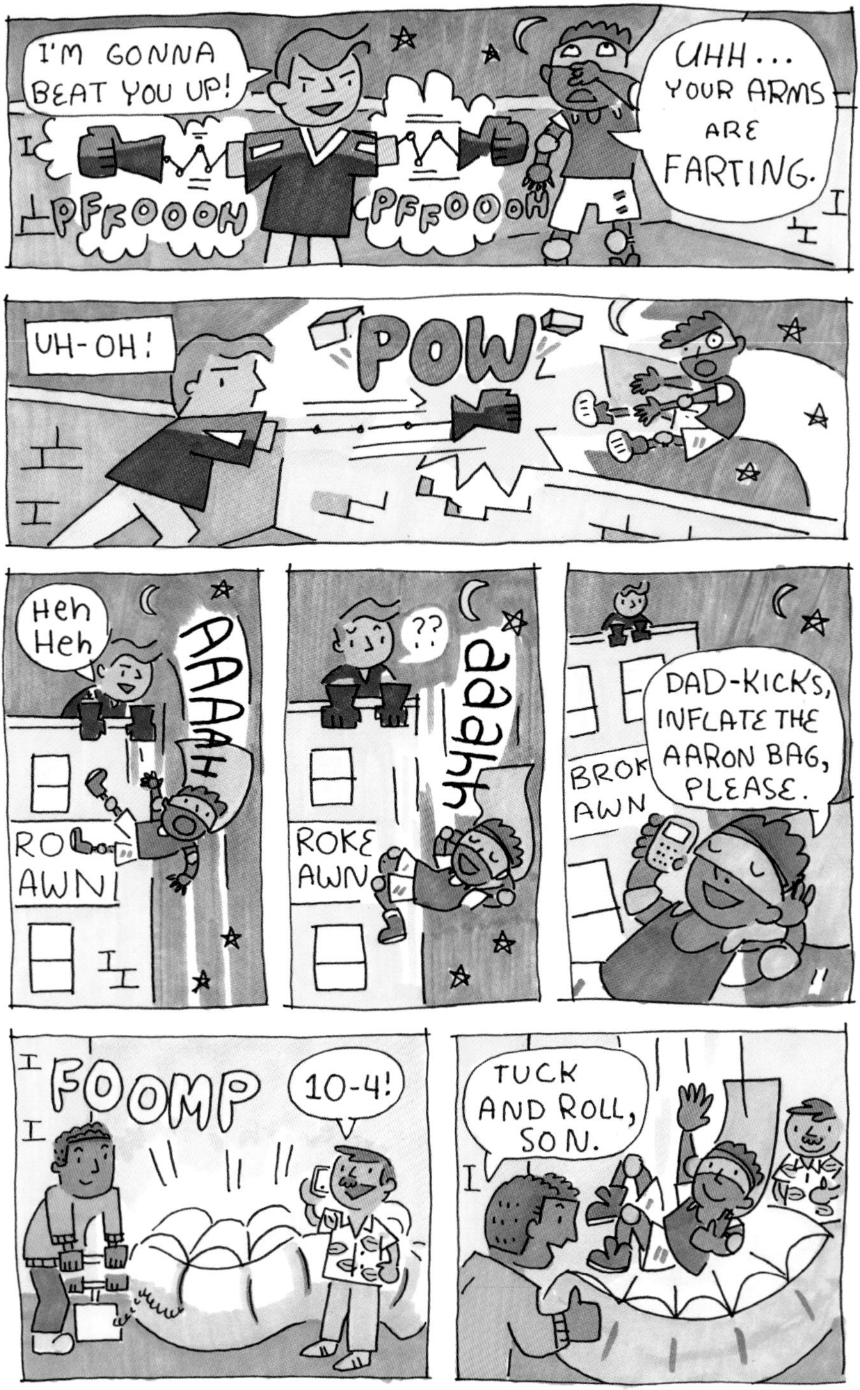
I'M GONNA BEAT YOU UP!
PFFOOOH
PFFOOOH
UHH... YOUR ARMS ARE FARTING.
UH-OH!
POW
Heh Heh
AAAAAH
??
aaahh
DAD-KICKS, INFLATE THE AARON BAG, PLEASE.
FOOMP
10-4!
TUCK AND ROLL, SON.

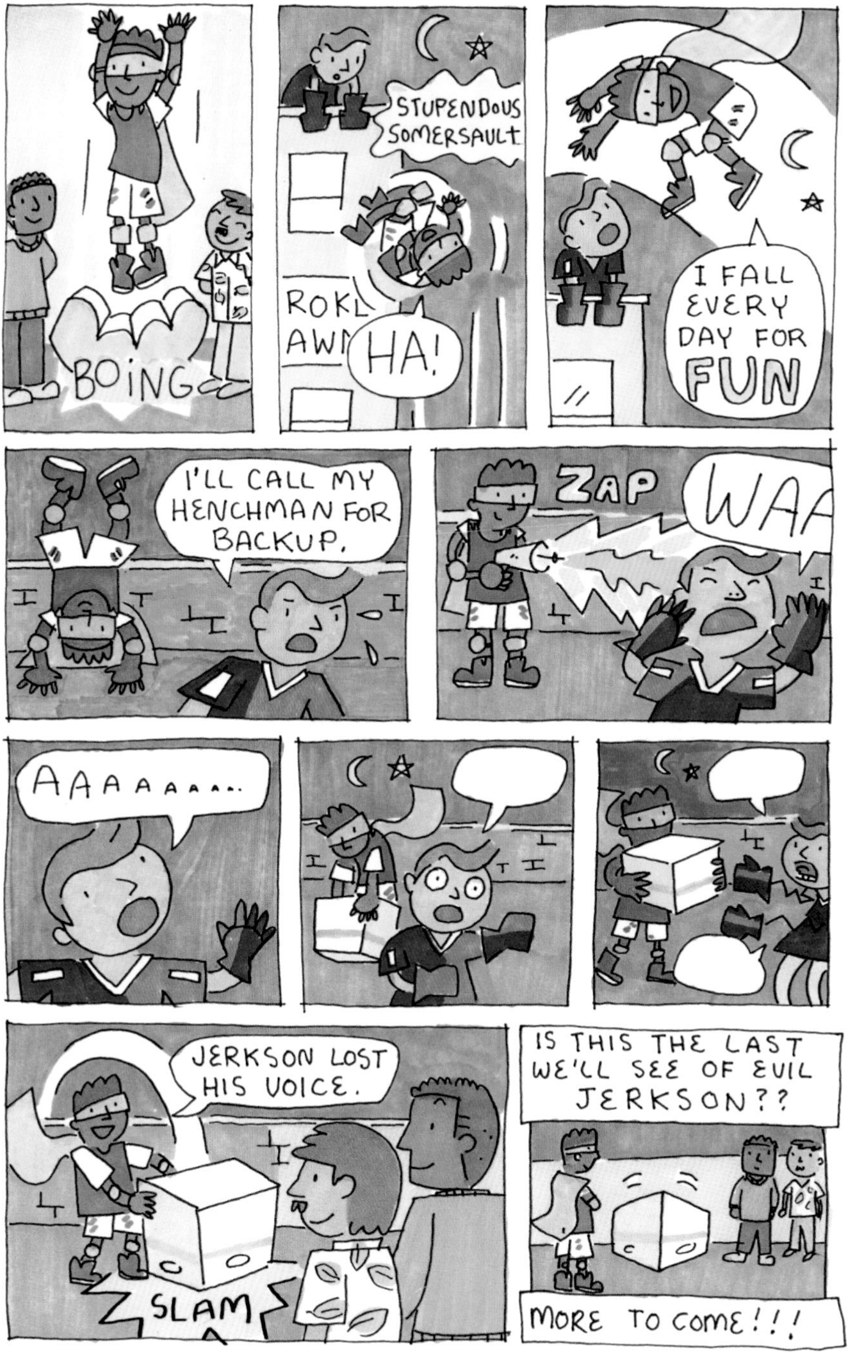
BOING
STUPENDOUS SOMERSAULT
HA!
I FALL EVERY DAY FOR FUN
I'LL CALL MY HENCHMAN FOR BACKUP.
ZAP
WAA
AAAAAAA...
JERKSON LOST HIS VOICE.
SLAM
IS THIS THE LAST WE'LL SEE OF EVIL JERKSON??
MORE TO COME!!!

CHEF CATE'S SCHOOL LUNCH REVIEWS

1 fork = try again 2 forks = ok I ate it. 3 forks = Mmm not bad. 4 forks = BRAVO! OMNIVORE

CORN DOG

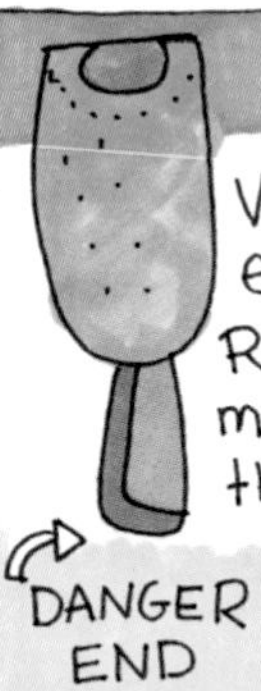
DANGER END

Very tasty. Do NOT eat while laughing. Riley almost poked my eye out with the stick end.

3 FORKS

FRITO CHILI PIE

Spoke to management. This is no pie. She said "Some folks call it WALKING TACO." Not a taco. Doesn't walk. Call it FRITO CHILI PILE.

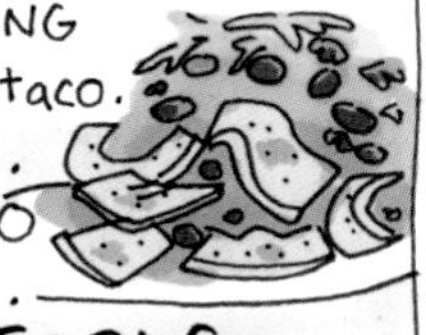

3 FORKS

CHEESEBURGER

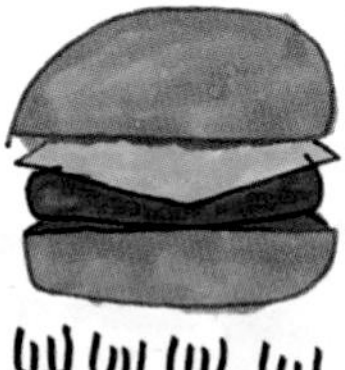

The best hamburger? No. The best school lunch? MAYBE.

3.5 FORKS

SALISBURY STEAK

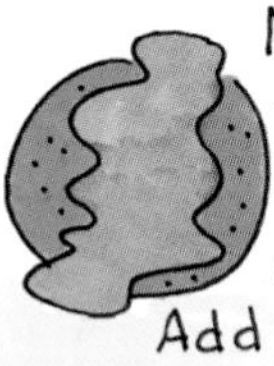

Not a fan. I suggest these changes: wipe the gravy off. Add cheese. Add a bun. VoilÀ, now I can eat it.

1 FORK

TURKEY A LA KING

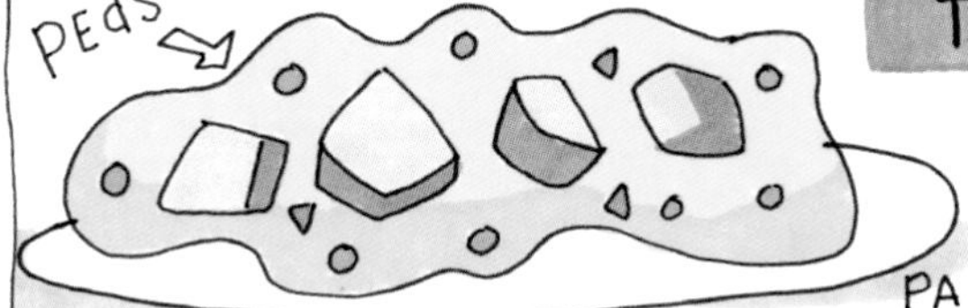
PEAS?

This lunch is the same color as GLOW IN THE DARK PAINT. We think it's made from ELECTROMAGNETIC GHOST PUKE. Riley can't even draw it without running to go hurl. If I were KING, I would decree that no one ever eat this.

NO FORKS GIVEN

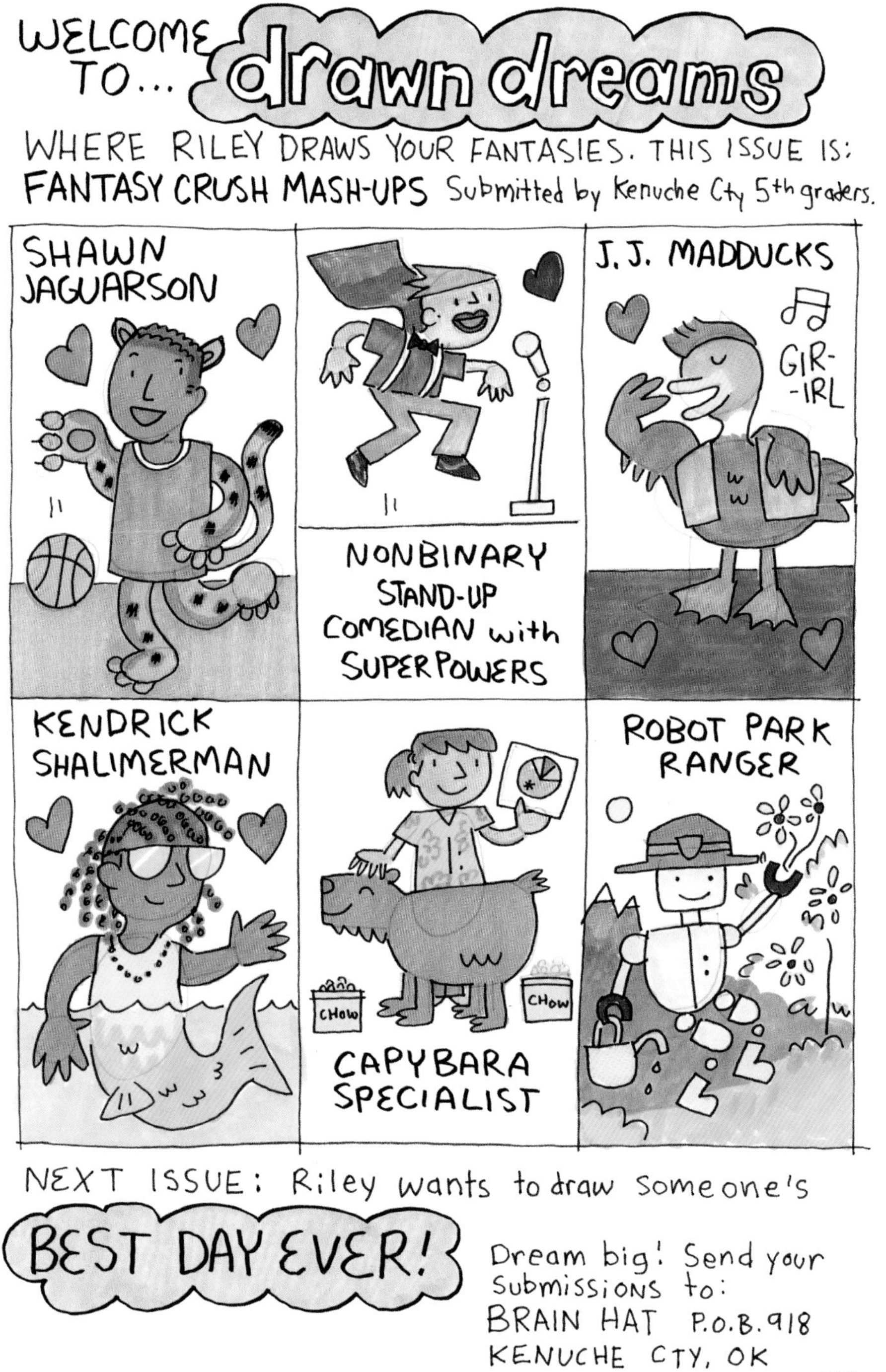
WELCOME TO... drawn dreams
WHERE RILEY DRAWS YOUR FANTASIES. THIS ISSUE IS:
FANTASY CRUSH MASH-UPS Submitted by Kenuche Cty 5th graders.
SHAWN JAGUARSON
NONBINARY STAND-UP COMEDIAN with SUPERPOWERS
J. J. MADDUCKS
GIR-IRL
KENDRICK SHALIMERMAN
CHOW
CHOW
CAPYBARA SPECIALIST
ROBOT PARK RANGER
NEXT ISSUE: Riley wants to draw someone's
BEST DAY EVER!
Dream big! Send your submissions to:
BRAIN HAT P.O.B. 918
KENUCHE CTY, OK

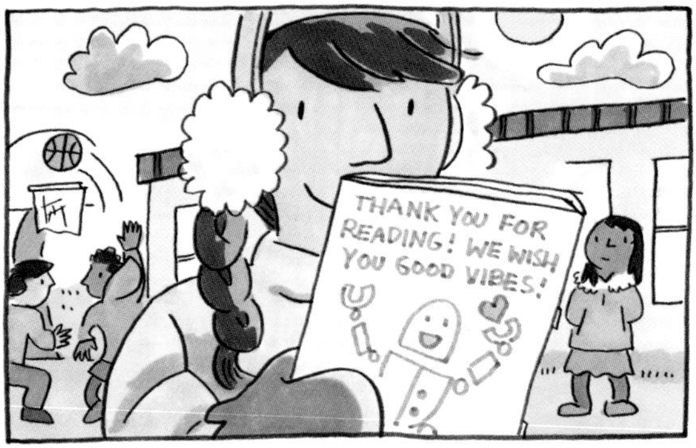
THANK YOU FOR READING! WE WISH YOU GOOD VIBES!

Aaron's dads sell *Brain Hat* at their shop for $2.00. That money pays for printing and supplies, so we can give it away free to kids at school.

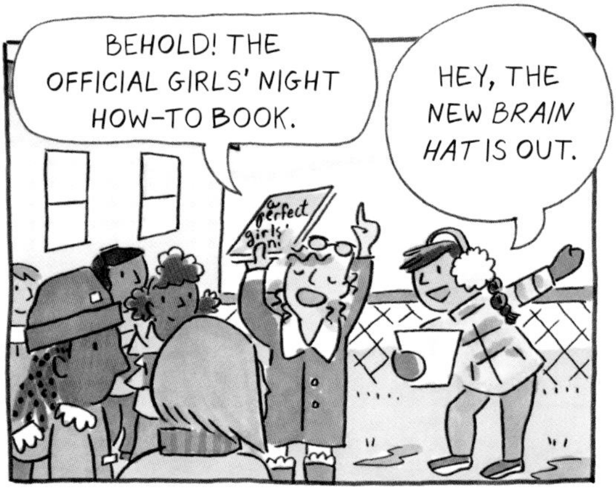
BEHOLD! THE OFFICIAL GIRLS' NIGHT HOW-TO BOOK.
HEY, THE NEW *BRAIN HAT* IS OUT.

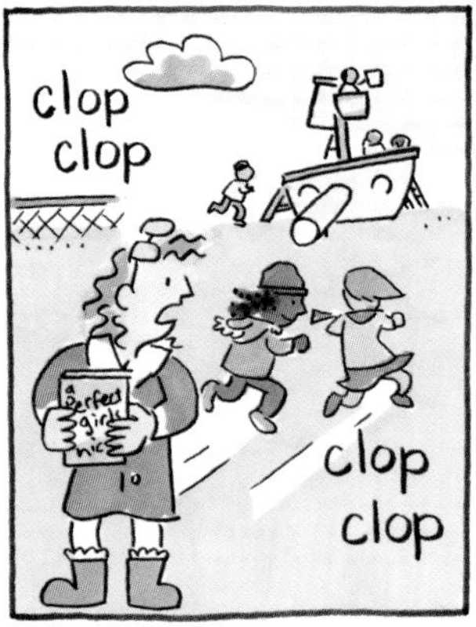
clop clop
clop clop

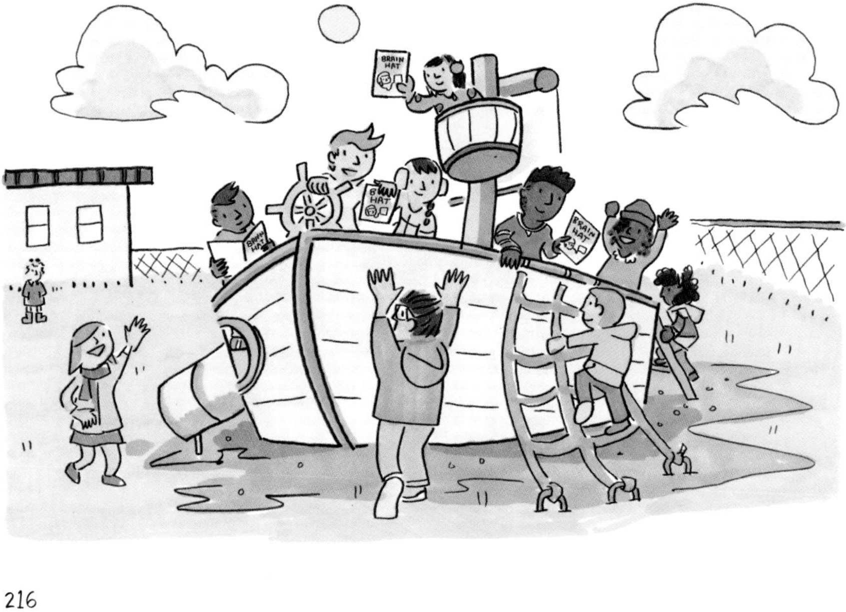
BRAIN HAT
BRAIN HAT

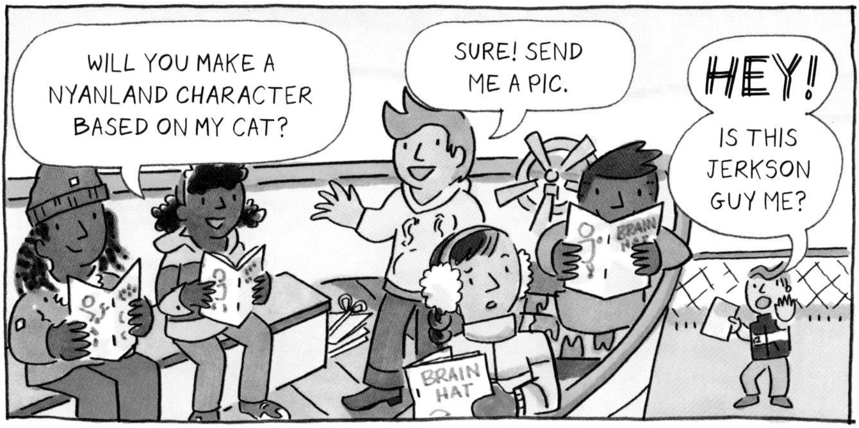
WILL YOU MAKE A NYANLAND CHARACTER BASED ON MY CAT?
SURE! SEND ME A PIC.
HEY!
IS THIS JERKSON GUY ME?
BRAIN HAT

Sure, not everyone is a fan. That's fine with us.

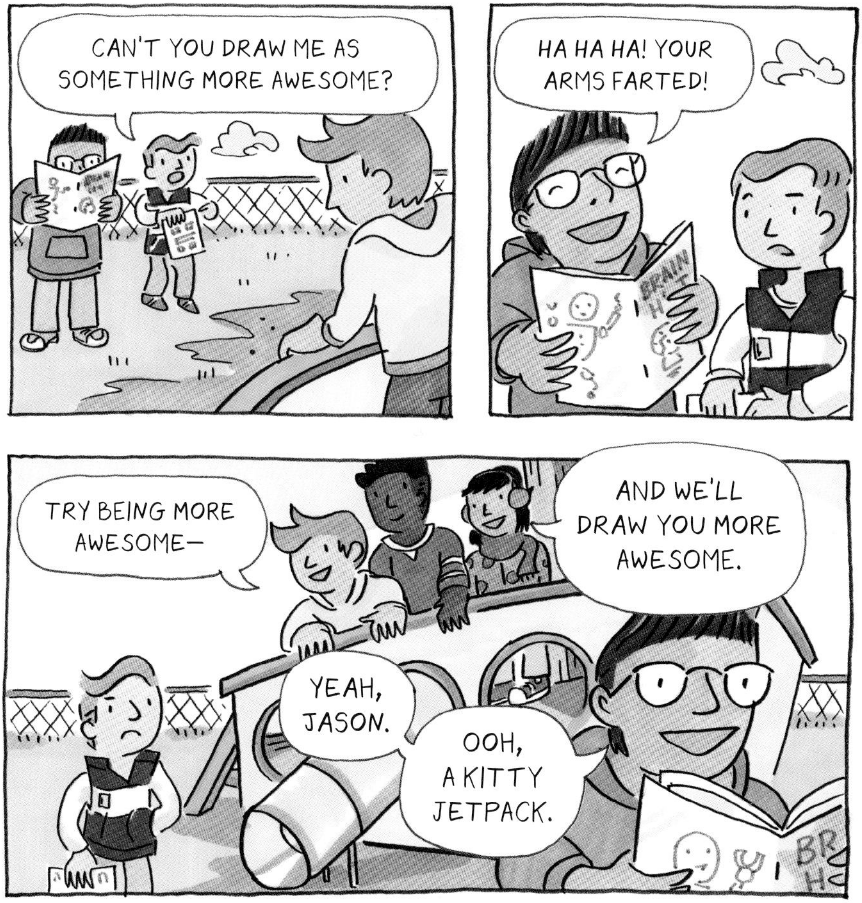
CAN'T YOU DRAW ME AS SOMETHING MORE AWESOME?
HA HA HA! YOUR ARMS FARTED!
TRY BEING MORE AWESOME—
AND WE'LL DRAW YOU MORE AWESOME.
YEAH, JASON.
OOH, A KITTY JETPACK.

It's worth it to find the few people who truly get you.

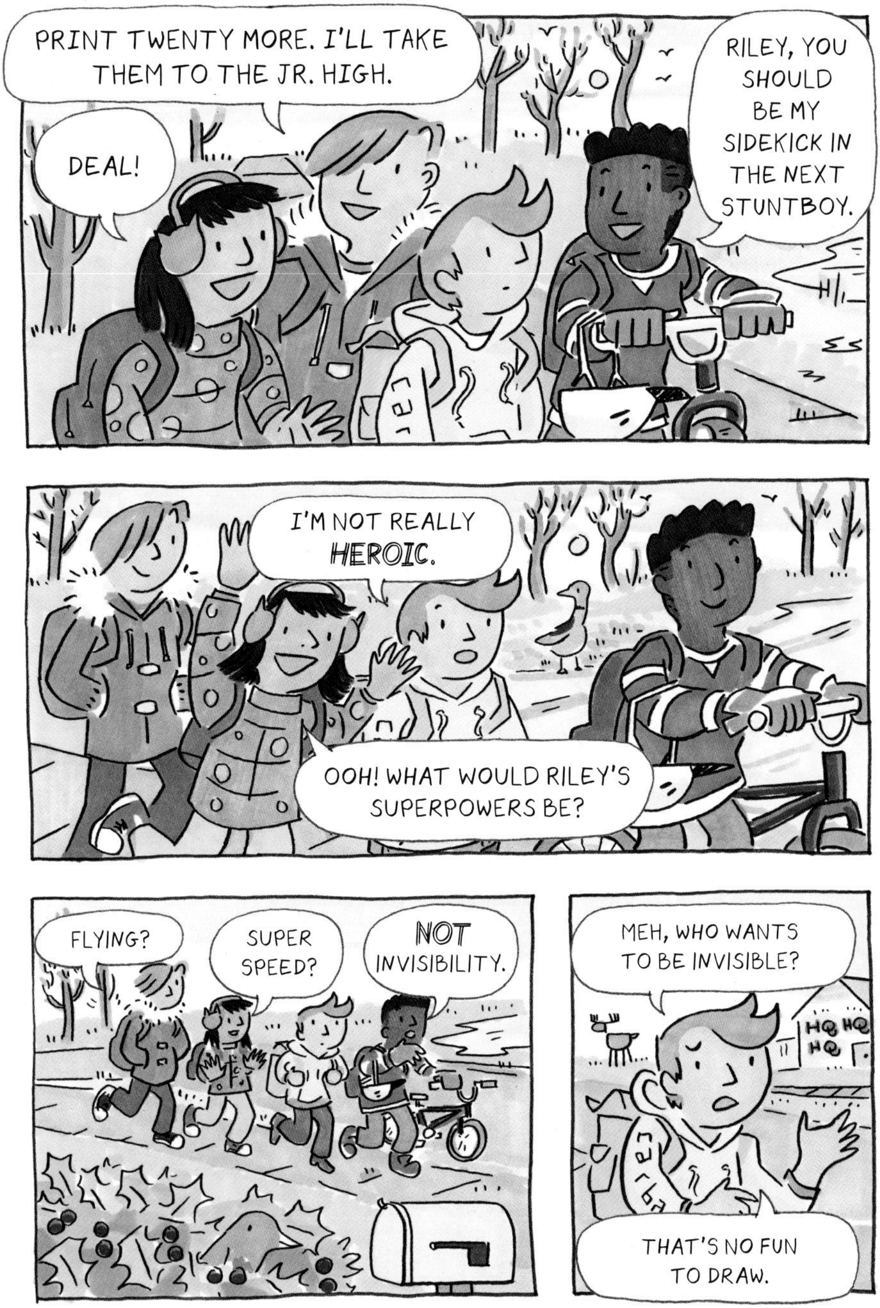

PRINT TWENTY MORE. I'LL TAKE THEM TO THE JR. HIGH.
DEAL!
RILEY, YOU SHOULD BE MY SIDEKICK IN THE NEXT STUNTBOY.
I'M NOT REALLY HEROIC.
OOH! WHAT WOULD RILEY'S SUPERPOWERS BE?
FLYING?
SUPER SPEED?
NOT INVISIBILITY.
MEH, WHO WANTS TO BE INVISIBLE?
THAT'S NO FUN TO DRAW.

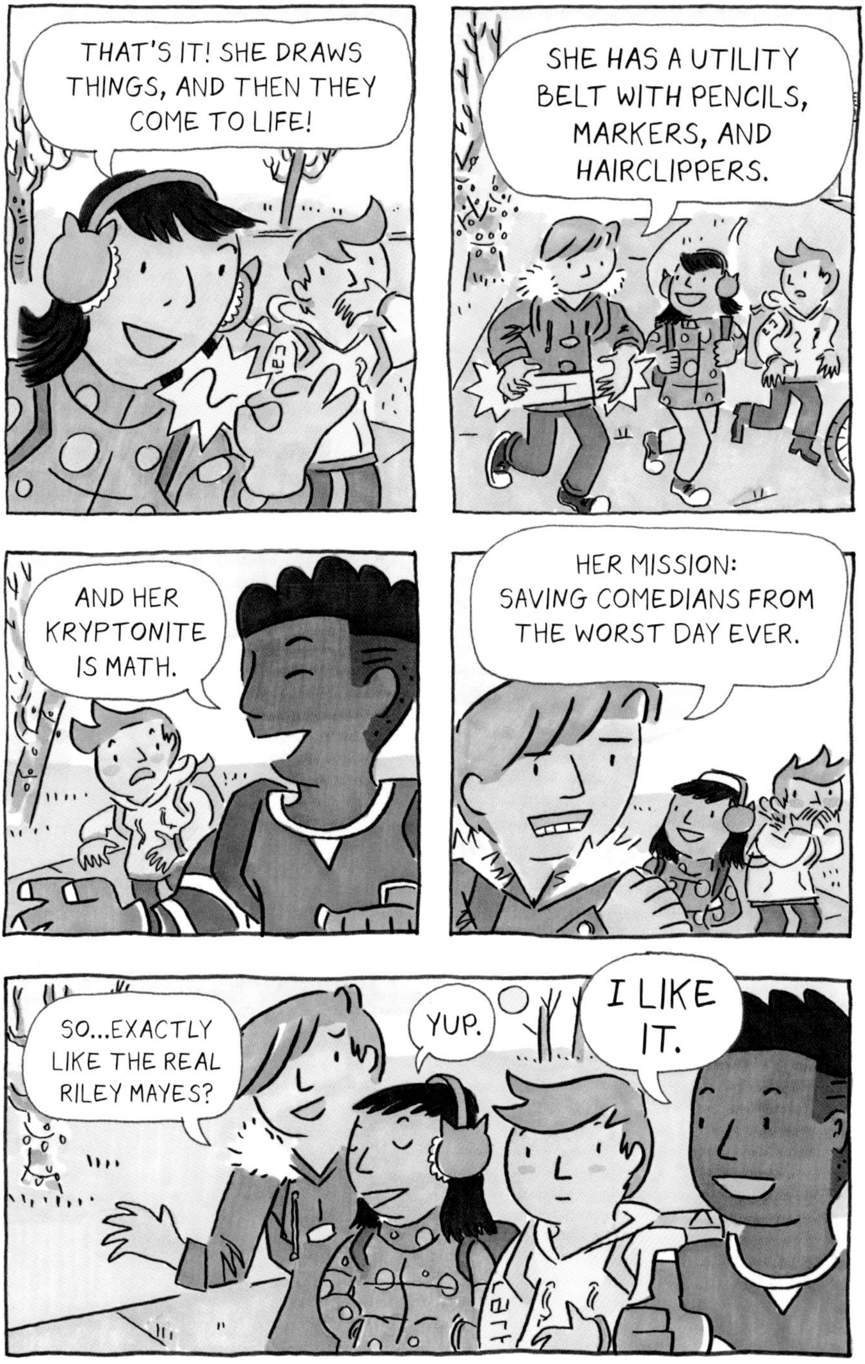
THAT'S IT! SHE DRAWS THINGS, AND THEN THEY COME TO LIFE!
SHE HAS A UTILITY BELT WITH PENCILS, MARKERS, AND HAIRCLIPPERS.
AND HER KRYPTONITE IS MATH.
HER MISSION: SAVING COMEDIANS FROM THE WORST DAY EVER.
SO...EXACTLY LIKE THE REAL RILEY MAYES?
YUP.
I LIKE IT.

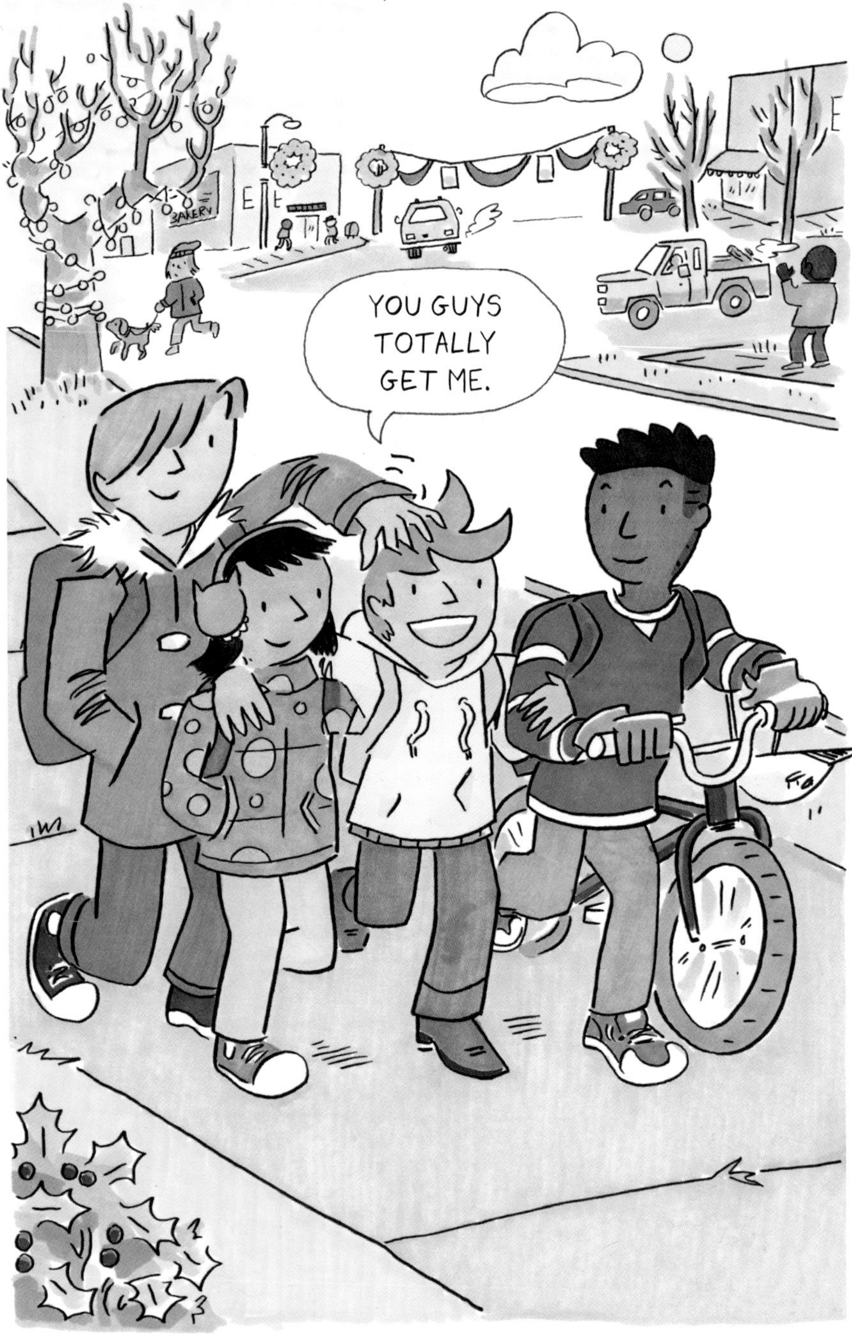
BAKERY
YOU GUYS TOTALLY GET ME.